"A good book takes us places we can't reach without a transport: a remote locale, an alien culture, another time, or into the heart and mind of a remarkable character. Pattison provides truly remarkable transport . . . it's a riveting story but it's also a great deal more. Pattison's narrative is filled with ritual, portents, and even demons, and somehow imbues the harsh Tibetan gulag with moments of eerie beauty and serenity." —*Booklist* (starred review)

"Set in the mountainous regions of Lhasa, this first novel is a stark and compelling saga . . . As in Tony Hillerman's Navajo mysteries, Pattison's characters venerate traditional beliefs, and mystical insight as a tool for finding murderers. Pattison writes with confident knowledge and spare, graceful prose." —*Library Journal*

"Eliot Pattison has hit a home run with his first fiction outing. Pattison's writing is lyrical and suffused with energy: a perfect combination for a thriller set in the mysterious and ancient land of Tibet . . . Pattison skillfully creates a picture of modern-day Tibet . . . Altogether, this is not a book you'll soon forget." —*Writers Write*

"A full-tilt thriller that exhibits a profound feel for Buddhism and how it manifests in a particular corner of the world . . . Pattison's novel uses the lens of thriller fiction to illuminate brilliantly the state of a (to Americans) little-known culture . . . Not only an exhilarating read, but an important one, politically and morally." —*Tricycle: The Buddhist Review*

WATER TOUCHING STONE

ELIOT PATTISON

WITHDRAWN

St. Martin's Paperbacks

To Barbara

A glossary of frequently used foreign words
is provided at the back of this book.

ACKNOWLEDGMENTS

For insights, information, and inspiration about life in the lands encompassed by modern China, I am indebted to the many Tibetans, Kazakhs, Uighurs, and Chinese who have quietly shared their stories with me during the past two decades. For reasons that should be obvious, they must remain anonymous. For their steadfast support and sage counsel in navigating the mazes of publishing. I am grateful to Natasha Kern, Michael Denneny, and Kate Parkin. Special thanks also to Christina Prestia, Dr. Scott Pattison, and Ed Stackler.

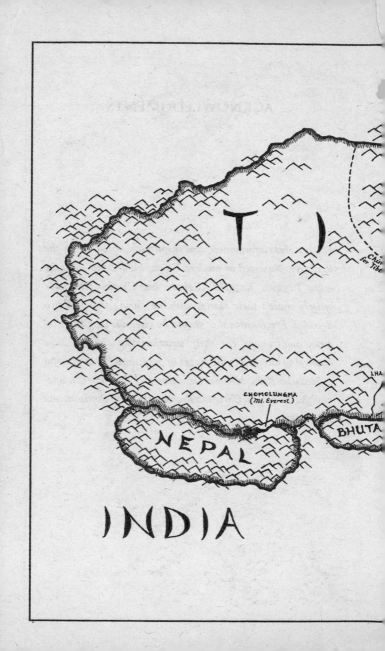

B E T

Political Autonomous Border Region

KHAM PLATEAU

LHADRUNG

BURMA

Saskya Gompa

Khartok Gompa

Ragyapa
Village

Jade
Spring
Camp

Lhadrung

Valley

Lhadrung Town

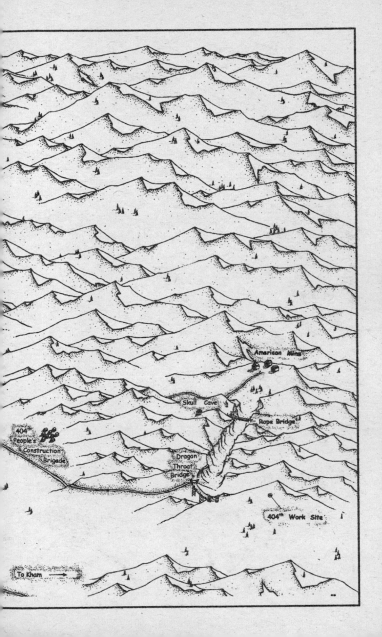

American Mins

Skull Cave

Rope Bridge

404's
People's
Construction
Brigade

Dragon
Throat
Bridge

404th Work Site

To Kham

CHAPTER 1

Everything in Tibet starts with the wind. It is the wind that offers up prayer flags to the heavens, the wind that brings cold and warmth and life-giving water to the land, the wind that gives movement to the mountains themselves as it sends the clouds careening down the ranges. As he looked out from his high ledge, Shan Tao Yun remembered a lama once suggesting to him that the human soul first became aware of itself in Tibet because the wind never stops pushing against its inhabitants, and it is in pushing back against the world that a soul is defined. After nearly four years in Tibet, Shan believed it. It was as though here, the highest of all lands, was where the planet, gasping and groaning, began its rotation, here was where it learned to move, here was where it was the most difficult for people to hold on.

There was an exercise for enlightenment Shan had learned from the lamas that was called scouring the wind. Extend your awareness into the air and float with it, become mindful of the world it carries and absorb its lessons. He and his companions had hours before darkness fell, before it was safe to travel again, and he sat cross-legged on his high perch and tried it now. Drying heather, Shan sensed. A hawk soaring high over the valley. The sweet, acrid scent of junipers, tinged with the coolness of snow. The distant chatter of ground squirrels on the rock-strewn slopes. And suddenly, before a spreading plume of dust in the north, a single desperate rider.

As Shan shielded his eyes to study the intruding figure,

a sharp syllable of warning cracked through the air. He turned to see Jowa, his Tibetan guide, pointing to an old man in a broad-brimmed brown hat walking toward the edge of the ledge, staring up the valley.

"Lokesh!" Shan shouted and leapt to grab his old friend, who seemed not to notice when Shan grasped his arm. He was blinking and shaking his head, staring at the figure approaching from the far end of the valley.

"Is it real?" Lokesh asked in a tentative tone, as if uncertain of his senses. The day before, he had seen a giant turtle on the top of a hill, a sign of good luck. He had insisted that they take it an offering and apologized because it had turned back into a rock by the time they had reached it.

"It is of this world," Shan confirmed as he squinted toward the horizon.

"He's frightened," Jowa said behind them. "He keeps looking back." Shan turned and saw that the wiry Tibetan had found their battered pair of binoculars and was studying the figure through the lenses. "That horse is dead if he keeps it up." The Tibetan looked back to his companions and shook his head. "Someone is chasing him," he said in a worried tone as he handed Shan the glasses.

Shan saw that the rider was clad in a dark *chuba*, the heavy sheepskin robe worn by the *dropka*, the nomads who roamed the vast plateau of northwestern Tibet. Behind the dropka's horse the dust was so thick that Shan could see no sign of a pursuer. He scanned the landscape. Snow-capped peaks edged the clear cobalt sky for miles in three directions, towering over the rugged grass-covered hills that lined the opposite side of the valley. Neither the long plain below them, brown with autumn-dried grass, nor the narrow dirt track from which they had retreated at dawn, gave any sign of life other than the solitary rider.

Shan could see the man's arms now, flailing his reins against the horse's neck. He looked down at their battered old Jiefang cargo truck, hidden behind a large outcropping a hundred feet from the road, then handed back the binoculars and stepped into the shadow of the overhanging rock where they had taken shelter after their night's ride. Ten feet away, where the shadow was darkest, Shan dropped to his knees. By the ashes of the small fire where they had roasted barley flour for their only hot meal of the day, a solitary stick of incense had been thrust into a tiny cairn of stones. A blanket of yak felt had been folded and laid on the ground, and on the blanket, sitting silently in the cross-legged lotus fashion, was a man in a maroon robe. He had close-cropped graying hair, and his thin face would have been called old by many, but Shan never thought of Gendun as old, just as he never thought of mountains as old.

The lama's eyes were mostly closed, in what for him passed as sleep. Gendun refused to rest during the night, while they traveled in the old truck, and he did not lie down in the daylight rest shifts taken by his three companions but only drifted off like this, after Lokesh had made sure he had eaten.

"Rinpoche," Shan whispered, using the form of address for a revered teacher. "We may have to leave," he said. "There is trouble."

Gendun gave no sign of hearing him.

Shan looked toward Jowa, who was using the binoculars again to survey the landscape beyond the rider, then turned back to Gendun, noting for the first time that the lama had arranged his fingers in a *mudra*, one of the hand shapes used to focus meditation, a symbol of reverence to the Buddha. He studied the lama's fingers a moment. The wrists were crossed, the palms held outward, with the little fingers linked to form the shape of a chain. Shan paused and stared at the hands. It was an unusual mudra, one he had never seen Gendun make. The Spirit Subduer, it was called. It chilled Shan for a moment, then he sighed and rose with a slight bow of his head, stepping back to Jowa's side.

The young Tibetan was looking up the slope above them, as though searching for a way to climb over the mountain. They both knew that there was probably only one reason the rider was so scared. Shan looked once more at the truck. Their only hope was that it would not be seen. It would be a bad finish, to be stopped here, high on the remote plateau, short of their destination. Not simply because of the suffering they would face from the Public Security Bureau, but because they would have failed Gendun and the other lamas who had sent them.

Lokesh sighed. "I thought it would be longer," he said, and touched the beads that hung from his belt. "That woman," he said absently, "she still has to be settled in."

Settled in. The words brought back to Shan how different they all were, how differently they seemed to view the strange task that had been set for them. Gendun had been with the lamas who had summoned Shan from his meditation cell in their mountain hermitage, seated on cushions around an eight-foot mandala that had just been completed that afternoon. Four monks had worked for six months on the delicate wheel of life, composed of hundreds of intricate figures created of colored sands. Fragrant juniper had been burning in a brazier, and dozens of butter lamps lit the chamber. A low rumble like distant thunder rose from a chamber below them, the sound of a huge prayer wheel that required two strong monks to turn it. For a quarter hour they had gazed in silent reverence at the mandala, then Gendun, the senior lama and Shan's principal teacher, had spoken.

"You are needed in the north," he had announced to Shan. "A woman named Lau has been killed. A teacher. And a lama is missing." Nothing more. The lamas were shy of reality. They knew to be wary of facts. Gendun had told him the essential truth of the event; for the lamas everything else would be mere rumor. What they had meant was that this lama and the dead woman with a Chinese name were vital to them, and it was for Shan to discover the other truths surrounding the killing and translate them for the lamas' world.

He had not known how far they would travel, and when he had arrived as instructed at the hidden door that led to the outside world, he had assumed that it would be to the north end of the Lhadrung valley, to the settlement nearest the hermitage. Nor had he realized that Gendun was to accompany him. Even when Gendun appeared at the door, Shan had thought it was to bid him well or offer details of his destination. He had even assumed that the canvas bag of supplies the lama had brought was for Shan. But then he had seen Gendun's feet. The lama had removed the sandals he always wore under his robe and replaced them with heavy lace-up work boots.

They had walked until dawn, when they had met Lokesh at the ancient rope bridge that spanned the gorge separating the hermitage from the rest of the world. Lokesh and Shan had embraced as old friends, for such they had become during their time together in Lhadrung's gulag labor camp, then the three had walked another hour until a truck had stopped for them. Shan had thought it was just a coincidence, just a favor from the driver. But the driver had been Jowa, and after Gendun had examined the vehicle with wide eyes, having never been so close to a modern machine, the lama had blessed first the truck, then Jowa, and climbed inside. Jowa had eyed Shan resentfully, then started the engine and driven for twelve hours straight. That had been six days earlier.

Shan had been confused from the outset, waiting each day for the clarification from Gendun that never came. But Lokesh had never seemed to doubt their purpose. For Lokesh their job was to resettle the dead woman, meaning that they must address her soul and assure that it was balanced and ready for rebirth. For Lokesh, the woman had to settle into her death the way the living, after a momentous change, had to settle into life. Not her death, really, for to Lokesh and Gendun death was only the reverse side of birth. But a death not properly prepared for, such as a sudden violent death, could make rebirth difficult. When a monk in their prison had been suddenly killed by falling rocks, Lokesh had carried on a vigil for ten days, to help the unprepared spirit through the period when it would discover it needed to seek rebirth.

Shan gazed toward the valley floor again. The rider continued his breakneck speed, bent low now, as if studying the ground.

Shan looked at his companions with grim frustration.

"Perhaps," Shan said to Jowa, "it is one of your friends." Jowa had been a monk once himself. But the Bureau of Religious Affairs had refused to give him a license to continue as a monk, and a hard shell had grown around the monk inside him. Jowa wasn't worried about resettling a soul. A teacher had been killed and a lama was missing, things that the Chinese did to Tibetans. Jowa had simply understood that they were being sent against an enemy. Shan studied him now as Jowa unconsciously rubbed the deep scar that ran from his left eye to the base of his jaw. Shan had known many such men during his years in Tibet. He knew the familiar hardness of the eyes and the way such men turned their heads when encountering a Chinese on the street. He knew the scars made by the Public Security troops, the knobs, who were fond of wielding whips of barbed wire against public protesters. The hard labor brigade from which Shan had been released four months earlier had been heavily populated by men like Jowa.

It had taken less than a day on the road from Lhadrung, however, for Shan to understand that the essential truth about Jowa was something else. As the former monk had stealthfully exchanged passwords with the horsemen who had taken them away from the Lhasa highway, Shan had realized that Jowa was a purba, a member of the secret Tibetan resistance, named for the ceremonial dagger of Buddhist ritual. He had replaced his monastic vow with another vow, a pledge to use up the rest of this incarnation in fighting to preserve Tibet.

"No, not one of us," Jowa replied curtly. "Not like that," he added enigmatically. "If it's soldiers I will go to the truck," he said in a low, urgent tone. "I will lead them away on a chase to the south. Gendun and Lokesh cannot move fast enough. Just climb higher and hide."

"No," Shan said, watching the rider. "We stay together."

Lokesh sat near the edge of the ledge and stretched, as if the approaching threat somehow relaxed him. He pulled his *mala*, his rosary, from his belt, and his fingers began reflexively to work the beads. "The two of you have strength," the old man said. "Gendun needs you, both of you. I will stay with the truck. I will tell the soldiers I am a smuggler and surrender."

"No," Shan repeated. "We stay together." As much as he needed Jowa for his wisdom of the real world, the world of knob checkpoints and army patrols, he needed Lokesh for his wisdom of the other world, the world the lamas lived in, for while they had to traverse Jowa's world to get to the place of death, once they arrived Shan knew he would be seeking answers in the lamas' world. Lokesh would have been a lama himself except that long ago, before the Chinese had invaded, he had been taken from his monastery as a novice to serve in the government of the Dalai Lama.

Shan watched Jowa remove the canvas bag that hung over his shoulder and his thick woolen vest, then wrap his hand around the pommel of the short blade that hung at his waist. Jowa would not speak about the priest within him, but at their campfires he sometimes spoke proudly about his bloodline that traced back to the *khampas*, the nomadic clans that tended herds in eastern Tibet, a people known for centuries as fearless warriors. Jowa no longer watched the rider but the cloud of dust behind him. Soldiers would have machine guns, but, like thousands of Tibetans before him, Jowa would rush them with only his blade if that was what it took to remain true.

"But the road," Shan said suddenly. "Why is he staying on the road?"

Jowa stepped to his side and slowly nodded his head. "You're right," he replied in a puzzled tone. "If someone chased one of the nomads, first thing he'd do, he'd get off the road." As he spoke, he swept his hand toward the wilderness that lay beyond the rough dirt track. They were in the wild, windblown changtang, the vast empty plateau that ranged for hundreds of miles across central and western Tibet, a land where the dropka had hidden themselves for centuries.

Lokesh cocked his head, then looked toward the opposite end of the valley, to the south. "He's not running from someone. He is running *to* someone."

They watched as the rider sped past the outcropping that hid their truck, reappeared, then abruptly reined in his horse. As the horse spun about in a slow circle, the dropka studied the road.

"I thought you hid the tire tracks," Shan said to Jowa.

"I did, for Chinese eyes."

The rider dismounted and led his mount toward the outcropping. Moments later he stood by their empty truck. After tying his horse to the bumper, he warily circled the vehicle, then climbed to the edge of the open cargo bay, his hand on one of the metal ribs designed to support a canvas cover over the bay. He stepped inside and lifted the lids of the barrels that stood there, then jumped out and studied the slope above him. Most of the slope was covered with loose scree, fragments of rock broken from the ledge above. Winding through it was the solitary goat path which they had climbed after leaving the truck at dawn.

"Sometimes the soldiers have Tibetan scouts," Jowa reminded Shan.

He touched Shan on the shoulder, motioning him into the deep shadow of the overhanging rock.

The dropka began climbing the path at a fast trot. Shan fought the temptation to pull Gendun to his feet, to scale the ridge and disappear with him. The others could explain themselves, they had identity papers. But no one could explain Shan or Gendun. Gendun, who had lived so hidden from the rest of the world that Shan had been the first Chinese he ever met, had no official identity. Shan, on the other hand, had suffered from too much official scrutiny. A former government investigator who had been exiled to slave labor in Tibet, his release from the gulag had been unofficial. If captured outside Lhadrung, he would be considered an escapee. Jowa pushed Shan against the rock in the darkest part of the shadow, beside Gendun, and waited in front of them, his hand on his blade again.

The man reached the ledge where they hid, took a few steps in the opposite direction, then turned and came straight toward them. When he reached the rock, he stepped toward the shadow and shielded his eyes to peer inside. "Are you there?" he called loudly, in a voice edged with fear. The man was of slight build, wearing a dirty fleece hat over a mop of black hair and a faded red shirt under his chuba. He twisted his head and squinted, as though still uncertain of what lurked within. Predators made lairs in such places, and so did the demons that lurked in mountains. He looked back toward the northern reach of the road, as if searching for something, then pressed his palms together in supplication and stepped into the darkness.

"We say prayers for you," he called out, still in his loud, frightened voice, then halted with a sigh of relief as Lokesh took a step forward. His mouth moved into a crooked shape that Shan thought at first was a smile, then he saw that the man was choking off a sob. "For your safe journey."

Lokesh was the most emotional Tibetan Shan had ever met, and he wore his emotions like other people wore clothes, in plain view, never trying to obscure them. In the prison barracks Shan had shared with Lokesh, one of the lamas had said Lokesh carried embers inside him, embers that flared up unexpectedly, fanned by a rush of emotion or sudden realization. When the embers flared, snippets of sound, in croaks and groans and even squeals, escaped him. The sound he made now was a long high-pitched moan, as if he had seen something in the man that scared him. As the sound came out he shook his hand in front of his chest, as though to deny something.

Jowa stepped beside Lokesh. "What do you want?" he demanded loudly, not bothering to hide his suspicion of the man. No one was to have known about their journey.

The man looked at the purba uncertainly, then took another step toward them. But as he did so Lokesh shifted to the side and the dropka was suddenly face to face with Shan, who stood in front of Gendun, hiding him from the man's view.

"Chinese!" he gasped in alarm.

"What do you want?" Jowa repeated, then stepped out into the sunlight, looking warily up and down the valley.

The herder followed Shan and Lokesh out of the shadows, then circled Shan once and looked back at Jowa. "You bring a Chinese to help our people?" he asked accusingly.

Lokesh put his hand on Shan's shoulder. "Shan Tao Yun was in prison," he said brightly, as if it were Shan's crowning achievement.

The anger in the man's eyes faded into despair. "Someone was coming, they said." His voice was nearly a whisper. "Someone to save us."

"But that's what our Shan does," Lokesh blurted out. "He saves people."

The man shrugged, not trying to conceal his disappointment. He looked up the valley, his right hand grasping a string of plastic beads hanging from his red waist sash. "It used to be, when trouble came," he said in a distant voice, as if no longer speaking to the three men, "we knew how to find a priest." He picked out a brilliant white cloud on the horizon and decided to address it. "We had a real priest once," he said to the cloud, "but the Chinese took him."

His expression was one Shan had seen on many faces since arriving in Tibet, a sad confusion about what outsiders had done to their world, a helplessness for which the proud, independent Tibetan spirit was ill-prepared. Shan followed the man's eyes as they turned back up the valley.

Someone was emerging from the dust cloud, a rider on a horse that appeared to be near collapse. The animal moved at a wobbling, uneven pace, as if dizzy with fatigue.

"When I was young," the man said, turning to Lokesh now, with a new, urgent tone, "there was a shaman who could take the life force of one to save another. Old people would do it sometimes, to save a sick child." He looked back forlornly at the approaching rider. "I would give mine, give it gladly, to save him. Can you do that?" he asked, stepping closer to study Lokesh's face. "You have the eyes of a priest."

"Why did you come?" Jowa asked again, but this time the harshness had left his voice.

The man reached inside his shirt and produced a yak-hair cord from which hung a silver *gau*, one of the small boxes used to carry a prayer close to the heart. He clamped both hands around the gau and looked back up the valley, not at the rider now but at the far ranges capped with snow. "They took my father to prison and he died. They put my mother in a town but gave her no food coupons to live on, and she starved to death." He spoke slowly, his eyes drifting from the mountains to the ground at his feet. "They said no medical help would be given to our children unless we took them to their clinic. So I take my daughter with a fever but they said the medicine was for sick Chinese children first, and she died. Then we found a boy and he had no one and we had no one, so we called him our son." A tear rolled down his cheek.

"We only wanted to live in peace with our son," he said, his voice barely audible above the wind. "But our old priest, he used to say it was a sin, to want something too much." He looked back toward the second rider, his face long and barren. "They said you were coming, to save the children."

A chill crept down Shan's spine as he heard the words. He looked at Lokesh, who seemed even more shaken by the man's announcement. The color was draining from the old man's face.

"We are going because of a woman named Lau," Shan replied softly.

"No," the dropka said with an unsettling certainty. "It is because of the children, to keep all the children from dying."

On the road below them, a hundred yards before the outcropping, the second horse staggered forward, then stopped. Its rider, wrapped in a heavy felt blanket, slumped in the saddle, then slowly fell to the ground.

The herder let out a sound that wasn't just a moan, nor just a cry of fear. It was a sound of raw, animal agony.

Shan began to run.

He ran in the shortest line toward the fallen rider, darting to where the path met the ledge, then leaping and stumbling down the loose scree of the slope, twice falling painfully on his knees among the rocks, then finally landing on all fours in the coarse grass where the valley floor began. As he rose he glanced over his shoulder. No one followed.

The exhausted horse stood quivering, its nose, edged with a froth of blood, nearly touching the ground beside a mound of black yak-hair felt. Shan slowly lifted an edge of the blanket and saw dozens of hair braids, a bead woven into the end of each. It was an old style for devout women, one hundred eight braids, one hundred eight beads, the number of beads in a mala. The woman was breathing shallowly. Her face was stained with dirt and tears. Her eyes, like those of the horse, were so overcome with exhaustion that they seemed not to notice Shan. Inside the blanket she had used as a cloak was another blanket, around a long bundle that lay across her legs.

He looked back. Jowa and Lokesh were slowly working their way down the path, Jowa leading the herdsman by hand, Lokesh thirty paces behind leading Gendun, as though both men were blind.

Shan raised the second blanket and froze. It was a boy, his face so battered and bruised that one eye was swollen shut. He slowly pulled the blanket away and gasped. Blood was everywhere, saturating the boy's shirt and pants, soaking the inside of the heavy felt.

He tried to lift the boy with the blanket, to take the weight from the woman, but the blanket was twisted in the reins. He tried to pull the reins away and found they were connected to the woman, tied around her forearm above her wrist, because her hand was useless. The wrist was an ugly purple color, and the hand hung at an unnatural angle.

As Shan lifted the boy out of the blanket and laid him on the dried grass, the boy's mouth contorted, but he made no sound. The boy, no more than ten years old, had been savagely mauled and slashed across the shoulder, through his shirt. He was conscious, and though he had to be in great pain, he lay still and silent, his one good eye watching as Shan examined him. The eye showed no fear, no anger, no pain. It was only sad—and confused, like the look on the herdsman's face.

The boy had fought back. His hands were cut deeply in the palms, wounds that could only have been made if the boy had grabbed at the thing that had slashed him. His shirt had been ripped open at the neck, the buttons torn away. Shan clenched his jaw so tightly it hurt. The boy had been stabbed lower on his body, a blow that had penetrated the ribs and left a long open gout of tissue that oozed dark blood. His pants too had been ripped in the fight, a long tear below the left knee. He was missing a shoe.

Shan looked back at the solitary, unblinking eye that stared at him from the ruin of the boy's face, but found no words to say. He gazed at his hands. They were covered with the boy's blood. Overcome for a moment with helplessness, he just watched the blood drip from his fingertips onto the blades of brown grass.

Lokesh appeared at Shan's side, carrying one of the drawstring sacks that contained their supplies. Producing a plastic water bottle from the bag, the old Tibetan held the water to the boy's lips and began to utter a low, singsong chant in syllables unfamiliar to Shan. Before he had been plucked from his gompa, his monastery, to serve the Dalai Lama, Lokesh had intended to take up medicine. He had apprenticed himself to a lama healer before being called to Lhasa, then continued his training during his decades in prison by ministering to prisoners, learning from the old healers who were sometimes thrown behind wire for encouraging citizens to cling to the traditional ways.

The old Tibetan nodded to the woman as he chanted, and gradually the words seemed to bring her back to awareness. When her eyes found their focus and she returned his gaze with a pained smile, Lokesh leaned toward Shan. "Her wrist is broken," he said in his quiet monk's voice. "She needs tea."

As Lokesh sat with the boy, Jowa settled Gendun into the grass by the truck, then brought a soot-covered pot and a piece of canvas stuffed with yak dung for a fire. When the pot was on the low blue flames, Lokesh looked up expectantly and Jowa motioned for Shan to help with the larger blanket. They untangled it from the woman, and Shan, following Jowa's example, secured the blanket with his feet so that, with both men holding the top corners of the long rectangle of felt, they created a windbreak. Lokesh needed still air for his diagnosis. As soon as the blanket was up he stopped his healing mantra and raised the boy's left hand in his own. He spread the three center fingers of his long boney hand along the wrist and closed his eyes, listening for more than a minute, then lowering the arm and repeating the process with the right arm as he tried to locate the twelve pulses on which diagnosis was based in Tibetan medicine. He finished by clasping the boy's earlobe with his fingers, closing his eyes again, and slowly nodding his head.

The boy just watched, without blinking, without speaking, without giving voice to the pain that surely wracked his body. The herdsman knelt silently beside him, his hands still tightly grasping his gau, tears rolling down his dark, leathery cheeks.

Lokesh finished and stared at the boy with a desolate expression. As if the motion were an afterthought, he slowly, stiffly raised the torn fabric of the boy's pants leg and looked at the skin underneath. The swing of the blade that had apparently slashed the fabric had not touched the skin.

"We can't stay in the open," Jowa warned, with nervous glances along the road.

"We could all have been killed," the dropka said in a hollow voice. "It was death on legs."

"You saw it?" Shan asked.

"I was bringing sheep down from the pasture. She was making camp. When I got to camp the dogs were barking on a ledge below. I followed the sound, with a torch. One of the dogs was dead, its brains scattered across a rock. Then I found the two of them. I thought they were dead too."

The woman's eyes opened as Jowa held a mug of tea in front of her. She raised her right hand with a grimace of pain. Jowa held the mug as she drank.

"Tujaychay," the woman said in a hoarse voice. *Thank you.* She took the mug with her good hand and drained its contents.

"The boy was bringing water from a spring down by the road," she said, her voice now stronger than her husband's. "He was late. I heard the sheep coming down the mountain. I needed to begin the cooking. Then the dogs started, the way they shout at a wolf." Jowa began fashioning a sling for her arm out of the canvas. "I ran. I saw it first from a ledge above, as it was attacking Alta. It was standing on its two rear legs. It had the skin of a leopard. I ran faster. I tripped and hit my head. I ran again. It turned as I came. Its front legs had paws like a man's hands, and one held a man's knife. But it dropped the knife and picked up a shiny stick, like a man's arm. It picked up the stick in both paws and hit me as I raised my hand. I fell and my hand hurt like it was in a fire. I crawled to the boy and covered him with my body. The thing came at us, waving the stick, but lightning called it back."

"Lightning?"

"In the north. A single lightning bolt. A message. It is the way that demons speak to each other," the woman said in a voice full of fear. "The thing looked at the lightning bolt and began backing away. Then I remember only blackness. When I awoke I thought we had both died and gone to one of the dark hells, but my husband was there and said it was just that the sun was gone."

"You saw its face?" asked Shan.

The woman's eyes were locked on the boy she had

called Alta. She shook her head. "The thing had no face."

The announcement brought a low moan from Lokesh. Shan turned. The old Tibetan was holding the boy's wrist but gazing forlornly up the road, as if expecting the faceless demon to appear at any moment.

Shan bent over the boy. "Alta, did it speak to you?" he asked. "Did you know who it was? It was a man. It must have been a man."

The boy kept staring, his eye like a hard black pebble. He gave no sign of having heard Shan.

"It was in leopard shape," the dropka woman said. "If it needs a man shape," she added in a haunting tone, "it becomes a man shape."

"There is a demon from the old days," the herdsman said in his distant voice. "Hariti the child eater. Sometimes," he added, his voice fading as if he were losing all his strength, "it just gets hungry. After the first kill, it can't stop itself." Hariti was a demon of old Tibet, Shan knew, for whom monks once set aside a small portion of their daily food to slack her hunger for children.

His eyes rested on Lokesh, who stared at the boy. Lokesh laid his hand on the boy's scalp for a moment, then reached into his sack and produced a leather pouch, inside of which were several smaller pouches. He opened three of the small pouches, placed a pinch of powder from each into his hand, and emptied his hand into the steaming pot. "For the pain," Lokesh said. "He is in great pain."

"What can we do?" the woman asked.

Lokesh looked forlornly at Shan, then turned slowly back to the woman. "There are words that must be spoken," he said in a cracking voice.

The announcement seemed to strike the two dropka like a physical blow. The woman groaned and bent over, holding her abdomen. The herdsman's head sank into his hands. There are words that must be spoken. Lokesh meant the rites for the transition of a soul. The boy just kept staring at Shan with his confused, fading eye.

Suddenly the woman gave a frightened gasp. Shan looked up to see her staring over his shoulder. Gendun was there, wearing his Buddha smile. The herdsman called out in surprise and knelt with his forehead on the grass at Gendun's feet.

Shan realized that neither the herder nor his wife had noticed Gendun before. They might have thought that he was an apparition or that he had been spirited there by Lokesh. The lama put his hand on the herdsman's head and offered a prayer to the compassionate Buddha, then did the same with the woman, whose eyes, though still forlorn, grew calmer. *We had a real priest once*, the man had said. *But the Chinese took him*.

Gendun knelt by the boy and held his hand. Then Lokesh sat beside him, and Gendun put his free hand on Lokesh's head in a blessing for the healer. The lama gazed at the boy in silence for a long time as Shan began to wash the wounds.

"I have no prayers for this boy's god," he said to the woman in a soft, apologetic tone.

She cast an anxious glance at her husband. "We are teaching him our ways. He has a mala." With an effort that caused her obvious pain, she leaned forward and pushed the boy's sleeve up. She looked at his naked wrist in puzzlement. "It's gone. The demon took his rosary." She lowered her eyes from the lama, as if shamed. "He has wished to make the ways of Buddha his ways."

"But does he pray toward the sunset still?" Gendun asked.

The woman looked to the ground, as if frightened by the conversation. She shook her head slowly. "He said that that god let his clan die."

Shan stared at Gendun in confusion. The boy was Muslim. But how had Gendun seen it?

Instead of touching the boy's head, Gendun gently raised the back of the boy's hand to his own cheek. "Then I say a prayer that whatever god resides in this boy's heart gives him strength against the pain he knows from now and from the past and mindfulness for the path he must now follow."

In the silence a raven croaked nearby. They turned to see it sitting on top of the outcropping, studying them intently. The herder took a step forward as if to say something to the bird, then looked back at Gendun and remained silent, as if the lama would not approve.

"We have to leave," Jowa said hesitantly. "Go north. Into the Kunlun mountains." He cast an uncertain glance toward the herder.

"These people need help," Shan protested.

"Go north," the herder said, nodding his head vigorously. "We heard about the killings, it is why we fled across the mountains. They said you were going there, to save the children."

Jowa's eyes were full of impatience as he looked at the herder. Shan understood. Jowa knew that the dropka in this far corner of Tibet lived in a world of superstition, not far removed from the days before Buddhism when shamans ruled the land. Something terrible had happened to the boy, but to such people a falling rock could be an angry demon and a man shape with fur could easily be a wolf or a leopard. "We're going about the woman," Jowa said.

The dropka nodded again. "About Lau," he said. "Our Alta, he is one of her students."

Lokesh gasped and turned to Gendun. "Lau was this boy's teacher?" the lama asked.

"One of the zheli." The man nodded. "Lau introduced us when we said we wanted to help the children." The dropka kept his eyes on the boy as he spoke.

"The zheli?" Shan asked. It was not a Tibetan word, though the herder spoke in Tibetan. Nor was it Chinese.

But the man seemed not to have heard. Lokesh sighed and helped the boy drink the tea, then they carried the boy to the shelter of the rock, out of the wind, in a patch of sunlight. Lokesh listened again, at his heart, his shoulder, and his neck, then the old Tibetan shook his head and gazed at the boy, tears welling in his eyes.

They sat without speaking, helpless, as the light faded from the boy's eye. For an awful moment there was terror in his eye, as if suddenly, at last, he understood his fate. A sound came from the boy, one syllable and nothing more. It could have been the beginning of a question, or a prayer. It could have been simply an expression of pain. But there was no more, as if the effort had sapped the last of the boy's strength. The woman, crying, held the boy's hand to her cheek.

Shan knelt by Alta and leaned forward, struggling to find

words of comfort. But after a moment he dropped back, unable to speak, numbed by his helplessness and the cruelty that had been inflicted on the boy.

A hard dark silence descended over the dropka man, who kept opening and shutting his mouth as if he too wanted to speak, but grief had seized his tongue. At last, as the boy shifted his gaze to meet the herder's eyes, the dropka found his voice and began softly speaking about going to spring pastures and of finding flowers and young birds on the southern slopes, about nothing in particular, only pleasant memories of the dropka life. The boy's face grew peaceful as he listened.

Jowa, his face drawn with sorrow, left to keep watch on the rocks. Gendun and Lokesh offered prayers. The herder kept speaking in a near whisper, leaning over the boy. And in an hour, with a long soft groan, the boy named Alta died.

No one spoke for a long time, then finally the woman wiped the boy's face and covered it with the blanket.

"The custom of his people," Shan said slowly, not certain how the two dropka might react, "would be to bury him before sunset."

The dropka nodded, and Shan retrieved a shovel from the truck. As he dug, the woman gathered small rocks for a cairn to mark the grave. While the boy was laid to rest in his blanket, Gendun spoke in soft tones, using a Buddhist prayer for the dead.

The dropka man stood for only five minutes, then sighed heavily and stepped away to retrieve their horses.

Shan helped the woman stack the rocks at the head of the small mound. "It's a Kazakh word," she said to him when they had finished, referring to one of the Muslim peoples who lived on the northern side of the Kunlun range. "A zheli is a line tied between two trees, or two pegs, to tether a line of young animals. It's how the young ones learn about each other, and the world. Lau used the word for her classes with the orphans, her special children. Her tether for the orphans."

"Your husband said we were coming to save the children. Did he mean the zheli?"

The dropka woman nodded. "When that other boy died,

we knew to flee. But not," she sighed, with her eyes on the grave, "not soon enough."

A moan came from beside Shan, and Lokesh leaned forward. "Another boy?" he asked urgently. "Another of Lau's boys?"

"First Lau," she said. "Then a Kazakh boy near Yoktian town."

"Do you remember his name?" Lokesh asked in an urgent tone. Shan looked at his friend in puzzlement. It sounded as though Lokesh was interested in one particular boy.

The dropka shook her head. "There are twenty, maybe twenty-five children in the zheli. Kazakhs, Tibetans. And Uighurs," she added, referring to the largest of China's Muslim minorities. She turned and nodded at her husband, who led both horses forward. Their saddles had been removed. The man was looking to the north, toward the snowcaps of the Kunlun. "Alta," she said quietly. "Our Alta was a Kazakh."

"A lama," Shan said. "Do you know about a missing lama?"

The dropka shook his head. "Lamas have been missing here for many years," he said, obviously not understanding Shan's question. His gaze stayed on the mountains. "You must hurry," he added abruptly, in a hoarse, urgent tone. "Death keeps coming. This demon has found its way into the zheli and it won't stop killing."

Shan stared at the man in silence.

"Alta's soul is at risk," the dropka continued in his forlorn tone. "A boy like that, so unprepared." A gust of wind swept across them and seemed to snatch the man's words away. He stopped speaking and only looked toward Gendun. The dropka meant the boy's soul would be wandering, lost, without an anchor of faith or family, easy prey for the things that devoured souls.

Gendun returned the man's gaze for a moment, then spoke with Jowa, who brought him a piece of canvas and a broken pencil stub, the end of which Jowa charred in the fire. The lama retreated around the far corner of the rock and began chanting a mantra as he worked with the stub. Jowa listened and watched, then retrieved a tattered broom from the cargo bay and, wedging the head under a wheel, snapped off the handle.

When Gendun returned, he laid the cloth on the ground in front of the herders. The herdsman uttered a groan of surprise and pulled his wife's head up to see what the lama had brought them as Jowa began tying it to the broom handle. It was a charm, a very old charm, seldom used, a drawing of a scorpion with flame in its mouth. On the shoulders of the scorpion were heads of demons, with words along each side of the figures. A charm against demons, a charm that had been empowered by the words of a lama.

The man stood and nodded solemnly. "We will ransom a goat, Rinpoche," he said. "Our old priest, he would tell us to ransom a goat." Removing an animal from those readied for slaughter, usually by marking it with a ribbon around its ear, was a way of placating the deities that predated the Buddhists in Tibet.

"Then certainly," Gendun said with a somber tone, "ransom a goat."

As Jowa readied the truck, cranking the old engine to life and moving it onto the road, Shan looked up to see Gendun move back around the rock. He followed and found the lama seated on the grass, looking to the south, toward central Tibet and the hermitage where he had spent nearly his entire life.

"I fear it has already begun," the lama said, gesturing for Shan to sit beside him. "We have entered it, but we are too late."

"Entered what, Rinpoche?" Shan asked.

The lama looked over the mountains and sighed. "It has no name," Gendun said. "The home of demons who would seek to kill children." His voice was like shifting sand.

It was not an actual place, Shan knew, but a state of mind that Gendun spoke of, a place in a soul full of hate, a place a man like Gendun could never understand.

"It's a lonely land," Gendun said as he surveyed the windblown plateau. "It's where I was born," he declared.

"Here?" Shan asked, following the lama's gaze. "In the changtang?" Of all the wild, remote quarters of Tibet, the changtang plateau was the wildest and most remote.

Gendun nodded. "In the shadow of the Kunlun mountains. But when I was young, Xiao Shan, my parents gave me to monks because war came, and the monks took me to Lhadrung." Xiao Shan. Gendun used the old Chinese form of address for a younger person, the way his father or uncle might have called him. Little Shan. The lama looked toward a black cloud moving along the slope of the mountains, a snow squall perhaps. "I remember a happier place. Now"—the lama gestured toward the track and sighed—"now I think this road will take us to a place you should not be, Xiao Shan." It had the sound of an apology. What Gendun was saying was that so many murders meant the government would be involved. "I know how it is between you and the other Chinese," the lama said.

Three days earlier, Shan had returned with fuel for a campfire in time to overhear Jowa pleading with Gendun to send Shan back. "He was never released officially, just given permission to be free in Lhadrung County," the purba was explaining to the lama. "Outside Lhadrung he is still a criminal, an escapee. They can check things." When Gendun had not responded, Jowa raised his voice. "They will take him behind their jail," he said in an impatient tone. "They will put a bullet in his head. And the rest of us will be guilty of harboring a fugitive."

"Would you imprison us all with fear, then?" Gendun had quietly asked Jowa, then nodded as Shan approached with his armful of dung chips.

"It's just the government's way of honoring me," Shan had observed with a forced grin, thinking of the monks and lamas in the gulag who sometimes thanked their jailers for providing them with such an unrelenting test of their faith. The conversation had ended there, and Shan had dropped his own idea of asking Jowa to take Gendun back. Certainly Shan knew what the government would do if it captured him. But he also knew what it would do with Gendun, who did not simply have no official identity, but was practicing as an outlawed priest. There were special places for people like Gendun, places without light and heat, places where they sometimes did medical experiments, places where Party psychiatrists attempted techniques for molding grateful new proletarians out of reactionary priests.

I know how it is between you and the other Chinese.

Gendun was not just referring to the physical danger. Shan remembered their last lesson together, as the two sat on a rock outside the hermitage. For four months Gendun had been speaking to him about how release from prison was a relative thing, how three years of slave labor had made scars on his soul that would never fully heal, how the greatest danger to Shan was acting like an escapee, for an escapee was only a prisoner without a cell. When the lama had reluctantly suggested that the quickest way to recover would be for Shan to leave China, to go to a new land, Shan had shared with him a letter from a United Nations official dated two months earlier, offering to sponsor Shan for political asylum in the West if he would be willing to give public testimony about the slave camps and Beijing's systematic destruction of cultural artifacts. If Shan could get out of China. They might find a way out for him, said the purba who secretly brought the letter, but it could take a year, maybe two.

Shan extended his hand, still stained with the boy's blood. It was how they often spoke to each other, not with words, but with gestures and symbols. Children are dying, he was saying, and Gendun nodded in sad understanding. If Shan left now, he would never, no matter how far he ran, escape the haunting image of the dying boy, staring at him in silent, terrified confusion.

"The way that is told is not the constant way," Gendun said. The words had become something of a personal mantra between them since the first days they had spent together, when they had discovered that the words were not only in the Buddhist teachings of Gendun's life but also in the Taoist lessons of Shan's boyhood. Together they had recognized that Shan's path was far from anyone's constant path, that the withered spirit he had brought from China had for now found new roots in Tibet but, when the dead pieces were trimmed away, some of the old roots remained, tangled around the new. The way that is told is not the constant way. Gendun had sensed it too when sitting with the dying Muslim boy. They were on a path for which there was no map.

Jowa honked the horn on the truck. Gendun seemed not to hear. Shan saw that his hands were clutched together, the palms cupped as though cradling something.

The lama extended his hands, and as Shan offered his own hand, palm upward, Gendun dropped something into it. A feather. A two-inch-long feather, delicately patterned in brown and black at the base and snow white along its top half, the end faintly mottled with black spots, as if someone had sprayed it lightly with ink. Gendun watched, fascinated, as it drifted onto Shan's palm, then rose and walked to the truck.

Jowa drove the ancient truck relentlessly, as if being chased, bouncing over washouts, sliding in and out of deep ruts, stopping with an abrupt shudder when small boulders, released from the slope above, appeared before them in the illumination of the parking lights. Jowa refused to use the headlights. Soldiers sometimes patrolled the mountains at night.

Shan had put the feather in the gau he wore around his neck and now, as the truck lurched through the night, he sat with his hand around the gau, thinking. Was it a clue? A bidding of good fortune? As he looked at the dying boy in his mind's eye he realized that no, it may have been just a token of beauty to be carried as he moved closer to the ugliness of murder.

Hours later, as Shan and Lokesh climbed into the rear cargo bay after pushing still another boulder aside, Jowa joined them. He checked the barrels lashed to the metal frame of the bay. Most were filled with salt, a vital trading commodity of the region, taken from the salt beds of the central plateau that had supported trade in the region for centuries. Directly behind the cab, under a pile of oil-stained canvas, were two empty barrels, the barrels where Shan and Gendun would hide if they were stopped by a patrol. This was their third truck, for twice they had had to cross over ranges on horseback, led by guides who would speak only to Jowa. Each of the trucks had contained similar salt barrels and two empty ones, with skillfully made inserts that allowed three inches of salt to rest on top once the barrel was occupied. The cover of salt traders might be sufficient for Lokesh and Jowa, who had their papers, but Shan and Gendun would have no chance unless they hid.

Jowa helped wrap a blanket around Lokesh. Although

there was room in front, the old Tibetan had chosen to stay in the cargo bay with Shan for most of the journey. As Lokesh settled with his back against the cab, Jowa moved to the rear of the truck. He stood for a moment before stepping down, his hand braced against one of the ribs of the bay.

"Before sunrise," Jowa announced through the shadows, "someone will meet us."

"Who?" Shan asked.

"Someone to take us there," Jowa replied in the distant, almost resentful tone he always used with Shan.

"Where?"

"Where we have to be."

Shan sighed. "You still don't think I belong here."

"They told me to bring you. I am bringing you."

"Why?"

A shallow, bitter laugh escaped Jowa's lips. "You know them, maybe better than I. There is no why with the old lamas. The woman was destined to be killed. You were destined to go."

"No. I mean, why you? You could have said no."

"I know this region. Years ago, I helped watch the army up here."

"You could have said no," Shan repeated.

It took Jowa longer to answer this time. When he spoke his voice was softer, not friendly, but not resentful. "The lamas grow old. I do not know what Tibet will be without them. In twenty, thirty years, who will go and sit in the hermit cells, who will go to live inside a mountain because the land's soul needs help?"

"Maybe you will."

"No. Not me. Not those like me. The Chinese have taught me new ways. I am contaminated with hate," he said matter-of-factly, as if speaking of a physical handicap. "I have fired a gun." He looked at the moon, and for the first time Shan thought he saw sadness on the purba's face. "How could I go and sit in a mountain if I have fired a gun?" It was a question Jowa had obviously asked himself many times. "And who's left?" He stepped out of the truck but lingered in the moonlight. "When they took my monk's license away, and I began to resist," he said, speaking toward the moon, "I thought then that the whole problem with Tibet was not enough resistance. It's like we talk ourselves out of so many fights that we no longer stand for anything." He shook his head and looked away, toward the darkened peaks. "Now . . ." He shrugged. "In prison I decided that there weren't enough of us left to fight, that all we could do was see that the lamas would be protected, so Beijing would not kill the old ways. But I didn't stop to think. The old ways are the lamas, and the lamas are as mortal as the rest of us. We can try to stop Beijing but we can't stop time. If the lamas don't survive, if what they do doesn't survive, then what's the point?"

Shan realized that in his own way Jowa was indeed explaining why he was escorting the unlikely trio on their enigmatic mission. Through the moonlight Shan could see him shrug again. "They almost never ask us for anything. It is impossible to say no."

But Shan knew that Jowa understood something else— that nothing the lamas did was random, that they didn't ask Jowa because he could drive a truck or even because he was a purba who knew the region, but because he was Jowa.

"The herdsman and his wife," Shan said as Jowa turned to leave. "How did they know? It's supposed to be a secret. I thought the purbas brought the word to Lhadrung, and only they knew we were coming."

"They did. The purbas know how to keep a secret."

"They said we were coming to save the children. Two boys have already died."

"An old woman died, and a lama disappeared. That's all I was told." Jowa disappeared around the corner of the truck. A moment later the heavy engine roared to life.

Shan retrieved a hat from the floor, a tattered quilted army hat with heavy earflaps. He pulled it over his head and settled against one of the barrels on the side so he could watch the moon. The purbas had brought the secret of the woman's death. But now there was another secret moving south through the dropka, a warning about children and death and about the strangers from Lhadrung coming to help.

They passed by a waterfall that glistened like diamonds

falling through the night. A small throaty buzz came from nearby. Lokesh was sleeping. Shan put his hands deep in his jacket pockets, for warmth, and his right hand closed around the small jar Gendun had given him that night when they began their journey, a jar of the consecrated sand taken from the mandala. He gripped it tightly as he gazed into the sky.

The moon that Shan watched was not the same moon he had known in the lands below, in the China of his first life. Like so much else in his second life, his Tibetan re-incarnation, the moon was more absolute than the one he had known in Beijing. In Tibet it was so brilliant and pure, so close that one could believe the old tales that drifting souls sometimes got caught in its mountains.

There were nights when he could get lost in such a moon, let himself be absorbed for hours in its beauty. But tonight the dead boy haunted him and kept him from the beauty. *You must hurry*, the man had said. *Death keeps coming.* To anyone else the words would have been a warning to flee, to run away from death. But for Shan they had meant hurry, go to meet it. A wave of helplessness swept over him, and he knew that his face wore the same sad confusion the Tibetans sometimes wore. Even some of the lamas had shown it when they had dispatched him seven nights before. They might as well have used the same words as the dropka, for all they had told him, for all Gendun still told him. *You must hurry. Death keeps coming.* That was all the lamas understood. Murder was an unknown land to them, and Shan was their ambassador.

CHAPTER 2

After midnight, as they stopped once again to move rocks from the road, Shan thought he heard something. A metallic rattle, a machine noise, coming from far ahead of them. He heard only a snippet of sound, then it was gone, so quickly he wasn't sure he had heard it at all. Sound traveled unpredictably in the high, rarified atmosphere. It could have been a truck on the lonely road ahead of them. It could have been a helicopter behind them. It could have been a plane in the far distance. No one spoke about the noise, but when they finished Jowa checked the two empty barrels with his hand lantern and insisted that Gendun switch places with Lokesh. If he slammed the brakes hard three times, it was the signal for Gendun and Shan to hide.

But when the need arose there was no time for a signal. Shan woke from a deep slumber as the truck lurched to a stop, then heard Jowa calling out in anger to someone on the road.

He quickly helped Gendun into one of the barrels and covered it, then peered over the top of the truck cab as Jowa switched on their headlights. Half a dozen men stood by a heavy red truck, the size of their own, though much newer. The engine hood of the truck was braced open, and strewn across the road were a spare tire and metallic objects that could have been engine parts.

They were not Public Security, Shan saw with relief, nor the army. He could see Jowa speaking with one of the men, a big, broad-shouldered Han Chinese wearing a white shirt.

Jowa was pointing at the red truck and at the road, which was blocked by the tire and parts.

Two of the men, in light brown shirts and pants of matching color, bent over the tire in the road, glancing frequently toward the man in the white shirt. Another stood with a foot on the bumper of the red truck, watching the sky. And a pair stood just behind the man who spoke with Jowa. They were all Han, and though they did not carry themselves as stiffly as soldiers, they had the quick, hunting eyes of soldiers. Shan looked back at the truck. An emblem was on the driver's door, what appeared in the dim light to be two outstretched arms, joined at the top.

Shan silently climbed down in the shadows and inched his way along the far side of their own truck, out of the strangers' view, until he reached the passenger door, where he ventured another look over the hood. What was it, he thought, what was so peculiar about these men? They were well dressed. They all wore the same trim brown clothing, except for the white-shirted man speaking with Jowa. They had no visible weapons, but three had large wrenches extending out of their pockets, and one held a ball-peen hammer. Two had heavy wooden sticks like truncheons hanging from their belts. Inside the cab of the truck he saw a figure in the passenger seat, the face lost in the night. A bright orange ember moved to and from the face. A plume of smoke rose from the window. Shan looked back at the man who watched the sky. The demon had been called away by lightning, the woman had said. Demons used lightning to speak with each other.

They needed a few more minutes to complete repairs, Shan heard the white-shirted man explain to Jowa. But no one seemed to be working on the engine. The man asked where Jowa was heading. North, was Jowa's reply, north to sell salt. The two men behind the speaker began to move away, distancing themselves from Jowa as though wary of his reach, then circling about, toward the Tibetans' truck.

"Can we help you?" Jowa asked loudly, watching the two men as they approached his open door.

"Nothing up north," the stranger in the white shirt observed in an accusing tone, still the only one of his company to speak. "Nothing but bandits."

Lokesh climbed out of the truck and stepped to Jowa's side. The man in the white shirt stared at him intently, surveying him from head to toe.

Shan realized he could be mistaken. Public Security didn't always wear uniforms. But Public Security carried submachine guns, not wrenches.

"You a bandit, old man?" the big-shouldered Han asked with a lightless grin. His deep voice echoed off the rock-face. "Where you going, sneaking about like this in the middle of the night?"

"Salt," Lokesh replied in a dry, croaking voice, and Shan saw him do something he had often seen him do in prison. He began shaking his head, and then his arm, as if he could not control it, as if he suffered from a disease of the aged. "Good Tibetan salt. Going as far as it takes to sell our salt," Lokesh said. Still shaking, he stepped toward the man, who retreated a step as if scared of him. "You should buy it so we can turn around and go home. This old truck hurts my bones," Lokesh groaned. "I want to go home."

The Han walked a complete circle around Lokesh, studying him again, then gave a shallow laugh. "Takes papers to sell things, old man. Bet you don't have papers. That's why you travel at night."

Shan's mind raced. If the strangers were bandits, what did the Tibetans have of value that might appease them? An old pair of binoculars. A week's supply of food. Perhaps the truck itself, and its barrels of salt. He had a nightmarish vision of the strangers driving away with Gendun still in his barrel.

The two men continued to circle the truck, aiming hand lanterns into the cargo bay. The man in white glanced back at the cab of his truck, toward the glowing cigarette that hung in the shadow.

Suddenly Shan was in the beams of the two brilliant lanterns held behind him. He stood like a dumb animal trapped by the light and let himself be led, one man pulling each elbow, to the man in the white shirt.

The man circled Shan as he had Lokesh, then stood in front of him, disappointment obvious on his face. He leaned close to Shan's ear. "Don't turn your back on the damned locusts," he said in a low voice. "They'll hit you with a stone and call it an avalanche." Locusts. The term was an epithet used by the Chinese for Tibetans, for the sound they made when chanting their mantras. The man looked back with a broad smile, apparently pleased with his suggestion, then stood in front of the three men.

"Don't think we can let you go north tonight," he announced. The men who had pretended to work on the tire rose, as if the words were a cue.

Shan glanced at Jowa, whose body was tightening like a coiled spring.

Shan put his hands in his pockets and shuffled forward, standing in front of Jowa. "You'll have to," he said in a good-natured tone.

The man in the white shirt seemed amused by Shan's announcement. He pulled a pack of cigarettes from his pocket and lit one. "Why so, comrade?" He turned his body sideways, as if to make sure Shan saw the men assembled behind him.

"Because the People's Liberation Army is chasing us," Shan said matter-of-factly.

The man's smile broadened. "The three of you and an antique truck," he said with a skeptical air.

"You know the army," Shan shot back. "Sometimes they just do it for practice."

As Shan returned the man's steady gaze his smile began to fade. He nodded at one of the men beside him, who bolted toward the truck, disappearing into the shadows by the passenger's door. He surveyed Shan, Lokesh, and Jowa once more, as if being sure he could remember their faces, then looked at the cab a moment and snapped his fingers.

His men leapt into action. In less than a minute the road was cleared.

"Be careful, comrades," the man warned in an icy voice. "Bandits are around every corner."

Jowa stepped toward the cab with a sideways motion, his eyes jumping from man to man. Shan pulled Lokesh back to the truck, and seconds later they were in the cab and driving away.

They drove up switchbacks over a high ridge for a quarter hour, then stopped just past the top to help Gendun out of his barrel. As Lokesh slid out of the cab, Jowa touched

Shan's arm. "I don't know who they were," he said. "I thought soldiers at first."

Shan realized Jowa was asking him to explain. "We're close to India and the road to Pakistan. There are smugglers. Maybe they were waiting for a shipment." Jowa pulled out his map and climbed out to study it in the parking lights. Shan turned to look through the rear window. No one was in the cargo bay. He looked in the side mirror. In the moonlight he saw Lokesh, sitting alone on the ground. Shan jumped out and jogged to the back of the truck.

Lokesh was holding his beads near his chest, counting them quickly. Shan climbed into the cargo bay. The hiding barrels were empty. Gendun was gone.

Shan stood with his hands clenched on the side of the barrel they had hidden Gendun in, his heart pounding wildly. A small white square of cloth was tied to the board above Gendun's barrel. A khata, a prayer scarf. Shan untied it and stared at it in confusion.

"Where is he?" Shan called out in alarm and darted to Lokesh, shaking his shoulder.

Lokesh looked up to the sky, slowly surveying the stars, as if they might show sign of Gendun. "He is gone now," he observed in a tiny voice.

Shan ran up the road a hundred feet and called Gendun's name, twisting the khata around his fingers. The sound flushed a bird from its roost and it flew across the face of the moon. He turned and saw that Jowa was in the bay now, staring at the empty barrels. Shan jogged back and squatted at Lokesh's side. "Where is Rinpoche?" he repeated desperately. "Was he taken by those men?"

"Lokesh, you must understand—" Jowa called out from behind Shan, "he's our—" His voice drifted off as he looked at the dark horizon. The wind seemed to rise, a cold wind that hinted of snow.

"He could be lost," Shan said in a brittle tone. "He could have fallen out of the truck on the steep slopes."

"He must have been taken," Jowa declared. "The bastards in the red truck. And we just drove away."

"Sometimes," Lokesh said with a long sigh, "a lama just gets called away." His voice was calm, but his eyes were forlorn. He saw the khata in Shan's hand, its end fluttering in the wind, and reached for it. Shan let it go. The old Tibetan laid it on his thigh and stroked it with a small, grateful smile, as though he needed reassurance that the Gendun who had traveled with them had been the flesh and blood Gendun. Shan dropped to the ground beside Lokesh, but his heart felt too heavy to pray.

Gendun was with the strange men in the red truck, the ones who acted like Public Security, who could chew up and digest a man like Gendun in hours if they chose. At best, Gendun was alone in the wilderness of mountains. Gendun, who had hardly known the outside world until seven days before. With a pang he remembered the first time he had met Gendun, hidden away in his hermitage. He had marveled over the watch on Shan's wrist. When Shan had let him examine it, he had listened to it, and shook his head, not just for the wonder of its workings but that people would think they needed such things. "You Chinese," he had said with a grin and a shake of his head.

Jowa turned the truck around and drove slowly in the direction they had come as Shan stood on the sideboard and held onto the mirror mount, calling out Gendun's name. Jowa turned on the headlights. They drove for a mile, then Jowa stopped and turned off the engine. Jowa sat at the wheel, gripping it tightly, torment twisting his face. Shan looked at him a moment. Did Jowa's pain come because he was a warrior who could find no enemy or because of what he had said before, that if the lamas didn't survive, there was no point in continuing?

"What if it just ends like this?" Jowa asked in a near whisper. "The last of the old ones just disappears. And the world stumbles on, a body without a soul." He looked out at a tall precipice that rose toward the heavens, a vast, darker shadow in a landscape of shadow. "What if he were the last one?" he asked the mountains, so low Shan barely heard.

"They said a lama was missing," Shan reminded Jowa. "Lau was killed and a lama was missing."

Jowa gave a small, stiff nod. "So your demon's appetite just gets bigger and bigger," he said in a hollow voice. "Three killings now, and two lamas gone."

They drove slowly back to Lokesh, who still prayed at the roadside. Jowa got out and sat with him in the moonlight, lighting a stick of incense as Shan climbed into the cargo bay.

"What is it?" the purba called out when he saw Shan emerge with the tattered canvas bag that carried his meager belongings.

"I will go back," Shan said. "I will go no further until I am sure he is safe."

"You can't," Jowa said.

"I have to." Shan squatted by Lokesh, who looked at him with pain in his eyes.

"You can't because they sent you," Jowa protested. "Because Gendun said you're needed in the north."

"That woman and the boys are dead," Shan said. "They are dead, and Gendun is not. Not yet."

Lokesh, his eyes now locked on the ember at the tip of the incense, slowly shook his head. "Those evil men were meant to be on the road tonight," he said. "And Gendun was meant to disappear tonight."

"And maybe I too was meant to disappear," Shan suggested.

"No," Lokesh said. "You are meant to go on." The certainty in his voice rang like a bell.

"Lokesh, my friend," Shan said, and he knelt now, putting his hand on Lokesh's shoulder. "I have been torn apart and patched back together so many times I am like a ragged old quilt. There are still so many pieces of me that don't fit together that sometimes I wonder my soul doesn't burst apart." He sensed the anguish in his voice, but he could not hide it.

"And you think Gendun has to put them together, Xiao Shan?" Lokesh asked.

"I don't know." He looked at Jowa, who stared at him, his face seeming to swirl with emotion. "But I know that of all the world I have seen, the lamas are the best part of it."

Shan stood, holding the straps of his bag, which still sat at his feet. He looked over the mountains, the snowcaps glowing in the moonlight. The wind blew steady and cold, reminding him that Gendun had nothing but his robe and a thin piece of canvas against the elements. An animal howled in the distance.

"We will wait here for Xiao Shan," Lokesh said to Jowa, as though Shan had already left, and raised the stick of incense in his hand as if it were a torch. "Xiao Shan will come back." He spoke as though Shan had already gone. "Because somewhere, on a high mountain, he will realize something. We are not responsible for Gendun. Gendun is responsible for us."

Shan realized that his fingers had closed around his gau, the box that carried his prayer and his feather. Gendun had sensed something that afternoon when he had given him the token, when he had emphasized to Shan that their trip could end in unexpected ways. Slowly, almost unconsciously, he sat down with his companions.

They prayed until the stick burned out, then they climbed back into the truck. Shan stood in the back, fiercely gripping one of the ribs of the bay, watching the blackened mountains as they moved on into the night.

He slept fitfully, often awakened with nightmarish visions of Gendun in peril, Gendun lying broken at the bottom of a cliff, Gendun in the hands of Public Security, interrogators standing by with electric cattle prods. He was roused when the truck made a sudden, wide turn onto a rough gravel track, then drifted off again, the eastern sky already grey with the hint of dawn.

It wasn't the morning light that broke the deep slumber that finally came, nor the stopping of the truck, but the braying of a large animal at the side of the vehicle, a sound so explosive that Shan sprang out of his sleep and slammed his head into one of the opposite barrels.

"End of the road," Jowa called out from behind the truck, where he stood with Shan's canvas bag. Shan stumbled to the open tailgate, holding his throbbing head, and nearly stumbled onto Lokesh as he stepped down. The old Tibetan was bent over at the rear of the truck, peering around the corner with a glint in his eye. He acknowledged Shan with an anxious nod and looked back around the truck.

As he surveyed the new landscape, Shan touched his forehead, absently noting that the fingers came away with a trace of blood. In the dim dawn light he could see that they were in what seemed to be a maze of huge boulders and outcroppings. Pockets of snow lay scattered among the rocks. No, not snow, he realized as he stared at one of the bright patches. It was sand.

He stepped around the truck and froze. Standing eight feet away was a tall brown creature with a long face and two large humps on its back, wearing a leather harness. A Bactrian camel. Lokesh ventured forward, shielding himself behind Shan as he peered over Shan's shoulder. The camel looked up at them, snorted, emitted another loud bray, then shook itself, creating an unexpected jingle. Small bells were fastened to the ends of the harness.

Lokesh burst into a low, wheezing laughter. Shan turned and stared in confusion at his old friend. The laughter could mean that Lokesh was scared, or confused, or even, on rare occasions, that he was filled with joy.

An angry syllable shot out from the shadows behind them. The camel seemed to recognize the voice or the word, and took two steps forward with an expectant look. Shan looked back for the source of the voice. He could see past the boulders more clearly now, into a gravel wash that descended slowly through the maze of outcroppings toward a series of smaller rocky ridges and long, low mountains covered with gravel and clumps of grey-green vegetation.

"Ai yi!" Lokesh exclaimed in a loud whisper, and stepped closer to Shan as though for protection. The smaller boulders were coming to life. The rising sun had given shape to several of the patches of darkness Shan had seen by the rocks. They were flesh, not stone, silent figures huddled under cloaks of gray and brown. They began to rise slowly, hesitantly, as if the sun's warmth had stirred them from hibernation. But as the faces drew up Shan could see they were not sluggish, only wary.

"Jowa!" one called, and stood up straight, throwing off his cloak. It was a Tibetan, a man several years younger than Jowa, wearing a strip of maroon cloth tied around his sleeve. It was a mark of defiance for monks broken by the government, a swath of color marking the robe that only those with a certificate from the Bureau of Religious Affairs were legally permitted to wear. The Tibetan looked from Jowa back toward a tall man in a fleece vest whose thick black hair was speckled with grey and partially covered with a brimless brown cap. Lingering in the shadows at the tall man's side was a third figure, thin as a post, a man with a stern face and restless eyes, who was wearing denim jeans and canvas running shoes. His nose was crooked, as if it had been broken.

The young Tibetan sprang forward and embraced Jowa, who quickly turned and pointed over the mountaintops, toward the direction they had come. Jowa produced a stub of a pencil from his pocket and began marking on a crude map the youth pulled from his pocket. The youth nodded when Jowa was done and climbed into the driver's seat of the truck. A moment later the engine sputtered to life, and with a reluctant groan the old Jiefang edged forward, then gained speed as it maneuvered up the twisting track that led back over the mountains.

"He will watch for Gendun," Jowa said to Shan in a hollow tone. "If he sees Tibetans on the road, he will ask them to watch also."

As the truck disappeared, Shan fought a wave of emotion. The truck was his last connection to Gendun, the last link to the new life he had built in the high ranges of central Tibet, to the monks who had become the only real family he had known since the Red Guard had killed his father more than thirty years before. It was time for Shan to leave the mountains, one of the monks had told him that night at the mandala. Not forever, perhaps, but for a while, to gain distance. To understand who he was, the monk had meant. Shan wasn't a monk, though he lived with monks. But he also wasn't Chinese anymore, not a Beijing Chinese. Consider it a pilgrimage, another monk had said. But Buddhists were sent to the sacred peak of Mount Kalais or other holy sites where the spirits of deities resided. Shan's pilgrimage was to death and confusion, to places where perhaps only sorrow and distrust resided.

They had meant to honor him with their trust, he knew. But in that moment he felt no honor. He felt only fatigue and fear. Fear for Gendun. Fear for the boys who had been killed for reasons no one knew. Fear that he would be stopped before he fulfilled the trust. Imagine you are in a spirit palace, one of his Buddhist teachers had once said, with a hundred doors before you. Only one door is yours, but how long will it take to find it? He sensed the hundred doors today, and all but one led to failure. He fought the tempation to run for the truck, to catch it and climb back into his barrel.

The two strangers stepped forward, then froze at the sound of hooves rushing on the gravel slope below. A rider wearing a tattered felt coat and red wool cap appeared on a brown and white horse, dismounting in a fluid vaulting action before the horse had stopped. The rider stood silently in front of the front of the older man, offering a respectful nod, then pulled off the cap. It was a young woman, with black hair tied in two short braids behind her ears. The camel brayed, then bolted toward her, pushing past Shan and Lokesh so abruptly that Lokesh was knocked to the ground. The woman gave the camel a brief but affectionate stroke on its head, then trotted to Lokesh, extending a hand to help him to his feet.

"Grandfather," she said softly in Tibetan, using the term in the old style, as a form of respect for elders. "Please forgive her, she is but a bata, a yearling, and still has much to learn." Her voice was filled with a quiet strength.

The high-pitched wheezing laughter seemed to overtake Lokesh again. "I saw one in a painting once," he said, still sitting in the dirt, shaking the woman's proffered hand as if she had intended to introduce herself. "I said it was one of the mythical creatures, a shape some deity had taken in someone's vision." His grin seemed to encompass his entire face. "My wife said no, it was just a horse with a broken back."

"Oh no, grandfather," the woman said, with twinkling eyes. She was young, Shan saw, no more than twenty-five, and where the rising sun hit her hair there seemed to be red in it. "She's just a donkey who ate two turtles."

The woman gently lifted Lokesh by his shoulder, brushing away the gravel from his back. The two remaining men began moving quickly, retrieving another camel and several small, sturdy horses from behind the rocks. The older man checked the saddles of two of the horses, then led the animals toward Shan and Lokesh, but stopped as he reached the woman's side. "You can't be here, Jakli," he said sternly. "It is too dangerous for you."

The woman he had called Jakli took one step toward him. "She was my friend, Akzu," she said soberly. "She was my teacher."

The words brought a wince to the man's face. "You owe that woman nothing," he said. "Look at what she did to you."

"I still owe her much, despite things," the woman called Jakli said, with a strange combination of defiance and pain in her voice.

The man called Akzu gazed at her for a long time, then a sad smile grew on his face. "Come here, girl," he said, and opened his arms. "Damn them all for keeping you from us. It's been too long."

As the woman embraced him, Akzu still smiled, but his face clouded, as if her presence reminded him of something he had hoped to forget.

Shan studied their new guides as Akzu began to load their bags onto the young camel. The animal had been a shock to Shan, not because he had never seen one, but because he had not appreciated how far they had traveled. This land was different. The people were different. Neither of the two men had the features of Tibetans. They had gone north, Shan reminded himself, so deep into the Kunlun mountains that they had reached a new people. As if in confirmation, the man at the camel called to the man with the bent nose in a language unintelligible to Shan. It was a dialect of the Turkic tongue spoken by the Muslims of China's far west. They were Uighur, Shan thought, or perhaps Kazakh, like the boys who had died.

The man with the bent nose stepped closer, his hand on the neck of the camel. "You're the one," he said in Mandarin to Jowa. "The one who knows about Public Security?"

Jowa glanced at Shan, discomfort obvious in his eyes.

"They told us—" the man pressed, "they said that you know the secrets of the Public Security Bureau."

Jowa frowned. "The last time I was in prison," he said

in a reluctant voice, "my cell mate had worked for Public Security. In Lhasa—part of an experiment in bringing Tibetans into their ranks. The experiment failed, and they had to put him somewhere. He knew it would be years before he was freed, and he decided to share his knowledge so his time as a knob wouldn't be wasted."

The man laughed, as if it was a good joke. "They say you destroyed a convoy of Public Security trucks."

"They happened to be parked in the wrong place. An avalanche started."

"But you did it."

"It was the rocks and snow that did the damage," Jowa said soberly. "Sometimes the mountain spirits get angry." The man laughed again. Jowa cast another awkward glance at Shan. The purbas had painfully learned not to ambush the Chinese overtly or commit obvious sabotage. There was always severe retaliation, and almost always it was against the innocent.

"They say you can beat Public Security checkpoints," the man continued, stepping to Jowa's side, helping to lift his bag onto the camel. "Even electronic checkpoints."

The words seemed to surprise Jowa as much as Shan. The man was traveling in the style of the seventeenth century and speaking of computer software security systems from the twenty-first century.

"Invisible checkpoints are not much different from physical ones," Jowa replied, still with his hesitant tone. "You just need to know how to find them." Shan watched in confusion from the shadow by the truck. Only Jowa and the Tibetan who had driven away were purbas, but the others knew purba secrets.

The camel shook its head, pulling the reins from its neck.

"Good for you," the man said, slapping Jowa on the back. "Good for us."

As the man with the crooked nose bent to retrieve the reins from the ground a paper fell from his pocket. A map. The wind tossed the map into the air, then dropped it into the circle of sunlight at the center of the clearing a few feet from Shan. He stepped into the light and picked it up. As he did so a brittle silence descended over the two

Muslim men, who seemed to notice his features for the first time. He extended the map to the man with the crooked nose, who merely stared at him with anger in his eyes. Akzu muttered a curse under his breath. Shan stuffed the map under a harness strap on the camel and stepped back toward his bag. He had taken only two steps when the man with the bent nose blocked his path.

"Who's this then?" the man snapped, speaking to Jowa but staring at Shan. He aimed a thick finger at Shan like a gun, then raised it and pushed Shan's hat off his head.

"My name is Shan."

Shan retrieved his hat and placed it back on his head. The man knocked it off again.

"You're Chinese," the man said in an accusing tone.

"In some ways," Shan answered calmly. He picked up his hat again. As soon as he pulled it over his ears the man knocked it off a third time.

"He's the one we're bringing," Jowa said, but he did not move from the side of his horse. "Because of the woman Lau."

"No one said anything about a Chinese coming."

"And I never expected a Uighur," Jowa rejoined. "They said Kazakhs would be here."

The man gestured toward the older man. "The Kazakhs and the Uighurs have many mutual interests. And we both have many mutual interests with the purbas."

Akzu stepped between them, alert, his eyes shifting from Shan to the Uighur. "We have more important work now," the older man said to the Uighur and gestured him away from Shan. Shan stared at the strangers. They wanted Jowa, he realized. Jowa who knew how to beat Public Security patrols.

"We can find our own way," a calm voice said behind him. It was Lokesh. He retrieved Shan's hat from the ground and held it.

"Fine," the Uighur said, and pointed his arm toward the foothills below them. "Northwest. Just keep calling and Lau's ghost will find you."

No one spoke as Shan and Lokesh shouldered their bags and began walking in the direction the man had pointed.

Jowa muttered something under his breath and began to follow.

The young woman retrieved her horse's reins and jogged to catch up with Shan. "My name is Jakli," she said, taking Shan's bag. "I will take you to Auntie Lau."

Shan offered a grateful nod. "I need to understand how she died."

Jakli nodded. "She drowned in the river, that's what the prosecutor thinks." She cast an uncertain glance toward the older man. "But it's not true," she said quickly. "Lau was shot in the head like an execution. The prosecutor would just make lies about it if she got the body. So we hid Lau. It would be the place for you to start."

Before Shan could reply, a horse shot past them. The Uighur, now mounted, blocked their path. "You have enough trouble, Jakli," he said to the woman. "You can't share secrets. You don't know this Chinese."

"If the old priests sent this man, then he is the one we need," Jakli said to the rider. The determination in her voice seemed as sharp as a blade.

"Old priests get soft," the man muttered.

Jakli's eyes flared. "After decades in prison for defending their faith they get soft? After watching their gompas leveled to dust they get soft? After their thumbs are cut off to stop them from doing their rosaries they get soft?" She touched Lokesh's arm and looked into his eyes. "Grandfather," she said. "You were a priest."

"For a while," Lokesh said, studying the woman with a toothy grin.

"Tell him. How many years in prison?"

"Thirty," he said, still grinning.

Jakli took his hand and held it in both of hers. She gazed at Lokesh, who stared at her in surprise, then she looked at the Uighur. "They don't get soft," Jakli said, the challenge still in her voice. "They get wise. They learn to see things. And if all our priests are gone, then we have to borrow our wisdom."

"I see things," the man said sourly.

"No. You are blind." She turned toward Shan. "This man is called Fat Mao," she said, gesturing toward the thin Uighur. "He thinks his enemy is the Chinese. But our enemies are murderers and tyrants and liars, whatever they look like." There was a cold fury in the woman's words that surprised Shan. But it did not seem to surprise the man on the horse. He winced, as if recognizing the fire he had ignited. With a pull on his reins he retreated a few feet.

"Shan has ways about him," Lokesh declared. "He can see through to the truth when others cannot."

"Great," the man on the horse ventured, keeping his distance from Jakli. "People are dying. The clans are being destroyed, and you bring us an oracle."

"He used the truth to free this man from prison," Jowa said, gesturing back toward Lokesh. "And last spring when a monk was about to be executed for murder, Shan found the truth. Because of what he saw the monk was freed and the real murderers were executed."

"You mean he got more Tibetans executed."

"No. Those executed were Chinese officials and Chinese soldiers."

The Uighur stared at Jowa, then at Shan, as if uncertain whether to believe the words. Lokesh nodded his head vigorously.

"Still," a voice came from behind them. It was the old Kazakh, the one called Akzu. He stepped to the side of the Uighur's horse. "There is no kindness in your voice for this man," he said to Jowa.

Jowa looked toward the ground. "The Chinese destroyed my family and killed my lama," he said tersely. It was the first time Shan had ever heard Jowa speak of his suffering. "But I know the lamas who asked for him to come here. If they asked, I would escort the Chairman himself."

The old man sighed audibly. "But we cannot take you to Lau. It is unimportant now. Lau will forgive us."

"I will take them, Akzu." Jakli said. "I said so."

"I know what you said, niece, but things are different now. We need this man," Akzu said, nodding toward Jowa.

"I mean, I said it to Auntie Lau," Jakli said. "I vowed it after her death."

The announcement brought a grimace to Akzu's face. He rubbed the nose of the horse, then looked at Jakli with pain in his eyes.

But before he could speak the Uighur called out in

alarm. "Soldiers!" he shouted, and in the next instant Shan heard what had alerted him, a low, rapid throbbing in the sky that was rapidly increasing in volume. Akzu darted to the camels and grabbed their reins, urging them back into the shadows between the rocks as Jowa and the Uighur did the same with the horses. Jakli leapt off her own mount and grabbed Lokesh's hand, pulling him urgently between two large boulders. Shan glimpsed the machine as he joined them in the shadows, one of the sleek grey helicopters of the People's Liberation Army. It flew low, following the contour of the mountains, and passed only two hundred yards overhead as they hugged the rocks.

No one spoke for a long time after the machine disappeared over the next ridge. "The bastards," the Uighur said at last, then glanced at Akzu. "We'll take the short way home."

Shan saw that Jakli remained frozen, staring at the horizon, fear in her green eyes, but he sensed that the fear was not for herself, but for others, others who might be caught exposed in the mountains.

"I am sorry, niece," Akzu said to her, putting his hand on her shoulder. "I know we said we would help about Lau when we laid her to rest, but things have changed. The Red Stone clan is betrayed."

The announcement shook Jakli from her paralysis. "Betrayed?" she asked, worry creasing her face. "Betrayed how?"

"That pig of a man named Bajys. He took our hospitality and lied to us. He killed the boy with him and ran to the Chinese." Akzu threw a meaningful glance at Fat Mao. "He will tell them things, to buy their protection."

"A boy died?" Shan asked. No one seemed to hear him.

Jakli collapsed onto a nearby rock, her face draining of color.

"Not one of our clan," Akzu said to her. "One of Lau's children. A good boy, named Khitai, only nine years old. The horses liked him. Bajys shot him in the head."

A sharp, painful gasp came from Shan's side. Lokesh was holding his belly, as if he had been kicked. "The boy Khitai?" he asked. He put a hand on Shan's shoulder as though he were in danger of falling. His face seemed to sag. "The boy Khitai was with you?"

Jakli and Akzu looked to Jowa, then Shan, for an explanation. The first boy to die had been with Akzu's clan. When the dropka had spoken about the first killing, Lokesh had asked the name of the boy. Now when Akzu spoke it, he recognized the name. As if perhaps Lokesh had come because of Khitai.

"It was a Kazakh boy," Akzu said with a confused look at Lokesh.

Lokesh seemed not to have heard. He made a small moaning noise and drifted away.

"I will take you to Lau," Jakli said to Shan once more. "Akzu will take your friend Jowa to the Red Stone camp."

Shan turned toward Lokesh, who knelt on a rock now, facing the snow-capped peaks, surveying the skyline. Shan knew somehow that he was searching for Gendun, that suddenly Lokesh needed Gendun. It had already begun, Gendun had said. He must have meant the killing of children, as if he had expected it, or as if he had hoped for Shan to stop it by explaining Auntie Lau's death.

As he approached his old friend he saw that Lokesh had his hands together, and he thought at first it was a mudra offering. But it wasn't a mudra, he saw as he knelt beside Lokesh. The Tibetan was simply twisting his fingers in some silent agony that Shan could not understand. Shan put his hand on the old man's back and spoke comforting words. But Lokesh seemed not to hear him.

"This boy," Shan said, turning back to Jakli. "He was one of the zheli?"

She looked at him in puzzlement. "Yes. He was one of the orphans, part of the zheli class Lau organized from the school in Yoktian. They're more than orphans; not only do they have no family, they have no clan left. But the zheli is not officially part of the school. More like a substitute clan, in place of the ones they lost."

Shan turned to his old friend. "Did you know this boy? Did Gendun know this boy?"

Lokesh slowly shook his head from side to side, still looking to the mountains with a desperate expression.

Jakli looked from Shan to Lokesh, her face clouded with confusion.

"Khitai," Lokesh blurted out in a despondent tone, but this time it was not just another expression of pain. It seemed he was trying to call the dead boy, with the anguish of a father calling a lost son.

"Why a child?" Shan asked in an anguished voice. "The children are just—" His tongue failed him.

When he looked into Jakli's face he saw anger growing on it. "They are all that's left," she said—meaning, Shan knew, all that was left after the torment and persecution that had destroyed their clans.

"I never believed in demons," a brittle voice said over his shoulder. It was Akzu. He was looking at Lokesh with a sad, knowing expression, as if he recognized something in the old Tibetan's countenance. "My grandfather told me demons slept in the earth, that sometimes they awoke with a blood hunger that could not be stopped, that there were seasons for demons and destruction, just as there are seasons for flowers and creation, and when their time came they could not be stopped any more than the rising sun could be stopped, that all you could do was suffer and wait for them to satisfy their appetite. I told him I didn't believe in demons, that it was just the myths of the old ones.

"But then when my grandfather wouldn't move his herds from the pastures our clan had used for five centuries, so that Chinese farmers could come with machines and rip up the land, I learned differently. A demon came and threw grenades in his tent while he and my grandmother slept, and it machine-gunned all the herd, killing everything, even the lambs." Shan looked about and saw Jowa and Fat Mao standing close now, listening with grim expressions. "I was the one who found the bodies, when I rode to sing songs with my grandfather. Their valley ran with blood. Since that day I believe in demons," Akzu said, in a calm, matter-of-fact way that chilled Shan. "The demon is released and it wants the orphans. I think it wants to finish what it started with their parents. Twenty-three orphans Lau had," he announced with foreboding in his voice, and looked toward the northern horizon. "Only twenty-one now," he added with a whisper.

46

He wasn't simply speaking of the traitor Bajys, because a man like Akzu understood that it was never just one man. The demons of modern China were the irrational, unpredictable political fevers that struck and infected some with hate and others with such fear that it drove them to betrayal and murder. Maybe Shan had been sent to track the demon that had killed Lau, but it could be the same demon that was now killing her children. He put his hand on Lokesh's shoulder and looked to Jowa, then Akzu. "We must go with you to this camp," Shan told the old Kazakh. "We must go to where this boy Khitai died."

Akzu stared hard at Shan, then turned to Jakli. "It may be that this demon is going to kill them all. I will not put our clan in its path," he said to her with a fierce glint in his eye, then turned back to Shan. "And if you get in its way," he warned, "it will kill you too."

CHAPTER 3

It comforted Shan that there were places on earth like the terrain they now rode through, places that could never be tamed. Some said such places were good for the planet, others that they were good for the soul. But Shan had met an old priest of a tiny, nearly extinct Tibetan sect who had insisted that such distinctions were misleading, that souls could not thrive unless the land thrived and that where the land deities had been shackled souls became grey, hollow things. The lama had lived all his life in the high ranges, but said that he had seen how Chinese made roads of asphalt and concrete. He had professed quite confidently that man, without knowing it, was making shackles of asphalt around the entire planet. When the last link of asphalt completed the last connection across the continents, he said, the world would end.

They rode for three hours in the shadows of rock walls, dashing over low passes where the sunlight exposed them, circuiting the perimeter of a vast grassland bowl because, Shan realized, there was no cover for riders who moved across it.

As they rode Shan asked Jakli about Auntie Lau. A teacher, she said, and until recently a member of the local Agricultural Council, a body which advised the local government on agricultural policy, elected by the local agricultural enterprises. Lau had been perhaps fifty-five years old, an orphan herself, without a family "but a mother to everyone," Jakli said, pushing her horse forward as Akzu turned with a chastizing frown. Sound carried far off the faces of the rock, and Shan had not missed the anxious way the old Kazakh studied the landscape.

A grim silence had descended over Akzu and Fat Mao as they trotted down the trail. At first Shan had thought it was still resentment over his presence, but then at a fork in the trail where Akzu led them down the least used of the two paths, he had seen that it was skittishness, even fear. Even the horses seemed reluctant to take the path and had to be reined tightly, before the riders could pull them between the two boulders that marked the trailhead. Akzu had dismounted to cut the bells from the harness of the camel.

Jakli rode in front of Shan. "A shortcut," she called back. But Shan saw the skittishness in her eyes too.

As they rode in the shadow of another rock wall he studied the five-mile-long valley it surrounded. It was not as fertile as the valleys in central Tibet but still held enough vegetation and water to support the small flocks of the dropka. There should have been herds, he knew. There should have been sheep or goats or yak, even the low-slung felt tents of a shepherd's camp. But it was empty, barren of life, as if somehow it had been sterilized.

The trail rose toward the crest of the ridge that defined the south end of the valley, and a small cleft in the rocks at the top appeared. Akzu signaled for the column to stop, then dismounted and led his horse to the opening. He pressed himself against the side of the cleft and peered through it. A moment later, visibly relaxed, he stepped quickly past the cleft and signaled for them to dismount and proceed. Shan awkwardly slid off his mount and followed their lead, but paused as he moved past the opening.

The object of their fear dominated the landscape beyond the ridge, a compound that, although at least two miles away, was clearly of huge dimensions. A long line of high wire fence, punctuated at intervals by guard towers, surrounded a complex of low, gleaming white buildings and cement bunkers.

"When I was young," a soft voice said behind Shan, "there was a nest of scorpions on the next hill from ours at our summer pasture camp. My brothers always wanted to kill them."

Shan looked at Jakli in confusion, then back at the complex. He knew what a Chinese prison looked like, and this was no prison. It had many guard towers but was too new and clean; too much of Beijing's money had been spent on the facility for it to be simply part of the gulag. But it also wasn't like any army base he had ever seen. Everything seemed to be made of cement. He saw nothing that looked like barracks. There were small buildings, the size of tool-sheds, at regular intervals inside the wire.

"No, my father said," Jakli continued. "Let them live. I would not have you walk the land without fear."

As he shielded his eyes from the glare of the sun, now high in the sky, Shan could see a large radar antenna sweeping the sky from the center of the compound. Brilliant white domes were arrayed beyond the antenna. Satellite communications links. The small buildings were not sheds, he realized, but entrances to an underground complex.

"We call it the Mushroom Bowl. One night I saw them do a test," Jakli said. "It went far into the sky, like a shooting star going back to its home."

A shiver swept down Shan's spine, and he could bear to look no longer. "I'm sorry," he said, without knowing why.

Jakli returned his gaze with a small, wise smile. "It is just our nest of scorpions."

The main purpose of Tibet and western China was to act as a buffer, Shan had once heard a top general opine at a Beijing banquet, a staging area and shield against the next wave of aggression. Which meant, more than anything, that the vast wilderness was the hiding place for the country's most important weapons. Many politicians boasted in the capital that Tibet received the equivalent of billions of dollars from Beijing. All but a fraction of that money went to hollowing out mountains for troop garrisons and building secret nuclear missile installations like the one Shan had just seen. The Mushroom Bowl. Named for the white domes that had sprouted there after Beijing's invasion and perhaps also for the specter of the warheads inside its missiles.

The wilderness had been tamed after all, he thought.

Maybe the old priest was right. When a sacred land got harnessed this way, it could mean the end of the world. The People's Liberation Army had its secret, buried ways to protect the world, or at least Beijing's world. For some reason he remembered the low rumble that was always present at their Lhadrung hermitage, the sound of the giant prayer wheel, kept moving by two monks at all hours, in a small chamber carved into a nameless mountain in remote Tibet. The lamas' secret, buried way to protect the world.

Now he understood the vacant grassland. Such bases were surrounded by military zones that would be patrolled by PLA commandos. In the imperial days there had been many places reserved exclusively for the emperor's family and high officials. To enter into them, sometimes to even look into them, meant instant death for any commoner. China still had its Forbidden Cities. There would be no excuses for a civilian caught in such a zone.

Another shudder moved down his spine. He wished he had not seen the base, wished he had not looked. It made a cold, hard, black place in his heart beside the many scars already there. After building installations like this, how could Beijing ever leave Tibet?

As he pulled his eyes away he saw that a large rock on the slope by the cleft had been painted red, and then saw another on the slope at the end of the bowl. It was a traditional way to mark the homes of the protective deities that lived inside mountains, the local land gods. At great risk Tibetans had painted the rocks, as if to fence in the base with watchful deities.

"Such danger," Shan said to Jakli, "just to save us time." His words were barely above a whisper, as if the Mushroom Bowl cast its shadow from miles away.

"You heard Akzu," Jakli said soberly. "We will take as many shortcuts as we need to, until the treachery stops." She gazed back toward the bowl. "The patrols are lazy. This time of year, they are mostly interested in animals."

"Animals?"

"With no herders here, it is like a giant game preserve. Generals come from Beijing, to shoot ibex and antelope. Snow leopards, sometimes."

"But still, if you are discovered—"

"Then we become the game," she said with a forced grin, and placed her open hands around her neck to give the impression of a head on a wall. "Mounted in some general's tearoom in Beijing. Rare counterrevolutionaries bagged in the wilderness."

Shan looked at Jakli, trying to understand how she fit into the complex puzzle of the group led by Akzu. "Akzu is your uncle," he said. "But you don't live with your clan."

"Sometimes. Right now I live in town. In Yoktian. I have a job in a factory. Making hats."

He asked her about the clan and Akzu. The question seemed to make her sad. After a moment she explained that the leathery old Kazakh was their headman, the elder of what was left of the Red Stone clan. Once the Red Stone had been a mighty clan with vast pastures in the north. But it had lost all those pastures to the government, and its people had been dispossessed. Akzu and Jakli's father had come thirty years before with a hundred surviving members to the borderland along the Kunlun, where the land and climate were so harsh that the population was sparse and nearly forgotten. They thought they could live without interference, out of sight in such a place. Now all that was left of the clan was one camp, and three families, coaxing a subsistence living out of the lands at the edge of the desert. And Auntie Lau, Jakli explained, was no one's aunt, not a part of the clan, but a Kazakh woman who had brought the zheli under her wing, a kind, wise, soul loved by everyone.

Almost everyone, Shan nearly added. "I thought you were from Tibet at first," he said.

"It's a border land, has been for thousands of years. Many bloods get mixed here. My father was Kazakh. His brother was Akzu. My mother was Tibetan. She died when I was a baby. My father disappeared ten years ago," she said with a slight shrug. "I ride with my father's clan when I can. In the spring I like to go to the oasis in the desert to train the camels."

"You speak Tibetan very well."

"My father loved my mother very much. He encouraged me to keep her ways alive. Auntie Lau helped, when she learned about my mother."

"She gave you Buddhist teachings?" Shan asked.

"Not really. She said discovering my personal god, that was for me to do privately. But she knew Tibetan things, like she knew Kazakh and Uighur things. She said it was important to understand what the government said about new ways but that the old ways should not be forgotten."

Shan studied the woman, wondering whether the words had been Lau's or were simply Jakli's. Understanding what the government said was not the same as heeding it. "I did not know that Kazakhs lived in Tibet."

Jakli smiled and flashed her green eyes at him. "Some do, I suppose." She shifted in her saddle and pointed to the line of mountains they were leaving, the wall that separated them from the missile base. "But that last ridge is the border. We are now in the Xinjiang Autonomous Region."

Shan halted his horse and surveyed the dry, rugged landscape. The sky was a brilliant cobalt. Behind him the majestic snow-covered central peaks of the Kunlun connected the eastern and western horizons. In a gap between the peaks he had earlier glimpsed the vast Karakorum mountains that, rising out of the northern end of the Himalayas, created a nearly impassable border with India and Pakistan. To the north lay a brown haze that he now recognized as the beginning of the vast desert, the Taklamakan, that dominated the geography of southern Xinjiang.

He had been taken to that desert nearly four years earlier, and the haze sparked disjointed images of sand and razor wire and hypodermic needles. The Kazakhs might use the desert to train camels, but the Public Security Bureau used it for other purposes. They had beaten him and questioned him and drugged him and questioned him until he was a hollow, shriveled thing, more dead than alive, then discarded what was left of him in a lao gai hard labor camp deep in Tibet.

"Have you visited Xinjiang before?" Jakli asked, as if recognizing something in his face.

"I don't know Xinjiang," Shan said quickly and urged his mount forward, fighting an unreasonable fear that the men who had tortured him in the desert prison would reappear at any moment. Shan had had a cell mate for a few days while he had been with the knobs, an escapee from one of Xinjiang's infamous lao gai coal mine prisons, caught fleeing through the desert. The man had no papers, and they hadn't bothered to track down his genealogy, meaning, in the knobs' parlance, to cross-check the tattoo that was his lao gai registration number to its source, to the history of his political infidelities and the gulag camp he belonged to. One of the knob officers had called the man a "free one" for the new recruits. The last time Shan had seen him he had been crouched in the corner of his cell, naked, covered in his own filth, drumming his head against the wall.

Two hours after the Mushroom Bowl, their mounts found a new energy, quickening their pace as they descended into a small green valley lined at its edges with pines and poplars. A dog barked in the distance. The horses and camels began to trot. As they cleared a bend in the trail, the Red Stone encampment came into view.

Three round tents of heavy felt lay in a clearing at the bottom of the fertile valley. Beyond them, against a steep slope, were ruins of two stone structures that had been spanned by canvas tops to shelter livestock. They were not the ruins Shan was accustomed to seeing in central Tibet, not the scorched rocks and bricks pockmarked from the bombs and shells of the People's Liberation Army. These were the remains of ancient buildings, overtaken only by time and nature.

Their small caravan was seen first by a lamb frolicking up the trail, then by the adolescent girl who was chasing it. Both lamb and girl gave a bleat of surprise, then turned and scurried back toward the tents. Four large dogs, one of them a big black Tibetan mastiff, barked in warning, then ran to greet the riders as they emerged from the trail.

Akzu and Jowa had already disappeared inside the center tent by the time Shan and Lokesh dismounted. The girl reappeared, her eyes round with excitement. Three women, one with grey hair tied in a red checked scarf, and two others a few years younger, looked up from blankets spread on the ground, where they were crumbling pieces of soft cheese to dry in the sun. The older woman called out excitedly to Jakli, as one of the others leapt up, grabbed a white dress hanging from a tree branch, and darted inside the center yurt. Two men with strong, leathery faces and thick black moustaches appeared at the flap of the center tent, smiling at Jakli, then casting suspicious glances at Shan. Akzu's sons, Jakli explained after she had greeted each of them.

"Jakli!" a youth of perhaps twelve or thirteen years exclaimed from the nearest of the stables as the woman entered the clearing, walking her horse. A tiny goat lay draped across his shoulders. He gently deposited it beside an older goat, then ran to Jakli's side and embraced her.

"My youngest cousin," Jakli explained to Shan. "Malik. He stays with the animals so much we call him Seksek Ata sometimes. The protective spirit for goats," she added.

The boy's smile faded and tension crossed his face as he hugged her again. This time it was not for joy, Shan saw, but for solace, for comfort.

Jakli held him tightly against her shoulder, planting a light kiss on the top of his head. "Khitai was your friend," she said in a melancholy tone.

An angry shout rose from the tent on the left. A disheveled, wild-eyed woman stood in the entrance, pointing at Shan and yelling in her Turkic tongue. Jakli stepped in front of Shan as though to shield him from the shrill woman, then pushed him away, toward the stables. The woman took a step into the sunlight, still shouting at Shan.

"She's crazy," Jakli said in a low voice when Shan asked her what the words meant. "Something about children." Jakli frowned as she saw that Shan would not turn away. "She says you always want the children. She says you killed the children." Jakli pushed his arm but Shan did not move. "Years ago she was pregnant. They told her she had to go to a government clinic to give birth. When she went, they gave her a needle that made her sleep. When she woke up the baby was out of her, and it was dead. Later she found out that she had been sterilized."

The angry woman picked up pebbles and began throwing them at Shan. "She changed after that," Jakli continued. "In winter, she sits with a rolled blanket and sings a besik zhyry to it."

"Besik zhyry?" Lokesh asked as he watched the woman.

"Kazakhs have songs for everything. Weddings, births,

horse races, the death of a friend, the death of a horse,"
Jakli explained, and thought a moment. "She sings cradle
songs. The songs that Kazakh women sing to babies."

They stood in silence. Several pebbles hit Shan in the
leg.

"Every time a child dies," Jakli added quietly, "she
thinks it was hers."

In the light Shan saw the woman's clothing was covered
with dirt. Bits of dried leaves clung to her shoulder-length
braids.

Shan let Jakli pull him away as a larger stone hit his
knee. But a moment later Jakli stopped. Malik was waiting
for them on a path on the slope above the stables. She
looked back at the crazed woman, as if maybe she preferred
to face the woman than to follow Malik, then sighed and
gestured Shan toward the path. As they approached the boy,
Shan saw that he had a sprig of heather in his hand. Jakli
bent and picked a sprig for herself, then Shan did the same.

As they followed Malik, a dark form rushed past them.
The woman's anger seemed to have disappeared, replaced
by sobs that sounded almost like the bleating of one of the
animals.

They made a silent procession up the path: the dark,
wild-eyed woman, then Malik, followed by Shan and Jakli.
After perhaps a hundred paces they entered a small hollow
near the top of the hill, a sheltered place closed to the north
by a huge slab of rock, open with a view for miles to the
south, into the Kunlun, toward Tibet. At the back, in the
shadow below the rock slab, was a five-foot-long mound
of earth.

To the left of the grave was an indentation of packed
earth. The wild-eyed woman, he realized, had been sleeping
by the grave. Strips of bark lay at the head of the grave,
bearing offerings of food. Two large feathers and twigs of
heather had been pushed into the earth at the foot of the
mound of earth. Shan and Jakli followed Malik's example
and offered their sprigs in the same manner.

The woman sat at the head of the grave, rocking back
and forth, her face now twisted with grief, singing a soft
song, giving no acknowledgment of Shan.

Feeling helpless, not knowing what to do, Shan knelt at

the foot of the grave. A moment later Jakli silently knelt beside him and began murmuring under her breath in the Kazakh tongue. Malik stood behind Jakli, his hand on her shoulder. Shan became aware of movement behind him and turned to see Lokesh, Jowa, and Akzu approaching the grave.

Lokesh sat and placed a palm on the grave. "Khitai," he said in a low, doleful voice, and stared at the freshly turned earth, his jaw open. As the others watched in silence, the old Tibetan's other hand found his rosary and, leaning back, he began a low mantra. Jowa sat beside him, then hesitantly produced his own rosary and joined the mantra.

The woman at the head of the grave blinked several times and rubbed her eyes as though awakening from a trance. She looked uncertainly about the circle, as if wondering how so many had joined her, or perhaps who was mortal and who was visiting from another world. Her eyes fixed on the rosary beads, first Jowa's, then Lokesh's, and light seemed to return to her face. She spoke to Akzu in their native tongue. The Kazakh headman looked at the two Tibetans and replied to her, then turned to the visitors. "She said it is good to have a mullah at last. I said you are not mullahs, you are Buddhists, but you are holy men nonetheless."

The woman was nodding vigorously, then patted the dirt the way she might a sleeping child.

"Who did he belong to, this boy?" Shan asked. "He was an orphan, but where was the rest of his clan?"

"Gone. Extinct, probably. We do not know the details of his birthing. Nor did he. He was from the zheli," Akzu said, as if it explained much.

Shan watched the haggard woman in silence, then pushed back from the pile of earth to stand beside Akzu. "You mean he lived here, but Lau was his teacher."

Akzu nodded. "Lived here for a short while. Some children have to be taken care of by everyone. He wasn't any trouble," Akzu said. "One of the zheli often comes and stays a month or two. Lau didn't like them staying in the town all the time. In the warm weather she arranged for them to go to the clans."

"But Khitai, he was new?"

"New to us. He had not stayed with the Red Stone before. But sometimes, when we took one of the orphans to Lau's meeting place, we would see him. Always smiling. He was luckier than most, because he at least had his companion, this man Bajys." He winced as he spoke, as if understanding the irony of his words.

"So Bajys was an orphan too?" Shan asked.

"Yes. But older, so he didn't go to school. They said the two of them had discovered years earlier they were from the same clan in the north and had promised to watch over each other. Bajys taught Khitai things."

"What happened to their clan?" Shan asked, remembering Akzu's words at the trailhead. Maybe the demon was finishing something started years before.

Akzu shrugged and stepped away from the grave as if leaving, then stopped in the center of the clearing and stared out over the hills to the south, toward the high plateau of Tibet. Shan followed him. "All the clans have been troubled since it began," Akzu said.

"The murders, you mean."

Akzu did not look away from the hills. He offered a sour smile, as if Shan had made a joke. "Sure, the murders. All the murders. All the arrests. Since I was a boy, when all the green shirts arrived."

Akzu was speaking of the People's Liberation Army and their invasion of the western lands fifty years before, when the region had been absorbed into the People's Republic. The story had been spoken of so often by some of Shan's former cell mates, the captured warriors, that it had been turned into a song which they whistled sometimes in front of their guards. The PLA had taken Xinjiang; then, after training on the Muslims, they had started on Tibet. Xinjiang had taken a year to subjugate, Tibet nearly a decade.

"Many old clans disappeared entirely," Akzu said, "lost forever. Others were broken up, separated by lines on Chinese maps." He looked back to Shan. "Emperors from Beijing had come to Xinjiang many times. They wanted to buy our horses. They wanted to guard their own frontiers with advance garrisons. Their armies stayed a few years and went home. It didn't affect the Kazakhs or the Uighurs who lived here. But Emperor Mao was different." He shook his

head. "We have always been nomads. The green shirts sent
by Mao drew boxes on maps and gave us papers that permitted us to live only in those boxes. We laughed. Obviously the Chinese didn't understand the way of the herds,
or of our people. But when we traveled outside their boxes
they sent us to prison. Or worse."

"You're saying the boy was displaced somehow."

"Displaced," Akzu spat. "You sound like Beijing." He
sighed and looked toward Jakli, as if reminding himself that
he had to get along with Shan. "The restrictions are not
being enforced as much today," the headman offered. "We
get visitors now, people roaming in search of family they
haven't seen for twenty, thirty years because they were assigned to live in different boxes on the Chinese maps. Lau
was like that at first, but she decided to stay in Yoktian
County to help all the others that wandered through."

"Khitai and Bajys came like that, looking for family?"

"Mostly, now, the orphans just try to find places to fit
in, try to make a new life. Auntie Lau said maybe we
should get to know Khitai. She said he was better suited
for the smaller clans, the ones that stay in the higher pastures away from town. We said of course he and Bajys
could come. Many such people never find their home
hearths. Things have changed so much. The children are
not permitted to learn the old ways." He shook his head
slowly. "I got a letter last year from a cousin who married
into a clan in the north. She said things were so much better
that Chinese come to their camp and pay to sleep in their
yurts and eat food from a wood fire. Tourists. I wrote a
letter to say that doesn't mean it's better, that if it feels
good to have them come and treat us like their pets, like a
circus show, then you have lost the why of it, you have
forgotten what being Kazakh is supposed to feel like."
Akzu shrugged. "I didn't mail it. Sometimes Public Security stills reads letters.

"But when travelers like Khitai come, we must make
room for them. We lost many from our own clan in the
struggles. Maybe some are still alive, in the north perhaps,
or even in Kazakhstan," he said, referring to the independent Kazakh nation to the west of China. "Sometimes broken clans go to a town to start a new life, like Lau. But

some just wander. Maybe we have family wandering too. We would want them to find friends along the way." Shan looked to Jakli. Her father had disappeared, she said. Akzu's brother. The headman sighed heavily. "We will know ourselves what it is like soon enough, what it is to be orphans."

Shan was about to ask him what he meant when Jakli stepped to his side. "Uncle, how long was this boy here?"

"Nearly three weeks. Before the last full moon. Khitai was quiet. A good boy. Mischievious sometimes. Once he climbed a tree near camp and threw nuts down on everyone who passed, making sounds like a squirrel. Always wore a red cap, his dopa, like a good Muslim. Stayed with Bajys working in the hills except when he played with Malik. We were glad to have them for the autumn chores. We were cutting hay for the winter." He cast a bitter glance at Jakli as he spoke the last words, as if cutting hay for the next winter had come to represent a cruel joke.

"How did the boy die?" Shan asked abruptly.

Akzu sighed again. "One of the old families visited that day, not a clan, the remnants of clans. The shadow clans, we call them. They're distrustful of everyone, wary as deer. They stay off roads whenever possible, just herd enough sheep to feed themselves. Usually stay in the highest pastures where no one else ever goes, near the ice fields. If they need supplies they come to one of the small camps like ours to trade. Some took children from Lau too. She said it helped keep the shadow clans connected to the world," Akzu added, gazing back at the woman at the head of the grave. "We made a meal together, then they moved on at dusk. Malik was away, so Khitai played with the boy from the other family, one of his friends from the zheli. They played in the hills most of the day. The other zheli boy was happy, he told me at the meal, because his shadow family didn't speak the Turkic tongue so well, or Mandarin."

"They weren't Kazakhs?"

Akzu shook his head. "Dropka, Tibetans. One of the border families. Many of the dropka on this side of the border worked with Lau."

Shan closed his eyes as a new surge of grief swept

through him. To stand at two children's graves in just two days was as hard as anything he had faced in the gulag. "We saw them," he announced after a moment, having a hard time forming the words. "We buried their boy," he said, and explained what had happened on the changtang. Jakli gave a small moan. Akzu lowered his eyes and spoke several words in his native tongue that sounded like a prayer.

"Where was Bajys that day?" Long ago Shan had learned not to believe in coincidence. The killer had targeted both boys and killed both, two days apart. "Why would he turn on Khitai this way? And why Alta, afterward?"

Akzu looked solemnly at Jakli before speaking. "The day before, Fat Mao was here, to ask if we would help when people came from Tibet to help about Lau." As he spoke, the headman glanced at Lokesh, looking old and frail at the edge of the grave, then glanced at Shan, and finally Jowa. An aged Tibetan, a Chinese exile, and a sullen, unhappy warrior. Not, Shan suspected, the help Akzu had anticipated.

"Bajys was there? He knew about Lau's death?"

"No, Lau's death was kept a secret from the zheli. At most they just heard the rumors from town, that she had disappeared. But Bajys came into the tent and stared at Fat Mao. We asked him what he wanted, but he just stared at Fat Mao, then turned and ran away. He must have understood, must have eavesdropped, maybe he knew Fat Mao from town. It's the kind of information that could change a man's life. For certain men it would be like finding gold lying on a trail. Go to the prosecutor, tell about the secret resistance, give some names. Get a reward, get a new job somewhere, a new life. I think Bajys told the boy that day what he was going to do, and Khitai resisted it, said he would tell Fat Mao, that he would stop him. But Bajys had no kind of life. It was the biggest opportunity he might ever hope for. That other boy, he must have heard too."

"Did Bajys have a gun?"

"Apparently. Lots of Kazakhs keep guns for hunting."

"Where did it happen?"

"Here, in this same clearing. We found the boy sitting

against the rock, not far from where he is buried."

"Who, exactly, found him?"

"The next morning Malik went to look for him when he didn't come for breakfast. The boy passed much of his time here. It's quiet. He had lessons here with Bajys. Malik went up the path at dawn and came back running, shouting for us. It had to be some sort of terrible accident, I thought at first. He had found a gun and was playing with it."

"But there was no gun," Shan stated.

Akzu shook his head slowly.

"Did anyone examine his body?"

"We have no holy man nearby. No mullah. We must bury our dead quickly, before sunset. My wife came up here and washed him and placed him in a shroud. She didn't know Khitai well." Akzu sighed. "But she knows how to bury children. We sang songs, but such songs should be sung about the dead one's life, and no one knew what to sing." He looked at Jakli, as though to reassure her. "So we sang about riding horses in the high pastures and how eagles fly." He cast a meaningful glance at Shan. "It was one bullet in the center of the forehead," he explained in a lower voice. "A small gun. The bullet did not have much velocity. Quiet. No one heard the shot." Akzu gazed at Shan, as though challenging him to ask how the headman had knowledge of weapons. "No wound in the back of his skull. The bullet stayed inside."

"Nothing else? Any sign of a struggle?"

"His clothes were torn. Shirt ripped open, and one of his pants legs got torn. A shoe was missing." Akzu's eyes shifted toward the hills, his gaze returning tinged with worry. There was something else on his mind. Akzu had intended to bring only Jowa to his camp, Shan recalled. Because he knew about Public Security.

"But you said Bajys and Khitai were related, the last of their clan. They had been together so long."

Akzu shook his head slowly. "Bajys was unsettled. Some people are always nervous around children. Sometimes he was like an uncle to the boy. When we ate, he would remind Khitai of his manners. Sometimes he was like a teacher. But sometimes it was like he was scared of the boy."

"Scared?"

"Not scared." The headman frowned. "I don't have words. Sometimes it was like Khitai was the older brother. Bajys was nervous about pleasing him." Akzu stared at the sky a moment, then shrugged. "When a colt grows up without a herd, it is always skittish."

"Orphans have reasons to be skittish," Shan suggested.

Akzu nodded. "But the dogs liked Bajys," he added in a confused tone, as if that were the greatest mystery of all. He shrugged again. "We will find him if he ever leaves the Chinese town. The clans won't go to the government about it. We find our own justice. But he knows we can't go to town to take him. Too many knobs there."

"Your own justice?"

"We know the killer," the headman said with a chill in his voice. "He will be found eventually and he will pay the price of all killers."

The words surprised Shan, who had lived in Tibet for so long. Revenge was not something that Buddhists sought. But they were in a Muslim land now, and Muslims believed in retribution.

"What about Lau's other children, the rest of the zheli?" Shan asked. "Have they been warned? Until the killer is found, until we understand why he is killing, they are all in danger." Akzu's words from the trailhead still haunted him. Maybe the demon is going to kill them all, the headman had said. Twenty-three orphans, and only twenty-one left.

Akzu and Jakli exchanged a worried look. "Word has gone out," Akzu said in a pained tone. "We do what we can."

"It's not easy," Jakli said. "It's why Lau called them her zheli. Those children are like wild horses, scattered over the mountains, always moving, always wary."

"But surely their homes are known. Their foster families."

Akzu shook his head. "Homes? They're with nomads, traveling with their flocks until winter, bringing the children together only for Lau's classes. Sometimes they pick up mail at farms, or in town. People know the names of the clans, maybe know the pastures they traditionally use. We knew where two zheli girls were staying, in a valley near here. They're being kept in their tents now, with someone always watching." Akzu looked out over the mountains. "Since she retired from the Agricultural Council, Lau was going out alone into the ranges, giving the children medical exams, bringing food to the poorest families, teaching special lessons. I think only Lau would know where all the children might be at any one time. Maybe that will save them, their secrecy."

"So Lau knew Red Stone clan was here, at this camp?"

Akzu nodded. "She knew we come here in the autumn, knew we use it as a base to gather our flocks for the winter. But it's not important what Lau knew. Bajys was here." Akzu gazed back at the mound of fresh earth. "The only children killed were one at Red Stone camp and one who visited Red Stone camp," the herder said somberly, and began walking back down the trail.

The front flap of the center tent had been tied back when they returned to camp, and as they approached a grey-haired woman appeared at the flap. She studied them with strong, proud eyes, then gestured them inside. Shan followed the example of Jakli and her uncle, rinsing his hands in a basin of water by the front flap, then sitting on a cushion near the center of the heavy carpet that served as the floor of the tent as the woman handed them small, chipped porcelain cups filled with steaming liquid.

"My wife is baking today," Akzu announced as the woman leaned over a brazier where a kettle simmered. Beside the brazier sat a clay pot of yogurt and, on a large flat stone, a stack of *nan*, the flat bread favored by China's Muslims. "You will sleep with our clan, in the tent near the stables."

The woman smiled shyly as Shan nodded in greeting and sipped his cup. It was not tea, as he had expected.

"Warm goat's milk," Jakli explained. From behind a rug suspended at the back of the tent Shan heard voices. The two other women he had seen earlier peered out from the edge of the carpet and looked at Jakli with small, expectant smiles, then disappeared.

The milk was surprisingly bitter, but the liquid filled him with warmth as it hit his stomach. "Had he been away, this Bajys?" Shan asked.

"Away?" the headman asked. He drained his cup, then reached behind him and produced a small drinking skin. With a slight bow of his head he extended it to Shan with both hands.

Shan held the skin without looking at it. "Auntie Lau died more than a week before. Could Bajys have killed her as well?"

Jakli's head snapped up with sudden interest, as if she had not considered the possibility.

"No," Akzu said after a moment. "He was with the clan for the past month. That place in the desert where she died, Karachuk, to go there and back would be more than a day. He was never gone more than four or five hours, when he went with Khitai to the high pastures." The headman nodded at the skin. "Kumiss," he said. "Drink."

So there were two killers, Shan thought. And Bajys was only part of the answer. "Karachuk?" he asked. "Why was she there?"

Jakli and Akzu frowned into their cups and exchanged a glance. "An oasis place, that's all," he said enigmatically, then steered the conversation away from Lau and the dead boy, speaking instead as a host spoke to his guests, following the code of hospitality Shan had experienced in nomad tents in Tibet. He showed Shan how to twist the wooden plug off the skin and raise it to squirt into his mouth. Shan did so uncertainly, for he had not seen such skins in Tibet, then nearly choked as the acrid liquid hit his palate.

Akzu grinned. "Fermented mare's milk," he explained, then accepted the skin back from Shan and took a long swallow of the pale white liquor. He sighed with satisfaction, then spoke of how the horses were growing heavy coats, the sign of a harsh season to come. After a quarter hour Jakli rose and stepped behind the carpet partition at the rear, triggering a hushed, excited chatter from the women behind it. After a few minutes she reappeared, flushed with color, as though embarrassed, then retrieved Shan's drawstring bag where it sat by the entrance. Shan offered his gratitude to Akzu's wife, then followed Jakli to the tent by the animals.

Malik appeared, holding the flap open as if he had been waiting for them. But Jakli lingered, looking toward the tent on the opposite side of the camp, then handed Shan's bag to the boy and silently moved into the third tent. Shan hesitated, wondering if Malik would explain. But the boy shrugged and moved back behind the flap. Shan followed Jakli and heard a strange, irregular clicking sound as he approached the third tent. Five faces looked up at him as he stepped inside. Jowa, Jakli, Fat Mao, and Akzu's sons.

Jakli sat with Jowa near a small smoldering brazier. The Uighur and the two Kazakh men were kneeling behind them, a sheen of excitement on their faces, looking at a small portable computer in Jowa's lap.

Jakli looked up, startled. "By the stable. There is a pallet for you in the tent with Lokesh."

But Shan stepped closer. One of the Kazakhs muttered a curse as he approached. Jowa seemed undisturbed. He glanced at Shan and kept working, tapping the keyboard, reading the screen with intense curiosity.

Jakli stood, uncertainty on her face. "It's only some records about agricultural production units. Jowa is helping with the computer."

Shan stepped to Jowa's side and studied the screen as the purba slowly scrolled through a computer file. The data was in Chinese, with the same heading on each screen, "Agricultural Production Inventories, Yoktian County." There were subheadings for cotton, wool, barley, and wheat, each with production records. Over seventy percent of the production was credited to the People's Construction and Development Corporation. Other, smaller entries, were for the patchwork of collectives and family enterprises comprising the remaining participants in the local industry.

Jowa stopped at the screen for wool production. One of the Kazakh men hovering over his shoulder pointed to an entry at the bottom of the screen. "Red Stone," it read. "That's us," the man said. "Red Stone Herding Enterprise. The clan enterprise."

Jowa highlighted the name and tapped a button. A five-year record of production from Red Stone appeared, with a graph at the bottom. The clan's wool production had steadily declined. Jowa tapped another button, producing a screen for five-year comparisons with others in Yoktian

County. Red Stone had the lowest productivity in every year and by far the lowest cumulative total.

Jakli leaned over Jowa and translated what the screen said. While most of those present clearly understood Chinese, few, apparently, could read it. When she had finished, one of the Kazakh men spat a curse. "The Brigade," he said. "They beat us down for years, treat us like slaves in our own land, and still they are not satisfied."

"The People's Brigade, they call it," Jakli explained to Shan. "It was Beijing's first stage of settlement. Many of the soldiers sent here as occupation troops were given economic incentives to stay and develop the land. A company was formed for them and land grants made to the company. They took prime pastures and plowed them under for cotton and other crops. They became bigger and bigger. Now the Brigade is practically as powerful as the government. Runs schools. Runs local clinics. Even operates some of the prisons, on contract to the Ministry of Justice and Public Security. Thousands of workers. Hundreds of enterprises. We could never compete."

"The Brigade and the army, they are the same?" Shan asked. China's military had a long tradition of investing in commercial companies.

"Five years ago the Brigade was privatized," Jakli explained. "But it's still run like the army. Run by Han Chinese who used to be generals."

"Like a kingdom," someone said in a bitter tone from behind them. Akzu had entered the tent. "A separate kingdom within the country, supported by Beijing."

"But what are you—" Shan began.

"They say production must be more efficient," Akzu said bitterly. "They say small clans are no longer cost effective."

"Cost effective?"

"The Poverty Eradication Scheme, they call it," Jakli said. "A government policy, implemented by the Brigade."

"But what does it have to do with your clan?"

Jowa interrupted by closing the screen with a loud snap. "The smallest producers are being bought out," he explained. "The Brigade is identifying the least efficient producers and will integrate those workers into more efficient production. Higher value added, they call it."

"You mean the clan is getting new lands?"

"No," Akzu said. "Our clan runs its business through a company with shares, something the government established several years ago. Now the Brigade is buying all the shares."

"But if you didn't agree to it—" Jowa began.

"There's a term I heard in the town," Jakli interjected. "A hostile takeover. Everyone kept repeating it, like they thought it was funny, like something you read about in American magazines."

"But just having its shares bought shouldn't affect the clan," Shan suggested.

Jakli grimaced. "To them, we aren't a clan, just new employees. The Brigade already has plans for Red Stone. Everyone will be assigned to towns, different towns, to break up the clan. Apartments will be given to parents with a child. Others will live in workers' dormitories." As she spoke a shudder seemed to move through her. She clutched her chest as though short of breath.

The headman pulled a folded envelope from inside his coat as he sat by his sons. "We received a letter last week. We are to deliver our herds, our horses, our dogs, even our tents to the Brigade by the end of the month. In ten days, just after our autumn horse festival, our nadam. All members report for reassignment." He gestured toward a stack of papers by the computer. "Final inventory of assets required. Every sheep, every lamb, every damned spoon and pot."

"Poverty Eradication Scheme," Jowa said in a hollow tone. "The bastards are liquidating the clan."

In the heavy silence that descended over the tent, nothing could be heard but the breath of the horses tethered outside.

"No one's said it like that before," Akzu said.

Fat Mao stood. "But it's the truth. This Tibetan speaks the truth. They've done it to Uighur farms. They've done it to Kazakhs in the north." His eyes narrowed and he looked at Shan. "Poverty Eradication Scheme." He spat the words and grimaced. "It's not about economics. It's about politics. People in Beijing planned it all. They want to make it impossible for a Uighur to be a Uighur, or a Kazakh to be a Kazakh." The man's eyes drifted toward Jowa. "The Chinese are very clever. They study a people and determine what is most important of all to that people, then they find a means to hollow that thing out, to first take away its power, then eventually remove it completely. In Tibet they take your holy men. Tell me, friend, without your holy men can a Tibetan be a Tibetan?"

Jowa looked away, then his eyes met Shan's. They had already lost their holy man. Jowa's hands closed tightly around the corners of the computer screen. "I grew up in the grasslands, with the herds," he said suddenly. Everyone stopped and looked at him, surprised by the sudden anguish in his voice. "It was like that in the valley where my family lived. They came in big trucks one day. They loaded everyone in two trucks, about fifty of us. Said that because our family owned land we were reactionaries. Said that the land needed Chinese technology, that they were going to bring tractors and plant Chinese wheat. They sorted through everything in the camp as we watched. Anything that was used for taking care of the herds or moving camp, even the carpets used in my family for eight generations, they put inside the main tent. They collapsed all the other tents and threw them on the big one. Then they set it on fire.

"My mother screamed. A soldier hit her with the butt of his rifle and knocked out four teeth. My sister ran to embrace her pony so they shot the pony. My father said a mantra to the compassionate Buddha and they grabbed his rosary, a coral rosary from the time of the Seventh Dalai Lama, and cut it so the beads were lost in the grass. My aunt jumped on the back of a soldier, screaming, scratching at his face." Jowa's voice drifted off.

"If your enemy leaves you only your hands," Akzu observed with a chill in his voice, "then you scratch them with your hands. If they take your hands and only leave your teeth, then you bite them." The words had the tone of an old war song.

Jowa nodded slowly. "But some soldiers took her out in a pasture." The anguish was back in his voice. "They did things to her, and then she died. They threw her body in the fire and then they drove us away. In the trucks they sang songs in praise of the Chairman. They hit us with rifles until we sang too."

"It's not so bad now," one of the Kazakhs said, but his voice lacked confidence. "Not so violent."

Jowa gave an angry snort. "Now they do it with computers and bureaucrats. And corporations." He turned to Akzu. "You think they'll send all of you to one place, mothers and fathers with their children? It didn't happen that way in Tibet. The families would arrive at a new apartment and the next day a Chinese comes for your child. Has to go to a special school, they say. A boarding school, far away. They learn to sing out of a little red book. And when they come back they all have Chinese names and mock all your old ways."

Akzu looked like he had been kicked in the belly. He held his hand tightly over his abdomen and slowly rose, as if with great effort. Without looking back, he walked out of the tent.

"Until last night," Shan said in the silence that followed, "we had a holy man with us. Then he disappeared."

Jakli sighed heavily. Fat Mao seemed to visibly stiffen. "Who took him?" he demanded.

But Shan could not reply. Just saying the words had filled him with fear again. He felt a desperate compulsion to run, to return to the mountains and find Gendun. The lamas hadn't understood, had expected too much of him. He didn't know the Muslims. He didn't know Xinjiang. He could do nothing about these Kazakhs who were being killed. Someone had been mistaken. None of this was about Tibetans.

Jowa quietly explained what had happened the night before.

"Uniforms?" Fat Mao asked.

"None."

"What color was the truck?"

Jowa looked at Shan. "Hong," the purba said. Red.

The Uighur and Jakli exchanged a glance of alarm. Fat Mao spat a curse.

Jakli looked at Shan. "The Brigade," she said slowly. "They drive red trucks." She looked back at the Uighur with question in her eyes. "But they can't be in Tibet.

They're not authorized." She grimaced, as if realizing as she spoke that formal authority was unimportant to the Brigade. "I mean, they've never been there before."

Shan found his voice again. "If they took him," he said urgently, "if the red truck drove Gendun Rinpoche back to Xinjiang, where would they go? Where would they hold him?"

The Uighur slowly reached into his jacket and pulled out an envelope, from which he produced a computer disc. "On to Glory," he said with a sour smile.

As Shan watched in confusion, Jowa accepted the disc and inserted it into the machine. When the screen lit again, it was dominated by huge Chinese characters that had once been part of Shan's daily existence as an investigator in Beijing. *Nei Lou*, it said. Classified. Internal government use only. A fire seemed to grow in Jowa's eyes as he stared at the screen.

The Uighur leaned forward and tapped the keyboard several times.

"Glory to the People Reeducation Facility," Jowa read out loud as the screen changed. "Lao jiao Camp 947." Lao jiao facilities were reeducation camps, jails for lesser offenders than those sent to the gulag, used to punish minor political sins. Admission to lao jiao was administrative, meaning that citizens could be sentenced on the authority of a single official, without a judge, without a trial.

"The Jade Bitch," Fat Mao said in a low voice.

Shan looked up at him.

"The prosecutor in Yoktian. Xu Li," the Uighur explained. "As cold and hard as jade. Glory Camp is her personal dungeon. Pass gas near her and off you go to eat rice for a few months in Glory Camp."

"Recent admission records," Jowa read off the screen. "But it's too soon," he said. "The disc is—"

"Up to date as of six o'clock last night," Fat Mao announced in a conspiratorial tone.

"Gendun was only taken last night."

"Keep looking," the Uighur said, nodding toward the screen.

"Unassigned numbers," Jowa read in a puzzled tone.

"Right. She always has a few numbers assigned to the

others authorized to use the camp. The knobs. The army. The Brigade security teams. Her obsession with efficiency. Open prisoner registration files without names, based on anticipated arrests. They order food, arrange bedding, and staff assignments based on all the files. The Brigade can just take someone there and fill in the name at the gate. Sometimes she lists the reasons in advance. Youth gangs. Cultural recividists."

"A few files?" Jowa asked. "Thirty or forty you mean."

The Uighur bent over the screen in alarm. *"Ta ma de!"* he spat. "Damn it! What is she up to?"

They scrolled back and forth between recent admissions and the open files. After several minutes Fat Mao stood up with anger in his eyes. "Usually, Glory gets maybe five, six new inmates each week. A week ago she established forty open files. Gave ten to the Brigade to fill, ten to the knobs. Kept twenty for herself. Three days later half of the files are filled. Twenty new inmates. Yesterday six more, then—" He stopped in midsentence and pointed halfway down the screen. "And there's something new," he said. "Six more open files created yesterday. Assigned to the Public Security Bureau."

"But you said the knobs already get—" Jakli interjected.

"No. The local knobs, I meant," Fat Mao said in a low voice, like a growl. "This is different. This says Public Security Headquarters. Boot squads. Working for the bastard kings in a bastard government."

The words cast a pall over the company. They stared at the screen without speaking.

"Nothing about monks," Jowa said finally in a low aside to Shan. "Nothing about Gendun or Tibetans."

"Headquarters," Jakli repeated the words. "It could mean regional headquarters in Urumqi," she said, referring to the capital city of Xinjiang, six hundred miles to the northeast. "Or it could mean Beijing." She looked about, wide-eyed, as if she had seen a phantom. In either case it meant someone else was watching Yoktian County, from high above. Jakli moved as though to rise but seemed to have lost her strength. She sat back heavily and stared at the screen.

Shan stood suddenly. He felt short of breath. He stepped outside and breathed in the cool air. It had been Public

Security headquarters in Beijing that had sent him to the gulag. He had assumed that the very worst that could happen to Gendun would be capture by the local knobs. But the headquarters knobs had university degrees and high ranks in the Party. The boot squads were their special soldiers, always led by a political officer. They would see Gendun differently. He would be an experiment. They might seek to use him, after breaking him with technologies not even the most serene mind could resist. They had done it before, more than once. They had even taken the Panchen Lama, the highest of all reincarnate lamas after the Dalai Lama, and imprisoned him for ten years in a maximum security prison near Beijing after he had spoken out for Tibetan independence. He had emerged a different man, married to a Han Chinese woman.

Inside the tent by the stables Shan found Malik kneeling by his bag, smoothing out a pallet consisting of three small carpets stacked together. Lokesh was sitting cross-legged on a similar pallet facing an assortment of objects that lay on a small red carpet, a Muslim prayer rug. He was holding the stub of a wooden pencil in his palm, in front of his chest, his eyes closed.

Shan's foot brushed against a tin can containing small bits of glass that lay at the edge of the red carpet. It tipped over, making a tinkling sound that snapped Lokesh out of his trance.

"He didn't have much," the old Tibetan sighed, gesturing toward the objects before him.

"These were the boy's?"

Lokesh nodded and stared inquisitively at the objects. The tin can with glass baubles. Three pencil stubs. A small, lute-like instrument with only two strings. A braid of leather straps that showed signs of having been repeatedly braided and unbraided, as if in practice. A single jade ball, the size of a large marble. Five pieces of dry, brittle wood with black marks that could have been writing on them. A young boy's treasures.

Malik raised the lute and plucked a string absently. "A dombra," he said sadly, "for singing the old clan songs."

Shan knelt and lifted one of the pieces of wood.

"We found them, that day," Malik said, looking at the

pieces with a puzzled expression. "It had been smashed, the pieces scattered around his body."

What had been smashed, Shan almost asked, but he began fitting the pieces together and soon saw that the object was composed of two pieces, a flat bottom frame into which a wedge slid. The top of the wedge held two lines of text written in small fluid characters that resembled Sanskrit, the nearly extinct language of the lands south of Tibet. When it slid open, the flat surface inside, complete except for a large splinter missing from the center, was filled with writing in the same script. Like a letter, he thought, with the address on top.

He looked up to see Lokesh staring intensely at the collection of objects. Like an investigator, Shan thought. No, not exactly, he realized as he watched Lokesh slowly extend his hand and brush his fingertips over each item, for the old Buddhist would never see the collection as physical objects, as the meager trail of a young life. He would see them as the vestiges of a young soul, as signals for the boy's spirit, the tracks of the boy's inner god. Lokesh seemed to no longer be aware of Shan, as if once again the unpredictable embers within had ignited. The old Tibetan stared at the jade ball and slowly leaned toward it, as if it beckoned him. Shan picked it up and extended it toward Lokesh. They were in the land of jade. China had always obtained its jade from the Turkistan kingdoms north of the Kunlun. The Jade Bitch, the Uighur had called the prosecutor. Shan saw that the jade was delicately carved with tiny lotus flowers, with a hole running through its center. A bead. He dropped it into the Tibetan's open palm.

"What is it, old friend," Shan asked. "Who was the boy? Did you know Khitai?"

Lokesh sighed. "Not this boy," he said, as if there were multiple Khitais, then stared at the bead as a single tear rolled down his cheek.

It was almost dusk before Shan was able to return to the boy's grave, having finally left Lokesh in Jakli's care. His friend seemed to have gone into a strange trance, staring at the jade bead for more than an hour, during which the wild-eyed woman had reappeared, with a quiet, morose air, and sat beside the old Tibetan. When Shan had left the tent, the woman was patting Lokesh on the back like a sick child, humming one of her cradle songs as Jakli tried to coax him into eating some buckwheat porridge.

The last rays of the sun washed the back of the clearing, causing the grave to glow with an eerie pink light. Inside the rock enclosure the air was deathly still. A solitary cricket chirped.

Shan moved slowly along the edge of the rocks, then dropped to his knees beside the small mound of earth. He placed his palms on top of the loose soil, then stroked it, realizing after a moment that he was repeating the motion of the crazed woman, rubbing it the way a parent would smooth the blanket of a sleeping child. He had a son somewhere, not seen in years. With a stab of pain he realized that he didn't know if his own son was still alive. The possibility of his son's death had never occurred to him. But the tides of insane violence that had surged through his country did not discriminate between young and old. Children died for the sins of their parents, sometimes quickly, sometimes by the slow extinction of being abandoned. No, that was history, a voice in his head argued, and Shan's son would have the protection of his mother, a high cadre in the Party. Then he looked back at the grave under his hands. Khitai no doubt had thought himself well protected with the Red Stone clan. Children still died.

Was that indeed why he was here? he wondered. Was there something historic in the death of the woman Lau, something sensed by the old lamas that signaled a new tide of destruction, that meant a new demon of repression had been unleashed?

He absently scooped some of the loose earth from the grave, then slowly sprinkled the soil back over the mound and patted it smooth again. What was it about this homeless Kazakh boy that made him suddenly so dangerous to Bajys that he had to be shot? Had he indeed tried to stop Bajys's betrayal of the clans and the secrets of Fat Mao? Had he stolen something? Was it punishment? A mischievous boy who wandered from camp to camp might learn things, might be tempted by things that in turn could tempt Bajys.

But what? The meager possessions of impoverished no-mads? And what could he have that Bajys did not also have? Both boys, he remembered. Alta and Khitai had played together and had then been killed two days apart. One beaten and shot, the other beaten and stabbed. Maybe the boys had known something, had discovered something so dangerous to their killer they could not be left alive. They lived in a land of secrets. Secret families. Secret dissidents. Secret army bases.

As he idly stroked the earth, his fingers brushed something hard. He probed the soil and retrieved a curved piece of wood, small enough to fit into his hand. It had been crudely carved into the image of a bird in flight. It could have been one of Khitai's toys. It could have been a religious symbol. He pushed his fingers into the sandy soil and dragged them along the length of the grave. Near the head of the mound they touched something else, a five-inch splinter of wood. It was the missing piece from the strange wooden letter, containing a single line of the Sanskrit-like text. What did it mean? Was it an epitaph? Could the killer read the strange text? Did it contain a message that had caused the boy's death? He laid the two objects, the splinter of text and the crude bird, before him. Had they been buried by the same person? Perhaps they were both just offerings, or mementos. Did they mean something when put together?

He stared at them a long time, then scooped out two small holes and reverently returned the bird and the splinter of wood to the grave.

The cricket chirped again. Crickets were supposed to bring good luck. But they had brought none to Khitai. And none to Red Stone clan.

He rose and paced about the darkening clearing, considering it not as a graveyard but as a killing place. Bajys could have come up from the encampment or climbed along the ridge, over the rocks, into the clearing. He had come near the end of day, the end of a day when Khitai had been playing with Alta, the boy with the dropka. He had shot, but no one had heard a gun.

He realized the wind that coursed over the rocks could mask such a sound. As he paused to listen to its low moan, Shan felt something black and icy surge within him. It came like this sometimes, a dark coldness welling within, and when it did he had to stop and fight it. Sometimes it came on him with a spell of shaking, other times as a burning spot on his arm where he wore his lao gai tattoo, or along his spine where the knobs had used cattle prods. It was black and shapeless, and he had no name for it. It wasn't fear, or hate, it was just the thing that lingered from his years in the gulag, especially from the first weeks when all he could remember was a miasma of pain and people shouting at him. He closed his eyes and remembered the first time he had met one of the lamas, when the old Tibetan had pulled Shan's face out of the mud as he lay beneath a raging guard, about to suffocate. The lama had straddled Shan's body to take the baton blows meant for Shan. He remembered the serene smile on the lama's face as the guard beat him, and his weakness passed. He put a hand against the rock wall for a moment to steady himself, then continued around the clearing.

As he walked he found a place in the wall opposite the entry path where a thick slab of rock had tumbled from above, creating a small sheltered alcove. He stepped into its shadows and struck a match. A white cylindrical object lay at the base of the rock, partially covered with sand. He reached for it and found that it was a candle, which he lit just as the match flickered out.

Protected as it was from the wind, the sandy floor of the little enclosure still showed shallow indentations where two people had sat, facing the flat rear wall. On the wall, inscribed in chalk, was a circle eighteen inches wide. Only a circle. It could be a drawing game played by children. Shan's mind drifted to other circles he had seen on walls, those drawn on prison walls to symbolize a mandala, which always began with a circle to focus the mind into awareness of inner space and emptiness. Some circles were drawn to help focus meditation. But that was in Tibet, not in a Kazakh herding camp.

He held the flame higher and saw more writing on the adjacent wall. Two horizontal lines intersected by two perpendicular lines, with two Xs and two Os in four of the boxes formed by the lines. A drawing game popular in the West, played by Shan with his father when Shan had been

Khitai's age. He looked back at the circle. No doubt it too had been part of a game, perhaps simply a target for boys throwing stones. He turned to the line game. It had been interrupted. He shuddered as he saw in his mind the young boy playing his innocent game, only to be dragged away by someone intent on killing him. Did it mean Alta had been a witness, left sitting in the alcove? Or did it mean the murderer himself had been playing the game with Khitai? A murderer so heartless as to kill a child would be capable of anything, even luring a child to his death by an act of playfulness. What kind was it, Lokesh would have asked, what kind of demon had taken over Bajys? Hariti, the dropka had said. The child-eating demon.

As Shan descended the hill, Malik was sitting in the evening greyness at a small fire by the animal pens, the big mastiff lying beside him. He was studying the sky and seemed not to notice when Shan sat beside him.

The sky was still and vast, dominated by a brilliant half moon. From a distance an animal howled. On the far side of the fire Shan saw a large peg in the ground from which a rope extended into the darkness. Tethered to the rope were several young horses.

When he had been released from prison, he had spent many nights like this, under the stars in secret meditation places shown him by the old lamas. Sometimes one of them, usually Gendun, had sat with him, trying, he eventually realized, to draw out the torment that resided in his soul. They had reconstructed his life year by year, sometimes month by month, having him speak over an old ceramic urn decorated with a simple line drawing of the Compassionate Buddha.

"The pot is now full," Gendun had said when they had finished, and he had capped the vessel with a ceramic lid. He had handed Shan a rock and one of the small, melodic bells used in the temple, then left Shan under the stars without further explanation.

Shan had been on an open ledge, so high that the sky had been almost as broad below him as above him. Once he had tried to move the urn and it had seemed incomprehensibly heavy. After several hours, in the darkest of the night, Shan had shattered the urn with the rock and picked up the bell. He had rung the small bell, making a sound like a brilliant vibrating crystal, until the sun rose.

He fingered the tiny shard of the urn that he still carried in his pocket. He had returned days later to retrieve it, for there was one piece of his prior life he could not leave behind. His son.

When Malik reached over to nudge his leg, the touch was so unexpected that Shan jumped. "Do you think he went there?" the boy asked quietly. "Last year, when a baby died, my uncle said they go to a beautiful valley on the moon."

Shan followed his gaze toward the moon. It made his heart ache, that the boy was so familiar with death. "I don't know," he said. "Maybe. It is very beautiful."

"It's so white," Malik whispered. "It must be the color of their sand." He was silent a moment, then asked another question. "Where would they get water?"

"Perhaps," Shan suggested, "they need no water."

The comment seemed to confuse the boy. He looked into the flames. "Water is life," he said, sounding very wise. "Is that how you know you're dead? You have no more thirst?" When Shan didn't answer he slowly bent and lifted something lying at his feet. A knife. And a thin piece of wood that widened into an oval at the end. He began slicing away slivers of the wood, aiming the cuttings into the embers where they curled in the heat, then flashed into a quick, hot flame.

"A spoon," Malik volunteered. "A present for Jakli and—" he paused. "A present, for the horse festival."

Shan watched him work the wood with firm expert strokes. "I saw the bird you gave him," he ventured quietly.

The boy showed no surprise. "My mother asked me to carve one when the baby died last year. To help guide him through the sky, she said. This time no one asked but—" Malik shrugged. "The zheli are younger than me. It made me sad, to know they had grown up always running. Khitai, he had no *ashamai* saddle, no *sundet* horse."

"I don't understand."

"Those orphans, they never have a real home. Khitai said when he was young people passed him around, to protect him. Sometimes he was in the mountains, sometimes in a city. Once he spent a year living in a cave. He said it was better with Bajys and Lau, but growing up like that, it meant he didn't know the old Kazakh ways. I was sorry he had no saddle." Malik paused and glanced at Shan. "When a boy is five years old he can ride alone," he explained, "and is given a special soft saddle, an ashamai saddle, decorated with feathers and red paint. Later, when a mullah pronounces him ready to start the road to manhood, there are ceremonies and a feast and he gets a sundet horse, his first horse. But Khitai never had any. Not a saddle, not a horse. He said it was all right, that he loved all the animals, and they taught him things. He climbed a tree to see baby birds once. He followed butterflies."

"Were you good friends?"

"We only knew each other a little while and only were together two or three times a week. Sometimes he helped me tie the zheli out at night," the boy said, and gestured toward the line of tethered horses. "He spent most of his time with Bajys, looking for sheep on the high slopes or in their spot above the camp."

"What did they do there?"

"Talked, mostly. I think Bajys wanted to tell Khitai all the things he could remember about their old clan, so the memories wouldn't die too."

"Why would they go away like that?"

"Clans have secrets. There are memories that can't be shared in front of strangers."

Shan leaned forward and pushed a stick into the fire. "You and Khitai, what did you do together?"

"We played when we could. Sometimes we would climb into the lamb pens and laugh because they would try to nurse on our fingers. Sometimes we would go on walks and pretend things."

"What kind of things?"

"You know. Shooting soldiers."

The words made Shan look back at the yurt where Jowa and Fat Mao still sat with the computer. "Does Fat Mao come here a lot?"

"Not often. He's a soldier too," Malik said, as if understanding why Shan asked. "A special kind. *Lung ma*," he whispered with awe in his voice.

"Lung ma?" It was an old term, from the ancient courts. It meant *horse dragon*, a mythical beast, part horse, part dragon, that protected the common people from injustice.

"Sure. Like your Tibetan soldier."

Like Jowa. The lung ma, Shan realized, was a counterpart to the purbas.

"They all call themselves Mao. Like a joke. You know this Mao, that Mao. Too dangerous for real names, he told me once. They make things happen to the government sometimes," Malik declared with a knowing nod.

"Did Khitai know about them?"

"No. It's a secret. Fat Mao made me promise. Says if I can keep the secret maybe someday I can be one too," the boy said, and it saddened Shan somehow. Did Lau know about the lung ma, he almost asked, then realized he didn't need to. Fat Mao had sent the message to the purbas about her death. If Lau had been part of the lung ma she may have been killed for it. The main job of boot squads was to stamp out resistance, and nowhere in China was there more violent resistance than in Xinjiang.

"Did you know Lau?" he asked.

"Sure. She brought medicine for the animals sometimes."

"Did you hear she was dead?"

"Only yesterday. It was a secret until then."

"Do you think she was killed for what she did for the orphans?"

Malik took a long time to answer. When he did, he looked toward the young horses. "She didn't do anything for them that I don't do for our zheli," he said, and there was an edge of fear in the boy's voice. He spoke several Turkic words to the horses, calming words that had the rhythm of a song, then suddenly turned to Shan with an expression of pain. "If they take us to the city, we won't know who we are. We won't have horses. We won't have tents, maybe not even dogs." He fell silent for a long moment. "And what will happen when I am old? There will be no more clan. No one to carve me a bird when I die."

Shan cradled the boy's hand in his own. "You are strong. A strong spirit will always find the way."

They sat in silence. How long had it been since he had

talked with his son like this? Years. No, never like this. Shan's wife, the dutiful Party cadre, had raised their son hundreds of miles from Shan and jealously guarded the boy when they were together. He had always told himself that it would be like this one day with his son, but that had been just one more of the lies that had kept him alive during his Beijing incarnation.

A shooting star blazed across the sky in the direction of the moon. Another child perhaps, going to the beautiful white valley.

"Were you with Khitai when he played his line game on the rock?"

"We played those games sometimes. He knew games I had never seen before. But not that last day. A late lamb had been born in a grove of trees two miles from here. It is my job to watch the babies, or they could die. I had to stay with the lamb all day. Then I could be sure it knew the scent of its mother and that it was strong enough for me to bring it back to the other lambs."

"Until that night?"

"When I returned at dusk I was going to go up to Khitai's spot, to look for him. But one of the young rams got caught in a vine and cut its leg. I had to put on salve. It was crying. I spoke to it. *Khoshakhan, khoshakhan*, you have to say to lambs. It's an old word, like a charm. It's how they know you love them," the boy said, with the voice of an old man. He sighed. "It was dark. I stayed up late, because it was then that I began telling them why we have to leave them soon. The Brigade will take good care of the sheep, I said. What else can I say? All the lambs and young goats would have grown up with me in the mountains. And now none of us will. I have to at least leave them with hope." He looked at Shan with an empty expression and shook his head. "The next morning I asked my aunt where he was, and she said probably up in his place in the rocks."

"What was it like, when you found him?"

Malik looked at the moon. "It was still dawn. He was sitting in the shadows against the rock, near where he is buried. He seemed surprised."

"Surprised?"

"I couldn't look after the first instant. But when I first found him I thought he was looking behind me, in surprise, like someone was creeping up on us. I said, you look funny. And you have three eyes." Malik looked down to the embers. "But his eyes had no seeing. I called for Khitai and ran away."

As Shan repeated the boy's words in his mind the dog's head shot up. Shan looked in the direction of the dog's gaze to see Lokesh standing in the shadows, looking as frail as a stick figure. The Tibetan sat down beside the dog, which immediately laid its head on his leg.

"I don't understand," Shan said to the boy. "Why did you call for Khitai?"

Malik frowned and looked back toward the moon.

"Because this boy," Lokesh answered Shan in a trembling voice, "the boy in the grave, he is not Khitai."

Malik sighed, as though with great relief, and nodded.

Shan looked back and forth from the boy to the old man. For a moment he felt as though he was not in the middle of a murder investigation but in a teaching, as if he sat between two lamas who were asking him to explain impossible contradictions.

"I told Akzu it wasn't Khitai," Malik blurted out. "Those things in the tent, the dombra and the jade bead, they weren't Khitai's. It was the other boy of the zheli who had visited that day, whose name was Suwan. He just had Khitai's red cap on. Akzu wasn't certain. The boy's face was so bruised and swollen. Akzu didn't know Khitai well, he's been away many times these past weeks. He said Khitai was the name of the boy Lau had sent, that whichever boy it was, Bajys had killed him, that if Khitai had gone with the other clan to escape Bajys, then may God protect him. He said I should not tell this to others, because it would just add to the sorrow of my aunts. He said either way an orphan had died, that a good Kazakh boy had been buried, and that was the end of it. I was not to tell the secret."

But now, Shan realized, Lokesh had divined the truth, and spoken it first, so Malik could explain.

The dog's head shot up again, and its tail wagged. Shan looked over his shoulder to see Jakli standing with the tethered horses, listening.

"Do you know Khitai?" Malik asked Lokesh.

The old Tibetan shook his head slowly.

Malik stared at Lokesh with round eyes, feeling, Shan knew, the same emotion as Shan himself, a confused awe of the strange magic that seemed to be working in the Tibetan. Shan had been wrong. It had not been Alta who had visited the camp but another family, another dropka family with a boy named Suwan, who had taken his belongings into the Red Stone tent, as if moving in. Khitai had changed places, switched positions on the zheli tether, with this boy, who had complained that his foster family couldn't speak his native tongue.

"Did Khitai speak Tibetan?" Shan asked.

"No. He was Kazakh," Malik said with a puzzled tone. "But he wanted to go higher."

"Higher?"

"Deeper into the mountains than Red Stone goes. The season is almost over, and the herding families live close to town in the winter. But word came that the Brigade was breaking up all the clans, that maybe the zheli would be broken up and shipped away to Chinese places. Khitai was very scared of the Chinese. I think they did bad things to his people when he was young. Khitai talked about getting away, to the last range, we call it. The highest part of the Kunlun, where the glaciers live."

They watched the fire in silence.

"Did you return that piece of wood to his grave?" Shan asked at last.

His words seemed to frighten Malik. He squeezed Shan's hand tighter, as if to remind him that he was not an old man after all, just a boy who kept burying other children. "I found it the next day," Malik said. "My aunt had collected all the other pieces and put them with his things. I was going to bring it to the tent too. But I didn't want to touch it so I pushed it into the grave with a stick."

"Why?"

"Maybe that was what had called to the demon. The killer broke the secret writing apart. Maybe that's what had made the killer so angry."

"You mean Bajys?"

Shan saw Malik nod in the dark. "The thing that Bajys

became, my uncle said." The boy was quiet a long time, watching the dying flames. "I know there are protective deities, like those that watch over animals. I know, because I have seen how lost babies find their mothers on the far side of a mountain. And if there are protective deities then there must be the opposite kind," the boy said in a knowing tone, as if he had often thought about the possibility.

A destructive deity, Shan thought. A demon.

"And it's still out there," Malik said in a haunted voice. "The thing that kills children."

"We have to leave as soon as possible," Lokesh announced suddenly in a weak voice. "We must go and talk with Auntie Lau."

Shan looked at his friend with worry. Something inside Lokesh seemed to have been collapsing since he had first heard Khitai's name. "Do you know about lamas here?" Shan asked Malik. "Was there one who was a friend of Lau's perhaps? One who is missing?"

"Holy men?" the boy asked. "No. That Prosecutor Xu in Yoktian, she would never allow it. She gives speeches sometimes. She hates Tibetans. She says they are all traitors." Malik thought in silence for a moment. "She wouldn't kill them, though," he said with a certainty that chilled Shan. "But she would take them to a place where it is easy for a holy man to die."

CHAPTER 4

The rising sun washed the peaks in a blush of gold and pink as they rode down the rough northern slope of the Kunlun mountains. The light seemed to revive Lokesh, and he broke into one of his traveling songs, praising the deities who preserved mountains. Akzu and Jowa rode ahead, out of earshot, speaking in the same urgent tones they had used in the yurt with Fat Mao the day before. Every few minutes Jowa stood in his stirrups, looking ahead as if searching for something. Fat Mao, perhaps. The Uighur had been gone when they awoke.

Suddenly Akzu raised his hand in warning. As they stopped, the sound of hoofbeats came from higher on the slope, from a trail that ran along the crest of the ridge above them. A small rider appeared on a loping grey horse. Shan heard Akzu curse, then call out to the rider, who wheeled the horse to a halt fifty feet above them. It was Malik.

"The zheli have to be warned!" the youth called out to his uncle. "Khitai is still alive. The thing that is Bajys will come for him too, and maybe the others!"

Akzu cast a worried glance toward Jakli. "We need you, boy," he shouted in reply. "You don't know where to seek. This is not the time." Anger seemed to enter his voice as he spoke. "I am head of Red Stone clan. I tell you no."

The young Kazakh gazed out over the mountains for a moment. When he turned back toward his uncle Shan saw pain in his eyes. "And I tell you I am tired of digging graves," he called back, then kicked his horse into a sudden gallop.

Shan watched Akzu as the headman gazed toward the boy and saw his face shift from anger to fear and then pride. "Go with God, boy," the old man offered quietly, then muttered to his horse and continued down the trail at a fast trot.

Half an hour later, at the top of a ridge that descended sharply in a series of switchbacks, Jakli pointed to a ribbon of grey on the northern horizon. "The highway," she said, "four hundred miles west to Kashgar."

Shan leaned forward in his saddle and pointed toward a huge rock formation a quarter mile to the west. It stood like a massive sentinel, towering three hundred feet above the ridge. At its top, fastened to a long pole held fast with a cairn of rocks, was a large square of ragged red cloth, perhaps six feet to the side. It was a huge *lungta*, a Tibetan prayer flag. In front, Lokesh stopped singing and stared toward the cairn, his hands cupped around his eyes. As he recognized the flag he began to wave, first at Shan, then toward the flag.

Shan studied the towering rock. It seemed impossible to climb. But someone had done so, as if daring the Chinese to risk their own lives to take it down. Not just someone. A Buddhist. It was a border land. Many different peoples lived here, Jakli had said. But Tibetans, Malik had warned, were singled out by the prosecutor for special treatment. Border lands had people of mixed blood. Like Jakli herself, part Kazakh, part Tibetan. Mixed blood and perhaps mixed allegiances. Like Lau, perhaps—the mysterious woman with a Han name whose death had so stirred the lamas, the dead woman Jakli was taking him to visit.

"*Lha gyal lo!*" Lokesh called out in his loudest voice, causing Jowa to spin about with an angry glare. The old Tibetan ignored the purba. "*Lha gyal lo!*" he repeated. "May the gods be victorious!"

"Your friend," Jakli said, looking at Lokesh, who waved at the flag again. "Is he crazy? I'm sorry—is he touched from old age, perhaps?"

"Senile?" Shan smiled as he studied his old friend. "If senile is being unaware and lost and unable to connect things, then Lokesh is the opposite of senile. He has seen too much. All he wanted was to be a monk, a monk healer. But he so excelled at his lessons that his gompa sent him to work for the government. Then Beijing came and said he couldn't be a monk anymore. After a few months he got married, to a nun who had also been expelled. Two weeks later he was thrown into prison for being a government official."

"For thirty years," Jakli recalled.

Shan nodded. "Every visiting day his wife would come. Usually she wasn't allowed close enough to talk, so they would wave at each other, just wave for hours. And two days after he got home his wife died."

Jakli's eyes had grown moist as Shan spoke. She looked at Lokesh, then turned away, into the wind, and urged her horse forward.

They rode for another hour, descending constantly, until they reached the junction of several horse trails behind a long narrow structure at the head of a gravel road. The three-sided building was constructed of cinder blocks that had begun to crumble into dust. At one end the wall had partially collapsed, causing a sharp dip in the corrugated tin roof. To avoid total calamity, stout logs had been braced on sheets of plywood that pressed against the exterior walls. As they dismounted and walked around the end of the building, Shan saw half a dozen trucks in various states of disrepair, sitting in the shadows of the building. The garage and its motor pool was operated on Ministry of Agriculture subsidies, Akzu explained, for the small farming and herding enterprises in the region.

A small cubicle had been constructed of plywood in the rear corner of the building, at the end where the wall was intact. On a crude door cobbled together of wood and cardboard was a faded poster of a dozen young men and women representing some of the scores of ethnic groups that had been liberated by Beijing. Clad in the blue uniforms of the proletariat, they all joyfully raised wrenches and hammers toward the sky. *Cultivate the Wealth of the Minorities*, the caption read.

Past the door sat an emaciated short-haired dog and a short dark man with several days' growth of beard and stains of motor oil on his hands and arms. Reading a newspaper at a rusty metal desk, the man glanced up as Akzu appeared, offered a grunt of greeting, and pointed to a board from which five nails extended, each holding a ring of keys.

"Leave quickly, uncle," Jakli said softly as she approached the door. "The clan needs you."

The man's head snapped up at the sound of her voice. He looked at Jakli with a frown, then back to Akzu. "Checkpoints," he muttered. "Four miles up the road to Yoktian, then out on the main highway, going west."

"Jakli is taking them—" Akzu began.

The man interrupted Akzu with an upraised hand. "Don't want to know where, old friend. Too many people asking too many questions these days. Just a mechanic, that's all I want to be." He picked up the paper, revealing an open ledger book underneath, then slammed the ledger shut and gazed at the board of keys.

"Take the turtle," he said, pointing to the last set of keys in the row. "We never officially acquired it, so it's not on the books. Don't have to record anything."

Akzu tossed Jakli the keys and pointed toward the last bay, which held a small sturdy truck that appeared to have been assembled from parts of other vehicles. It had wide tires, a short cargo bay constructed of rough cut lumber, an oversized gas tank that extended along the frame, and a long cab, so large it accommodated a narrow rear seat. The high, rounded lines of the cab did indeed resemble a turtle shell.

"Who?" Akzu asked the man.

The man frowned again. Too many questions, he had said. "Grey," he offered with a tone of resignation, and Shan realized Akzu meant, whose checkpoint? Grey was the color of the Public Security troops, the knobs. The army wore green. Traffic police wore blue. "But she's not there. Too busy elsewhere. Grabbed four yesterday. Three the day before, I hear, from town. Some teachers from the school. Motor pool. That's how I heard. They took a driver."

Jakli, who had just gestured for Shan to join her at the truck, stopped abruptly at the announcement. She stepped back toward the cubicle. "On what grounds?" Jakli asked in a raised voice. Shan had begun to understand something about the spirited Kazakh woman. If Lokesh sometimes unexpectedly overflowed with sorrow, then Jakli was subject to attacks of defiance in a similarly unpredictable manner.

"On the grounds that she is the prosecutor," the man replied, but he looked at Akzu, as if he were not inclined to converse with Jakli. "It's about that woman, Lau, someone said. They're taken for questioning about her disappearance. You knew Lau. They could take you too."

"But she drowned," Akzu said, exchanging a worried glance with Jakli. "People say she drowned."

"So I heard. But no body was found. Anyway, must have been a slow time in town."

"What do you mean?" Shan asked.

The mechanic looked at him with the same reluctance he had shown with Jakli. "Army shoots someone, that's national defense. Public Security knobs shoot someone, that's for public security, by definition. We shoot one of them, that's assassination. Simple. Like inserting pegs on a board. They have forms all printed up. But this one, just an old Kazakh woman disappearing? A Kazakh or Uighur here or there, usually she doesn't care."

"But this time," Shan observed, "the Prosecutor is putting up checkpoints and picking up witnesses."

"Not witnesses," the mechanic shot back. "The actors in her latest production. The political gallery."

Shan studied the man. He suspected the man had not always been a mechanic. "The prosecutor is using it," he said, nodding his agreement.

The mechanic held up his hand again, as if signaling that he would hear no more of such dangerous talk. Akzu gently pushed Jakli out of the cubicle as the mechanic went back to his paper.

Moments later Jakli stood at the driver's door as Akzu showed her a map pulled from the visor of the truck and pointed to several dotted lines that wandered back and forth across the dark line that represented the Kashgar highway. "Go with speed, niece," the headman said. "Then back to town. You will be missed at the factory. You take too many risks. Remember Nikki. Remember your aunts."

Nikki. Shan remembered Malik, speaking of the present

he was carving. There had been another name which the boy had been wary of speaking.

"Always," Jakli said with a shy smile that encompassed both Akzu and Shan. "Watch for Malik, Uncle," she added. "Watch for the children." She gave Akzu a quick embrace, then froze.

A bright red truck was skidding to a halt in the loose gravel in front of the garage. Shan recognized the gleaming vehicle as one of the four-wheel-drive trucks produced by an American joint venture in Beijing, a factory he had audited once in his prior incarnation. On the front door of the truck was a large insignia in gold, a representation of the head and shoulders of a man and a woman, their arms crossed over a rising sun, one hand holding a hammer, the other a wrench. Below the sun was an oil derrick, a tractor, and an animal that may have been a sheep. Shan realized he had seen it before, two nights earlier, on the truck that had stopped them in the Kunlun. The Brigade had arrived.

Akzu quickly stepped out of the garage, into the sunlight, in front of the red truck, as if to distract the new arrivals. As he did so a Han Chinese emerged from the rear seat, a man of perhaps thirty years, wearing a red nylon parka that bore a miniature version of the same emblem on its breast and sunglasses under an American-style front brimmed hat. He rapped a knuckle on the window of the front passenger seat and pointed toward the cubicle in the shadows. The two men in the front emerged, the driver holding a clipboard, the other a small calculator, and stepped briskly toward the cubicle.

Shan felt a tug at his sleeve. Jakli was pulling him back, behind the turtle truck. He let himself be eased into the shadow as he watched a second figure climb out of the back seat, a tall, lean man with a thin face and high cheekbones, wearing a brown suitcoat, at least two sizes too small, over the blue pants of a factory worker. Shan glanced at Lokesh and saw from Lokesh's sudden interest that his old friend had also recognized the man's features. The tall man was unmistakably Tibetan.

"Akzu," the man in the cap said as the headman approached. "An unexpected pleasure!" His voice was as smooth and polished as his face. An eastern voice. A university-trained voice.

"Ko Yonghong," Jakli whispered to Shan. "District manager for the Brigade."

Akzu greeted the younger man affably but slowly stepped around the red truck, even as Ko put his hand on the Kazakh's shoulder. Akzu wanted him away from the garage, away from Jakli and her companions.

The wind caught Ko's parka as he walked and opened it. He was wearing a white shirt. Only then did Shan notice that the two men who had gone to the desk wore light brown shirts, clean shirts with collars and cuffs, like uniforms, like those he had seen on the high road in the Kunlun. He glanced into the windows of the red truck, as though hoping for a glimpse of Gendun, then studied the district manager carefully. Ko Yonghong. Ko Forever Red. It was a name favored by parents who were ambitious Party members. The man who was liquidating the Red Stone clan.

Suddenly, before Shan or Jakli could restrain him, Lokesh stepped out of the shadows and raised his hand toward the tall stranger.

"Tashi delek," Lokesh said in an affable voice. Hello, in Tibetan.

Though softly spoken, as if not to be overheard, the words stopped Ko Yonghong, twenty feet away. He spun about and stared at Lokesh with intense interest for a moment, then paused to light a cigarette with a gold lighter and grinned at Akzu, as if the herdsman had presented him with an unexpected gift.

"Ni zao. Ni hao ma?" the Tibetan replied with an awkward smile and a quick glance at Ko. Good morning. How are you? in Mandarin. "I am called Kaju. Kaju Drogme."

The announcement instantly brought Jakli out of the shadows. At the same moment Ko stepped to Kaju's side, still studying Lokesh. He inhaled deeply on his cigarette, then gazed slowly down the line of trucks in the garage, as if looking to see what other surprises lurked in the shadows.

He wasn't the man who had challenged them two nights before in the Kunlun, Shan knew, but he could have been the man in the seat, smoking in the dark. Why would the Brigade be inside Tibet, why would it be waiting on a deserted road in the middle of the night? What had they done to Gendun, he wanted to shout. But why, he wondered in the same instant, why had they not just taken all of them, Jowa and Lokesh too, if the Brigade was so interested in Tibetans? Shan slipped around the front of the truck, into the light, suddenly feeling the need to protect Lokesh.

"Red Stone has no vehicles," Akzu said suddenly, and Shan understood what the men in the garage were doing. Taking inventory.

Two streams of smoke snaked out of Ko's nostrils as he stepped around Kaju to the front of the red truck, where he could see all of them at once. "You will be pleased to know the enrichment program has been expanded. We're privatizing the motor pool as well."

"Enrichment?" Akzu asked tersely. Shan could see that he was restraining himself, trying not to antagonize the Brigade manager.

"Poverty Eradication seems such a demeaning term," Ko said, sounding more like a political officer than a businessman. "Think of all the shares in the company you'll have, comrade. You'll be an owner of the garage now too. We will be launching stock exchange shares soon. We have special advisers working on it from Beijing. Consultants from America, even."

One of the men, Ko's driver, suddenly ran out of the end of the garage. A wrench flew past his head. Ko pretended not to notice. The man stopped and glared back into the shadows a moment, then moved to the rear of their vehicle and opened its hatch window. He rummaged through a large cardboard box and pulled out a carton of cigarettes, then ventured back into the garage.

"I'm so pleased that you have acquired your own consultants, comrade," Ko declared with a narrow smile, sweeping his hand toward Shan and his companions. Shan watched the man's eyes as he studied them with an unsettling air of satisfaction. Ko Yonghong, Shan decided, was a man who constantly looked for personal benefit, who sought to identify advantage or leverage in every new relationship. The director stretched his arms languidly and nodded slowly, as if making the point that he did not want to learn the identity of Akzu's companions. As if he had already decided who they were and had more to gain by not challenging them.

"You're the new teacher," Jakli said suddenly, looking at Kaju. "For Auntie Lau."

The Tibetan seemed relieved by the question. "We are expanding her good works, yes," he said in a thin voice, nervously glancing at Ko. "The Brigade has made a contribution to funding. Comrade Director Ko wants to bring the orphans into a more formal program. An official cultural integration program at the school in town. An assigned classroom."

"What she did for them no school could provide," Jakli shot back.

Ko stepped closer and raised his hands as if in surrender. "Not traditional school," he offered in an earnest tone. "Just make the Brigade resources available."

"It's not Brigade resources they need," Jakli said with a spark in her eyes.

Ko cocked his head as he examined Jakli, and leaned forward. "You're very pretty," he offered, still in his earnest voice. "I could get you a job."

Jakli ignored him. "The Kazakhs and Uighurs can take care of their own orphans."

Ko raised his hands in surrender again. "Please. I am a friend of your people," he said with a smile. "We could organize a sports team for them, be sure they receive necessary testing. Put them on the rolls for eligibility in our special youth programs." Ko patted Kaju on his back. "But it's all up to our new teacher. We don't want to scare them off. Whatever they're comfortable with. Above all, it must be a process of consensus. It will be traumatic for them at first, when they learn of our loss."

"Our loss?"

"Surely you understand that Lau was valued by all of us. A treasure. We can offer special counselors, if they need them."

"We're going ahead with the classes. I don't want them to miss a session," Kaju said softly. "They need to keep progressing, keep learning about the new society. It's what she would want."

Jakli appeared surprised at the man. She had wanted to

be angry, Shan sensed, to resent Lau's replacement. But the young, nervous Tibetan seemed genuinely concerned about the children.

"You came quickly," she observed.

"I was already here."

The mechanic emerged into the sunlight, holding the carton of cigarettes. He retrieved his wrench from the dirt and sat against a tree at the end of the building, opening the carton with obvious relish and lighting a cigarette.

"I don't understand," Jakli said.

"Kaju graduated from a special university program in Chengdu. A facilitator in intercultural relations," Ko explained. "We're very proud of his work. The way of the future. Privatization, integration, the path of a strong nation."

Shan began to recognize a new species in Ko. Shan had been raised in a world which revolved around Party rank, a world so structured around political rank that officials sometimes carried their office chairs into meeting rooms as a form of intimidation, because even office furniture was allocated according to which of the twenty-four grades of the Party a cadre belonged to. But Ko was not in the government. The cool sneer of a Party official seemed to lurk behind his every expression, but he was a businessman.

Akzu was staring at the ground. He had seen the path mentioned by Ko. The liquidation of Red Stone clan. Shan remembered the agony on his face when he had heard how their children would be sent to memorize Party scriptures.

"You'll see, comrade. We only want to help. If the Poverty Scheme doesn't work, come and tell me," Ko said, resting his hand on Akzu's shoulder again, then stepped to the vehicle that Jakli had been about to drive away. He opened the door and gestured for Shan to step inside. "Meanwhile," he said, looking at no one but Jakli. "You and your special friends no doubt have important business. Do not let us delay you."

Ko kept smiling. He seemed very pleased to have discovered Shan, Jowa, and Lokesh. Pleased, and not at all interested in stopping them or intimidating them. And that, more than anything, scared Shan.

As Jakli and Jowa moved around to the driver's side,

the Tibetan teacher followed them, wearing an uncertain, nervous expression.

"Why are you here?" Jowa growled to the man, in Tibetan.

"I am a teacher. I told you," Kaju replied in Mandarin.

"I mean here, today, in this garage."

Kaju looked back at Ko. "I asked to come," he said in Mandarin, refusing to reply in the language in which Jowa addressed him. "Here, in the shadow of the Kunlun, there are places to hide. I want to explain how hiding helps no one."

Jowa's eyes narrowed, more suspicious than ever.

"Who's hiding?" Jakli asked, watching Ko, who was leaning against his own truck now, out of earshot, still wearing his satisfied smile.

"Maybe not hiding. Running away, perhaps. Maybe you could help."

"Who?" Jakli pressed.

"The children, of course. The orphans," Kaju said. "Lau's children. My children now. We have to reach out to them, help them understand why they have a new teacher, why they must move on. Dealing with death is a learning experience too."

The flash of anger in Jakli's eyes was unmistakable.

"I want to help them," Kaju offered, "We can't stop the classes, or we will lose them, lose all her good work. But only half came to the last session after her disappearance. We must all strive against distrust."

A special university program, Ko had said, Shan recalled as he watched the Tibetan. Kaju had clearly mastered the vocabulary. He wondered if the Tibetan was capable of conducting a conversation without resorting to political slogans.

Jowa pushed Jakli into the driver's seat and shut the door behind her. He stared at Kaju. "Because they're being killed, you bastard," he said under his breath, in Tibetan, so low that Shan barely heard.

But Kaju had heard. His jaw dropped open. His face paled. He stood there, confusion gripping his face as Jowa and Lokesh climbed into the back of the truck. Jakli eased the vehicle out of the bay and was halfway across the garage yard when she slammed on the brakes. Another vehicle was emerging from behind the poplars that lined the road, a boxy black sedan. With a sinking heart Shan recognized the car. A Hong Qi, a Red Flag limousine, perhaps fifteen years old, the kind passed on to senior officials in remote corners of China after being retired from use in the eastern cities. Jakli made a small choking sound and her hand jerked to the door handle as if she were going to run.

They watched as the limousine stopped directly in front of the Brigade truck, as though to block it. A brawny young Han man climbed out of the driver's seat, then opened the rear door. A woman wearing a dark blue business suit emerged. She was in her forties, with the high cheekbones and broad face of northern China. Her eyes were hard, her mouth set in what looked like a well-used expression of disdain, and her hair was tied in a tight knot at the back of her head, underscoring the severe cast of her face.

Shan watched Ko Yonghong as he stared sourly at the new arrivals and uttered something to Kaju that caused the Tibetan to disappear into the shadow of the garage. Then, as the woman turned toward him, a cold smile rose on his face and he gave a small nod of greeting.

Shan looked back at Jakli, who still stared nervously at the woman. He did not need to ask her who the woman was. The Jade Bitch. Prosecutor Xu Li.

"You said she was using Lau's death," Jakli whispered. "What did you mean?"

"Picking up Lau's acquaintants. Erecting checkpoints. It's a campaign, not an investigation. I knew a senior Party member in Beijing who said that crime should never be seen as a social problem but as a political opportunity, and that murder was the best opportunity for any law enforcement official."

"Opportunity?"

As they spoke neither moved their gaze away from Prosecutor Xu. She stood beside her car, looking at Ko Yonghong expectantly, waiting for him to come to her.

A third figure climbed out of the Red Flag. A lean man with a pockmarked face, wearing a trim grey uniform bearing four pockets on his jacket. A officer of the Public Security Bureau.

"Sui," Jakli hissed. "Lieutenant Sui. From the barracks in Yoktian."

"There was a murder in Beijing years ago," Shan continued, watching the knob officer as he spoke, "a youth without a job who stabbed a street vendor, an old man who sold noodles. The killer was arrested at the stand, eating a bowl of noodles beside the body, blood on his shirt. But after a week of analysis Public Security announced that the vendor had been from a family of landowners and that he had failed to state this when his family background was requested on his license application. A political review had been conducted, and it was concluded that the vendor had still been victimizing society by lying to get a license, that his antisocial deception inevitably attracted violence. Citizens were invited to amend their registration forms to correct incomplete data or, better still, to inform on any other former landlords who tried to conceal their class history. Long essays in Party newspapers, speeches on television. Thirty or forty were arrested and sent to prison."

His gaze drifted toward Ko. The sour expression was gone. He was glaring at the knob officer with obvious resentment. Ko did not like Public Security, or at least did not like Lieutenant Sui.

The knob officer stood at Xu's side for a moment, surveying the compound with a predator's eyes, then stepped into the shadow of the garage.

"But the killer was punished, surely," Jakli said.

"Sent to work camp for a year, for not having a residency permit."

"This is different. Lau's death was not political."

"Her death?" Shan asked. "You said the prosecutor doesn't even know she's dead for certain. All she has is a report of her disappearance." A movement at the end of the garage caught Shan's eye. Akzu was quietly leading his horse around the building, behind Xu's back. "What is her biggest political complaint?"

"The border clans. She says they are irresponsible. They foment unrest. They're reactionary."

Shan nodded his head grimly. "Lau was a teacher. A moderating influence. Trying to bring the orphans of the clans into the social fold. So the border clans thought of her as an enemy."

"Impossible! She was one of us. Never did we—"

"By failing to engage in the socialist dialectic," Shan persisted, explaining the likely mindset of the prosecutor, "the border clans have cut themselves off from the moral nourishment of the state. They breed animosity and social irresponsibility." As he spoke Shan continued to look at Xu. "She must hope Lau is dead. Proof that the clans are destructive of society and must be eliminated."

Jakli said nothing. He looked at her. She was biting her lip, her eyes moist, still staring at Xu.

Ko also wanted the clans gone. The Poverty Eradication Scheme was accomplishing that goal. But somehow the prosecutor and Ko seemed to have little in common, as if they wanted the clans gone for entirely different reasons, or perhaps in entirely different ways. The Prosecutor's way, Shan suspected, was much more absolute than Ko's. Ko might be little more than a good soldier in the former army brigade. But the prosecutor had more authority. Ko answered to a corporate office in Urumqi. Xu Li answered to Beijing.

Suddenly there was a tap on the driver's door. Jakli turned and gasped. Lieutenant Sui glared at her through the glass, his face as thin and hard as an ax. As her arm shot forward to lock the door, Shan reached out to restrain her. She resisted a moment, then relented and opened the door as Sui pointed toward the front of the truck.

Moments later Lokesh, Shan, Jowa, and Jakli had been herded into a line before the knob lieutenant. He didn't ask for papers but simply wrote in a tablet, wearing a victorious expression, looking up to study each of them in turn, as if meticulously recording their descriptions. Shan turned his head to see Akzu with his horse, standing by the end of the garage, his face drained of color. The mechanic sat nearby, shaking his head grimly.

"Public Security has amended the Poverty Scheme," Sui suddenly announced. His voice had a hollow, metallic quality to it. "The wild herds are to be rounded up. The horses represent a security threat." He swept them with the cool, slow stare that seemed to be a trademark of every Public

Security official Shan had ever known. "They are to be rounded up and brought to Yoktian with the remainder of the livestock." His gaze settled on Shan for a moment, examining him in pieces, settling for a moment on Shan's close-cropped black and grey hair, then the loose end of the frayed belt, several sizes too big, that protruded from his narrow waistband, then finally his cheap vinyl shoes, cracked and caked with dust.

"They're not yours," Jakli said in a brittle tone, looking at Sui's chest, as if she were trying to detect a heart. "The horses belong to the Kazakh tribes; they always have since the time of the great khans."

"Exactly," Sui said with a lightless smile, as if Jakli had proven his point. "We know what the khans did to China."

Shan stared at the man in disbelief. It had been a thousand years since the khans, progenitors of the modern Mongols and Kazakhs, had invaded China, displacing the Sung dynasty and establishing the Yuan court. He saw movement from the edge of his eye and turned to see Akzu edging forward, leading his horse toward the knob with fire in his eyes now, as if the leathery old Kazakh was going to attack Sui.

"You'll never find all our horses," Akzu said in a venomous tone from ten feet away.

"Not so hard to round them up with helicopters," Sui answered with a sneer that exposed a row of yellow teeth.

"Chinese don't know horses," Akzu protested. The reins slipped from his hand to the ground and he stepped closer, his fists clenched.

"Harvesting of unutilized agricultural resources," came an icy voice from behind Akzu, "is a long-standing policy of the People's government." As the prosecutor spoke she stepped toward them, her driver towering just behind her.

Akzu's shoulders slumped and his chest sagged forward, as if he had been stabbed in the back. He didn't turn to face the woman, but simply stood, staring at the ground.

Shan's heart raced as he sensed Jowa tense, as though ready to spring at the knob. Then suddenly Ko Yonghong passed Xu Li and stood beside Akzu as though to protect him. "These people are enrolled in the Poverty Scheme, Comrade Prosecutor," he declared in a frustrated tone.

Xu seemed not to hear him. She touched her forehead and Sui stepped forward and with two quick motions knocked off the hats that Lokesh and Shan wore, then moved back for Xu to see.

"You mean the Kazakhs, Comrade Director," she said to Ko as she strutted forward, her escort still hovering a step behind. Her small black eyes glanced at Jakli, who seemed unable to raise her face toward the prosecutor, then studied Jowa and Lokesh with a sour expression. Xu hated Tibetans, Malik had said. She considered them all traitors. Her gaze finally settled on Shan.

Ko retreated, yelling orders at the men conducting the inventory, kicking a stone into the air that landed near the mechanic, who sat with a disinterested glaze on his face, smoking another cigarette. Akzu remained frozen in place, silently watching the prosecutor.

Xu paced along the gravel in front of them, still watching Shan, then gestured her escort toward the limousine. She followed him there and conferred with him in low tones, then the man jogged to Sui and spoke into his ear. The knob frowned, then moved backward, watching their small party warily, as if expecting an ambush. "The People's government appreciates your contributions," Xu's escort said in an oily tone and gestured them toward the turtle truck. Jakli grabbed the hats from the ground and pushed Lokesh toward the cab as Jowa and Shan climbed into the rear.

As the engine roared to life Ko approached Akzu, put his arm over the headman's shoulders, and guided him back to his horse. Jakli waited until Akzu disappeared around the building, then put the truck into gear and sped past the poplar trees that marked the entrance to the garage. Shan watched in the side mirror as the compound disappeared in the distance, then felt Jakli's glance. No one followed. The Prosecutor and Public Security were zealously filling up Glory Camp but still had let them go.

They drove for over an hour, twice detouring along dry stream beds in order to avoid checkpoints. As they passed a sign announcing five more miles to Yoktian, Jakli slowed, studying the willow trees that lined the road. She nearly stopped, then, checking to see that no other vehicle was in sight, abruptly turned into an opening in the trees. The route was more of a broad trail than a road, and the sturdy little truck bounced and heaved as they crossed ruts and holes that would have stopped lesser vehicles. After a few minutes the track reached a small stream flowing from the south and followed it toward the mountains. The Kunlun were in full view now, and Shan could see the high peaks that marked the Tibetan border.

Suddenly Jakli stopped the truck. "It's your lama, isn't it?" she asked as she followed his gaze. She was silent a moment. "I could take a different road if you wish. If you wish, I will take you as close to Tibet as I can. He is your friend. Your lama. Lau will wait."

Shan offered a grateful smile and shook his head. "I will go to meet Lau. It is why he asked me to come."

But now Jakli was studying the snow-capped peaks. "When I was young, people stayed away from the high mountains. They called them the edge of beyond, as if there was a totally different world on the far side, or maybe the world just ended there. Then I learned it was my mother's world, on the other side. Now—" She shook her head slowly. "The high plateau up there, where the dropka live, it's one of the last free places, beyond the reach of evil. Like *beyond* means *safe*. Many days, it's the only place I want to be." She was silent a moment, then put the truck back in gear and drove on.

"The edge of beyond." Shan repeated the words like a prayer. It was true. Gendun, as always, was at the edge of beyond.

After a quarter hour, Jakli pointed to a grove of trees at a bend in the stream and leaned forward in anticipation, then eased the truck to a stop under the shade of a grove of poplar trees. There was a small log building near the water, a tiny cabin with a porch, a single plank door and no window.

"It used to be a herder's hut, for the summer when the high pastures are green," Jakli explained as they climbed out. "One of Auntie Lau's favorite places."

"She lived here?"

"Sometimes. She had a room in Yoktian for many years, in the unmarried teachers' quarters. Officially, she lived there. But she stayed here in the warm weather, after the herds got so small the pastures here weren't needed. This was like a—I don't know. A retreat. A sanctuary, in a way. She came here years ago to help a flock of sick sheep. She kept coming back. Not so far from the highway to be inaccessible by car or truck, but far enough to be quiet, to be a world apart."

Shan saw the fond way Jakli looked at the cabin and the meadow beyond, filled with heather and asters in brilliant autumn hues, surrounded by rhododendron with leaves of crimson. It was like an oasis in the high dry mountains, the long slope above facing south so that it was protected, capturing more heat and water than the surrounding landscape. "It was that kind of place for you too," Shan suggested.

She nodded. "Auntie Lau taught me many things here."

"About animals?"

"About animals. About nature. About medicine. About people. About the stars. She was full of knowledge. Sort of overflowing with knowledge. I never knew anyone like her. Everyone, all the Kazakhs and Uighurs loved her. She was from nobody's family but everyone's aunt. It's why she got elected to the Agricultural Council."

"She brought the zheli here?"

Jakli nodded again. "Several times a year. Sometimes for what she called a reverence day."

"Reverence day?"

"Sort of meditation all day, whatever kind of quiet each of the orphans felt comfortable with. Some drew pictures. Some wrote letters. Some stared at flowers."

"What did Khitai do?"

Jakli considered the question for a moment. "I was there at the end of the day the last time. I think he climbed up the trail and sat near the top of the hill. Yes. I remember him. He was on a rock ledge," she said, pointing toward a slab of rock that jutted from the hillside. "Like an old goat, looking out over the mountains. Not with pride, just lost in the beauty."

Shan looked at the empty ledge. Was Khitai sitting on some other rock today, watching? Did he even know a killer was coming? Had Malik found him? With a shudder he realized that, by seeking out the zheli, Malik might be putting himself in the path of the killer.

Jakli stepped onto the narrow porch of the hut. "This place was like a shrine when she was here."

"A shrine?"

"A mosque. A temple. A religious place, is all I mean. You wanted to think big thoughts, just to please her." She opened a wooden latch on the door and led Shan into the cabin.

It was indeed as sparse as a temple inside. A small table, a chair, two benches, and a bedframe made of hand-hewn timbers comprised the only furnishings. Its walls were unfinished logs, many still holding their bark. A tin basin with two cups sat on the chair and a felt blanket lay folded on the bed. In the center of the table sat a single pine cone.

Shan stepped to read a sturdy piece of paper pinned to the log wall. It contained two flowing Chinese ideograms, one over the other, elegantly drawn with brush and ink. The liquid strokes combined the image of a bird flying away into the sky and the symbol of two hands struggling for a single object. It meant *do not contend* and was associated with the Eighth Chapter of the Tao te Ching, the greatest of the Tao teachings he had learned as a child. The characters brought a momentary aching to his heart, for the Eighth had been his father's favorite verse. Shan knew the passage well:

The greatest good is like water
Which benefits all things
And yet it does not contend
It stays in places that others disdain
And therefore is close to the way of truth

The verse was used to describe how enlightened individuals found contentment by not struggling, by staying in lonely, quiet places where truth, like water, was more likely to be found. Sometimes the final words of the passage were translated as the way of life. Truth or life. Perhaps, he thought, looking back at the ideograms, for Lau there was little difference.

He touched a corner of the paper with his fingertips, then

pulled them quickly away, as if he were intruding on Lau.

"She was like that," Jakli explained from his back.

He turned and nodded. "I need to understand something," Shan said as she roamed about the small room, gazing upon its contents. "Yesterday when you came to us, Akzu said you didn't owe Lau anything, after what she had done to you."

Jakli turned from the opposite side of the table. "I never understood. A misunderstanding of some kind, I guess. I was in a camp, for reeducation. Lau wrote a letter to the prosecutor, saying I should not be released as scheduled, that I should serve extra time on probation at the factory in Yoktian they use for former prisoners. The hat factory. When they told me why I couldn't go back to the clan I didn't believe it. But they showed me Lau's letter." Jakli sat in the chair and cupped her hands around the pine cone. "It's okay," she said in a confused tone, toward the cone, as if somehow it were a vehicle for reaching Lau. "Just a mistake, I know. She had been nervous lately."

Shan heard someone enter behind him. "There's no sign of her. Nothing that speaks of her," Jowa said over Shan's shoulder.

"Maybe that is her sign," Shan suggested, looking at the paper on the wall, "the simplicity."

Jakli led them to a trail at the far end of the meadow. As she disappeared into the brush, Lokesh halted in front of Shan. A small waterfall could be seen at the edge of the woods. Birds sang. "It's the kind of place where the soul of a boy could linger," Lokesh said with a sigh, then excitedly called Shan to watch a large beetle crossing the path.

Their small procession followed the stream above the meadow for nearly a mile on a foot trail that wound its way through more rhododendron thickets and stands of tall evergreens. He studied the path. It was little more than a game trail, but judging from the many recently broken plants and seedlings at its side, it appeared to have seen heavy recent use.

The path opened into a small clearing bordered on the opposite side by a rock wall that rose vertically nearly fifty feet. From the lower limbs of an ancient pine that towered over the wall, something man-made dangled in the wind. It was a diamond-shaped frame of sticks bound with twine, with strands of brightly colored yarn connecting the sides. A spirit catcher, a talisman used in many of the nomadic cultures, to trap the devils that fly in the air.

Jakli stopped at the foot of the wall and motioned her three companions toward the far side of the tree. Shan stepped forward. In the shadow of the tree was a darker shadow. It was a hole in the rock, a narrow cleft perhaps six feet high and wide enough to slip through sideways.

Shan followed Lokesh's eyes toward a small pile of brush at the side of the hole. No, he saw, it wasn't a pile of brush, it was flowers, bundles of flowers dropped at the side of the opening. They were mostly asters, the autumn wildflower that was in bloom on the slopes. Some looked so fresh they could have been dropped an hour earlier; others were dried and brittle. Beside the stack were over a dozen crude animal shapes of twigs bound with brown twine and vines, creatures with long legs that Shan took to be horses and creatures with short legs that might have been sheep or goats. Beside the stick creatures were several small clay objects, in the shapes of pots and bells. As he bent to examine them more closely, the air suddenly chilled. A frigid draft swept over Shan, raising the hairs on his arms. It was coming from the cave.

Jakli appeared beside him. She stood in the chill wind with her eyes closed, reverence on her face, as though praying. He had heard of such caves. Some said that death lived in these frigid places and that such wind was its breath. Some of the old Tibetans said such places were portals to the eight levels of cold hells that were taught by the oldest of the Tibetan sects.

Jakli reached into her pocket and produced a small battery lamp that she handed to Shan, then reached behind the pile of flowers and retrieved two sticks saturated with resin at the tips. She handed them to Jowa, produced a box of wooden matches, lit the torches, then took one for herself and stepped into the cave. Shan followed her closely, his throat suddenly dry. They were going to visit Auntie Lau.

After half a dozen steps, the passage widened to ten feet, but the ceiling dropped so low they had to bend over, holding their lights extended at their sides. The cold wind seemed to increase, dampening the light of the torches. Moments later they emerged into a larger chamber, perhaps fifty feet wide and three times as long, with a twenty foot ceiling. The air was more still, but even colder. Jowa uttered a gasp of surprise as he extended the torch over his head. The ceiling was glowing. Long stalactites of crystal hung down. It was ice, Shan saw. The entire ceiling was coated with ice.

"It wasn't so long ago that the glaciers left these hills," Jakli explained in a low voice. "Their roots are still here." She led them across the chamber to a five-foot-wide opening, which led into a smaller chamber with the same high ceiling but no more than twenty feet long.

In the dark and the cold, Auntie Lau was waiting.

She lay on a knee-high rock slab at the rear of the chamber, her hands on her stomach, her face so peaceful it seemed she was only napping.

Jakli knelt at the dead woman's side. Shan watched as she pulled a sprig of heather from her pocket and dropped it on the slab beside the body.

"I met her when I was just a girl that first summer she appeared. I was just eight or nine years old. My horse had a stomach sickness. I heard a healer was at a sheep camp so I was going to walk my horse to her. But after three or four hours my horse would go no further. He gave a long bellow and stood, weak and aching. I sat and made a fire, and suddenly she was there. She said she had heard a sick animal call. But she wouldn't give it medicine, not right away. She wanted to know about my horse, about how long we had known each other and where it had been born and how it acted in the rain. Then she touched the horse in many places and spoke to it. Finally she mixed some herbs and told me to stay there that night and sing to it. In the morning he was better, so strong he wanted to run all the way home."

Lokesh sat beside the slab, giving Jakli a small nod as if to encourage her to continue.

"One of my cousins said she must be some kind of sorcerer, when I told him," Jakli recounted. "But I said she laughed too much to be a sorcerer. I saw her many times after that, often unexpectedly, in the mountains, in the desert, wherever. Once she was healing a small squirrel that had been dropped by an owl. She said it was her duty to heal all the injured and the sick but that the greatest duty of a healer was to the smallest and the weakest."

"What do you mean, she appeared?" Shan asked.

"You know. One of the homeless. Her family had been lost too. She was like a wandering healer. We were fortunate she decided to stay in Yoktian County."

Lau's hair, black with a few strands of grey, had been set in two short braids tied with dark red ribbon. She was dressed in a long grey robe embroidered with flowers along its edges, her legs wrapped in red woolen leggings that covered the tops of a pair of small, well-worn leather boots. A red scarf, embroidered with flowers and leaping deer, covered most of her head, pulled low over her brow. Someone had dressed her for the cold.

"How far away is the place where she was killed?" Shan asked.

"Karachuk? In the desert, many miles inside the desert. They used her horse, then a truck to bring her body. Half a day's travel."

"Did you bring her?"

Jakli nodded. "From the road. The Maos came and told me at the factory, and I met them at the road."

"So the Maos were at this Karachuk when she was killed?"

"No. Some others, who went to the Maos." Jakli returned his steady stare with a cool, determined expression. There were secrets she would not tell.

"And she told you she wanted to be left here? Is this the Kazakh way?"

"No. But she had ideas. I mean, she lived her life in her own way. I think she wanted to leave it in her own way as well. She said to take her to this cave above the cabin."

"Who?" Shan asked. "Who did she ask?"

"She told her friends. About three months ago, she told her friends this is where she wanted to go."

The body had been kept remarkably fresh by the cold. It could stay like that for months, he thought. Maybe years. "It's a lot to ask of friends."

Jakli looked at Lau with a sorrowful smile. "It wasn't any trouble."

"But the way you speak about her, she wasn't the kind to put burdens on her friends."

Jakli knitted her brow, as if trying to understand Shan's point. "Lau was only going to die once," she said slowly.

But why this cave? Shan asked himself. It was as if the cave itself meant something. But what? A place where demons lived. Or maybe a place that demons feared. He walked slowly around the slab of rock, studying the dead woman. "If she was an outsider, without papers for a work unit here, how could she have been elected to the local council?"

Jakli shrugged. "She was checked, no doubt. She was Kazakh, and the herders loved her. As I said, she was everyone's aunt. And it was only the Agricultural Council. No real power."

"But the authorities. To get on even such a council a background check would have been required."

Shan could see in Jakli's eyes that she understood. Lau's family could have been lost in many ways, for many reasons. If it had been imprisoned, officially disbanded, or executed, its members by definition were bad elements in the eyes of the state. Holding office even in a lowly Agricultural Council was a privilege denied bad elements. He remembered Akzu's suggestion at the grave of the boy buried by the Red Stone clan. The demon wants to finish what it started with the parents of the zheli. Lau too had been from a lost clan. The secret that bound the victims could be from decades earlier, when the Kazakhs and Uighurs were being subdued by the People's Liberation Army.

"She was rehabilitated. I don't know. The people wanted her. The government is more forgiving now." Jakli spoke the last words without conviction, while looking at the slab of ice that covered much of the wall behind Auntie Lau.

Shan knelt by Lokesh, at the woman's head. The light of the torches gave her bloodless flesh an orange glow, adding to the sense that she was only sleeping. It seemed that at any moment the woman might sit up and chide them for disturbing her rest.

"We had to let people think there was an accident," Jakli

said. "There had to be an explanation. We couldn't report her murdered and have the government involved."

Shan looked up. It was as if Jakli had waited to explain, so there would be no secret from Lau.

"A riding accident," Jakli continued, looking at Lau now. "We arranged for your—" She paused and drew in a deep breath. "We arranged for her horse to be found walking along the high road that follows the Yoktian River. The next day, someone at school reported her missing. She had a jacket, given her by the Agricultural Council, with her name on it. Fat Mao dropped it in the river. A woman found it floating downstream, near town."

Slowly, as reverently as he knew how, he eased the scarf above her forehead. A hole, over a quarter-inch wide, was at the hairline. He brought his lantern closer and saw dark smudges around the wound. It had been done at close range, execution style.

"Do you think it will keep growing?" Jakli inquired. She was looking at the ice patch again. "Maybe it will reach out and cover her. She could last a long time like that. Thousands of years."

Shan rose with a reverent bow of his head and noticed Jowa standing at the entrance. The purba had not ventured further into the chamber, as if he had decided to stand guard. Or was frightened.

On the wall that curved away to the left, toward the entrance, Shan noticed dark shapes in the ice. He extended his electric torch toward them and saw that they were hands. At least a dozen hands had been pressed into the ice and left their unique indentations on the wall, like farewell salutes.

A tomb of ice, Shan thought. A guardian to the cold hells. What had Auntie Lau's final hell been like? She had not been killed randomly. She had been sought out. But why?

He gave voice to his thought. "Could she have been robbed of something?"

"She owned almost nothing," Jakli said. "The Brigade school gave her a room and an office."

Shan stepped to the end of the platform and knelt. "When she was prepared, before she was brought here, did anyone see—" As he slowly, painstakingly unwrapped the leggings, he answered his own question. "Ai yi!" he gasped under his breath. Bruises and welts, never healed, were on top of her feet. She had been beaten, beaten long enough before dying for the bruises to appear.

"We saw," Jakli said, her eyes welling with tears. "She must have been in such pain." Her hand shot to her mouth and she turned away. "But she wouldn't have talked. She was strong."

Shan nodded, not because he understood Lau but because he understood interrogation. Either she would have talked after the torture on one leg began, or she would have kept silent through the torture on both legs. He moved to her side after quickly covering the legs again and slowly rolled up the sleeve on Lau's lifeless right arm. Inside the elbow was another welt, centered over a tiny red spot.

"I saw that also," Jakli said over his shoulder. "Just a bruise. Nothing," she said in a cracking voice, a voice that told Shan she knew what it meant.

There was a movement at his side. Jowa had approached to look at the arm. "Injection," he announced solemnly. "She was injected with something when the beating didn't work." The purba exchanged a knowing glance with Shan. It meant her killer knew interrogation technology and had access to the drugs that were used by government interrogators. She had been killed for something she owned after all. She had been killed for information, tortured to reveal something.

Lau seemed more a mystery now than before he had visited her. Shan turned toward the entrance, then hesitated and stepped to the left wall. On an impulse he pressed his palm into the ice, near the impressions of the other hands.

"Why," he asked, feeling the numbness spread through his fingers, "did she stop serving on the council?" He pulled his hand away and studied his ice print. It was deeper than the others.

"When we did that," Jakli said, nodding at the hand-prints, "Akzu said that if the ice doesn't shift, the hands could be preserved for centuries. He said it would be the only evidence that we ever existed." She looked at the prints, then fitted her hand into one near the center as if confirming it was hers. "Just an emptiness in the ice in a dark cave on a forgotten mountain."

Shan looked at the woman, startled by her words. Jakli kept facing the wall. "I washed her at the stream," she said in a whisper. "I keep thinking of the terrible pain she died in." She pushed her hand more firmly into the ice, as if to create a greater emptiness. "Lau was disqualified some-how," she continued in her whisper, as if worried Lau might overhear. "Four months ago someone said she was no longer eligible to hold office."

"Someone?"

She shrugged. "The rules change all the time. The Brigade has taken over many of the functions of the old councils."

"But someone announced that Lau could no longer serve."

"I don't know, I guess. She just was gone. Someone else just started attending instead of her."

"Who?"

Jakli did not respond until she had stepped to the entrance to the larger chamber. "Ko Yonghong," she said in a brittle voice. "Comrade Managing Director."

"Was Lau told the reason?"

"If she was, she never told anyone else."

"You never thought it was odd, the timing?"

Jakli shook her head, confusion clouding her face.

"It was not long after that she asked for her body to be taken here," Shan reminded her. "As if it was only then that she became worried. Why, do you think?"

Jakli looked back on the dead woman, biting her lower lip. She looked as if she were about to ask Lau herself. Then she shrugged and turned back to Shan. "She associated with undesirables."

She was referring, Shan knew, to herself, and Akzu and the nomads. Perhaps even the Maos.

"But who was closest to her? Did she have a helper? Perhaps she was training someone. I need to know what her reaction was, when she heard she could no longer serve. Angry? Scared? Relieved?"

"No one."

"No one? Or no one you want me to see?"

Jakli seemed to consider his words as she bid farewell to Lau with a nod of her head, then stepped back into the larger chamber. "It's complicated," she said. "I want you to find the killer. But this is a land of secrecy. The Chinese make it that way. There are things that could be dangerous for you to know."

"Dangerous to whom?"

"Me. You. Others."

"You mean the resistance? The lung ma?"

"Resistance? There is no real resistance. Just intelligence gathering. How can we resist the People's Liberation Army or the Security Bureau? The Tibetans tried it, using flint-locks and swords against machine guns. A million of them died. Not resistance. A preservation movement, that's the best anyone can hope for. It's what Lau told the zheli a hundred times. Preserve what is good for the day when the bad goes away."

A minute later they were nearly at the mouth of the tunnel. Jowa and Lokesh could be seen outside by the old pine, straightening the stick-figure offerings. Shan paused at the entrance, holding his light close to the wall. There was something he hadn't seen before, a drawing made in chalk, a series of lines within a six-inch circle. At first it appeared to be an egg with a small plate on top, capped with something like a button with a flower growing out of it. Below the egg shape on either side were flowing, curving lines, like a banner blowing in the wind.

With a flash of recognition Shan pressed the light closer. It was in white chalk, recently laid on the rock.

"Do you know it?" Jakli asked over his shoulder.

"A *bumpa*, it's called, in Tibetan. A sacred treasure vase. One of the eight sacred Buddhist symbols."

"A vase?"

"An urn. A sacred receptacle," he said, his brows wrinkled in confusion. "It means hidden treasure."

Jakli stared at the chalk drawing a moment, then slowly stepped outside, leaving Shan alone. As he stood there, a particularly strong gust of cold air hit his back. Lau's breath.

Outside, he found Lokesh kneeling by the old pine, righting the stick animals that had fallen over, arranging them in a semicircle around the entrance to the cave, facing outward. The old Tibetan sang one of his old songs while he worked, sometimes pausing to admire the handiwork of one of the figures.

As Jakli bent to help Lokesh, Shan touched her shoulder and gestured toward Jowa, who stood nearby, facing the thicket on the opposite side of the clearing. One hand was behind his back, a finger raised toward Shan, signaling him to wait. The other hand hovered over his blade.

The wind died, and Shan realized what had alarmed Jowa. There was a sound coming from the thicket, an animal sound, like a low-pitched growl. Shan stepped to Jowa's side, No, it wasn't a growl, he realized as he moved closer to the sound, it was more like a moan.

Something moved in the thicket. Jowa ran.

The thing flashed into view between two rocks, a low, dark shape trying to escape beyond the wall of rock. Jowa disappeared into the thick rhododendron and Shan followed. Jakli streaked past him with the speed and stealth of a seasoned hunter.

The creature ran hard. Shan saw it again as it scrambled across rocks in a pool of light fifty yards ahead. It was black, but its two rear feet were bright red. It was making another sound now, a wrenching howl, a sound of new fear. Shan ran faster, ignoring the branches slapping his face, stumbling twice on the loose rocks, leaping over beds of moss, pausing once to listen, then sighting Jakli again and darting toward her as she disappeared back into the dense undergrowth.

Then another sound split the silence of the forest. Jowa had caught the thing and was shouting for them.

Gasping for breath, Shan arrived in a small clearing to find Jowa and Jakli looking down at a dark figure that cowered at their feet. Shan wondered where they had found the large black chuba which covered the thing, then realized that their quarry was wearing the chuba.

Jakli lifted an edge of the sheepskin robe and exposed two human feet, clad in bright red, ankle-high athletic shoes. She gasped, as if recognizing the shoes. Her eyes flared with sudden anger and she pulled on the chuba, struggling to lift it for a moment, then wrenching it free to reveal a small man, quivering with fright. She paused a moment, her eyes full of fire, and pounced on the man, pounding his back with clenched fists.

Jowa and Shan exchanged a look of surprise, then bent to pull her away. She would not relent. "Traitor!" she screamed, still hitting the man. "Murderer!"

They had to forcibly lift her, one under each shoulder. When she was off the man's back she lashed out with her feet, kicking him on his arms and legs.

The man did not fight back. He seemed not to have noticed the blows. He lay curled up, making the same low moaning noise they had first heard from the thicket by the cave.

"Don't you understand?" Jakli cried in frustration. "It's Bajys! The child-killer!"

Shan rolled the man over. The face that looked up was contorted with fear. Bajys kept his hands locked about each other, as if he had to stabilize himself even though lying on the ground. His eyes blinked open and shut. Tears streamed down his face.

Jakli shouted at him in the Kazakh tongue. The words were unintelligible to Shan, but the sharp, accusing tone was unmistakable. The man looked at her in confusion, then looked to Jowa and began speaking.

"Help me. Help me, brother," he said, his chest heaving with sobs. "The monster has been loosed. There is only death. The world is ended. I cannot find my way out."

Something was wrong. Shan, Jakli, and Jowa exchanged a confused look. Bajys was speaking Tibetan.

Jakli spoke to him again, in the language of their clan, not shouting this time but still in anger. Bajys just looked at Jowa with pleading in his eyes. Jakli's rage evaporated into bewilderment. "It can't be," she said to Shan in Mandarin. "He's a Kazakh. He's never spoken Tibetan." She spoke to Bajys again in her Turkic tongue, but the man stared at her dumbly, then looked at Jowa.

"Tell this woman," he said in a trembling voice, "I do not understand her. She confuses me with someone else. Tell her not to waste her time in anger. There is only time for prayer now. All we can do is pray."

Jakli's face seemed to go limp. She looked to Shan as

if he could explain, but he shook his head and helped the little man to his feet. They made a slow procession back to the clearing, Jowa and Shan supporting Bajys, Jakli behind, a numb, confused expression on her face.

Lokesh showed no surprise when they led the little man into the clearing. He took his hand and led him to a log in the bright, warm sun in the center of the clearing, then sat with him.

"Are you a priest then?" Bajys whimpered to the old Tibetan.

Lokesh gestured for Jowa to join them, then placed his own rosary in the man's hands. "We both trained at gompas," Lokesh said, nodding toward Jowa. But Jowa remained standing, as if unable, or unwilling, to console the man. "I have seen them," Lokesh offered with a sigh. "I have seen demons in my lifetime too." His voice was serene, as if in prayer.

"He couldn't—" Jakli said to Shan as they watched. "Sometimes I prac..ce my Tibetan, sing Tibetan songs. Bajys never understood. He's a Kazakh, a Muslim. He can't speak Tibetan." Her voice drifted off as she looked at the diminutive man. He was holding the rosary tightly wrapped around the fingers of his left hand, his right hand clasped over them, rocking back and forth, murmuring a mantra in Tibetan.

But Jakli would not give up. "Where did you go?" she demanded again, now in Tibetan. "Why did you run away? They are certain you killed the boy—" Confusion seemed to grip her tongue.

"She used to go to the old place in the sand," the little man said suddenly, in Tibetan. "When I saw that Khitai was dead I had to find her." His voice was barely above a whisper. "When she wasn't at the cabin, I went out on the sand. All day and part of a night I walked. I went to the *lhakang* place, the sanctuary place." He raised his hands in front of him as though to defend against something invisible to the others, then pushed the beads against his forehead so hard they pressed into his flesh.

"Khitai isn't dead," Jakli said. "It was the other boy."

But Bajys seemed unable to hear her. "I looked in the huts away from the lhakang," he continued. "But there was only dead people. Everyone dead. Like in the old thangkas," he said in his trembling voice, referring to the religious paintings that often hung in Tibetan temples, "where the demons are eating human limbs." He stared at the ground, his eyes wild. "People were in pieces. A leg. A hand. Dead hands."

They stared at Bajys in horror.

The little Tibetan seemed not to notice them, as if he were lost in his vision of death. Surely, Shan told himself, it was only a vision. Not a memory.

"We'll go below," Shan said quietly to Jowa and Lokesh. "We'll make a fire. Come when he is ready."

But Bajys spoke again.

"Then I remembered the special place inside the mountain," he said in his tiny hollow voice. "So I came back here. I sensed her here. I shouted for her with great hope. But she wasn't in that place. She was just in the back place, the ice room, and when I found her she had no voice left for me."

Shan sprang up, grabbing the battery light, and ran back into the cave. Moments later he stood at the front of the wide chamber, Lau's burial room opposite him. Lau had a place in the mountain, not the burial chamber where Bajys found her. A special place. He played his light along the walls at floor level. To his right the wall was solid, dropping straight to the stone and clay floor without interruption. He began walking along the left wall, the base of which was obscured at several places by slabs of rock that had shifted from the ceiling. He explored each slab, shining his light into the shadows where they had fallen against the wall. After fifty feet he stopped. There was something in the air, the vaguest hint of incense and singed butter, a temple scent. In the next pocket between the rocks there was no sign of an opening, but the scent grew stronger. Then around the next slab he found a small gap at the floor, big enough for a person to crawl through. The clay floor below had been worn smooth. He dropped down and crawled inside. After ten feet the passage opened into a chamber slightly larger than Lau's burial room.

Shan had been in shrine caves before, where Buddhist artifacts and relics were secreted, sometimes centuries old, and when his light played upon a small golden Buddha he thought he had found another. But it wasn't a room of Buddhist treasures he had found. The Buddha, at the far wall, was on a small altar of hand-hewn timber, joined with pegs. Around it were seven containers, representing the seven offering bowls of Buddhist worship. But the bowls did not match. Some were not even bowls. There was a chipped teacup in the row, and a tin mug of the type Shan had used in prison. Yet they held the traditional Buddhist offerings. The first, second, and sixth were filled with water, the third with flowers, the fourth with incense, the fifth with butter, the last with aromatic chips of wood. On the Buddha's shoulder a prayer scarf had been draped. Beside the foot-high statue was a small ceramic stand to hold stick incense, partly covered with ashes. Six feet in front of the altar was a large tattered cushion, then a single, smaller cushion five feet beyond it. For a teacher to sit with his student. Beside the smaller cushion was a brazier with two charred stubs of wood, the remnants of a fire.

A log had been wedged into a crack in one wall, and hanging from it was a painting on cloth, a Tibetan thangka, so worn it was threadbare in spots. Shan studied the painting, holding the light close. The central image was a fierce woman mounted on a horse, robes swirling about her as if blown by a wind. It was a rendering of an obscure figure seldom seen in temples. But in the prison barracks, when the winter storms had kept the prisoners from work, the old lamas had taught about such figures and the lost gompas that had revered them. It was a protective goddess, in the form known as Magic Weapon Army.

Another light flickered behind him. Jakli appeared, carrying her torch. She stood in a numbed silence, in apparent disbelief at Shan's discovery, then her eyes filled with wonder as she stepped tentatively toward the small Buddha. She studied the room for a long time before she spoke. "I have visited the cabin more than a score of times with Lau," she said at last, confusion in her voice again. "Once we even came to the cave, to see the ice. But I never . . ." Her voice drifted off. She sat on the student's cushion and picked up a piece of chalk lying beside it, rolling it in her fingers as she gazed around the room.

Shan cast his light along the rear wall. There was a stack of folded blankets on a straw pallet and several ceramic pots beside a small pile of split wood for the brazier. Above them, where the wall presented a flat, even surface, were marks in chalk, words in the graceful Tibetan alphabet. Although he was still being taught the written language of Tibet, Shan recognized several simple figures in a row along one side. *Chig, nhi, soom, shi, nga, trook, doon, gyay, gu, ju,* he read. One, two, three, four, five, six, seven, eight, nine, ten.

"When I was young," he said to Jakli, surprised at how the secret chamber moved him, "my father would take me into the closet of our apartment whenever the Chairman gave speeches. My mother played the radio as loudly as possible, and he took out secret books, old textbooks, and he would teach me things. English. The history of America and Europe. The Declaration of Independence. He made me memorize the American Declaration of Independence."

"He could have gone to prison."

"He already had. He had been a professor of Western history. A Stinking Ninth," Shan said, referring to the lowest rank of the Nine Bad Elements identified as enemies of the people by Chairman Mao. "The very worst kind, since he had American friends. This was after prison, after his release. Even after our family had been sent for reeducation at an agricultural collective." He sighed and looked around the chamber again. Lau taught here. Bajys knew about it. Which meant Khitai knew about it. Maybe others of the orphans. It was an illegal place. A Buddhist place.

"How many Tibetans are there," he asked, "among the zheli?" He looked at the cushions. One for a teacher, one for a student, only one student at a time.

"Several of the shadow clans that help are Tibetan, dropka families. But among the children, two or three at most. The zheli are Kazakh and Uighur. Maybe one or two Tadjiks."

"Kazakh like Bajys?"

Jakli's only answer was a confused frown. She walked around the room, touching things with the tips of her fingers. "A secret room," she said. "For secret Buddhists."

"For children," Shan said, looking back at the simple numbers written on the wall. Or one child.

"She taught me Buddhist ways," Jakli said. "Quietly, at private places. But not here." Her face was clouded with emotion.

"I think this was different. I think someone else came here," Shan said. "Not Bajys. Maybe not just Lau. Maybe another teacher. A Buddhist. I think it's why Lau asked to be taken back here. For a final meeting."

"But she was dead," Jakli said in confusion.

Shan walked around the room. He stood in front of the Buddha, placing his palms down on the makeshift altar, then stepped back to the chalk writing. He recognized several other words. He saw the six syllable mantra, *Om mani padme hum*, invoking the Compassionate Buddha, and below it the twelve syllable mantra, *Om ah hum vajra guru peme siddhi hum*, invoking the blessing of the holy teacher Guru Rinpoche. The top rows had been written very high, several inches higher than he could reach. He stretched his arm overhead to prove it to himself, then surveyed the chamber once more. "Nothing to stand on," he observed. "No stool, no bench."

"What do you mean?" Jakli inquired.

"Lau was no taller than me. I don't think she wrote this."

Jakli studied the writing for a moment. "She didn't. I know her hand. She is teaching me—she was teaching me to write Tibetan." She looked back at Shan, wide-eyed, as if just realizing the meaning of her words. "Someone else was here," she whispered. "Someone else was the teacher here."

Shan nodded. He had not found the missing lama, but he had found the lama's home. He stepped to a cluster of simple, familiar drawings on the adjacent wall. From over his shoulder Jakli pointed to the first image on the left side, a vertical line with something like a bloated figure eight at the top. "A monk's stick," she said.

"A staff." Shan nodded. "A mendicant's staff," he added and explained that the grouping depicted the prescribed possessions of an ordained monk. He pointed each out. The staff for walking and shaking in a prescribed fashion when asking for alms. A water pot and a water sieve, to prevent the drowning of innocent insects, then an alms bowl, a blanket, three outer robes, two underrobes, a sitting mat, and sandals.

He stared at the drawings, then back at the numbers on the wall and the thangka. The chamber was for a child and not a child. And it was Tibetan but very old Tibetan, from a teacher rooted in one of the oldest of the Buddhist sects. He stepped to the pallet and found a perfectly folded maroon robe. He carefully lifted it. It was a monk's robe. It was clean. He looked back at the tunnel leading to the chamber. The robe had no marks from the clay. It was for use inside the chamber only. Beside where it had lain on the pallet was a large pair of sandals, larger than Shan would wear, larger than Lau would wear.

Jakli stepped back and sat again on the student's cushion, and he knelt beside her, realizing after a moment that they were both staring at the empty cushion by the altar. The missing teacher. They were waiting to be taught, but there was no one to take the cushion.

"Messages," he said at last, giving voice to his speculation. "The trail lies in all the messages." He felt Jakli's gaze but did not look away from the cushion. "Lau's coming here in her death was a message, her way of sending a warning to someone unknown to anyone else. If she were killed she wanted the teacher who used this room warned away from the danger. But she couldn't risk divulging his or her name, not even to you. Even if she took such a risk, who should she tell? It was too unpredictable, where and when she might die."

"But she knew," Jakli said slowly, studying the piece of chalk intensely, as if hoping it might begin writing answers for her. "She knew that she was in danger, didn't she? She knew months ago that she was in danger. I never thought of it."

"And she knew that, no matter what, no matter how or where she died, certain friends would honor her last request," Shan suggested, and Jakli offered a sad smile in reply.

"There were other messages," he continued. "It was the purbas who brought word to the lamas about Lau. The Maos knew of her, or someone connected to her knew the

Maos. The Buddhist who taught in this room perhaps. But why?" He turned toward her with a sudden thought. "Or was it you? You know the purbas. You know the lung ma."

"No. I was in town, making hats. Fat Mao sent for me."

Shan nodded. Fat Mao knew. Because the lung ma sent the message to the purbas. "But why?" Shan repeated. "It's not just that what went on in this room was Tibetan, or even that it was secret. There was something else, so important that word went to Lhadrung." Why Lhadrung? Why Gendun and Lokesh? he asked himself silently. It wasn't just that Gendun had been born in the region but that Gendun was involved in the mystery, part of the greater secret.

"Lau," Jakli said. "Lau was the secret."

"No. Part of it, yes. But the killing didn't stop with her. There is something else, an evil still unfolding that we have to stop. Something connected with the children."

Jakli bent forward, plucked something from the edge of the cushion, and held it up in her fingers. A small clump of brown fibers. "Wool," she said, rubbing it between her fingers. "Full of lanolin. Unwashed. Like from a herder's vest. Or a sheepskin blanket." It told them little but set the image, that of a student on the cushion, huddled in a sheepskin against the cold air, facing the teacher who sat before him in his robe.

"The teacher," Jakli said. "Maybe it's the teacher who the killer wants. From Lau the killer learned where the students were. The zheli. So he attacks the students to find the Tibetan teacher who uses this room."

Shan slowly nodded. The Muslim boy Suwan had been killed first. But the next boy killed had been Alta, the Kazakh boy being raised by Tibetans, a boy being taught the Buddhist way, a boy whose rosary had been stolen by the killer. Then there was Khitai, whose name Lokesh somehow knew yet didn't know. He rose and walked along the wall again, then stopped and faced the long mantra on the wall, written by the secret teacher.

"There was another message," he said. "Not so secret. After the killing at the Red Stone camp, warnings went out. And about us coming. The dropka on the road knew."

"Many people would have heard about that killing," Jakli confirmed. "The clans have their own ways of spreading news. Herders meet in remote places. Notes are left on trees. Some old clans send dogs with letters on their collars. People were told to watch for the killer."

"But not just a general warning." He told her what the dropka had said, on the high road entering the Kunlun. *You are going there, to save the children.* "Lau died, then Suwan died, and someone decided the children were in danger. The teacher who used this chamber. Perhaps he warned one of the herders. That would have been enough to start the warnings, to cause the dropka to flee."

"Many people knew about Lau, about the zheli," Jakli said. "When a mother ewe dies, the lambs are always in jeopardy. And some said the zheli was always a dangerous thing, that there were those in the government who opposed it."

"Is that why she was forced from the council?"

"I don't know. I don't think so. You heard Ko today. People became accustomed to it. People support the zheli program now."

People, Shan thought. Meaning the Han who were quietly building a little kingdom in Yoktian.

Jakli stood and stepped toward the tunnel. "Did they ever find your father out?" she asked, as she bent to her knees by the tunnel. "In his secret classroom."

Shan stopped and looked at the writing on the wall. What kind of world was it where in order to be enlightened you had to hide? "No," he said in a wooden voice, still looking at the wall. "They would have eventually, but the Red Guard came one day, just because he had been a professor. They beat him and broke things in his body. My mother and I were held and forced to watch. He didn't die then, but when he breathed little bubbles of blood came to his lips. The next day they came back and made a bonfire of all his books in the street. He watched from the window because he was in too much pain to move. He watched them in horror and I watched him and slowly he just stopped breathing."

He stood in silence, looking at the secret writing on the wall.

"But the books from the closet," Jakli asked softly. "Did they get those too?"

Shan looked back with a sad grin. He shook his head slowly. "Afterward, I just went in alone, with a candle."

As she disappeared down the tunnel Shan hesitated, then picked up the chalk she had left on the bench. Quickly, in small Chinese ideograms, he wrote near the entrance. *The way that is told is not the constant way,* he wrote. His message for Gendun, who had ways of finding secret treasures. As he looked at his words a realization swept through him. Perhaps the room was no secret to Gendun. The hermitage in Lhadrung was populated by secret teachers. This chamber was home to a secret teacher. No one knew about the teacher who used the room. But Gendun had told Shan that Lau had been killed and a lama was missing. The purbas had only known that Lau was dead. The fact that the message had come that way had been a message in itself, meaning that the lama who used the chamber was gone, unable to communicate with Lhadrung directly. So Gendun had inferred the second part of the mystery, that someone had taken the lama.

They walked past the clearing without speaking to Jowa or Lokesh, who still sat with Bajys as he swayed back and forth, reciting mantras with the two Tibetans. At the cabin they lit a fire in a circle of stones.

"No one will believe it about Bajys," Jakli said as she made tea in a dented pan she had retrieved from under the porch. "I don't know if I believe it. It doesn't make sense."

"You mean they will still hunt him as a killer?"

She nodded. "Maybe he is. I know people who say it is possible to be possessed," she said, remembering Malik's words. "Maybe in killing the boy, something possessed him, then left him afterwards."

"Something that taught him to speak Tibetan?" Shan asked. "Something that made him recite Buddhist prayers?"

"He could still have killed the boy."

"The man we found up there is no killer."

"But he lied to us. He's no Kazakh."

"Did he lie? Or just not tell all the truth? You said it before. Some secrets are too dangerous to tell," Shan reminded her.

"He didn't kill the boy," Lokesh said confidently. "He didn't kill Auntie Lau."

"You think they are the same? I mean, one killer?" Jakli asked, looking from Lokesh to Shan. "He has to speak to us, tell us what happened."

"He might not know," Shan said. "Maybe it was seeing the dead boy that did this to him. He had built something around his Tibetan self. A Kazakh shell. And the shell was shattered, lost forever, when he saw the dead boy."

"An old shaman told me once of souls getting confused when death was close," Jakli said. "Getting mixed up, being lifted out, then going back to the wrong body."

"And whose soul does he have now? The killer's?"

"I don't know. I just know that he's not Bajys but he has the body of Bajys." Jakli sighed, then looked up into Shan's eyes. "And they will still kill him. You don't know the old clans. They have their own justice. The government won't help, even if someone asked. If the clans are convinced Bajys is the killer, they will punish him. When I was young two horse thieves were caught near our camp. They were hung from two limbs of the same tree. I went out looking for lambs and saw them. All purple and bloated." A visible shudder moved through her body.

"Who among Lau's friends were Tibetan?" Shan asked.

"No one," Jakli said. "Me, I'm the closest to being Tibetan. I've known her all these years and I've never seen her with a Tibetan except the dropka who watched the children, and they usually stayed away, bringing the children and then hiding until Lau was done."

"She was Kazakh," Shan said with a hint of skepticism, "with friends who were Han Chinese and Uighur. But she had no Tibetan friends. Even with the Tibetan herders wandering the hills below the Kunlun."

"Tibetans aren't given papers for Xinjiang. Very few are classified as natives here. They're treated—" She shrugged as if it was painful to finish the sentence and busied herself with the tea.

"Badly," Shan said, finishing the sentence for her.

Jakli nodded. "Speeches are given by the prosecutor, by Public Security officers. Tibetans are always the example of the uncooperative minority, of the reason why assimilation of the country has taken so long. In Yoktian, a friend showed me something on a computer, an image taken from phone lines. It was from somewhere outside China, and it was a film of a Chinese flag being burned. A Tibetan child appeared and lit it on fire. When it was ashes, the film repeated. Again and again."

"You mean Tibetan friends would have been politically dangerous to Lau."

She nodded again.

"Then why did she learn Tibetan?"

"I don't know. She knew lots of languages. Tadjik. The people's Mandarin. The Party's Mandarin. English."

"English? Why English?"

Jakli looked up as if surprised by the question. "This is China," she said with a small, chastizing smile. "People sit in closets and learn things." She looked up the mountainside. "Lau taught people what they needed. She sometimes taught about Buddha. But she also taught about Mohammed. If she had Han children in her zheli she would have taught them about Confucius and Lao Tze. That's what she did."

"No. In the cave, it was different."

"I don't think so. Why would you believe—"

"Because," Shan suggested, "she never took you there." His words brought a small, nearly silent moan from Jakli. He had seen many things in Jakli's eyes when she had entered the cave chamber and sat, stunned, on the student's cushion. Wonder. Confusion. Reverence. Sadness. But also pain. "You were a friend, and a student too. She taught you about Tibet and Buddhism. But she hid this place even from you."

"But you said there was someone else. Another teacher."

Shan nodded. "A friend who was Tibetan, who does not appear Tibetan. Who else came to this place?" The chamber had not been just for talking about Buddhism. It had been for teaching the Tibetan language and other things Tibetan. The things lost, or nearly lost, to the two generations born since the Chinese invasion.

Jakli looked for a long time into the fire. "There were herders sometimes, passing through. A crazy Xibo who watches the water. In his fifties maybe. They say he's a lunatic." The Xibo were a Manchurian people, uprooted from their homelands nearly three centuries before and sent west to fight the Muslims on behalf of the emperor.

"The water?"

"The Agricultural Council gives a small stipend to make sure key streams are kept open and not contaminated. Many of our streams only flow in the spring. Only a few are constant. So they have people, usually retired herders, who watch the water, keep dead animals out, clear fallen trees from it."

"Who else?"

"Her drivers. And people at the school in Yoktian may have visited here sometimes. Others from the Agricultural Council, maybe."

"Drivers?"

"Sometimes. She couldn't drive a car. So when she was on business for the Council, she used the vehicle pools."

"But not since then, not since she left the council?"

"Sometimes one of the drivers still helped. A Kazakh from the motor pool."

"Would he have known where she was the day she died or who she had been traveling with?"

"I don't know. Maybe."

"Do you know where he lives?"

"In town, probably. But now at Glory Camp."

"Glory Camp?"

"You heard Fat Mao. Prosecutor Xu stopped at the motor pool in Yoktian."

Shan studied Jakli. "She didn't pick you up. Even though you're a friend of Lau's. Because," he suggested, "the prosecutor knew exactly where you had been when Lau died." He paused and studied Jakli, who seemed to have little concern about being absent from her probation job. "Were you there, at your factory?"

Jakli grimaced and nodded, still staring at the fire. "I left for a day when we brought Lau to the cave. Then I left when I heard you were coming. It's mostly Kazakhs and Uighurs who work there. I have friends there. They cover for me. It's not strict. Not usually, as long as enough hats are being made."

"Prosecutor Xu saw you today. Does she know your face?"

She looked up at him with a frown, but before she could

reply Jowa called from the trail. Bajys was emerging into the meadow, supported by Lokesh and Jowa. He seemed barely to have the strength to stand.

"Bajys will have to be protected," Shan said.

"There's a place deep in the Kunlun," Jakli said readily, as though she had been thinking the same thing. "A Tibetan place. Jowa must know about it."

Shan studied her. "You mean, a place where purbas hide?"

"A secret place."

"Are you one of them?" Shan asked abruptly, before the three men were in earshot.

"A purba? Tibet is their cause."

"But not yours?"

"I struggle for my people," Jakli said with a sigh. "For Kazakhs. For Tibet, when I can." She darted forward to help Bajys onto the porch, then took control with a matronly air, sending Shan for water, Jowa for firewood, and Lokesh for dried grass to make a pallet for the ragged, wasted little man.

Bajys sat limply, his eyes unfocused, as she pulled off his shirt, wiping his body with the cold river water. He seemed not to notice any of them.

They drank tea, sharing the two cups from the cabin, and waited until Bajys began to look about, as if finally recognizing where he was.

"It's me, Bajys," Jakli said in Tibetan. "From Akzu's camp."

He looked at her without expression.

"What happened, that night in the rocks?" Her voice was slow and tentative, as if it were not anger but fear she now felt. "Were you with the boys? We need to understand. Do you know that it wasn't Khitai?" Jakli asked.

"Where would he go?" Lokesh interjected. "Where would Khitai run to?"

Bajys twisted his head one way, then the other, as he stared first at Jakli, then Lokesh. "I heard the shot. I saw him lying there, with his red cap, and ran. He's dead." The little Tibetan stared toward the door of the cabin, as if seeing someone there invisible to the others. "That was the one I loved," he said in a hollow voice. "That was the one

I was to keep safe. He'll be dead again. But that was the one I knew."

Shan stared at him, trying to make sense of his strange words. "Why did you come here?" he asked. "When the boy died, you fled to Lau. Why?"

Bajys's gaze roamed around the campsite before he spoke again. "Sometimes it comes like this, like a dark cloud. And people just die. It can't be stopped." A rattling noise came from his lap. His hand with the beads was shaking.

"Wangtu knows," he said suddenly in a small, quivering voice. "Wangtu told me. Lau was being stalked, he said."

Jakli greeted the words with a frown. "Wangtu doesn't know," she said with abrupt annoyance. "He just talks."

Bajys looked at her and shook his head. "Wangtu knows," he said mournfully. "The world is ending." He seemed to be shrinking before their eyes, growing smaller, hollowing out. Shan had seen it before, even in brave men, and he shuddered to think of the ugliness that caused it. Bajys had gone from the horror of finding the dead boy to see the wise, gentle Lau and instead found human limbs scattered about, a place of terror and death.

"You know this Wangtu?" Shan asked Jakli.

Her frown returned. "I told you about him. Lau's driver. I knew him when I was young."

"That one at Glory Camp?"

"Not for long. She'll question him, he'll offer something unrelated, he'll be released."

"What do you mean?"

"Don't you understand? That's her game. Throw as many as she can in the camp, let them sweat. They can always think of somebody's sin."

"But for how long?" Shan asked. "When will he be released, so I can speak with him?" The prosecutor, he realized, may have deprived him of the only witnesses who could make sense of Lau's death.

"A week, maybe two."

"Too long."

She looked at him and sighed. "You want to get into Glory Camp? Go to town. Burn a copy of the Chairman's speeches in the square."

"I don't want a one-way ticket."

"No way to see him that doesn't involve going into the prison."

A tremor crept along Shan's arm. His right hand clamped over his left forearm, over the number he wore there, the number tattooed on his skin by his prisonkeepers in Tibet. Talk of a prison, even a low security lao jiao camp, seemed to cast a chill over the group. Shan moved closer to the fire.

A hawk screeched overhead. Red and gold leaves danced across the ground, scattered by the late afternoon wind.

"It wasn't supposed to be me at all," Bajys said suddenly, barely above a whisper. "The oldest son goes, that's the way it always was."

Shan and Lokesh exchanged a glance. There had been a Tibetan tradition of centuries, now shattered, like so much else touched by Beijing, that the oldest son of each family would be sent to train as a monk.

"I was just a dropka, I just wanted to stay with the herds. But my brother was back from a month at the gompa," Bajys said, his voice weak but steadier. "He was getting ready to return for six years of study. We were celebrating Losar, the new year festival, and saying goodbye by playing in the snow one last time. There was a place on the mountainside with a creek that became a long ice slide in the winter. We would sit with a sheepskin on the ice and slide, a hundred, two hundred yards, down to the flat ice where the river was. My brother slid down as I watched and laughed. But when he got to the bottom a black hole in the ice opened up. He shot into the hole and was gone. We never saw him again. No struggle. No body. Hardly a splash. At first I thought it was a good trick and I laughed. But it wasn't a trick. He was gone, laughing with me one second and gone the next. Like he never existed. Even before the Bardo, before the death rites were done, they cut my hair and sent me to the gompa in his place."

His face contorted with pain, Bajys looked into each of their faces, as though inviting any of them to explain it to him. But no one spoke. They sat silently watching the fire.

Shan studied his companions. He knew without asking

that they had reached a common understanding. A killer had to be stopped. Khitai and the rest of the zheli had to be saved. The missing lama had to be found. But first Bajys would have to be taken to shelter by Lokesh, who could protect his soul, and by Jowa, who could protect his body. They would go deep into the mountains. And Shan would stay, because Shan had to go back to prison.

CHAPTER 5

There was a mountain before him, and on the mountain was a squirrel and on the squirrel was a flea and on the flea was an eye that watched the sky, the flea wishing for wings. Shan kept his focus high, on the horizon. The mountain was there, but the rest was in his mind's eye only, his way of keeping distracted as the truck moved to the end of a long flat valley tucked into the north slope of the Kunlun. He shifted his gaze from the horizon to the floor of the truck, not daring to look at the huge barbed wire compound they approached.

He knew he had to speak to Lau's driver, Wangtu, and any other of Xu's recent detainees Jakli might find. But as they had driven into the arid valley that contained Glory Camp, the black shapeless thing—his legacy of the gulag—had crawled into his gut again, and he had fought a sudden urge to leap out of the truck. No, it's only a reeducation camp, he told himself, not one of the gulag prisons where they trained you with electric shock and ball peen hammers, where misfits like Shan were sent to have their souls splintered and their bodies battered. Not a real prison. Only a reeducation camp, he told himself again as they approached the mile-long row of barbed wire that defined the front of the compound. But when he looked down he saw that his hands were shaking. He placed his right hand over his left forearm and squeezed, trying to control the reaction. Then he noticed the spot his hand covered and squeezed even tighter.

"Are you in pain?" Jakli inquired, with a motion of her hand that caused Fat Mao to slow the truck.

No, Shan was tempted to say, I am not in pain, I am in weakness. If he were caught and they checked the tattoo numbers, they would classify him as an escapee. What had Jowa said to Gendun? They would simply take Shan behind a rock and shoot him. He felt as though at any moment he would lose control of his body and it would fling itself out of the truck. But he just stared at the floor. On the floor was a pebble and on the pebble was a lichen and in the lichen lived a mite.

Jakli had driven from Lau's cabin to a small compound of windblown structures on the Kashgar highway consisting of a shed with a bank of gas pumps outside it, a larger garage building surrounded by vehicles in various states of disrepair, and, on the opposite side of the road, a square cinder block structure, painted yellow, with a large glass window and a hand-lettered sign that said only *Tea*. She made a series of phone calls from a phone by the gas pumps, and an hour later a delivery truck en route to Glory Camp had stopped for them. Three men were inside, Fat Mao at the wheel and two Kazakhs with heavy moustaches whom Shan recognized as Akzu's sons. The Kazakhs had climbed out onto the burlap sacks in the back of the heavy open bay vehicle to make room for Jakli and Shan in the cab. A fourth man had climbed down from the sacks, a sullen, broad-shouldered man with cold eyes and a gutter of scar tissue on his neck that could only have been made by a bullet. Jakli had introduced him as Ox Mao. Ox Mao had silently climbed into the turtle truck and driven away with Jowa, Lokesh, and Bajys.

Jakli silently placed her hand on Shan's white knuckles, then slowly pried his fingers and moved his hand away. She rolled up the sleeve of his shirt and traced the tattooed string of numbers with her finger. "I have other friends who survived the gulag," she said with a sigh. "But they always show it on their faces. I have never seen it on your face. You did well."

"No one does well," Shan whispered, looking at the tattoo. Four guards had held him down when he had resisted the ink needle. Finally they had lost patience and held his nose and mouth until he fell unconscious. When he had awakened, the numbers had been completed, and a political officer had been standing over him, gloating. "Wear it proudly," the officer had barked, "it proves the state still cares about you."

Jakli spoke in her Turkic tongue and Fat Mao reached under the seat, then handed her a small medical kit. She extracted a large adhesive bandage, peeled away the backing, and placed it over the tattoo. "There," she said, and rolled down his sleeve. "Just like us now."

Strangely, the coldness began to recede. He recalled her words. Other friends, she had said. As if Shan were a friend too.

The single guard at the small hut by the gate recognized the truck and began to open the gate before they reached the outer wire. They coasted through without stopping, slowing enough for Fat Mao to toss the soldier an apple. A faded banner, frayed at the edges, hung between two posts. *Become Liberated from Feudalism.*

Shan's prisoner-eyes took over for a moment. The gate was not well maintained, its hinges loose and rusty. Much of the wire in both the gate and the perimeter fence also appeared rusted. The guard himself was overweight and middle-aged, not one of the crack People's Liberation Army or Public Security troops that controlled hard larbor prisons, and his carbine looked older than the guard himself.

Wangtu would be on trusty duties, Fat Mao explained, since he was only being held for questioning, which meant he would be excused from camp routine to unload the weekly food delivery at the camp warehouse. Jakli pointed to the warehouse, a big square building between the perimeter fence and the inner wire that contained the prisoner barracks. They drove slowly toward the structure, past the low L-shaped building that housed the administrative offices for Glory to the People Camp. Several men in brown shirts and pants stood on the steps of the office building, watching their truck. He had not seen the men before, but he had seen the brown clothing, in the mountains before Gendun had disappeared.

"Brigade security," Jakli explained. "A small garrison of

soldiers remain, but last year the Brigade assumed responsibility for administration of the camp."

Beyond the warehouse Shan saw a huge pile of coal and a small boiler building, marked by a fifty-foot-high smokestack. There were gulag prisons in Xinjiang, Shan knew, that were giant coal mines, where men and women led brutal lives extracting coal with hammer and chisel, providing coal to sister prison facilities and shipping the remainder to eastern cities.

Past the boiler was a cemetery.

After he climbed out, Shan looked back at the long rows of sun-bleached planks that served as markers, with the odd realization that he had not seen a cemetery for years. In Beijing land was too scarce to waste on the dead. Only the most important Party members or the wealthy were granted permanent graves. Others could pay for the right to be interred for a few years, to allow family a chance to visit, but when the contract expired the bodies were dug up and burned. The Buddhists he had known in Tibet still practiced sky burial, leaving the dead for the vultures, the quickest way to return the body to the circle of life.

Suddenly a harsh voice erupted from the loudspeakers arrayed on poles around the compound, announcing in Mandarin that Sessions in Praise of Party Heroes would commence in ten minutes. Shan surveyed the compound inside the inner wire fence as it came to life. Barracks—most constructed of cement block with tin roofs, others of plywood whose layers were peeling away—lined three sides of a square nearly a third of a mile on each side. The U-shape they formed opened at the front, toward the administrative complex where the truck now sat. At a second, inner gate that led to the barracks two more guards could be seen, one leaning against a post as if asleep. One of the buildings, the nearest to the inner gate, had heavy wire covering its windows and four guards sitting on a bench by its door. Shan studied it closely, suddenly aware that Gendun could be inside.

Past the barracks, at the end of the inner compound, Shan could see fields, empty except for one large plot with scores of cabbages. Beyond the wire to the south and east were brown, grass-covered hills on which scattered sheep grazed.

With painful memories he watched as hundreds of grey-clothed prisoners scurried toward their assigned political education classes. No one could be late. A lao jiao inmate did not suffer the deprivations of the gulag prisoner, but discipline was still strict. Shan's eyes drifted back toward the cemetery and studied the long rows of markers. Lao jiao prisoners were typically short-termers, sentenced to a few months or a year. That should mean that few would die during their term.

"They contract contagious diseases sometimes," Jakli said as she followed his gaze. "And two years ago there was a drought. People in the towns got the priority allocation of food. Next in priority were the agricultural enterprises, then the livestock. Then came the prisoners. Older prisoners died of malnutrition. They ate their belts, they ate their shoes, they ate bugs and worms. But they died anyway," she sighed. "And the Brigade sends lao gai prisoners who are too ill to work, just sends them here to die. They hate having underproductive workers lying around the coal mines. Sometimes," she added, "the boot squads bring special prisoners here, because it is so far from anywhere, so secret."

The truck backed toward a large plank building with a loading dock. As it stopped a figure wearing a white shirt and tie emerged from the administrative building and waved a clipboard at them. Jakli gestured Shan toward the cargo bay.

They had agreed in advance that Shan would push the sacks from the top, the position least visible to the guards, handing the sacks to the others until Jakli found a way to take Wangtu aside. PRODUCT OF GUANGDONG PROVINCE, Shan read on the burlap bags as he climbed to the top. It was another of Beijing's cruel jokes. The Tibetans and the Kazakhs, as well as the many other minorities of the western reaches, traditionally ate barley and wheat as their staples. But Beijing arranged for much of the local grain production to be shipped east for livestock feed and exchanged for rice, the staple of the Han Chinese. Explanatory tracts, written by the central government, were distributed among the local populations to demonstrate that rice was healthier. Rice, some even claimed, was what made the Han people smarter than others. An American acquaintance in Beijing had once laughed at Shan for being upset at a poster saying that Rice was the Food of Patriots. Just a marketing slogan, he had said.

From his perch on top of the rice bags Shan surveyed the camp again. He could see the graveyard clearly now, including several mounds of fresh dirt at the far end, and quickly calculated that it contained at least two hundred markers. A new building came into view—a shed for tools, perhaps—located between the boilerhouse and the cemetery. A movement at the side of the shed caught his eyes. As he watched, a figure stepped into view at the corner of the building, and the chill returned to his spine. The figure was a soldier but not one of the lazy, ill-equipped guards that stood at the wire. Even from over fifty yards away Shan recognized the uniform and the swagger. The man was from Public Security, a knob, and the weapon cradled in his arm was not an outdated rifle but a compact submachine gun.

"Are you ill?" Jakli called out for the second time that day, and he realized he had flattened himself against the sacks. Prisoner instincts died hard. "We must move," she explained as he rose and shook his head. She stretched out an arm to help him down from the truck.

Back in the cab of the truck Shan's fingers wove themselves into a mudra, his hands clasped together with the middle fingers pointing upward. Diamond of the Mind. Clarity of purpose. Remember your goal. Preserve mindfulness. He looked up from his hands just as the truck passed through the inner wire.

"I thought you meant we would leave!" he gasped.

"The loading dock is closed today," Jakli said as she looked back at the dock with a puzzled expression. "We have to unload half directly at the kitchens, then the other half tomorrow morning at the dock. We'll find Wangtu," she assured him, "one place or the other."

But in that moment Shan was not worried about finding Lau's driver. His tongue was so dry that he couldn't speak, or he might have shouted in protest. He was being taken back into prison after all. Had it all been some dreadful trick of his former jailers, to ensnare him behind government wire for a few more years?

Jakli placed her hand over his forearm again. "What were we to do? It would be more suspicious if we refused. You will be safe, I promise."

He realized he was sliding down in the seat, as if his body had willed itself to hide. He was being taken back into prison, and this time there would be no Buddhist monks to heal him when the jailers had finished with him.

A squeeze from Jakli's hand brought him back to reality. "It's only when you act like a prisoner that you become one," she observed in a calm, sober voice.

Her wisdom struck him like a fresh, cool wind, and it shamed him. He slowly sat up in the seat and said no more until they approached the long building at the base of the compound that served as kitchen and mess hall.

"I'm sorry," he said, fighting the temptation to again hold his tattoo.

Saying the words out loud somehow gave him strength but also heightened his shame. *There is nothing to fear behind the wires.* The words came back to him as starkly as when they had been spoken to him years earlier by a serene old monk serving his thirty-fifth year in the gulag. *For no jailer who ever lived can imprison the truth.*

He stepped out and stared at the first of the barracks, the special detention barracks, two hundred yards away. "Do they bring those prisoners out for exercise?" he asked Jakli.

"No. People here call them the invisibles," she said with a sigh. "Special cases. Usually nothing to do with Yoktian."

Shan stared intensely at the building, as though willing himself to see inside its walls.

"Your lama," Jakli said with sudden realization. "You think he's inside." She stared with him for a moment, then pulled his sleeve. "It's dangerous to appear too curious," she warned.

Shan fought a new urge, a compulsion to run to the sealed barracks and pound on the door, calling for Gendun. For a moment nothing seemed more important than hearing the sound of the lama's voice.

A door opened at the side of the mess hall and several

men wearing loose-fitting grey tunics emerged. Jakli leapt out and disappeared into the building. Shan looked around the compound, nearly empty again now that the prisoners had joined their classes, then climbed down and joined the line of men forming to carry sacks of rice into the kitchen. He gazed at the barracks with the wire windows, futilely looking for any sign of who might be inside, then accepted one of the heavy bags and followed the line through the door, dropping it onto a stack under the supervision of a cackling woman in a brown dress who waved a wooden spoon with an air of authority. A tall man with a scar on his cheek stood at a sink, washing pots. He was doing so with only one hand. Shan stepped closer and discovered the reason. The man was chanting under his breath. His second hand was at his belt, counting a string of yellow plastic rosary beads. Another man, older than the first, stood beside him, drying the pots, though he seemed to be having trouble handling them. He was balancing each one on his palm to dry them, then placing them on a wall shelf by clamping them with his middle fingers. His thumbs were missing. Another Tibetan. Shan had seen it before. Not a week had gone by during his imprisonment when he had not heard guards cruelly joke about Tibetans being pruned. For several years it had been one of the favorite forms of punishment by certain knob officers, who used tree pruners to clip off the thumbs of monks to keep them from their rosaries.

Shan looked out through a set of double doors over the long rows of empty plank tables. One of the political classes had convened at the far end of the mess hall. A large Han woman in another brown dress was pacing inside the seated circle of prisoners, her hands clasped behind her. For one brief moment she faced the double door and Shan heard her call out, so loudly that for a chilling moment Shan thought she was addressing him.

"Who is the great provider of the people?" she asked in a shrill voice.

"The Party is the great provider of the people," the prisoners responded in chorus. It had a familiar, singsong ring to it. A mantra for the Chairman.

Shan looked from the hall back to the Tibetan at the sink, who seemed unaware of the activity around him as he offered up his own silent chant. A mantra for the Compassionate Buddha.

Outside, as Shan accepted another sack off the truck and moved back toward the building, a voice from behind him repeated the slogan the instructor had chanted. But then Shan realized the words were changing each time the man repeated the chant.

"Who is the great shoemaker of the people?" the man sang. "The Party is the great shoemaker of the people." His voice was soft, but loud enough for the men around him to enjoy his performance. "Who is the great barber of the people? The Party is the great barber of the people." Some of the men laughed. Others looked about nervously to see who else might hear.

Shan had to pause at the small flight of stairs leading to the door to wait for the older man in front of him, who seemed to be having difficulty carrying the bag up the stairs. He looked back at the man who was mocking the political instruction. A tall, large-boned man with a thick, well-groomed moustache and a sour smile returned Shan's stare. "Who is the great zookeeper of the people?" the man asked, nodding toward Shan. Shan said nothing. The man repeated the question.

Shan nodded back without shifting his gaze from the man's taunting eyes. "The Party is the great zookeeper of the people," Shan replied quietly.

The man's smile broadened and Shan saw that he was looking past Shan's shoulder to Jakli, who had appeared at the top of the short flight of stairs. "Allah be praised," he gasped under his breath. Jakli nodded and gestured them toward the shadow on the far side of the truck.

"So you've met," she said as she joined them.

"Not exactly," Shan said.

"Wangtu," Jakli said, touching the man on the arm as she spoke. "This is Shan. He came about Lau and the children."

But Wangtu seemed to have forgotten Shan. He looked at Jakli's fingers, still resting on his arm. "I thought you were gone," he said, the self-assurance suddenly gone from his voice. "They said the Jade Bitch had it in for you." He glanced at the supply truck. "You're free? You're out?"

"Mostly," she said and explained why Shan was there.

Wangtu shrugged. "Don't know about children," he said in an earnest tone, as if children didn't inhabit his world. While he studied Shan he worked his tongue against his cheek, as though searching for something in his mouth. "When boys die, that's for their parents."

"These had no parents," Jakli threw back in an impatient voice. "Lau's orphans. One lived with Bajys. You know Bajys."

"I could get you things," Wangtu said to Jakli. "I could come see you. I live in town."

"You live in Glory Camp right now."

"This?" Wangtu said with a dismissive wave of his hand toward the barracks. "Vacation. Sing a few songs, see some old friends." With these last words he sobered and gave Jakli a meaningful stare.

"How did you know Bajys?" Shan asked.

Wangtu sighed. "He and that boy, they help bring wool to town sometimes. For this clan or that clan. You know, they stay with different clans. A few weeks here, a few there. That was Lau's system. I see people, at different places. When the Brigade doesn't use me for the school, I drive trucks for the wool processing plant. They clean it and bale it and I drive it to the carpet factories in Kotian," he explained, referring to the large city over a hundred miles to the west that had once been a Silk Road trading center.

Shan looked back at Jakli. "The school is run by the Brigade?"

"The school, this camp, soon the whole world," Wangtu said in a thin voice.

"But you told him something," Jakli pressed. "You told Bajys that Lau was in trouble."

"Your father," Wangtu asked. "Did he ever come back?"

The question seemed to catch Jakli off guard. She didn't return his gaze but looked to Shan. "Wangtu and I," she explained, "we went to school together."

Wangtu grinned, as if grateful for the acknowledgment.

Jakli glanced at the truck, which was being rapidly unloaded. "Quickly, Wangtu. Why did you warn Bajys?"

The Kazakh studied the compound as if trying to remember. "I didn't, exactly. I just told him Lau was walking with the blue wolf." He cut his eyes toward Jakli as he spoke.

The announcement brought a hard glare to Jakli's face. "A jinni," she explained to Shan, as she kept her eyes on Wangtu. "A blue wolf is a very bad type of jinni. An evil spirit."

"For Kazakhs," Wangtu added. "For old Kazakhs, anyway."

"Tell us," Jakli said impatiently. "Why would you say a blue wolf shadowed her?"

Wangtu seemed not to be listening. He was looking over her shoulder. "I could get you that," he said with a wistful nod toward the wire.

Jakli turned and froze. Pleasure flashed across her face. In a rope pen between the inner and outer fences was a magnificent white horse.

"We used to walk together, Jakli," Wangtu said with an odd melancholy in his voice. "I sang songs at your camp."

The woman seemed not to have heard. She took a step forward, as though drawn by the graceful animal that pranced about the makeshift pen.

"I could get white horses for your clan," Wangtu suggested.

"Why did you say it to Bajys?" Shan pressed. Jakli broke from her trance and stepped behind Shan, as if Wangtu's offer of the white horse somehow scared her.

Wangtu sighed. "I hear things, okay? I heard a new teacher was coming. I heard Lieutenant Sui in the back one day, telling the head of the school that Lau had been reported by another teacher, who said that at one of her classes Lau read off a list of names from the five twenty-ninth, and later from 1997."

"Dissidents," Jakli offered quickly to Shan, and glanced at the truck. "But she wasn't arrested. She was murdered."

Wangtu snorted and opened his mouth as though about to laugh. "Murdered? No. Disappeared, near the river. She could still come back."

"Disappeared with a bullet in her head," Shan said. "We've seen her body."

Wangtu looked at Jakli, who confirmed Shan's words

with a nod. He grimaced, then studied Shan with suspicion on his face. "Who sent you?" he asked Shan.

"Priests," Jakli said quickly, as if worried that Shan might speak first. "Priests said he should come."

"Priests? Priests?" It was Wangtu's turn to be confused. "You mean a mullah?"

"It doesn't matter," Jakli said, impatience back in her voice. "There are no bad priests."

"Sure there are. The priests that run this camp." Wangtu's voice was hollow now, and his eyes flared. "What was it the Chairman said? Religion poisons the people. So he got rid of the other religions and sent out his own priests." He looked back at Shan. "All the prosecutor says is that Lau disappeared. She spoke to us, all the ones detained. She said maybe reactionaries did something to Lau, maybe kidnapped her. They do that sometimes, she told us, hoping to trade for one of their own in prison. Maybe one of us would think of something helpful, she said."

"I saw Lau," Jakli said coolly. "She's dead, Wangtu, but the prosecutor mustn't know. It won't help anyone."

A low whistle came from between Wangtu's teeth, and he shook his head slowly. "I liked Lau." The Kazakh's eyes drifted toward the old man who had struggled on the steps. He was leaning against the wall by the door, gasping for breath.

Shan studied the man on the steps. "He's old for a rice camp," he observed. The People's reeducation resources were seldom wasted on those who had little left to contribute to the proletarian effort.

Wangtu frowned at Shan, as if perhaps Shan, or all Hans, were responsible for the man being there. "He's a teacher. Forty years in a village near Kashgar, then they put him out, told him to go to some rest home built for pensioned teachers. Instead he started unofficial classes among the clans, riding from camp to camp, taking payment in food and a pallet. Got reported for teaching ancient history."

"Ancient history?" Shan asked.

"You know, before 1949. The Republic of East Turkistan, the kingdoms of the Silk Road. When this land was independent. I tell him he's got to stop. I tell him he's too old. He's on his third bowl."

"Third bowl?" Shan asked.

Wangtu cast a surprised glance at Jakli as he spoke. "Third lao jiao term. Each time you arrive at the camp they give you a tin bowl, for washing, for eating, drinking, everything." His eyes drifted back to the old man on the step. "After three bowls, it's hard labor if you're picked up again."

Shan looked back at the old teacher. "He wouldn't last a month in the gulag," Shan said.

Wangtu's feet shifted, and his eyes slowly surveyed the length of the wire along the side of the compound. A small vehicle, looking like an ancient armored car that might have been used in the original Eighth Route Army, drove slowly along the wire. "He won't last a month at Glory Camp, not this time. Life's cheap here since the Brigade started running the camp." He didn't seem to be speaking to them anymore but to someone else toward the office compound. Shan followed his gaze. He was looking at the cemetery.

"A Mongol," Wangtu said, "just a teenager, had a magazine with color pictures of horses. Against the rules, but so what? Just horses. Every day he'd look at the pictures and say he was going to have a herd of horses someday. At a class the instructor for his barracks pulled the Mongol's magazine from the back of his pants, where he hid it during the day. This instructor, she said the barracks needed it because the latrine had no more paper. When the Mongol leapt at her the instructor hit him in the head with a shovel. It made a crunching sound, like stepping on a rotten log. The boy sat on the ground with his head in his hands and the instructor circled around him and gave a speech on the evils of hoarding property. When she finished she yelled at the Mongol to apologize to everyone. He wouldn't reply, so she kicked him. He just rolled over. He was paralyzed. He just lies on his bunk now. The instructor took his magazine to the latrine."

Jakli put her hand to her mouth as if to hold back a sob.

Wangtu winced, as though reproaching himself for upsetting Jakli.

"But why would you warn Bajys?" Shan asked. "Why

did you suspect trouble would come to Lau? Who was the evil spirit with Lau?"

"We were friends, Lau and me. She was the only one who ever sat in the front of the car with me. She used to bring me medicines, and she gave me special teas from herbs she found in the mountains." Wangtu pointed for Jakli to look back at the white horse, as if it might comfort her. "Things were happening to her. Fired from the Ag Council. The report to Public Security." Jakli turned away now, looking at the faces of the other prisoners. "That Tibetan," he continued, to her back. "I told her about that Tibetan."

Jakli spun about.

"Kaju. I didn't know his name then, but I told her, maybe three months ago, about the Tibetan Director Ko was bringing for the zheli. She didn't know. I told her I heard Ko talking in a car one day, I said to her I guess they think you're leaving."

Three months ago, Shan remembered, was when Lau had begun explaining where she wanted her body taken. "What did Lau say?" Shan asked.

"She just smiled at first and patted my arm. Then she said yes I guess they do, and she sighed and said she never should have gone to Urumqi. She always talked with me, but that day she was just quiet until the end of the trip."

"Gone to Urumqi?" Shan asked. "What did she mean?"

"I never knew." Wangtu shrugged. "Some trip to the capital."

"What else did she say?" Jakli asked.

"When she left that day she said maybe she shouldn't bring me teas anymore, that later people would say we were friends because of it. She said we could still be friends in our hearts but that she wouldn't want me hurt because of it. I said I don't care what they say, and she said you have to care, because this is China." Wangtu looked back at the white horse with a pained expression. "After that she always seemed to be in a hurry, no time to talk. I didn't drive her much afterward. Haven't seen her for a month." He shifted his gaze toward the horizon with a thoughtful expression. "Where she died, who was there?"

"That's what we want to find out." Jakli said.

"No. I mean, who did she go see? It's important. Lau, she had only certain people she trusted. She would only stay where one was close. She moved from one to the other, like from one oasis to another. Where she went, you should ask them there."

Shan and Jakli exchanged a glance. Lau had died in the place in the desert which Jakli seemed unwilling to speak about, the place where Bajys had his nightmare vision of dismembered humans.

"The prosecutor," Jakli said. "The prosector doesn't know," she reminded him.

"All I know," Wangtu said with a forced grin, "is that she didn't know how to swim." He cast a hopeful glance toward Jakli. "I wouldn't tell all this to anyone. But I did to you, Jakli."

Jakli looked at him in obvious discomfort. "I am getting married, Wangtu," she announced quickly, then leaned forward, kissed his cheek, and stepped away toward another prisoner she seemed to have recognized.

Married. Shan gazed after Jakli, feeling foolish for not having understood before. The hushed, excited conversations at Red Stone camp. The dress being whisked away by the older women. Malik's secret gift for Jakli and someone else, whose name the boy was reluctant to speak. Nikki, the name Akzu had mentioned when parting from her at the garage. Other women would have joyously shared the news. But Jakli's marriage was wrapped in secrecy. Shan understood, for he too had grown up in a world where you said the least about the things that were most important to you, for fear that they would be taken away.

Wangtu stood, crestfallen, as he watched Jakli begin talking with a short plump Han man. "You have to keep her out," he said, then repeated the words more urgently, as if Shan might not have heard.

"Out?" Shan asked. Shan looked at her again. What an odd time to be getting married, when the clans were being disbanded, and children were being killed. But Shan had learned years ago how difficult it was to translate the language of another's heart.

"Out of Glory Camp. Out of prison. Some of the guards hate her because she talks back to them, because she resists.

She's not made for a cage. Like the Mongol boy." His disappointment seemed to have turned to worry. His mouth opened again but no words came out. He looked to Shan and then to the ground. "I would have done her time for her if I could," he said quietly. "She belongs in the mountains, on a horse." Then he drifted away, as if he had forgotten Shan stood there.

"Comrade Hu," Jakli said as she brought the short Han toward Shan. "Chairman of the Educational Committee for the school in Yoktian."

Hu touched his thick-rimmed glasses and gave a shallow smile. "Former Chairman, I guess," he said.

"Not necessarily," Jakli said reassuringly. "It's just Prosecutor Xu's way, to intimidate witnesses."

"I told her," Hu said. "I witnessed nothing. Lau was not on our official staff. We had no official responsibility for her. Once she received a small stipend but that stopped years ago. We just gave her an office, let her know our schedules so she could coordinate. Let her use our drivers sometimes."

"So you spoke to Xu already?"

"This morning. She told me to think about it, after I said I knew nothing. Good jobs are hard to find in Yoktian, she reminded me. She looked at my file and reminded me that I have a family. I told her there were no secrets about Lau. She was an open book. Maybe too open. That's all it was, she was too blunt with the wrong person. Some of the herders have tempers, some still have one foot in the age of the khans, when there were blood feuds." He looked over the prison grounds. "I offered to instruct classes while I was here," he declared, as if he suspected Shan might be a political officer.

Shan's attention drifted away. Comrade Hu, he had quickly decided, was not the type that Lau would have confided in.

He sensed that Wangtu was right, that Lau was someone with great intuition about people, who moved from one she trusted to another she trusted. But what did she leave with them? Secrets. Secrets are what you give to those you trust. She had gone to the place in the desert, to the place called Karachuk, not to die but to share a secret.

He noticed another man, sitting in the shadows against the wall of the mess hall, facing the open yard of the camp but casting occasional glances toward Shan and Jakli. He was nearly bald and had so little flesh on his face that the contours of his skull were unmistakable.

His eyes made momentary contact with Shan's, and as they did so his eyelids seemed to droop and his fingertips touched the ground, as though the man had grown sleepy.

"A waste of time," Jakli declared as she followed Shan's gaze. "Go ahead," she said with a shrug, "but you'll make no sense out of what he says."

Shan cast her a puzzled glance as she continued to speak with Hu.

"The Xibo," she said in an aside to Shan. "The waterkeeper."

"What's his name?"

"I don't know. He's always just the waterkeeper. He just mutters nonsense and drools. He speaks only the tongue of the clans and the old Xibo words."

Confirming that Jakli remained occupied with Hu, he stepped toward the bald man.

The waterkeeper gave no acknowledgment when Shan squatted in front of him. He just shuffled sideways, as if Shan had blocked his view. Shan matched his movement, then sat on the ground. The two men said nothing. Shan stared at the waterkeeper. The man stared over Shan's shoulder as if not noticing him, sucking something, perhaps the shell of a nut, or a pebble. A thin line of drool hung from the corner of his mouth.

Shan had spent his childhood in Manchuria. He had known Xibos, and the man in front of him was no Xibo. Nor was he in his fifties, as Jakli had indicated. He was older, perhaps much older, though only his rheumy eyes and the rough yellow ridges on his fingernails showed it. The man looked down at the dirt in front of him and made a grunting noise, an old man's noise. But Shan believed none of it. Not the absent, drooping eyes, not the drool, not the muttering.

It was the fingers he had noticed first, while still standing by Jakli. The fingers weren't just drooping down, they were carefully aligned, with the left hand flat in the lap, the right draped on the right knee, palms inward, fingers aimed down, thumb slightly apart. It was a mudra, the Earth Touching mudra, invoking the land deity, calling it to witness. And between the fingers of the right hand was a small dried flower.

There was a connection Jakli had apparently overlooked. The waterkeeper was hired by the Agricultural Council. And Lau had served for years on the council.

Shan began arranging his own fingers carefully, in a fashion he had learned in Lhadrung, with his hands cupped, pressed together, the fingertips touching, the thumbs pressing against each other.

The waterkeeper's eyes drifted, passing over Shan again as if he were not there. The last of the bags for the kitchens was unloaded, and the men began to bunch up near the stairs, watching the loudspeakers as if expecting new instructions.

Shan did not move. He fixed his eyes on those of the waterkeeper.

Finally the man's eyes found Shan's hands. His head made a quick, trembling motion as if his mind itself were blinking. With one glance Shan understood. The man saw what Shan had made, a mudra, the mudra of the Treasure Flask, the sign of the sacred receptacle. He saw what it was, and he saw that Shan knew he had seen.

The hoods over the waterkeeper's eyes slid away. His eyes did not move in their sockets, but his head rose slowly until he met Shan's gaze.

"I have been to your cave, Rinpoche," Shan whispered in Tibetan. "I am going to help you. I am going to help the children."

The waterkeeper did not reply, but after a moment took Shan's hands and squeezed them slowly, but hard. "Even if you find the one, you can't take it back." The words came so suddenly, in Tibetan, and in such a low, whispered voice that Shan almost thought it was only in his head. But the man's moist eyes grew wider, and his mouth moved again. "You can only take it forward," he said hoarsely, and his eyes shifted toward the mountains, towards the Kunlun and Tibet.

The memory of Bajys's words flooded over him. *That*

was the one I loved, he had said of Khitai, as if there were many Khitais. *That was the one I was to keep safe.* Bajys hadn't understood, or if he had understood, hadn't cared, that Khitai was still alive. What had broken Bajys, what had sent him fleeing, whimpering, raving, toward Lau was a broken trust. Someone had discovered a momentous secret, Bajys's secret, and because the secret was known, Bajys's world was ending. Now the teacher, the old lama who was the waterkeeper, was speaking in the same riddles. Maybe Bajys had not been speaking of a boy after all, but of an object. *You can't take it back. You can only take it forward.*

Suddenly the truck engine roared to life. The old man rose, his eyes assuming their drowsy, half-wit glaze again. He stumbled over his own feet as he headed toward the mess hall. The prisoners at the door laughed at him.

An instant later the loudspeakers crackled to life again. The men gathered around the mess hall and straightened their tunics, then started moving into the throng of prisoners that began filling the yard. It was their turn to be blessed by the political priests.

Moments later Fat Mao eased the truck past the inner wire. But as they tried to leave Glory Camp they found the main gate secured with a chain and padlock, no guard in sight. They waited nervously for ten minutes, then Fat Mao inched their truck toward the administration building. A figure emerged, not a guard but a Chinese clerk in a white shirt frayed at the cuffs.

"You were told what to do," the man said in shrill voice. "The rest of the cargo is unloaded tomorrow."

"So we will be here tomorrow," Fat Mao said. "At dawn if you wish."

A sneer rose on the clerk's face and he unfolded a slip of a paper from his pocket. "We are authorized to receive one shipment a week," he squeaked. "You are authorized to be paid for one shipment a week. The full cargo was accepted by signature at the kitchen." He waved the paper near Fat Mao's face. "You think you'll come back tomorrow and be paid for two shipments? Not a chance."

"Don't be ridiculous. We only get paid for shipments we deliver."

"Exactly," the clerk said with a victorious wave of his hand. "And you propose to deliver only a half-loaded truck tomorrow." He raised his nose and seemed to point it at Fat Mao. "There are campaigns against corruption."

Shan watched the Uighur's jaw tighten as he tried to control his anger. "Then we will unload the bags on the dock. Tomorrow you can move them inside."

"Your payment is for delivery inside the warehouse. Cheating on labor is another form of corruption," the clerk snapped back.

"So open the warehouse."

"The warehouse is closed by order of Major Bao of Public Security. You have been permitted to use the repair bay tonight." He pointed to a tall structure beyond the office that was nothing more than a high roof supported by four posts, with a workbench at one end. "But I warn you," he added in his shrill voice, "we have a complete inventory of all tools."

"We are supposed to be back with our families tonight," Fat Mao protested. "Our people expect us in Yoktian."

"We all must make sacrifices. That is the essence of Glory Camp," the clerk said happily, as if grateful for the chance to offer political advice, then spun about and marched toward the office building.

Fat Mao stared venomously at the clerk, and then, with a glance toward Jakli, put the truck into gear and drove toward the repair bay. "Campaigns against corruption," he muttered. "How about a campaign against stupidity?"

Shan remembered the knob guard. "He mentioned Major Bao," he said to the Uighur. The Brigade ran the camp, the prosecutor kept it filled, but the knobs apparently used it at their convenience.

Fat Mao grimaced. "Head of Public Security in Yoktian. Lieutenant Sui's boss. The two people you never want to cross in this county are Major Bao and Prosecutor Xu."

The Uighur and the Kazakh men rearranged sacks of rice in the cargo bay into makeshift beds and immediately lay down to sleep. Shan stepped toward Jakli, who stood by one of the posts supporting the roof, staring toward the prisoner yard.

"I never expected this. I'm sorry," she said. "Jowa spoke

to me at Lau's cabin. He told me they were working on a way out for you, out of China, that there are people at the United Nations who would take care of you once you crossed the border. I wasn't thinking. That kind of opportunity never comes for most of us. We never should have asked you to take this kind of risk."

"It's just kind words they speak to me sometimes," Shan said. "Just their way of giving me hope. It will be years. Most likely, it will never happen." He stared toward the mess hall where he had last seen the waterkeeper, then toward the barracks with the wire windows, the special holding cells. He had forgotten to ask the waterkeeper a question. Did he know Gendun? "And no one forced me here," he added, trying to force a smile.

Jakli shifted her gaze back toward the prisoner yard. Not the yard, Shan saw after a moment, but the wire, or the rope corral adjoining the wire. "There used to be more horses," she said in a sad tone. "They take horses in trains to the east from Kashgar now. There are factories there that do nothing but kill horses. They put the meat in cans. So the government can boast about how well the people are fed. Now they want all the herds, even the wild ones."

Jowa had been right, Shan thought. The Poverty Scheme was a liquidation program. In the name of liquidating inefficient assets, the government was liquidating the entire nomad way of life. A private, politically correct scheme for achieving the final stage of what Beijing had started decades earlier.

"Why a white horse?" Shan asked.

"White horses are for gifts."

"Wedding gifts, you mean?" Shan asked, turning to look her in the eyes.

"Not only weddings. Namegiving days. Special festivals," she said, shifting her gaze back toward the horse. "But especially weddings," she added with a shy but determined smile that said she would say no more about the topic.

"And Wangtu talked about Lau reading names from the five twenty-ninth and—"

"And 1997," Jakli finished. "Political demonstrations. The five twenty-ninth means the May 29 uprising in 1962. Kazakhs and Uighurs fought against the government, in

Yining. Many were killed. The government never reported the deaths. But we know the names. We honor the names, by reading them out loud at clan gatherings. Then in 1997 there was more fighting. The PLA was called in. Machine guns were used. Bombs went off in Urumqi."

"Was Lau a dissident?"

"Someone who reads the names of heroes to children, is that a dissident?"

"You know what I mean. Was she marked for criticizing the government somehow?"

"No." It seemed to take a great act of willpower for Jakli to turn away from the horse. She pulled a piece of paper from her pocket. "Otherwise, we wouldn't be here. There would be no murder to investigate. There might have been an announcement about a political correction. Maybe a lie about her being transferred. But just no more Lau." She pulled a folded, tattered envelope out of her pocket, then stepped to the cab of the truck and climbed up, as if to read its contents.

Shan realized that if he climbed the remaining sacks of the cargo bay into the deep shadow cast by the roof of the repair bay, he would have a clear view of the administrative compound without being visible from the outside. He nestled onto the sacks at the top and did what he did best. He watched.

The warehouse, apparently usually open, was locked for some reason. There were no windows on the three sides he had observed thus far and only the single set of doors at the loading bay. The compound was quiet. The afternoon classes were in session. The only sign of life came from the boiler building, where several men hauled coal from the pile, and the small shed, where the solitary knob guard stood, occasionally pacing around the structure, sometimes raising and sighting along his weapon toward the horizon. The administration building remained quiet, although the sound of music drifted out of an open window. It was a military march, from a badly scratched recording, played again and again.

He drifted into sleep. When he woke, a new car was parked by the administration building—a Red Flag limousine. The music from the administration building had stopped, but there was no sign of activity from the new arrival. Inside the inner wire a few prisoners drifted around the mess hall. A class sat outside now, around the pole in the center of the prisoner compound that held the red flag of the People's Republic. The door of the warehouse remained closed. The workers at the coal pile still fed the boiler. But the guard at the shed had brought a chair to the front of the structure. He was slumped in it as though asleep, his weapon hanging from the back of the chair.

Slowly, his eyes shifting from the guard to the administration building and back again, Shan climbed down from his perch. Jakli had joined Fat Mao and her cousins and was sleeping, the tattered envelope held between her palms as though she had been praying over it.

He walked toward the warehouse, fighting the urge to run, watching the door by the empty limousine and, in the opposite direction, the solitary sleeping guard. It was indeed locked, but as he pressed the latch he thought he heard a voice.

"Who is it?" Shan whispered, first in Tibetan, then in Mandarin.

There seemed to be a reply, a low sound, but whether it was a word or simply a moan he could not tell.

He could not risk attracting attention. Shan quickly stepped away from the doors and moved around the edge of the building, hoping to find a window in the far end. There was none. He turned to face the boiler house and beyond it, the cemetery. The shed was quiet, the administration building still, the gate unmanned. He set a course toward the shed with the Public Security guard. Thirty feet away, close enough to hear deep snoring from the knob in the chair, he veered toward the boiler house.

A small column of greasy smoke rose from the chimney, drifting toward the mountains. Half a dozen men labored at the mound of coal adjacent to the structure, loading oversized wheelbarrows that they pushed through the open front of the buildng and dumped at the boiler, where another man shoveled the coal into the fire.

The six men were different from the other prisoners. They did not wear the coarse grey uniforms of the men inside the wire, and though their clothes were stained with coal dust, the colors of their shirts and vests were still bright enough to mark them as recent arrivals. Perhaps, Shan considered, they were more of Xu's special detainees. But they seemed somehow different. Wangtu and the others had been given light duties. These men had the hardest labor in the camp, as if they were destined for the harshest fate. But the faces of the men seemed to say otherwise. There was no surrender, none of the bitter resignation to surrendering a piece of their lives to the political officers. They were rough men, thick with muscle, none of them Han. They did not seem to take their labor seriously, as though they could be relieved, or even freed, at any moment. But they expected no relief from Shan. Three of the men glared at him and looked away. The others continued their work while silently frowning at him. Then he remembered the computer data that Fat Mao had shown them. There were other reservations at Glory Camp, for the Brigade, and for the special knob boot squads whose job it was to fight reactionaries and insurgents.

Shan moved into the shadow under the roof and looked back. Nothing had changed. The limousine was still at the office. The knob was still asleep. He studied the building. It contained only machinery, the boiler and the small old turbine generator it powered. There was a workbench with mechanic's tools by the generator. No one else was in the structure except the man at the open boiler door. He stopped, silhouetted by the intense fire, and leaned on his shovel as soon as he noticed Shan.

As Shan nodded awkwardly and ventured a step closer, the man wiped the soot from his brow. Shan froze in confusion. The man's skin was white. The stranger pushed back his filthy cap, revealing a swath of long blond hair. A flicker of interest passed over his face as Shan approached, and with a heavy Western-style hiking boot the man kicked the boiler door shut, muting the roar of the furnace.

"Hello, your excellency," the Westerner said in a mocking tone. He spoke in English, with an American accent. "Did you bring me some tea and cakes?"

As Shan took another step forward a hand closed around his upper arm, a rough painful grasp that pulled him backward so hard he almost fell. Shan turned to look into the face of the beefy Public Security guard, who had clearly awakened in a surly mood. His weapon hung forward from his shoulder, his fingers resting near the trigger.

"No damned access!" the knob snarled. "No one! No time!" he barked, then roughly pulled Shan toward the sunlight.

"Yo!" the tall Westerner shouted in farewell, with a mock salute. "Let's do lunch sometime!"

Shan let himself be led toward the center of the yard, craning his neck to watch the American as the man made an exaggerated shrug of disappointment toward the men at the coal pile, who laughed, then lowered his cap and resumed shoveling the coal.

As Shan turned back to the guard his face tightened in fear. He had not simply been stopped in his investigation of the men working at the boiler, he had been exposed. He was being escorted by a knob. Knobs did not take you where you wanted to go. They took you where Public Security wanted you.

But as they proceeded across the empty yard the guard's resolve seemed to dissipate. His steps became shorter, and he released Shan's arm. He looked at the shed where he had been posted, then glanced back at the administration building and turned uncertainly toward Shan. Suddenly his head snapped back toward the office building. A figure had appeared on the steps of the building, a woman in a black suit. Prosecutor Xu Li.

The guard looked from the woman back to Shan, then spoke nervously. "No one is to go near the boiler house crew, that's all," he said, then brushed the shoulders of Shan's threadbare jacket with a sheepish, deferential look, and jogged back toward his shed.

The woman stared at Shan in expectation. She was waiting for him. She did not need to summon him with a guard holding a submachine gun. Her severe stare was weapon enough.

With a quick glance he saw that no one was stirring at the repair shed. Would he at least be given a chance to say goodbye to Jakli, to get a message to Lokesh? No, he realized, he could do nothing that might implicate Jakli and the others. His mind raced. He would have to say he tricked Jakli and Fat Mao, that they knew nothing about him.

He put his hand on his chest, over the gau around his neck, then took a deep breath and with small steady steps went to surrender to Prosecutor Xu. He let his prisoner's instincts take over, as a way of fighting the cold fist of fear in his belly. Would they take him back to Tibet? Would they send him to the special interrogation place he had visited in the desert? Or would they decide he wasn't worth the trouble and dispose of him right there. At least, a detached voice called out from somewhere in his mind, you'd get a real grave.

As he approached her he studied the woman's spare, stern face. Surprisingly it didn't show the contempt of a jailer for a prisoner. It didn't show suspicion. It only showed impatience.

He was almost at the stairs when she spun about and stepped inside, leaving the door open for him. He followed her.

The interior was like a thousand other government offices Shan had seen. Most of the space was devoted to one large open chamber with two rows of metal desks, the majority of which were unoccupied. A young woman of Kazakh or Uighur blood, her hair bound into two small pigtails, looked up from a computer terminal, then quickly, nervously, averted her eyes. Someone called out a whispered warning, and Shan saw two other office workers scurry away from their desks, toward another woman who motioned them into a back room. As if they had detected volcanic signs in Xu and were expecting an eruption.

Xu Li waited for him at the door of a meeting room, pointing to a chair at a large metal table.

He sat. She stepped to a thermos and poured two mugs of tea, placed one on the table barely within Shan's reach, then sat opposite him.

"I know what you're doing here," she said brusquely.

It was over, before it had really started. Children were still dying. Gendun was lost. The waterkeeper lama was imprisoned. And Shan would never have his chance to help them, nor his chance to leave China. He locked his hands around the steaming mug. There were tricks prisoners played, to endure. Many of them had to do with simply getting through the next moment, not thinking about the suffering to come, only dealing with the present suffering. Had his hands instinctively begun playing the old game, he wondered, fixing on the searing heat from the mug, focusing on one sense in order to evade as long as possible the flood of pain to come? The monks in his gulag barracks had taught him that such concentration was not the best answer, that he shouldn't seek concentration but mindfulness, to steer his mind to a place interrogators didn't occupy. But he had no time to prepare, and if such concentration was the only crutch he could find, he would use it. His eyes lost their focus as he stared into the mug, absently considering how it would be years before he had real tea again if he were being returned to the gulag. Sometimes, when there was hot water, he would put a weed in it and call it tea.

"My name is Xu Li," the woman announced. "From the Ministry of Justice. I am the prosecutor for this county."

Jade Bitch. Shan almost said the words out loud. There was another trick he had learned for interrogations, not from the monks but from the khampa warriors who had shared his gulag barracks. Preempt the fear. Preempt the pain. If they were going to threaten something awful, imagine something even more terrible. If they were going to hurt you, then try to inflict greater pain on yourself. He raised the mug to his mouth and swallowed half the scalding liquid, raising a long stab of pain from his tongue to his belly. He lowered the mug and stared at the prosecutor without expression.

The action seemed to unsettle the woman. She raised her own mug, then put it down quickly as the heat singed her tongue. She frowned. "I know you are from Beijing. I don't know your real name." Her voice was smooth and supremely confident, a voice long accustomed to being in complete authority. "I don't want to know your name."

It seemed impossible. How could she have known his background already? Had he been so careless? Had everything since he arrived in Xinjiang been an elaborate trap?

"Nobody asked me if I approved of what you are doing.

No one is going to. It's all Beijing, I can smell Beijing all over it," she added, as if it explained much.

Shan looked around the room. There was a chalkboard on one wall, with a number scrawled near the top. Nine hundred forty-eight, no doubt the number of citizens undergoing reconditioning at Glory Camp. There was a faded poster with a collage of bright young Chinese faces, with the caption *Destroy the Four Olds*. It had been one of the more enduring campaigns started by the Red Guard many years earlier, part of the insanity that had swept his father away. Destroy old culture, old ideology, old customs, old habits. It had been a particularly intense spasm of pain inflicted on the Tibetans, Muslims, and other minorities. Old books, traditional clothes, and religious artifacts had been consigned to bonfires. Entire fires had consisted of nothing but braids of hair worn in the old fashion.

Fire. If he set a fire, he thought, looking at a trash basket overflowing with paper, maybe in the confusion Jakli and the Kazakhs would be permitted to evacuate without questioning.

"But," Xu Li said tersely, "I am still the prosecutor."

Shan brought his eyes back to the woman. Why was she being so indirect? "I've seen your camp," he said tentatively.

"My chop is on file here. Glory Camp is a resource utilized by many counties in Xinjiang and Tibet."

What game was she playing? Saving him for someone else? Baiting him before moving in for the kill? "I do not doubt you are a zealous guardian of the people, Comrade Prosecutor." He returned her steady gaze.

She extended her mug as though in salute to Shan, then sipped it as she contemplated him. "I have served the people of this county for many years. I am not ashamed of my service. I could have gone back to Beijing when my first tour was finished. I asked to stay. I have received many awards from the Party and the Ministry for the progress we have made here."

He raised his own mug in salute. How, exactly, do you measure progress? he wondered. In the number of citizens sent behind wire? The size of the prison cemetery?

"I believe in the order of law," Xu continued. "I know

you have a job. But I must tell you, Comrade, I am not afraid to do my job. I will enforce the law against anyone who breaks it." Xu stared at him malevolently, then abruptly rose and left the room, leaving the door open.

Shan stared after her, dazed. There were spirits in the Buddhist mythology that one might meet while traveling. They would speak in strange words, and they might bare their teeth at you, but if they moved on without eating you, meeting them was considered a blessing.

The workers in the outer office did not look up as he moved through the room. No guards came. No doctors with syringes poised. He paused for a moment, still in shock, until the faces began to turn toward him, then he quickly stepped to the door.

Outside, the limousine was gone. Jakli and her cousins were still asleep. He checked the compartment under the dashboard of the truck and confirmed there was a flashlight, then climbed into the rear of the truck and settled back onto the sacks of rice, gradually falling into a slumber troubled by visions of dead children.

When he awoke it was night. Dim lightbulbs affixed below the speakers of the public address system were the only illumination in the administrative compound. Jakli and the others were squatting by a small fire made of scraps of lumber. They had impaled several small apples on screwdrivers and were roasting them over the flames. Jakli pushed one of the apples onto an oily rag and extended it to Shan.

He accepted the apple and tossed it from hand to hand to cool it. "Did they tell you why the warehouse is closed?" he asked.

"On the orders of Public Security, nothing more. Sometimes they fumigate. Poison gas, maybe."

"I think there are people locked inside."

Jakli shrugged. "This is a prison."

He nodded his head toward the smokestack. "Where did those men go? They were carrying coal." There was no sign of activity at the boilerhouse.

"Gone," Fat Mao said. "We were asleep."

"Why would they need a Public Security guard?"

Jakli's head jerked up. "Knobs? There's knobs here?"

She stepped backward, so her face was in shadow. The others looked up, suddenly alert. Her actions needed no translation.

"I saw one." Shan glanced toward the shed, which appeared abandoned. "By the boiler." A wisp of smoke rose from the boiler chimney. The coals had been banked and left to burn slowly. The demand for electricity and heat would be lower at night. Jakli moved to one of the support posts and leaned against it, her eyes sweeping across the compound.

Shan stepped beside her. "And I saw the prosecutor," he added.

"She has much business here," Jakli said, not hiding her bitterness.

"I mean, she spoke to me." He explained the strange encounter with Xu.

Fat Mao pressed close and asked him to repeat Xu's words. "She thinks you're someone else," the Uighur gasped in confusion.

"More precisely," Shan said with a chill, "she thinks I am someone who would be with Kazakhs and Uighurs, a Han working with herdsmen." He looked into Fat Mao's face as he spoke. "A Han whom the prosecutor herself is wary of challenging."

"From Beijing," Jakli added in a low voice.

Fat Mao cursed. "There were six reservations made," he reminded her. "For arrests by knob headquarters. Headquarters uses spies sometimes. Undercover agents."

"What does it mean?" Jakli asked.

"I don't know," Shan said. "Except that the clans of the borderlands are in perhaps even greater danger than we thought. The knobs wouldn't send a spy just to help with the Poverty Scheme. Where else do the clans gather? Where a stranger might find his way among them?"

Jakli thought a moment. "Karachuk. Where Lau died."

Shan nodded. Lau had gone to the desert with her secrets, and someone had infiltrated her place of trust. "Tell me how to go."

"I will take you."

"No. You must return to town. Your probation."

"I made a vow to Lau."

"It is not what Lau would want, to have you back in prison."

"Sure, I'll go make hats," Jakli said in a taut voice. "Bright red hats with beads. Purple hats with sequins. While the children die and Red Stone is ripped apart." She broke away and stepped to the back of the shed, leaning against one of the posts as she gazed into the darkness.

He realized that she was not looking at the compound but at the distant patch of shadow where the white horse was penned. In the distance he could hear its hooves as it nervously pranced about its pen. As he approached her she began a low song in the tongue of her clan. Shan recognized a word, repeated many times. *Khoshakhan*. The way you tell the animals you love them.

"It's for the horse, isn't it?" Shan asked when she was done.

She started, as though she had not known he was there. "Yes. It says—" She thought a moment. "It says you are made of wind running. I will tie owl feathers in your mane, and we will ride like an arrow into the mountain clouds. My great uncle taught me. He was a *synshy*—a knower of horses, it means. He could speak with horses."

"You said owl feathers?"

"Owl feathers bring good luck. And wisdom."

Shan realized his hand was on his gau.

"On my naming day, a beautiful black and white colt was born, and my father promised it to me. We grew up together. Zharya was his name. We won races, many races. We went to high meadows and he listened as I played my dombra." There was a whisper behind them, and Shan turned to see that the others were listening too.

"Is he in the Red Stone camp still?" Shan asked.

She made the song again, only humming this time. "No," she said in a taut voice, just when Shan had decided she had not heard. "Once, when I knew an army truck was coming, Zharya and I dragged a heavy log across the road." She took a step away, into the darkness, but spoke again after a moment. "We rode up the mountain and watched from a cliff where the soldiers could never catch us. We were laughing, Zharya and I, standing side by side as the soldiers tried to move the log. Then Zharya groaned and fell down and there was a cracking sound from below. They had shot him with a rifle." She looked back into the darkness. "It took him all afternoon to die. He just lay there with his head in my lap, looking at me like it was all a bad joke."

A gust of wind moved through the silence, a dry, cool wind, smelling of coal dust.

"But you have a new horse now," Shan offered at last.

"That one? Just from the Red Stone herd. I don't have a horse life anymore," she said with great sadness, then climbed back onto the sacks for sleep.

Shan leaned against the pole, watching for another quarter hour, then followed the others onto the sacks. But Shan did not sleep. He watched.

The compound was empty but the lights were on at the guard towers, which switched on spotlights at irregular intervals to sweep along the fence. There was no chance of sneaking through the wire to find the waterkeeper, no chance of searching for Gendun in the special detention barracks. Shan looked back at the boiler. Electricity was still being used. Someone would have to go to the boiler to stoke the coal.

He watched the moon rise and listened to the national anthem played over the public address system to signal curfew. What was the curfew discipline in a lao jiao camp, Shan wondered. Surely it could not be as severe as that at his gulag prison, where questions were never asked. Gulag prisoners caught out after curfew were shot on sight.

He must have dozed, for when he looked up he saw the smoke from the boiler was much heavier. The boiler had been replenished. There was no sign of the workers. He waited another quarter hour, then quietly climbed past his sleeping companions and retrieved the flashlight from the cab. Its batteries were nearly exhausted, its light barely reaching three feet. Perfect for his needs.

Walking slowly, heart pounding, he crossed the compound and circled the little shed by the boiler house. There was a window at the rear. Locked. He put his face to the glass but could see nothing. From the front corner he surveyed the compound. A single vehicle with brilliant headlights moved along the outer wire, a truck on patrol.

Shan waited for the truck to pass along the front of the compound and turn down the far side, then tested the front door. It was open. There were two small rooms. Inside the first was a collection of shovels and rakes and brooms, with a long bundle wrapped in burlap on the floor. Shan had seen such bundles before, in carpet markets. The looms of Xinjiang, especially of this far southwestern corner of the region, had been providing carpets to China and the rest of the world since the days of the Silk Road.

He moved into the rear chamber, which was larger than the first. In rows stacked five and six high were cardboard boxes. Most of them were glued shut, fresh from the factory, but the dim light of his hand lantern revealed their packing labels, in English and Japanese. Radios were inside, and tape recorders, and video cameras. And more than thirty small boxes containing a machine called a disc player. Two airtight metal ammunition cases held bottles of pharmaceuticals, in their original factory packages. Some he recognized as antibiotics, others bore English trade names that meant nothing to him. He pulled a small pad of paper from his pocket and listed the contents of the inventory, then quickly scrawled at the top of the pad, *Glory Camp, Black Market Goods*.

Preoccupied with speculation over why the knobs had been guarding the goods—were they merely protecting evidence, or were they protecting their investment?—Shan stepped back into the entry chamber and knelt at the carpet, which no doubt was part of the same hoard of goods. The flashlight fell and rolled onto the floor as he leaned over. Not bothering to pick it up, he placed his fingers inside the bundle to feel the density of the weave, for an indication of its value. He recoiled in horror.

A feeble cry escaped his lips as he threw himself backward. His chest heaving, he crawled to the doorway. Cracking open the door, he lay there, gulping in the cool night air to calm himself. It was several minutes before he had steeled himself enough to return to the bundle.

It was not a carpet. He found the flashlight, then folded back the sacking and studied his grisly discovery. A young man stared back at him, surprised and lifeless. His skin was covered with soot, his hair jet-black. The body had not been lifeless long enough to be cold. He saw moisture on his own hand and leaned closer. The man's left ear had been severed. It was an old form of torture that had been popular during the Cultural Revolution. When a prisoner refused to divulge information, refused to implicate others with information he had heard, the ear was severed. If you will not share with us what you have heard, then what value are your ears, Red Guard interrogators would shout. The face wore the remains of a grin. The great sadness that had descended on Shan flashed into horror again as he brought the failing light closer to the man's open eyes. They were blue.

He rubbed a corner of the sacking on the scalp and it came away with a greasy black smudge. He smelled it. Shoe polish. He wiped more of the man's scalp, exposing hair the color of broom straw. He dragged a fingernail over the deep layer of soot that covered the man's face, leaving a white track. It was the stranger from the power plant, the American who had taunted him at the boiler.

Lowering himself into the lotus position, he extinguished the light, leaving the room lit only by the rays of the half moon that floated through the open door. It wasn't death that weighed so heavily on him, but that death was so familiar. Since he had left his former incarnation in Beijing, death had seemed to be everywhere. Perhaps it was what one of his teachers had said, that death was the final measurement in the dimensions of souls. Maybe that was what unsettled him so, that death seemed to amplify how incomplete most humans were, and that the closer to death he got, the more incomplete he felt.

Shan did not know how long he sat in the moonlight with the dead man. When he surfaced to consciousness he realized he was reciting a Buddhist prayer for the passage of souls. He sighed and began to unwrap the body of the Westerner, switching on his light again. On the left hand was a line of clean white skin where a ring had been removed. The right hand still bore a ring. Shan eased it off, a simple circle of steel with a crude hatchmark design scratched in its surface, which no doubt remained only because of its negligible value. The pockets of the man's shirt were empty. He opened the shirt. A scar creased the upper right shoulder. A large oval birthmark lay above the right hip.

The man's denim pants bore an American label. Levi's. Their pockets appeared empty. His expensive American hiking boots had been removed. He pushed his fingers to the bottom of the pockets, and from the right rear pocket extracted a rolled up piece of paper pressed against the bottom, where it had been overlooked by whomever emptied the pockets. A series of abbreviations were written on it in English, arranged in five rows. *FBP* it said, then *SBRF, SSCF, TBLF,* and on the final line only *C.*

He knelt at the American's head and stared intensely into the man's eyes, as if he could will them to life again. He knew nothing about the man, except that he had been young, and strong, and jovial. And far from anywhere that might have been called a home.

The knobs did this. The knobs had killed an American, he realized suddenly. What was it the American had done that made him so dangerous? Even for the knobs, killing a foreigner was profoundly dangerous. And what was the American doing that was important enough to risk his life in such a faraway, forgotten place? Sometimes the boot squads brought special prisoners here from far away, Jakli had said, secret prisoners.

Shan slowly rewrapped the shroud, then stood, took two steps, and clutched his chest as the helplessness surged through him once more. He darted outside, moving to the rear of the small building, where he leaned against the wall in his weakness, gulping the fresh night air, trying to purge himself of the smell of death. As he sank to his knees he heard the haunting voice again, as clearly as if the forlorn dropka had been standing behind him. *You must hurry. Death keeps coming.*

CHAPTER 6

The turtle truck lurched across the desert like a small boat on a rough sea, rocking and pitching as it broke across the waves of sand. Jakli worked hard at the wheel, frequently adjusting the angle against the dunes, dodging patches of light-colored sand, always warping back in a northeasterly direction, toward the heart of the desert. She had stopped as she had left the road, looking at Shan with a grave expression. "The Taklamakan," she said, gesturing toward the endless expanse of sand. "It's an old word, from before the time of writing. Because so many people have died out here. It means once you go in, you never come out."

But Shan already felt mired in a place with no escape. The American was not his responsibility, he kept telling himself as he gazed at the desolate landscape, not his mystery to solve. He had Lau and Gendun and the dead boys and now the waterkeeper, and he had no room on his back for the dead American. It was only by some grim chance that he had stumbled upon the body. The American had nothing to do with Lau and Khitai. Perhaps his death was part of the strange game between the knobs and the prosecutor or even connected to Ko Yonghong, who had boasted about his American consultants. More likely, it was the work of the boot squads, who brought subversives from all over China to a place like Glory Camp. But still the death of the American hovered near like a dark shadow. He had begun to accept what the natives of the region kept telling him, that it was a shadow land, a forgotten place, a

Jakli began to walk toward an opening between
wall and the largest, most intact of the structures, a
rectangular building of stone blocks with high narrow
dow openings almost as high as the wall. A barracks
haps, Shan thought. Short stumps as thick as his arm, bak
rock-hard from the centuries of dry heat, poked out of th
sand at regular intervals beside lower walls that might have
been the ruins of personal dwellings. There once had been
free peaches for the thirsty traveler.

As they passed the large stone structure Shan saw the
remains of wood beams protruding in a row from the outer
wall, supports for roofs long gone. At one of the ruins the
walls remained high enough to hold the beams in their orig-
inal position, giving an idea of how the street would have
looked eight or nine centuries before. Shan cautiously
stepped into the doorway. He started and leapt back at the
sight of two large eyes staring at him. Jakli laughed, and
he peered back inside to study the life-sized mural painted
on the interior wall. Although cracked and disjointed where
plaster had fallen away, he could plainly see the figure of
a leopard feeding on a small brown animal. The colors had
bleached away to mere tinted shadows, but the savage emo-
ion of the cat's eyes seemed as vivid as the day when they
ad been painted centuries earlier.

As he backed away a sound came from nearby, the bray-
g of an animal or perhaps just the wind playing with the
ins. After another hundred paces their path opened into a
urtyard with several misshapen stone columns arranged
a circle. Jakli stopped and pointed at the columns. As he
proached them he saw features in the wasted stone, a
nd here, a graceful leg there. It had been a garden of
tuary.

They climbed half a dozen stone steps from the ruined
den to the top of a small knoll, the highest point within
walls. The reclining Buddha dominated the scene be-
d them. The figure appeared so relaxed, so natural a part
he rolling landscape that it seemed at any moment the
e might stand and start walking toward the Kunlun. At
far end of the ruins, to the north, at least three hundre
s away, more ruined statuary stood in a line in the san
Sentinels," Jakli explained as she pointed to the

land between worlds, where people lived like ghosts in
shadows and life was very cheap.

"You seem to see things I do not," Shan observed, un-
certain whether it was anger or just a hard-edged alertness
that had settled into Jakli's eyes. Even after she had agreed
to take Shan to the place where Lau died, Fat Mao had
argued against it, complaining that she had to return to the
hat factory, that the place called Karachuk would be too
dangerous for Shan. Fat Mao had returned them to the ga-
rage by then, where Akzu had been waiting, sharing a skin
of kumiss with the surly mechanic. Akzu had pointed to-
ward the high ranges and raised his voice. Finally, when
Jakli had promised to return to the factory after delivering
Shan to Karachuk, he had embraced his niece and knelt to
pray facing west, toward the Muslim holy city.

"By rights, we should not be in the desert in a truck,"
she said after a moment. "Only with camels is it safe, and
even then the inexperienced often die. But we have only a
short distance, and this close to the mountains we can drive
most of the way on the old riverbed," she said as she guided
the vehicle down a short bank of sand onto a wide, level
channel of packed sand. "The key is to avoid the soft
spots."

"If we don't?"

"The desert can swallow a truck as easily as a man or a
camel." As if on cue a pile of white bleached bones ap-
peared on the bank of the dead river. It contained a long
skull and heavy ribs and was pointed in the direction of the
snowcapped mountains. "It's always been this way, since
the early Silk Road. Some people got wealthy from the
passage. Some people just died."

After almost an hour Shan discerned a line of shadows
on the horizon. Irregular and large, they seemed like mis-
shaped buildings one moment, eroded rock formations the
next. For a moment, from a distance, Shan believed that
they were creatures bent under heavy loads.

At a curve in the riverbed Jakli accelerated and shot
straight across the bank, directly toward the formations,
then, half a mile away, turned ninety degrees to drive par-
allel to them toward the south. "The Silk Road," she said
abruptly. "Do you know much of it?"

"The school texts," Shan said with a shrug.

His words brought a grimace to her face. "They will tell you it was a region of terrible class struggle, of great oppression, of temples for the worship of wealth built on the backs of slaves," she said, slowing the vehicle to steal a glance at the mysterious shapes. "Our history texts," she said, slowly shaking her head, "they are like studying beautiful paintings from the back of the canvas." She gestured toward the shapes. "The glorious Karachuk. Ignored by our teachers because it was not Chinese. But it is because of places like this that I have learned not to curse the Taklamakan. The very elements that make the desert so treacherous have preserved its treasures."

Jakli's expression grew lighter as she eased the truck toward a low, flat ridge. Following her gaze Shan saw an ancient wall. "Karachuk was an oasis on the southern arm of the Silk Road," she explained, "when the ice fields in the mountains still fed the river enough to keep it flowing all year. A major city once, praised for its fertility and hospitality in the ancient texts. Uighurs lived here, and Kazakhs and Tibetans. Life was so pleasant that many travelers lingered for months or years, even for the rest of their lives. The old writings spoke of it, but it was lost centuries ago in a grandfather sandstorm, a *karaburan*. Then ten years ago another storm came and the top of it was swept clean."

Shan could clearly see now that the shapes were the remains of man-made structures. A pressed earth wall the color of the sand rose in spots to a flat top and elsewhere had crumbled, revealing in its gaps small sand hummocks whose orderly placement suggested buildings. As Jakli crested the dune that extended south of the wall like a giant drift of snow, a huge form of distinctly human features greeted them. It was a statue of a reclining Buddha, twenty feet high at the shoulder, leaning on an elbow to face the southern mountains, toward Tibet. Most of its head was gone. Only the mouth, curved in a serene smile, remained above the neck.

"I had forgotten that the Buddhists were here," Shan said slowly. Buddhists. Perhaps he had begun to find a trail after all, a trail of hidden Buddhists. The Muslim boy who wore a rosary. The secret Tibetan classroom in Lau's cave. The waterkeeper in the rice camp. A headless Buddha in the desert.

"It was all Buddhist, for hundreds of miles north and east. Then Muslims came from the west and Chinese came from the east," Jakli explained. "I have read the journals of a traveler from the east," she continued after a moment. "Xuan Zang, his name was. He passed through the kingdom of Karachuk on a pilgrimage to India, as an envoy from your emperor. Twelve hundred years ago. The kingdom census showed five thousand souls living here, in a luxu[ry] and peacefulness unknown in what was then China. Gra[pes] hung from arbors above every doorway. Households [had] peach and pomegranate trees near the street, and the k[ing] ordered that a passerby had the right to pluck a ripe f[ruit] for refreshment, but only one." Jakli looked in his direc[tion] with a wry smile. "Now that was enlightened communi[sm.]"

She pointed toward the south, where the tops of the [mountain] ranges could be seen on the horizon. "But they owed e[very]thing to the ice fields in the mountains, which fed the [rivers] and irrigation channels that flowed here. Then the ice [fields] began to shrink. People began to move closer to the m[oun]tains as the water disappeared. By the time the sand s[torms] came it was already mostly deserted. I remember wh[en the] storm uncovered the city. People said it was the w[ork of] God, to remind us of who we are. Others said it v[as the] work of the desert spirits, who were inviting us bac[k."]

There was one more dune, smaller, that ran dia[gonally] along the southern end of the ruins, in front of a ga[p in the] old walls near the Buddha. Jakli accelerated over [the] mound. The front wheels of their vehicle left the s[and and] with a heavy lurch they landed in the ghost city [of Kara]chuk.

The ruins cast a spell over Shan the instant h[e climbed] out of the truck. They were in a small courtyard s[urrounded] by vague shapes of buildings constructed of [mud] bricks, their color and texture so much like th[at] the entire landscape was a patchwork of brown[s.] The twisted, desiccated remains of trees climbe[d out of the] sand here and there. The top of an arch protru[ded from the] desert thirty feet away.

"covering the northern approach. Stationed at the top of the city wall." She turned and gestured toward a shape closer to them, on the long, low dune that covered the western wall. The helmeted head of a warrior emerged from the sand. Beside it the top half of a hand protruded, held up as if in warning.

The sight brought an unexpected grin to Shan's face. He felt an odd peace in the presence of such ancient beauty and mystery. He had seen statues like these at other ruins in China and Tibet. But always before they had been pockmarked with bullets or scorched from explosives. The army had been fond of using such statues for target practice. Most ancient fortress walls had been brought down because they symbolized imperialism or could be used by rebels. The huge national libraries, some filled with manuscripts dating back over two thousand years, had been destroyed by the revolutionaries. Temples, not only in Tibet, had suffered the same fate. As a student Shan had been bused to one of the old imperial tombs to watch the Red Guard conduct a criminal trial for an ancient Ming emperor, disinterred from his tomb. The emperor had been convicted of a lengthy list of crimes against the people, and his body burned with the artifacts from the tomb.

But Karachuk had evaded the hand of Beijing by sleeping under the sands. Shan could have contemplated the scene for hours. He saw the same grin on Jakli's face and knew she felt it too. He realized that the things he enjoyed the most in life seemed to be those which had been forgotten, overlooked by modern Chinese society. The hidden monks of Tibet. The old Taoist texts taught by his father. The hand of an ancient warrior rising out of the sand.

They continued down the path, away from the wall, descending gradually toward a large bowl below a long, high outcropping of rock that defined the eastern boundary of the town. Shan paused to study the collection of buildings below the center of the outcropping, a dozen small structures which were in far better repair than the others. They were constructed of the same pressed earth and mud brick walls as the other structures, but their walls, though cracked, were still intact, and they had roofs, capped by grey, sun-baked tiles that had been covered with sand and

pieces of rotten wood. Beyond the huts was a larger building consisting of a square end joined to a round domed
structure, which also appeared to have survived the centuries without serious decay. Or perhaps, Shan considered, as
he studied the structure, it and the smaller buildings had
been artfully reconstructed to appear as ruins to the casual
or distant observer. Behind the domed building, in a corral
consisting of three stone walls abutting the face of the outcropping, stood several long-haired horses of the short,
sturdy breed that had once conveyed the soldiers of the
khans across two continents. In front of the large structure
Shan noticed a small ring of stone above which hung a
tripod of weathered beams. A well.

Shan became aware of Jakli standing apart, gazing at
him uncertainly. "I don't know what they will do. It's a
dangerous place, like Akzu said."

"But Lau died while visiting here?"

Jakli nodded.

"Meaning she had friends here. Like Wangtu said, people she trusted."

Jakli nodded again.

"If Lau had friends here, then I am not afraid," he said,
hoping his voice did not betray his uncertainty.

She seemed about to answer when her head snapped up.

A man was walking away from the large building in an
erratic, weaving motion toward the corral, as if drunk. They
watched from the shadows as he quickly saddled one of
the horses and trotted down a path that led through the
north end of the ruins.

Jakli was still watching the man as Shan moved down
the trail, past the huts to the plank door of the large building. The horses silently watched him. A faint scent of
smoke hung in the air. He paused at the door, glancing at
Jakli, who lingered on the hill, surveying the little village
nervously, as if she had decided after all that it had indeed
been a mistake to bring him here.

Suddenly the door exploded outward, propelled by the
weight of a man who collided with Shan. The two men
landed in a heap in the sand and the stranger seized Shan's
throat in both hands and began to squeeze. Shan gasped
feebly and tried to buck the man off. His assailant re-

sponded by releasing his throat and pounding Shan's chest with his small, hard fists as Shan twisted and turned, trying to escape.

"Thief!" the man shouted at Shan in a shrill voice.

Two more hands appeared, grabbing the man's shoulders as Shan slid away. Jakli held the man for only a moment, then he squirmed from her grip and crawled toward Shan, his eyes wild and murderous.

"Hoof!" Jakli screamed. "You have to stop!" She kicked the man's back, without effect, then kicked again, harder, knocking him prostrate on the sand.

The action brought the man to his senses. He pushed himself up on his hands, looked around with a blank expression, then slowly rolled over and sat up, gazing at Shan and Jakli in confusion.

"Ah, it's you," the man called Hoof said dully to Jakli, and his gaze drifted toward the door. "I didn't see you," he muttered. His confusion seeemed to fade, replaced by something that Shan thought might be disappointment.

Shan felt moisture on his hand where he had tried to push the man away. "You're bleeding," he gasped, suddenly afraid he might have injured the man.

The expression on the man's face as he looked at his wounded right shoulder was not alarm, but disgust. "Robbed, and stuck in the bargain," he groused in a high voice. "Nothing but bad joss here." He had a huge nose and pale skin, with spots on his cheeks that might have been freckles. His small features came to life as he sat and studied Shan. "No one wants you here," he said with an odd hint of hope in his voice.

"You should clean that cut," Shan said, exploring his pockets for something to help the man.

"You'll have to go before—" The man's warning was cut off by the appearance of a figure in the doorway, a tall man wearing an embroidered skullcap and a brilliant green shirt from which the sleeves had been torn. He held a glass, which he was wiping with a scrap of cloth.

"Damn you, Osman!" Hoof squealed. "Some dog's whore stole my pouch." As if having an afterthought he raised a hand, which was red with his blood. "And stabbed me. A man isn't safe!"

The man he had called Osman grunted, and his eyes lit as he saw Jakli. He raised his head with a broad smile, then noticed Shan. The smile disappeared. He threw the rag at Hoof and stepped back into the shadows.

"Sons of pigs!" Hoof cursed and threw the rag back at the door.

Shan tore a strip from his undershirt and tied it around the man's wound. As he did so the man's expression softened. "You'll need to leave. I could help you," the man said in a new, confiding tone. "I am called Hoof. I'm a good Tadjik. I know the desert. I have Chinese friends. I'll take you to town. You'll be safe in a town."

"He's safe where he is," Jakli said, stepping forward so that she towered over Hoof, who was still sprawled in the sand.

"Sure he is, sure he is, if he's with you." Hoof scuttled backward on all fours, crablike, out of Jakli's shadow, then leapt up and darted back into the building.

Shan looked after him. "His name is Hoof?" he asked Jakli.

She sighed, watching the doorway with worry in her eyes. "It's a way of some of the old herding clans. A baby is named after the first thing the mother sees on the morning after the birth." She motioned him toward her, as if to lead him away from the building.

But Shan followed Hoof inside.

At first it seemed he was entering a cavern. He stepped into an unlit corridor five paces long, with deeper shadows that hinted of alcoves on either side. In the dim light he studied the sand floor of the corridor as he moved down it, trying to understand what had just happened to the Tadjik. A stone wall faced him at the end of the hallway. A ghost wall. The hands that had constructed the structure had been guided by a geomancer, one of the shamans who were more important than any architect or carpenter in building even the simplest stable in the traditional kingdoms of northern Asia. Practicing his art of feng shui, a geomancer had long ago directed the placement of a wall facing the door, because evil spirits only flew in straight lines. The main entrance itself, Shan realized, opened to the south because those same spirits lived in the north.

The scent of lamp oil and and cinnamon hung in the air. He heard laughter and a loud voice telling a ribald joke in Mandarin.

At the wall he turned to the left, into a short corridor that ended in a small arched doorway. Shan stood in the arch and stared through a miasma of tobacco smoke into what appeared to be the public room of an inn. The chamber was illuminated by a dozen large candles and four kerosene lanterns, two of which were suspended from the wooden beams over a large table by loops of what looked like telephone cable. The table, which stood ten feet away, had been raised by piles of flat stones under its legs, so that it stood at the waist of the man who had briefly appeared in the doorway, the tall man called Osman. He was leaning on the makeshift bar beside a basket of dried figs, a stack of flat nan bread and a collection of bottles containing liquids, most in various shades of brown. Drinking glasses, many of them cracked and dirty, were stacked precariously at the edge of the table. Behind Osman a large shaggy grey dog lay on the floor, asleep.

A dozen men were scattered around the room, seated at several large wooden crates that functioned as makeshift tables. The wounded Hoof shared a bottle with another man at the table furthest from the door, holding his arm, scowling at Osman as he muttered something that made his companion laugh. A small, exquisitely carved table stood in the center of the room, unoccupied. On it stood an ornate chess set and beside it was a large, filthy, overstuffed chair that had the appearance of a pincushion from all the straw that had been jammed into the holes in its upholstery.

The clamor of voices abruptly ceased as he stepped into the room.

Shan was the only Han.

With the eyes of half the men fixed on him, Shan moved uncertainly to an upended box beside the bar. As he sat and reached for one of the figs, his observers turned away. The volume of conversation rose again. Two men rose to refill their glasses, giving the stuffed chair a wide berth. Shan saw that the sleeve of the bright red shirt worn by one of the men appeared empty, and he looked closer. The man was missing an arm below the elbow.

Through the smoke Shan studied a mural painted on the wall behind Osman. It contained figures with long faces and beards, the faces of Europeans or perhaps Persians. They were riding donkeys with heavy packs toward a man who awaited them under a grape arbor. One of the figures had its eyes scratched out, a familiar sight in the lands of the Muslims, whose holy law forbade images of humans. A nail had been driven into the plaster above the mural to support a small framed black and white photograph of a horse. In a niche beside a curtain that hung at the opposite end of the bar was a stone Buddha, badly cracked, into whose pursed lips a cigarette butt had been jammed. A hand-lettered sign hung on the wall above it, proclaiming *This Bar is Nei Lou.* On the wall past the curtain was suspended a white flag with a crescent moon and a single star.

"Do you have tea?" Shan asked.

"What you see is what you can have." The man called Osman held up a leather drinking bladder. "Kumiss," he said, then pointed with it toward the bottles. "Bai jin. Mao-tai. Beer. Vodka." He had a gravelly, impatient voice. "Two yuan."

"Two yuan?" Shan asked in disbelief. Two yuan would buy a meal for an entire family in many parts of China.

"Our special rate for eastern visitors."

"I'll just have water."

"Three yuan."

Shan felt someone at his shoulder. "Two teas, Osman," Jakli said.

The bartender frowned. "He's with you?"

"With me. A friend of Auntie Lau."

"He's here on your word?"

Jakli said nothing. She stared at him for a moment, then stepped to the wall and pulled the cigarette butt from the Buddha's mouth, throwing it to the floor. "Two teas."

Osman considered her silently, then leaned down and pulled a large black thermos from the floor. He filled two of his glasses with steaming black tea.

"Nikki?" Shan heard her ask in a quick, anxious tone as he surveyed the room. "I don't see his men."

The question seemed to put Osman at ease. "Not yet. Tomorrow, maybe. One last caravan. Soon, be sure of it."

The tall Kazakh studied Jakli's face, which had suddenly clouded with worry. "He's fine, girl. You have my word. No one catches Nikki," he added with a smile that exposed a silver tooth. "No one but you." He poured another tea, then raised it to his own lips in a toast. "To dark nights and sleeping sentries," he said with a small grin.

Shan looked back at the one-armed man as he returned to his seat with his glass refilled. He had heard in prison about men escaping the gulag and chopping off their own arms above the tattoo to destroy the proof of their genealogy.

Jakli pushed her stool closer to Shan, as though to shield him, and they quietly drank their tea while Osman wiped glasses at the opposite end of the bar. As Shan surveyed the occupants she quietly explained the rules of the community. No one removed artifacts from the sand, unless they were to be kept and used at Karachuk. No one built anything that might appear like modern construction to aerial surveillance. No one built anything, period, without Osman's approval. No one burned wood from the ruins, for fear of telltale smoke, and for the need to preserve what was there. He asked about the flag. From the Republic of East Turkistan, Jakli explained, in which Osman's grandfather had served as a vice-governor in Yoktian.

"This is Osman's town, then?" Shan asked Jakli in a low voice, keeping his eyes on the man behind the bar.

"My ancestors lived here," Osman interjected loudly and stepped closer. "It's my right." His eyes locked with Shan's, as if he was waiting to be challenged, then after a long moment he turned to Jakli. "Where's Akzu?" he asked.

"With the Red Stone. The Poverty Eradication Scheme. Less than two weeks now."

Osman grimaced. "The bastards. I told him. Bring the clan here." He clasped his hand tightly around a bottle and for a moment he stared at it. "This is the way it ends," he said grimly, "with corporations and Chinese giving speeches." He looked back up at Jakli. "I told him, better yet, bring me Director Ko. We'll make him right at home." The men at the nearest table laughed and Osman acknowledged them with a thin smile, then turned back to Shan. "You have business with Nikki?" he asked in a voice that was filled with suspicion. "Something special to buy?"

"I came because of Auntie Lau," Shan said. "She was—" But he saw that Osman was not listening. The bartender had sensed something, a movement, a shadow nearby. He was slowly turning toward the curtains that hung at the far side of the bar, his hand moving under the table, as though reaching for something. The grey dog was on its feet suddenly, growling.

The room grew silent again as a whispered warning shot through the crowd and the occupants of the tables looked up anxiously at the rear curtain. A finger, a very large finger, appeared near the top of the curtain and slowly began to push it aside.

Osman instantly relaxed. He brought his hand back from under the table. Several of the men in the room gave a small cheer. A bald man wearing a fleece vest rose and made an exaggerated bow toward the curtain. Others raised their glasses over their heads. The dog shot forward, wagging its tail.

"Marco!" Jakli exclaimed with sudden joy and ran to the stranger's outstretched arms.

Shan would have been at a loss to describe the man who entered the room. Many might have simply used the words big and Western. But to call the bearded man big would have been like simply describing a bear as big. And certainly he had the face, the features, the build of a Westerner, but there was something in the man's countenance that was not of the West. His eyes were blue, but they roamed across the room with the same hard, wary intelligence Shan had seen in Akzu and some of the other men of the clans. His skin bore the same leathery creases Shan had seen on the clansmen. There was one obvious difference, however. The stranger's face carried lines around his eyes that said he was a man who often smiled.

"Comrades!" the man thundered in a boisterous, mocking tone as he released Jakli from his hug and pulled her with him toward the bar. "Your commissar has arrived! I am going to instruct you in good socialist thought! I am going to clamp your loins so you don't have children! I am going to ration your belches, your bottles, and breaths! I am going to register your lice and tax your horses' piss!

And you'll crave every minute of it because it is all for the beloved People's Republic." He spoke in perfect Mandarin, and pronounced the last words like shots from a cannon. His audience laughed raucously.

A huge grin settled onto the face of the man Jakli had called Marco. He reached into the deep pockets of the massive overcoat he wore and produced two bottles of vodka with Cyrillic labels.

"But first we drink!" The bottles were corked. He produced an expensive Swiss army knife and opened its corkscrew.

Osman tossed him a glass. "What do we celebrate now, you old bear?"

"Sure we celebrate! Because I'm alive and you're alive! Because Jakli is so beautiful and Nikki is so bold. Because we've all beat the odds and seen another harvest season. Because I'm bringing enough vodka to the horse festival to stay drunk for a week!"

Every man, even the sulking Hoof and his companion, rose and converged on the bar as Marco filled their glasses. "To smugglers!" he toasted when all the glasses had an inch of vodka in them, *"Wan sui!"* His shout shook the lanterns. "Ten thousand years! Wan sui for all smugglers, the most honorable of all professions." He considered his glass a moment. "We don't pretend to obey rules we don't believe in," he declared with exaggerated solemnity. "And we always give people what they want." The men at the bar slapped the big man on the back and snorted with laughter as he taunted them with a pair of worn ivory dice.

At last his eyes came to rest on Shan. "Who's this ragged little thing, Jakli dear?" he asked, with a smile that had lost its light.

"He's come to help. About the killings."

Marco's nostrils flared. "God's breath, child!" he growled in a low voice. "Surely you didn't—"

"He's not from the government," Jakli interjected quickly. "He's from Tibet."

Marco frowned, then studied Shan with a cold gaze. "A hard place, Tibet," he said after a moment.

Shan nodded. "Especially for Tibetans."

Marco gave a bitter grin and a nod of acknowledgement. "Where in Tibet?"

"Mostly, the 404th People's Construction Brigade. At Lhadrung."

"Lao gai." Marco spat the words like a curse. He swallowed what remained in his glass, then stepped to Shan's side, gripped his forearm in his huge hand, pushed up his sleeve, and examined his tattoo.

He pressed it and stretched it, then nodded his approval, as though a connoisseur of such marks. "Before that?"

"Beijing."

Shan's announcement silenced every man within earshot.

The brawny man poured himself another shot of vodka but left it on the bar as he examined Shan more closely. "A silk robe!" he exclaimed with false warmth, referring to the mandarins who had run the empire during the dynasties. Amusement was in his voice but not in his eyes. He lifted his eyebrows in mock bewilderment. "Or perhaps a palace eunuch?" The men yelped with laughter.

"I am called Shan Tao Yun," Shan said quietly.

Marco raised his glass. "Welcome to the Karachuk Nationalities Palace, Comrade Shan," he said, referring to the gaping halls built in provincial capitals for the glory of the country's multiple cultures. Low snickers rose from the tables.

"You—you are a visitor as well, I see," Shan said awkwardly, still confused by the man's Western appearance.

Several of the men laughed again.

"By the spirit of the Great Helmsman, you offend me!" Marco boomed. "I am the best damned socialist in the land! If anyone ever gave me a passport, which they won't, it would be red. With a big yellow star and four small ones," he said, referring to the emblem of the Chinese state. "I am as stalwart a citizen as can be found in Xinjiang."

"That's not saying much," Shan offered. It was a dangerous game they were playing, especially because he did not understand the connection between Marco and Jakli, and how much her protection accounted for.

Marco's grin returned. "A silk robe with a sense of humor." He leaned toward the man behind the bar. "Must be true what they say, Osman," he said in a sober tone, his eyes twinkling. "The worker's paradise just keeps getting better and better." He shifted on his seat, causing his heavy wool tunic to fall open. Two objects became plainly visible to Shan. One was a heavy silver chain, attached to a large pocket watch. The other was the biggest pistol Shan had ever seen, a revolver that looked like it had been made in the nineteenth century.

"I didn't hear the rest of your name," Shan said to Marco.

The big man looked hard at Shan. He was clearly not accustomed to being pushed. "I am called many things. But I was baptized, Comrade," he said in a taunting tone. He seemed to enjoy the look of confusion that flashed across Shan's countenance.

"Yes, baptized. By an old priest who once gave communion to the Czar. My mother chose the name, for the many strange lands she expected me to see. Marco Polo Alexei Myagov. A member of one of our country's honored minorities. The most loyal white Chinese in the land."

An Eluosi. Shan had almost forgotten they existed. Most of the Russians who had fled the Bolsheviks eastward across the Pamir or Tian ranges eight decades earlier had moved on to Shanghai, then eventually emigrated to Europe or America. Some twenty or thirty thousand, however, had stayed in Turkistan, even when another generation of communists had annexed it as Xinjiang. He had heard once that visiting certain villages in the far north of Xinjiang was like paying a visit to Czarist Russia. A few thousand of the Eluosi were still scattered among the population of Xinjiang and had even been granted special privileges for hunting and fishing on the lands originally purchased by their forebears from local warlords. Otherwise, they were a people lost to the world.

"It's many a year, I wager, since anyone has visited Karachuk from Chambaluc," Marco observed, using a name for Beijing Shan had not heard since he was a boy, the name given to the city during the Yuan dynasty, when the khans, linked by blood to the Turkic peoples of Xinjiang, controlled all of China. It was, Shan realized, the name many of the original inhabitants of Karachuk would have used. Marco's voice was warmer but his eyes remained suspicious. "What did you do there, before you earned your tattoo?"

"I was with the Ministry of Economy," Shan said self-consciously. "An inspector."

"But you inspected the wrong people."

"Apparently."

Marco's laugh was too large for the room. It rattled the stacked glasses. He poured himself another vodka and gestured toward Shan's still untouched glass.

"Well, Comrade Inspector, here we're all just faceless members of the glorious proletariat. *Gan bei*," he toasted, and drained his glass.

Shan stared at his glass, then lifted it under his nose. It was the closest he would knowingly get to tasting the hard liquor. It was not because it would violate the vows of the monks, which he had not taken, but because somehow it felt as though it would violate his teachers who still sat behind prison wire in Lhadrung.

Marco surveyed the room as he drank. Suddenly his glass stopped halfway to his mouth and he spat a curse, then sprang to the chess table in two long strides. He let out a second sound that was not a word, but a roar. "She's gone!" he barked.

Osman trotted to the table. "Impossible. Your empress was there last night. I was sitting here, thinking about my next move."

Marco's head swayed like that of an angry bull as he surveyed the room. "Osman and I have played this game for six months," the Eluosi declared loudly, to no one in particular. "In the winter, I sometimes bring food and fuel and stay for a week, at this table."

Shan stepped to his side. The game pieces were of ancient bronze. One army was red, one green, identified by small rubies and emeralds inlaid on the head of each figure. The stones were heavily scratched. Shan did not have to be told that the figures had been dug out of the desert sand.

"My empress!" Marco bellowed again. Shan saw that the ruby-capped counterpart to the green queen on Osman's side of the board was missing.

Osman leaned toward Marco's ear and spoke quietly, nodding toward Hoof.

"Mother of Christ!" Marco exploded as Shan retreated toward Jakli. "Two thefts! You swine!" he shouted at the general population of the room. "Lau's body barely cold, and now this! I won't have it. I should kick every man jack one of you to whatever hell you believe in. We have honor here. Shepherds. Caravan men. Smugglers. We treat you like brothers and sons. Where in hell do you think you are? Urumqi? Yoktian?"

"That Xibo from Kashgar was here," Osman offered anxiously. "Just released from detention. Probably it was him. Nobody followed Hoof out. But the Xibo left five minutes before Hoof. Probably took the queen, then jumped Hoof for his pouch. Miles away by now."

"The thief is still here," Shan said, very quietly.

Marco did not seem to hear him. He moved to the bar and took a deep drink directly from his bottle, then turned to Shan as he wiped drops of vodka from his beard with his sleeve. "Again."

"I believe the man who did this is still here," Shan said in the same low, self-conscious voice.

Marco stared at him in brooding silence. "An inspector, you said. So just like that, the inspector knows who the criminal is." He looked out over the men in the room. "This isn't Beijing, you know. People are not simply guilty by decree here."

"It's just a matter of understanding the facts," Shan offered. "When the facts are properly understood, justice may find a way."

"Justice?" Marco asked incredulously, his thick brows rising. "Did you say justice?"

Shan looked at Jakli, hoping for help. But she was staring nervously at Marco.

"Here is a strange creature for you, Osman," Marco said, his voice as sharp as a razor. "A silk robe who worries about justice." He put his hand around the nearly empty bottle and turned to the tables. "Gentlemen of the court! We have an entertainment. The renowned detective Shan Tao Yun from the court of Chambaluc is about to show us astounding feats of reasoning and deduction! No doubt he is a descendant of the great Judge Dee, magistrate of the Tang dynasty," he barked out, referring to the legendary investigator whose exploits had been the subject of folktales for centuries.

Marco whispered to Osman, who retrieved a long club of black wood from the corner behind the bar, then stood by the corridor to the front door.

"But I can't—" Shan protested, thinking of making a dash for the door himself.

"More crime has been committed among our own," Marco spoke in a tone that told everyone that the joking was finished. "As if what happened to our Lau wasn't enough. There will be an end to it," he vowed with a sound like a snarl.

Shan realized that he was not being offered a choice. He stepped back to the bar, his eyes on the little Buddha. "I would like," he said in a tentative, uneasy voice, "another cup of tea."

Osman smiled, as though pleased with Shan's discomfort, then stepped away from his post by the door long enough to pour the tea.

"I don't wish that anyone be hurt," Shan said after a sip from the cup. This was Turkistan, he reminded himself, where retribution was always a few steps ahead of forgiveness.

Marco merely stared at him.

Shan sighed. "Something happened in here a few minutes before I arrived. An alarm. A signal. A new arrival, perhaps."

"Nothing," Osman said in an impatient tone.

"Sophie," the bald man in the fleece vest called out. "I said I heard Sophie coming."

Marco raised his eyebrows toward Osman.

"True enough," Osman said. "But no one else heard anything. We didn't expect you."

Shan looked at Marco. There was someone else with the Eluosi, someone with the improbable name of Sophie. "The possibility that you were coming scared Hoof," he said.

"Because?" Marco asked.

Shan replayed the events in his mind. Hoof had not simply been trying to flee. He had been wounded and then had lied, trying to blame Shan, and then had given up when he saw Jakli. Shan had not understood the disappointment on the Tadjik's face. "Perhaps because he had taken something. Because he had to lose it, or hide it now that you were coming. He only had a few moments."

Hoof had stood and was inching closer, his companion behind him. "I've ridden with Nikki," the little Tadjik blurted out. "I have groomed your animals. This Han insults me. He hates our kind."

Marco silenced him with a raised hand, then turned back to Shan.

"All right, tai tai," Marco said. *Tai tai*, esteemed one, was a form of address reserved for the most venerable of the mandarins.

"Where does Hoof wear the missing pouch?" Shan asked Osman. Hoof retreated to stand with his back against the wall, looking toward his companion, who seemed to be edging away, back toward their table.

"It was big," Osman answered, "it hung from his belt. His left side."

Shan nodded. "Perhaps this is what happened. Hoof had the empress in his pouch. When Marco was coming he had to be rid of it, because Marco of all people would notice it gone. Get rid of it but not get rid of it. Hide it, so he could get it later. He cut off the pouch and hid it in the corridor. Through the opening in the door he saw me, a Han, coming. Thinking he could blame it on me, he cut himself and threw himself on me as I opened the door."

"Someone could have been waiting with a knife in the corridor," Marco suggested. "The Xibo."

"Exactly," Hoof said eagerly. "He stood in front of me, he rushed me." His eyes did not move from Marco.

Shan shook his head. "That floor in the corridor had half an inch of sand," he observed. "It would have left signs of a struggle. But look at it, you won't see any. And he blew out the flames on the oil lamps as he went down the corridor, to make it appear an ambush had been set. The lamps had just been extinguished when I entered. I could smell the oil."

"True," Osman added. "They were dark when I went out to see who was shouting."

"But surely he wouldn't cut himself," Marco countered.

"Not a bad cut, just enough for blood to show," Shan said and saw that Marco was not convinced. "This is how it happened. The cut was on his upper right arm. A thief's knife would have been low and to Hoof's left, to cut away the strap of the pouch, not high and to the right. Hoof held the knife in his left hand and cut his own right arm. I was watching everyone drink. Hoof is the only man in this room who is left-handed."

Osman nodded. "Bad upbringing. A good Muslim is always trained to use his right hand."

"So what?" Marco asked.

Shan extended the index and middle fingers of his left hand like a blade and made a chopping motion on his upper arm. "He cut himself like this. A thief would have swung low, cut his belly on the same thrust maybe, but not the upper arm." Shan shrugged, and looked toward the shadows of the front corridor. "There must be shelves in there or niches for the oil lamps."

Osman nodded, pulled a lantern from its hook, and led them into the corridor. The original builders had provided four deep concave shelves for lamps. The first two niches were nearly obscured by cobwebs behind the lamp. At the third the webs had been recently broken. Marco reached in and pulled out a pouch. Making a small, angry growling noise, he marched back into the room and snapped out Hoof's name.

The Tadjik stood with his back to the wall, alone, abandoned by his friend. Marco held the pouch by the man's nose for a moment, then reached into it and pulled out the emerald queen.

Hoof's hands began to tremble.

Marco upended the pouch on the bar and out tumbled two large round objects, both the same size, each wrapped in white paper. Marco shook one and an apple fell out. "You stole from me," Marco growled as he extended the queen toward the Tadjik. "You stole at Karachuk. You stole when we were still mourning our lost aunt."

Hoof looked back at his companion, who stared at him stonily.

"Say it," Marco boomed. "Say you stole."

"I st—stole," the Tadjik murmured.

"Why?"

"Last year, you hit me. I was unconscious for an hour. My head hurt for a month."

"You insulted my camel," Marco shot back.

No one laughed.

Shan picked up the second round object. He pulled on the edge of the paper and a ball rolled out, a three-inch white leather ball joined by heavy reddish seams. Although Shan had never seen such a ball before, it looked vaguely familiar. He stared after it as Osman picked it up, shaking his head at Hoof, and placed it on top of one of the glasses, then tossed the crumpled paper into a basket that was nearly filled with empty bottles.

The men in the room began moving out, trying to look inconspicuous, their heads turned away as though they had seen something in Marco's face and were scared of it. Only six remained by the time Marco noticed. "No!" he called out. "Stay and witness!"

The big Eluosi pointed to the floor in front of the bar and Hoof stepped forward, cowering, his arms half raised as if he expected to be struck. "Here is what you will do, Hoof the thief," Marco announced as he paced around the Tadjik. "The uncle of Osman, he has a camp near the Wild Bear Mountain, at the ford of Fragile Water Creek. You will go there. You will tell them my words. They lost a son to fever this spring. They are outside the county, not in the Poverty Scheme. Which means they are going to winter camp soon. They will need help to gather fodder, to milk the goats. If you leave before they take the herds to spring pasture, I will know it. We will all know it, we will understand that you are indeed someone without honor. And then you will have no protection. Do you understand?"

Hoof lowered his arms and nodded slowly, then more vigorously, as though grateful for Marco's mercy.

Shan stared in confusion. Marco had just sentenced the man as surely as if he had been in a courtroom before armed guards.

At the corridor Osman spoke with Hoof's companion, who grimly nodded and escorted his friend out of the building. Shan stared at the empty doorway. It had been foolish, what the Tadjik had done, almost unbelievably foolish, as though perhaps he had had another motive they had not seen. He picked up the ball and tossed it from hand to hand, until he noticed that it had words imprinted in English. "Made in America," he said to Jakli, translating to Mandarin. He used the traditional Chinese words for America: *Mei Guo*, Beautiful Country.

"Beautiful ball for a beautiful country," a deep voice said from behind him, in English. Shan turned with a start to see a tall man in his mid-forties, with sandy-colored hair turning to grey. A pair of bright blue eyes stared at Shan from behind gold wire-rimmed glasses. The man raised an oversized leather glove in his left hand, punched his right fist into it, and opened the glove toward Shan. "That would be mine," he said, his eyes full of challenge.

Shan weighed the ball once more, remembering at last what it was, then tossed it into the glove. "Baseball," he said in English, in an awkward rhythm. The last time he had pronounced the word out loud had been with his father, over thirty years before. He returned the stranger's steady stare. "You're American," he added, as an observation, not a question.

"Dammit, Deacon," Marco muttered. "You don't know him."

"He's with Jakli," the man said. "That's good enough."

Meaning what? Shan wondered. That the American was usually hidden from strangers. But also that Jakli had a much closer connection to the two strange men than he had thought. Shan studied the man named Deacon. There had been another American hidden away, inside a burlap death shroud.

"Jacob Deacon," the American announced, extending his hand to Shan. "Just Deacon will do. You're a friend of Nikki's?"

Shan returned the handshake uncertainly, looking at Jakli.

"A friend of some Tibetan priests," Jakli said.

"Okay," Deacon said with a small smile. "I believe in Tibetan priests too." He looked at Marco. "How about you?"

The Eluosi frowned. "I've known priests and mullahs.

And I've known commissars. Commissars are easier to deal with."

Deacon laughed and pounded Marco on the shoulder, then pulled a bottle of water from a carton behind the bar. He poured a glass for Shan, then one for himself. "The real thing. And it's free." Shan studied the man. Had he been listening from the rear corridor the entire time?

"When is Nikki coming?" The question burst from Jakli with a sudden energy that caused Shan to look back at her.

"Caravans are unpredictable." Marco shrugged. "Maybe he decided to hole up in Ladakh for a few days because of patrols." He placed one of his paw-like hands on top of Jakli's head for a moment, the way a father might touch a daughter. "He'll bring you something bright and shiny. Or maybe something soft and flimsy."

Jakli's face flushed and she good-naturedly batted Marco's hand away, then quickly grew serious again. "Shan needs to know about Auntie Lau. Two of the children have died now too." Osman cursed. Marco raised his head with a growling sound, suddenly very sober, as Jakli explained about Suwan and Alta. "Shan thinks it started with Lau. He needs to know who might want to kill her. What happened before she died."

"A good woman," Marco said solemnly. "A bad death."

"Why would someone do this to an innocent woman?" Shan ventured.

"Innocent?" Marco asked. "That's more than I know."

"You don't consider her innocent?"

"Of course not. Are you? I sure as hell am not. Osman's not. My camel's not. They've proven Jakli's not innocent, three times over." The words brought a bitter smile to Jakli's face. Marco looked over to Osman. "Ever meet an innocent person, old friend? I haven't. Hell, Osman's got a niece six months old, still at her mother's breast. She's not innocent. She's Kazakh."

"You're saying Lau was killed because she was Kazakh?" Shan asked.

"No. But maybe in the end that's what it was. What being Kazkah made her do. The bastards."

"What bastards?"

Marco poured the remains of the vodka into a glass. "Just bastards in general," he muttered.

Shan turned toward the rear corridor. The American was gone. He felt Marco's gaze.

"You'd be wise to be gone yourself," the Eluosi observed in a dangerous tone, wiping his mouth on his sleeve. "It's a bad place to be asking questions."

"If you would talk with him," Jakli suggested, "maybe he wouldn't have to ask so many."

Marco sighed. He stepped behind the bar and retrieved three of the flat nan breads. He tossed one to each of them, then mounted a stool and chewed meditatively on the third as Osman collected glasses from the tables. "It was just before Nikki took the last caravan out," Marco said. "We had to pick up some men. Lau rode in that evening, all excited about something."

"Alone?" Shan asked.

"Alone. Her horse was so exhausted we were scared it would die. Osman stayed with it, rubbing it, walking it, making sure it was cooled down before drinking."

"Who did she speak with?"

"No one. Everyone." Marco stared at his crust as he spoke, then looked up with a new sadness in his eyes. "They say she was a healer, but many didn't understand the most important thing she did, the most important healing." He paused to bite off a piece and chew. "There's a little brown mouse in the desert," he said in a contemplative tone. "It collects things, like a pack rat. But where the mouse lives is so harsh that it usually just collects thorns and sharp pieces of crystal and small dried dead things. Lau was like that, with people's troubles. People would tell her their nightmares, their painful memories, their fears, and they would feel better, like she had taken them away, collected them inside herself, so they could heal."

"You're saying people confessed things to her?"

Jakli nodded. "It's true. I keep wondering. What if someone told her something, a secret she wasn't supposed to know? What if they changed their mind later and decided she had to be silenced? People get drunk and talk. She had a way of getting people to talk."

"No," Marco disagreed. "You didn't see her that night.

The way her legs were beaten. If you want to stop her from spreading your secret, you just shoot her. If you want to pry out someone else's secret, you beat her first."

Shan took a bite of his bread and looked up. "You mean, you saw her."

Marco stared at his piece of bread. "I mean I found her. Nikki and I. Nikki first, at the quiet place she liked to go to. Only she and Jakli were the ones who usually go." He glanced at Jakli. "Nikki missed you. I think he went there because it reminded him of you. But when he went inside he found her tied to the old statue. He came and got me, with tears in his eyes." The big Eluosi looked down into his hands. "His mother taught him that, that sometimes it is all right to cry." Marco raised his eyes to Jakli, who seemed to be fighting back her own tears.

"I used to see it a lot, when the Red Guard were roaming the land," Marco said with a bitter tone. "They would break bones in the feet with a hammer. If you do it just so, it makes the skin agonize to the touch. Then they hit the feet and shins with a stick. Doesn't take much force to create a lot of pain. Sometimes they just used chopsticks, snap the skin with chopsticks. Do one foot, start with the second if they still don't talk. Afterward, you would see them on the street. The knobs would laugh and call them drunken foot, because they couldn't walk in a straight line anymore. The ones that held out, they did both feet. No one did much walking after that. Her killer, I don't think he intended that she leave the room, no matter what she told him."

Jakli tore away with a sob and ran out the back passageway, followed a moment later by Osman.

"Maybe she didn't talk," Marco suggested. "She was a tough one." He poured them both some tea.

"She talked," Shan said, and told Marco about the bruise on her arm, the place where a syringe had been inserted.

Marco sighed heavily. "What's the point of beating her, then?" he asked into his glass.

Shan looked up into Marco's eyes and knew he didn't have to explain. The injection meant that the killer was someone experienced in interrogation technique. Those who were hardened to it sometimes developed appetites for watching people in pain.

Marco was silent a long time. "We would have seen a knob or a soldier," he said in a low, angry tone.

"Not if he was well trained. Or if he was disguised," Shan suggested, and related what Prosecutor Xu had said to him at Glory Camp, how she had mistaken him for a knob agent.

"God's breath," Marco said, and shifted in his seat to face the empty tables, as if trying to fix in his mind each of the faces of the men who had occupied them. "It's a bad time."

Shan watched the brooding Eluosi. A bad time just because of the treachery, he wondered, or bad timing for the treachery, because of something else?

"Why here?" Shan asked. "You were here. A few others. This settlement here, it's not a big place, not easy to hide in. I think the killer took a big risk, killing Lau here. But he had to, because suddenly it was urgent. He couldn't wait."

"Nothing's changed."

"Not yet," Shan said and saw Marco clench his jaw. "What if the secret she died for was your secret?"

Marco drained his tea in one long gulp and fixed Shan with a stare. "You should go home, Comrade Inspector. I will get the bastards."

"You sound as if you know who did it."

"Not yet. But it's what I do. I get bastards." He spoke in a stark, haunting tone, as if it were a threat against the entire world, including Shan. "My hobby," he said with a thin smile. "I remember. I watch. I make sure others don't forget."

Shan considered Marco. A forgotten man of a forgotten people, without legal travel papers, without hope of ever getting legal papers. Not unlike Shan. Maybe that was all that Shan was about too, about getting the bastards, whomever they were. He recalled what Marco had done to Hoof. He had gotten the bastard.

Marco suddenly appeared very tired. He stretched and lifted his heavy frame from the stool, then moved to the center of the room and collapsed into the overstuffed chair. He shut his eyes and quickly drifted into the deep slow breathing of slumber.

Shan sat silently, trying to make sense of Lau's killing, trying to keep at bay the question that lingered constantly at the edge of his consciousness, the question of Gendun and his safety. From the basket he retrieved the paper that had been wrapped around the ball, flattened it, and sketched on its clean back a rough map of Karachuk, to have a context for the location of Lau's killing, to fix the spot when Jakli finally showed it to him. Lau had not died in this room, or in the nearby huts. He remembered Bajys's words. He had gone to the place of sands to find her, to the lhakang there, the sanctuary place, which, Shan knew, must be the quiet place Marco referred to, the place where Lau's body had been found. But he had been too late. He hadn't found her in Karachuk. He had only found pieces of bodies. She had died tied to a statue in the quiet place, Marco had said. Shan sat on the floor by the bar, in the cross-legged lotus style, contemplating his map, then finally rose and moved out the rear corridor.

The passage led down a curving hall to a small plank door that opened to the east, at the back of the makeshift community, onto a sandy swath, across which stood the rock outcropping that defined the eastern boundary of the ancient city. The sun was low in the sky. A cool breeze was blowing. There was no sign of life, except in the corral, where the horses had been joined by half a dozen camels, including one huge silver creature that seemed to study Shan as he moved.

Shan climbed halfway up the rock, stopping when he was just above the domed building. He sat and leaned against the warm rock, drained mentally and physically. Someone had tortured a woman here, a healer and a teacher. She had been killed for a secret, but in order to find her, her killer had penetrated another secret, the secret of Karachuk. Because she had not been just a healer and a teacher. Lau had lived in many worlds, it seemed, just as Shan had traveled through many worlds to arrive here, at this ghost city in the desert where the gentle Lau had met her violent end.

He pulled out the paper he had taken from the dead American and studied the strange combination of letters. FBP the first line said. Could it be a code for numbers, with

F meaning six, for the sixth letter of the English alphabet? He quickly calculated that FBP would mean six, two, and sixteen. Meaning what? An address? A phone extension? Or were the letters geographic abbreviations? FBP could mean Frankfurt, Beijing, and Paris, or a thousand similar combinations. He sighed and took comfort from the knowledge that the paper wasn't for him, not part of the mystery he was meant to solve.

His eyes fluttered with drowsiness. For a moment he saw Karachuk the way it had been, smelled the spices brought by the caravans, heard the creaking of well ropes, the laughter of youths dead all these centuries. It was still an oasis after so many years, it still attracted refugees from a harsh world outside. Perhaps the very fact that its current inhabitants were outcasts from politics and technology meant that they were much like the original citizens of the town. A dog barked from somewhere, whether from his dreams of the past or from the present he could not tell. The wind blew a sheet of sand around the shoulders of one of the stone sentinels on the distant wall, making it appear as though it were wearing a cape that flapped in the wind.

A small sad smile rose on Shan's face as he looked out over the ruins and contemplated not the mystery of Lau's death, but the mystery of life. He closed his eyes and let the timelessness of the place seep through him. A fragrance of spice wafted through his imagined caravan city, like the ginger he always smelled in those rare, perfect moments when he was able to conjure up a vision of his father. But when he opened his eyes to a dusk sky streaked with vermillion, the smell was so pungent that he stood to look for its source. It wasn't spice, he realized after a moment, but incense, and he followed the trail of the scent toward the top of the rocks.

The outcropping was wider than he had thought, easily a hundred feet across at the top, and in a shadow near the center he discovered steps that descended into a cleft in the rock. He followed the carved steps, worn smooth and hollow by centuries of use, and as he descended he heard a woman crying.

CHAPTER 7

The gap between the rocks quickly closed up to form a passageway—not a cave, but a structure created long ago by building a roof over the cleft and squaring the walls with plaster. The first thirty feet were deep in shadow. Wary of falling into a concealed crevasse, Shan was about to retreat when the passage curved and he saw the small pool of light cast by a flickering oil lamp. The flame illuminated a dim image on the wall, the head of a bull with angry eyes, wearing a necklace of skulls. A Buddhist image, the shape of Yamantaka, king of the dead. Shan followed the path lit by another lamp ten feet away, then another, studying with reverent awe the paintings of wild animals and landscapes that came into view on the walls. After the fourth lamp, past a patch of naked rock where the plaster had crumbled away, the paintings changed. There was a gentle-looking deer, an image that had grown familiar to Shan in his visits to gompas, the symbol of Buddha's home in India, followed by scenes from the life of Buddha.

The winding tunnel opened into a broad chamber, which he realized had been a bowl in the outcropping that was covered by a roof. A dozen lamps set in wall niches illuminated what had once been a magnificent painting on the walls, a long continuous scene of a journey through an ancient land. To his left were sheep under willow trees, which grew along a road that linked the scene together. The road passed through low wooded mountains, and horses appeared, ridden by archers. The painting faded into the shadows at the back of the chamber, then emerged on Shan's right with scenes of camel caravans moving on sand toward snow-capped mountains.

Beyond a heavy table near the center of the room were several crude benches and sitting cushions arranged on an old carpet. Jakli sat on one of the cushions, staring at a lamp in her hands. She did not seem to notice as he stepped to the table. On it lay six long rectangular sandalwood boxes, plainly but expertly crafted with delicately fitted joints. Pechas, they were called, the Tibetan books that consisted of unbound pages of silk or parchment stacked inside a wooden case. One was open, and several of its pages were arranged in front of it as if it were being read. Behind the books was a bronze statue of Buddha, a foot high, and beside the large figure were several smaller figures of Buddha in gold, none more than three inches high. Below the table was a wooden box covered with dust-caked cloth. Shan pulled up a corner of the cloth. Inside was a jumble of spindles and cylinders, pieces of the prayer wheels used by Tibetan Buddhists.

He sat beside Jakli. "This was the place, wasn't it?"

She was weeping. No longer with the wracking sobs he had heard outside, not even with great emotion, but as she gazed silently into the lamp, he saw two tears roll down her cheeks. She looked up without embarrassment and nodded toward a pallet near the wall, in the darkest shadows of the chamber. He lifted a lamp and stepped toward the pallet. It was drawn up against a large object, covered with a cloth. He pulled on a corner of the cloth and it slowly slid away, revealing a three-foot-high Buddha carved of stone. The plaster just above the Buddha's left shoulder showed fracture lines extending from a single small hole. Down the left side of the statue a rust-colored stain ran to the floor.

"She started bringing me here years ago, whenever we happened to be at Karachuk together."

"She read the Buddhist books with you?"

"Sometimes. But mostly we sat and talked. It was just a quiet place." She looked about the room with a fond but melancholy expression. "For some people, once they knew about this place, this is where they would always go." Shan understood. He felt the reverence of the chamber. It was a place where he would go. Jakli looked back at the flame. "Sometimes she taught me things about healing. Sometimes, after she had gone to her council meetings, she told me about the silly things people do in towns. Ever since she learned my mother was Tibetan, she helped me keep her memory alive."

"Did you want to become a Buddhist?"

Jakli's eyes had drifted back to the stain on the statue. "Lau would never put a name on it. It was so I could worship my inner god, is what she would say." She held the lamp up, as though to better see Shan's eyes. "It is not a bad thing, to be a Buddhist."

"No, it is not," Shan said with a sad smile and followed her eyes toward his hand. It was wrapped around the gau that hung from his neck.

"Are you one, then?" she asked in a puzzled tone.

Shan thought a moment. "When I was young my father took me to the old Taoist temples. Then they were destroyed. When I was older," he said with a sigh, remembering the secret altars made of sticks in his prison barracks, the rosaries of seeds and fingernails and the prayer wheels made of tin cans, "I was taught by Buddhist lamas. But I keep the Taoist verses alive inside me, for their wisdom, and for my father." He looked at the mural on the wall. And I keep the Buddhist verses in my heart, he almost said, because they brought me back to life after I had died. "I guess I am like you," he said. "A little bit of a lot of things." He looked at the small Buddha. Once, in a prison barracks, he had seen an altar consisting only of a series of curved lines scratched on the wall, representing the outline of a seated Buddha.

"I was never sure. I worried about betraying one of them, my mother or my father," Jakli said in a distant voice. "But coming here—it was Marco who showed me Karachuk, when Nikki and I were children. We would sit on the rock and watch for ghosts. We weren't scared. For centuries Karachuk was inhabited only by ghosts. In the old Karachuk it was different. Look—" She rose and carried her lamp to the fresco on the far side of the table, near the desert caravan scene. It showed a domed building that appeared to be a mosque, with men in the red robes of Buddhist clergy standing in front of it, apparently conversing with mullahs. "Here, the Buddhists and the Muslims learned to live together, to share their wisdom."

He turned back to Jakli and saw her staring at the pallet where Lau had died. "I told her so many things," Jakli said, another tear escaping down her cheek. "What if Lau died because of my secrets?"

"Are your secrets so dangerous?" Shan asked in surprise.

"Maybe."

Shan remembered Marco's words at the bar. *They've proven that Jakli's not innocent, three times over.*

"Because of the things you went to rice camp for?" he asked quietly, looking at the fractured plaster above the statue. There had been no exit wound from the bullet that killed Lau. Her killer had fired another bullet over her head, into the plaster. To secure her, perhaps to make her sit still while he tied her to the Buddha.

Jakli shrugged. "You know how it is. Chinese pest control. All it takes is a few strong words to be sent behind the lao jiao wire."

"Three times," he said. Three bowls, he thought, remembering Wangtu's words.

"First time, I told a Chinese teacher that she was wrong to say Kazakhs and Uighurs were descended from Chinese. She took me to the headmaster. He hit me with a bamboo stick and I apologized. But when I left, there was a rally outside by the Muslim students. The headmaster said it was my fault, that I had organized a political protest. Eleven months in Glory Camp, memorizing the Chairman's verses. They never let me back into school after that."

"But that was only the first."

Jakli's eyes settled on the oil flame again. "At a collective meeting the Chinese birth inspectors announced a new campaign of enforcement. I stood up and asked them what right they had. We produce plenty of food to feed our families. There's plenty of land. I said they limit the number of babies and keep all the good doctors for the Han. Many more of our children die. It's just slow genocide, I said."

"You said that?" Shan asked in disbelief. "Genocide?"

"That was twelve more months, at a camp in the desert.

Everything was full of sand there. It was the truth, what I said."

"I know," Shan said somberly. "But I never heard anyone say it in public."

"Then there was a campaign against smugglers. A tent at our clan's camp was found with boxes of Western medicines and portable tape players. You know, with the little headphones. They had no evidence, didn't know whose tent it was. I told them it was my tent."

"But you weren't smuggling."

"No. But the tent was my uncle's, and the goods were from Nikki. I couldn't let either of them get arrested. My uncle, he has to watch over the clan. And Nikki, they would be tough on him. He would be like a caged tiger if they put him behind wire. For me, all they could charge was concealing evidence. So I got ten more months in reeducation."

"But after three terms, it's hard labor," Shan said soberly. "The gulag." He remembered Akzu's warning when she had first appeared at the trailhead. It's too dangerous for you, he had said to his niece.

Jakli nodded slowly and pushed back a loose strand of hair. "But that won't happen now. Nikki will protect me."

"Nikki. He is Marco's son."

Jakli nodded again and turned her face to Shan's, suddenly smiling through her damp eyes. The strand of hair fell back, and she curled it around her finger with the shy expression of a young girl. "We're going to be married—at the nadam, the horse festival."

Shan looked away self-consciously. He did not know what to say. Marriage, and all it implied, was so distant to him it seemed like some vague concept he had read about in an old book. He looked back silently for a long moment. "But he is away."

"On the other side of the border. One last trip."

Shan nodded. The son of Marco the smuggler was a smuggler himself. "And Lau knew about your marriage."

Jakli nodded, still fingering her hair. "She was filled with joy when I told her. Nikki was always one of her favorites," she added, and her eyes drifted back to the flame.

Jakli was going to marry a young Eluosi, the tiger for

whom she had gone to jail. He studied her. The longer she sat looking at the flame, the more frightened she appeared to be.

Shan looked about the chamber again. Lau had been there alone in the flickering light when Nikki had found her body. "Who was here that night, at Karachuk?" he asked, staring at the stained Buddha. He walked slowly along the wall, feeling one moment warmed by the simple beauty of the ancient painting, the next chilled by the thought of the violent death Lau had met there. She moved from one person she trusted to another, Wangtu had said, as though from one oasis to another.

Jakli sighed. "Marco was here, Nikki, and Osman. Others, drinking at the inn. When we took her body to the cave we asked all the obvious questions. For hours we talked about it. No strangers were here. No one even saw a strange horse or camel. A vehicle would have been heard. Osman said it was the ghosts. Everyone laughed, but he wasn't joking."

"A horse could have come," Shan suggested. "It could have been left on the far side of the wall and not have been noticed. Or the killer could have left the horse on the far side of the rock, and climbed over without going inside the old city."

She nodded slowly. "Lau came on her horse. You heard Marco. Her horse was all lathered, she had been riding hard across the desert."

"Because she was rushing to see someone?" He stopped by the table and looked into the box of religious artifacts again. Something glinted in the light. He reached down the side of the box and pulled out a long cylindrical object, capped by a needle. A disposable syringe.

"No one," Jakli said in a faint voice. She was looking at him with a stark, frightened expression. She had seen the syringe. "No one knew she was here."

"The killer knew." Lau was running from someone, Shan thought. And came to Karachuk for sanctuary. He looked back at the statue. In the dim light it looked like the Buddha had been shot and had bled its heart onto the floor.

He stared at the syringe in his hands, then abruptly let go of it, as if it could strike him of its own will. It dropped into the shadows and he stood staring at his empty hand. He paced around the chamber, studying the old painting again, somehow sensing something of Lau. An old monk had told him that sometimes when people died in great pain little pieces of their soul broke away and wandered aimlessly about. "Do you know now why she wrote that letter to the prosecutor?" he asked.

"She didn't mean it," Jakli said.

"No. She did mean it. I think I understand. It was her gift, like trying to protect Wangtu by not giving him any more teas. She was worried about you. Three bowls of lao jiao. Ready to be married. She wanted to be sure you were protected, safely held in probation, so you couldn't get arrested again. It would have caused her pain, but she did it for you. She would have sacrificed much, even your feelings toward her, if it meant you would be safe." Despite what Lau had done, Jakli was defying her probation, as if she didn't care, as if she were out of the prosecutor's reach, or would be soon. He looked at Jakli. She was biting her lower lip, tears on her cheeks again, staring at the lamp. He sighed and slipped away.

All traces of the sun were gone as Shan stepped out of the cave, but the sky was brilliant with trembling stars and a rising two-thirds moon. A chill wind blew, the kind some monks called a soul-minding wind from the way it made the spirit wary and instantly alert. From across the desert came the howl of a night animal and, much closer, the chirp of a cricket.

He found his former perch overlooking Karachuk and turned up his collar against the cold. There was no activity, no sign of life, except a few glimmers through the thin cloth that hung in half a dozen windows. His fingers absently ran through the white sand by his leg. He longed to return to the dreamlike state he had felt when he first sat on the rocks, but the vision of Lau dying in the Buddha's arms had burned too deeply. His fingers made random shapes in the cool moonlit sand. Then he stopped, wiped the sand smooth, and made a two-part ideogram. The top was a small cross mark whose ends swept into right-facing curves, with a long tail to the left. It symbolized a high barren plateau and implied emptiness. The bottom half had two Y-shaped figures standing on a curved line, showing two humans standing back to back on a mound. The ideogram meant *openness* and was the sign his father always used for Chapter Eleven of the Tao te Ching. *Using what is not*, it was called:

Thirty spokes converge on a hub
What is not there makes the wheel useful
Clay is shaped to form a pot
What is not there makes the pot useful
Doors and windows are cut to shape a room
What is not there makes the room useful

He mouthed the words silently, then heard the last lines in his mind so crisply it was as if one of the Taoist priests of his childhood were reading beside him:

Take advantage of what is there
By making use of what is not.

What was not there, he knew, was the motive, for the motive was the connection that had driven Lau to Karachuk, where smugglers hid, where the American waited—the connection that had taken the killer from Lau to the boy Suwan at the Red Stone clan, then to the boy Alta in the high Kunlun. And on to where? Back to Karachuk? If the motive was simply to find secret Buddhists, the killer might be seeking the waterkeeper. If the motive was to find and kill particular children, then the zheli was the trail, the chain that guided the killer, a chain the killer destroyed as he followed it. Unfinished business, Akzu had said. The clans of one or more of the zheli might have been targeted years earlier, and the killer might have reappeared, as though awakening from a long hibernation, to stalk the last survivors. Kazakhs and Uighur clans had fought soldiers years earlier and been destroyed or dispersed in punishment. But they had inflicted significant losses on the army, and perhaps somewhere had kindled a lust for revenge that had smoldered for decades. Lau may have been alive during those terrible years, but not the zheli. What kind of blood-lust burned so deep it drove the killer even to the offspring of his enemy?

A movement below broke the spell. A dark, hulking shape, barely lighter than the shadows it moved in, stole along the back of the domed building. It made no sound, and the animals in the pen ignored it, almost as if they could not see it. Ghosts roamed the Taklamakan. For centuries Karachuk had been a city inhabited only by ghosts, Jakli had said.

The phantom glided toward the rocks now, stopping every few seconds as if to listen or watch. Lau's killer had moved like this, unseen in the night. And Lau had not been killed by a ghost. It could be the killer again, he thought, or a thief. But who would risk the wrath of Marco?

The figure should have been close enough for Shan to hear its feet on the gravel at the base of the rock, but there was no sound except the crickets. The thing bent over on all fours and moved closer to the outcropping, only fifty feet from Shan now. Suddenly a brilliant light flashed from the shape, followed by a sound of glee, then the light disappeared and the grey thing hurried back toward the compound.

Shan launched himself from his perch and ran down the path, jumping onto the sand and darting to the shadows at the rear of Osman's inn just as the figure disappeared around a hut at the far side of the corral.

The horses trotted away from him as Shan approached. They had not been frightened by the figure who had gone before, only by Shan. The big camel, so silvery in the moonlight that it too seemed like an apparition, made a sound that started as a snort and ended in a low, throaty grumbling sound, as if first it were alarmed and then just angry at being disturbed.

The hut had no window. As he approached it Shan saw that its plank door was ajar, and he gently pushed it open a few inches. A thick rug had been hung over the inside frame, concealing a dim light from within. He slipped inside and saw to his surprise a wall of neatly trimmed boards that had been expertly fitted into the structure only three feet inside the entrance. A narrow plank door with a hasp for a lock hung open enough to leak the brilliant white light of an incandescent bulb along its edge.

Shan waited in silence for several minutes, then laid a finger against the wooden door. It swung inward a few inches, enough for him to see a table nailed together of rough planks, stacked with books.

"It's open," someone said in Mandarin.

Shan pushed the door and stepped inside. Deacon, the American, was standing at a workbench under a naked lightbulb, examining something under a large magnifying lens that was suspended by a swinging arm clamped to the table. Without turning around, he gestured toward a bottle on the table. "Help yourself to the vodka."

Shan silently surveyed the room. The electric line for the bulb ran to a wooden box in the corner, containing a series of heavy batteries. The books, in English, German, and Chinese, appeared to be textbooks on anthropology and archaeology. Another volume, thicker than the others and leaning open at the back of the table, seemed to be on a different topic. It was held open by a heavy spring clip to a diagram of a human skeleton.

"If you've grown particular, there's a clean glass on the shelf above the door," Deacon said, then glanced over his shoulder. He paused and raised an eyebrow, then returned to his work. "It's you," he said impassively. "Expected a Russian."

Shan did not immediately reply, for, an instant after Deacon had noticed him, his own eyes had found a shelf hung above the bench where Deacon worked. It held half a dozen small cages, all different but each one constructed of finely worked wood. They all glowed with the patina of great age. The largest, perhaps six inches long and four in height and depth, was made of thin slats of sandalwood. The smallest appeared to have been crafted out of a solid piece of fruitwood, hollowed out and carved into the shape of a temple.

The cruelest thing they had done to him in the gulag was to steal his memories. The pain from his repeated interrogations, from batons sometimes, and drugs, and electric prods, had dulled his memory, had made certain parts of his brain seem inaccessible. It was part of the Party's master plan, a cell mate had said, to cauterize the brain so it could not remember that once things had been better. But on seeing the cages something vague had jarred loose in the back of his mind.

At least three of the cages appeared occupied.

Deacon had followed Shan's gaze. "Marco laughs at me, but I tell him every proper town needs its own orchestra."

"You were outside," Shan said, then added with sudden realization, "you were gathering singers."

Deacon looked at the cages with a satisfied grin. "Got him, finally. Old Ironlegs, we call him. Makes a rasping sort of song, like his leg is made of metal." He turned to Shan. "You know crickets?" he asked in English.

Shan looked at the American in silence and slowly grinned. It seemed a wonderful question. "When I was young," he said, awed that the memory should have leapt out and found his tongue after being lost for so many years, "my father would take me to an old Taoist priest who had avoided all the suffering in the cities by fleeing to the mountains. He lived alone and spent most of his time weaving baskets and meditating on the Taoist scriptures. The only other thing I remember about him is that he collected singers. He taught me about them." How remarkable, Shan thought, to be in the desert, with a strange American, looking for a killer, and suddenly have one of the darkened doors of his memory opened.

Deacon smiled. "My first trip to China, I went to a market and saw a vendor selling insect singers. Had maybe fifteen species. A horse bell. A stove chicken, with the big antennae. Some of the black ones, ink bells they're called. And a weaving lady."

Somewhere deep inside Shan, something warmed as he heard the names, names he had first heard with his father, decades earlier. "I remember one called a *cao zhong*," he said. The words came unexpectedly, on a flood of recollection. "A beautiful one, loud but perfectly pitched. I don't know the English."

"A grass katydid," Deacon said. "God, I'd love to have a katydid. Too dry here." The American's eyes filled with pleasure as he gazed at his cages. "That street vendor, I sat with him for two hours as he explained how each had different songs, how their diet could affect their song, how the emperors used to have tiny furniture made for their favorite crickets. Next trip, I took my son Micah to see him again. All Micah did was grin, the biggest, most beautiful grin I ever saw on his face. We were hooked." Deacon looked with pride at his collection of cages. "The vendor told us they bring good fortune."

Shan nodded. "Because their song is so alive and bright. Living music, the old priest called it. Because you can't control them. If a cricket chooses to bring his living music to your home, then nature has indeed blessed you." Shan pried the door of his memory open further. "I remember one called a blue bell, and a painted mirror." He rushed the words out, as if scared of losing them again. "And a bamboo bell."

"With Ironlegs my chorus is complete. He's a watchman. *Pang t'ou*, they call it. Watchman's rattle. Full moon in ten days. My son and I will take them out into the dark at midnight and listen to their chorus. We'll watch for shooting stars. One of the old Kazakhs told my son that some crickets can do that, call in shooting stars."

"Your son?" Shan asked. "Your son is here?"

"Not here, but in Xinjiang."

For an agonizing moment Shan's mind raced. No. Deacon couldn't be old enough to be the father of the dead American at Glory Camp. "How old is he?"

"Ten." The American pushed the lens away and surveyed his cages again. "They'll attack each other if you don't keep them separate," he said, as if eager to shift the conversation from the boy called Micah.

"The old priest had a lot of antique cages, like yours, and some made of gourds," Shan recalled. "Others he made of bamboo splints or reeds."

"They're hard to find, the old cages. What happened to his?"

Shan smiled sadly as that part of the memory flooded over him. His father had left him with the old man one night, and they had stayed up until the crickets stopped singing in the early hours of the morning. "One of the few people who knew about him was a shepherd boy who brought rice cakes to him on festival days. But the boy joined the Red Guard and had a quota of reactionaries to arrest."

"Christ," Deacon muttered, as if he recognized the story.

"One day the boy came and told the old man that he would have to tell his platoon leader about him, that they would come the next day to take him away."

"Jesus. What did the old man do to the boy?"

"He thanked the boy for showing him respect," Shan said with a sigh. "That night, because the cages were from imperial China and he knew they would be crushed by the Guard, he freed all his singers. Then he waited until the moon rose and he burned all the cages. I know because my school class was required to go to the trial. The Guard was furious, because he refused to condemn the Taoists, and he only talked about that perfect moment, in a serene voice, about how the crickets had stayed and watched the fire and sung their most beautiful song ever as the cages burned. We were forced to leave, because the old man didn't follow the script." There had been another trial later, he recalled, when the Red Guard had begun to exhaust the supply of ready victims. They had arrested a vendor of crickets and put the insects on trial for contributing to the reactionary tradition. In the end they had roasted all the crickets on tiny spits and made the man eat them.

The laptop computer beeped and the screen went blank. Deacon took a step toward the workbench and closed the cover.

"I didn't know there was electricity," Shan said. "There wasn't any at Osman's."

"Only here. A portable solar rig. Charges the batteries enough for four or five hours' use."

Solar cells and crickets. A computer in an ancient Silk Road hut. An American hiding in a Chinese desert, drinking vodka with a Russian renegade. Jakli had taken him to another world, or several other worlds, none of which seemed connected to Lau or Gendun or the dead boys.

Shan could see the back table now, where Deacon had been working. The lens had been over a piece of cloth, an old faded textile with a crosshatch pattern of threads colored in shades of brown, yellow, and red. Deacon stepped forward, blocking his view of the table.

"Why are you here, Mr. Deacon?" Shan asked.

"Deacon. Just Deacon. I told you. Collecting crickets."

"I mean here, in Karachuk. In the Taklamakan. In Xinjiang."

Deacon smiled thinly and looked up at his crickets. "Maybe because of that grin on my boy's face. Hard to come by, back home." He looked at Shan. "Or maybe for the same reason as Marco, and Osman, and Jakli, and Nikki."

"You mean to hide?"

The American shook his head solemnly. "To the contrary. We came here to stop hiding. Here is where no one can hide."

"We?" Shan asked. "You and your son?"

Deacon frowned. "My wife and I."

"I thought that hiding was the point of Karachuk. Smugglers. Outcasts. They come here to hide."

"Then you don't get it. I've been everywhere, on every continent, even the Antarctic. This is the only place I know on earth where you're totally responsible for yourself. No police. No soldiers. No goddamned government to tell you what to think or to make it easy for people not to think. You have to be somebody here. You have to trust and be trusted."

Shan stepped closer to Deacon's worktable. Deacon moved to block him. "You have to trust," Shan said, repeating the American's words.

Deacon frowned. "You didn't say what happened to that old priest with the crickets."

Shan looked at the cages once more. "They beat him at the end of the trial. Then they forced other priests to beat him. He died and they burned his body, all on the same day they took him from the mountain." Shan sighed and looked at the cricket cages again. "My father got some ashes from where the fire was and he took me back there, to where the priest had lived. We made a secret shrine for the ashes. When we left at dusk the crickets were singing for him."

The American stood still and let Shan push past.

It was indeed an ancient textile Deacon had been studying, a piece of thickly woven reddish-brown fabric. The cloth was wrapped around something cylindrical, covered at one end with a bit of canvas. To the right was a small binocular microscope.

"Textbooks say you can only dye white wool, wool without natural pigment," Deacon said over his shoulder. "But in the Taklamakan they never read those books. This is wool from a brown sheep, with most of its threads colored with a red-purple dye through some process we don't understand yet." Deacon pointed to the crosshatch pattern. "Here, they wove with strands of undyed white wool and white wool dyed red."

Shan looked at him in confusion. Surely the American hadn't come halfway around the world to secretly study cloth.

Voices suddenly broke through the silence outside. Multiple voices, a commotion of running and shouting. Someone called for Marco. Deacon looked back at his door but seemed reluctant to leave Shan alone.

Someone shouted the American's name. The door swung open, but no one was behind it. As Deacon stepped toward the opening, Shan quickly pulled away the canvas at the end of the textile.

He stared in disbelief, fighting a sudden nausea. The fabric had been a pants leg. Extending from it was a human foot, small and shriveled, but unmistakably a foot.

"Shit," the American muttered, his eyes moving from Shan to the door.

Somebody shouted again and Marco's huge frame filled the doorway. He gestured for them to come out and retreated far enough for Shan to see Akzu behind him, looking so exhausted he could barely stand. Jakli ran up, holding a blanket around her shoulders.

"Someone killed a Public Security officer," Akzu gasped. "Lieutenant Sui. The knobs will be crawling all over the county in a few more hours. They will declare martial law." The Kazakh pronounced the words like a death sentence, then turned to Shan and the American as though further explanation were required. "Arrests will made, lots of arrests. Soldiers will sweep everywhere. Everyone must flee. They're going to take our families."

CHAPTER 8

In the early morning light the stone sentinels of Karachuk seemed to have crouched, as though coiled for battle, sensing an approaching enemy. Indeed, the news brought by Akzu seemed to have transformed most of the town's inhabitants. The bright clothing Shan had seen the day before had been replaced by shades of brown and grey that blended with the desert. Long knives had appeared on many belts and, to Shan's great discomfort, rifles were slung on the shoulders of some of the Kazakhs.

He found Akzu and Osman at the corral, speaking in hushed, hurried tones.

"Where was Sui killed?" Shan asked. "Usually these things happen in the cities. Surely they wouldn't suspect the herdsmen."

"On the Kashgar highway," Akzu sighed, "twenty miles outside of Yoktian. No one lives there but Kazakh and Uighur herders. You know what the knobs will do. Sweep the camps for political undesirables. Curfews will be imposed. Four years ago when an army sergeant died martial law was declared for six months. Suspects were sent directly to the coal mines, their families to Glory Camp. The fools who did it have no idea of the suffering they will cause."

"What fools?" Shan asked. "You know who did it?"

Akzu was gazing toward the mountains. "Malik is still out there. He brought a boy back to us, then left again. Now my sons have gone too, to gather those of the zheli who can still be found." He turned to Shan as if just hearing his question and shrugged. "The Maos. It's what they do. That's who did it four years ago. The hotheads. The ones who think change can come overnight."

"Think?" a loud voice interjected over Shan's shoulder. "They don't think. They're just arrogant predators, as bad as the knobs sometimes. An easy kill comes along, bang. They just satisfy their appetite and move on." Marco didn't seem frightened like the others. He only seemed angry. "The whelps! How dare they do this to us!"

Surely the murder would mean added pressure from Public Security. But Marco's rage seemed more focused, as if the incident meant interference with a particular plan.

The Eluosi's fury choked off as he looked in the direction of the outcropping. His oxlike breathing dominated the silence. Shan followed his gaze toward the highest point. Jakli was sitting there, arms around her raised knees, watching the western horizon.

"Mother of God," Marco said, his voice suddenly soft and pained.

"She fears for her—for your son?" Shan asked awkwardly.

"Not that," Marco muttered. "Nikki is fine. Nikki is invincible." He kicked the wall of the building. A piece of the old mud stucco fell away.

"Something else," Osman explained. "If the knobs mobilize, they will check all undesirables. She is supposed to be at her factory job in town. A violation of probation, not to be there. Her friends cover for her, because her friends know it is for Auntie Lau. Everyone loved Auntie Lau. Normally the knobs won't bother to check there. But now, with Sui dead, they are bound to look everywhere. No one can cover when the knobs come looking for her. If they arrest her," he said, turning to speak toward the distant mountains, "she won't be at the horse festival. She won't be getting married. They'll take her to one of the coal mines. I was at a coal prison once, delivering food with some Maos. Hammers and chisels is all they get. No gloves. No mining machines. Never enough food. I saw prisoners whose hands were nothing but bone and skin, like skeletons." He looked back at Jakli. "So young," he said in a near whisper, "so full of life. A few months in a coal mine and she'll be old and empty."

The silver camel in the corral made a snickering sound. Shan moved to the corner of the building just as Osman led two horses behind the nearest hut, one saddled, the other bearing a heavy load of crates with canvas lashed around them. Where was he going? To warn his family? To make a suicidal dash across the border? He studied the others, nearly all mounted now. They looked more like a raiding party than a band of refugees.

A gust from the east blew a sound toward him. He turned and saw that Jakli was standing now, waving at someone. It was a mounted man, trotting briskly toward the north of the compound, toward the heart of the endless desert. Shan caught movement out of the corner of his eye. Osman appeared, nodding toward Marco. Shan swung his head back toward the rider. It was Deacon. The American was trotting alone into the desert, leading the pack horse.

Shan quickly walked to the hut the American had been using. Two men were in front of it, shoveling sand against a barrier of sunbleached planks that had been set against the entrance, which itself was now blocked by a heavy beam, arranged to look like it had dropped from the roof. The hut was being transformed back into a ruin.

Shan paced around the building. It had no other opening, except a small chink in the wall at ground level where, he surmised, the conduit for the solar panels had run to the batteries. As he stared at the hole one of the men threw a shovelful of sand to cover it. No, Shan almost protested, there are singers inside. Old Ironlegs had to be fed. But in the same instant he knew somehow that Deacon had taken the crickets with him. In the few minutes Shan had spent with him he had sensed that there were few things more important to Deacon than the date he had with his son, Micah, the rendezvous to sit with their singers under the full moon.

But was the other thing still inside? The appendage, the human leg. What had the American been doing with it? Dissecting it? Gloating over it? Whose leg had it been? Shan realized that perhaps it had not been as old as it first appeared. This was the desert, where things became desiccated almost overnight. Perhaps it had been someone who had died recently. Perhaps Deacon was doing his own detective work. Only then did he remember Bajys's words about his desperate search at Karachuk. About how he had found pieces of people, like in the paintings of demons.

Shan saw that all of the huts in the hollow had been reduced to apparent ruins by the addition of sand and ancient planks to blend in with the rest of Karachuk. As he watched the evacuation sadness flooded through him again. He had been mistaken, of course, to think he had arrived in another world. This was the same world, the world of knobs and bloodstained Buddhas.

He felt a sense of loss, a sense of defeat, as he absorbed the news of Sui's murder. It meant he would be unable to travel anywhere, that everyone, including the murderer, would drop into holes, doing their best to disappear for what could be weeks, even months.

Marco was with the silver camel at Osman's door when Shan rounded the corner of the building. Shan had not really studied the animal before, but as he looked at her he realized she was unlike any of the creatures he had yet seen in Xinjiang. Her eyes were bright with intelligence, her hair lustrous. Her head was bent to one side as she looked back at him, as though cocked in curiosity. To his surprise he saw that her left ear was pierced with a small, elegant silver ring.

Shan stepped forward as Marco hoisted a simple wood-frame saddle between the animal's humps. The camel bent her head still further, then pushed her nose into Shan's hands and licked them.

Marco stared at her uncertainly. "Sophie! You harlot!" he barked and scratched the camel between the ears. "She doesn't do that," he said with a puzzled expression. "Only for family. For me and Nikki. And Jakli," he added.

"She's handsome."

Marco hugged the camel. "She's beautiful. Like a beautiful woman. The Emir of Bukhara," he said, referring to the ruler of one of the ancient walled cities of central Asia, "had a stable of two hundred racing camels until the Bolsheviks laid siege to his city. For three years the Emir fought from the city walls. The Bolsheviks built a damned railroad right up to the walls while he watched helplessly. Had to feed most of his camels to his troops. But when the Bolshevik troop trains began arriving, he made the bastards promise safe conduct for the surviving twenty camels and their grooms before his surrender. He refused to let the invaders in until he saw the camels were free. Sophie came from one of those survivors."

Shan dared to put his hand on the camel's neck. Sophie pushed against him as though asking for him to rub it. He did so. "I thought Karachuk was safe."

Osman carried out two large pannier baskets stuffed with smaller boxes and bundles wrapped in cloth. "The safest of places," Marco agreed. "Next to my home. Which is why we won't risk it. Knobs never venture this far onto the sand. But when this kind of trouble hits they call in helicopters. They see us down here and—" He shrugged and looked at Osman. "Then no more week-long chess games, right, old friend?" He stepped to a smaller camel standing behind Sophie and helped Osman tie the baskets to her pack frame.

Jakli appeared behind Sophie, looking worn and fretful. She was carrying Shan's drawstring bag.

"You need to go home, Chinese," Marco said.

"I have no home."

"All right, Back to Tibet."

"I am not finished."

"Sure you are. The knobs are finishing it." Marco seemed to see the determination in Shan's eyes. "The hornet's nest has opened up. You don't want to push another stick up it."

"I cannot stop unless asked by those who sent me here," Shan said quietly.

Marco shook his head. "They don't know this land. You don't know this land." He looked past Sophie's neck toward the desert. "It's the way it has always been. Like a tide on the great sea, the beast comes. People build a good life around a herd, an oasis, a small valley in the mountains. Every few years it is swept away. They know it. They come to expect it. Long ago, when Karachuk was fertile, sometimes locusts came and ate everything green for a thousand miles. Sometimes, before the desert finally consumed everything forever, it was a giant sandstorm, a karaburan, the kind that can blow for days and destroys anything softer than a stone. Sometimes it's an army. The Mongols invaded. The Chinese invaded. The Persians invaded. They say the Romans invaded once. If you believe all the stories, even an army of tigers invaded, ridden by monkeys." He looked back at his knots, gave them a final tug and unwound Sophie's reins from her neck.

"Monkeys on tigers, knobs on tanks, it's all the same. If you want to live and keep those important to you alive, you fade away. Become invisible. Go underground. Go to the high mountains. Just get out of the path of the beast."

Shan well knew the beast Marco referred to. He had been swallowed into its belly for over three years. "The beast doesn't always have to win," he said stubbornly. Jakli was near him now, looking anxious to be gone.

Marco stared soberly at Shan. "That," he said after a moment, "depends on how you define winning." He turned and nuzzled his face into the thick hair on Sophie's forehead, as if consulting the animal. "Look, Comrade Inspector," he said, lifting his head, "Jakli says you have no papers at all. Let her take you back to shelter. Wait a week or two at least. Go to Red Stone clan. Count the sheep."

Shan did not move, did not take his eyes off Marco. "Red Stone has enough troubles of their own."

The Eluosi frowned and shifted his gaze to Jakli. He stroked his beard and glanced at Osman, as though remembering the innkeeper's warning about the coal mine prisons. "You have to hide, girl. Come with me. Don't get taken now, not so close to the festival."

Jakli smiled and, standing on her toes, kissed Marco on his cheek. "I'm staying with Shan," she declared brightly. "I made a promise to Lau."

But you also made a promise to Nikki, Shan almost said, then he looked into her eyes and realized it wasn't simply defiance he saw there. She had made a vow not just to Lau but to herself. She had to find justice for Lau before she was married.

Marco stepped back, rubbing his hand on his cheek where she had kissed him. The boisterous Eluosi seemed at a loss for words. "Damn it," he muttered, "then take him to Senge Drak," he said to Jakli. "Shan's their problem, not ours."

"Senge Drak?" Shan asked, looking to Jakli.

"In the Kunlun," Marco said, and paused with a meaningful look at Jakli. "Whoever killed Sui could be there," he said to her in a quizzical tone, as if the thought had just occurred to him. He turned back to Shan. "You want to stop the beast? Then take Sui's killer to the knobs."

The whinny of a horse interrupted Marco. They turned to see the remaining men of the compound mounted and moving in single file up the path that Shan and Jakli had taken the day before. The riders at the top of the column had stopped and were waving.

As if understanding the distant gesture, Sophie knelt in the sand for Marco to mount. The instant he was in the saddle she leapt forward at a trot. An energetic laugh escaped the Eluosi. "May the god of all creatures watch over you, Chinese," he called out. "Since I cannot." In a few seconds he was at the head of the column.

A strange emotion surged through Shan as he watched the line of riders and pack animals file out of the compound. It was a sight out of the past, out of the Silk Road, out of Karachuk as she was meant to be. A caravan of adventurers heading toward dangers known and unknown.

Jakli steered in a new direction as she drove the truck away from the ruined city, straight south, toward the high peaks that were the walls of Tibet. Toward the edge of beyond. Shan watched the barren landscape, fading in and out of wakefulness as the truck rocked along another riverbed. After an hour Jakli stopped in a grove of willows and poplars by the Kashgar highway and asked him to climb out to confirm that no other vehicles were in sight. He waved her across, and they followed another streambed for a mile until, with a lurch of speed, Jakli shot over the bank and onto a track just wide enough to accommodate the truck.

Shan studied the map on the seat. "It's not far to Glory Camp," he observed.

"Too risky for that again," Jakli said, shaking her head. "Not with knobs watching. Not after what Xu did with you."

"There were sheep on the hills over the camp," he said, and explained what he wanted to do.

Jakli sighed and stopped to study the map again. Half an hour later they had parked in a clump of trees and were climbing over a low ridge that ran along the east side of the rice camp. Halfway up, Jakli stopped him with a hand on his shoulder, then whistled sharply. Thirty seconds later a huge dog appeared above them, followed by a man whose face showed no sign of welcome. They approached the man, who acknowledged them with a conspicuous frown, then bent over the dog and ordered it away with a low command.

The shepherd pulled a pair of high-powered binoculars from his neck and handed them to Jakli, then spun about and led them up the trail. As they passed under a large poplar tree near the crest of the ridge, the man muttered a word of the Turkic tongue, and the same word was called back from above. Shan looked up to see a second man perched with another set of binoculars. They weren't shepherds. They were Maos.

Jakli handed the glasses to Shan as Glory Camp came into view and motioned him into the shadows of a large shrub. Nothing unusual was happening yet, Shan heard the man report to Jakli as he surveyed the compound. No more truckloads of detainees. The prisoners were in class. The grounds were empty. The building with the holding cells appeared quiet.

"Nothing," the man repeated impatiently to Shan's back.

But there was something. At the flagpole in the center of the compound, a grey shape that could have been mistaken for a rock. He pointed at it.

"Him?" the Mao asked. "Been there all day. You think he's suffering? He's not suffering."

Shan extended the binoculars to Jakli. Was the man being punished? he wondered. Had he chosen to sit for hours in the sun and wind?

"It's nobody," the Mao said. "You couldn't recognize anyone from here anyway," he added and stepped away.

But Shan did recognize the man.

After ten feet the Mao turned. "You can't break them out," he called in a surly tone. "People get killed trying to break out," he warned and continued down the trail.

"I don't understand," Jakli said. "You know him?"

"You didn't know he spoke Tibetan, did you? You didn't know he used the cave."

She leaned forward with the binoculars, trying to see the man better.

"When he stood that day, did you see how tall he was?"

She lowered the glasses and searched his face, then drew in a sharp breath. "The waterkeeper," she gasped. Her lower lip went between her teeth and she raised the binoculars once again. "All those times," she whispered. "I could have asked for a blessing."

He looked at her, worried.

They walked back in silence and drove away.

As they climbed the long gravel-strewn slopes that led to the mountains, Jakli's mood lightened, and she spoke of familiar sights, pointing out where her clan had once camped, where she had once rescued a stranded lamb, where Lau had once shown her a nest of pikas. Once she stopped and pointed, almost breathless, toward movement on a hill in the distance. A small herd of wild horses. She climbed out and called something in the tongue of her clan, words lost in the wind. A horse prayer, she explained with a sheepish grin when she returned, to keep them from the Brigade.

They reached another road, which she eased onto warily, her eyes restlessly watching for approaching traffic, then slowly began climbing toward the snow-capped peaks as Shan continued to fade in and out of wakefulness. Once he awoke and the truck was stopped at the base of a huge grey cliff, with a meadow of asters on the opposite side of the road. Jakli was kneeling at the roadside, looking up at the tree-topped cliffs, holding a handful of flowers. He watched as she bowed her head and laid the flowers at the base of the cliff. When she returned he pretended to be still sleeping.

He faded back into slumber, and when he awoke it was late afternoon. They were driving in an unfamiliar landscape, amid mountains framed by a sky of deepening purple. He studied the ways the mountains folded into high mysterious valleys, the crags that spun upward as though they were giant hands pointing to heaven. He opened the window and tasted the chill rarefied air, fresh from icefields above. His memory did not know the terrain but his heart recognized it.

"How long have we been in Tibet?" he asked Jakli.

"The border isn't well defined here. Maybe five, ten miles ago."

"You must be exhausted. Let me drive."

"You don't know the way. Not much further."

They topped a high ridge and slowed to gaze on its fifty-mile view of the changtang plateau. In the far distance a large brown shape shifted and flowed across the grassland, a herd of wild animals. Antelopes perhaps, or even *kiangs*, the fleet mulelike creatures that still roamed the plateau. A few minutes later Jakli stopped the truck and stepped out into the wind. "I haven't been here in four years," she said. "There are no maps for it. Do you see it?"

"I've never been there," Shan said, and he turned to look toward the north. A pang of guilt swept through him. He had left the waterkeeper, and the zheli children, and Gendun.

"Senge Drak," Jakli explained. "It means *lion rock*. Shaped like a lion."

They studied the surrounding peaks, then climbed back inside, and Jakli eased the truck onto a narrow track that mounted the next ridge in a long, low ascent. At the top she stopped again and pointed. The mountain they were climbing unfolded to the south in a long U shape. They had reached the center of the ridge and were facing the opposite arm, a long bare ridge that ended in a huge cliff with the contours of a face. On top of the face were two outcroppings that might have been ears. Far below a small ridge jutted along the edge of the base, giving the appearance of a leg at rest.

In another hundred yards the track ended and Jakli parked the truck under a huge overhanging rock. Together they covered the truck with a dirty grey canvas she found in the cargo bay and began walking along the narrow goat path that traversed the steep slope. After a few steps she stopped and threw a pebble into the shadow of a second overhang. The pebble bounced back with a metallic clank.

A second truck had been hidden at the head of the path.

Shan detected a subtle pattern of shadows on the face of the cliff as they approached it. Not all the shadows were just clefts in the rock, some were openings, portals that had been cut out of the cliff face. The Lion Rock, Shan realized, was an ancient fortress, one of the *dzong* that once guarded Tibet. The dzong had been built into the formation, utilizing the lines of the towering rock to blend with the mountain, which commanded a view far out into the changtang and the pass through the Kunlun.

"It was so far away from the heart of Tibet that the government overlooked it," Jakli explained. "Or maybe the PLA just didn't think it worth bothering with. Couldn't be bombed from the air like most of the dzong. And it had been abandoned for centuries. No invaders would come from this direction. No meaningful armed resistance could be mounted from it. It doesn't stand in the way of anything."

They hiked to the end of the path as the remaining daylight quickly faded. Jakli paused to gaze at the last blush of crimson to the west, as if sending a silent prayer that way, then led Shan into a darker patch of shadow that was the entrance to the dzong. Following the dim light of butter lamps, placed at long intervals along an entry corridor, they arrived at a narrow door of heavy hand-hewn timber. As Jakli pushed it open, its iron hinges groaned loudly.

"Their alarm system," she said as she bent and led Shan through the door. Not just an alarm system, Shan saw, as he studied the door. It was so low that most of those entering would need to bow their heads, exposing their necks to a defender's blow, and so narrow that no more than one intruder could enter at a time. In an age when soldiers fought with swords and arrows, one or two defenders could hold off a small army at such an entrance. Jakli put a restraining hand on his arm after two steps. They would wait in the room.

The empty chamber was perhaps forty feet wide, the far side lit by a dozen butter lamps on a long table of handhewn timbers. To the right the wall sloped with the natural curve of the rock, as if the room had once been a natural cave that had been expanded. The wall beyond the table was hung with old carpets, which were slowly moving. From the draft that flickered the lamps Shan surmised that the carpets covered openings to the outside, the portals he had seen from the path.

He walked slowly along the hanging carpets. Some weren't just carpets, he discovered, they were thangkas depicting scenes of life in a monastery. The hangings by the portals were nearly threadbare, eroded by the wind. In one space a simple black felt blanket had been hung. Suddenly the hairs on Shan's neck moved. Someone was watching, from the other end of the room. Seeing nothing but shadow he lifted a lamp and ventured toward the darkness.

After five steps he froze. Two huge unblinking eyes stared back at him, level with his own. The serene head of the figure was slightly cocked, as if in inquiry, and one of its hands clutched a bell. It was a seated Buddha, carved so as to appear to be rising out of the living rock, so that although the head was nearly complete in circumference, at the bottom, where its legs were folded into the robe, the remarkable Buddha was little more than a bas-relief.

As he approached he saw that the rock on which the Buddha sat had been sculpted to simulate an altar, on which the figure seemed to be resting. On either side large niches were carved to receive offerings, their tops coated with the black soot of torma offerings, the butter figures that were burned on festival days.

Jakli stepped past him and placed a lamp in one of the niches. "The soldiers who built this place," she explained, "they were from the Tibetan empire period. Warrior monks. Sometimes they fought under the same lamas who led them in worship. We found an old writing about life at Senge Drak." She raised her hand to the head of the Buddha as she spoke, not touching it but following the gentle contours of its face with her fingers. "The monks were fabulous archers. They would not practice like others by shooting birds or deer or other living creatures, for they believed in the sanctity of life. So the archers would stand at the open portals and their teachers would drop paper birds into the wind for them to shoot."

"If all armies were like that," a familiar voice added, "war would be obsolete."

Shan turned. It was Lokesh, wearing his crooked grin. His eyes twinkled and he stepped forward to embrace Shan.

"But not every army shoots only paper birds," said another figure, emerging from the shadows as he spoke. Jowa. He seemed less happy to see Shan.

Lokesh winced, as though disappointed at Jowa for intruding.

"Are they here?" Jakli asked abruptly. "Did they come to celebrate while everyone pays the penalty down below?"

Jowa looked at her in confusion and seemed about to ask her a question when another figure emerged from the shadows. It was Fat Mao. Jakli bolted across the room, launching into a tirade in their Turkic tongue, raising her hands, not to strike him but to pound the air in front of the startled Uighur.

"Sui was a son of a bitch working for a bigger son of a bitch," Fat Mao said in Mandarin, and stepped closer to Shan and Jowa, as if he needed protection. Shan studied the Uighur. He seemed exhausted, and his clothes were soiled and torn in places. He had been traveling too. Perhaps fleeing. "He deserved to die. But I didn't kill him."

"Maybe not you," Jakli snapped, "but the other Maos. At the worst possible time. You're not warriors, you're just predators. Make a kill and run away. Let everyone else pay for it—" Her voice choked with emotion.

"It was not a Mao," Fat Mao insisted.

"You don't know that," Jakli shot back.

"I know it," the Uighur said. "If it happens in Yoktian County, I know it. Sui was being watched, whenever possible. But no one—no one of us—killed him. I know what you think. The knobs will think the same thing."

"Saving Red Stone clan. Finding Lau's killer, the killer of the children—" She stopped as if about to add to the list, but did not. "Impossible now."

Was that why? Shan wondered. Had someone killed Sui to distract the knobs from something, or, knowing how the knobs would react, to keep their little group from proceeding with their own investigation of Lau's disappearance?

Someone else stirred in the darkness. A short, slender figure appeared, carrying bowls on a wooden plank. *"Jah,"* he announced in Tibetan. Tea. It was Bajys. Not the terrified, ranting Bajys, but another Bajys, or the beginning of another Bajys, for he still had the hollowness, the emptiness in his face that Shan had seen at Lau's cave. As Shan accepted the bowl from Bajys, he saw that the man's hand was steady, but there was a tremble in his eyes.

Jowa took a bowl and sat on the table, away from them, drawing a paper from his pocket to read, as if uninterested in further conversation.

Shan felt a tug at his sleeve. "The Maos must know something, if you were watching Sui," he said to Fat Mao. He turned and saw Lokesh beside him, pulling his sleeve, urging him toward the shadows.

"The first man to find the body was a Uighur truck driver," Fat Mao explained. "Driving alone with a load of wool for Kashgar. Sui's body was propped up against a rock at the side of the road."

"The killer made no attempt to hide it?"

"More like an attempt to make it conspicuous. The trucker saw him clearly in his headlights, thought he was sick or hurt, so he stopped. But Sui was shot through his heart. Twice. A quick death."

"You mean the body was arranged afterward."

"Exactly. In the sand beside the body a finger had written *lung ma*. No way Sui wrote it. He would have dropped like a stone."

"The knobs found him like that?"

"Not like that," Mao said. "The driver wasn't sure what to do, wasn't sure who Sui was."

"Sui was a knob. Everyone knows the uniform."

Fat Mao shook his head. "Sui wasn't in uniform." He looked from Shan to Jakli, letting the words sink in. "But Sui had a pistol in his belt. And then the next person on the road helped."

"Someone who knew Sui?" Shan asked. He turned toward the shadows. Lokesh had disappeared.

"Someone who was looking for Sui. Who erased the words in the sand. A Mao. He was going to hide the body, but there was no time because of traffic coming on the highway. All he could do was put Sui behind some rocks."

"You mean a Mao was following Sui?" Shan asked.

The Uighur nodded. "One of us had been watching Sui

but lost him in Yoktian. Sui was to meet Prosecutor Xu at Glory Camp, so the follower drove in that direction."

Fat Mao stared at Jakli with a grim expression. Perhaps Xu had decided to meet Sui early, on the highway, to dispose of him for some reason.

"Sui's pistol," Shan asked, "what type?" The knob had died with his pistol in his belt, as though surprised by his killer.

"Not official. Small caliber, like a target gun."

"The size of the bullets used on Lau and Suwan, at the Red Stone camp," Shan sighed. Jakli sat down heavily at the table. "What happened? Why were you following Sui?"

"When the trucker understood who Sui was, he had no interest in staying. He drove away. After he spat on the body."

"Thank you," Shan murmured, "for that important detail."

Fat Mao shrugged. "We were watching because that's what we do, whenever we can. To warn people. To learn things." He pressed the heel of his hand against his temple. The Uighur's head was hurting, Shan realized. He wasn't used to the altitude.

"The Poverty Eradication Scheme," Jakli said. Her words brought a look of reproach from Fat Mao, but she did not stop. "Public Security is involved somehow. Sui came that day at the garage, when Ko was there for inventory."

"You mean Sui was working with the Brigade?" Shan asked.

The Uighur sat at the table, elbows on the table, and lowered his head into his hands.

"Probably," Jakli said. "Maybe just to make sure there's no dissension, make sure the clans get moved when they've been told to move, make sure no one evades the scheme."

"It was Sui who said the Brigade was going to collect all the wild horses," Shan reminded her.

Fat Mao raised his head. "Sui was following Director Ko," he announced.

"You mean, to Glory Camp?" Shan asked.

"I mean, to lots of places. For the past three weeks, at least. Like Ko was under suspicion by the Bureau." He pressed his hand to his temple again, then shifted on the bench and lay down upon it.

Shan looked about. Lokesh had not returned. Bajys had disappeared as well. He took a step into the shadows and discerned the outline of a doorway. He stepped through it into another tunnel, lit by small lamps. After thirty feet he stopped, confused by a new sensation. Not really a sensation, but a beginning of awareness, a glimmer of realization. He steadied himself with a hand on the rock wall, closed his eyes a moment, then suddenly opened them and began to run.

After a hundred feet, the corridor divided into two passages in front of a large wood pedestal holding a three-foot-high prayer wheel. Without hesitation Shan followed the left tunnel and came to a timbered door. The door was open far enough for him to see a square chamber of perhaps thirty feet to the side, softly lit by a ring of butter lamps in the center. It was a soft, silent room, lined entirely—floor, walls, and ceiling—with planks of fragrant wood. It was the kind of chamber built in temples to hold treasure. Shan stepped inside.

Lokesh was sitting near the lamps beside a man in a monk's robe, who was settled in the lotus position, his elbows on his knees, his fingers spread out to support his bowed head. Shan struggled to calm his racing heart. It was Gendun.

Shan joined the two Tibetans by the circle of light and sat silently, breathing in the scent of the old wood. He picked a flame and stared into it, seeking to focus himself, to cleanse his mind for Gendun. If what you selected was pure enough, absolute enough, you could immerse yourself in it; it could become your shield from distraction. Anything could work—a ball of mud, a drop of blood, a tiny heather flower—as long as it was pure.

"I met a hermit once," said a voice that drifted into his consciousness. "He claimed to have been reincarnated from a juniper tree. He said he could hear wood speak." The voice resonated in his heart and filled Shan with warmth. "He said we were all trees once in the past. I said I didn't think so, that I was still striving to become a cedar."

Shan blinked away from the flame and looked up to Gendun's broad smile.

The lama pressed his palms together over his heart in greeting, then stretched out his palms, forearms extended from his knees. It was his way of embracing Shan.

"Rinpoche," Shan said slowly. "We have come far from your mountain at Lhadrung."

"As long as I have a mountain to sit inside of," Gendun said, "there will be my home." His voice sounded like sand falling on a smooth rock.

Shan smiled. Gendun had meditated for so many years inside his rock hermitage that all those who knew him believed he could sense the life force of mountains.

"Have you been well?" he asked Shan.

"I have been confused."

Gendun smiled. "So have I, my friend." He fell silent again, but his smile did not fade as he looked from Shan to Lokesh.

"We thought those men took you that night," Shan said.

"The mountains here," Gendun said with a tone of wonder. "They have a different voice. Have you noticed? My eyes see them as a stranger, but in my heart I know them, from all those years ago."

Shan could only smile in reply. "Have you been here all these days, Rinpoche?" he asked after a moment.

"He left the truck when the Brigade stopped us," someone replied from behind him. Shan turned to see Jowa in the doorway.

"I came two days later," another voice said, and the youthful purba who had driven the truck away after they had met the Kazakhs appeared. The young Tibetan stepped past Jowa and into the room, his eyes wide as he looked at Gendun. "Just sitting right here, alone. He wouldn't leave."

Jowa lingered at the door, as if reluctant to approach the lama.

"How far, from where we stopped on the road?" Shan asked.

"Fifteen, maybe twenty miles." The young Tibetan shook his head. "But Senge Drak is secret," he said in a tone that suggested a question, as if asking Shan to explain it. "He had never been here. There were no trails from where he left the road."

Gendun gave no sign of having heard the conversation. He had already explained it to Shan. The mountains had their own voices.

Shan looked at Jowa, not the young Tibetan. Jowa looked not just tired, but uncomfortable, as if Gendun, one of the holy men he fought for, somehow intimidated the purba.

"We have told him about the second boy," Lokesh said in a suddenly somber tone.

Told him what? Shan wanted to blurt out. How would Lokesh have described Suwan's murder? Another young soul has gone beyond sorrow, perhaps.

But then Gendun spoke. "Have you come far?" he asked Shan.

Feels like far, Shan almost said, thinking of the grave at Red Stone, Lau's cave, the rice camp, and Karachuk. Feels like I've traveled a year in the last four days. "I met Auntie Lau," he offered.

"Do you like her so far?" Gendun asked with twinkling eyes.

"I think she honored all the worlds she lived in."

As Gendun nodded he slowly opened and shut his eyes.

"And I met an old waterkeeper."

Gendun nodded again and made a tiny flicker with his eyebrow. Shan recognized his question. "He is still in this life," Shan said. "In prison, but not suffering." His eyes moved from Gendun to the flame of the nearest lamp. "I am going to get him released."

Some things are not real until they are said out loud. Gendun looked at him, but not as intensely as Shan looked at himself. The words, though unexpected, though unintentional, rang like a bell. It took only a moment for Shan to realize, as some unconscious part of him already had, that in the miasma of people and events he had encountered since arriving in Xinjiang the only certainty was that the waterkeeper, the old lama with whom he had spent no more than two minutes, had to be freed from prison. And Shan was the only one who could do it, for only Shan understood.

The bell in his mind rang again. It grew louder. Not a bell, he realized, but the delicate tingling of *tsingha*, the small circular brass chimes used in Tibetan temples.

Bajys appeared at the door, smiling shyly while he rang the tsingha twice more, as if just for the pleasure of doing so. "There is food," he announced and turned back down the tunnel.

They followed the sound of the chimes down the hall to another large room cut into the living rock, nearly as large as the entry chamber, with similar portals opening to the sky. Shan realized they were on the opposite side of the cliff face now, the other side of the lion's head. The room was brightly lit with kerosene lanterns and butter lamps, and beside a timber table a brazier burned, fueled by large chips of yak dung. Fat Mao and Jakli were already at the table with another Tibetan, a large man with a heavily scarred face, who greeted Jowa and the young purba with a familiar nod. Shan looked back at Fat Mao. He had traveled hard that day, ever since Sui had died. But doubtlessly he had other, easier places to hide. He had rushed to Senge Drak to see the purbas.

Bajys waited until Gendun was seated at the center of the table, then retrieved a pot of barley porridge from the brazier. No one offered introductions.

As they ate, the three purbas and Fat Mao spoke in hushed tones about the death of Sui, and Shan explained the killing to Gendun.

"I am sorry a government man had to die. We must be hopeful for his soul," the lama said quietly.

Fat Mao reacted to the lama's words with an exaggerated wince. His gaze moved along the faces of the purbas as he shook his head, as though to express his frustration that they should have Gendun among them. "We should just be hopeful for all those who are going to suffer now. The innocents. The families. The old people. Hope they hide well. Hope the monster eats its fill quickly and moves on."

"The pain will come," Jowa agreed. "Which is why we are going home. When the jackal comes to eat the turtle, the turtle must go inside its shell. We must protect ourselves. We must protect Rinpoche."

The lama tilted his head toward Jowa. "I don't understand your word. Protect?"

"We can do more good alive, and free, in Lhadrung," Jowa said. "The danger will pass. If you wish to return when it is safe here again I promise I will bring you. In a month, maybe two."

Jakli pushed her bowl to the center of the table. "Somebody in the purbas or the Maos knows what happened to this knob Sui," she declared sharply. "There are only a few who would ever touch such a man. People move to the other side of the street when they see such a man approaching. They avert their eyes. Men like Sui are like the dragons that roamed the land in the lost ages, inflicting random terror. The people don't seek out dragons. There were only special soldiers, sanctified by priests, who fought dragons." She glanced at Shan. "Warrior monks. Only they dealt with dragons. And if in killing one dragon they provoked a whole nest of dragons they still stood between the dragons and the people."

A sneer rose on Fat Mao's face. "And who is fool enough to stand before these dragons? These are Beijing dragons. Cut off a head and two heads grow back."

"There is no magic weapon," Shan said in the silence that followed. "There is only the truth. Whoever killed Sui must accept responsibility for the action."

"You mean, go to the nest of dragons and be eaten," Fat Mao shot back.

"If that is what is necessary to protect the innocent."

Jowa stood with a sour expression and gestured for the other two purbas to join him. "We're leaving. All of us. My job is to keep us safe. All of us. That means all of us go back to Lhadrung. We're not going to die for someone else's fight. I fight for Tibet. I fight for Tibetans."

Gendun's eyes settled on Jowa. "It is only the chance of birth that made you Tibetan in this life," he said in a tentative tone, as if puzzled by the purba's words. "You may be Chinese in your next. You may have been Kazakh in your previous."

"It is enough, just to watch out for this life," Jowa said sharply, but as the words left his mouth regret was already in his eyes, as if he had forgotten whom he was addressing.

"Rinpoche," he added in a low, awkward voice. His hand went to the dagger at his belt, not in a threatening way, but self-consciously, as if to hide the weapon.

Gendun frowned. A fresh silence descended on the room. The lama stood and filled everyone's tea mug. He moved to Jowa, who still stood, and slowly lifted the purba's hand and placed it, palm open, over his own heart. Shan had seen it before, among the more orthodox Buddhists. It was how some lamas conveyed truth to a student.

"We do not struggle for Tibet or Xinjiang or for any other lines on a map. We do not struggle for Tibetans or for Kazakhs. We struggle for those who love the god within and for those who can learn to do so." Gendun withdrew his hand and looked into Jowa's determined eyes, then into Shan's and Jakli's. He moved across the room and stood near one of the portals, where the covering had been tied back, and faced the open sky, the wind rustling his robe.

"If I had killed a man like Sui," Jowa said to Gendun's back, a pleading tone in his voice, "I would not hide. I would give them my head proudly. But it was not me, and so I will not offer my head." He looked toward the floor. Despair passed over his face, then his eyes grew hard again. "We have to return to Lhadrung. There are other fights to wage. Fights we have a chance of winning." His eyes shifted toward Shan, then he looked back at Gendun and hesitantly pulled a paper from his pocket, the one he had been reading earlier.

"And you," Jowa said to Shan, with an expression that seemed to mix resentment and pride, "you have been rescued. You have an appointment at the Nepal border." He sighed loudly and waved the paper toward Shan. "A UN inspection team got permission for a quick tour of gompas south of Lhasa. We have a way to get you across with them when they leave, and they will take you from there." He unfolded the paper and extended it toward Shan.

"You won," Jowa continued, a trace of bitterness in his voice. "A chance in a million. But we have only eight days to get you there. Barely enough time to make it." He looked about the room, surveying the faces of the Maos and Jakli, then back to Shan. "No need to worry about other people's business now."

Shan gazed at his companions. Jakli was smiling brightly at him. Lokesh was nodding. "It is everything you need," the old Tibetan said. Gendun just smiled at him.

"Our truck is at the head of the path," Jowa explained. "There are barrels in the back, and blankets, like before. Everyone goes, including Bajys. When the moon rises we will all go to the truck and sleep there tonight, and we will begin before dawn." He drained his cup of tea and looked at Shan as he laid the paper on the table. "If we see any dragons on the path we will be sure to wake you," he added in a taunting voice. Jowa's companions joined in his laughter and followed him out of the room.

Gendun wandered into the shadows of the corridor, followed a moment later by Bajys. Shan poured more tea for Jakli and Lokesh.

"I had a teacher once," Lokesh said after a moment. "He didn't believe that the human incarnation was particularly important in the chain of existence. He said humans come and go, they throw off faces all the time, that the whole purpose of humans was to keep virtue alive, to be a vessel for virtue. He said that if you lived enough lives that way, you became virtue, and then you had a chance at true enlightenment."

Jakli, Shan, and Fat Mao sat in silence, considering his words. Certainly Lokesh was right about one thing, Shan thought. Humans were throwing off faces all the time. Somehow life seemed even cheaper in Yoktian county than in the gulag. Jakli picked up the paper and read it, then pushed it toward Shan, with wide, excited eyes. He scanned it quickly. It was true. Someone had put a new life together for him. He was to be reincarnated once more. There was a community of Chinese exiles in England who would welcome him. He was to live with a professor of Chinese history in Cambridge until he was settled. Eight days. It would take six days of hard travel to arrive at the appointed place near Nepal.

A low rumbling sound rose from the corridor. Shan recognized it immediately. The prayer wheel.

"Bajys," Lokesh explained. "That first night we came he was still incoherent, and he barely had the strength to walk. But then he saw the wheel and began turning it. He was crying at first, then laughing, and he kept turning it all night long." The old Tibetan's eyes were wide and bright, as though he were describing a miracle.

They listened to the rumble for several minutes without speaking. Maybe all would be right, if Bajys just kept turning the prayer wheel. Some of the old lamas might have said that Shan's work was indeed finished, because he had found someone to turn the wheel that had not spoken for centuries.

Finally Lokesh rose. "I must prepare Rinpoche's blankets for the truck," he said and left through the rear doorway.

Shan found Gendun in the room of fragrant wood.

"It is right that you come back with us," the lama said. "This was all a mistake. We didn't understand. We will go to Lhadrung together. We can watch the moon from the truck, like before, and you can go to your new life."

"I have only just begun here," Shan said woodenly. It was happening too fast.

The lama shook his head. "Even without the letter Jowa gave you, you should have gone back south. The thing that dwells below, it's like a cloud that covers a beautiful moon. I have no words for it, except death. But that is too simple a word. If you were lost, Shan, without your soul in balance . . ." He studied his clasped hands a moment, then looked up with wide eyes. "It would be worse than losing Lau."

"Because she was prepared?" Shan asked.

Gendun nodded.

"Not just prepared," Shan suggested. "She expected it. She expected to die for her secrets." Gendun turned his head toward Shan as if about to correct him. Shan exchanged a long silent look with the lama. "Not her secrets, really," Shan said. "Her faith. She was Tibetan, but not just Tibetan. I think she had religious training. I need to know for certain, Rinpoche."

"It seems you already know, my son."

Shan nodded slowly. "She was an *ani*, a Tibetan nun."

Shan heard a sound behind him, a small murmur of approval. Lokesh was there, and came forward to sit with them.

Gendun offered a sad smile. "Once she was a nun, but her convent was destroyed."

"I have known many monks who lost their gompas to Chinese bombs," Shan observed. "Some said, Without my gompa, I am no longer a monk. Others said being a monk had nothing to do with a building. An old monk in my prison said it best. I carry my gompa on my back. It's all about serving the inner god, he said, and no bombs can destroy the god within. I think Lau found a way to serve her inner god in Yoktian."

Gendun didn't just look at Shan. He seemed to be watching him, as if something important was happening to Shan.

"She lived a Kazakh life these past years and was buried in Kazakh clothing," Shan continued slowly, "But she asked to be laid to rest near the teaching room of the old lama who posed as the waterkeeper. She taught Jakli the old Tibetan ways. She helped the lama with his secret teaching."

There was another sound at the door and movement behind him. He did not turn as the figure sat beside him. He knew it was Jakli.

"We used to meet on festival days," Lokesh said in a faraway tone. "The monks from our gompa and those nuns. Lau came from a small sect, from a tiny gompa built near a glacier north of Shigatse. We would unfurl a giant thangka down the hillside—a hundred feet long, it was. There would be archery contests and acrobats who climbed to the top of huge poles to bring back prayers tacked to the top. The nuns would sing to us, and we would serve special tsampa we made with cardamom spice." As he extended his long bony hand, spotted with age, toward the lights, Jakli reached out and clasped it between her own, as if to thank Lokesh. Or perhaps comfort him. "Later," he said with a sigh, "people came and burnt her gompa." He began humming one of the old songs as they watched the flames of the lamps, then paused. "It was a long way she went," he added, "to die like that in the desert."

"Now they have sent another Tibetan to teach the orphans," Shan said.

"Is he not also in danger, then?" Gendun asked.

No, Shan started to say, because Kaju works for the

Brigade. "No," he said instead, "because the killer already found the orphans."

"You mean, at the camp of the Kazakh clan."

"And after that, the boy we buried by the road. First Lau, because Lau had to tell the killer about the orphans. Maybe," Shan said in a grim voice, "the killer is after all the orphans. The old Kazakh says it is a killer from the old days, returned to destroy the children of his enemies."

Lokesh shook his head, with a tiny, almost imperceptible motion. But Shan noticed.

"Or maybe he asked Lau about one boy, but then that boy was unexpected, was not right," Shan suggested. "The killer tore each boy's shirt open. He tore the pant leg. First with Suwan, then with Alta." He looked at Lokesh, still trying to understand. "He had gone for a boy at Red Stone camp, but the boy didn't have what he wanted. Maybe the killer was looking for something, perhaps something of Lau's that she had entrusted to an orphan. If he had found it, why would he go on to attack the second boy?"

"Maybe," Lokesh said slowly, "the children did something Lau, or her killer, never expected."

Shan looked at his old friend and nodded.

"If it is true, then maybe the demon isn't after all the children," Jakli said. "Just always the next one, until he finds what he needs. Or she," she added with a glance toward Shan.

They stared at the flames. A deep groan seemed to come from somewhere. It could have been the wind. It could have been the mountain, trying to make itself understood.

"You have the solved the mystery of Lau," Gendun said with a slow nod, looking back toward Jakli as he spoke. "That is enough, perhaps. To reveal Lau's secret teaching."

Jakli spoke Lau's name with a sound like a sigh and looked up with a nod. "Her path has been identified," she agreed. "Lau's truth can be told to those who were close to her, to close the circle of her life. She was a secret Buddhist. It should be enough to know that." Jakli looked at Shan and shrugged. "We know who is the enemy of secret Buddhists. I think it will be enough to persuade more herders to protect the zheli, to hide them for the winter at least." The demon was the government, she meant, and no one could stop the government. "It is all any of us can do," Jakli said to Shan, biting her lip as if she were in pain. "Now you can go on to your new life."

Gendun's eyes moved toward the floor and took on the distant look of deep meditation. Lokesh began counting his beads, appealing to the Compassionate Buddha.

The two Tibetans would not hear Shan even if he pressed on with the questions that burned on his tongue. Jakli too seemed lost in her own sort of trance, watching the two Tibetans so intensely she did not appear to notice when Shan rose. He picked up his lamp and wandered out, into the dark, silent corridors of Senge Drak. He longed to see all of the remarkable dzong and regretted that he had only a few hours to experience it. He passed down a long row of tiny rooms carved out of the rock, several with shreds of cloth hanging in front of them. Meditation chambers. He walked for over fifty yards without seeing an end to the rooms, and stopped, awed by the sheer number of the cells. Some fortresses had training grounds for their garrison. Senge Drak had meditation chambers.

He stepped to a cell that had most of its covering intact, slipped inside, and settled into the lotus position with the lamp at his side. He closed his eyes. He might not be able to speak with the mountain, but he could feel its serene power. The suspicion and fears, the possibilities swirled about his mind. He was more confused than ever. Everything was too unfocused. There were too many disconnected people, too many disconnected forces pulling him apart. Someone was going to rescue him, to give him a new life. Everything he needed, Lokesh had said. But that wasn't justice for Lau or her boys. Who would find her killer? Who would save the waterkeeper?

He put his hands in a mudra, the Diamond of the Mind. He had to explain things to Jakli and the Maos, but he did not understand them himself. He had to simplify, to focus on the simple explanations, for they were usually the right ones. Prosecutor Xu hated Tibetans. She was the likely one to have discovered that Lau was a Tibetan nun and, if so, was tracing any of the zheli with Tibetan roots. She or her enforcer had gone to the Red Stone camp and killed the first boy, who had been with Khitai. They said Khitai had no Tibetan roots, but they had said the same about Bajys. Or perhaps Khitai, who had been the first target when the killer had extracted information from Lau, was just a Kazakh boy who had the Tibetan thing that Gendun and Lokesh were so concerned about—Lau's treasure, the thing that now was being passed from orphan to orphan, one step ahead of the killer.

When he opened his eyes he noticed something in the corner, a long piece of coarsely woven woolen that might once have covered a meditation cushion. He lifted it and saw with a start that it covered an artifact of Senge Drak. It was a graceful bow, unstrung. Pulling the cloth entirely away, Shan found a small bowl of camphor wood, carved with intricate geometric designs. He lifted its top and found, lying in a neat curl, a bowstring, exactly as its owner had left it—when? A century ago? No. Jakli had said the dzong had been abandoned for centuries. Two or three hundred years, perhaps. He picked up the bow and laid it in his lap.

He retrieved the covered bowl. There were four rows of repeating designs, two on top, two on the bottom. He and his father had passed many hours exploring the Tao te Ching by using throwing sticks or dice to randomly identify verses. But their favorite method was finding patterns in their environment and reading the patterns to derive tetragrams, the four line combinations that, in the charts memorized by all students of the Tao, referenced one of the book's eighty-one chapters.

Shan counted by sixes along the top rows of tiny triangles. After the final set of six, three remained. Three was represented by a broken line of two parts in the system, the base of the tetragram. He drew the line in the dust of the floor with his finger. After counting the second row, comprised of tiny flowers, two remained, meaning a solid line for the next segment of the tetragram. The third row, of miniscule circles, added up to ninety-seven, leaving one, which in their improvised system meant another solid line. The last row of little squares yielded five at the end, for a line broken in thirds. The tetragram he had drawn in the dust was a line of three parts over a solid line, then a second solid line, over a final line of two parts. In the Tao te Ching chart the tetragram translated to fifty-six. He smiled sadly.

The verse had been inscribed on the door of the secret temple he had frequented in Beijing during the years when the government had kept temples closed. He recited it out loud, whispering it the way a warrior monk in the cell might have whispered his rosary.

Those who know do not speak
Those who speak do not know
Block the passages
Close the door
Blunt the sharpness
Untie the tangles
Harmonize with the brightness
Identify with the way of the world

Shan contemplated the aged bow a long time after he finished. Then, slowly, with a tremble in his hands, he unrolled the ancient bowstring and fitted it to the bow. Why weren't bows used in all meditation? he wondered. So perfectly flexible, so perfectly taut, so perfectly focused. He remembered a blizzard day in his prison when a lama had issued all the prisoners imaginary bows and had them shoot imaginary arrows for hours, until no one could tell if they were drawing the bow or the bow was drawing them. He drew the bow back and held it, reciting the Tao chapter again and again. He held it until it hurt, until he knew what he had to do, and longer, until the danger of the thing he had to do was out of his mind and the bow was drawing him. Then he closed his eyes and in his mind took aim at a paper bird.

CHAPTER 9

The truck bound for central Tibet departed when dawn was but a hint of grey on the horizon. One of the purbas sat on the hood with a small flashlight to avoid the telltale glare of headlights. Shan watched the truck from the rocks above as it coasted down the long slope, slowly climbed the next ridge, and disappeared into the vastness of the changtang, then slung his bag over his shoulder and starting walking.

He could tell from its birthing that the day was going to be clear and crisp, and he walked with vigor, his feet watching the path while his eyes watched the stars as they twinkled out. The air seemed to murmur, though he felt no wind. A nighthawk called. Something started in the rocks in front of him, fleeing with a clammer of small hooves.

In his mind he heard the Tao verse, as crisp as the call of the bird. Those who know do not speak. Those who speak do not know. Auntie Lau knew but she could no longer speak. Perhaps the dead American had known something, something about a broader conspiracy that was reaching into Yoktian. The dead boys could not speak, but sadly, he suspected they had known nothing at all about why they had died. The purbas and Maos were not shy of speaking, but their words were too often clouded with bitterness and hate.

As he walked with the sun rising over his right shoulder, he consulted the mental map he had made of the route Jakli had driven through the mountains. It was frustratingly short. He had slept too long in the truck the day before.

Where his map ended, he would just keep moving north, toward the haze of the desert.

He walked two hours to the main road, and it was another hour more before the first vehicle approached. He jumped behind a rock and watched as a minibus, its sides badly dented and scarred as though it had barely escaped an avalanche, passed. In its windows he saw sheep standing on the passenger seats. Half an hour later he was walking on a steep curve around a high rock wall when the sound of another motor echoed down the road. He wedged into a split in the wall and watched a small car, its engine sputtering and belching greasy smoke, roll past. He eased out of the opening as it disappeared and found himself in the path of a truck whose approach had been masked by the car. As it pulled to a stop he recognized the odd-looking vehicle.

He sighed, then sat on a rock and put his bag on his lap. Jakli turned off the engine, climbed out, and sat beside him without speaking. The wind began to blow. A few small cotton-bright clouds scudded across the peaks.

"Sometimes on special days like this," she said after a few moments, "when it's so clear and deep, like a lake in the sky, you hear things. Groans and rumbles, the sounds of the earth. When I was young my Tibetan grandfather said it was the sounds of the mountains growing."

They watched the clouds.

"I said if they would just grow high enough, maybe everyone would just leave us alone."

A small grey bird landed and looked at them. "Why won't they leave us alone?" Jakli asked the bird in a voice that suddenly seemed to have the fatigue of an aged woman. She offered Shan her water bottle. He drank and handed it back, watching the bird as it watched them.

"This road," she said, with a vague gesture around the curve, "it goes north, out of Tibet. Not to Nepal, just back to Xinjiang."

Shan nodded. "I have eight days to get to Nepal. I am going back to Xinjiang first," he said softly, not wanting to frighten the bird.

"You have two days," Jakli corrected him. "After that no truck could get you there in time."

"I'm not going far, just to Yoktian. To the office of Prosecutor Xu."

Jakli considered his news a long time, then sighed. "If you confess to the killing of Sui," she said matter-of-factly, "just to call off the knobs, then I will stand up in the town square and say you're lying. I'll say that I did it."

He offered a small grateful smile. "I would give up much to keep the knobs away," he said. "But I will not give up the truth." Shan had simply realized that of those who knew but would not speak, the Prosecutor and her files perhaps knew most of all. "If Xu had discovered that Lau was a Tibetan nun," he said, "it would explain much. Why she has reacted so severely, made so many arrests. It would mean a campaign not against her traditional targets, but against Tibetans. And it would mean Kaju, the new teacher, must be one of the agents working secretly."

"But even so, what could you do?"

"Find proof about Kaju and expose him. Then even if we can't find them the children will stay away from him. He'll have to leave."

They watched the clouds. The sun emerged and lit the nearest of the snow-capped peaks so brilliantly it hurt the eyes.

At last Jakli sighed. "Where you go," she said, pushing her windblown hair from her face, "I will take you. We will find a way for you to leave in two days."

"No. You have a job, making hats. If you can make it to the factory, it's the safest place for you."

"It's a town job. I don't like it. They didn't ask me if I wanted to work in the city. I served my time behind the wire. They can't imprison me in a town too." She stretched, pushing her hands toward the sky. "Besides, I *am* going to my factory for a while, if the patrols don't block us. Check in, make some hats, just for fun." She pulled the bag from her lap and rose.

"It's too dangerous for you," Shan said, realizing that he had heard Akzu use the same words with Jakli. "I don't want you involved anymore. Please. You have a new life planned."

Jakli seemed to find the words amusing. "I could say

the same about you," she said with a twinkle in her eye
and stepped to the truck.

He followed her reluctantly and climbed in the passenger
door. "If I write a letter," he said as the truck pulled away,
"could you get it delivered to Lokesh? I left my blankets
stuffed with sacks to fool the purbas. He was asleep under
his already."

"Sure," Jakli said agreeably. "Just write and give it to
me."

Shan retrieved his pad and opened it to a blank page.
"He has no address," he added. "The purbas will know
where he is."

"Actually, they don't. But I know the address. Kerriya
Shankou," she said.

"Kerriya Shankou?"

Jakli waved her hand toward the rugged windswept landscape. "This pass. Entrance to Xinjiang. Postal code is the
back seat."

Shan turned in confusion. The back seat was covered
with a tarpaulin. He raised one corner. Lokesh was underneath, sleeping.

"He said he hoped you wouldn't be disappointed in him,
that he was sorry to play a trick on you with his blankets.
Looks like you all played a trick on the purbas."

"What do you mean?" Shan asked, looking at his old
friend with a frustrated grin.

"They left in the dark, thinking all of you were under
the blankets as they had instructed. But when I rose after
dawn I heard someone outside, shutting the heavy door at
the top of the rock. There's a flat rock there called the
sentinel stone, between the lion's ears. I found Gendun on
it. An hour later Bajys walked in. Said he jumped out of
the truck because he discovered Gendun was missing."

"But Lokesh should stay with Gendun," Shan said.

"He said he has to go to the school in Yoktian. He said
he would walk all the way if he had to." Jakli kept her eyes
on the road but Shan saw her smile. "Said he didn't want
you involved anymore, that he felt better knowing you were
safe and going to your new life."

"Why the school?"

Jakli shrugged. "Because of Lau. Because of my friend

the Tibetan nun." She mouthed the last words slowly, as if getting used to their sound.

The Ministry of Justice office in Yoktian had been built to palatial dimensions. Indeed, Shan realized as he studied the two-story structure's tiled roof and balconies from a bench in the town square, it probably had been built as a palace, though early in the last century. He remembered the crescent moon flag he had seen in Osman's inn. Yoktian had been a regional capital in the Republic of Eastern Turkistan.

As he sat and waited he watched a team of municipal workers progress along the stucco wall that surrounded the Ministry building. The three men in blue coveralls were attacking a series of posters that appeared to have been recently glued to the large bulletin boards that hung on the face of the wall. Not a series of posters, he saw, but at least twenty of the same poster. It held the image of a red-haired woman with light skin and large round eyes. Along one side of the poster was a line of Chinese ideograms, along the other a matching line in the Turkic alphabet. *Niya Guzali*, the poster said. Then, below that, *Niya is our Mother*.

The crew was stripping the posters away. Where the poster hung tight, they unrolled and pasted another poster over it. *One Heart, Many Bodies*, it said in bold Chinese ideograms, with no Turkic counterpart, then *Achieve Success by Building Socialism with Chinese Characteristics*. One of the men, as he finished pasting a poster to the wall, looked nervously about, as if he feared something or someone in the crowd that milled about the square. Shan surveyed the square. With a chill his eyes settled on two grey uniforms, knobs holding automatic weapons standing on the far side of the square, watching the work crew. Or perhaps protecting the work crew.

Nowhere else had they seen knobs. No arrests were being made. There had been no roadblocks to finesse. No camps were being raided for undesirables. The seemingly inevitable reaction to Sui's murder had not come. Surely the body had been found. Scavengers would quickly draw attention to it. Sui had been going to see Prosecutor Xu. She would have been the first to miss him, the likely one to find the body. But she had not raised the alarm.

Someone else settled onto the bench, facing the opposite direction, and placed a plastic bag between them. "Shoes," the figure said in a loud whisper. Shan looked at him uncertainly. He wore a purple dopa, set back on his thick black hair, and two gold teeth gleamed from his mouth. "My name is Mao," the man said as though to explain. "It's clear," he added hurriedly. Jakli had promised to confirm whether the prosecutor's car was parked anywhere near the Ministry building.

Jakli had first driven to the edge of the town, parking outside a complex of windblown buildings made of corrugated metal. She had run inside, under a frayed banner that proclaimed *Hats for the Proletariat, Hats for the World*, then emerged a few minutes later with a white shirt and grey pants. He had quickly changed in the truck, but when she had arrived at the Ministry building she noticed his tattered shoes and complained that they would betray him. Depositing him on the bench, she had driven away. Now, twenty minutes later, new shoes had appeared. Shan eased his old shoes off, slipped on the black shoes from the bag and then, without looking back, walked across the street. He carried a thick envelope, the kind a case file might be carried in. Jakli had bought the envelope at the post office and stuffed it with a newspaper.

He walked into a large two-story entry hall, with a high vaulted ceiling pockmarked where pieces of plaster had fallen away. A graceful wooden stairway curled up one side of the hall toward a set of double doors crowned by an ornate plaster archway. On either side of the entry hall the lower walls were covered with painted murals of beaming proletarians. The paint was cracked and peeling, leaving many of the figures without faces, some without heads, but all their fists were intact, raised in salute to the red flag of the People's Republic. A brown beetle was crawling across the nearest of the murals.

The floor of the room had been spared revolutionary fervor. It was an intricate mosaic installed many years earlier, with scenes of horses and mountains and bowmen that, though cracked in places, was still beautiful. A desk sat at the base of the stairway, and from behind the desk a pair of legs protruded. A bald, middle-aged man lay on the floor, snoring, his head resting on a folded jacket. As Shan had expected, government decrees seeking to break the tradition of after-lunch napping would mean little so far from Beijing. It was the slowest part of the working day.

He moved up the stairs at a deliberate, businesslike pace and explored the empty corridor before entering the arched doors. Two lavatories. A janitor's closet. Two small meeting rooms, both empty. A door to a back stairway.

Pushing open the door under the arch, Shan entered a large square central chamber containing four desks for clerical workers, two on either side of a central aisle that led to an ornate wooden door. There were two smaller doors on either side of the square. Only one worker could be seen, a thin young woman sitting at one of the desks closest to the ornate door, looking at her reflection in a hand mirror as she held a tube of lipstick near her mouth. He quickly saw what he was looking for, a small sign by the first door on the left. Records.

He squared his feet between the first two desks and stood, arms akimbo, waiting for the woman to turn. She saw him first in the mirror and spun about, her face flushed. She trotted to his side and greeted him with a quick, deferential bow of her head. She was Han, with her hair in an elaborate braid down her back, and she wore a red blouse that appeared to be silk, over which a gold necklace hung. Three of her fingers were adorned with gold rings. Expensive ornaments for a government office worker.

"Someone," he said, trying to muster the smug, impatient voice of Beijing officialdom, "was supposed to be here to help. Is that you?" Gendun had told him that no one was ever totally rid of prior incarnations, that vestiges of them lurked invisibly in the background of the current one. It disturbed Shan that the voice came so readily, that the old incarnation seemed so near now. The lower life form from which he had evolved.

The woman looked at one of the side doors, where others, Shan suspected, lay napping. "The prosecutor is out," she said meekly.

"Meaning what? That inspectors from Beijing must just wait at her convenience?"

The woman's eyes widened at the mention of Beijing. "No—no! Of course not, comrade. I am sorry. I am just the prosecutor's secretary. I'm sure she would want someone to—but I'm not supposed to leave the office unattended."

Shan tapped the envelope in his hand impatiently. "I have no time to wait. Bring my tea to the records room."

The woman winced, then bowed her head and scurried toward a bench at one of the rear corners of the room where two large thermos jugs sat.

Shan decided he could risk no more than a quarter hour. He spent the first few minutes of them studying the system used for organizing the cabinets that lined three of the room's walls. A cabinet of papers with a label "Reports to Central," arranged chronologically, held what appeared to be monthly reports to Urumqi and Beijing, dating back several years. Most of the remaining file drawers were devoted to two other categories: "Citizen Reviews" and "Proceedings."

No file for Khitai. No file for Bajys, or Alta or Suwan. No file for Kaju Drogme. For Lau there was a half-inch-thick folder in the Citizen Reviews, the kind of background file that would be compiled for anyone in political office, even one as low as the Agricultural Council. He scanned it quickly, starting with the back, the earliest material. Most of it consisted of a standard form completed on the basis of interviews with Lau and a dozen acquaintances, signed by a Public Security case handler with a copy to Prosecutor Xu. He wrote the name of the case handler in the notepad from his pocket, then read the details. She had described herself as orphaned during what the handler called the "period of violent anarchy preceding assimilation," which Shan took to mean the arrival of the Chinese army, and had been assigned to an agricultural collective in the north, in the Ili Kazakh Prefecture. Her birth records had been lost in the fires that swept public buildings in 1963, during the "Period of Adjustment." Shan paused at the term. He had heard many labels of the bloodbath years of the Cultural Revolution, when he had lost his father and uncles, but this was a new one. Period of Adjustment. An image flashed through his mind of violent clockmakers sweeping the countryside, replacing gears in the back of people's skulls.

At the bottom of Lau's form was a list of questions, with boxes to be checked for yes or no. Did the subject serve a period of patriotic service in the People's Liberation Army? No. Does the subject regularly read publications of the Communist Party to stay informed of the progress of socialist thought? Yes. Has the subject been observed in practices of the religious minorities? No. Does the subject have relatives living outside the People's Republic? No. Identify the *cheng fen*, the class background, of the subject. Not verifiable, although no reason to refute subject's statement that her family worked as farm laborers, it said. Farm laborers were the most revered of class categories. Lau had understood her audience. There was a brief memo near the top of the file, dated only three months before. It was written by Prosecutor Xu to Lieutenant Sui of the Public Security Office:

> *I attach no importance to the absence of comprehensive registration files for Comrade Lau. Comrade Lau like many of us merely suffers from the disarray in government administration that plagued Xinjiang until recent years. Her records for the past decade are complete and have been verified. Where records do not exist, our long practice has been to conduct ad hoc verification of political reliability, which was done in her case. Additional verification will be conducted pursuant to the procedures of this office. There is no basis for the suggestion that she be reclassified as a cultural agitator.*

Shan read the memo twice. The words were plain enough, but what was important was what was not written. What the memo meant was that Sui had questioned Lau's reliability, not long after Lau had learned she was being dismissed from her Agricultural Council post. Someone had sent information against Lau to Public Security, information that might suggest she should be politically reexamined, possibly be reclassified as an undesirable, not a criminal but sufficiently suspect to be barred from a position of trust. And Xu had decided to intervene, to defend Lau. The prosecutor seemed to have no suspicions about Lau. He read the memo once more. Sui was suggesting that Lau should be confronted politically, and Xu was saying no, as if perhaps she had some other purpose for the hidden nun, some other goal that Sui was interfering with. There were no records beyond the ten years during which she had lived in Yoktian County. The murdered boys had been approximately ten years old. Could Lau's entire existence in Yoktian have been planned as a cover for raising the orphans? Or at least certain orphans? The memo had been copied to someone named Bao Kangmei. He had heard the name before. The warehouse at Glory Camp had been closed by order of Major Bao, who must be Sui's superior officer. He read the last last two sentences once more. They read like a reproach, as if Xu was chastizing the knob officer.

The last entry in the file was a copy of another form, captioned "Report on Missing Person," signed by Prosecutor Xu Li, and showing that a facsimile of it had been sent to the same Bao Kangmei. Shan quickly scanned the form. The first report of Lau's absence had come from the school, then soon thereafter her horse had been found wandering along the river trail, and her jacket had been found in the river. Only the last paragraph had new information. Lau's identity papers had been turned in by a citizen to Lieutenant Sui, who personally verified that they had been found in the mud on the riverbank near town. Sui had questioned Lau's political reliability, then had become involved in the investigation of Lau's disappearance.

He paused, then searched again for a file on Kaju. Nothing. He pulled the folder on Wangtu. Ten pages long, filled with routine entries. He dug deeper into the Citizen files. There was a file for Akzu, thicker than that for Lau. An ink stamp had been used on the cover. *Cultural Agitator,* it said in red ink. He scanned the file. It told the story of a peasant landowner who, like thousands of others, had been stripped of his property, then gradually rehabilitated. A memo dated six months earlier reported that Akzu had been singled out in a criticism session for failing to produce his clan's quota of wool. An agricultural expert had even testified that Akzu's stubborn adherence to outdated production techniques deprived society of valuable meat and wool. The most recent entry, dated a month earlier, was a memorandum from Brigade headquarters in Urumqi listing over fifty names of Kazakhs slated to go to a special year-long political education program upon implementation of the Poverty Reduction Scheme. Shan found Akzu's name halfway down the list.

He returned the file and stood sipping the tea that the nervous secretary had delivered to him. He had hoped for more, but what? A file on an anonymous American executed at Glory Camp? He opened the drawer on Citizen Reviews and found, to his surprise, one marked simply *Mei guo ren*. Americans. Inside were half a dozen memos from the prosecutor, all of them short, formal approvals for travel plans for American tourist groups. No, he saw, one was not a tourist group but a scientific delegation. Two years earlier a group of American archaeologists and anthropologists had come to the region under the wing of the Museum of Antiquities in Urumqi. There was a list of names and credentials attached to the memo, as well as a handful of photographs. Nothing that could be linked to the young blond American he had seen at Glory Camp. Shan recognized one name. Deacon. But it was a woman, Abigail Deacon, from Oklahoma, author of a book on ancient textiles. The files on the Americans ended with a date one year earlier. Stapled to the front cover was a stern note from the Public Security Bureau ordering that all reports on Americans henceforth be forwarded, without retention of copies, to Bao Kangmei.

He pulled another file, under Proceedings, for Jakli. There was a strip of yellow tape affixed to the edge of the file so it could be flagged easily when searching the drawer. There were other strips of yellow tape, not many. He quickly checked several. One was for a man who had been sentenced to life imprisonment for assaulting a birth inspector and who had escaped the year before. Another was for a man convicted and sentenced to ten years' lao gai for conducting a Lui Si remembrance ceremony. Lui Si, Six Four, was a reference to the 1989 disturbance in Tiananmen Square which occured on June 4. The yellow tape meant criminals with particularly dangerous politics.

He looked back at Jakli's file. It held copies of school files reporting classroom disciplinary infractions. A long report had been written by a political officer indicating that she had been a model student and targeted for communist youth camp. But then at age twelve that had changed. At age twelve, the officer wrote, she had come under the influence of reactionary culturalists. Meaning Kazakh sheepherders. When Jakli was twelve, Shan recalled, the army had shot her horse. The story ended two years earlier. No copy of Lau's letter to the prosecutor. He looked at the label again. *Part One of Two*, someone had scrawled on the file cover. But part two was not in the drawer. He looked on the table where a few files awaited refiling, then the Citizen Records in case it had been misfiled. Nothing. Someone else was interested in Jakli's current file.

Quickly he searched for one more file in the Citizen Reviews. Marco Myagov. Nothing. Then at the end of a drawer he saw a red-marked file, just labeled *Eluosi*. Six pages dealt with others, a form for each man and woman mentioned, rejecting requests for external passports. The remainder of the half-inch file was on Marco. Several applications for internal travel and work permits. He read the first one, dated nearly sixteen years earlier. Marco had applied for his young son and himself to travel north to Yining, to see an uncle who was dying. A large red stamp had been affixed to the front. Denied. Another, six months later, to attend the funeral. Denied. And another, to investigate a special school for his son. Denied. Request for a work permit. Denied. A dozen more requests, for a variety of reasons, all denied. The last was dated over ten years before. After that the material was all reports from Public Security suggesting his political unreliability, even suggesting smuggling activity. But nowhere was there mention of Marco being sentenced, not even to a rice camp, or any suggestion of hard evidence against the man. Shan moved to the most recent entry, a memo from Lieutenant Sui, copied to Prosecutor Xu. Interviews suggested Marco had organized one of the caravans that were still used to supply the high mountain villages at the top of the Kunlun and beyond, in Aksai Chin. Aksai Chin. Shan stared at the words. It was the disputed border zone, a barren, windswept territory claimed by both India and China, although controlled by the Chinese military. But Marco's caravan had gone out with eight riders, an informer reported, and returned with only four riders.

Shan quickly finished his notes and opened the door. The nervous secretary was at the nearest desk now, working at a computer console. A young man with the look of a soldier, though dressed in a business suit, sat at another desk reading a magazine. A bald man stood by the wall with a cup of tea, the man Shan had seen sleeping in the lobby. Shan hesitated, then pulled his notepad out and wrote on a clean sheet the name of Kaju Drogme. He stepped to the console and bent over the shoulder of the secretary, showing her the name. "I need to know who this man works for," he said.

The woman's face flushed, and her eyes flickered toward the man at the adjacent desk. "From the Brigade," she said in a self-conscious whisper. "Urumqi, I think. But here, it is Ko he reports to. Ko Yonghong." She looked up with a new air of self-importance. "Everyone knows Ko. He gives me rides in his new red car, one without a top. You know, like on American television."

Suddenly the arched outer doors burst open and Prosecutor Xu appeared, framed in the doorway. Shan bent lower, trying to hide his face behind the computer monitor. "Loshi," Xu called out as she stepped toward the secretary. "I need—" She stopped in midsentence. She had seen Shan.

He slowly straightened. She stared at him coldly, then looked at the young man at the desk, who had dropped his magazine and stood, suddenly alert, watching Shan with a predator's eyes. Shan realized he had seen the man before, driving the prosecutor's car at the motor pool.

"Thank you, Miss Loshi," Shan said. He returned the stare of the man he took to be the prosecutor's enforcer without blinking, then waited as Xu stepped toward the heavy wooden door at the rear and held it open. He turned and silently marched into the prosecutor's office. Xu stood aside to let him enter, stepped to Loshi's desk, and asked a question Shan could not hear. Loshi raised a sheet of paper to her chin, like a shield, as she nervously responded, then Xu returned to her office, closing the door behind her.

The room had been built as a sleeping chamber. Prosecutor Xu's desk was on a short platform that rose out of the rear center of the mosaic floor, extending in a broad rectangle to the back wood-paneled wall, just the size for a large bed. Several chairs were arranged in a semicircle on the platform in front of the desk. Not exactly a desk, Shan saw, but a heavy table of dark wood, its edges carved with the shapes of birds and flowers, similar to the designs on the floor. Another artifact of the building's past, the kind of remnant that would have been thrown onto a bonfire years earlier if it had been found in the eastern cities. Shan settled into the center chair.

Xu sat at her table and folded her hands in front of her. "Not even an inspector from Beijing has the right to use my office without my permission," she growled.

"Your office, Comrade Prosecutor, belongs to the Ministry of Justice," Shan said, surprised again at how easily the words rolled off his tongue. Not surprised, he thought after a moment, but frightened, that the old Shan, the one-time Inspector General of the Ministry of Economy, lurked so close. He clenched his jaw and tapped the envelope. "Ministry representatives are always entitled to access if they are looking for corruption, say, or abuse of office."

The words had the desired effect, silencing Xu for a moment. Shan had little hope of defusing her anger, but he might deflect it, might at least stall it on the chance, however improbable, that an escape presented itself. And if he could not escape, he might use her arrogance to at least get her to admit what she knew about the killings.

Xu's lip curled up as if she was about to snarl, but she looked into her hands, not at Shan. "I have nothing to hide. I have nothing to fear from—" Her words were cut off as the door was flung open and a thick bull of a man burst into her office.

"Call them off!" the man shouted at Xu. "Order your damned whelps off or I'll call Beijing! You are endangering my investigation!" His heavy cheeks were flushed with color. Drops of saliva shot from his mouth as he shouted.

Shan didn't need to see the grey uniform to know what the man was. The Public Security Bureau had arrived, and if he had had a slim chance of escape a moment earlier, he had none now. He rose slowly, fighting the knot that was tying itself in his abdomen, and silently pulled a chair from the side of the desk and sat again, facing the knob officer, as if he were with Xu. The prosecutor did not seem to notice. The action took Shan out of the line of fire between the two and gave him a clear view of the furious stranger.

His hair was close-cropped and speckled with grey, like Shan's. His face had the broad, flat features of the southeastern coast, a region known for its fishermen and pirates and the difficulty of distinguishing between the two. As his barrel chest heaved up and down, Shan saw a bulge on the left side of his uniform, below the armpit. A pistol, strapped under his tunic.

"You will have to be more specific, Major Bao," Xu said icily.

Major Bao. It was the knob officer who had demanded all reports on Americans be sent to him, the one mentioned at Glory Camp. Lieutenant Sui's commanding officer. Shan remembered what Fat Mao had said. The two people in the county to stay away from were Prosecutor Xu and Major Bao.

"Specific, hell!"

"Major, you're overwrought." Xu seemed accustomed to his fury. "Sit down."

Shan studied the two in confusion. They should have started their feeding frenzy by now. They should have begun the process of dissecting and digesting Shan. But Xu and Bao appeared to be little interested in cooperation. Lieutenant Sui, who must have reported to Bao, had been with Xu at the motor pool. Bao Kangmei had also been the name copied on Xu's memo about Lau. Shan looked at the knob again. His hands were like cabbages, his eyes like dirty ice. Bao Kangmei. Resist America Bao. It had been a popular name during the struggle with the Americans in Korea.

Bao made a sound like a growl and dropped into the center chair just vacated by Shan. "Your damned investigators are spooking everyone," he said in an icy tone. "Everyone's running to cover. The caravans will stop moving. If you ruin my operation, I'll ruin you."

Shan studied the knob. Bao didn't want to stop the caravans, he wanted them to keep moving. Shan remembered the black market goods at Glory Camp, in the shed guarded by the knob guard. In the shed with the dead American. Was that all it was? Was Bao just a black market businessman? Perhaps the American had simply been an unlucky merchant, in Xinjiang to buy carpets on the black market, perhaps even to trade for electronic goods.

Xu sighed as if she were sympathetic to Bao. But her face showed no warmth. "My team has never been closer to a breakthrough. The Poverty Scheme is what we have waited for all these years. I will not call them off a real case so you can chase phantoms."

"Not phantoms, Comrade Prosecutor. Enemies of the state. Enemies of Beijing."

"It's your crutch, isn't it, Major?" Shan looked up in surprise at Xu's words. Never had he heard anyone speak in such a tone to a knob. "You're the only one who speaks of Beijing so often. But I am the one who catches criminals. Beijing knows that."

Bao glared at her.

Xu's face seemed to soften, now that she had scored against him. "Surely a few minor inquiries in the mountains can't upset an important Public Security operation, Comrade Major."

But Bao did not seem to have heard. His oxlike head was turning to the side, looking onto a huge table, bigger even than that used as Xu's desk, which was pushed against the wall. It seemed conspicuously oversized, as though ready at any time to receive a banquet or a body, at Xu's convenience.

A single cardboard box sat in the center of the table. On it, written with a broad black marker, was a name. Lau.

Bao exchanged a silent, meaningful look with Xu, then rose and stepped to the table. Xu stared after him with an icy expression. By the time she had joined him Bao had dumped the contents of the box on the table. Shan stood to see better, then glanced at the door. He might make it if he walked quietly away, without attracting those in the outer office. But he turned back to look at what Xu had collected from Lau. Three books. A short, narrow knife, like a dagger. A wooden box, the size of a shoe box, though half as high. Several notebooks. A small jade statue of a horse. A simple white metal box, dented from long use, inlaid with a row of pink coral squares on its top—a pen case, of a type often seen in Tibetan instruction halls.

Oddly, the discovery seemed to have subdued Bao. He stared at the evidence, then at Xu. "You have been sharing the results of your investigation with my office, no doubt."

"We have no official investigation results yet, comrade. Just a missing persons review, after all. These are simply personal effects. In case we ever identify her family. Things from her room in the teacher's dormitory. Space is in short supply. Her room was cleared out for another teacher."

"But still," Bao said in a taunting tone, "here they are, on your evidence table."

Shan quietly inched his way toward the table. He stood back, out of Bao's reach, but close enough to see the objects clearly. The books were poetry. The top one Shan readily recognized, the works of Su Tung-po, a broken Sung dynasty official who had written beautiful poems about living in exile.

"Even in death you are too kind to her," Bao said as he picked up the knife and waved it in the air, as if it proved a point.

"A letter opener," Xu shot back, not bothering to hide her impatience.

As the major clamped his huge hand over the wooden box, Shan saw that it was of rosewood, a superbly crafted container carved with delicate flowers along its rim. Bao raised the box and shook it. Something rattled inside. He turned the box over, looking for a latch.

"A puzzle box," Xu said tersely. "Ching dynasty."

Shan saw that she was right and realized with pleasure that it was a very old piece, one of the wooden puzzle boxes that had been popular in China two centuries earlier. No two would be alike, and each would be opened by pressing a certain point or sliding a series of pieces out in the right order. He realized with surprise that Xu might have been saving it, as Shan would have, to discover the right combination of pressure and pushing which would unlock its secrets.

"You really don't understand, do you?" Bao observed in a gloating voice. He looked at the prosecutor with a strange pleasure in his eyes, then laid the box on the table and with an abrupt hammerlike movement of his fist smashed it open.

He ignored Xu's glare as he picked through the shards of wood. There were two pieces of metal inside, one a two-inch trapezoid of bronze, engraved with a figure of a flying bird, a hole at each end. The other was a brilliant gold coin.

Bao extracted the gold piece from the splinters and extended it like a trophy. It was a Panda, the one-ounce gold coin minted by Beijing for the international collector's market. The Major gave Xu a victorious glance and, still extending the coin in front of his chest, returned to his chair. As Xu turned to follow Shan quickly pocketed the bronze medallion.

Bao let the prosecutor wait and watch as he set the coin on the desk in front of him, then slowly, clearly relishing Xu's discomfort, he produced a pack of cigarettes and lit one. "Maybe," Bao suggested as he exhaled a sharp stream of smoke, "you don't always catch the criminals, Comrade Prosecutor."

"Lau labored for many years," Xu said in a smoldering tone. "A model worker. There is no crime in saving wages."

Shan stood by the table, looking at the coin in front of Bao. It was worth more than some herders made in a year.

"Your model worker had secrets. Good citizens don't keep secrets. A true believer in the socialist imperative keeps no secrets." A row of yellowed teeth showed as he offered a narrow smile. "There are those in Yoktian who want to unravel the fabric of society. It all starts with a few loose threads."

"What do you imply?" Xu shot back. "She was one of those holding it together. We needed her."

As Bao shook his head he exhaled, creating a cloud of smoke about him. Then his gaze settled on something under a piece of paper on Xu's desk. He leaned forward and snatched it up. Shan instantly recognized it, a wedge-shaped tablet like that in Suwan's belongings. Not the same, for this one had a crosshatch design across the top edge, but bearing the same Sanskrit-type writing. Bao slid the top out, then slammed it shut and stood. "Where did you find this?" he demanded.

"Lau's things." The prosecutor lit a cigarette, inhaled

deeply, then shot a stream of smoke toward Bao. Like a duel of dragons, Shan thought. He found himself stepping closer, looking at the wooden tablet.

Bao's eyes widened for a moment, and he looked back at the items he had scattered across the table. He said something to himself in a low venomous tone, so low Shan was not sure he had heard correctly. "Bitch," it sounded like, "the traitorous bitch." Then he met Xu's puzzled gaze. "You haven't called anyone about this?" Bao barked. "The Ministry? The Antiquities Institute?"

Xu shot an uncertain glance toward Shan, then slowly shook her head. "Just a toy of wood some children made."

Bao's eyes closed to two narrow slits. "Fine. Keep thinking that, comrade," he spat. "Treason all around and you only see toys." He spoke to the wooden wedge now. "Think of all the work that has been done, all the sacrifices we have made to establish the most glorious society on the planet. The government gives us everything. We owe it everything. To think that there could be those in this very county who seek to tear our state apart, it sickens me," the knob growled. "You're wrong about her, Comrade Prosecutor. She wasn't who she said. There is no lower life form than those subversives who seek to undermine the state. Insects. Maggots, all of them, especially Westerners who foment it. We will crush them. And I will also crush those who stand in our way." He stuffed the wooden tablet into the big flapped pocket at the bottom of his jacket.

Shan found himself standing at the desk. He quickly sat back in the chair near Xu.

Xu's face drew tight as she stared at the pocket where he had stuffed the tablet. "I thought we were speaking of caravans." Did she recognize the dangerous ground Bao was pushing her toward? Shan wondered. Or was she simply reacting to the wild gleam in his eyes?

Bao's hand moved to a breast pocket, from which he extracted a folded piece of rice paper. "You've never seen this, I suppose?" He unfolded it and extended it in his hands a moment, then turned it over. It was a strip sixteen inches long, a poem inscribed in a child's hand, in Mandarin on one side and Tibetan on the other. *Master's gone to gather flowers*, the first line said. *Pollen on his funny robe.*

"Discovered hidden in her quarters," Bao stated. "Fortunately Public Security was able to intercept it instead of another office," he added pointedly, then folded the paper and stuffed in back in his pocket.

"A child's imagination," Xu offered stiffly, though the writing seemed to shake her.

Shan stared at the floor, avoiding eye contact with either. The poem was written about the waterkeeper. Bao suspected there was a lama somewhere, an illegal lama, and that Lau had been connected to the lama.

"I was in Turfan too," Bao said, giving no sign of having heard the prosecutor. "I heard the speeches. Some have lost sight of their essential duties. If you neglect your essential duties, no matter how hard you work, you are a liability to the state." It was a familiar code Bao was using now, speaking in political slogans.

As the major finished, his gaze rested on Shan for the first time. "Do you know your essential duties, comrade?" Bao asked him with a narrow, lightless smile. "Do you recognize treason when you see it?"

"I remain ever mindful of what I owe the state," Shan said woodenly. He fought the almost overwhelming urge to bolt. Xu's enforcer was outside the door, then the man at the stairs, perhaps others who had returned from their rest. With luck, Shan might get past them. But Major Bao was not the type to travel without an escort. There would be more knobs outside.

Bao let the smoke drift out his mouth so that it curled around his cheeks. "Tell your prosecutor to do the same."

Shan clenched his jaw so tightly his teeth hurt.

"I am not his—" Xu began. Shan turned toward her with an empty expression, resigned to his fate. Xu locked eyes with him for a moment, then looked back at Bao, without continuing.

"I do not consider Prosecutor Xu a woman who forgets her duties," Shan offered.

Bao gave Shan another narrow smile and leaned toward him. "I thought I knew all of the trained hounds here. You're new?"

His incredible luck had failed. For a moment there had been hope that both would end the meeting with mistaken assumptions about him. But now there were only two ways to leave the room. With Xu or with Bao. He couldn't say he worked for the knobs, as Xu had assumed. He couldn't say he worked for Xu, for any disclaimer from her would mean immediate arrest by Bao. Shan's only hope was to give Xu something, perform for her now, make her curious enough that she might offer him cover.

Bao stared at him with sudden, intense interest.

"I am new," Shan said. "I am from Beijing."

"Who are you?" Bao pressed. "Your name."

"Someone who is wondering why you seem more concerned about smugglers than the murder of one of your officers."

Bao's eyes flared and his upper lip began to curl at one edge, exposing a large yellow tooth, like a fang. He stood and threw his cigarette, still lit, onto Xu's desk. "You don't know that."

"On the highway. Two days ago."

Bao did not take his eyes from Shan. "Accidents happen on the highway," he muttered.

"His name was Lieutenant Sui." Shan heard a sharp intake of breath from Xu, behind him. "Two bullets in the heart. Surely you have reported it. Beijing takes great interest in attacks on Public Security officers." Could it be possible that Xu didn't know about Sui?

Bao's face paled. His lip curled higher, toward his nose. It was not a sneer—more like the way some animals bare their teeth before tearing into the flesh of their prey. Without looking Shan sensed Xu's body tighten, but he did not take his eyes off Bao. The major reached Shan's side in two quick steps, then raised his open hand and slapped him, hard.

"No officer was killed," he snarled. Then, in his next breath, as only one trained in the peculiar logic used by political officers could do, he asked, "How do you know this? This is a Public Security matter." His furious question was directed at Shan but Bao's eyes came to rest on Xu. Then, as if his remark needed further punctuation, he raised his thick pawlike hand and slapped Shan again.

Shan tasted blood from the inside of his cheek. He would sit there and let Bao slap him all day but he would say no more. Shan had found a place inside, an oddly serene place, a little room he had constructed in prison and not visited since. Some prisoners had called him the Chinese Stone for never breaking from physical punishment. Some of the Tibetans had said it was because his soul had sufficiently evolved so that he was always prepared to leave his body. He had never thought they were right. He only knew that he had evolved sufficiently that, no matter what, even under the threat of death, he would not cower before men like Bao. It didn't mean much to the world if such men couldn't get what they wanted from physical torture, for they could usually obtain it through chemicals. It only meant something to Shan.

As he braced for another blow Shan reminded himself of the Tibetan prisoners who, after all the torture, the starvation, the freezing, even the amputations, thanked the Lord Buddha for allowing them the opportunity to test their faith.

Through a fog of pain Shan heard Xu push back her chair and step away from her desk. He had lost. She was going to join in Bao's fun, he thought numbly.

"This is Prosecutor Xu Li of Yoktian County," he heard her say in a loud, professional tone, the way she might speak before a tribunal. "In the name of the Ministry of Justice I am demanding that Major Bao immediately desist."

Bao had found a place within himself too. Not a place of serenity. Perhaps the opposite of serenity. As the Major looked toward Xu he made a sound like a snarl, a sound of disgust. Shan followed his gaze. He had to blink hard to focus on the prosecutor, blink several times before he fully understood what she was doing. Xu stood with a video camera. She was recording Bao's actions.

Bao picked up a tea mug and threw it, not at Xu, but at the wall beyond Xu, who kept filming as the mug shattered behind her. Then he grabbed the gold coin, spun about and marched out of the room, slamming the door behind him.

A brittle silence lingered in the office. A thin line of smoke rose from Bao's cigarette, still on Xu's desk. Xu approached her desk and stood looking at the door, then looked at Shan. She raised the smoldering cigarette with the paper it had landed on and dumped it into a mug at the side of her desk, then picked up the phone and asked Loshi to bring in two teas.

The prosecutor circled her desk twice, her arms folded over her chest, not speaking until the tea arrived.

"I could have you behind the wire at Glory Camp before nightfall," she said.

"I've been to camps," Shan said quietly, returning her stare over his steaming mug. "Good exercise, bad food."

"I thought you were working for Public Security when I met you. One of the new agents brought in for the project."

"The Poverty Eradication Scheme?"

Xu did not respond. "Let's say you're not Public Security. Let's say you're not Ministry of Justice, not here on a corruption investigation. Just theoretically. But you know that Sui was killed, a secret kept even from me." Xu had not challenged Shan's announcement about Sui. Bao's reaction, he realized, had been confirmation enough. And Shan had been wrong. Xu had not known about Sui's death, he was certain. But Bao had. The knobs knew one of their own was murdered, and they were doing nothing about it.

"Walk around one of the markets and listen for twenty minutes. You'll see how big a secret it is."

She still ignored him. "So let's say you were associating with bad elements. Say, independence-minded herdsmen. Maybe subversive hatmakers."

The words hit Shan harder than Bao's hand ever could. Xu had seen Shan at the garage with Jakli, maybe also checked at Glory Camp for the names of anyone on the rice truck known to the guards. He glanced across her desk, looking for the second half of Jakli's file, the active half.

"I don't wear hats," he said weakly.

"Then maybe you're with the smugglers. We'll have lots of time to decide."

"I'm not with anyone."

"But you are from Beijing. I can tell. Your accent maybe. Or your arrogance in getting around my office."

"As I said, I am an investigator. My name is Shan. And I am from Beijing."

"But not investigating for Beijing. Surely not an independent investigator? Please, comrade. This is not some American movie."

"I am retired."

Xu studied him over the top of her teacup. "And you say you've been in camp before? Maybe you were forcibly retired."

Shan raised his mug. "I salute your deductive powers."

"And what? You're investigating as a pastime?"

"I was asked by friends to look into something. Nothing that concerns you," he offered, though he didn't believe it.

"Except you wind up breaching security at Glory Camp, then rummaging through my files."

Shan looked into his mug. "I have interesting friends."

Something that might have been amusement passed over Xu's countenance, then her features hardened again. "If I weren't so overworked I could spend hours just thinking of all the charges against you. Entering Glory Camp, a state security facility, without authorization, breaching the security of my files, that's a few years right there. But I think we'll keep it simple." All she had to do was to ask for his papers, for the required identity documents he did not possess, or the required travel permit. Then she would order him to roll up his sleeves, and find the tattoo on his arm.

Shan fixed his gaze on a carved bird at the edge of the table. "I am here about the children," he said quietly. "The children who are being killed. Lau's children."

Xu stared at him in silence. She seemed about to speak more than once but reconsidered each time. Then she slowly stood and walked to the shelf behind her desk.

With a chill Shan saw the tiny red light that indicated that the video camera, now on the shelf, was still operating. She had been recording their conversation. But now she retrieved the camera, shut it off, and returned it to the shelf, facing the wall.

She came back to sit not at her desk but in the wooden chair beside Shan. "What children?" she asked. Her voice was still hard, and filled with suspicion.

"A boy named Suwan, nine years old, shot in the head. A boy in the Kunlun mountains, named Alta, beaten and stabbed to death. The same age. Both part of her orphan class."

Xu frowned. "You're desperate, comrade." She had apparently decided not to believe him. "There have been no reports."

"They were with nomad families."

Xu's eyes seemed to drill into his skull. He broke eye contact and stared at the bird again. "Impossible. You should investigate a bit more before concocting your stories. The orphans have a new teacher. Everything continues as normal. But of course you know that. You asked my secretary about him."

"Yet, Comrade Prosecutor," Shan said very slowly, "you are concerned about Lau. About how she died." He glanced back at the evidence table. "She was murdered. And now her murderer is killing her children."

Xu frowned again and sighed. "Fiction. Concocted by the reactionaries, to make the people fear the assimilation programs. Lau died in an unfortunate accident. When the river waters recede this winter we will find her body." She opened a desk drawer and retrieved a pad of paper. "Write your statement, comrade," she said. "You've done it before, no doubt. We will consult it in your sentencing." She paused a moment, then tossed the pad toward him. "Maybe you did think the children were in danger. Say that. It could be useful. Bad elements put the children in danger. They engage in the patterns of feudalism. Distrust of authority. Blood feuds. Obsession with icons of dying cultures," she suggested. "Reactionaries, all of them. Those who resist our efforts to integrate all peoples."

Shan did not touch the pad. "Is it possible she was a friend of yours?" he asked tentatively. Xu had written a memo to defend Lau.

Xu did not answer.

"I saw her body," Shan said. "She was beaten on her shins. Tortured, before being drugged and shot." He paused to let the words sink in. "What are you going to do about her children?"

This time when Xu stared at him her eyes blinked, then she looked down. For a fleeting moment there seemed to be a glimmer of uncertainty on her face.

"She was getting old," the prosecutor said. "She was having trouble with her heart."

"Who told you that?" He realized she had not answered a single one of his questions.

"There was a meeting of the Agricultural Council, after we decided she had died. It was mentioned in a speech honoring her on her death."

She stared at him as he shook his head slowly. "Maybe you should ask your friend Bao about the orphans," Shan suggested.

"What do you mean?"

"I had an old friend in Beijing. Forty years with the Ministry of Justice. Said I should always assume that Public Security knows ten times more than they tell the public, five times more than they tell their colleagues at other government offices, and twice as much as they tell the Chairman."

Xu acknowledged the point with a sour smile, then pulled a form from a pile of papers on her desk and began writing on it with the stub of a pencil. "Maybe I will find time to explore your imagination further, comrade. Not today. At Glory Camp. They will hold you in a special place, alone, so you can more clearly consider all you will need to confess to."

"I have a better idea. Let me go."

Xu gave a cold smile and kept on filling out the detention form. "Shan," she said without looking up. "A common name. It tells me nothing."

"You know Bao is lying to you," Shan said. "You just don't know how much. You think you should do something about Lau. What if what happened to Lau is connected to Sui being killed? Let me go and I will find out. I promise to meet you again, soon. Here. You think because Bao is Public Security that there is nothing you can do. But there is. You can let me continue."

Xu's pencil stopped writing. "Maybe I was wrong about you," she said. "The Brigade runs a lao gai camp deep in the desert. Maybe that is where I should—" Her words were cut off by a woman's scream. There were shouts from the outer office, and the pounding of running feet. There was another high-pitched scream, then another. Xu stood at her desk, then quickly stepped to her door and opened it. The outer office was empty. At the sound of one more scream she ran to the corridor and down the stairs toward the sounds. Shan followed her, then stopped in the corridor and ran to its end, where he quickly found the back stairway.

In less than a minute he was running down an alleyway. He emerged onto the street a hundred feet from the Ministry office. Traffic in the street was stopped, the cars and trucks abandoned by their drivers. A crowd swarmed around the front of the Ministry building. Shan edged forward and stood on the running board of an abandoned truck to see over the crowd.

"Murder!" someone shouted.

He saw the prosecutor emerge from the building, followed by Miss Loshi and the lean man from the outer office. On the steps in front of Xu a man and woman in herders' clothing stood, the man holding a bundle in his raised arms, a bloody blanket wrapped around a young boy. The boy was dead.

CHAPTER 10

Someone grabbed his arm and began pulling. He stood, resisting, staring at the dead boy. The woman beside the man with the boy began shouting at the prosecutor. Then she turned and began shouting at the rapidly growing crowd. Some people were fleeing, Shan saw, trying to urgently weave through the crowd, to escape the square. Han. The Han Chinese were fleeing.

"Niya!" someone shouted, and the crowd began to loudly chant the name. "Niya! Niya! Niya!" The name from the posters, the name of the red-haired woman he had seen on the posters.

The knobs, he suddenly remembered. There were knobs with machine guns. He turned and saw the two grey uniforms on a balcony overlooking the far side of the square. One appeared to be speaking on a portable radio. The other held his gun at the ready.

On the Ministry steps the herder with the boy still stood, silently holding the boy as though presenting the body to the prosecutor. He was crying. The dead boy's eyes were partially open, as if the boy were squinting, trying to see something in the distance. His shirt was torn and stained with blood. There was a hole in the center of his forehead.

Someone grabbed Shan's arm with two hands now and would not let go. It was Jakli. He looked back at the dead boy and let himself be pulled down from the truck and led away.

They walked fast, though not so fast as to attract attention, past four blocks of pressed earth and cinder block structures in various stages of disrepair, the shops, garages, restaurants, and dreary offices with grey metal shutters that kept Yoktian alive. He asked her who the boy was but she said nothing. He asked who Niya was, and then he saw she was choked with emotion, her eyes moist, her jaw clenched as though to stifle a sob.

Jakli led him into a compound of four one-story buildings surrounded by a waist-high wire fence. A concrete walkway, so badly buckled and split that Jakli stayed on the dirt beside it, led to the mud-walled building that sat in the center of the compound, flanked on three sides by identical structures. Shan stopped at the entrance and looked at the wooden sign that had been fastened over the doorway. It had once held a slogan, but half the sign had blown away, so that all remained were the words *Strengthens Children*.

Jakli did not realize he had stopped until she was twenty feet down the darkened hallway. She turned with her hands on her hips, waiting.

"Was the boy from the zheli?" Shan called out.

She looked up and down the hall with worry in her eyes, then stepped closer. "An orphan, yes," she replied in a taut, melancholy voice. "His name was Kublai. Staying with a clan about twenty miles into the mountains. He was watching sheep and didn't come back. When they went to look they saw his body below a cliff, with a dead lamb in his arms. He had fallen, they thought, probably while rescuing the lamb. But when they retrieved the body they saw he had been shot. The lamb," she added with a sudden, deep despair, "the lamb was shot too."

"Who is Niya?" Shan asked again. "What does she have to do with the boy?"

"My cousins reached four of the zheli families and warned them away," she said, looking at the floor. "Malik brought a second boy to hide at Red Stone. The boy had tied two mastiffs to him, as if they would stop the killer. Some Maos are there at Akzu's camp now, guarding the boys. Other Maos are looking in the mountains too. The children are so hard to find."

"Are the boys connected to this Niya?"

But Jakli seemed not to hear again. She turned and

walked, more slowly, stopping at a door near the end of the hall. Someone sat on the floor beside the door. The Mao with the gold teeth, who had brought the shoes. As Jakli bent to speak with him, Shan pushed the door open.

Inside, Lokesh looked up from a simple wooden table and offered a silent nod of greeting. It was a small room, with a window that looked over the schoolyard toward the south, toward the snow-capped Kunlun. Its walls were lined with photographs, at least two dozen. There were horses, many pictures of horses. There was a picture of a large Buddha statue, photographs of mosques, and even a reproduction of an old painting of Lao Tzu, the sage of Tao, riding an ox. At the top of a tall metal bookcase a string of prayer flags had been fastened, which draped down the side of the shelves.

Lokesh held a bell in his hands, an old bell cast of bronze, the tip of its handle ending in a familiar scepter-like shape. It was a dorje bell, used in Tibetan ritual.

"She forgot her bell," Lokesh said grimly, with a meaningful glance toward Shan. The peal of a dorje bell was said to drive away evil. Beside the bell on the table was a ball of thread, perhaps three inches in diameter, with red, green, and yellow threads intertwined. Not thread, really, Shan knew, but a sacred emblem used by some Buddhists to wrap around ritual implements as a means of invoking wisdom. One of Lokesh's hands left the bell and stroked the ball of thread. Further down on the table was a large book, a Koran, and a black dopa, one of the Muslim skullcaps.

"What is it you seek, my friend?" Shan asked the old Tibetan. His words came out almost as a sigh, cast out on the wave of emotion he still felt from seeing the third boy. He knew Lokesh had come down from Senge Drak, had chosen not to go back to the safety of Lhadrung, because he was looking for something, something he had hoped to find at the school.

"It is hard to put into words," Lokesh said in a hoarse voice, shaking his head, as if something was telling him not to speak. He gripped the bell with both hands. "In its physical emanation it is the Jade Basket. But it is said to be able to transform itself, if it needs to, for protection."

"Protection of what?" Shan asked.

Lokesh's brow wrinkled. "On the outside," he said with difficulty, as though the words caused him pain, "the last time anyone saw it, it looked like a silver gau. Open it and there is a finely carved basket of jade, and inside that a place for a prayer."

The last boy's shirt, Kublai's shirt, had been torn, he remembered as he played the image from the Ministry steps over in his mind. Like that of Alta and Suwan.

"That's what you came for?" Shan asked. "This Jade Basket? Is that what you must take back?" Is that what Lau died for? he almost asked. For an artifact? There were symbols, he knew, objects of great power, of great veneration, for which devout Buddhists would gladly give their lives to protect. Indeed, dying for such objects would add great merit for the next incarnation.

"It's not safe to speak about it," Lokesh said, still shaking his head. "If you don't know how to approach it, then the closer you get, the farther it is." He looked up at Shan, clearly struggling painfully with something inside. "Don't—" His voice choked off and he stared at the bell with a doleful, perplexed expression.

"Did Lau have it? Is that why you came here?" Shan asked.

But Lokesh just stared intensely at the bell in his hands. He seemed beyond hearing again.

Shan walked about the office, then stood in the doorway, surveying it. Xu had been here. Public Security had probably been here. Managing Director Ko had certainly been here. Xu had taken what seemed to be Lau's personal effects. But Lokesh had found two more, he believed, the ball of thread and bell. They had been hidden in plain sight, camouflaged with her cultural instructional materials. From behind him in the hallway he heard the Mao speaking to Jakli, pointing to something on the office door opposite Lau's. He stepped to the other side of the hall to investigate. The Mao was pointing to a handwritten sign taped to the glass on the door. In two-inch characters someone had written one of the Great Helmsman's most famous slogans. Religion is the Opiate of the Masses. There was a nameplate on the door. Committee Chairman Hu, it said. Shan remembered the plump, worried Han teacher he had met at Glory Camp.

Shan wandered back into Lau's room. From the end of the table he picked up a piece of paper. A printout of names.

"The zheli," Jakli explained over his shoulder. "A list from the computer of all the orphans she worked with, and the zheli class schedule." She pointed to three names on the list. Suwan, Alta, and Kublai.

"Did Lau use the computer?" Shan asked.

Jakli paused and pulled the list closer. "No. She didn't like computers."

"Or, at least, didn't trust them," Shan suggested.

Jakli nodded as she examined the list. "Someone else did this."

"It makes it easier," Shan said in a low voice and saw the question in Jakli's eyes. "For the killer." The killer had the list, available at any Brigade computer, and only needed the location of the zheli members. Which was why he had tortured Lau. He studied the schedule. The zheli had two class meetings left for the year, one in a week, and the other five days later, both at a place called Stone Lake. He pointed at the entries.

"At the edge of the desert," Jakli explained. "It was a tradition of Lau's, to end the season of classes with two sessions there. To understand the desert better, she said. It's too hot to go there in the summer."

"The boys," Shan said. "Which are the boys? I wasn't certain before, but now it seems clear. The killer is only attacking boys."

Jakli studied the list and pointed out nine more names. She held her hands together and twisted her fingers as she stared at the names, as though she had seen a ghost. It was not a student directory. It was a death list.

There were notes fastened on the wall, torn from student workbooks. *Thank you, auntie,* one said, *for showing me that the desert is still alive. My baby bird sang a song today,* another said. Two seemed to be poems. *While my horse drank,* it said, *I saw an old farmer, so asleep a mouse nibbled at his whiskers.* Another was written with a more mature, artful calligraphy. *In the mountains*, it said, *old men wait, with the wisdom of snow.*

Shan looked out the window. The building across the courtyard to the south had low drifts of sand along its walls. Beyond them, he gazed at the Kunlun, toward Senge Drak. Jakli had left Gendun there that morning, sitting on the sentinel stone on top of the mountain.

He sensed someone step behind him. He did not turn but saw the tumble of long dark hair from the corner of his eye. Jakli silently reached onto the wall and removed the second poem that he had admired, the one about wise old men. She folded it, and put it inside her shirt. He watched as she retrieved a chair from the table and studied the montage of photographs on the wall. After a moment she set the chair down in front of the wall, climbed it, and pulled down a photograph of the Great Hall of the People in Beijing. She handed it to him with sad smile and stepped down. The photograph was stiff and heavy. He turned it over. On the back was affixed a photograph of a red-robed, balding man with spectacles, wearing a serene smile. The Dalai Lama. Jakli used her fingernails to slit the tape that held the secret photograph and put it in her pocket.

Suddenly the light in the office was switched off. The Mao with the gold teeth was at the door, silently pointing out the window. People had begun filing into the courtyard, arranging themselves along the wall of the opposite building. Jakli froze, then darted to the wall, and pressed against it, as if to hide.

It was knobs, herding children out of the school. Thirty or forty students had apparently been pulled out of classrooms with their teachers, who cowered in the doorway to the courtyard. The students were being arranged in a single line along the wall. One knob officer was shouting at them to be quiet, while another stood with a video camera, sweeping its lens along the faces of the children. As they watched, the youngest children, perhaps seven years and younger, were dismissed and sent running back to their teachers. Another group of older children, teenagers, was dismissed a moment later. The knobs began talking to the fifteen or twenty children who remained, one man speaking as another recorded the interview with the camera.

"It's all right," the Mao said. "Just stay quiet."

"They know the zhelis are not here," Jakli said.

"Sure," the Mao said, "But some of the children may know how to find them. For the Poverty Scheme, the knobs are probably saying. Have to round up the orphan children, for their own good. Like the wild horses," he added bitterly.

Shan looked back toward the table. Lokesh was watching the children with anticipation in his eyes, as if perhaps he was thinking of going to them. Had the Mao told him about the third child? Shan wondered.

As if reading his mind Jakli stepped to the table and sat across from Lokesh. She placed a hand over his and shook it until Lokesh looked at her. "Another boy," she announced gently. "Another boy has been killed in the mountains."

When she had finished explaining what she knew, Lokesh sat staring at the dorje bell, lost in his thoughts again, more forlorn than ever. Shan leaned over Jakli. "The boy. Was he missing a shoe?"

"I don't know. Is it important?"

"The other two, they each had a missing shoe."

"What kind of shoe?"

He shrugged. "Just shoes." He thought a moment, then told her about the wooden tablet Bao had found and his reaction to it. "Suwan had one," Shan said. "It was shattered by his killer."

Jakli looked up with new worry in her face, then stood and stepped to the bookcase. She retrieved a photograph of a horse with a wooden frame from the top shelf. Not a frame, Shan saw as she held it out, but a flat piece of wood onto which the photo had been carefully taped to give the appearance of a frame. Jakli turned it over to reveal the wedge shape on its reverse side. Another of the tablets with the ancient writing.

"It's called Kharoshthi, this writing. From the people who lived here two thousand years ago. Sometimes the tablets are uncovered in the desert."

He reported Bao's reaction when he had found one of the tablets on Prosecutor Xu's desk and how Xu also had several of Lau's personal effects.

Lokesh looked up. "What? What did she have?" he asked in a strained, hurried voice.

"Not a gau," Shan said. "Books. A little jade horse. A pen case."

"A pen case?" Lokesh asked urgently, leaning forward. "Copper? With turquoise circles?"

Shan shook his head and studied his friend in confusion. "White metal. With coral."

Lokesh grimaced as if in pain and looked back at the bell.

Shan's eyes drifted back to the wooden tablet in Jakli's hand. He asked what Bao had meant when he had asked about the Antiquities Institute.

"The People's Antiquities Institute," she said. "It's a group of government scientists, archaeologists with Party memberships."

"I don't understand," Shan said. "Why would he say it has to do with Westerners?"

Jakli looked up with new alarm in her eyes. "Westerners? He said that?" She shook her head slowly. "It was the Americans who gave the tablets to Lau, enough for her to distribute them to the zheli. It was part of her helping them understand who we are."

"But to Major Bao it is an act of treason," Shan said, his mind suddenly racing. He had been wrong about Xu. She had not known about Sui, nor about the two dead boys. It could have been Bao all along, Bao and the boot squads searching for those he considered traitors to China. He must have found a link between Lau and the Americans and might be following the zheli to the Americans. Shan remembered the poem about the lama and Bao's reaction to the wooden tablet on Xu's desk. Evidence of treason. To Bao, finding traitors would be more important than finding Sui's killer, at least temporarily, if he were on the verge of closing in on his traitors. Shan and Jakli exchanged an alarmed glance.

"The Americans have to be warned," Jakli gasped. "They go to the zheli class sometimes."

"To the zheli?" Shan asked in disbelief. "Surely it would be too dangerous."

"I was there with Fat Mao when Lau tried to talk them

out of it. The Americans said they wanted to talk about their work to the children, to the next generation, to let them know there are other people on the planet who care about them."

Their work. What was it the Americans were doing that could so infuriate Bao? Digging up ancient tablets? Looking at old cloth?

"They said it was worth the risk," Jakli added, "to have children listen."

Shan remembered Deacon's strange words. He and his wife had come to Xinjiang to stop hiding. "Maybe you should go to the Americans," he said. "I must help the children."

Jakli gazed at him, her eyes widening in realization. "But what you said about Bao, it means that it is all about the Americans, about following a chain of Lau's students to the Americans. The children are hiding. You will never find them. But if we can't find the children, then we must go to the other end of the chain and work backwards. Find the Americans, and trace back their link to the children. Cut off the trail that Bao is following. It's what we have to do. And then," she added with a determined glint, "then we get you back in time to cross to Nepal."

Suddenly a figure appeared in the doorway, a thin young woman in the grey uniform of a knob. They froze, all except Lokesh, who stood and rang the dorje bell, the bell that drove away demons. He rang it loudly, repeatedly, stepping forward while extending the bell toward her, and with each of his steps the woman retreated, until finally she turned and bolted down the hall. Jakli grabbed Lokesh, who was laughing now, and they ran down the hall in the opposite direction.

Karachuk felt different this time, Shan thought. There was still the excitement, the feeling of entering a lost century, but there was also something else. Not fear, but close to fear. A sense of foreboding in the wind.

Jakli seemed to sense it too. She had maintained a brooding silence for much of the journey to the lost city and now paused warily as they passed out of the corridor of ruins and saw the domed building where Shan had met Marco. She looked at the sky, which was grey and unnaturally dark for mid afternoon, and frowned, then nodded toward a small spiral of dust, a tiny whirlwind that was scudding toward the wall behind them. "See one of those wind demons at night," she said, "when the moon is just right, and you'll be sure you've seen a ghost." She offered a half smile as she spoke, but it did little to ease the tension from her face.

Lokesh, standing in front of them, stared at the spinning zephyr. "When I was a boy," he said solemnly, "an old man told me that whirlwinds are one of the ten thousand forms that spirits may take. It is the way some souls move about. Inside, there is a brilliant seed of awareness." He studied the wind devil intently, as though trying to recognize something within it. "They can appear suddenly, like a thought, and then just"—Lokesh shrugged as the spiral passed over the outcropping and was gone from view—"just pass us by."

Shan looked at the path of the wind devil. It seemed the story of everything that had happened since he had left his mountain in central Tibet. Awareness passing him by.

Through his strange mix of emotions, Lokesh had understood they had to move quickly. There was no doubt now that the killer was still at work, and the remaining zheli boys had to be found and protected. The Mao with the gold teeth had also understood, and as soon as they cleared the school, he had jogged away toward town. But Jakli was right. If Shan had less than two days, he had to focus on the Americans. If Bao was the killer, he was only interested in the zheli and the Jade Basket as a way of finding subversives. Ultimately his goal would be the illegal Americans and those who helped them. If so, that was where the answers lay, with the Americans.

The ruins were empty. They walked stealthfully, like thieves, wary of the slightest sound and movement, sometimes starting from the occasional gasp of excitement from Lokesh as he gazed on the ruins. Jakli led Shan with short uncertain steps into Osman's inn. The stuffed chair and tables were still there, even the chess set, but all sign of recent use had been removed. Sand had been thrown on the tabletops. A search party would know it had been inhabited more recently than the remainder of the city, but would not know if it had been last week or ten years before.

No one had reclaimed Karachuk since the hurried exodus only forty-eight hours before. "Wasted. We wasted the trip," Jakli said in frustration as they stepped outside. "No one's—" She stopped as Shan pulled her arm and pointed to the corral, where Lokesh stood near the fence. He was holding a dark brown lump in his palm, wearing a victorious grin. "It's fresh," he called out, putting the lump under his nose. "Today!" It was camel dung.

As they hurried toward the corral Lokesh cocked his head toward the rocks at the back of the corral. "This place," he said with the same enthusiasm, "it is wonderfully full of spirits!" It took a moment before Shan could discern the object of his friend's attention, in the shadows near the top of the rock. A large grey creature, watching them intently.

"Not a spirit," Jakli said with new energy in her voice. "Osman's dog." She eagerly scanned the rocks. "Osman didn't go. He's the protector of Karachuk."

They found the dog's master in the temple, lying on a pallet below the rough-hewn altar. Only two candles lit the large room. The big dog, having greeted Jakli by burying his muzzle in her hands, had followed them into the chamber, then stepped in front of them and pushed Osman with his nose.

"All right, all right," Osman mumbled to the creature and sat up. As his eyes cleared he made a sudden motion toward something lying at his side, then relaxed as he recognized his visitors.

"Sorry to disturb your dreams," Shan said.

"Not sleeping, exactly," Osman said gruffly. "Listening." He spoke quietly into his dog's ear, and the animal trotted away, down the tunnel. Back to its post.

"Listening?" Shan asked.

Osman nodded and gazed down the dimly lit corridor. "For the wind. For helicopters. For spirits." He was in a dark mood. He seemed to be waiting for something evil to arrive.

"Any sign of Nikki?" Jakli asked softly.

"Of course not, girl," Osman grunted, rubbing his hand

over his face. "He's too smart to come out of the mountains now. Probably go straight to the horse festival," the Kazakh added, casting a small, expectant grin toward Jakli.

Lokesh stepped to the altar and lit one of the butter lamps with a candle, then gestured for Shan to do likewise, paying homage to Buddha. As Shan stepped over Osman's pallet a glint of light caught his eye. On the floor, beside the pallet, was a long chopping knife, nearly as big as a sword.

"Too early to come back," Osman growled. He spoke to Jakli, but his eyes were fixed suspiciously on Shan. "The knobs could still come."

"We're not staying," Jakli replied. "We came to learn the way to the American. Deacon. He went into the desert. Which oasis?"

"No oasis."

"He has to be at an oasis," she said impatiently. "We must find him, Osman. There is no time to argue."

Shan looked about the room, which was growing increasingly brighter as Lokesh lit more lamps. The statue of Buddha had been covered again with the canvas. There were wooden crates stuffed with liquor bottles, a basket full of glassware, and in the farthest shadows something else. Cardboard cartons. Shan took three steps toward them before Osman warned him off with a raised palm. "Too much curiosity can be a dangerous thing," the grizzled Kazakh said.

But Shan had seen enough to recognize the cartons. He had seen identical cartons before, the new cartons of electronic goods from Glory Camp. In the hut with the dead American. On top of the cartons was a small, high-powered portable radio transmitter.

"Go back," Osman said. "Wait a few days. Deacon will return here."

"There may be no time to wait," Jakli said, her voice rising. "The Americans may be in danger."

"No one will welcome you, even if you find it. And if you don't find it, the desert will eat you. Nikki, he would kill me many times over if I sent you out there and something happened."

"Which is why you must give us very good directions,"

Jakli said, folding her arms with a determined stare.

Muttering under his breath, Osman produced a bottle of vodka from his pallet. As he reached for glasses, he studied his visitors again, then returned the vodka and pulled out a bottle of water. He filled a glass for each of them and motioned for everyone to sit on the floor. "You go due east ten miles, with your shadow always in front of you, then exactly northeast, through the Well of Tears, between the two walls. Then three miles due north. Sand Mountain, it is called," he began, drawing with his finger in the sand on the floor, describing the landmarks they would see. It was the old way, Shan realized, the way of the herders, imparting information orally, before everyone, so together all the details would be remembered. "If you had horses I'd say don't go today. Bad day on the desert, maybe. Smells wrong. With a truck, maybe, I don't know. Not the best sand for a truck." He shrugged and shook his head. "No. Wait here tonight. Tomorrow will be better."

Jakli exchanged a glance with Shan. Before they had left Yoktian she had arranged for a Mao truck to meet him on the road outside of town by evening of the next day, to begin his journey to Nepal. It was all they could hope for, she had said on the drive to Karachuk, to protect the boys and shield the endangered Americans. Then Shan could go on to his new life. Osman looked up at the glint in Jakli's eyes and sighed, then retrieved an old compass from one of his baskets. "Make it in less two hours," the Kazakh said as he handed Shan the compass. "Go like hell. There is no place of safety on the way."

Osman's ominous tone made no sense until forty minutes later, as the rugged little truck lurched across the sands. Then, as Jakli slowed to check first the compass, then her mirror to verify that she was navigating in a straight line, a small cry of distress escaped her throat. Shan followed her gaze toward the northwest. A tiny piece of the sky was missing. On the horizon, framed by dark clouds on either end, a green-black hole seemed to hover above the desert.

Jakli pushed the accelerator. "A storm," she said with alarm. "That color. It is the seed of a death storm. A kar-aburan."

"But it is too far away," Shan said. "It could blow in any direction. No need to—" He stopped as he saw the grim set of Jakli's eyes and silently accepted the compass as she put both hands on the steering wheel.

Minutes later Lokesh began chanting. But it wasn't a prayer, Shan realized after a moment. He was chanting the directions to the Sand Mountain. There was a long, treacherous gully, the Well of Tears, down which they would drive, then it was a sprint of three miles north until they reached the Claws. "How will we recognize the Well?" Shan had asked. Osman had only laughed, as though it were a foolish question.

"It's just a storm," Shan said, without conviction. He had never seen a sky like the one in the north. It didn't simply look like a hole in the horizon now. It looked like a huge mouth, and the mouth was clearly getting closer, like a predator that had somehow sensed their presence.

"It's why he said to hurry," Jakli said. "Osman has the old desert senses. He smelled something in the air." She gripped the wheel with white knuckles. Her foot held the accelerator to the floor. The rear axle fishtailed when it hit patches of soft sand. They crested a small dune and the front wheels left the sand, spinning in the air before dropping into the desert with a sickening digging sound as they landed. The sturdy little truck hesitated, then lurched forward again. At such a speed, they could land the wrong way and roll the vehicle. And an immobile truck in a sandstorm would be like a boat on a beach as a typhoon approached. Before long it would simply be engulfed.

"The Well!" Lokesh called out from the back, and his hand shot between Jakli and Shan to point to a long low ridge in front of them that seemed to have split apart at the center. "Straight northeast, into the Well of Tears," he recited in a singsong fashion. "Out of the Well, three miles north like an arrow," he continued, repeating the words exactly as Osman had last spoken them.

The Well was a gully between two walls of rock and gravel, and as they neared it the pathway grew more stable. Their wheels did not slip as much. But the walls seemed to go on endlessly, as far as the horizon. Had Osman said how far? No, just all the way through.

"Maybe the storm will go west of us," Shan offered.

"Maybe," Jakli said, but there was no sign of hope in her voice. The color had been slowly draining from her face.

"This canyon," Shan said as they entered the walls, "surely it will protect us."

"The storm comes from the northwest," Jakli said, her voice rising. "It builds its force below the western mountains, then grows as it eats the heat of the desert. Bigger and faster. A caravan in such a place might escape if the wind is right. If the wind is wrong, the wave of sand breaks over them. Or the canyon can act like a funnel, like a narrow bay in a storm that suddenly surges with a wall of water. They can be buried twenty feet under in minutes."

From inside the walls they could no longer see the storm. But there was something else. Shan opened his window an inch. There was a low steady groan, above which were cries and moans in many voices.

"Ai yi!" Lokesh cried out. "The misery!"

Certainly it could only be the rising wind playing on the strangely formed fingers and crevasses of sandstone that topped the walls, but the sounds seemed so human that a chill crept down Shan's spine. The Well of Tears.

"They come here," Jakli said, leaning forward in her seat as though she could make the truck move faster by sheer force of her will. "The souls lost in the desert for all the ages. The weak ones, the young ones, who have no direction, no strength to guide themselves to the next life. They gather here, pushed by the wind, trapped forever."

A strange, haunting feeling gripped Shan as he looked at Jakli. "You mean, the old legends say that," he said. Or had he just thought it? His tongue felt strangely thick, his mouth so dry he couldn't move his lips. Jakli wasn't sure they were just legends. Lokesh, sitting at the edge of his seat, his face nearly pressing against the glass, seemed to have no doubt. He knew they were not legends.

"Do you feel it?" the old Tibetan moaned, in a voice Shan had never heard from Lokesh, a voice of agony. Lokesh began doing his beads with one hand, his other hand pressing against the glass as though to reach out to the lost souls. His chant had changed now, and his mantra grew in volume. He wanted the Compassionate Buddha to hear above the din, to come and rescue all the stranded souls, those lost in the past and those about to be lost in the present.

Jakli was no longer able to hide her fear. Her hands began to tremble. A thin sheet of sand began blowing over the gully, creating an eerie, shifting ceiling ten feet above the truck. She pressed on. "Get it ready!" she cried above the rising sound of the wind.

Shan looked at her in confusion, then saw that his hands seemed to have understood her on their own. They held the compass close to the dashboard. The desperate travelers would have only one chance, one sprint across the desert to the Sand Mountain, a place they had never seen, a place they might not even recognize, a place that might even be buried by the storm by the time they approached it.

Would the compass work in the storm? he wondered. Would the rock walls interfere with it? Would the lost souls, eager for company, misdirect the needle?

The needle swung wildly back and forth until he realized it was because his hands were shaking. He clenched the instrument tightly and the needle began to stabilize.

Suddenly the sand sheet overhead dropped almost to the roof of the truck, then the walls disappeared. The truck shuddered as a blast of wind hit it, and Jakli struggled to align the wheel with Shan's arm, which he threw out in the direction of the needle. He glanced at the odometer. Three miles was all they had to cover. Three miles to outrun the storm and avoid death.

Jakli's head began to turn toward the storm.

"No!" Shan shouted. "Don't look at it!" He did not want her to see what he himself saw now, did not want her feeling the terror that now gripped him as he stared at the maelstrom. The storm covered the entire western sky, and the giant black-green mouth was open, moving directly at them. No, he saw, it wasn't that the storm covered the sky, for everything, above and below them, seemed the same disturbing color. There was no longer a sky, no longer a ground. The whole world was turning into a chaos of churning sand. This was the way it would feel, something said in the back of his mind, to face a tidal wave on a tiny island in the middle of the sea.

Lokesh shouted his mantra louder than ever, as though warning the storm away.

"Two more miles!" Shan shouted, glancing at the odometer. His arm ached with the tension as he continued to point with the needle. A tear rolled down Jakli's cheek. A mile and a half. Maybe they could do this, maybe they could beat the monster. A mile and a quarter.

Then Jakli was sobbing and Shan realized the truck wasn't moving. The wind gave the impression of movement, but the big wheels of the truck had bogged in the newly churned sand and were spinning uselessly, the odometer still turning. Then the engine coughed and died.

With the mechanical noises gone, there was only the howl of the wind. The truck rocked, like a small boat in high seas. Jakli stared outside a moment, then turned to him with a strange calmness. "That little pad," she said in a tiny voice. "May I borrow it?"

He handed her his pad and pencil, and she quickly wrote something, tore out the page, then folded it into the tattered envelope he had seen her with at Glory Camp, then put them inside her shirt, against her skin.

Shan could not see what she had written, did not want to see. But when she handed the pad back with a sad smile, she had pressed so hard that the indentations on the page below were clear. "Don't stay, Nikki. I'll be with you in the beautiful country. I love you forever," it said in English, and Shan was shamed to have seen it.

"We could run," he said. Somehow he remembered that she had warned him. The Taklamakan. It meant, once you go in, you never come out.

Lokesh's mantra had grown softer now.

"A lot of good people are out here," Jakli said in a hollow voice, still wearing her small smile. "Warrior monks. Merchants from the Silk Road. Pilgrims. I never thought. . . ." Her voice drifted away, and she settled back into her seat, watching a small stream of sand particles that had begun to blow in through a crack in the rubber that sealed the windshield. She began singing a song in Tibetan. Shan had heard it before, a very old song called a spirit wedding song. It was for loved ones separated by death.

A distant feeling seemed to settle over him as he looked toward the maw of the storm, as if he were somewhere else, just watching. He opened the pad to an empty page in the back. *Spilled ink in the sky*, he saw himself write. *Coming to drown me.*

He watched his hand take the slip of paper and put it in his pocket. Then he, Shan, was back. "No!" he shouted to the storm, putting aside the part of him that was ready to die. He was not going to spend eternity in the Well of Tears. His door was in the lee of the wind. He tied the string of his bag to his arm, then opened the door and stepped out. The sand was nearly over the wheel wells now. He tried to read the compass but could not hold it steady, so decided to walk in the general direction the truck was facing. The wind beat him back after two steps. It clawed at his face, the sand stinging like hornets. There were storms, he had heard, in which the sand blew so hard that it etched the skin and flesh from the faces of living men. He remembered the statues at Karachuk. Maybe he would end like that, gnawed to ruin by wind and sand, a mere suggestion of a human.

Something was forcing its way into his mouth and nose. It was gritty and tasted of salt. He realized, from a strange distance, as though he were watching someone else, that he had fallen. He lifted his hand to his head, which was against the bumper of the truck and throbbed with pain, and his hand came away wet and red. Then he discovered with mild surprise that his legs were gone. No, not gone, he decided, just buried in the wave of sand that was rapidly moving up the body of the truck. Half a grave. Is there such a thing as half a grave? he considered dully. A sound like the croak of a dying frog escaped his throat, then he shook his head violently. "No!" he shouted. "Gendun!"

He dragged himself along the truck until he found the door and with great effort pulled it open far enough to slip inside.

Lokesh was singing with Jakli now, not a mantra, but the spirit wedding song, and Shan lay in his seat, gasping for air, listening. Then the others grew strangely silent.

"The old ones," Lokesh said in a whisper not of fear,

but of awe. "They are coming for us, to take us to the Well." He started singing again, his voice calmer.

The rubber sealing began to crumble, eaten by the wind, and sand began churning through the truck. But Shan no longer heard the wind. There was a chorus of soft voices and he recognized each one of them, the lamas who had saved his soul. He wasn't going to have a new life. He was reliving old lives. An image flashed through his mind like a dream. He was on the Silk Road, and he was losing the emperor's treasures. He smelled ginger. His father was close.

Then he heard a strange sound, like a laugh, from behind him. He blinked the sand from his eyes and saw an exuberant smile on Lokesh's face. "I had always hoped it would be like this," his old friend said, "to be able to see them when they came for me."

And indeed, out of the maw of the storm two phantoms appeared, shrouded in black, faceless, arms extended toward the truck to receive them. The old ones had come for their souls.

There were many kinds of hells, the old Tibetans taught, but the atmosphere in all was the deepest of black. The tiny dull hint of consciousness, all that remained of Shan, clung to that thought. There were many kinds of hells, as there were many kinds of sin, but the worst were the cold hells, and the one Shan had gone to was surely the coldest and the blackest.

There was nothing, only the cold and the black, and the silence to let him agonize over all his failures. He had abandoned the children, who would now die. He had abandoned Gendun, who would be captured and devoured by the knobs. He had lost the waterkeeper, who would just fade away among the political priests who had captured him.

His agony ebbed and flowed with his consciousness. Whenever he was aware, he was aware of pain. And when he tried to conjure faces, they were always the faces of dead children.

Once something soft touched his head. His eyes fluttered open and saw a blurred flame, and for an instant he seemed to see a woman with wise green eyes leaning over him. Her face, lit by the flame, seemed to be made of fine porcelain. He knew her skin would squeak if he touched it. Then the light went out and he was back in his cold hell.

After some time—hours, days, years, he could not tell—the visions sometimes became beautiful, with faces of sacred figures, sometimes one of the many Buddhas he had met in Tibet, sometimes Lao Tzu, the sage of the Tao, who centuries earlier had himself disappeared into the western desert. Sometimes he seemed to be in a great warehouse of the Silk Road and heard the braying of camels and excited voices in many tongues calling out, then he was being condemned for losing the emperor's caravan and was being tied to a post for the death by a thousand slices.

Once in his visions a man with light skin sat before him with a brilliant lantern, reading from a large book in a rich, deep voice, and the words he read were in English.

"The tent," the voice said, "the tent in which the Great Khan holds court is grand enough to accomodate one thousand princes. Each hall of the tent is supported by columns of spicewood skillfully carved, and the outside is hung with lion skins. Inside the walls are all of ermine and sable . . ." The words were strange, yet familiar—as though he had heard them before, but in a different language, and in another lifetime.

What were the stages, he tried to recall, the stages of Bardo, when the spirit drifted until it saw the path to rebirth? Ignorance at first, clinging to the illusion that the body still lived, then realization that death has occurred—the Glimpsing Reality stage, the lamas called it, when uncertainty and hallucinations of the past lives might pull the dead back, delaying the final realization that there was no path possible but rebirth.

He fell back into the dark, silent hell, then smelled ginger in his hallucination. His father was walking in the shadows ahead of him, excited because they were going to watch the sun rise from an old Taoist temple. They met a kind old Englishman whom his father introduced as a professor of Chinese history, who joined their journey. Later his father stopped and asked if he were tired. He rubbed

Shan's cheek with his hand. His hand was wet. It was rough. It smelled foul.

Shan opened his eyes and cried out. The tongue of a silver camel was licking his face. Then he sat up, awake in his old body, and the animal twisted its head and looked at him with an expression of disbelief. With a gasp of unexpected pleasure, Shan realized that somehow he knew the animal's name: Sophie.

A figure appeared at the entrance to his chamber, then stopped and ran away, calling out excitedly.

A moment later Jakli ran in, Lokesh two steps behind her. His old friend knelt and clasped his frail hand over Shan's own, a huge smile on his face. Jakli held a large dipper to Shan's lips and insisted he drink again and again.

"How?" he asked, and found his throat was rough and gravelly, unprepared for speech.

Both his friends explained at once, and gradually he understood that it had not been the old ones they had seen but Marco and Deacon, wrapped in heavy felt blankets, tied to Sophie, who lay like an anchor on top of the nearest dune. It was an old trick of the desert clans. The anchor had to stay on top, where the wind hurt the most, because below, out of the strongest wind, was where the sand filled, where everything was buried. Marco and the American had pulled them inside the shelter of their blankets, then followed their ropes to Sophie, where they had waited for three hours, using Sophie as their windbreak, all five rolled in the blankets like a giant cocoon. When the howl of the wind had stopped, they had looked out to find themselves on a flat expanse of sand, the nearest dune a quarter mile away. The truck had vanished.

"Thank your god," Marco said, "that it was only a little one, just a small storm."

Jakli poured water on a cloth and wiped Shan's head. "You hit your skull on the truck," she explained. "A concussion, against the bumper."

"How long?" he asked in confusion.

She sighed and shook her head. "Almost two days. I'm so sorry," she said with pain in her eyes.

He wondered about her apology a moment, then realized she meant it was a day too late. He gazed at her dumbly, his mouth open. He would not be going to Nepal and a new life, he would not meet the old professor after all. "And this place?" he finally asked.

"Sand Mountain. Marco was already here. Osman called him on the radio and said to watch for us because of the storm."

"The radio?" Shan croaked. His throat still felt parched despite all the water.

But no one seemed to hear. They were looking up at the entrance to thé chamber, where Marco stood with a lean sandy-haired man. Jacob Deacon.

"Is the great investigator ready to talk?" the Eluosi barked out from thirty feet away.

"He's too tired," Jakli protested.

"It's all right," Shan said and extended his hand to Lokesh. But as he started to rise dizziness overwhelmed him, and he dropped to his knees.

Marco walked to his pallet and stood over him, stroking Sophie's neck.

"A few more hours' rest," Jakli said. "This afternoon."

Marco nodded reluctantly. "If Sophie and Jakli say wait, I wait. But a few more hours only." He moved back into the shadows.

"This afternoon?" Shan asked. "But it is night."

"This is a cavern," Jakli explained. "A water station. A monastery even, long ago."

"A water station?"

"The aqueducts under the sand. The *karez*—they brought water from the mountains when there were still huge ice fields. The textbooks from Beijing say that engineers from Nanjing and Sian built them but the old stories and the walls say otherwise. Men from Persia came to build them during your Tang dynasty, in exchange for the precious stones and fruit from our land. The walls have paintings of them."

A thick, worn book lay beside his pallet. "Someone was reading to me," he said. He picked it up. *The Travels of Marco Polo*, in English.

"I was," Deacon said. "Warp's idea, she says it helps bring an injured brain back."

"Warp?"

Jakli put a finger to his lips. "There will be time later for explanations." She handed him the ladle again.

Shan drank. His thirst seemed unslakable. "The water still flows from the mountains?"

"A trickle, enough to keep Sand Mountain alive."

"But it must have been a thousand years."

Jakli nodded and pushed him gently back down on his pallet. "Now sleep again. We will be near."

But when he awoke the chamber was empty. Carefully, wary of summoning the pain that came with sudden movement, he picked up the clay lamp by his pallet and began to explore.

The chamber was roughly forty feet on each side. Two of the walls had been plastered and held life-sized paintings of stern men with blue eyes and long reddish hair and beards that were squared at the bottom. Their faces somehow reminded him of the woman in the poster, Niya. They were offering gifts to other figures who stood in front of horses, scores of tiny horses painted out of scale. Down the tunnel that led out of the room he saw half a dozen meditation cells. He looked in one and stepped back quickly. Two figures lay asleep under blankets of rough sacking.

The tunnel parted. To the right he saw lights and heard several voices. He stepped to the left and soon emerged into another large chamber. Sophie stood there with two other camels. On the sand floor beyond was a bright patch, reflected from a passage at the end of the chamber. Sophie greeted him with a soft wickering sound, and he rubbed her neck a moment, then followed the curving passage for twenty feet and emerged into brilliant sunlight.

Shielding his eyes, he stepped into the desert. The sky was a brilliant cobalt, devoid of clouds. He quickly discovered that the Sand Mountain was a long outcropping of sandstone, much bigger than the one that held the temple at Karachuk, perhaps two hundred feet high and over half a mile long. There was a ruin near the top, an old sentinel tower of cut stone. He walked halfway up the path that led to the tower and sat on a rock, then stretched and filled his lungs. The air was pure and clear, with no scent of the death it had carried two days earlier. In the far south a long line of white hovered on the horizon. Not a cloud, he knew, but the high Kunlun, where Gendun sat inside the mountain, waiting.

Two days, he thought. In two days the killer could have found another boy.

When he went back inside, through the small fissure hidden in shadow, Jakli was sitting at the entrance, bent over a wooden bowl, rubbing something with a brush of brass wire. She did not notice him until he knelt beside her.

"I'm sorry," she said, lowering the brush. "I should have taken you back to Senge Drak. You had a new life to go to. It is my fault."

"I think in that storm," Shan said after a moment, looking out the opening toward the desert, "in those moments when the blackness overtook us, I think I gave up that life."

She looked up and nodded solemnly, as if she perfectly understood, as if it had been the bargain Shan had made with the deities of the desert, the price he had paid to keep them all alive.

He gestured toward the bowl and she gave a sigh of exasperation, then rubbed the object in her hand with an oily cloth and held it up for Shan's inspection. "Virtue medallions," she said. "Deacon uncovered them by one of the altars."

Shan saw that there were perhaps a dozen pieces in the bowl, some caked with dirt, others already cleaned and shining brightly in the light. Jakli held the one she was working on in her open palm. It was a two-inch trapezoid made of bronze, slightly curved at the ends, which were punctured with small holes and inscribed with intricate ideograms.

"For the warrior monks," she explained. "We found references in some of the old books. Today, soldiers receive awards for valor. But valor was taken for granted in the old armies, in the monk ranks. It was virtue that was sought. Maybe a soldier made an act of sacrifice for his parents. Maybe he dedicated his life to the perfection of his archery. Maybe he spent all his off-duty hours writing the nine million names of Buddha, or performed great feats for the cause of truth. He would be rewarded with a medallion from his general."

"They must be centuries old," Shan said in an awed tone.

"From the Tibetan garrisons that were here. Eleven, maybe twelve centuries ago."

"They belong in a museum."

The words brought a strangely emotional reaction. Jakli clenched her hand around the medallion. "Not with the communists," she said in a fierce tone, then calmed. "Virtue shouldn't be locked in museum."

"No," Shan said, not certain what he meant. He knelt and reached into the bowl, picking up two of the restored medallions. Half of those in the bowl, all the clean ones, were tied in pairs with waxed string. Each pair matched. In his hand was a pair of two rectangles, inscribed with lotus flowers running across their faces. There was a round set, with an eagle's face, and another pair with a running horse.

"Auntie Lau," Jakli said. "She once told me that such treasures belong to no one, that they are entrusted from time to time to an honored few, then passed on like a force of nature."

Shan remembered that Lokesh had used similar words, about virtue. "But where do such things go?" he asked, reaching into his pocket to touch the medallion there, realizing now that Lau had possessed one of the ancient tokens. He began to pull it out, to show Jakli.

"The people of the desert are the ones to decide how to share the secrets of the desert," a woman's voice said at the edge of the shadows, speaking in English.

Shan dropped Lau's medallion back into his pocket and pulled out his hand.

"Warp!" Jakli exclaimed as a woman with long black hair tied in a single braid at the back emerged into the light. She wore heavy black-framed spectacles and was older than Jakli, and shorter, so small-boned that she seemed lost in the oversized green smock she wore. It was the kind of smock doctors wore, or laboratory workers.

"And the dead will walk again," the woman said, with a narrow smile toward Shan. She extended her hand as Shan rose. "We were very worried about you," she said, now speaking in fluent Mandarin. "Abigail Deacon."

"Professor of Cultural Anthropology," he said in English. Her grip was firm, and as she squeezed his hand the woman stared intensely at him. Her skin was olive-colored, and her eyes, though brilliant blue, had an almond shape, the hint of an Asian heritage.

"Shan Tao Yun," the American woman shot back. "Formerly of the Chinese government."

Shan nodded slowly, with a quick glance at Jakli. "Good," he said. "There is no time for anything but the truth."

"Is he always so serious?" Abigail Deacon asked Jakli with raised eyebrows.

Jakli smiled at Shan, who stood uncomfortably between the two women. "Sophie licks his face," Jakli offered in reply.

The American nodded thoughtfully, as though acknowledging the point, then wiped her spectacles on her smock and studied Shan carefully. "Jakli said you lost a chance at a new life, by coming to warn us."

Shan shrugged. "All I know for sure is, I gave up a hard week's ride in the back of a truck."

The American woman smiled. "The least we can do is invite you to dinner," she said, then turned and stepped back into the shadows.

"In his hut at Karachuk," Shan recalled after a moment. "Deacon was studying old cloth. Is that what his wife is doing here?" He didn't ask Jakli the rest of the question. What had Deacon been doing with a human leg?

Jakli nodded as she scrubbed another medallion. "Abigail is an expert. She sees things in cloth no one else can see."

"Why here? Why so much secrecy?"

"Here is where the cloth is. In the desert. In the ruins. It doesn't travel easily. So it's better to study it here."

"But there are museums of antiquities. In Lhasa. In Urumqi."

"What she does is special," Jakli said enigmatically.

"You mean political," Shan said in puzzlement. The Americans clearly were in China without permission. Surely they hadn't put themselves at risk of capture by a man like Bao over pieces of cloth.

Jakli kept cleaning a medallion without reply.

"What could be political about cloth?" he pressed.

Jakli frowned without looking up.

"I was sent on a path leading from the murders. The only way I can get to the end of it is by understanding everything I encounter on the way."

She cast a peevish frown his way, then covered the bowl with an old towel and stood with the bowl balanced against her hip. She led him down the tunnel, past the corridor to the room where he had slept. They pushed aside a heavy felt blanket that had been hung in the corridor, then a second, lighter cloth that was tacky to the touch, as though designed to catch dust and flying insects. They entered a well-lit room that seemed half laboratory and half library. Eight tables, made of planks on trestles, were arranged in two rows. One, against the wall, had a series of smaller trestles and planks that had been stacked to form shelves for dozens of books. Two tables held binocular microscopes, like the one Jacob Deacon had used at Karachuk, with a sophisticated camera beside one. Scattered about were large clear plastic envelopes holding bits of cloth. A balding man, with several days' growth of whiskers, was bent over one of the microscopes, manipulating a piece of cloth with two metallic probes. Abigail Deacon sat at a computer console surrounded by pieces of cloth in long transparent envelopes. Incandescent bulbs hung from wires strung across the ceiling. Shan followed the wires to a bank of batteries, larger but otherwise identical to the solar power system he had seen at Karachuk.

The older man's head jerked up. He muttered a syllable of alarm and Abigail Deacon turned. Her frown was not one of anger, only irritation at being interrupted. She turned for a moment to make several strokes on her keyboard, then removed the computer disc and inserted it into a plastic case. Shan counted a dozen similar cases on the table, all with discs inside. She spoke to the older man in the Turkic tongue, then turned to Shan.

"My husband said you would have questions. Lots of questions," the American woman sighed. She rubbed her eyes a moment, then motioned to a large thermos, from which she poured tea into three mugs, setting two on the table by the second microscope. "Sorry," she said. "Chairs are in short supply. We don't bring many nonessential goods this far. Take mine," she said with a gesture toward the stool at the computer console.

Shan shook his head. "You speak both Mandarin and the tongue of the clans," he observed, question in his tone.

The American woman nodded. "My grandmother was a Kazakh. Married an American archaeologist when he was here exploring the Silk Road early in the last century. Kept the languages alive in our family."

Shan's eyes fixed on the nearest envelope of fabric, a strip of vivid and jagged red, yellow, brown, and blue lines, like lightning bolts. It was frayed at the edges and had several small holes, but the colors were vibrant and the cloth looked strong. "You find cloth, Mrs. Deacon," he said uncertainly. "You make records about types of cloth."

"Warp," the woman said. She smiled when she saw Shan's confusion. "My husband is Deacon. I'm not Mrs. Deacon. Or Dr. Deacon. And not Abigail. Just Warp, like on a loom. Nickname from college." She made an up-and-down, swimming sort of motion with her hand, and Shan understood it to mean the motion of thread being woven through a loom.

"Warp," Shan said slowly, and the American smiled.

"Before we began paying attention to the Taklamakan," the American began, "there was only one place on the planet that gave us worthwhile samples of ancient textiles: Egypt. Always a problem for archaeologists, because it means a huge gap in understanding ancient cultures. Textiles played such an important role in life. Always a major industry. Typically textile production consumed more labor in ancient society than production of food, and always it reflected religion and culture. In Egypt we can use textiles to place a person's social status, his job, sometimes even his or her personal hygiene."

"But in Egypt," Shan said, "the fabric must be two, three thousand years old." He looked back at the sample. "This looks much more recent." As his gaze drifted across the laboratory, it paused on the top shelf of books. One end had been cleared away to make room for half a dozen cricket cages. He recognized them—Deacon's treasured cages from Karachuk. On another shelf were stacks of the wedge-shaped wooden tablets.

"We date with radiocarbon, using wooden artifacts found with the samples. Hairpins, utensils. Wooden jewelry. Wooden letters, sometimes," she said, nodding toward the stacked tablets. The American woman pointed toward the textile sample in the envelope by Shan. "That's about a thousand to twelve hundred."

"Sung dynasty," Shan said, wonder in his voice.

The American shook her head. "One thousand B.C. Your Shang dynasty."

Shan looked up in disbelief.

"The sands. The dryness. Exactly like in Egypt," she explained. She pushed another piece of fabric toward Shan, showing him its subtle design of sheep in several colors. The border of a robe, she explained.

"But this should be celebrated," Shan said. "I've never heard—" He broke off in confusion at the sad glance exchanged between Jakli and the American.

"These textiles and the others we have, they span over two thousand years," the American continued. "They share nothing with the lands east of here. Many designs coincide with Persia, even Macedonia. And this—" Warp pointed to a plaid with blue, yellow, and brown. "This twill is a direct match to shreds preserved in salt mines in what is now Austria, made by ancestors of the Celts.

"Dr. Najan," she said, nodding to the balding man at the microscope, "is retired from the museum in Urumqi. He has deconstructed the weaving of several pieces and can tell you exactly how the looms were built to produce such weaving. They were primitive looms of a kind still used today in Turkey and Afghanistan." There was a glimmer of challenge in the American's eyes now. "The evidence is irrefutable. When we publish we'll have enough to fill five volumes."

The People's Republic, Shan knew, was itself the oddest of fabrics, a patchwork of peoples and cultures and histories woven together and compelled to stay together by force and doctrine. History books were crafted in Party workshops to validate that patchwork, and the annexation of the vast lands of Xinjiang and Tibet had been politically justified by pronouncements that the native peoples had always been part of the Chinese people. Every few months headlines proclaimed more Party-sponsored research that proved the common roots of the Chinese and the Tibetans, or the Chinese and the nomads of Xinjiang. A favorite of Party bosses was a permanent Chinese chromosome project designed to prove scientifically that Tibetans and the other minorities all descended from Han Chinese stock. Shan knew about such studies, had even known some of the scientists involved in Beijing, for the same scientists sometimes worked on forensic teams. First came the doctrine, and the science was designed to accomodate the doctrine. It was not unlike his own work in Beijing, where in every investigation he had been assigned a political mentor and where it was even possible for investigators who defied doctrine to be accused of the crimes they were investigating.

Abigail Deacon seemed to be reading his mind, "Party scientists have announced with great fanfare that Tibetans and Han Chinese share 99.9 percent of the same DNA material," she said with a sour smile. "Likewise Kazakhs or Uighurs with the Han. What they don't tell anyone is that Han Chinese and Nigerians, or Amazon Indians, or Scottish Highlanders also share 99.9 percent of the same DNA. Because we all happen to be the same species."

Shan looked silently from Abigail Deacon to Jakli, to Dr. Najan, who was now looking at him with a defiant stare, then raised his teacup in salute. The painstaking research was for their science. The secrecy was for the independence movement.

"The woman," he said, remembering the square in Yoktian, "the woman on the posters. Niya."

"Niya Gazuli?" Jakli asked. "It means the Beauty of Niya, from the ruins of ancient Niya where she was found. In the desert, less than two hundred miles from here. They found her mummified remains after a storm uncovered a burial site. Dr. Najan was on the recovery team. She's at least twenty-five hundred years old. Red hair. A robe decorated with figures of horses and birds. And not a drop of Chinese blood in her. She's become a symbol, a rallying cry. Posters. Songs. Mother Niya, who taught us that the government lied. The government seized the research after word leaked out," she said with a meaningful glance at Dr. Najan. "Since then—" She shrugged.

"We know of at least one instance," Najan continued the story, "where the government confiscated mummies and destroyed them. They control research much more tightly now. Foreign involvement is suspect. Some scientists from Kazakhstan and Europe gave speeches and were condemned by Beijing as subversive agents, trying to meddle in the internal affairs of China." Bao had a term for such scientists, Shan recalled. The insects he intended to crush.

"But Beijing has no right to these treasures," the American interjected. "No one owns knowledge. It doesn't belong to Americans or Europeans or Chinese. We take small samples and return the specimens to the desert, to places only Kazakhs and Uighurs know."

"Are there others in Xinjiang?" Shan asked, remembering the steel ring in his pocket, where he had kept it since the night at Glory Camp. "Other American scientists?"

The American woman tightened her brow, as if uncertain how to reply. "Probably. We hear rumors of others. A German graduate student was discovered conducting an unauthorized excavation with Uighur students a few years ago. He disappeared, never heard of again, here or in Germany. Now everything is secret, compartmentalized for security. We only know about our project," she said.

Shan looked back around the lab, then at the two scientists, staggered by the size of the effort and the size of the risk. Bao had a scent. The Americans wouldn't be deported if found. They were illegals, invisible to officialdom. Bao would know that the best solution would be to make them disappear. Like another American who had been captured by the knobs and brought to Glory Camp.

Did they truly understand the danger? he wondered. With a chill he remembered that special knobs from headquarters were in the county. They didn't come for dead boys or a missing teacher. They had come for foreign subversives. They could arrive by helicopter at any time—the next hour, the next minute. He surveyed the resolute scientists as they returned to their work. Jakli understood. Surely Najan understood. If the knobs landed in airships they would have incendiary bombs, special bombs that could suck all the oxygen out of a place like this. They might take the trouble to march through and shoot each of them in the head. Or they might just seal the cavern up and let them all die more slowly. The knobs would have many options if they discovered Sand Mountain, but none would include taking prisoners.

"Your son," Shan suddenly remembered. "Your son is here," he said, instantly regretting the alarm in his voice.

Abigail Deacon searched his eyes for a moment. "What about him?" she asked.

"Is he here, at Sand Mountain?"

The American looked at Jakli. "He's safe. Not here, in the Kunlun."

"What do you mean?" Shan asked.

"With some herders. Lau arranged it, as if he were another of her orphans. One of the border families, a shadow clan, Lau called them. She said it was the safest place he could be."

"The zheli?" Jakli gasped. "Your son is with the zheli?"

Abigail Deacon didn't know, Shan realized with a chill as the woman looked at them in confusion. She had sent her son to safety in the mountains. But now the American boy was on the zheli death list.

CHAPTER 11

Shan touched his finger to his left temple, where a low throbbing had started again. Before he could speak Jakli's hand was on his arm, pulling him away, guiding him back toward his pallet.

"They need to understand. Their son is in grave danger," he said through his pain as she led him down the tunnel.

"The family he's with, they're wary as leopards. No one sees them unless they want to be seen," she said but did not sound convinced. She gave him more water and lit the small lamp by the pallet, then left him to sleep.

He did sleep, at least he thought he slept, but not for long. Sounds in the tunnel brought him to full wakefulness, the throbbing not gone but subsided. He picked up the clay lamp and rose, then listened to the sounds and returned the lamp to the floor. There were voices speaking in the herders' tongue. He could not recognize the words, but they were nervous and harried, filled with the urgency of a task at hand.

Shan ventured toward the sounds, edging around the corner where the tunnel entered the chamber, where he saw two men, wearing the woolen vests and caps of herdsmen, carrying something into one of the meditation cells. A third, dressed in the same garb, held a bright kerosene lantern. The bundle carried by the first two was long and narrow. They carried it gingerly, as if it could break.

The men disappeared into the cell, then quickly emerged without their bundle and jogged down the corridor. He was about to move toward the cell to investigate when another light appeared. Jacob Deacon approached, carrying a bag like a doctor's kit, accompanied by Dr. Najan, who still wore his lab coat, and carried a bright battery-powered lamp. Speaking in low tones, they entered the same cell. Shan inched along the wall for a better view. Deacon was kneeling at the blanketed bundle left by the herdsmen, with a large syringe. He pressed it into an opening in the blanket, handed it to Najan, and accepted a second syringe from Najan. The American repeated the process with the syringe, then both men quickly rose and retreated back into the darkened tunnel.

He realized now that it was a person they had carried into the cell, an ill person who needed the American's medication. He waited five minutes, then retrieved his lamp and returned to the entrance of the cell. He recalled that this was where he had previously seen two sleeping forms. Were they all sick, perhaps injured like Shan in the karaburan? He stepped into the cell and saw three blanketed forms on the floor.

Each was wrapped in a heavy felt blanket, with a small roll of felt for a pillow. On the blanket of each an embroidered scarf had been carefully laid, smoothed out so its pattern of leaping horses and large trees was clearly visible. Careful not to wake the sleepers, he moved the lamp closer to the first figure and froze. There was something terribly wrong with the face. The man had no nose. With a trembling hand Shan moved the lamp directly above the face. He had no eyes. And the man, Shan realized as he studied the dried, mummified features, had not seen for centuries. The sand and dryness preserved things, Abigail Deacon had said. He had thought she was only talking about textiles. Shan gently pulled the blanket open to reveal a brown twill robe and understood how she received her textile samples. The burial clothes, worn by the mummies of the Taklamakan.

After the first moment of fright, Shan felt no fear, no revulsion. Quickly he looked at the other two figures, a woman with long brown hair in two braids, in the fashion of Niya Gazuli, and a man so complete, so well preserved he appeared in the dim light to be sleeping. The man was extraordinary, a visitor from a lost world. His face, though leathery, was light in color, and his thick, long, dark hair had a distinctly reddish hue, as did the man's thin beard. A cord of woven multicolored yarn connected his wrists, placing his long, delicate fingers in a reverent repose. He wore a heavy woolen shirt with cuffs that reminded Shan of the strip he had seen in the laboratory. On his feet were boots of thin leather, perhaps deerskin, and felt leggings extended to his knees.

He meant to leave, to go on to avoid detection and not to disturb the mummies further, but something held him back. He dropped to his knees by the bearded man and with a slow, tentative motion touched the cloth of his sleeve. Perhaps the man was a builder of Karachuk, Shan thought with a strange excitement. Perhaps he had plucked an apricot and sat to eat it in the shadow of the reclining Buddha. The serene face of the dead man seemed to hold great wisdom, and the man seemed to be challenging Shan to discover it.

He did not know how long he knelt, contemplating the figures. Eventually he became aware of cigarette smoke. He looked up to see Dr. Najan.

"You've met our silent partners," Najan observed quietly.

"How is it possible? Where—"

"The tracks of all the dead rivers are well known. All the old settlements were on the rivers, that's where we always look. The oldest burial grounds can be easily identified, because burials were made inside circles of logs, built like a small fortress. After a big storm, sometimes a ring of logs is exposed. There are a few old Kazakhs and Uighurs who know the desert ways, who aren't afraid to camp in the desert at night."

"With three, you are able to determine so much?"

"Three? These are only the latest, exposed after the karaburan. Over fifty have been collected. Another thirty have been examined in situ."

"Fifty mummies are here?"

"We take our samples, take photos and videos, then return them to their sleep. If we feel the site has become known to looters, we bury them in a new, secret location."

As the scientist gazed upon the three mummies, Shan saw a strange, sad pride in his eyes. "We have words we read over them, to apologize for disturbing their rest, to let them know we have not forgotten."

Shan remembered the syringes of Deacon. "You take samples of tissues," he said, "not just samples of textiles."

"Whenever possible. Only a tiny sample of tissue, to be sent to labs in the United States and Switzerland that are secretly helping us. We need a statistically significant set of DNA data." Najan squatted and leaned against the wall, looking at the mummy Shan had exposed. He felt the spell too. "We don't think they would mind. The first time, we had a Kazakh here, one descended from the people of Karachuk. He went inside, alone, while his grey dog kept watch outside. He said words over the dead ones and explained to them. He said afterward that the old ones would be proud to help."

Shan smiled. He had met the one who spoke to the dead. Osman.

"It is so dangerous, what you do," Shan said after a long silence. "They would call you a traitor. They would say you are collaborating with foreigners to undermine the state. Don't you have a family?"

A sad smile grew on the scientist's face. "I come from a Uighur clan. When I was young, I had uncles, many uncles. I loved my uncles and aunts and cousins. My uncles would sit around the fires and drink kumiss and tell stories of the clan from back to the time of the great khans. We rode fast horses on festival days and performed ceremonies that had been done for a thousand years. They taught me the names of the spirits that watch over animals and how to hold their eagles."

"Eagles?"

"Hunting eagles. My clan was famous for its hunting eagles. They were raised from hatchlings, as part of the family." The Uighur drew deeply on his cigarette. "But there are no more uncles and aunts. I have only one child, because the government said so. My daughter will be permitted by the goverment to have but one child. Without brothers and sisters there are no more uncles and aunts, no cousins. Festival days aren't the same, some are even forgotten altogether. My uncles are dead. No more hunting eagles. No one remembers all the stories. Maybe I do it for them." Najan pulled on his cigarette, then nodded at the mummy with the beard. "This one, he was someone's uncle."

They walked back down the tunnel together. Najan showed Shan a second row of cells, containing another dozen mummies. They were arranged by age. One cell held those known to be from a two-thousand-year-old burial site, another even older mummies. Or parts of mummies, for most of the cell's contents were pieces of bodies, all that were left in some graves after the storms, and time, did their work. The first cell, where Shan and Najan had sat, contained bodies from a known Tibetan garrison town, from the end of the first millenium.

"I was frightened at first," the Uighur said. "Now, I just come sometimes and sit with them. I know that these people lying here, they would approve."

"Do you know the old tablets?" Shan asked after a moment.

Najan put his palms together horizontally and slid them apart, as though opening one of the wooden tablets. "The Kharoshthi texts? Sure. They were first uncovered a hundred years ago, by European archaeologists working the ruins of Niya. We found dozens here, in a cell at Sand Mountain."

"Public Security knows about them," Shan told him.

The Uighur scientist shrugged. "It was just a matter of time before they found out."

"They're looking for a trail to get to the source, to get to the rebels working with foreigners. Major Bao thinks that maybe he found a connection through Lau."

"But Lau has gone beyond speaking."

Except, Shan reflected bitterly, in the last few minutes of her life, when she had undoubtedly spoken through a haze of drugs and pain. It seemed more certain than ever that this had been the secret her killer had wanted, that Bao was on a relentless, bloodthirsty drive to expose the dissidents and their foreign collaborators. And if so, Bao wasn't after all the zheli, but only the boys, finding and killing the boys, because it was a zheli boy named Micah who was the link to the American scientist.

"Bao spoke about the Antiquities Institute."

Najan gave a bitter smile as he finished his cigarette. "They tried to get me to work for them once. Wanted me to prove to the world that the Kharoshthi writing is actually a form of ancient Chinese. They're not scientists, they're propaganda agents, dedicated to fostering the myths. They tell the newspapers that Niya Gazuli was faked by foreign subversives. They would try to prove that cavemen in Africa ate with chopsticks if they thought they could get away with it." He shook his head sadly, then nodded toward Shan and headed back in the direction of the laboratory.

The cell with the thousand-year-old Buddhists had a new visitor when he returned. Lokesh had brought in several lamps and uncovered all the faces. He was reciting a mantra, a prayer for the souls, Shan thought at first, then he saw the joy in his friend's eyes. It was a celebration, not a mourner's chant.

Shan sat across from Lokesh, one of the mummies between them, the man with the dark red beard. Around the man's neck was a chain, bearing a gau that lay on his chest. He wore a heavy vest, with a small pocket from which a cup made of cow horn protruded.

Lokesh looked up with a huge grin. "He waited a thousand years so we could meet him."

Shan started to say that the man's soul had long departed, but he knew his friend understood. It wasn't that he was paying homage to souls that may have been reincarnated twenty times since leaving these frail bodies. It was just that these people were so real. In that moment, if the man had sat up on his blanket, Shan would not have run. He would have wanted to clasp the man's hand.

"Look in the blanket, Xiao Shan," Lokesh said excitedly, lifting a corner of the felt covering the man's lower body. "I know him."

Shan studied his friend uncertainly, then looked back at the mummy. "I don't understand."

"I mean, I know he was man of good deeds. He was a man who had suffered and didn't mind the suffering. He was a man who understood the things that we understand. Look."

As Lokesh raised the felt Shan saw that around the mummified wrist was a string of beads. A Buddhist rosary. Lokesh pulled the blanket away further and pointed to two thick rectangular objects with cracked leather straps, placed beside the man's hips, where the man's hands could reach them if he extended his arms. They were the hand blocks used by pilgrims, the smooth wooden blocks with leather straps into which a pilgrim inserted his hands to protect them while making ten thousand prostrations on the ground each day. Shan had seen identical blocks used by pilgrims along Tibetan roads, along the sacred Barkhor path in Lhasa. From a standing position they would kneel, then place the hands on the ground and drop to a completely prone position, reciting a mantra as they did so, then rise, take one step forward, and repeat the process.

"There's writing on the blocks," Lokesh said. "Tibetan, in the old style. I studied it. It tells his story. This man"— Lokesh seemed almost overcome with emotion as he spoke—"he was going to Mount Kailas," he continued, referring to the holiest of Tibetan places, the father mountain at the edge of the Himalayas. The first of the mountains, the Tibetans called it. "He was going to leave these blocks on the mountain after completing a circuit of prostrations around it, as an offering for the spirits of his daughter, who had died falling from a horse, and his wife, who had died giving birth to his daughter."

Lokesh looked at Shan and sighed. Something had happened, something had stopped the man hundreds of miles from his destination. "He had come far," Lokesh said, admiration in his voice. "His home, it says, was Loulan, one of the old cities, gone now, at the eastern edge of the desert. He had come almost halfway."

It could have been a sandstorm, Shan thought, or the bitter cold of the winter desert that stopped him. It could have been the arrow of a bandit. Or a Chinese soldier.

They sat in quiet reverence for several minutes, with Lokesh sometimes making soulful moaning sounds.

"Do you sense it, my friend?" Lokesh asked. "It makes some part of me feel alive like never before." The old man seemed to struggle to find his words. "It's as though when they were put in the ground they were wondering would the world survive, would people like us still be here. For all the pain, the wars, the famines, the sandstorms, the persecutions. And now they emerged to find out."

They fell silent again, in a strange communion with the thousand-year-old Buddhist, then a thought seemed to capture Lokesh. He sobered and looked up at Shan. "If I knew this," he said solemnly, "if I knew in a thousand years another human could reach and touch me this way, like a link in the chain of the goodness in souls, I would lie down and die right now."

Shan remembered Lokesh's words at Senge Drak. Maybe humans existed, he had said, just to keep virtue alive and to pass it on to someone else.

They ate outside, as the sun set, by a small brazier into which Deacon set a cannister of gas that burned like a stove. His wife made flat cakes of buckwheat flour, then fried together an assortment of canned goods that Deacon produced with a festive air from his rucksack. Bamboo shoots, bean sprouts, and even pineapple wound up in the same pan, served on the buckwheat cakes.

Shan was ravenous.

"So you had an audience with the Jade Bitch," Marco observed as he joined Shan on a flat rock. There were no plates, no chairs, no tables—nothing, Shan realized, that could not be carried inside quickly if an aircraft approached. Between bites Shan explained what Xu had said, and done, at her office.

"Why would she think you were from Beijing?" Abigail Deacon asked.

"Listen to his voice, woman," Marco interjected. "It has the tones of Beijing."

"That," Shan agreed, "but mostly because she expected someone from Beijing. From Public Security headquarters."

"The boot squad reservations at Glory Camp," Dr. Najan muttered.

Shan looked at him, considering the implications of his words.

"You have friends who watch over you," Shan suggested. "Friends with laptop computers."

The Uighur nodded soberly. "Brave friends. Named Mao."

"Xu had evidence in her office," Shan said. "Lau's things, from the school."

"But Lau drowned," Marco said. "That is what Xu thinks."

"The prosecutor had looked at the evidence," Shan said. "The statement that she failed to report to the school. The horse on the trail. The jacket. And her identity papers."

"Identity papers?" Jakli said with alarm in her voice. "We never—"

"Public Security reported them turned in the day the jacket was found. Taken out of the mud on the riverbank near Yoktian."

"Who turned them in?"

"Lieutenant Sui."

"The killer!" Jakli gasped. "Lau's murderer planted the papers with Sui, to complete the story."

"Or Sui was the killer," Marco said grimly. "I've seen him on a horse. He could ride well."

"Impossible," Jakli argued, "the knobs would have been all over Karachuk if he had seen things there."

"Not if it was just one knob," Shan suggested, "on a special mission. Sui, or one like him. Xu thought there were secret knobs operating in Yoktian," he reminded them.

"A secret mission to kill a teacher?" Deacon asked.

"A special mission to kill a Tibetan nun," Shan said.

"A nun who becomes a teacher," Jakli observed, "not such a strange story in the border country." She said it tentatively, as if trying to convince herself. "There are more Tibetans here than people think, they change their identity to be safe. They have good reasons."

"Some can leave their past behind," Shan said. "Some can't. And it wasn't just about her past. Perhaps something from her past was the link, the trigger that got the knobs interested in the zheli, a way to find what the knobs were already seeking. What boot squads were seeking," he added in a near whisper.

No one spoke for a moment. No one needed to be told

what the boot squads were looking for. They watched the blaze of crimson that was all that remained of the day as it faded into pink and gold and then grey. The American woman rose, then settled on the sand in front of her husband, who rubbed her shoulders.

"Three boys dead," Marco said gravely.

"Micah's out there," Abigail Deacon said, worry in her voice now.

"He's all right, Warp," her husband said reassuringly. "He's in the high mountains. Untouchable. Not long until the full moon, and we'll be together. A new performance."

Warp wrapped her arm around his leg. "You and your damned crickets," she said. "Micah's going to wind up with a bedroom full of insects when we go home."

"Good company. Smarter than fish," quipped Deacon. "Good joss."

His wife laughed, a soft infectious laugh. "My father kept crickets one summer," she said, "used them for fish bait." Deacon, who seemed to have heard the story before, lowered his hands over her face, and she playfully batted them away. "My mother hated them but she let him keep them so long as they were away from the house. One day he left a can of them in the bedroom, while he took a shower, and forgot them. A few days later he puts on his underwear and it falls to pieces. Every pair, full of holes eaten by the crickets. He never said anything. But he got rid of all the crickets that day."

"See?" Marco said with a laugh. "Good luck. Good luck for your mother."

They laughed. They all laughed, even Shan made a sound like a laugh. Marco told a story of how a pet squirrel had made a nest in his mother's only surviving dress from Russia, and they laughed again. Jakli explained how Nikki had once caught an albino mouse for her, and when he got to her camp it had given birth to five tiny pink mice in his pocket. Dr. Najan spoke of a pet pika that always chewed off the buttons of his mother's clothes and took them to his box as treasure.

As he listened a little lump grew in Shan's throat, and a stranger feeling in his heart. What was it? They were happy and he was happy for them. But there was something else. Something they were doing had reached a place inside, a hollow place, another of the chambers that had been unoccupied for so long he had forgotten how to open it. But once it had been full, once it had been overflowing. He recognized the place at last, in a pang of emotion. It was family, it was the way they spoke so openly and laughed so readily, the way Marco and the Americans and even Jakli were so familiar and confiding of the little things, the personal things. Long ago, Shan had shared it with his father and mother, but never with his wife, never with his son.

"How about you, Inspector?" Marco asked in a jovial tone. "Ever have a pet?"

It took a moment before he realized the Eluosi was speaking to him. Shan looked out over the dunes, mottled in evening shadow, like a rolling sea. It seemed like he spent a long time, exploring the forgotten chamber, but they all waited in silence.

"Not a pet," he heard himself say in a near whisper. "In the China of my boyhood you never had enough food to keep your own belly full. Pets never survived. But when I was young my father and I would go to the river and watch the world go by. In the fall farmers would bring ducks to market from far inland. They would clip the wings of the ducks, thousands of ducks, and herd them downriver like vast flocks of sheep, the shepherds in sampans wearing black shirts and straw hats. Once I cried because I realized all the ducks were going to be killed and eaten." He sighed and looked toward the stars. "My father said don't be sad, that for a duck, it was a grand adventure, to float hundreds of miles out into the world, that the ducks would have chosen the river even if they knew their fate. Then he looked all about, very serious, to be sure no one listened, and told me a big secret. That sometimes ducks escaped and made it all the way to the sea and became famous pirate ducks."

No one spoke. No one laughed. He glanced at Marco, who was just nodding toward the horizon, as if he knew all about pirate ducks.

"After that," Shan continued, "every time we went to the river we took paper and inkstones and brushes. We wrote poems sometimes, about the grandeur of the river and how the moon looked when it rose over the silver water. Sometimes I just wrote directions to the sea. Then we folded the paper into little boats and sailed them into the duck herds."

They watched the stars. After a few minutes Marco outlined with his finger the constellations and challenged the Americans to tell the English names. The Northern Bushel they instantly knew as the Big Dipper, and the White Tiger as Orion the Hunter. The game continued good-naturedly. The Porch Way was Cassiopeia, and the Azure Dragon, Sagittarius.

Lokesh wandered from the group and sat on the sand twenty feet away, facing the darkness. He seemed to be looking at something, or at least toward something. Shan considered the direction and noted the position of the small mountain they sat beside. His friend was looking toward the Well of Tears. Lokesh had heard lost souls there.

"Xu had a file on Americans," Shan said suddenly. He was reluctant to break the mood, but the words had to be spoken. Everyone seemed to freeze, and they all watched him intently now. "A list of visiting groups." He looked at Abigail Deacon. "She has your name."

She shrugged. "I was in a delegation. A group of professors, looking at the ruins of the Silk Road market towns. The Marco Polo tour, they called it."

"But only one name was circled on the list. Yours."

The American woman looked at him uncertainly, almost resentfully, as if Shan were accusing her.

"There could be a dozen reasons, Warp," her husband said. "Your flight connections were delayed."

"Sure," Dr. Najan confirmed. "They had to arrange a special car for you to catch up. That's when we first met, the day you caught up with us. Warp, she always wanted to do things not on the itinerary. Asked for a guide to take her to some of the old watchtowers on the mountains. Asked for special food." He looked at Shan as if scolding him. "So they circle a name. Lots of reasons."

"Lots of reasons," Shan agreed woodenly. Good reasons. And bad reasons. He surveyed the team that lived in the little outpost. So far from the world, so absorbed in the grand mystery of their science, it would be easy to forget the bad reasons. The Public Security reasons. The Ministry of Justice reasons.

"The killer," Marco said. "He's hiding far away by now. With Sui murdered, he'll know the knobs will be angry as hornets."

"No," Shan said, and he pulled from his pocket the list of names that Jakli had retrieved from Lau's office. "He killed a third boy," he reminded them. "He has a plan." Shan handed the paper to Deacon, who produced a tiny flashlight. His wife held the paper as Deacon held the light and the others gathered around.

"Twenty-three names," Shan explained. "The zheli. The list is from the school records, the official roll of participants. Anyone could get it. You could print it from a government computer in Urumqi or Lhasa or Beijing if you wanted. Eleven girls. Twelve boys, nine left alive. First Suwan—" Shan pointed to the center of the list, then to two others. "Alta, and Kublai."

"But there's no logic, no way to know what the killer is thinking," Marco said.

"Wrong." Shan pulled a pencil from his pocket and reached for the paper, then handed pencil and paper to Jakli. "Eliminate the girls," he said.

She studied the paper and quickly drew lines through eleven names.

"Then Suwan," he said, and she put an X by the boy's name. "And the boy with the dropka parents who was killed—" Jakli made another mark. "And then Kublai." She made a third mark and returned the paper to the American woman.

The first X was on the center of the page. The next two were the top two names of boys.

"That's his great logic?" Marco asked skeptically, as if he thought little of Shan's discovery. "Just go down the list?"

"He targeted Suwan, and when Suwan proved not to have what he wanted he started from the top of the list."

Abigail Deacon gasped and grabbed her husband's leg tightly. "Micah!" she said in alarm, pointing to a name midway down the list. The fourth boy from the top. After Kublai came a boy named Batu, then Micah Karachuk.

"You can't run to him," Marco warned as he watched the Americans. "It may be what the knobs expect. They're watching everywhere. It must be why they haven't acted on Sui's murder, hoping you'll come out of hiding. You're too conspicuous. You'd be seen in the mountains, reported. Then Micah—" Marco shrugged. "Micah needs you to stay where you are."

Deacon nodded. "We made up the name," the American said in a near whisper as he stared at the list, then began to explain their decision to entrust their son to Lau. Soon after they had arrived in the desert it had become clear that their cavern at Sand Mountain was no place for a ten-year-old. He had met some of the zheli, had met Khitai, at a horse festival in the spring. Micah spoke Mandarin, as did most of the children, and was quickly picking up enough of the Turkic tongue to get by. He loved animals. The zheli was the perfect answer. He would be well protected, watched over by Lau and the nomads. "Besides," Deacon said, trying to lighten his wife's mood, "he's such a mischievous pup, the discipline of the sheep camps would be great for him. He loves it. Been with four different families so far."

"Lau knew this?" Shan asked.

"She suggested it. But kept it secret from the others. So Micah was just a Kazakh boy from a distant part of Xinjiang. Several of the children only spoke Mandarin, because they had been raised in government schools, so his not speaking the clan's tongue was not suspicious."

"So none of the children knew?" Shan asked.

"Not supposed to. But you know ten-year-old boys. Last month, Lau told us Micah had bragged about his parents, then at a class he handed around a jar of American peanut butter. We didn't know he had taken one. Then when I went to see him, he surprised me with three of his friends. Made me promise to come to some classes just before we left Xinjiang, to talk about our discoveries."

Shan stared at Deacon a moment. The Americans were planning to leave soon. Had the boys' killer learned this, and been forced into desperate action?

"He's made some good friends, better friends than in America," the boy's mother added. "Especially Khitai. Micah asked if Khitai could come to our moon festival, to hear the singers." There was no fear in her voice now, which comforted Shan. She had decided her son was safe.

"Stone Lake," Deacon said. "The next two classes are at Stone Lake. Lau always took the children there in the fall."

"If he comes," Jakli said. "Warnings have been going out. Some of the children may stay hidden in the mountains."

"The people he's with now," Deacon said, looking at his wife, "they are as hidden as hidden can be. Not a clan, just two men, a woman and two children. No assigned lands. No contact with the Brigade. The other children don't know where they are. Not even Lau knew all their hiding places. They just stay high up, until winter, roaming just below the ice fields. Lau said we shouldn't expect Micah to see us or anyone else, except on the class days."

"But the others," Jakli said in a forlorn voice. She read the next few names on the list. "They are in danger. The killer could be stalking them. Tonight."

The color had faded from the sky. A cricket sang from the rocks above. Lokesh took another cup of tea and sat, as if listening to something in the darkness. Then, from the edge of the little circle Lokesh spoke, unexpectedly, still looking out into the desert sky. "They say the Jade Basket can vanish, when evil draws near."

"What do you mean, Lokesh?" Jakli asked.

But even if the old Tibetan had been speaking to them a moment earlier, which was far from certain, he was conversing only with the stars now.

Shan realized that Marco had gone, then turned toward the entrance and saw him standing above, on a tall boulder that gave him a perch to see far out into the desert. And he was looking, looking hard. It was for Nikki, Shan realized, his son who was on caravan, smuggling goods across the border. Nikki, who was going to change Jakli's life forever. Shan saw that Jakli had noticed too. She followed Marco's gaze for a moment toward the darkness, then quickly turned back to the others.

"My cousins and the Maos won't find them all. We have to be there to warn them," she declared urgently. "They're supposed to be at Stone Lake in five days. Kaju is going there." She looked back at Shan. They had no vehicle, he realized. They were stranded in the desert.

"That Tibetan?" Najan asked. "He's one of them. Works for Ko. For the Poverty Scheme. Who best to trap the zheli than their own teacher?"

The words seemed to create a stillness in the air, like the calm Shan had felt before the horrible sand storm.

"No," Jakli said slowly. "The Brigade is only conducting business," she said uncertainly. "It has to be the knobs. Or Xu."

"Either way," Deacon said heavily, "the other boys have to be protected. They're in greater danger than Micah."

"A boy named Batu," Shan said toward the night sky. "Next on the list."

Marco appeared, his eyes still watching the desert. He poured himself a mug of tea, drained most of it in one gulp, then threw the remainder into the sand. "It's a clear night. With the stars out, we can navigate. I leave for the Kunlun in three hours. Sophie and I, we'll take you as far as town. The Maos are there, they can get you a truck."

"Then I suggest we get some sleep," Jakli said. She walked over and put her hand on Lokesh's shoulder. The old Tibetan turned his head, still wearing his distant expression, then rose and silently let her lead him inside.

Shan did not feel like sleeping. He had slept for two days already. He helped the others remove the cooking implements to one of the cells that had been converted to a pantry, then wandered along the murals on the walls. Lokesh was right, Shan felt it too. Never had he been anywhere where he felt so connected to the ancient world. It wasn't a quality of history he felt, nothing like the distance created by museum displays. It was a direct, visceral quality of continuity, of the great chain of life. No, perhaps it was only the chain of truth he sensed. Or maybe even simpler, a realization that people always had done good things, and it was only good things, not people, that endured.

But Shan was not sure what good things were anymore, or at least how he connected to good things. He was adrift, without answers to save the boys who were dying. His friends seemed to have secrets they could not share. His enemies seemed everywhere, yet impossible to find. His government would like nothing better than to put him behind prison walls again.

He found an oil lamp and wandered outside, climbing up the narrow trail that led to the top of the rocks. He lay back on a flat rock and mingled with the stars for several minutes, then lit the little lamp and took out his notepad and pencil.

Dear Father, he started. *I have found a place from a different world, where I made a thousand-year-old friend.* He should have been using an inkstone and brush and was shamed that he had only his pad and a stub of a pencil. *Now I am supposed to provide everyone's answer,* he wrote, *but instead it feels like each person's tragedies and sorrows, now and in the future, cast a shadow and I attract the sorrows of all I meet, until I stand in the one place where all the shadows intersect, the darkest place of all.*

I travel, but I have no destination. I have no family. I have no home to long for. I can only long for the longing. This is not what I expected my life to be, Father, when you and I wrote poems to the ducks.

Come closer, Father. Help me watch the stars.

He read it twice, then signed it. *Xiao Shan.* Little Shan, the way his father would have called him.

He would have liked to have bamboo splints and juniper, to make the kind of small fragrant fire that attracted spirits. But he had none. So he picked a few dried stems from the wiry bushes on top of the rock and arranged them in a small dense pile. He took a sheet of blank paper and folded it into an envelope, wrote his father's name on it, and set the letter on the twigs. It was a meager offering. He should have had rice paper, he should have spent an hour just practicing the rhythm of the ideograms before inscribing them in the bold flowing strokes his father had taught him. *Forgive me, Father, for these my shortcomings,* he said in his heart, and lit the fire with the little lamp.

The ashes floated upward, toward the heavens. For a fleeting moment they drifted across the Northern Bushel, then they were gone.

After a long time Shan wandered back inside. The tunnels were silent. Even the camels were sleeping. With his little lamp held in front of him, he found the cell with the ancient pilgrim and sat beside him, gently pulling open the blanket that covered him so that Shan could see his hands and the worn spots at his knees that were the signs of a pilgrim. More than ever the man seemed to be asleep. Sometimes, when the light flickered, it seemed his mouth moved. He had been exposed in the karaburan that had almost killed Shan, the one that had made it impossible for Shan to leave for a new life. The scientists would take their samples from the pilgrim and he would be returned to the desert, perhaps to be exposed by another storm in a thousand years. A messenger. Or still a pilgrim, Gendun would have said, brought back to visit important places of virtue, to stir mindfulness in others, across time.

"My name is Shan Tao Yun," he said quietly to the silent figure. "I was born in Liaoning Province, near the sea, more than four decades ago." The words just came out, suddenly, without conscious effort. "When I was very small we made sweet rice cakes on festival days and took them to the temple. But sometimes I ate one when my parents weren't looking. They never found out." He spoke on, of memories that he thought he had lost until that instant, of his forgotten cousins and the way his mother sang opera songs to goats when they had been sent to a work camp. He smiled as he spoke, because the ancient man had come back and unlocked more doors in chambers he had forgotten how to visit.

The man's hands were held together, as if in prayer. Shan realized there was something between them, pressed together in the palms, with a protruding end barely visible. A stalk of something. A piece of grass, maybe. Shan leaned over with the lamp. As he did so he touched the arm and the top palm lifted fractionally. With a choke in his breath, Shan recognized it. A feather. A feather had been placed in the man's palms, a thousand years before.

He settled back, his heart racing. Then, with a slow, reverent motion he reached out and pulled it from the pilgrim's clasp far enough to see it in the lamplight. It was an owl feather, desiccated, its shaft bare for a quarter of its length, but still almost identical to the one in his gau, the one Gendun had given him before they had parted. He stared at it, overcome with wonder. Time passed, and still he stared. Not at the feather. At the man's face. At his long delicate fingers. The man had not been a shepherd. He had been an artist, or a teacher perhaps.

Finally, with utter confidence in the rightness of what he was doing, he lifted the feather from his gau, then carefully extracted the feather from the pilgrim's palms and inserted his own in its place. He placed the pilgrim's feather, the thousand-year-old feather, into his gau, then gently closed the man's hands, unprepared for the wave of emotion that swept over him. His own hands trembled. When they calmed he saw that they had come to rest on those of the pilgrim.

He pushed the rosary down the man's wrist, to be close to the fingers. Then, without knowing why, he cried.

CHAPTER 12

They rode urgently through the night, the three camels in single file as Sophie and Marco led the way toward Yoktian. Marco invited Shan to ride double behind him, and though the Eluosi was silent for the first two hours, he began speaking to Shan of camels and the beauty of the high lonely places he called his home. Just before dawn, as they crossed the Kashgar highway and Sophie settled into a trot for the final miles to Yoktian, Marco began singing loudly: old songs, Russian songs, songs he said were for drinking on long winter nights.

The sun was an hour over the horizon when they arrived at a series of low sheds by the river, a large complex of holding pens for livestock shaded by a row of tall poplar trees in the golden plumage of autumn. The pens near them were all empty, but five or six at the far end, a hundred yards away, were full of horses. The Kazakh herds were being collected. Marco tied the camels in the shadows of the first shed, then led Shan up a small knoll. They were on the outskirts of the town, less than two hundred feet from the main road leading to the town square.

Half an hour later, Shan, Jakli, and Lokesh approached the low mud-brick buildings of the hat factory. Workers were on benches, milling at the gate, and as they stepped into the compound, someone called Jakli's name. Akzu sat on a nearby bench, smoking with one of his sons. Their hands were stained purple.

"You're making hats?" Jakli blurted out.

"Of course. Wonderful hats," he said with a nod to Shan and Lokesh. "The best hats. Always wanted to make hats, niece," he said dryly, looking at his stained hands. "Thank you for the opportunity."

"But why—" Jakli began, but did not finish her sentence. She had realized, Shan knew, that they were to cover for her.

"No sense in taking undue risk, not so close to nadam. The manager here is a Kazakh. He said he won't cover up for anyone if he's asked, but as long as production is above quota not many questions get asked," Akzu explained, standing and stretching. "As long as the boot squads don't come." He looked at a woman who appeared on the steps of the main building, holding a clipboard. "There's worker attendance forms inside the door, niece. Go sign a few."

"But the zheli—" Jakli began.

Akzu held up a hand to cut her off and looked about before answering in a low voice. "The clan still searches for them. And for Malik. We can't find Malik. He was seen galloping down a highway yesterday, as if in pursuit of someone." He looked toward the southern horizon. "I go back into the mountains tonight. One of your cousins will stay here until nadam."

As Akzu spoke a low moan came from a nearby bench. An old man with a long drooping moustache sat and stared at a piece of paper in his hand.

"Been that way for hours," Akzu said. "He came here to ask the manager to explain where his sheep were. He thought it must be some kind of map or directions to a pasture."

"His sheep?" Shan asked.

"It's a share certificate in the Brigade company," Akzu explained in a bitter tone. "He surrendered his sheep to the Brigade, and all they gave him was a piece of paper. Sixty years with his herd and just a piece of paper."

As Jakli took a step toward the man as though to comfort him, Akzu pulled her arm and led her to the gate of the compound. Her eyes never left the mournful old herder.

Ten minutes later Shan and Jakli were at the school compound. There was a ragged broom leaning against the crumbling concrete gatepost. Lokesh picked it up.

"Cleanliness is an overlooked virtue," he said with a twinkle in his eye. Shan nodded and smiled. Lokesh meant he would wait, and watch, at the gate.

Shan and Jakli stood in the shadow of the empty entry-way, checking for signs of knobs. Seeing none, they quickly moved down the empty corridor to Lau's office. They searched Lau's office again, looking for more information on the zheli. In her desk. In the computer. Under her desk drawers. Nothing. A number of the photographs had been pulled from the wall since their last visit, some ripped away, their remnants hanging loose. Someone else had come back to the office, searching. Looking for what? The photo of the Dalai Lama that Jakli had removed on their last visit? Jakli went outside, toward the class buildings, hoping to find children who might have word on the missing zheli. As she departed Shan saw that the light was on in the opposite office.

He stepped to the door, which was open a few inches, and looked at the little hand-lettered sign again. Religion is the Opiate of the Masses. He looked back. The sign would have been in front of Lau whenever she walked out her office. There were voices inside. As he pushed on the door, it swung open to reveal the short plump man he had met at the rice camp, Committee Chairman Hu, wearing a bulky, brown cardigan sweater. He was sitting sideways on his desk, facing the rear of his office as he spoke enthusiastically to a tall lean man who leaned against the rear window casement. Kaju Drogme.

They stopped speaking and looked at Shan as he took a step inside. The Han was holding something, explaining it to Kaju—a thin, sleek, grey box, curved at the front corners, with earphones hooked to its rear. The man raised his eyebrows toward Shan but his gleaming expression did not change.

Shan nodded at Hu. "Just looking at her office again," Shan said to the Committee Chairman.

Not only did Hu not seem surprised, he appeared to welcome the comment, as if it were an invitation. "A suicide, I told them," he said with an oddly bright tone. "Obviously it was a suicide. Disgraced from the loss of her council position. Facing retirement, with no prospects, no family."

Shan stepped closer to the man. The box was a music player of some kind. On the lid he saw a stylized logo for a Japanese company. A plastic bag with an instruction manual lay on the man's desk.

"Just the day before she did it, Comrade Ko came in and told her she would be welcome to move to Urumqi. Said there was a retirement complex, a high-rise building just for retired citizens. A number of heroes from the Revolution live there, they give speeches about the liberation battles every week. Said he was going to Urumqi and that he wanted her to go with him to see it. At Brigade expense." Hu shook his head, looking back and forth from Kaju to Shan. "But Lau wouldn't have it. Acted like Director Ko had kicked her. She sat down, out of breath. Too old-fashioned, she was. No flexibility." He lowered his voice and leaned toward Shan. "She had allowed herself to become isolated, cut off from the socialist fabric. A latent reactionary," he said in a knowing tone. "Go, I said, don't you recognize the offer? They are offering rehabilitation. I told them at the camp, wrote it all down for them."

Hu had become much more talkative now that he was out of the rice camp. He had a story now, and he had his job back. When Shan met him at Glory Camp he had said he had nothing to report about Lau. But Prosecutor Xu had kept him behind the wire, to think about things.

"You found a way to get out of Glory Camp," Shan observed. "Not really a place for a man like you."

Hu nodded energetically. "It was getting unbearable. Like an insane asylum with the patients taking over."

"What do you mean?"

"It was those men, the crazy ones who disrupted the camp."

"Disrupted?" Shan asked.

"One of the damned fools without thumbs. Or not him, really—he just translated."

Shan looked from Kaju to Hu in confusion.

"The senile old Xibo could make that man without thumbs understand him. Anyway, at three o'clock one morning they were all found sitting in a circle on the floor, the whole barracks, with the thumbless one and the Xibo sitting in front of them, chanting the political slogans they had been taught that day. When their officer stormed in and demanded an explanation, the old Xibo explained through the other. He said he was unfamiliar with the particular path to enlightenment being taught at the camp but that it was important to strive for perfection in its practice, since enlightenment must be the goal. Everyone in the barracks was different after that, obedient and polite, smiling like fools all the time. The officer was furious but the prisoners were doing nothing wrong. The guards kept the Xibo separated from the others after that, let him wander around alone. Mostly he sat at the bed of some Mongol boy who couldn't walk."

Shan sighed. He remembered the waterkeeper sitting alone at the flagpole. Maybe at least it might improve the chances for rescuing the waterkeeper, if the old man were able to freely move about the camp. He had vowed to himself that as soon as he knew all the boys were safe, he would return to Glory Camp and find a way out for the old Tibetan. Shan saw that Kaju was staring at the teacher with a puzzled expression.

"You mean there is a lama at the camp?" Kaju asked.

Hu laughed. "Not a damned lama. Just a crazy Xibo."

Kaju leaned forward and seemed about to correct the man, then shrugged and looked into his hands.

"What did you mean," Shan asked Hu, "that Ko was offering Lau rehabilitation?"

"People misunderstand Ko. He has the best of intentions. Comrade Director Ko was saying in his way that she was being forgiven for all the unauthorized teaching, for the misappropriations. Take the retirement flat, I told her. They'll have elevators there. Television."

"What kind of misappropriations?" Shan asked. Kaju still leaned against the window, gazing uncertainly at the Han teacher.

"Using Ministry of Education cars without permission. She took Ministry paper and pencils out of the school. Food from the school kitchen. Not to mention teaching unapproved curriculum or encouraging religious practices."

"Chairman Mao," Shan declared stiffly, "taught us to be vigilant. He warned us about religion."

"Exactly!" Hu agreed, and turned with a victorious smile toward Kaju.

"A good citizen like you would try to stop it, to do what you could," Shan suggested.

Hu nodded gravely. "I tried to warn her first. I've been teaching thirty-five years now. I went to university in Urumqi. It's not how things are done, I told her. She was never trained for teaching. What she did, it was never done that way."

Shan looked at the machine in the man's hand. "There're new ways now," he observed. There were crates at Glory Camp, he remembered, with the same logo. Crates he had seen with the dead American. And also crates with Osman, at Karachuk. Had Osman stolen from the knobs? No. It wasn't the knobs who were passing out machines, it was the Brigade. The Brigade was using the knobs' inventory, even though everyone insisted Ko and Bao never cooperated.

Hu followed Shan's gaze. "From Director Ko! Part of the new incentive scheme. We're not going to just punish bad actors, we are going to reward good behavior."

Kaju had one of the machines too, sitting unopened in its plastic bag on the window sill. He picked it up. "The orphans," the Tibetan said. "All the orphans who return to class, who enroll in our new program, will get a disc player. They—" He was interrupted by a loud buzz from the public address system in the hall.

Hu rose from his desk abruptly. "My class is starting," he announced, and pulled a cap with a snap-down visor from a drawer. "Political history." He pulled the cap low around his head and looked at Shan and Kaju as if about to ask them to leave.

"We'll just be a few moments," Shan said in a reassuring tone. "The investigation."

The man nodded soberly and scurried out of the room.

Kaju Drogme looked at Shan, then at the machine in his hands. He shrugged. "These children," the Tibetan said in a confused tone. "They hardly know what radios are. Maybe they've seen tape players, in town. Maybe even if they got to a city, some day, some year, they could buy a disc to play."

"If they had any money," Shan added.

Kaju gave a weak smile, as if thanking Shan for understanding a bad joke. "I have friends in Chengdu," he said, still gazing at the disc player. "Maybe they could send some old discs." He shrugged again and looked at Shan. "You were there that day at the garage. When the Tibetan warned about the boys."

"Why is Ko doing this with the orphans? What is the rush?"

"Not orphans," Kaju said. "There was a memorandum. We are to call them Emerging Members."

"Members of what?"

Kaju hesitated. "The memorandum didn't say. School. Society. Socialism." He shrugged once more. The movement seemed be one of his defining characteristics. "What he's doing is rewarding everyone, pursuant to new Brigade policy. Ko didn't decide it on his own. It came from Urumqi. But he wants this county to lead in the initiative." The Tibetan looked up with a self-conscious grin. "If I get all the children back within two weeks, he's going to give me a special apartment. One of those reserved for Brigade managers. And access to the motor pool. And a title, Director of Economic Assimilation."

"Economic?"

Kaju nodded. "He says that's why assimilation failed, because it was always made political. People don't understand that economics bring people together far more effectively. Use common cultural themes to build common economic interests to bind them together. That's how Director Ko defines my job. Ko said the Brigade itself is the best example. A company owned by Hans, Kazakhs, Uighurs, Kirghiz, Tadjiks, Xibo, Hui, probably ten other cultural groups. But everyone works together successfully. No one refers to Han shareholders versus Kazakh shareholders, just shareholders." Kaju looked back at his machine. "The disc players are not the right reward, that's all. He wants so much to help them, to bring them into the new society. His enthusiasm gets misunderstood sometimes. I will speak with him. Maybe new saddles. Maybe even foals from the Brigade herd." Kaju paused and nodded. "Foals would be perfect."

"Maybe not," Shan said. "I thought horses have been declared reactionary. They're all being arrested by the knobs."

The Tibetan's face clouded, and he shrugged again. "You just don't understand Ko. He wants to do the right thing. A few days ago he started a new children's health program, all on his own."

"Health program?"

Kaju nodded energetically. "Special help from local Brigade resources at the clinic, for newborns. Ko says it will build trust."

Shan looked at him in confusion. Was it possible that he had indeed misunderstood Ko? Ko, after all, was a creature of the new economy, a creature of a kind Shan had never known. "You said there was a memorandum from Urumqi?" he asked.

"Sure, about the gifts. Ko left a copy on all the teachers' desks today." He looked up at Shan and his brightness faded. He looked toward the door as if to confirm no one could hear, then turned back to Shan. "How did you know that day at the garage, that the boys were in danger? That Tibetan with you said they were dying. Then two days later one is killed."

"Two had already been killed. We had just come from one of their graves."

Kaju stared at him with a chastising frown, shaking his head. "No," Kaju insisted. "You don't understand. What you're talking about is just a blood feud. Ko said so at a Brigade briefing. He spoke to Public Security. Bystanders get caught in fights between rival clans sometimes. A vestige of the old ways. Proof of why the clans need to be brought in, need to enroll in the Poverty Eradication Scheme. If they don't, eventually Public Security will have no choice but to just take them away."

Shan looked out into the hallway, which remained quiet, and back to the Tibetan. "Kaju," he said very quietly, causing the Tibetan to lean toward him. "Lau was murdered. Tortured, and then murdered."

The Tibetan seemed to search for something in Shan's eyes, then he frowned and shook his head again, as if disappointed. "That kind of talk," he said, still shaking his head, "it just doesn't help anyone. Not the children. Not the clans. Not the assimilation effort." He stepped past Shan into the hallway, then turned and lowered his voice. "You sound like one of the radical elements, one of the lung ma. Don't let anyone else—" He was interrupted by another sound on the public address speaker, a two-tone chime. He glanced up at the speaker with a grateful expression. "I have a meeting," he said with a final shrug, then tucked the disc player under his arm and moved briskly down the hall toward the rear door of the building.

Shan waited a few seconds, watching Kaju cross the yard to one of the classroom buildings, then stepped silently toward the main entrance. Halfway down the hall, turning to confirm the hall was still empty, he stepped into a vacant office. There were two sheets of paper on the desk inside. A memo from Director Ko, attached to another memorandum from Urumqi—from Headquarters, People's Development and Construction Corporation. Regarding Economic Assimilation. Shan folded it and put it in his pocket.

Jakli was at the door, and Lokesh still swept at the gate, singing to himself. As the Tibetan saw them he retrieved a burlap sack from the bottom of the post and extended it to Jakli. "A man gave this to me for you," he said. "A Uighur, I think. He said his name was Mao."

Jakli accepted the bag with a tentative, outstretched hand, but as she opened it the caution on her face abruptly changed to joy. She pulled out a horse's bridle, a bridle of rich black leather studded with silver. "Nikki!" she exclaimed, and darted down the street.

"I spoke to the Mao," Lokesh said, leaning on the broom as he watched Jakli disappear in the direction of the livestock sheds. "The boy Kublai was buried outside of town. People came, a lot of people, chanting that woman's name. Niya." He gestured with a nod of his head toward the other side of the street, where a poster had been freshly pasted to the wall, another of the posters of Niya Gazuli Shan had seen at the square. "That Mao said to tell you something, that the boy was missing a shoe. He said you would understand." But Shan didn't understand. It was as though shoes were the artifacts being sought by the killer.

Lokesh looked back at the poster, as if he were conversing with the red-haired woman. "Knobs were there, at the burial," Lokesh sighed toward her. "Imagine that," he said, with disbelief in his eyes. "Knobs come, to bury a boy."

When they caught up with her at the sheds, Jakli was dancing a jig with Marco, as the Eluosi waved the bridle over his head. They stopped and embraced each other when Shan and Lokesh approached.

"It means Nikki is back?" Shan ventured.

Marco nodded vigorously. "Not home. But close, across the border now. The pack animals are slow. He sent someone ahead." He halted his dance and looked at Jakli, suddenly sober. "There's much work to be done. Only a week now." He began tightening the harnesses on the camels, humming a tune as he worked.

"It's going to be all right now," Jakli said, stroking Sophie, her face still aglow. "Nikki will know things. Nikki will—" The words died in her throat.

A figure had appeared at the front of the shed, a bedraggled boy with a tangled mop of black hair. His dirty red shirt was torn in several places and his face was gaunt, a mask of exhaustion and fear.

"Batu!" Jakli gasped, and stared.

"I just keep running," the boy said, breathing hard. "With no place to go. I just run. I stop and get some water, then I run again." His voice was shaking, and he looked over his shoulder as he spoke "I saw you on the street, and I followed."

Jakli leapt forward and put her arms around the boy. "The clan," she asked, pressing the boy's head against her. "Where is your clan?"

"I heard about the zheli boys dying. The last time a lamb was killed too," the boy said with a long dry sob. "If the thing comes looking for me I want it away from that clan. They've been good to me. And away from the lambs," the boy added as he looked at Jakli.

Batu. Shan didn't need to pull the list of the zheli from his pocket, because he had memorized the boys' names. Batu was the third boy from the top of the list. The next boy.

"I didn't do anything," the boy said, his voice breaking with a sob. "Why would they want to—" Jakli held the boy at arm's length as he spoke, then cut him off by placing a finger on his lips. She held him tightly and stroked his head. *"Khoshakhan, khoshakhan,"* she whispered. The word for comforting lambs. At last she looked from Marco to Shan, then Lokesh with a grave, determined expression.

"I must go," she said. "I must go to the Maos, help them find the others. I know places they do not." She looked at Shan. "Where the shadow clans may be."

"I'll go with you," Lokesh blurted out with great emotion. He was looking at the boy as he spoke. "I have to find it."

Jakli looked at the old Tibetan with moist eyes. For a moment Shan thought she was going to embrace Lokesh and murmur the lamb word again. "No," she said firmly, as she might with a child, and put a hand on his shoulder, pushing him gently toward Shan.

"I'll give you food for the boy," Marco offered and reached into one his saddlebags.

"But I'm staying in town," Shan said with a worried glance toward Lokesh. "I'll sleep here. I must see the prosecutor. I said I would."

"Impossible!" Jakli exclaimed, but then seemed to recognize the determination in Shan's eyes and frowned. She watched as Marco handed the boy an apple and he attacked it with ravenous bites. "No," she said, in a new, insistent tone as she looked in the direction of town. "Not back there, not in one of her traps. Tomorrow in the afternoon. Say three o'clock, at the highway station, where we met the rice truck. Our ground."

"I need food for the others," Batu said tentatively.

"Others?" Jakli asked then, as if grasping his meaning, she knelt by the boy, her hand on his arm. "You know where other zheli boys are?"

The boy looked about warily. "At a place called the old lama field. It is safe there, high in the mountains. I was going there. Khitai told us that it is protected by the mountain deities."

Lokesh looked up with a new alertness in his eyes.

"You mean he took you there?" Shan asked.

"Yes. Years ago, the first time, when he was only seven. He had never been there then, but somehow he sensed where it was. When he found it he kept laughing, like he had found an old friend. Just some ruined walls. But a beautiful painting. I think Khitai is there now. He might go for the flowers, the assignment."

"Assignment?" Shan asked.

"Lau's last assignment to the zheli. A collection of autumn flowers. The flowers were beautiful by the lama field, she always said so."

Shan looked at Jakli, remembering the flowers at Lau's cave. Some of the other zheli children had remembered their assignment.

"Khitai knows that one of the shadow clans tended sheep in the mountains above the field," Batu continued. "That is where he might go after getting his flowers, with the clan who watched over Suwan."

Lokesh stood up, erect, like a soldier preparing for action. Suwan had visited the Red Stone camp and died. But his clan might have left with another zheli boy, with Khitai, knowing that Lau sometimes let the zheli switch families, unaware of Suwan's fate.

Jakli went to the front of the shed and looked out, as if collecting her thoughts, then turned. "I know this place. It's near an old Russian lodge," she said, looking to Marco.

"Like hell—" the Eluosi sputtered.

"They have nowhere to go," Jakli pressed. "You can't stay here. The Brigade is bringing in horses all the time."

"I can't—" Marco spat, then he looked at Jakli and a low audible exhalation escaped his lips, not quite a whistle, almost a snort. He looked to Shan in exasperation. "May as well argue with a gnat up your nose," he groused. Sophie turned and made a snickering noise toward Marco, her tongue exposed. "God's breath," he muttered, "not you too."

And then Jakli took the boy's hand and suddenly placed it in Shan's.

The action shook Shan so greatly he almost jerked his hand away. He stood in silence, unable at first to even look the boy in the eyes, unable to understand the sudden acrid taste of fear in his mouth or the welling of emotion within.

Slowly he brought his eyes up and Batu looked at him with a small, uncertain smile. He knew children, he could talk with children, he had shared secrets with Malik. But this boy, he was Lau's boy. Shan had had such a boy once, a son, and he had lost him when he was Batu's age.

"This is Shan," he heard Jakli say. "A friend of Auntie Lau's."

Shan found himself on his knees in front of Batu and saw that he was tying the dangling laces of the boy's boots. His hands had taken him where his heart needed to be.

As Jakli tied the bag with the bridle to Sophie's saddle, Marco found a brown shirt in his saddlebag and told Batu to slip it on over his red shirt, then leaned into the camel's ears. The camel made a slow, snickering sound, then Marco straightened. "Okay, mount up," he said, with raised brows, as if expressing surprise. "She says okay. But"—he pointed to Shan—"you've got boots and"—he added, pointing to Lokesh—"you've got bags." He ignored the inquisitive looks on their faces and led Sophie out of the shed, then turned as he reached the sunlight. "One more thing. She says if any of you ever breathe a word of where you are going or how we get there, the blue wolf will track you down and put you in his belly."

Batu nodded solemnly and looked at Sophie with wide eyes.

Jakli hugged Batu again. "You're safe now," she said, then broke away with a quick glance at Marco and Shan. "Three o'clock tomorrow," she reminded them, then jogged away toward town.

As they led the camels away from the settlement, they passed a cemetery on the far side of the river. Near the bank was a fresh grave, with a small brown and white horse standing nearby, its head hung low. They paused to look at it.

"Most of the zheli didn't even have their own horses," Batu explained. "Kublai was singing for a month last year when they gave it to him." The Kazakh boy shook his head and sighed like an old man as he looked again at the animal waiting at the boy's grave. "Now look. It's hard on a horse."

* * *

The three camels moved quickly up the valley, along a trail that paralleled the river, then over a long ridge into a landscape that Shan recognized, the small valley where Lau's cabin lay. Shan kept his eyes on the wooded slope above as they passed the building, toward the cave where Lau lay waiting for her justice.

They quickly left the valley behind, and the sun had passed its zenith before Marco slackened the pace, pausing at a pool below a small waterfall. They were deep in the Kunlun, and the wind blew cool and fresh out of the icefields above them. Marco watched the horizon with restless eyes.

"If something happens," he said in a voice that seemed taut with premonition, "do what I do. Do it fast. Don't talk. Listen to me. Listen to the camels."

Batu rode with Shan, sitting double on the camel behind Sophie, and they followed the silver camel southwestward on a trail that opened to long vistas over the distant desert. Then the trail dropped abruptly into a long valley of brown grass and gravel, down which a swift stream rushed. The path through the landscape was surprisingly wide, as if cleared long ago for heavier traffic. Batu pointed out things Shan did not see. A pika stuffing its cheeks with grass to store in its winter den. An eagle soaring over the adjoining ridge.

Suddenly Sophie stopped. Shan clenched his jaw, but relaxed as he saw that Marco was not searching about for danger. Then he realized that the Eluosi was watching Sophie's head. The silver camel jerked her nose toward the western ridge and brayed. Marco shot out of his saddle. "Helicopter!" he roared and shouted several words in Russian.

The camels bolted off in different directions just as their riders began to climb down. They tumbled to the ground as the camels themselves dropped, folding their legs under their bodies, tucking their heads against their shoulders. From somewhere nearby Shan heard Lokesh laughing. He looked over the side of the camel to see Marco lying against Sophie, curled in the shadow of her body. Lokesh, still wheezing with laughter, was slowly doing the same. The appearance of the animals with their riders pressed against them would be that of three more boulders in the grey and brown landscape. It was why Marco had asked Batu to cover his red shirt. A surveillance team, flying fast, could easily overlook them.

A low ululating rumble rolled up the valley now, a sound that took Shan to the edge of terror, for fear that Lokesh and the boy would be taken. This was how the army and the knobs kept the nomads intimidated, by suddenly appearing out of the sky to check for illegal weapons or identity papers. You can't hide from Chinese, an old dropka had told Shan once. They have machines with guns that live in the clouds.

Shan caught a glimpse of the helicopter as it cleared the ridge. Then someone pulled his head down and pushed it against the camel. Batu.

Marco waited ten minutes after the whine of the engine had faded, then called a hasty word to the camels and the animals unfolded their heads. Moments later they were moving up the trail at a fast trot.

A quarter hour later Lokesh rose in his saddle and called out. "*Lha gyal lo!*" He waved to get Shan's attention.

"The field!" Batu exclaimed.

They had been to the lama field before, Shan saw as he followed Lokesh's pointing arm. The huge red prayer flag on the rock monolith was before them, rumbling in the wind.

Batu led them to a small outcropping three hundred yards from the monolith, where low mounds of rocks outlined the remains of a four-room structure. It had been built against the rock, facing the monolith. A place of hermits. "On the other side, there are more walls," Batu explained excitedly as they dismounted, "and you can see the faces of Tibetan gods." He ran toward the ruins, stopping every few seconds to call out that it was safe, that it was only Batu and their friends.

They caught up with the boy at the back of the rock, where a large room had been built against the outcropping, staring forlornly at the wall. As Shan approached he smelled fresh paint. There had indeed been a mural, no doubt a beautiful one, protected even after the collapse of the outer walls by an overhanging shelf of rock. But it was no more. The wall had been covered with black spray paint, and over the paint two posters had been freshly pasted. Escape the Chains of Feudalism, one said. The other, in fine Chinese print, was a copy of a state decree prohibiting religious practices which had not been authorized by the Bureau of Religious Affairs.

"The rocks," Marco muttered suddenly, and pointed toward Sophie. The camel had taken a step forward and was stretching her neck toward a large outcropping on the slope above them. The Eluosi jogged stealthily toward the rocks, gesturing for Shan to follow as he disappeared into a narrow opening between two huge boulders.

Shan caught up with him as he stood on the far side of the boulders, at the edge of a large clearing ringed with several rock cairns and the remains of a long rock wall consisting of hundreds of long thin stones. Shan recognized it, a sacred *mani* wall, each of whose stones was inscribed with a Buddhist prayer. They had found the lama field itself, and in the center of it was a single boy who knelt at a fresh mound of earth.

It was Malik, from the Red Stone camp, and he was stroking the top of the mound, speaking in a low tone.

Malik turned and gasped as he heard them approach, then leapt away, running toward another outcropping further up the slope, where Shan saw a grey horse tethered. He had almost reached the horse when he was stopped by a call from behind Shan.

"Seksek Ata!" a young voice called out. Shan turned to look at Batu, ten feet behind him. He had heard the words before, the name of the protective deity for goats, the nickname for Malik.

Malik turned and stared at them, not moving until Shan reached his side. The boy's eyes seemed glazed over with grief, and he looked not at Shan but at the mound of earth. "I came fast, because the other boys I found said Khitai might be here. But they were already lowering him into the ground when I arrived," Malik said, his voice cracking with grief. "If I had come a few hours earlier I could have taken him away to safety." The boy was swaying on his feet. His hands trembled. He seemed but a shadow of the sturdy youth Shan had met at the Red Stone camp. It had been nearly a week. The boy had been riding the hills, tracking the zheli, knowing death was lurking everywhere, desperately trying to do something to stop it. He had brought two boys back to the Red Stone camp, Jakli had reported. But when he had finally found another of the boys, the grave had already been dug.

Lokesh appeared and stepped to the side of the grave. A burlap sack lay on a rock ten feet from the mound of earth. Lokesh stared at the sack with wide, frightened eyes, then moved toward it in tiny, mincing steps. As Shan stepped to his side, Lokesh bent and emptied the bag onto the rock. His friend's face seemed to collapse.

On the rock lay a short chain of small iron links and a long tarnished copper case inlaid with turquoise circles—a pen case. A battered metal cup lay beside the case with several short strings of beads, different colored beads of wood and plastic and a single one of green jade. He looked back at the pen case. It was the one Lokesh had asked about in Lau's office.

Something had lodged in the mouth of the bag and Shan pulled it free. A wedge-shaped piece of wood with a top that slid open. One of the Kharoshthi letters.

The embers inside Lokesh had ignited and seemed to be consuming him from within. A noise was coming from his chest—it had the tone of a mantra, but it was just a long continuous moan, as if he had forgotten the words. The old Tibetan clasped the metal cup with both hands and he looked up at Shan with moist, forlorn eyes. For the first time since Shan had known him, Shan saw something else on Lokesh's face. He had seen the expression before, on Bajys's face when they had found him at Lau's cave, when Bajys had proclaimed that the world had ended.

"The herders thought he had fallen at first," Malik said from behind him, "that maybe he was trying to climb the rock with the god flag on it." Shan turned. The Kazakh youth stared stiffly straight ahead, like a soldier making dutiful report. His lips quivered as he spoke. "But his pants were covered with blood. It was because a knife had gone into his belly, up into his heart. His pants were ripped, and a shoe was off. They said his face was battered, like it had been kicked. I think Khitai fought back."

Batu stepped to Lokesh and began patting the old man's back.

"What was in his pockets?" Shan asked. "Did he have something around his neck?"

Malik still stared woodenly at the grave. "Nothing. His things were in his bag. Because they were getting ready to leave."

"The herders, boy," Marco said grimly. "Where did they go? What did they see?"

"Gone, back into the shadows. Those dropka came here for the day because Khitai said so, and left their sheep alone with their dogs. All they could do was say words over Khitai and hurry back to their flock. They won't come down for a long time." Malik looked at Lokesh as he spoke. The frail old Tibetan was rocking back and forth now, as if Batu's touch had set him in motion. "I asked. They didn't see anything. They left Khitai here, sitting at the painting while they checked the high pastures above here for strays. But it was that woman who did it, the one they call the Jade Bitch. I saw her later, after the herders left. I had told them that I would stay, because Khitai was my friend, that I wanted to talk to him a while, that I could say words for a Kazakh burial that dropka might not know. That's what I was doing when I saw her come back to blind the gods."

Blind the gods. He meant the spray paint on the deities, Shan realized.

Marco handed the boy a water bottle and a piece of nan, which he consumed ravenously. "God's breath," the Eluosi muttered to Shan. "They're practically babies. The bitch hunts them down like carrion." He put his hand on Malik's shoulder. "We have to go," he said, scanning the sky. "She knows this place."

Shan silently returned Khitai's possessions to the sack, prying the cup from Lokesh's hands as Malik and Batu helped the old Tibetan to his feet. He lingered at the grave as the small, sad procession disappeared between the boulders. Four boys were dead. A third of the zheli list had been extinguished. A wave of helplessness, as palpable as a blow to his belly, struck him, and he found himself on his knees, with his hands on the grave.

"I'm sorry," he heard himself say. He knew there were no words he could give the dead boy. What had Marco said—no one was innocent anymore. "I would have given my own life," he said in a steadier voice, "to keep more of you from dying." As he spoke he realized that Khitai had not been the next name on the list. Because perhaps he simply had the bad luck to be at the lama field when the killer appeared. Or perhaps, he thought, remembering Lokesh's reaction at the grave, Shan had been wrong, and the killings had not been about the Americans. Had Khitai always been the target? It was as if there were two motives, two killers, two mysteries at work.

He knelt in silence until he heard Marco call from below. Then, quickly, he ran his fingers through the loose soil. He found a familiar object at the head of the grave, a curved piece of wood carved to look like a bird. It was what Malik made for dead children. A few inches away his fingers touched something so hard and cold it made him start. He pulled out a black, hinged, metal container and opened it. It was a compass, an elegant device filled with oil and bearing a red cross on its face, above the words *Made in Switzerland*. He stared at it in confusion. Such an instrument cost more than most herders made in a month.

Marco called out again. Shan buried the bird and pocketed the compass, stood and paused. He ran to the mani wall, selected one of the stones inscribed with a Tibetan prayer and placed it at the head of the grave, then jogged back to his companions.

As he reached the others, Malik was pulling Marco away from a small boulder near the ruins. It had a hole at its base. "Don't go near that nest," Malik warned. "That pika, he has a demon in him now."

Shan and Marco exchanged a puzzled glance and stepped to the hole, around which dried grass and twigs had been stacked. Marco knelt and cursed as he looked into the shadow. Shan bent and saw it too, a gleaming red dot of light in the hole, like an angry eye. The Eluosi reached in and pulled out first the battered, lifeless body of a ground squirrel, then a small video recorder.

"Motion activated," Marco spat, as he pulled out the tape. He threw it high overhead, where it lodged on a shelf in the rocks, then slammed the camera against the boulder.

"When they left they tried to get the helicopter to land by the flag," Malik explained as they were poised to mount, "but the wind deities protected it. So they shot at the flag with a gun." The flag did indeed seem more tattered than when Shan had first seen it.

"But that's all right," Batu assured them. "That man Bajys, Khitai's friend, he told us old men come and fix the flag sometimes, that they have for hundreds of years. Old men," the boy repeated with a wise nod. "Or maybe they're mountain deities."

They mounted, with the younger boy riding behind Lokesh, and after crossing a low ridge soon reached the head of a deep valley. Marco dismounted. "It is dangerous now. Walk, and walk carefully." He checked the harnesses of each of the camels and tied the reins to the saddles. "The camels know the way." He patted Sophie's hindquarters and she bolted onto a side trail that led to what appeared to be the base of a cliff. Not a cliff, Shan soon saw as the camel began to climb a narrow switchback trail. It was a steeply sloped rock face. At the top, far above, Shan could see a chimney-like rock formation.

The arduous climb took nearly an hour. After they cleared the crest, Shan stood in wonder. Behind the crest was a small plateau, invisible from below. Thick clumps of conifers surrounded the bottom of the rock formation, which, he quickly realized, was man-made. An ancient watchtower. Two sides of the plateau were surrounded by steep rock walls rising to the summit of a mountain more than a thousand feet above them. Two hundred feet up the wall, a spring emerged, descending in a long crystal ribbon to a small pond. A grass-strewn meadow covered two-thirds of the plateau. Scattered across it were half a dozen Bactrian camels.

"The armies of the Tibetan empire," Marco explained as he joined Shan. "They built roads down the river valleys leading out of the Kunlun, then garrisoned troops where the roads could be defended." He gestured toward the old tower. "Shepherds rebuilt it. When my father tried to take our family out of China, into India, an army patrol chased him. We hid here while the soldiers searched. A week, then my mother got sick. A month, then the camels ran away. After a while my father just started building. 'Stay the winter,' he said, 'it's safe here.' 'Might as well stay the summer,' he said later, 'good hunting here.' " Marco shrugged. "Almost forty years ago. We just kept building."

As they led the camels past the base of the tower, a large structure of logs came into view. It had clearly been built from the tower in stages, with a chamber butting against the tower that led into three sections of varying height. Neglected flowerbeds sat on either side of an oversized wooden door with handwrought ironwork. At the end of the building, under the largest pine on the plateau, a large double-barred cross stood over three graves.

Shan and Marco pulled the saddles from the camels as Malik and Batu helped Lokesh to a stump, where the Tibetan sat with his head in his hands. He had not spoken since leaving Khitai's grave. Marco cast a sad look at the old man, then wrapped an arm around each boy and led them to the doorway. Stepping in front of them he made a small bow and with a sweep of his hand gestured them inside. "Welcome," he said, "to the Czar's summer palace."

The Eluosi escorted them into a warm, intimate room whose plank floors had been lined with thick carpets. On the front wall, flanking the door, hung the skins of several large animals. The afternoon sun that found its way through the open door reflected off a large brass samovar sitting on a table at the far side of the chamber. Shan moved toward the urn in admiration, but was distracted by several small, faded, black and white photographs hanging above it. They were of figures inhabiting a different world. From one yellowed photo stared an old man with spectacles and a long white beard; his eyes seemed to be animated with rebellion, or anger perhaps. In the next frame a man with a sharply trimmed beard stood beside a beautiful fur-clad woman with light-colored hair. A horse-drawn buggy and driver waited behind them. The woman's mouth was opened in a smile, as if she were announcing good news.

The man and woman appeared again in a photograph set in rugged mountainous terrain. They were dressed in simple woolen tunics now. The man's beard was no longer trimmed, and the woman's hair was in braids, the way female workers wore their hair in the fields. In the man's arm was a child, a boy who stared defiantly with a strength that seemed to have been lost in his parents. Inserted into a bottom corner of the frame was another photo, also faded but more recent. It was of another woman, with strong weathered features and light-colored hair tied in a scarf. Batu stepped outside and a moment later reappeared, leading Lokesh.

"Family," Marco said behind Shan, in a mellow voice. "In a better year. Near Yining, in the north." He stepped across the room to a large door that stood ajar, leading into a room of stone walls. The base of the ancient guard tower. "The best place for a Russian to be, where Moscow had forgotten you. But then in 1950 somebody in some god-rotten Party headquarters in Beijing opened a map and saw a big wide open space with not enough red flags on it. When they sent troops to Turkistan, they decided that the mountains to the west should be the obvious border. Yining was on this side so they shipped in a few thousand retired soldiers." He snapped his fingers. "Just like that, Yining was no longer a free White Russian town, it was a Chinese town. And the original inhabitants had only one right, the right to leave. Except there was no place to go by then."

"This is not such a bad place," Shan offered.

Marco shrugged. "Sure. Our own little world. The shepherds came, sometimes. My father traded furs for the things my mother wanted. We made a good life. Then a fever came. I was fourteen. There were no doctors for people like us. I awoke after my fever broke, in my bed alone. My father was dead, lying on a pile of fresh earth. I thought he had buried the family treasure. I uncovered it. He did bury our treasure. He had died burying my mother." Marco turned and disappeared into the tower.

Shan looked about to see Lokesh holding the tapestry that hung at the far corner of the room, looking down a dark hallway. Lokesh entered the hallway and Shan followed, leaving Batu and Malik staring at their reflections in the samovar.

The hall had three doorways framed in hewn logs. The first led to a large room with a small iron stove and a plank table surrounded by mismatched chairs, some made of sturdy tree limbs, others of fine carved wood with soiled, though once elegant, silk seat cushions. A dried shank of meat hung from the ceiling, as did small strings of onions.

Lokesh stood at the second doorway, studying the next room's contents with intense curiosity. Over his shoulder Shan saw that the walls of the room were covered with photographs torn out of magazines, images of horses and birds and Western actors and actresses, most with captions in English. From two heavy log beams overhead hung several pelts of fur. On one wall above a shelf jammed with books was a poster of a Hong Kong rock star. Near the door there was a sleeping pallet on a rough wooden frame. A row of military caps hung on pegs over the bed. Chinese, but also foreign army caps. Shan studied them. Indian. And Pakistani, and another he did not recognize. Below the caps was a single photograph of a girl on a horse, laughing. Jakli. On the upended log that served as a bedside table stood a cassette player, a tape box on top. *Advanced conversational English*, it said. Lokesh picked up a heavy walking stick leaning in the corner by the door and extended it for Shan to see. Carved along the length of the stick in English letters was the name Niccolo.

"It's not Russian," Shan said. "Niccolo. Not Russian, not Kazakh."

"Italian," came a bass voice from behind him. "Marco Polo visited strange lands, but before him his father Niccolo went down the Silk Road. He went to foreign lands first, before Marco. Niccolo Polo Myagov," Marco said with pride.

"And so history repeats itself," Shan ventured as he turned in the doorway. It wasn't just her marriage that Jakli was anticipating, and it wasn't just the marriage that Lau had wanted to protect her for by keeping her in probation. Nikki was making one last caravan, Osman had said. Shan had not at first understood what Jakli had written when the karaburan was bearing down on them, because she had

written in English. *I'll be with you in the beautiful country.*
She had meant *Mei Guo*, because it was translated as *beautiful country* in Chinese. America.

Marco's eyes widened as he studied Shan a moment,
then the Eluosi shrugged. Marco picked up one of the two
other wooden sticks that stood in the corner by the walking
stick, and examined it absently. It was tapered and smooth,
with a knob at the narrow end. For hitting baseballs, Shan
suddenly realized. "He wasn't sure at first. Even then he
had to convince Jakli. She said she didn't think America
had horses, that all Americans had two cars and wouldn't
want horses. But Deacon told her that people have horses
for pleasure. Said he has a ranch. Said he would buy horses
for them. So now they're getting out, thank God."

Getting out. For a while Shan had been getting out, or
at least could pretend he was getting out. The truck to Nepal
was gone. He had lost track of the days. Maybe today was
the day that someone on the border would be waiting for
him, waiting for an hour or two, perhaps the whole day,
before deciding that Shan had been prevented from being
liberated. Somehow his own failure to reach the outside
seemed to make it all the more important that Nikki and
Jakli succeeded.

Marco sighed and surveyed his son's room in silence,
then motioned for his visitors to follow him. "Time to earn
your keep."

He led them outside to Sophie, who was standing beside
Lokesh, her big moist eyes only two feet from the Tibetan's
own, staring intently at the old man. Marco pulled a small
metal hook from a nearby stump and handed it to Shan.
"Boots," he said to Shan, then extended a brush to Lokesh.
"Bags." The Tibetan seemed to awaken at the words, and
accepted the brush with a small grin.

Marco showed Shan how to use the hook to clean the
camels' feet of any stones or twigs that had lodged in their
hooves, then demonstrated on Sophie how Lokesh should
brush the thick hair on their humps. Then Marco produced
a handful of sugar cubes from his pocket and handed them
to the boys, who eagerly offered the treats to the camels.

As Malik moved away to offer the last cube to his own
horse, Shan followed. "I saw what was in his grave," he

said to the youth's back. The boy only nodded as he stroked his horse's mane.

"Was it Khitai's compass?" Shan asked.

"No," Malik said in a whisper, as if frightened to speak of the thing. "His zheli parents, they said they found it near his body, lying against a rock. Khitai must have knocked it away from the killer." Malik turned to face Shan. "In the old days if a warrior died in battle, you buried him with the trophies he had taken from his enemies." The boy shrugged and turned back to his horse.

They ate a vegetable stew prepared by Lokesh on the little iron stove. Afterward Shan wandered out toward the pasture, watching as the evening stars rose, listening to the serene sound of the waterfall, immersing himself in the peacefulness of the place. He saw a glimmer of light and discovered Marco with a lantern at the end of the cabin, talking in low tones to Sophie as he stroked her back. Shan sat on a log and watched, not thinking the Eluosi had seen him until a few minutes later, when Marco's hand swung out and gestured for him. "You can scratch her ears," he said. "She likes that, after a long day."

The two men worked on the animal in silence for several minutes.

"She's a handsome creature," Shan offered.

Marco nodded approvingly. "And smart as any two Chinese." A moment later he looked up, his mouth open, as though to apologize, but did not.

"Your son," Shan said. "He has his own camels?"

"He prefers horses. Grew up riding with the Red Stone clan. He rides a strong black mountain horse. His mother's stock had Cossack blood."

"Is she traveling too then?" Shan asked.

Marco grew silent. "Not here," he said in a tone that made it clear Shan had gone too far. Marco's parents had died at the cabin, Shan recalled, but there were three graves.

"I have a boy," Shan volunteered quietly. "He would be eighteen."

"Would be?"

"I don't know," Shan began. "I haven't seen him for eight years." Marco looked at him and seemed to recognize that Shan too had pieces of his life too painful to probe.

"Eighteen. Not a boy, then," Marco said. "A man. Not much younger than my Nikki. Did he have a horse when he was young?"

"No. No horses."

"A camel, perhaps?" Sophie stood with her eyes closed, but her ears moved as if she were following their conversation.

"No."

"Ah," Marco acknowledged with a sympathetic tone. "Not everyone gets to ride in this life." He produced a wooden comb, which he began to run through the hairs of Sophie's neck. He handed it to Shan after a minute and showed him how to use it, putting his huge hand over Shan's to pull it through the hair.

"My Sophie," Marco sighed, "she has a soul deeper than most men. I talk to her. She talks to me. Smells strangers from two mountains away. Damned few people I'd rather be with." He walked around the camel, as if making a final inspection, then looked at Shan with an expectant expression.

"Come with me, Mr. Shan. I've got something to show you."

Shan looked up in surprise. Marco was speaking in English.

"Shan. Sh-aann," Marco tongued the word as he led Shan toward the front door. "Not an English name. In English you should be John. Yes," he said with a look of satisfaction. "John. Johnny, they say sometimes."

Shan smiled. "Like an American movie," he said in the same language.

"Ah! Exactly. John Wayne!" Marco exclaimed, then returned to Mandarin. "You speak it better than I do."

"My father," Shan said, and Marco nodded, as if it were all the explanation he needed.

They stepped into the room at the end of the inside corridor, a large chamber with rough log walls and a huge bed constructed of split logs, piled with felt blankets and furs. Pelts hung from log rafters. A sword hung on the wall. Two old pistols with cylinder magazines hung from pegs near the door. Flung across a table by the bed was a stack of magazines, in English. Oddly, all seemed to be about ocean fishing. Shan picked up the top magazine.

"Do you know the ocean?" the Eluosi asked tentatively. He seemed reluctant to show curiosity in his voice, but his eyes betrayed it. For an instant Shan saw the eagerness of a schoolboy. On the wall behind Marco there was a series of old calendars, all with a single color photograph of an ocean beach or an island. The region Marco lived in, Shan suspected, was further from an ocean than any place on the planet.

"As a boy, I lived in Liaoning Province," Shan replied, "near the sea. My mother's family was from a fishing village."

"Beaches!" Marco exclaimed in English. "Of white sand, like warm snow. Water as far as you can see. And the tuna fish." He looked at one of his calendar pictures, of a rocky coastline containing conifers and a single log cabin with bright yellow shutters. "It can reach over one thousand American pounds," he said soberly. "A fighting fish that's not for the faint of heart or weak of limb." He looked back at his magazines.

Shan had a vision of Marco, lying on his furs as it snowed for days, memorizing passages from his magazines.

One of the calendars had a photo of a man in a brilliant white shirt landing a long silver fish on a brilliant white boat. "Not a man in my family for five generations has ever seen an ocean," Marco declared, with longing in his deep voice. "Salt water. It has fish, delicious fish, as heavy as mutton, as delicate as sugar cake." He fixed Shan with a stern gaze and leaned toward him, as if about to disclose an important secret. "There is a place called Alaska," he declared, lowering his voice. "It has mountains like here. It has ocean too. I have seen pictures. Nikki has books that talk about it. Monster fish. Fry them in butter. And you know what else, Johnny?" Marco asked with a spark in his eye.

Shan shrugged. "I have never been there."

"It has Russians. Emigres from the Czar's days. Russians who speak English. Who are free men."

Shan smiled. He realized that he liked the man not so

much for the boldness of his actions, but for the boldness of his dreams.

Marco pulled a thick book from a wooden crate, an album of old photographs, and gestured for Shan to sit beside him on the bed as he quickly leafed through the pages until he found what he was looking for: a brittle, faded photograph of a Bactrian camel draped in what looked like a silk banner. Holding the camel's head was a man with a thick moustache and a bald head. On the other side of the animal was another man, a European, wearing a heavy fur *ushanka*, the winter cap favored by Russians. On the European's coat was a shining medal in the shape of a star. Flanking the two smiling men were two stern guards in turbans, each holding a long rifle.

"Sophie's great-grandmother," Marco said proudly.

"I see a certain resemblance," Shan said, to be polite.

His words delighted Marco, who shut the book with a huge grin. He pointed to an object that hung from a leather strap around a bedpost and lifted it to show Shan. It was the medal from the photograph. "Given to my great-grandfather by the Czar himself," Marco explained proudly. It was a golden star with red enamel borders and the image of a mounted cavalryman in the center. Marco gazed upon it with silent satisfaction, then looked at the wall, as if consulting an invisible clock. "Time to go up. We always go up," he announced, then stood and left the room with long, deliberate strides.

Shan checked on the boys, who slept in Nikki's room, then found Marco on the tower, staring out over landscape as if searching for someone.

"It's a dangerous thing, your seeing the Jade Bitch," Marco said in a slow, contemplative tone without turning toward him. "You heard that boy. She killed Khitai."

"I don't know that. Malik just saw her the day after. You didn't see Zu's face when Kublai was brought to her door. She was horrified. It was no act."

"The worst thing you could do is to underestimate her."

"The worst thing," Shan countered, "would be for me to misunderstand her."

Marco offered a skeptical grunt in reply.

"Why would she go to that place twice? Why not apply

the spray paint the same time she killed Khitai?"

Marco threw his hands up in a gesture of frustration. "Didn't have the paint. Wanted to go back for that camera."

"I don't know. Maybe there wasn't just one killer," Shan said. "Kublai and Suwan were shot. Alta and Khitai were beaten and stabbed."

"Maybe it was four killers," Marco said darkly. "Someone declared an open season on boys."

"But they all had one shoe missing," Shan said in a distant voice. He had no answer. They watched the moon. He found himself listening for crickets. "When you arrived here today," Shan said after several minutes, "you thought someone might be waiting. Because of the silver bridle."

Shan could see Marco's nod through the moonlight. "Osman. With more horses."

"The silver bridle," Shan suggested, "it was a signal, it meant a new plan. A faster plan, for the next caravan."

Marco nodded. "The silver bridle was a gift for Jakli. For the wedding. It just means get ready, at the horse festival, at the nadam."

But Jakli wasn't making bridal preparations. She was in the mountains, evading the knobs, trying to save the lives of orphan boys. Maybe, he hoped, she would meet her Nikki in the mountains, maybe Nikki could persuade her to stay out of danger. "I don't understand something, Marco," Shan said after a long silence. "You are a smuggler, but you live over a hundred miles from the border."

"I would never live closer, too dangerous. Like lingering in the breath of a dragon." The Eluosi looked up at the moon and yawned. "You're too traditional. You think too much like a policeman. There're many kinds of borders. Over the next ridge, it's Aksai Chin. Disputed land. India says it's hers. Traditionally it was part of Ladakh," he added, referring to the border region between Pakistan and India that held the upper waters of the Indus river.

"But the People's Liberation Army controls it," Shan reminded him. "Soldiers everywhere. And villages. Muslim villages. Old Tibetan villages." He had been driven through the disputed zone in one of the armored cars used by the knobs to transport special prisoners. On a break, when they allowed him ten minutes of exercise, he had seen prayer flags for the first time, fastened to a distant cairn of rocks. He remembered thinking through a drugged haze that it must be some kind of festival day.

"I found something out, Johnny," Marco said in a conspiratorial tone. "Sometimes the more you watch, the less you see."

The edge of the moon appeared so brilliant, so crisp, that it seemed like a shining piece of porcelain. In the distance, high snow fields glowed.

"They have huge caves, the army," Marco said. "Brought in thousands of gulag slaves to hollow out entire mountains. Some say the whole Tibetan border is just a series of hollowed-out mountains, full of soldiers. They have their damned missiles and radar dishes. An Indian plane goes through, or a Pakistani, and they can shoot it down in seconds. But say an eagle goes through—they never see it, because they use machines to do the watching. They watch for metal things, not real things. You and I, we would watch the sky. But they just sit and watch screens inside the mountains.

"And if army trucks or tanks come across one of the passes, they see them on their detectors. But maybe not a camel or two. Elsewhere they have patrols, but in some places it's so important they use only electronic surveillance. A small group, if it's careful, can sneak through. Don't carry metal. Don't make sharp noises. Don't do it often, got to use different routes, many techniques." He sighed and pointed toward a falling star. "Things can be arranged from a hundred miles away. Sometimes a wise man may even find ways to smuggle without smugglers."

"I don't understand."

"Trucks, for example. Big market for heavy trucks in Xinjiang. So last year I brought in five heavy trucks, filled with Indian dyestuff for the carpet factories. The border patrol, they searched those trucks good, but everything is legal. Never realized I was smuggling in the trucks. Even had trucks going out, with the same paperwork. But they were twenty years older and about to fall to pieces." Marco chuckled to himself. "Even did it with a bus.

"And something else I have learned. When is contraband not contraband?" He turned to face Shan, leaning on the old stone parapet. "When the government brings it in."

Shan nodded. In his Beijing incarnation his main activity had been investigating corruption. Once he had discovered that an entire shipload of equipment had breezed through customs clearances because the smugglers had falsified papers saying it belonged to the Ministry of Petroleum Industry.

"Sometimes, if someone in the government has a shopping list, they won't ask where you got it. They may even be willing to turn a blind eye at a checkpoint."

"You mean, you work for the government sometimes?"

Marco spat a curse. "Never. I mean sometimes, if a certain greedy officer wants some Western goods, he may want to place an order, and may want to misdirect a patrol so his order gets through."

"And sometimes," Shan said, "people go out. People go out to stay. Nikki, he goes in and out."

"Sure. You can sneak past the missile silos, once in a while. And there are places you can use, between snows, high passes no good for trucks or Chinese soldiers. Places that only a few old hunters know about. Where you can die from the cold or wind as easily as a bullet. Nikki knows them well. He went across for horses. He knows a horse trader in Ladakh, across the border."

"White horses," Shan suggested.

"Right. For Jakli."

"For getting married. At the nadam festival."

Marco nodded. "All the Kazakhs will be there, the few old clans left here. Starts in four days. The last one for the clans in Poktian County," he added somberly.

Shan thought a moment. "Lau was going to be there, wasn't she?"

"Jakli asked Lau to stand for her. Lau was the closest she had to a mother."

"But why get horses if they're leaving?"

Marco grunted. "You can't stop, can you? Can't stop asking questions."

"Not while there is a murderer stalking boys."

Marco made a frustrated, rumbling sort of sound that Shan took to be a token of surrender. "Nikki has to get the horses. You have to understand about Kazakhs and their horses. Not like anything Chinese. Or anything Russian. Horses can be as important as family."

"Like some camels."

"Different than me and Sophie. The old ones, they talk about how the souls of horses and the souls of Kazakhs are intertwined. They name horses after their children, and children after their horses. The rite of passage for a Kazakh is when he gets his first saddle, meaning he is old enough to ride alone. They have a whole vocabulary for types of horses and movements of horses. They tell stories about horses that lived five hundred years ago. They have old shamans who can speak to horses. The old Kazakhs, they won't go near a Chinese clinic for themselves. But if their horse gets sick, they'll do anything, even ask a Chinese doctor for help. Nikki knew how important it was to Jakli, to observe the tradition by giving at least one white horse to the bride's family. To honor her, to honor Akzu. To honor her lost father. In the old days, there would have been many horse gifts, from friends and cousins. Once I saw a nadam camp with two hundred white horses."

"So Akzu gets the horses," Shan said. Akzu, whose clan was being dissolved, whose herds were being surrendered to the government. "But Jakli and Nikki, they are going. Out of China. To America. It's why she isn't worried about Prosecutor Xu anymore, only angry at her. But how? Out of Aksai Chin?"

Marco made one of his growling sounds. "Don't ask what cannot be told."

"This isn't about Lau anymore," Shan said. "It's about keeping Jakli and Nikki safe. About the boys. About the Red Stone clan."

Marco put both hands on the parapet and looked out over the moonlit range. "Okay," he sighed. "A special route. Foolproof. Can only be used once. By boat."

"But the rivers aren't navigable," Shan said in a puzzled tone.

"In the missile region they still use laborers to dig out mountains. Prisoners—Kazakh, Tibetan, and Uighurs, mostly. There's buses that take them, shuttle them in and out twice a month. Big project at the end of the road, past the main base at Rutog, in Tibet."

Shan knew about Rutog. About one hundred twenty miles from Xinjiang. Close to India. A nuclear zone, a missile command center.

"There's a village called Ramchang, on a lake about twenty miles long. The border with India, the real border, cuts right through the lake."

"Then the army must have surveillance."

"Sure. Electronic, it's so important. You know, in case the Indians launch a battleship at them. But we know a man there, a Tibetan hunter who was allowed to stay on the border because his daughter was in a special Party school in Lhasa."

"A hostage."

"Right. Except Lhasa forgot to tell the army that his daughter died in a traffic accident a few months ago. He's leaving, and he needs some money."

"Even if he takes you over the lake the army could detect—"

"He has stealth boats," Marco said with a hint of amusement. "Coracles, made of willow branches and yak skin. They can't be detected on radar. It works."

"You mean," Shan said, "that the purbas use them."

"A boy named Mao went too, with some scientific specimens. They have their own boats. We have the Panda boats."

"Panda boats?"

"That's what he charges. Four people in a boat. One gold Panda per boat."

Shan's hand clenched the stone wall in front of him. "Auntie Lau," he whispered.

"What's that?"

"Lau was going."

"It was for Nikki and Jakli. I arranged it. Part of my gift, for their new life."

"But Nikki and Jakli are going to America."

Marco sighed. "They weren't at first. But then they met the Americans. That Warp, she became like another aunt to Jakli. Warp was going out, with their son, back to start writing her book, to get him back in American schools. The Maos were working on it. Then Jakli spoke to Warp. Warp spoke to some Maos. Some Maos spoke to me. Before long they're getting a Panda boat too. Then Warp and Deacon, they offer for Nikki and Jakli to live with them. Nikki, he wants to go to Alaska, to build a cabin so I can come someday. But Warp says first come to their university, she will get them money to help with the translation and explain the research. The Maos want it too, now—they say Jakli can give speeches in America about what Beijing does in Xinjiang."

Shan told Marco about the gold Panda hidden in Lau's puzzle box. "Money for a boat," he said. "For Lau, to leave. Lau and someone else. Maybe Bajys and Khitai."

Shan looked at Marco, who stared with a frown at the moon. "What was it you said? I never stop? Like you never stop trying to hide things. She came to you at Karachuk, didn't she? She was frightened. She knew about Jakli leaving. And that night she asked to go out at the same time, because suddenly she knew she was in danger. But the killer had followed her there."

Marco made no reply. He seemed to be searching the moon for something to say.

Shan pulled the bronze medallion from his pocket. "This was with the gold piece. Half of a pair. I got it before Bao did." The light was too poor to show its details, so he pressed it into Marco's hand.

"God's breath," the Eluosi muttered, and sighed heavily. "No good, so many people talking about secrets. It's the ticket. That old Tibetan with the boats, he doesn't know anyone's face but mine. And I'm staying. He'll have the matching medallion from each set. They're unique, not available outside museums. Until Deacon found them at Sand Mountain. So the Tibetan is given the match to each pair, delivered to him by the Maos. Show the medallion, pay the Panda. No chance for him to be tricked."

The ticket. Lau had a ticket for freedom, for a new life. She had kept it in her office, before riding to Karachuk to be killed. "Where was Lau going? To America?"

"I don't know. I didn't want to know. She was a Tibetan nun, you said. Maybe Dharmsala. From the far end of the lake it's only two hundred miles away." Dharmsala, on the southern slope of the Himalayas, was the home of the Dalai Lama, the capital of free Tibet.

Shan found Lokesh in the entry chamber, sitting on the floor below the samovar, their blankets unrolled on the carpet. The old Tibetan was chanting his rosary, staring at a small mound of felt on the floor in front of him. Shan watched a moment, confused, then lowered himself beside his friend. He sat silently and soon realized that Lokesh was not chanting a mantra anymore, but a pilgrim's prayer, an invocation for the protective deities to watch over a pilgrim. Slowly, giving time for Lokesh to object, he raised the felt. Two blocks of wood lay underneath, two pieces of carved wood with cracked, dried leather straps fastened loosely over the top of each. With a flood of realization Shan recognized them.

"You brought them out," he whispered in surprise. "They're his."

"Yes," Lokesh said in a bright voice. "I am going to take them to Mt. Kailas. I am going to complete his pilgrimage around the sacred mountain, using his blocks, then leave the blocks as he promised."

Shan grinned at Lokesh's joke, then saw the strange excitement in Lokesh's eyes. "You can't," he protested as he realized it was no joke. "Even for a young man it would be difficult. Winter is coming. To circle the mountain on your hands and knees could take many days in the snow and wind." Perhaps weeks, he thought. Pilgrims sometimes took several days to complete the thirty mile circuit on their feet.

"I promised him," Lokesh replied in a serene voice.

Shan began to speak, but the protest died in his throat. Lokesh had made a promise to the dead pilgrim, to the thousand-year-old mummy. But as his hand closed around his gau and its feather he realized that somehow he had made a promise to the dead man too, to carry on the virtue. He fell silent and listened as Lokesh continued his prayer.

After a few minutes he moved to the kitchen table, and in front of two candles spread the meager possessions of Khitai. The strings of beads. The small length of chain. The pen case. The battered silver cup. He held each in his hands. Maybe it hadn't begun with Lau or the American boy. Maybe it had begun with Khitai. Lokesh and Gendun had come to find the Jade Basket, which had been entrusted to

Khitai. Why? Because he was a bright, resourceful Kazakh orphan, the last place an enemy would look? Or was the boy special for another reason?

He idly picked up the chain and saw that each of the small links had a tiny lotus blossom worked into the metal. Perhaps it was simply a random piece of treasure collected by a curious boy. Or it could be an artifact, he realized, like the twelve linked dorje chains sometimes depicted in the hands of Tibet's protective deities. He counted the links. Twelve.

He lifted the beads in his hand. Wood and plastic and one jade bead. Why was the string so long at the end of each set? What was the significance of several yellow beads among the brown ones? Why was one strand composed of ten smaller beads tied tightly together? He tied one strand to another and looked at it, trying to find a logic in the sequence of the colors or varying shapes of the beads. Then, more quickly, he tied the pieces together to make a loop, then fastened the smaller string of ten beads onto the string, so it hung down. With a tinge of excitement he counted the beads. The colored beads divided the strand into four equal sections. The smaller beads that dangled from the string were for marking tens and hundreds. In total there were one hundred eight on the loop. It was a mala. The dead Kazakh boy Khitai had a Tibetan dorje chain and a secret Buddhist rosary. He had found the waterkeeper's hidden student.

CHAPTER 13

Prosecutor Xu offered no greeting to Shan when she took his call. "I don't usually speak with fugitives," she said in a voice tight with anger. "Fugitives are a matter for Public Security."

Shan had called the Ministry of Justice from the phone outside the highway station, telling Miss Loshi that the prosecutor's friend from Beijing had to speak with her. "I told you I would return soon," he said. "That I would have more evidence."

"I never agreed," Xu shot back. "You made a suggestion. I suggested you should be in jail. Then you escaped from my custody."

"Three o'clock today," Shan said. He told her where the garage was.

"This is not a negotiation, comrade. You can surrender at my office. Or I can dispatch a truckload of uniforms to drag you to my office."

"Comrade Madame Prosecutor," Shan said patiently. "I told you children were being killed. You didn't believe me then. I thought perhaps you might have reconsidered the point by now."

After a moment Xu replied in a terse voice. "That particular message got through to me."

"Good. So perhaps you and I are working with a common goal."

"You and I have nothing in common. I have suspects in the boy's death."

"Meaning what?" Shan asked. Marco was ten feet away, pacing up and down the road like a sentinel. Jakli, who had been at the garage when they arrived, had found an orange soda for Batu, who kept looking toward the mountains. Malik had refused to leave the Kunlun and had ridden away to seek out more of the zheli. "That you and Major Bao struck a deal? Is that what justice is in Yoktian?"

There was a long silence on the receiver. Shan heard voices in the background. Perhaps the prosecutor was calling for her car. Perhaps she was calling for reinforcements.

"Fine," she said at last. "The highway. But not three. Three-thirty, perhaps. Four, maybe. You will wait."

Jakli frowned when he relayed the conversation. "It is what she would do, to spring a trap, buy some time to get others here first. Plant some enforcers. Get some in looking like truck drivers, maybe." She was obviously exhausted, having searched much of the night on horseback with the Maos. They had found another boy before dawn, cowering alone in a cave, and the Maos had taken him to the Red Stone Camp.

Shan shrugged. "Not so easy to do, this far from town."

Jakli gave him an impatient look that somehow seemed to fade into one of sympathy, the way a mother might look at a child. "Sometimes you make me think it's true what they say about Tibet."

"What's that?"

"That it makes people new, washes away all their prior experience. Sometimes I think you are so naive."

To be called naive was such a grand joke that Shan wanted to laugh. If someone wanted a word for all that was not naive, they could take his name.

Jakli stepped into the shadows between the garage and the smaller building that housed two old trucks, where Marco now stood with Sophie, Batu in her saddle. Jakli spoke hurriedly with the Eluosi and pointed to a large truck behind the buildings, where a man was laying long planks to form a ramp into the cargo bay. Marco gave a mock salute to Shan and turned toward the truck. In five minutes Sophie and the two camels they had ridden from his mountain home were loaded into the truck, and the truck pulled out, Batu waving from the window.

It occurred to Shan, as he surveyed the broken-down trucks, stacks of bald tires, the decrepit yellow tea shop and the cracked walls of the garage building, that all of Xinjiang seemed to be a series of ruins. Some were just newer than others. He stepped toward the wall of the garage, the largest building, feeling very tired. He had sat far into the night reading his notes and staring at the meager possessions of Khitai. They had mounted the camels before sunrise, taking a different trail out of the valley. Now he had over an hour to wait for Xu. He checked on Lokesh, who lay asleep on a blanket behind the garage, then sat down on a stack of tires by the wall and found them surprisingly comfortable. Leaning against the wall, he shut his eyes.

Images of the day's ride flashed through his mind. He and Batu had ridden beside Marco for hours and listened to long tales of Marco's youth, tales about vast gatherings of nomad clans, where scores of camels raced, and young girls shot arrows to win white horses. In the predawn light Marco had spoken about the stars, which he knew very well, a skill acquired over nearly thirty years of night caravans. Shan had been surprised to learn that Marco was his own age, and the Eluosi had mused how different their lives had been, living at opposite ends of the People's Republic. He drowsily remembered how Marco had taught them a song, a silly child's verse about camels flying like birds, and they had sung it until they reached the highway.

When he opened his eyes, it was after three. Somebody had been busy, rearranging the area between the buildings. Three tables, or a table and two upturned crates, had been brought out and two figures sat at each. Those at the table played chess, the other two, mahjong. Several more vehicles had appeared in the compound. They looked vaguely familiar. He studied them for a moment and realized they were the trucks he had seen in the motor pool. All of them, except the turtle truck that lay buried in the desert. He noticed the flash of gold teeth from one of the men playing mahjong. It was the Mao from town, who had brought him shoes. A woman in the long grey dress and cowl of one of the strict followers of Mohammed sat close to him, reading what might have been a prayer book. As he rose and stretched his arm, the woman also rose, then reached out and pulled his arm. It was Jakli.

"The prosecutor's car drove by fifteen minutes ago. She stopped and let someone out," Jakli reported, nodding toward the tea shop across the road.

Shan circled around the rear of the garage and crossed at the end of the compound to reach a small window in the side of the shop. A well-dressed woman sat at the table by the front window, the only one of the shop's tables which was occupied. In one corner an old man with a long thin beard and a black dopa cap sat by a small gas stove, leaning against the wall, asleep. Shan stepped inside and took the empty chair across from Loshi.

"It's Miss Loshi, I believe," he said. "My name is Shan. We spoke at the prosecutor's office."

The young woman, so engrossed in watching out the front window that she had not noticed him, gave a startled gasp. Instead of replying, she raised something from her lap, a small black oblong object with a two-inch stub extending from one end. A cellular telephone. She held it in both hands, her wrists on the edge of the table, extending it like a shield.

"In ten, maybe twenty years, they might get around to installing transmission towers for those phones in this region," Shan observed, attempting a good-natured tone. "Maybe longer. Public Security doesn't want them to become too popular in places like this."

Loshi looked at him, then glanced uneasily outside.

Shan studied the nervous young woman. She had heavy makeup on her eyelids, and an expensive gold chain hung over her bright red silk blouse. Prosecutor Xu's security.

Loshi moved forward on her seat. "I know that. It doesn't work in town either. But most people don't know. I was talking to a herder. It scared him. He said he thought it was just something that Han used to summon other Han. He said he's never seen anyone but a Han with one, except Americans on television," she explained with a satisfied air. "So, see. It works."

"You're the prosecutor's secretary," Shan said. "Did she have secretarial work for you on the drive here?"

But Loshi kept looking at her phone. "They work in

Shanghai. And Hong Kong. Everyone has them in Hong Kong. In Hong Kong you can send a fax with one."

"Or is it because she trusts only you?" Shan wondered out loud.

"You're not supposed to talk to me. Talk to the prosecutor."

"You are here. The prosecutor is not here."

"I know people too. Just like the prosecutor. I work for the Ministry of Justice too."

"A big responsibility."

"I get special awards sometimes," she said, as if hoping to intimidate him. "Secret awards."

Shan remembered something else about Loshi. Ko Yonghong of the Brigade was taking her for rides in his car without a roof, like in American movies.

"Do you know about the dead boys, Miss Loshi?"

The girl seemed to be struggling. She put the telephone on the table and pushed the buttons, then put it to her ear in a strange pantomime, as if practicing for when she arrived in the real world. "I liked Auntie Lau," she said into the mouthpiece, as though speaking to someone on the phone. "I was sick once, when I went to a council meeting with the prosecutor. Auntie Lau gave me some herbs and cured me."

"Did you see her only that once?"

"Sometimes she came to town. She was always smiling. She gave me a book of poems written by retired soldiers." Loshi put the phone down. "I guess I never knew anyone who smiled so much. Like an old beggar, she smiled. You know."

Shan looked at her uncertainly. Like an old beggar. She meant like one of the old nuns and monks who used to roam Chinese streets seeking alms. Did her whole generation remember the monks that way, just as beggars? He watched the street. Jakli was speaking with the men at one of the tables. There was a horse-drawn wagon parked in front of the garage now, partially loaded with hay. A man was pumping air into one of its rubber tires.

"Were you born here, Miss Loshi?" Shan asked. "In Xinjiang?"

She shook her head absently. "We're from the coast. The

ocean. North of Shanghai. Technically, I was born here, but we're from Shantung Province. My father was sent to manage a factory in Kashgar many years ago. Some day I'll go to Shantung. Prosecutor Xu says she could get me transferred, if we keep maintaining our quota of resolved cases."

"You'd rather be in the east?"

"Back home? Sure."

Home. Loshi had never been there, but Shantung was home. He should write to the Chairman. *Dear Esteemed Comrade. After fifty years we now have conclusive proof that the experiment of absorbing the western territories has failed. Because Loshi wants to go home.*

"What about the prosecutor? Does she want to get transferred too?"

Miss Loshi made a sly smile and opened a nylon case on the table beside her. She pulled out a pack of cigarettes and lit one. She hesitated, then offered one to Shan. He shook his head. "She's not going anywhere. I'm leaving soon. But Comrade Xu—" She shrugged and exhaled two sharp streams of smoke from her nostrils. "Longest serving prosecutor in all of Xinjiang, in one post. Twelve years. In Yoktian, of all places."

Shan wondered if the young woman understood what she was saying, or was it just because Yoktian, in Loshi's world, was not a fashionable place to be? Twelve years in her post meant Xu was in career trouble, that she had been sent here, or remained here, because she had fallen out of favor. He recalled Bao's tone when he had reminded Xu of political commentary made at a conference in Turpan. *If you neglect your essential duties, Bao had said, no matter how hard you worked, you are a liability to the state.* But Xu was a zealot, the Jade Bitch. She kept the rice camps full. She shot at prayer flags from helicopters. What essential duty had Bao been referring to?

Shan glanced at the cigarette package on the table. "They're expensive," he observed. They were American. *Loto gai*—Camels.

Loshi seemed pleased that he had noticed. "I got them from Ko yesterday. To apologize to me about the sports car. He had to give it to that Major Bao."

Shan almost asked her to repeat the words. "Major Bao?

He gave his sports car to Bao?" he asked incredulously.

"You know." Loshi shrugged. "Public Security. Ko said he would get another one soon." Her breath tightened and she leaned toward the window. A black car, Xu's Red Flag sedan, was pulling to a stop in front of the garage.

Shan stared a moment longer, unable to comprehend why Ko would give his expensive car to a man who was not even a friend, who was a rival in many ways. "I'll go around the back," he said in a conspiratorial tone, and stood. "I won't tell her we spoke."

Loshi gave him a nervous, uncertain smile, cupped her hands over the cell phone, and looked back out the window.

Shan watched from the side of the tea house as the chess players at the table scattered the instant the prosecutor stepped out of the driver's seat. She stood and surveyed the compound, hands on her hips, then sat at the abandoned table, putting a small canvas bag on the table beside her. Moments later Shan stepped around the corner of the garage and joined her.

"He came back that day and asked about you," Xu said immediately, venom already in her voice. "Major Bao. He was still angry. Not just angry. Enraged. Said he should have arrested you. I asked him why. Said you could jeopardize a confidential investigation. He demanded more information about you."

"What did you tell him?" Shan asked.

"That you were one of my informers," Xu said, and paused, as if for effect. "But he wanted your name, your work unit." The prosecutor lit a cigarette, a thick unfiltered kind, the sort factory workers smoked. "I told him it might jeopardize a confidential investigation," she said with a sour smile. She stared smugly at Shan as she let the smoke drift out of her mouth. "But I have a friend in the Ministry in Beijing. Nearly ready to retire. I called her. There was an Inspector Shan once, she said, Inspector General of the Ministry of Economy. A fighting dog sort of investigator. The kind everyone hates." She inhaled on the cigarette again and examined him. "You know. Impractical. Incapable of prioritizing for the socialist order."

It was a familiar phrase. One of the idioms of *tamzing*, the struggle sessions where individuals were confronted with their shortcomings as citizens and their remedies beaten into them, figuratively and otherwise.

Shan saw that his hands had done it again, unconsciously made a mudra, as if trying to tell him something. The fingers were clasped, the middle fingers raised upward. Diamond of the Mind. "Prioritization for the Party, prioritization for the state, prioritization for the workplace," he recited the equally familiar refrain that had been shouted at him more than once from political verse books. "I saw an advertisement for a book once in a Western magazine," he said. "Getting your office organized in ten easy lessons." He looked at her with a stony expression. "Kind of the same thing."

She offered an icy smile. "This Inspector Shan, he's said to have taken on Party bosses, maybe even investigated them. Said to have been made to disappear." She opened her mouth and let the smoke curl around her lips.

"The advantage of disappearing," Shan said, "is that afterward expectations are so much lower." He stared at his hands. "All the zheli boys are in jeopardy," he said. "More could be killed."

"This Shan. My friend called the Ministry of Economy. The main thing people say about this Shan is good riddance. He made everyone's life difficult. As hard as a senior Party member. But when he was offered Party membership he turned it down."

"The killer is after the boys. Only the boys." He looked back at the tea house, where Loshi sat watching through the window. Ko had given his expensive car to Major Bao. It made no sense.

"An investigator is supposed to find answers, supposed to make life easier for people," she continued, as if she had not heard any of his words.

Shan focused on the end of her cigarette. "Sometimes an investigator can do no more than remind people of their conscience."

Xu's lips curled, as if she found the comment amusing. "Your killer," she observed. "He may have been looking for that one particular boy. Kublai. Maybe it's over."

"Or maybe he wants them all dead," Shan said.

Xu winced. "Don't be ridiculous. No one could get away

with eliminating entire . . ." Her words drifted off, as her eyes drifted toward the horizon. She shook her head.

"What are you saying, Comrade Prosecutor? One or two boys, and who cares? But ten or fifteen, that would be what? Unacceptable casualty levels? Politically embarrassing? How about five or six? Maybe up to ten, and no one would really notice?" He kept his eyes on her as he spoke. "Just orphans, after all, just Kazakhs and Uighurs at that."

"Some people see conspiracies everywhere."

"This is the People's Republic, Prosecutor. Its lifeblood is conspiracy."

Her eyes flared, and she looked about at the other tables. No one seemed to be listening. "Be careful, comrade. I know my responsibilities to the state."

"Wonderful news," Shan snapped.

Her brow wrinkled in question.

"That you take your job seriously. The prosecution of crime, isn't that what it is?"

She frowned again and pulled on her cigarette.

"Maybe this investigator from Beijing," Shan said, "maybe he discovered the most important thing of all. That working for the government is not always the same as working for the people."

She surveyed the compound. Shan followed her gaze and saw another familiar face among the men at the mahjong table, despite the oversized Chinese army hat pulled low over his head. Fat Mao.

The horse cart pulled slowly away from the garage bay.

"I checked with all the Ministry offices from here to Kashgar and a hundred miles east. There have been no other reports of children being killed."

He stared at her. She did not blink, she did not look away. "Another boy was killed since the one brought to Yoktian," Shan announced. "The fourth boy."

"No." Xu glared at him resentfully. "I don't believe it."

"You said no once before, Comrade Prosecutor, when I told you boys were dying."

Xu frowned and said nothing.

"A boy named Khitai was killed near the giant prayer flag in the mountains. You know that flag."

"I know it," she replied stiffly.

Shan nodded. "You were seen there." A thought occurred to Shan. Batu had believed Xu had gone to find boys and kill them. But maybe she was following someone. She had left the camera for surveillance. He had thought it was to watch for Buddhists and dissidents. But maybe it was to watch for the killer.

Her eyes smoldered.

"Perhaps it means you are close to an arrest," Shan suggested, returning her angry gaze.

"A small group of herders had been seen there three days ago. We went to investigate. They may have been with one of Lau's zheli. Or perhaps they needed to be registered for the Poverty Scheme."

"Two days," Shan said. "The herders were there two days ago. The day the boy died."

Xu shook her head. "Three."

If she was right, Shan thought, then Batu had also been right. More than one zheli boy had gone to the lama field to complete his project for the dead teacher.

"Show me the body," Xu said tersely.

He shook his head. "Khitai is buried. He has been violated enough."

"Then only one boy died," Xu said. "That's all we know. One boy killed, that could be anything. We have an official investigation. Forensic exams shows a small-caliber bullet. Could have been a hunting accident. The clans are allowed to have small-caliber firearms for hunting."

"A hunting accident?" Prosecutor Xu, Shan decided, was a very complicated woman. "I thought it was feudalism, you said."

"Fine. Without question it demonstrates the corrosive influence of the old clan structures. Irresponsibility. Lawlessness in the mountains. This is the twenty-first century, comrade. It has to stop. I am always willing to throw the full weight of my office to assist victims of crime. But first they have to ask. Let them file reports if others died. I will not accept rumors. Not about Lau. Not about other boys. The resources of a great nation are theirs if they ask."

"Speaking statistically, Comrade Prosecutor, how many reports of serious crime do you receive from the nomads?"

"A few every year."

"How many from Han living in the district?"

"More than ninety percent of my reports are from Han."

"And the Han represent how much of the population?"

"Resettlement has been slow this far away." She shrugged. "Thirty-two percent is the official number."

"And you resent the Tibetans and Kazkahs and Uighurs for not reporting crimes."

"It's difficult enough, keeping such a vast country together. We all have to cooperate. A citizen who does not participate is not a complete citizen. People must be taught to come to us."

"Perhaps a giant tamzing. Bring all the herders in. And their sheep. Can't forget their sheep. The herds are so disorganized. Prioritization for the Party."

As Xu looked at the ember of her cigarette an expression of bitterness seemed to pass over her face. Could it indeed be true that she took her job seriously?

"There are some investigations," he ventured, "where you reach the end and wish no complaint had ever been filed. Because of what you have to report."

"Don't tell me my job. I've been prosecutor a long time, Comrade Shan."

"I know," Shan shot back. "Twelve years in Yoktian."

She fixed him with a frigid stare. "I meant, I know how to write reports."

He stared at her and saw the admission in her eyes. They both knew that in the People's Republic writing reports on criminal investigations was one of the highest forms of art. "Most times," he said very slowly, "you just have to write about who the criminals are. But sometimes there are cases where you have to write about who you are."

Xu didn't reply. She lit another cigarette from the first and stared at the makeshift tabletop, a piece of rough plywood, as though suddenly interested in its patterns of wood grain. "We have a file on the dead boy. Director Ko has suggested several suspects. I have been trying to find others who may have information. Apparently the children, the zheli, were very secretive. Lau didn't record their whereabouts. No one seems to know much."

"Director Ko?"

"The Brigade knows the clans better than any organization. They are at the forefront in implementing many social policies." She worked her tongue against her cheek, as if chewing on something. "It makes them a target sometimes. For resisters."

"Resisters?"

"Clan members who oppose the Poverty Scheme, for example. Someone sabotaged a Brigade truck yesterday."

"A truck?"

"A transport for livestock was stolen. A Brigade driver in a car gave chase into the mountains. On a curve, the truck rolled over and burned. Kazahks or Uighurs did it. We're investigating."

Shan stared around the compound again. Had the Maos stolen the truck, hoping to set up some kind of ambush?

"The Brigade is our engine of social change in Xinjiang. We all have to keep that engine running," Xu stated. It had the tone of a political mantra, preapproved by Party headquarters.

Shan recalled his last conversation with Kaju. "What," he asked, "is the Brigade doing with infants at the local clinic?"

Xu frowned again. "Now you're suspicious when someone helps babies? You're paranoid. Delusional. Maybe you feel so guilty about being a Han that you hate all Han. I can find"—She searched for a word—"therapists who could help with that. Everyone knows the newborn survival rate among the minorities is low. Ko wants to help."

Shan watched as the horse wagon stopped in front of the prosecutor's car. The driver unhitched the horse and led it away. He looked closer. There was no room at the front. The wagon blocked the car. He surveyed the compound. Jakli had said Xu might bring others, disguised as truck drivers.

"That's a Buddhist thing," she said suddenly, taking notice of his mudra.

Shan collapsed his fingers self-consciously, without answering. "Lieutenant Sui," he said. "Are they investigating his murder?"

"Bao's office said he is transferred out, a new assignment in Manchuria."

"But you didn't believe it."

She drew deeply on her cigarette. "It's not that simple."

"Of course it is. Sui is dead, or Sui is transferred. Did you try to verify his transfer?"

She frowned, as if she found the subject distasteful.

"There are two possibilities," Shan suggested. "Public Security is covering up, not telling the Ministry of Justice. Or Bao is covering up, not telling even Public Security." There was another possibility, which he would not give voice to. The killing was known to all, to Bao, to Xu, to Beijing, but not yet politically resolved.

"That day at the motor pool," he added. "Sui was with you, Kaju was with Ko. Kaju said he was looking for the boys, Lau's boys. Maybe Sui was too."

This time when she exhaled she blew the smoke directly into his face. "We were using the roadblocks for the missing person investigation. Public Security was cooperating. The Ministry and Public Security work hand in hand."

"Last time I was with you," Shan returned matter-of-factly, "Public Security was throwing a mug at you." For a second, and only a second, Shan thought he saw something that might have been amusement in the prosecutor's eyes.

"I have another idea about Sui," Xu said. "If he is dead, maybe Tibetans killed him."

Shan felt his throat go dry. He returned her stare and shrugged. "This is Xinjiang."

"This is borderland. This is everywhere and nowhere. When you drove away that day at the motor pool, Sui got on the radio with the roadblocks. He said to detain you. Not you, actually. He gave orders to stop the truck and arrest the old Tibetan with you."

Shan stared into his hands. Sui was looking for Tibetans. Was he the one who had found Lau? Out of the corner of his eye he saw a grey figure rise and slowly walk around the back corner of the garage. Jakli, going to where Lokesh slept.

"A harmless old man," Shan said.

Xu looked toward the Kunlun with a pained expression. "The one word I would never use for Tibetans," she said with a strangely distant tone, "is harmless." She gazed around the compound. "Everyone else we can talk with, we can negotiate with, we can educate, we can teach the wisdom of becoming something else." Her mouth twisted, as if she had tasted something sour. "But the Tibetans," she said slowly, "they just stay Tibetans."

"Which is why you attack prayer flags?" Shan asked quietly.

She silently stared at him for a long time, then looked down at the table. "I know at least one boy died," she said, just as quietly. "Sui implied that Tibetans were involved in some new conspiracy. I asked my investigator to watch, and listen, to find where in the mountains the zheli children might meet Tibetans. We heard about a small family at that place. We went to look. Now you say a boy died at the place," she added, as if it proved her point.

You went to blind the deities, Shan almost said. "You went with Public Security?"

"No."

"Meaning what? That Public Security doesn't care about boys but you do?"

She stared at him coolly without answering.

He pulled the black compass from his pocket, opened it, and placed it on the table. "Do you recognize this? Was it your investigator's? Bao's?"

"Not mine," she shot back resentfully, as if he had accused her of something. Then she stared at the device. "You found it there? My investigator wasn't there, before he went with me. He had just been asking questions, talked to helicopter pilots. It's not his. As for Bao, you'd have to ask him. I can arrange a meeting," she offered with a cool, thin smile.

Shan folded the compass but left it on the table between them.

"What if you had found a boy out there, what would you have done?"

"Take him into protective custody for a few days. Then give him back to the school program."

Shan was silent for a moment, considering her words. "Tell me, Comrade Prosecutor," he said as he pocketed the compass, "do you think Tibetans are guilty, just because Sui was looking for them?"

"Sui. And now Bao. He's erecting random checkpoints

throughout the county. Anyone with Tibetan papers is to be held for questioning, even anyone with a Tibetan birthplace. He's rounded up a few old men who couldn't explain their origin to his satisfaction."

The waterkeeper. She had not mentioned the waterkeeper. Because, he hoped, the lama had not been discovered. Maybe he was better off at Glory Camp, maybe he was invisible to Bao at Glory Camp. Though not if he continued to interfere with political officers.

"Because of a poem?" Shan asked. "Does poetry scare Bao so much?"

She frowned again. "Because he is a major in Public Security," she said, meaning Bao could do whatever he wanted. He owed an explanation to no one, including the prosecutor.

She stared at him and seemed to detect the pain in his eyes. "Your friend," she pressed, clearly enjoying his discomfort, "an old Tibetan traveling with a known fugitive. Think of the stories he will have when Bao picks him up."

Just an old man, Shan was about to repeat, but a question overtook his tongue. "Why did he radio the others? Why didn't Sui just take him there, at the motor pool?"

Xu opened her mouth as though to reply, but she had no words. She just looked back toward the Kunlun.

"Because," Shan ventured, "he didn't want Ko to know."

"Sui was angry when the patrols didn't find your friend. Issued a description to them, so he could be picked up later."

"There is another Tibetan," Shan said. "What do you know about Kaju Drogme?"

"I interviewed him before he started. He's different. A model for all the minorities. One of the few Tibetans who has recognized the challenges of balancing the needs of our society. There was a meeting about him, to decide on bringing him here. Ministry of Education. Bureau of Religious Affairs. Public Security. The Brigade."

"Why the Brigade?"

"Of course the Brigade. In this district, the government decides and the Brigade implements. They have a special office in Urumqi for this program, administering fifty or sixty teachers all over Xinjiang, all minorities trained in cultural assimilation. Got the attention of Beijing and of the top managers of the Brigade. The Brigade," she reminded Shan, "is one of the largest companies in China." She thought for a moment and shrugged. "Still, the program's only an experiment."

"You're not convinced."

"He goes too far sometimes. Lau, she was balanced. But this Kaju—I went to one of his classes. He was showing everyone how Buddhist prayer beads work, asking if anyone had beads when they were young. I called the Brigade office to complain. They said it was part of the program. Validate the ethnic roots. Make Tibetan children know it's all right to have beads, make the Muslims know it's all right to bow toward their Mecca sometimes. Then gradually make them see how old-fashioned it is, just a subtle form of mind control."

Shan looked at her without replying. Validating ethnic roots was also one way to identify hidden Tibetans. Mao tse-Tung had launched a campaign over thirty years earlier known as the One Hundred Flowers program. Let one hundred flowers bloom, the chairman had said, as a way of encouraging people to express diverse views, to criticize the government in public. It had been staged as a way of flushing out dissidents. After a few months the campaign was ended and those who had spoken out against the Chairman were arrested.

Shan saw that another vehicle, a heavy diesel truck, had arrived at the station. It was parking directly behind the Red Flag, so close the car was blocked between it and the horse cart. The engine did not stop as the air brakes hissed and the truck halted. The driver stayed at his wheel, watching someone, the mahjong player closest to the prosecutor. Fat Mao. What had Marco said of the Maos? He had called them predators, always waiting for an easy kill.

Shan unfolded the paper he had taken from the school and pushed it in front of her. "Are they so eager to get the children to confess religion that they must offer bribes?"

Xu didn't touch the memo but read it where it lay. A lip curled up, and he began to realize that the sour expression was a fixture, that perhaps she had been sour so long that it was the natural position of her face when it relaxed.

Shan watched her eyes drift over the names of those who had received copies of the memorandum from Ko announcing the gift of music machines. There were two names familiar to him—Bao Kangmei, Kaju Drogme—and a third unknown to him. Rongqi, Urumqi, it said.

Xu sighed and put the paper in her canvas bag. She held it by the edges as she did so, as if it were fragile.

"Thank you," she said. "I have you on videotape at my office. Now I have your fingerprints." A look of great satisfaction rose on her face. "Outside agitators always make good candidates."

"Candidates?"

"For anything. Murder. Even treason. Good for tying up loose ends in files. Maybe just breach of public security. That memo was for government workers only. You don't work for the government."

"Not for the government," Shan said. "It was for the Brigade."

She shrugged, as if it made no difference.

Shan stared at her. "Fine. Arrest me. The only thing I'm really good at, Comrade Prosecutor, is surviving. I'll go to prison. I'll survive. But they would have won."

"Who?"

"I don't know yet. Bao, maybe. Kaju. This Rongqi in Urumqi, maybe."

Xu lit another cigarette before replying. "I don't have to implicate you in anything. You're a weed. You don't belong here. By definition, weeds are guilty. I have a weed control program. One call and you're in Glory Camp for a year."

Shan ignored her. "Rongqi," he said again. Was she trying to avoid the name? "Did he know Lau?"

Xu hesitated. "A general. Former general. Now one of the top leaders of the Brigade. Second in command. He met Lau with me in Urumqi."

"She went to the capital with you?"

"Rongqi was the one to approve the new program for assimilation. I thought she was a model of the kind of person we need. The Ministry of Justice decided to support the program, to offer up its databases. I asked her to go, at our expense, to be recognized." There was something new in Xu's voice. An uncertainty, a hesitancy.

"But something happened."

"I don't know. Rongqi was cordial. They were talking, then she went cold. Said she was sick and excused herself. All the way home, she was quiet."

"This was before she was eased out of the council position?" The day before she had died, Hu had said at the school, Ko had tried to persuade her to go back to Urumqi with him.

"Maybe two or three weeks before." Her face hardened. "There's no connection. I know your type, Shan. The higher up someone is, the more guilty they are." She twisted the butt of her cigarette into the makeshift tabletop. "I have a riddle for you. When you're made to disappear once, they call it the gulag. But when you're made to disappear twice, what do they call it?"

Shan sighed and looked up at the sky. "I'll go to your office, in two days. Your territory. Arrest me then if you still want to."

Xu frowned but didn't say no.

"I don't believe Sui was with you that day just because of your missing person inquiry," Shan said. "Not if he was looking for Tibetans."

"He was working roadblocks for me, and for a Bureau case on smugglers. Jade thieves."

"Jade?"

"He asked me that day if I had seen any interesting jade. I knew what he was asking. This region is the source of all Chinese jade. Special licenses are given to those who extract it and process it. Special certifications are made by inspectors to assure its quality. Special fees are assessed. Sometimes people try to avoid the procedures and sell it cheap on the black market. It's one of the regular assignments for junior officers. He heard I was going to sweep roads, he thought he would take advantage to check for illegal jade. Tibetans with black market jade, apparently."

No, Shan was about to say. He was looking for the boys. He looked toward the rear of the garage, where Lokesh had been sleeping. Sui had been looking for the Jade Basket. He had been killed. Then Ko had given Major Bao his

expensive car. Not out of friendship. Because Ko was ob-
ligated to Bao somehow. Or out of mutual interest.

Xu was watching the compound. She looked from the
horse cart to the heavy truck that blocked her car. She
seemed to sense something. There was a flicker of ner-
vousness, then she swept the smoldering butt of her cigarette onto the ground and rose with a glare that caused all
around her to turn away. Shan saw Fat Mao make a motion
and the diesel truck began to back up, to make room for
the Red Flag to move.

"One last thing," Shan said. "Miss Loshi. Did you ask
her to come?"

"What do you mean?"

"I mean, her boyfriend is Director Ko. Did she ask you?"

Xu thought a moment. "My chief investigator is in the
mountains. She knew that. She offered to ride with me."

"And watch."

"And watch," Xu agreed with a sneer, then waved toward the tea shop. Loshi emerged a moment later, the cell
phone extended in front of her. Xu's protector.

Shan nervously watched as Xu placed her canvas bag
on the hood of her car. He saw a flicker of movement at
the corner of his eye. Fat Mao darted into the garage. A
moment later the Uighur reappeared, holding a folded piece
of white paper. Suddenly someone shouted from the far end
of the compound. An animal burst out from between two
trucks, a large ram, bleating, running wildly, butting its
head into the air every few steps as if battling some invisible rival. Several men shouted and ran toward the animal.
Others ducked into the buildings.

In the center of the road Miss Loshi stopped and made
a sound, not a scream, but a high-pitched yelp. She did not
run from the animal charging toward her, but stood still
and covered her eyes.

The ram seemed to take the motion of her hands as a
signal. It lunged straight at her, veering at the last moment
so that its heavy shoulder slammed into her knees, knocking her legs out from under her. She collapsed onto the
road and sat with an expression of shock on her face as
several men closed around the animal. Prosecutor Xu darted
around the limousine to help Loshi to her feet. In the same

instant Fat Mao ran to the limousine. Shan looked back to Xu as she led Loshi to the car.

The compound burst into activity as the Red Flag disappeared down the highway. The men at the tables stood. The driver in the heavy rig shut off his engine and climbed out. The man with the horse brought the animal back to its wagon.

Jakli reappeared, pulling off her cowl and shaking her hair free, Lokesh following a step behind, wearing a wide grin.

"It makes no sense," Jakli said, looking down the highway, where the car had gone. "What is she doing? She brought no one but her worthless secretary."

"She never expected to arrest him," Fat Mao said as he sat at the table beside Shan. "She wants to use him, and take him later." The Mao studied Shan uncertainly, then extended a piece of paper toward him. The memorandum Shan had given to Xu. "I replaced it with a blank page," he said with a thin smile. "Making her mad on purpose," he added, shaking his head at Shan. "You have no idea how dangerous that is."

Shan took the paper from him and folded it for his pocket. "The only thing I do on purpose," Shan said, "is to find the truth."

Fat Mao stared at him, displeasure on his face. "What if finding your truth puts all of us at greater risk?"

"The only ones at greater risk," Shan said as he looked with alarm at Lokesh, "are children and Tibetans."

CHAPTER 14

Fat Mao drove quickly, always south, faster than was safe on the rough roads. There had been no argument, no discussion. Shan would go no further until he saw Lokesh back to Tibet, safely away from the knobs. Fat Mao had grimaced but said nothing, just pointing to the smallest of the trucks. Lokesh had shrugged in disappointment and let Jakli help him into the vehicle.

As they had started down the highway Shan watched Jakli depart in the horse cart down a dirt track that led into the hills, sitting beside the driver as the man urged the horse to a fast trot. She wouldn't listen to Shan's entreaty to go back to her factory, where knobs were soon likely to notice her absence. The zheli were meeting in four days at Stone Lake. Major Bao knew it. Director Ko knew it. Prosecutor Xu knew it. It was in the Brigade computer. The whole world knew where the surviving boys could be found in four days.

The old Tibetan leaned his head against the seat and sang in a low voice as Fat Mao drove. He seemed to be losing strength, and not just since being told he had to leave Xinjiang. Since they had found Khitai's grave there had been times when Shan would look at his friend and think that he was somehow shriveling, as if something essential was going out of him. It was like a tide that coursed through the old man, for at other times he was still vibrant and strong. Yet the weakness seemed to plague him increasingly now, so that Shan had begun to worry that old age and the stress of their search was beginning to overwhelm Lokesh. He feared greatly for his old friend, and what could happen to him if they didn't finish their search soon. Shan had not put into words his other reason for returning to Senge Drak. He wasn't going just to assure Lokesh's protection. He had to solve the secret of the Jade Basket. And the answer was not in Xinjiang.

The sun was nearly on the western horizon when the truck approached the rough path that marked the final climb to Senge Drak. But Fat Mao could go no further, for he had urgent business below. He cautioned them against missteps in the evening light, then offered them blankets and told them where a small cave was, the safest place to go, to wait for the sun of the next day. But neither Shan nor Lokesh intended to wait. Fat Mao had no light to offer them and left with a warning.

"We never go in the dark," the Uighur warned. "You could fall, and no one would ever know. No one would come if you were injured."

A blustering wind blew off the changtang. The ends of the blankets, rolled and carried over their shoulders, whipped and fluttered. Shan's eyes watered sometimes, and he remembered Mao's warning. The Uighur warrior had sounded unnaturally fearful, as though Senge Drak was a phantom place that could not be found in the dark, that perhaps didn't exist in the dark. But, Shan mused as he led Lokesh around the bend of another steep switchback, Senge Drak didn't exist in the world most people inhabited. It didn't exist at all in the world of the communists and flatlands and empty people who chanted the Chairman's verses. It existed in the world of Gendun and Lokesh, whose weakness, Shan suspected, had something to do with being cut off from that world.

He turned and watched his old friend as he pushed against the wind, a smile on his face, one of the harmless Tibetans who somehow worried Xu more than all the others. He remembered the strange way she had looked toward the Kunlun, as if remembering something or seeing something she could not understand. Oddly, one question kept echoing in Shan's mind. What had it been like when she had sprayed paint over the faces of the Tibetan deities? Had she gloated? Or had she trembled?

But Shan was still caught between both worlds. And more than ever he knew that the reason he had been selected by the priests was because he belonged to neither. Something had shifted the delicate balance between the two, and people were dying because of it. The key to everything was understanding what there was of the priests' world that drew them to this strange, remote land. There were pieces of it, he knew, out in the desert, where pilgrims lay long dead. There were pieces in Senge Drak and in Karachuk, and with Jakli and the old waterkeeper. The Jade Basket was part of it, but still a mysterious one, for though he knew the Tibetans did not covet things, they seemed to covet the mysterious gau. The boy, Khitai, was part of it. The boy who had carefully hidden his rosary and dorje chain, and who, Shan was somehow certain, had sat in the teaching chamber with the waterkeeper.

Shan only had pieces. Pieces of the Tibetans' mystery. And pieces of the other, the Americans' mystery. But none of the pieces would fit together. Was it because he had confused the pieces, because some of those in the Americans' mystery belonged in that of the Tibetans?

A new light began to shine in Lokesh's eyes, a new bounce seemed to rise in his step. Their path wasn't just up the huge rock monolith that housed the dzong, it was to sanctuary. And Senge Drak was not just sanctuary, Shan knew, it was timelessness, it was mindfulness. Shan decided that perhaps as much as Lokesh he himself needed to partake of it. He walked as if in a dream, letting his feet drop as though in an act of faith, into the shadows that covered the narrow path. Timelessness. The great barriers to understanding, Gendun had once told him, were material possessions, which only built hunger for more, and time, which pushed so many to rush through life, fearful they would miss something if they slowed, as though, if they were quick enough, they could change their destiny. Time seemed so unimportant when sitting in a meditation cell or watching the night sky. Shan too could drift if he let himself, so that the thousand-year-old mummy, and Lokesh, and Buddha's deer on the wall painting, and the tiny autumn flowers that bloomed for a few days before dropping were all mingled in the same serene place that, for lack of a better word, was his life force.

But no, Shan thought, he could not drift. There was someone out there for whom time was important. Someone racing to kill young boys.

He became aware in the distance of the large blunt cliff face with two outcroppings on top. There was a thin line of shadow on its lower slopes that was the path into the tunnels, snaking along the side of the lion. Below them the huge gully dropped hundreds of feet to a dark tumble of rocks below, splinters that had sloughed off the mountain. They stood for a moment together at the edge, in the last dim light of dusk, the wind blowing hard against their faces. A large bird flew past and Lokesh cocked his head to watch it as it moved over the lion-shaped mountain and appeared to settle on one of the outcroppings, a small shadow on one of the lion's ears.

Without looking back at Shan the old man started walking toward the bird.

As they moved along the slope Lokesh led at an increasingly brisk pace, until Shan almost had to trot to keep up. It was indeed as though time had become something different for Lokesh, as though there was an old, weak Lokesh time and a stronger, younger Lokesh time and the two didn't proceed in any particular sequence or with any predictability. No, maybe it was predictable, Shan thought, remembering how energized Lokesh had been in the old dzong. Lokesh the younger was moving toward Gendun Rinpoche and Senge Drak. Shan had to find a way to keep him there, deep in the dzong or hidden elsewhere in Tibet, for that was the land of Lokesh the strong. If he went back to Xinjiang where the frail, weak Lokesh seemed to reside, the old man might not survive.

The dzong was empty as they entered. The brazier in the large room where they had eaten was cold. There was a half-eaten plate of tsampa on the table. They stood at one of the open portals, silently looking out over the vast empty plain until Shan became aware of a presence behind him.

It was Jowa, but not the proud purba he had known.

This was a subdued, haggard Jowa, looking half-dead with fatigue.

"You came back," Shan said. "You didn't go with the purbas." He remembered the boasting that last night they had been together, how Jowa the warrior had taunted even Gendun. And he remembered the confused Jowa on an earlier night when Gendun had first disappeared, the Jowa who had said fighting was futile if the lamas didn't survive.

Jowa seemed not to hear him. "I've seen them like this," he said in a haunted tone. "Three days and two nights now. Someone's got to stay with them when they're like this. He could try to fly out the window. His spirit wouldn't know what his body had done until it was too late."

Shan found a ladle of water on the table and handed it to Jowa, who seized it and swallowed the liquid in huge gulps that somehow seemed like sobs. Shan led him to a pallet in one of the cells. When the purba dropped his head to the floor he fell asleep so fast it seemed he had simply lost consciousness.

Lokesh was not in the hall when he returned. But Shan knew where to look. He stepped over the sleeping form of Bajys, sprawled across the threshold of the doorway to the fragrant room, and found Lokesh sitting beside a single oil lamp. With Gendun. The old lama had anchored himself with a *gomthag* strap, a strip of cloth used by hermits that ran around the knees and the back to prevent the body from toppling over while the spirit was elsewhere.

For Gendun was indeed not there.

Shan had seen deep meditation, had meditated himself for hours at a time, but never anything like this. The man's eyes were open, but he saw nothing. He seemed to have stopped breathing. Shan bent low with a lamp and watched his wrist. There was almost no pulse, only the barest of flickers every few seconds. The danger in talking to mountains, Shan thought, was that you could become one yourself.

They waited for an hour. Lokesh lit more incense and began a mantra. *"Om gate gate paragate parasamgate bodhih svaha,"* he chanted. Shan had been taught the ancient mantra in prison, though he had almost never heard it used. "Gone, gone completely, totally crossed over to enlightenment," Lokesh was saying. Gendun, like Shan, was seeking the truth.

Shan brought more lamps. Still, Gendun did not stir. Three days, Jowa had said. As strong as Gendun's spirit might be, his body was not young, and Shan feared for it. He rose and brought a ladle of water from the stone cistern at the back of the corridor of cells. But Gendun's mouth was closed, his head perfectly perpendicular to the floor, so Shan could not drip water into it. He dared not push Gendun's head back, dared not to touch his body, for a body in such a state sometimes had its own kind of fear. It could react to the slightest touch with spasms or flinch so violently it could harm itself. Imagine he is a ceramic pot, a monk had once said to him of a hermit in deep meditation, and your finger the sharp point of a nail.

Shan let the ladle drip on Gendun's hands. At first they did not react. Then slowly, like tendrils seeking a spring, his fingers unraveled and, as if with their own consciousness, searched the back of the hands for more. Shan let a few more drops fall, and the fingers found the moisture and brought it to the lips, which quivered at the sensation of the liquid. The fingers lowered and Shan repeated the process. Gendun's eyes did not move. He dripped the water a third time and finally there was a blink. He heard an audible sigh of relief from Lokesh, then raised the dipper to the lama's lips. At its touch they opened to receive the water. He offered a quarter of the ladle, then leaned back, sharing Lokesh's relief. It might still be an hour before Gendun returned but the water was bringing him back, reminding him that at least part of him was still bound to the earth.

They sat in the fragrant room until there was a sharp, audible exhalation from Gendun, the kind of sound monks trained in the old gompas often made when awakening from deep sleep. His respiration rose and his eyes began to flutter into focus. He gazed upon Lokesh and Shan for a moment as though he did not recognize them, then a serene smile rose on his face.

"You know," he said in a hoarse but casual voice, as if they had been speaking all the while, "I have an exquisite hunger."

They found barley kernels in a sack, lit the brazier, and

roasted the kernels for tsampa. Lokesh brought water from the cistern in a clay jar and Bajys, revived but as frail and exhausted as Jowa, found a ceramic pot filled with pickled turnips. They ate the simple fare with relish as a gibbous moon inched across the open portal, brilliant as a flame. At the far end of the table, where no one sat, Lokesh had arranged the items from Khitai's sack. The battered cup. The pen case, the iron chain, the beads.

When they had finished, Shan cleaned the pan and boiled water for tea. Lokesh discovered a bundle of incense and lit three sticks as Shan explained the death of Khitai to Gendun.

The lama sighed. "It is so difficult for a child to find its way," he said. His shoulders sagged, and he seemed a frail old man.

"I am going to talk with Jowa tomorrow, Rinpoche," Shan said to the lama as Bajys wandered out of the room. The diminutive Tibetan had frozen, barely breathing, as Shan had explained about Khitai's death. But he had not taken his eyes from the floor, had not shown any sign of grief, or even surprise. For him Khitai had already died, at Red Stone camp, where Bajys had found a dead boy and concluded that his world was ending. "The soldiers are looking for Tibetans," Shan continued. "Jowa knows the way of soldiers. You must let him take you somewhere safe." He heard the low rumble of the hallway. Bajys was turning the ancient prayer wheel. "You and Lokesh must go deeper into Tibet, away from the border." So difficult for a child. The words echoed in Shan's mind. Gendun meant, difficult for a dead child to make the progression to the next incarnation.

The lama looked at the patch of the night sky visible through the open portal. "I talked to a monk once who had spent years down below," he said, meaning the world outside the high ranges of Tibet. "He had gone away lighthearted and came back full of sad news. He said to me that many people had lost the way, that they ignored what was in their hearts because it was the safe way. He thought, incredible as it sounds, that there were millions of people down below who just wanted to live to be old, as if they were enslaved to their bodies."

Gendun lifted one of the sticks of incense and waved it slowly in the space over the table. "So instead of human beings fighting the wrong, he told me, they just say it is for governments to do so. And governments say we must have armies to be safe, so armies are raised. And armies say we must have wars to be safe, so wars are fought. And wars kill children and devour souls that have not ripened. All because people just want to be old, instead of being true."

"The history of the world," Lokesh sighed.

Shan poured the tea into three chipped mugs and they drank in perfect silence.

"I have never expected to grow old, Rinpoche," Shan said at last.

Gendun gave a small laugh. He studied Shan over the steam of his mug, then looked toward the open portal. "Sometimes I wonder, have I just been hiding all these years? Did I take the easy path, while so many have suffered?"

"There is no easy path in Tibet, Rinpoche," Shan said. With an ache in his heart he recognized, for the first time since he had met Gendun, something like regret in the lama's voice. "You were not hiding. You were being true." The old lama still stared out the portal. "There are people who are treasures, people who are irreplaceable. You are so vital to all of us that the right thing for me, for Jowa, and many others, is to protect you."

"I have lived in caves for many decades," Gendun said. "It never felt like hiding until now."

Shan wrapped his hands around his mug and looked at Gendun. "Auntie Lau was hiding, and what she was doing was the right thing."

Gendun turned to face him. "But she wasn't fleeing."

"No," Shan agreed. "She was protecting someone. The boy. Protecting him and teaching him."

Gendun and Lokesh did not respond immediately. Lokesh rose and filled their mugs again.

Shan moved to the portal and looked out into the night sky.

Lokesh began singing the old spirit wedding song in a hoarse whisper.

"The boy Khitai was not aware. He didn't know she was dead," Gendun said suddenly. "He is still looking for her."

He was. He is. Shan was there for the dead boy. Gendun and Lokesh were there for the living spirit, the thing that survived Khitai. A small boy spirit.

"The boy," Shan said tentatively. "The boy who was not a boy." He thought of the strange words uttered by Bajys. *That was the one I loved. That was the one I was to keep safe. He'll be dead again. But that was the one I knew,* Bajys had said.

Gendun slowly approached, carrying a stick of incense.

"It is a way of saying it," Gendun agreed. "But words of the tongue are not made for such things. I have searched, and I can find no words to explain it. All we knew was that Lau's death was of this world. All we wanted to do was protect the boy. We thought if you would find the truth about the killer of his teacher, then the truth would protect him." Gendun moved so close to the open portal that he seemed in danger of falling out.

"And the rest was—" Shan struggled to find the words. They hadn't intended to mislead him. They had not misled him. They had been unable to translate between worlds.

"Not secret," Gendun said, "just—" He sighed as he looked at a star. "Just not a thing of the world below." The wind tugged at his robe, giving it the appearance of a great rippling prayer flag.

Shan stepped to the portal and put his hand on Gendun's shoulder. "Rinpoche, I am trying to see to the other world, I must see to it. Because the answer lies where the two worlds intersect."

Gendun looked out into the night. A shooting star burst across the horizon below them.

"He was a friend of mine," Lokesh said in his distant voice. "Once, when I was a small boy, he saved me in a snow avalanche. He pulled me in and held me behind a rock as the snow tumbled over a cliff." He smiled. "After that we walked and found high places where we recited the sutras." He reached out and placed his hand around the battered cup from the boy's bag. "He carried this cup, and we would drink with it from mountain springs. We played with dogs and looked for caves. Sometimes we found things left by hermits."

"Khitai?" Shan said in a helpless voice.

Lokesh nodded and sighed with a strange dreamy expression. "Once on the Dalai Lama's birthday we climbed a mountain and threw paper horses into the sky," he said, referring to the old custom of sending paper horses into the wind. When they were found by needy travelers they would turn into flesh and blood creatures. Lokesh drifted back to the brazier and dropped in several juniper splints, then saw the confusion on Shan's face. "He wasn't called Khitai then. He was Tsering," Lokesh spoke with a satisfied smile, as if he had explained everything. "Tsering Raluk."

"And before that," Gendun prodded.

Lokesh shrugged. "Before that he was born in Kham, with the name of Dorjing." He looked at Gendun, who nodded for him to continue. "Before that his incarnation name was Ragta, born in Amdo. Before that, my brain is in shadows. In a long ago time I remember there was a boy in Nepal."

Shan found his way to the table and dropped onto the bench. "I don't understand. Incarnations have no prelife memories. They have no direction over where they re-emerge."

He looked at his two friends, who stared at him with wide smiles, like children sharing something wonderful.

"Ai yi," Shan whispered in realization. "He is a *tulku*." He never felt more ignorant than when the truth slammed into him, never more blind than when at last he could see. It wasn't a boy they were after. It never had been. He walked back to the exposed portal, and stood where the wind, now quite chilling, hit him with its full strength. He closed his eyes, his mind racing, and let the wind do its work, peeling away the chaff. A tulku was a reincarnate lama, a soul so evolved it could direct its reincarnation, could even have memories of its past incarnations.

"There was a gompa in the mountains halfway between Mount Kailas and Shigatse, for many centuries one of the largest in Tibet," Gendun explained. "The first abbot was a tulku, the Yakde Lama, the leader of one of the old sects, one of the lost sects." Although traditionally Tibet had been led by the Yellow Hat, the Gelukpa sect, many other sects had existed in the country, most small and nearly extinct, some tiny but still vitally alive after all the centuries. "Or nearly lost. The last Yakde Lama had a dozen gompas, small ones, mostly built during the old empire period. He had always trained at Shigatse as a young boy," Gendun said, referring to the huge Tashilhunpo gompa that had once dominated Tibet's second largest town. Only a small number of the reincarnate lamas survived in Tibet. But they were the essence of the church, for many Tibetans the most important leaders, the ones they rallied to.

"We can't let them do what they did to the Panchen Lama," a voice said from behind them. Jowa stood there, still looking haggard. But his eyes had fire in them.

Shan nodded sadly. The Tenth Panchen Lama, the highest reincarnate lama next to the Dalai Lama, the traditional head of Tashilhunpo gompa, had at first chosen to cooperate with Beijing, hoping to avoid bloodshed, accepting assurances that Beijing would preserve his gompa and the Buddhist traditions of Tibet. After he had been taken to live in Beijing, the army had imprisoned the four thousand monks of his gompa. Following years of indoctrination, he had been deemed sufficiently subdued to return to Tibet, but at a festival in 1964 he had discarded his speech prepared by the Bureau of Religious Affairs and shouted out his support for Tibetan independence before an audience of thousands. For that one act of defiance he had been sent back to Beijing in chains. After his death, under highly suspicious circumstances, the Bureau of Religious Affairs announced that it had found his reincarnation in the son of two Party members and took the boy into its custody for special education. The Buddhists, with the help of the Dalai Lama in India, using ages old divination practices, had separately identified a Tibetan boy as the rightful Panchen Lama, but the boy had been abducted by the government and not seen for years.

"I heard about a speech in Lhasa," Lokesh said with pain in his voice. "The government said it had been too tolerant, that they won't allow any more incarnations of senior lamas to be recognized. That there will be no more Dalai Lama after the fourteenth dies."

Gendun sighed. "Khitai was found when he was three years old," he explained, "by elders of his sect." There were special procedures, Shan knew, used for the identification of reincarnate lamas, each different according to the traditions of the sect. "The boy identified things from the lama's prior incarnations. The oracle lake gave a sign in the shape of his initials. He bore the birthmark, on his left calf. It was decided immediately that he must be kept hidden until he could assume the full role of the Yakde."

A birthmark. The dead boys had all had their pant leg sliced open.

"Lau, a nun from his order, had already been sent to make a place for the reincarnation when he was identified, in the north, in the borderlands. Then when the time came, Bajys accompanied him, because he had been a novice and because he came from a dropka family and knew the ways of herders."

Lau's records, Shan recalled, had been in order for the past ten years. It had all been for the boy lama, her settling in Yoktian, her election to the Agricultural Council, her adoption of the zheli. Not a mere ploy, for he knew she had loved the zheli, but an elaborate way to create a hiding place while still remaining true. "But Lokesh said he played with—"

Gendun smiled at the old man. "As Lokesh said, they used to play together. The one called Khitai was in the boy age of the last incarnation then, and Lokesh knew him in the boy age, the last time. Khitai would recognize him and know a friend had arrived." Gendun looked out the portal. "Or, if the worst happened, we would collect his artifacts, his special possessions."

Shan remembered Lokesh with Khitai's possessions at the boy's grave, staring at them as if they spoke to him.

"If Beijing understood," Lokesh said in a pained voice, "it would try to seize them, to forestall the selection process."

A chill crept down Shan's spine. "But you didn't find everything," he said to Lokesh. "You didn't find the Jade Basket."

Lokesh sighed. "No. We have the silver cup that my friend the Ninth used to drink from the oracle lake at their oldest gompa. We have the pen case. But not the most important of all, his gau. We need the gau. It is very old. It has always belonged to the Yakde Lama."

"The killer has it now," Shan said in an agonized voice. "He found Khitai." He stared down into his hands. "So I will find the killer, and I will get the gau."

"You'll never beat the government," Jowa said.

Shan looked up at him. "Is that what you think, that it's all of them together?"

"Sure. That's the way they work. Always directed from Beijing."

"I don't know," Shan said. "Some things have changed."

Jowa frowned and slowly shook his head.

Lokesh stood and placed his hands over the brazier, breathing in the fragrant juniper smoke. "So we must go," he announced, with a strange determination in his voice.

"Yes," sighed Gendun, rising from the table. He swayed, unsteady on his feet. "Perhaps I will rest a few hours first."

Shan looked with new hope at his friends. "You can be back in Lhadrung in a few days."

Jowa nodded heavily. "I will get a truck."

The two Tibetans looked at Shan with obvious bemusement in their eyes. "Not Lhadrung," Gendun said. "Down there, in the world. That is where we are needed."

"No, Rinpoche," Shan said in sudden alarm. "Please."

"Khitai is dead," Gendun said calmly, "and there is a boy spirit, undeveloped, unprepared, still trying to understand what happened. He needs our help. No one read him the Bardo rites. He will be confused. Even for a tulku it can be difficult if he had not obtained full mindfulness in his last incarnation. We will help him. A spirit who is uncertain may look for familiar faces. We must try to help him into the next life. And you must find the Jade Basket."

"Please," Shan asked in a desperate, pleading voice and stood, stepping toward Gendun. "What could you do? Nothing. The knobs are down there. The Brigade is down there. The prosecutor is down there. I can only find the gau if you go to shelter."

"Shelter?" Gendun said slowly, as if unfamiliar with the word. "We can go to the grave of the boy. We can pray and meditate. Then we will follow the signs."

You investigate in your world, Gendun was saying, and we will investigate in ours.

"No," Shan pleaded, his voice heavy with dread. "The place of his grave is watched by the prosecutor. You have no protection. No papers. You could never survive."

Gendun offered a patient smile. "We have our faith. We have the Compassionate Buddha."

Shan looked at Gendun, the reclusive monk who led a fragile existence in the cave hermitage of Lhadrung, who had never been in a truck until two weeks earlier, who did not know guns and helicopters and the electric cattle prods favored by knob interrogators. He stepped to the brazier beside Lokesh. "I promise you. If you return to the safety of Lhadrung, I will find the killer. I will bring back the Jade Basket, if I have to go to Beijing to do it. Get rest tonight and then go back to the fragrant room until Jowa arranges a truck. You can go home."

"Get rest tonight," Lokesh agreed with a nod. "Home would be good," he added in a contemplative tone. Gendun took Shan's hand and squeezed it, then the two Tibetans let Shan lead them to pallets in the nearest meditation cell.

But when morning came Jowa sat at the table, his face desolate. Bajys was running up and down the tunnels desperately calling out their names, his woeful voice echoing into the chamber. But they were not to be found. Gendun and Lokesh had left in the night. They had gone down to the world.

CHAPTER 15

Shan sat on the sentinel stone in a wind heavy with the scent of snow, letting it churn about him. Not just Gendun was lost this time but Lokesh too, wandering out into a world gone mad. He had left Jowa staring out of one of the portals with a blank expression. Bajys was walking about short of breath, as though constantly sobbing. Go back to the cell, Shan had told himself, sit with the ancient bow until you find a target again. But his mind had been too clouded, and he had climbed to the ancient sentinel post as the tide of sunlight swept over the vast open plain, sometimes watching for a glimpse of two figures in the distance, sometimes looking to the fast-moving clouds for answers.

A snow squall burst upon him, suddenly engulfing him in a fury of whiteness. He did not move, ignoring the cold, ignoring the particles that bit into his face. Perhaps it wasn't a storm, he told himself, perhaps he was looking inside his mind. It was all that he felt now. Confusion. A swirl of conflicting thoughts. Adrift between worlds. The coldness of death. Even if Khitai were the Tenth Yakde, why did he have to be killed so urgently? Why would the knobs let one of their officers be killed without reprisals? What was the nameless American doing at Glory Camp? Why had Sui wanted to arrest Lokesh, but only once he was away from Director Ko? Had they discovered the old waterkeeper? Was the serene teacher of the boy lama being tortured at this very moment? A patch of sky appeared through the snow, then as suddenly as the squall had started, it stopped.

And in the next moment he realized that he had at least one more piece of the puzzle and that he must act on it. He had been looking for clues in the world of Lau and the zheli boys. Now he had to look for clues in the world of the Yakde Lama.

When he went below Bajys had Jowa's coat on the table, brushing it with a tuft of horsehair, his hands trembling as he worked. Jowa sat nearby, staring at a map.

"There were gompas," Shan said to Bajys. "Gendun said there were still gompas of the Yakde. He said they grew out of the empire period, when there were armies that moved through this area. Meaning, maybe there were gompas established along the old empire routes here. How far is the nearest?"

Bajys just shook his head.

"If Khitai had lived," Shan pressed, "if you had known Lau was dead and had to take Khitai somewhere, where would you have gone?"

Bajys kept brushing. "Secret places," he said, looking over his shoulder toward the portals as if someone was hovering outside to overhear. "Lau knew them," he said, then glanced at Shan apologetically. "She was never going to die," he added in hollow tone.

Jowa looked at Bajys with a strange, expectant expression, as if at any moment to speak to him, to offer the words that might finally bring the tormented man's soul into balance. Or maybe just to embrace him, to comfort him and assure him that he had done no wrong.

"You mean, unregistered places," Shan suggested. No gompa was permitted to function unless licensed by the Bureau of Religious Affairs.

"I know about the Yakde gompas. I've read about them," Jowa said with a meaningful glance toward Shan. The purbas kept an ever-expanding chronicle of the atrocities committed by the Chinese, with copies maintained by purbas all over Tibet. "They were always in the remote places," Jowa said. "Out of touch with everything. Out of touch for years, sometimes. Places where no one would live, places where you would think no man could live. They were dying out, even when Religious Affairs started looking for them. Some were closed, their monks imprisoned.

But some were too remote, too tiny for the government to worry about. The air force made bombing practice on three or four, didn't bother with the rest. Word was that in some of them disease swept through and killed all the monks."

"But Bajys," Shan said, putting his hand on the nervous man, guiding him gently onto the bench beside him. "They must have told you. A place to take Khitai in case of trouble, in emergency. A dropka, like you, could find places in the mountains."

Bayjs pressed his hand against his forehead, as if it hurt. "Lau. I was to go to Lau."

"Did she ever speak of another place? Maybe she went there herself sometimes. Maybe the waterkeeper went there."

"A diamond lake," Bajys said. "All I know is she went there for strength once, to a place with a diamond lake."

Jowa's head shot up. "There's a lake, a shrine lake, an oracle lake, a few miles from here. I saw it once from a distance, with an old hunter. He said it froze much later than others, that deities must live in it because it always shined like a diamond."

They walked in silence for hours, through the high barren landscape, wary of any sound, dashing for cover even at a sudden roar of wind, fearful that it could be a plane or helicopter. Their paths were the trails of wild goats, their landmarks distant peaks that Jowa frequently stopped to study, as if he were mentally triangulating their postion. The purba led them around a valley where a small herd of antelope ran, then passed over a saddle of rock and began climbing a long ridge, always climbing, jogging along the bare places without cover, stopping twice to add rocks to the cairns built at high points as offerings to the mountain deities. A raven flew over them for an hour, watching them closely, circling back, roosting from time to time as if waiting for them. Bajys, whom Shan always kept in front of him, stopped often to stare at the creature, as if somehow he recognized it.

They went higher, over another pass, then up a steep trail of switchbacks. Shan found himself gasping for oxygen for the first time since acclimating to the Tibetan altitude years earlier. They found a stream of blue glacier melt and drank long. Jowa remained squatting by the stream. "I was wondering," he said to Shan, "did you tell Lokesh where the waterkeeper is?"

Shan rose and looked at the purba. "He listened while I spoke about it," he recounted slowly, then saw the concern in Jowa's eyes and understood. Gendun and Lokesh might try to find the waterkeeper, a link to the lost boy. Shan closed his eyes and fought the image in his mind's eye. If the lama decided Glory Camp was where he needed to be, he would walk right up to the wire, walk right up to the knobs and Prosecutor Xu.

Before they left Bajys had collected a dozen stones and built a small cairn, a tribute to the deity who lived in the mountain they climbed. It was to gain merit, Shan realized, part of atoning for losing Khitai. Bajys started down the path after he finished, but Jowa and Shan lingered, each adding several stones himself, sharing, Shan knew, the same silent fear of Lokesh and Gendun being captured at Glory Camp.

The further they climbed, the greater became Shan's sense of entering a different world. Bajys seemed to sense it too. He hung back, trying to let Shan pass him, to let him linger behind, but Shan pushed him on. A snow squall passed over them, obscuring Jowa but leaving his tracks outlined in white for them to follow.

"If Jowa is wrong," Bajys said as Shan caught up with him, sounding suddenly very confident, "we will die in the cold that dwells this high." They had a single blanket for the three of them, only a small pouch of cold tsampa to eat, and nowhere was there sign of fuel for a fire.

Abruptly the sky cleared into a deep, brilliant cobalt. Looking below, Shan saw that the snow had not stopped but that they had simply climbed above the storm.

They walked for another hour, over another ridge, then found Jowa waiting for them at the top of a small ledge that overlooked an extraordinary valley. They stood at the northern head of a mile-long expanse of gravel and dried grass that dropped between two long, massive rock walls with such perfect symmetry that they gave the impression of two monoliths that had once towered at the north end of the valley but that had been pushed over to shield the valley. Between them at the far end was a lake, still and clear, a piece of sky fallen to earth. The walls dropped at nearly identical angles toward the lake, each lined near its top with a tier of snow so perfectly straight that it seemed a baker had frosted them. Surprisingly, despite the cold and altitude, a few gnarled junipers grew at the edge of the water. And at the end of the valley, there was nothing but air. The world simply fell away past the strip of land that defined the end of the valley. In the far distance mountains could be seen, hugged by mist, but between the far peaks and the valley was only sky. Shan remembered stepping above the snow squall. It was as if they had arrived in a land that floated in the clouds.

"I thought this would be the place," Jowa said, with worry in his eyes. They would have no time to return to the shelter of Senge Drak before nightfall.

Shan moved to his side and looked down the face of the ledge they stood on. Three hundred feet below, past a series of ledges that jutted out like giant steps from the cliff face, there was a row of rocks. No, he saw, not a row, but a wall of rocks.

The silence was broken by a sudden hollow tapping sound from nearby, so loud it made him jump. A raven called as if in reply, and Shan looked up to see the large black bird land on a rock thirty feet away. Somehow he knew that it was the same bird that had followed them.

Jowa grabbed his arm, and Shan turned to follow his gaze toward Bajys, who had dropped to his knees by a flat rock that was immersed in the shadows. Bajys wore a look of wonder, the way Lokesh sometimes looked when his eyes saw between worlds. Shan took a hesitant step forward.

It was a rock, only a rock, or rather a large roundish boulder on top of a flat rock. But the rock had a smile on it.

They heard the hollow tapping again, louder, and it made Bajys crouch down, as if cowering. Shan drew closer, and the smile in the rock grew larger. Bajys wasn't cowering, he realized. The dropka was bowing.

A grey arm extended out of the boulder, holding the bottom of a short wooden staff, and as the base of the staff hit the rock they heard the tapping sound again. The raven spoke and hopped closer.

Shan knelt, then Jowa knelt, and as they watched, the boulder seemed to inch forward, its smile growing still bigger.

"Ai yi!" Bajys gasped.

The darkness above the smile stirred and two eyes appeared.

It was a man, an ancient man wrapped in a grey sheepskin cloak and a conical cap of the same material, shaped to cover the back of his neck and to hang low over his eyes, so that they were obscured when his head was bent. The eyes studied each of the three men in turn, sparkling with energy. The man tapped his staff again.

"After the snow my stick always rings," he said with amazement in his eyes, and he tapped it again for sheer pleasure. His voice was hoarse and slow, as if long out of practice. His skin was grey parchment, his fingers long and gnarled, as though made of jointed pebbles.

Shan looked at Bajys and Jowa. The Tibetans seemed overpowered by the old man.

The man's head drifted up and his eyes fluttered closed for a moment. "When the wind stops," he whispered, "listen to the water. You can hear it shimmering."

"We are looking for the gompa," Shan said with a quiver in his voice.

The man's head cocked to one side, and he laughed, a deep laugh that ended with a series of wheezing sounds. Then he abruptly rose, as if he had been pulled up by some unseen force. He stepped between Shan and Jowa and stopped, looking at the raven. The bird cocked its head at the man, turned toward the lake, and disappeared, not flying but jumping over the side of the ledge.

The man laughed again, stepped into a patch of shadow, and, incredibly, began to shrink.

Bajys gasped, then rose and stepped forward as if he might help the stranger. But the man had disappeared into the rock.

"A sorcerer," Bajys gasped.

"No," Shan said with slow realization. "Stairs."

They moved into the shadows and found a narrow set of steps, carved into the living rock and worn hollow in the center from centuries of use. Bajys darted forward and disappeared down into the shadows. Jowa and Shan exchanged an uneasy glance and followed.

It wasn't a cave they entered, as Shan had expected, but a dimly lit room of stone and mortar walls built against the cliff face. The light of a single butter lamp lit the room, below a long thangka of a brilliant blue Buddha. The Primordial Buddha, it was called—the Buddha of Pure Awareness. A brazier, laced with cobwebs, stood near the base of the rock steps. The wall opposite the rock face and the wall at the far end of the room each had a single heavy wooden door. Shan tried the nearest one. It opened slowly, with a groan of its iron hinges, into a chamber lit by a window that looked out over the valley.

From two wooden pegs driven into the mortar a rod was suspended, holding the remnants of an old jute sack over the stone window casement. There were cushions along the wall. On one cushion sat a small bow, like that he had used at Senge Drak. Though obscured with dust Shan could see that several cushions were made of silk, richly embroidered with shapes of conches, fish, lotus flowers, and other sacred symbols. It had the feel of a small *dukhang*, a monastic assembly hall, where lessons might have been given.

He stood silently as Jowa walked along the walls, feeling the reverence that permeated the chamber. "I think you have found it," Shan suggested. "One of the Yakde's gompas."

A small bronze Buddha, no more than eight inches high, had been placed on a stool near the window, facing the valley, as if to let him see the water that looked like sky. Or perhaps, Shan thought, so he could keep watch.

Jowa stood by the little Buddha. It too was covered with dust. He took the tail of his shirt and wiped clean not the Buddha but the stool around it, the way a monk would clean an altar without disturbing its sacred objects. When he was done he looked up at the door and back to Shan, both men realizing in the same moment that Bajys had not joined them.

They stepped back into the first chamber, then opened the second door. It opened silently into a dim passage. They followed it past half a dozen meditation cells and then descended another set of ancient stone stairs. The mountain, Shan realized, as he studied the steps and stone of the passage, did indeed descend in a series of huge stairlike ledges. What he had seen from the top had been the rock slab roofs of the structures built on those ledges.

A door at the bottom of the second set of stairs opened into a long passage, much warmer, its air hinting of incense and butter and the slightly acrid smell that came from braziers fueled by dried chips of animal dung. They passed more cells and opened a heavy timber door with ornate iron work, stepping into a large room that was brightly lit by two windows, one sealed with a frame of panes made of blown glass, uneven and bubbled, the other covered with a piece of transparent plastic sheeting that rattled in the wind.

There were half a dozen men in the room, all in faded maroon robes, seated in a circle around a large smoldering brazier. Several held the long rectangular leaves that came from pecha texts, and they appeared to have been reading to one another. One of them, now shorn of his cap and cloak, was the ancient man with the parchment complexion from above. Bajys, to Shan's surprise, was serving the monks tea, as if he were hosting them, as if he were a novice of the gompa, a familiar of the household.

Carpets, threadbare in spots, were laid on the floor, overlapping so that none of the stone floor was exposed. The walls were panelled in fragrant wood.

As Shan stepped forward, the men stared at him with wide-eyed expressions of curiosity. A bald man several years older than Shan but clearly the youngest of the group glanced at the back wall where clothing hung on pegs. The slight movement of his eyes confirmed Shan's suspicion that the monks were unlicensed. When Chinese came, the monks put on the clothes of peasants.

Jowa exchanged a glance with Shan. He had seen it too. The last gompa Shan had visited had a banner over its gate that read *Buddhism Must Resonate with Chinese Socialism*. It had been raised by the Democratic Management Committee of the gompa, the body appointed by the Bureau of

Religious Affairs to supervise the gompa's affairs. Committee members, carefully screened by political officers before being appointed by the government, were responsible, among other things, for assuring that all monks signed certificates promising not to take part in political activity.

The tension in the room broke as Bajys stepped forward with tea for Shan and Jowa, and they silently sat with the monks in their circle. This gompa had no Democratic Management Committee, no political certificates, no licenses for its monks. If discovered by the government its residents would be arrested and sentenced to hard labor. Some monks, like Jowa, walked away from their gompas instead of signing political certificates and applying for Beijing's permission. Shan knew many who had signed, strong, devoted teachers who argued that a piece of Chinese paper made no difference, and others who insisted that no one could ever be the same after signing, that the act was like a dark stone cast into the waters of their serenity, rippling outward, changing forever the face of their inner god.

As he surveyed the circle of monks a realization warmed his heart. Although these monks had been warned about Chinese and wearing robes, he knew by looking in their faces that they had no firsthand experience with licenses or government bureaucrats who pressed monks to report what their companions prayed for. Only the youngest of the monks had hesitated and looked at the peasant clothing. The monks in the circle were like the untamed, feral animals of the changtang, untouched and pure. A species near extinction.

The monks sat quietly, smiling radiantly at their visitors. "Welcome to Raven's Nest gompa," the bald monk said.

Jowa, to Shan's surprise, spoke first. "We are sorry for the intrusion," he said. "We came about the Yakde Lama."

To a man, the monks nodded and kept smiling.

"He lived here," the bald monk said. "He's coming back."

Jowa threw a triumphant glance toward Shan, then looked back at the bald monk. "The boy Khitai? He lived here?"

The monks looked at each other in confusion.

"The Yakde," the bald monk said with a shrug, as if not

understanding Jowa's questions. "He would sit and meditate in the middle of herds of wild antelope," the man said
in a bright tone. "He wrote a teaching on it. We have it, in
his own writing. That was the Second. The Fourth remembered and came to borrow it, and he took it to Lhasa to
show the Dalai Lama."

The Second Yakde, Shan quickly calculated, would have
lived at least three centuries earlier.

Jowa did not press. He did something truly remarkable.
He looked at the bald man and smiled—a serene smile, a
monk's smile.

"The Ninth," Shan said after a few moments. "Did the
Ninth come here?"

"Once," the monk said. "He spent some months here and
wrote a teaching about what we do here. The Souls of
Changtang Mountains, he called it."

Shan's mind raced. He should ask about Lau, about the
waterkeeper. But his heart had another question. "Did the
Yakde go south, beyond Lhasa?" he heard himself ask. "To
a place called Lhadrung?"

The bald monk readily nodded. The man must be the
kenpo, Shan decided, the abbot of the Raven's Nest. "The
Third did, and the Fifth. To a hermitage, deep in a mountain. And the last time an army came," the abbot said, "men
arrived from Lhasa. Wise men. They said, send your young
monks away, to hide. Some went to that mountain place.
The dropka brought horses and some of their children. They
were going to fight this new army, the dropka said, and
their children needed a place to go until the war was over."
The abbot sighed and sipped his tea. "The next year we got
a letter from one of our monks. They rode for weeks," he
recounted, "only at night. Near a city there was great fighting, terrible bloodshed, and the invaders shot cannons into
the mountains where our people were. In the end," he said
slowly, "three of our monks arrived in the Lhadrung hiding
place and two of the children. A young boy and a girl."

What had Gendun said—that he saw the Kunlun with a
stranger's eyes but that he knew it in his heart? When he
was young, his parents had given him to monks who took
him away.

A bell sounded from down another corridor, and the

monks handed their pages to the abbot and rose. Jowa stepped eagerly to the shelves, gazing upon the pechas, row after row of sutras and teachings. As the abbot arranged the pages into a stack and slipped them into a silk cover, he starting explaining details of the collection to Jowa.

Shan wandered down the corridor. A door to a room at the end was ajar. Bajys was inside, squatting before a long thangka that hung on the back wall of the room, an elaborate image of a man, not one of the Buddha forms, not even one of the many prominent teachers whom Shan had learned to recognize in such paintings. The floor of the room held a carpet far richer than those he had seen elsewhere in the gompa. Indeed, the entire room was appointed in a style far more elegant than elsewhere in the gompa. A robe with bright embroidery hung on one wall. A bronze figure of a lama, possibly the ancient teacher Guru Rinpoche, sat prominently on a table by the door.

"What is it?" Shan asked, not understanding anything Bajys had done since arriving at the gompa.

Bajys just smiled, the first smile Shan had ever seen on his face. There was a low wooden platform bed against the far wall. Bajys bent to straighten the bedding, then picked up a small bronze dorje, the small scepterlike object of Buddha ritual, on the table beside the bed and carefully wiped away its dust. He looked at Shan with surprise in his eyes, as if Shan had failed to see something important, something obvious to Bajys. He took Shan's elbow and guided him to the place where he had been squatting and nodded at the thangka.

Bajys had never been there before, Shan knew. He had not known about the gompa. But he had recognized the figure in the ancient painting.

"His eyes," Bajys said a tone of awe.

Then, with a catch in his breath, Shan understood. It was the Yakde. Bajys was looking at the boy lama in another body and had recognized him.

"It's his room," someone said over his shoulder. It was the bald monk, the abbot. "The room for when the Yakde visits."

Bajys looked at both men with a small, confused smile,

then looked at the dorje in his hands, as if not understanding how it got there.

"How did you know to come here?" Shan asked Bajys. He had not had time to explore the entire structure. Something had guided him to the room. "You were never here before. But you knew it was his room."

"It was just the place I was going to," Bajys began, struggling for words. "I couldn't know," he said, looking at the dorje as he turned it over and over in his hands. The dorje was called the diamond vehicle by many Buddhists, symbolizing the anchor of enlightenment, the indestructible power of Buddhahood. "My eyes didn't know," he said in a tone of awe, as if perhaps the dorje had called him. "But my feet did." He looked up, clearly pained by his inability to understand what had happened but unable to stop grinning.

The abbot took Shan down one more flight of stairs, past a storeroom that held baskets of grain and dried dung. Shan paused at the door to the room, and saw that only a tenth of the space was utilized. From pegs on one wall hung huge coils of ropes. He remembered what Batu had said at the lama's field, that Khitai had told him old men came sometimes to fix the flag on the huge rock tower. Shan followed his guide onto a long terrace that was covered by the ledge above but open on three sides, supported only by pillars of mortared stones. Along the inside wall was a long line of mounted keg-sized cylinders of bronze and wood—prayer wheels. At the far end stood a large four-legged brazier, for burning fragrant offerings. Below, on the valley floor, Shan saw the wall of rocks he had noticed from above, and he realized that it was an old corral. The Raven's Nest hung above the corral, clinging to the side of the mountain, separated from the valley floor by a precipitous drop of at least two hundred feet.

"It must be a difficult thing, to be the abbot of such a place," Shan said.

"I'm sorry?"

"Your job. To be responsible—"

The man smiled shyly. "But I am not the abbot," he said in a tone of apology. "I am just the abbot's assistant. While the abbot is away I do his job."

"Away?"

"On the other side of the mountains."

Shan stared at the brilliant waters. Maybe it was true. They brought visions of truth. "How long ago?"

"Not long. Five, maybe six years. But he's in good health. A nun came once and told us."

"What," Shan asked slowly, "what exactly did the nun do?"

"Gave us the message. No letter. She said a letter would be dangerous. She brought a dried flower, that's how we knew. Rinpoche likes to meditate on flowers. She smiled a great deal and gave us incense and bricks of tea and asked to go to the Yakde's room. She offered prayers there for a long time, and then she climbed down and sat by the oracle lake. She said she had always heard about this place, from her teachers, and she was glad to have seen it before she died. Then she asked for messages to the abbot from each of us and memorized our names and our messages. She said mostly she had come because the abbot was worried about us."

Lau had been there. Lau had sat in front of the thankga and no doubt had recognized the eyes as Bajys had. She had sat by the oracle waters after she had delivered the message from the abbot of the Raven's Nest, the waterkeeper who sat in Glory Camp. Shan vividly remembered the old lama's serene face and the dried flower in his fingers.

"Sometimes," Shan suggested, "sometimes you have other visitors."

"Herders come," the monk said, pointing out the narrow trail that followed the left side of the valley. "They bring grain and new blankets, sometimes. The herders have always kept the gompa alive. They say they can't bring their children for training anymore. But they bring us food." He looked toward a small ledge on the rock face fifty feet away. It held a nest. Three ravens sat there, all watching the two men intently. "Except, one day, the ravens were very scared, and one of the cloud riders came. Loud, like thunder."

Shan closed his eyes. "What did they want?"

"Up on his rock, Rinpoche, our old one, was rejoicing.

He said there were some Buddhas who flew like that. But the rest of us saw that they were just Chinese."

"They came to find you?"

"Not really. They paid us no attention at first. We watched from here for a long time as they worked by the lake. Then I put on the clothing of a herder and went down to the valley, and they met me. The man in charge said he knew we were illegal monks. He said that bad Chinese would arrest us, but that they were good Chinese and were our friends. He and his friends came back to the gompa and we offered them tea, and they gave us boxes of sweet biscuits. They asked about us, about who our leaders were, about our sect."

"You mean they were scientists?" Shan asked in confusion. "Professors?"

The monk was watching another group of ravens, flying in circles over the lake as if engaged in some aerial dance. Shan repeated the question.

"Not scientists," he said, still watching the birds. "Builders."

"I don't understand."

He turned back to Shan, puzzled, apparently trying to find words. "Wait here," he said and trotted back to the door, leaving Shan alone.

Shan looked out over the valley with an unexpected contentment. The Raven's Nest was so high, and the horizon so distant, that the clouds seemed to be moving below them, across the mouth of the valley. The place seemed disconnected from the planet, its remoteness a quality unto itself, as if a piece of the world had indeed broken off into the wind, unaffected by time, unaffected by the world below.

But then the assistant abbot appeared, with a satisfied smile, and in his hands was a red nylon jacket and on the breast of the jacket, where he pointed, was a gold emblem of a man and a woman reaching over an oil derrick, a sheep, and a tractor in a field.

Shan felt as though he had been kicked in the belly. He turned away for a moment, fighting a sudden flood of dismay and fear, the emotions of defeat. The world had found the Raven's Nest after all.

"It's a strong coat. We all got one," the monk said in a consoling tone, as if trying to convince Shan not to be worried. "When Rinpoche goes on top this winter he can wear it."

"When they came," Shan said with a sigh, "did they give names?"

The assistant abbot shrugged. "Our Mandarin is poor, I'm afraid. The one in charge smoked many cigarettes, and we couldn't see his eyes because he wore glasses that were very dark. He asked questions about the lake."

Shan looked out over the shimmering waters. "What about it? What kind of questions?"

"When did it freeze, how deep is it, did we drink the water ourselves, where were the sources of the streams that replenished it."

"You said he worked at the lake, before you went to talk. What did they do?"

"I don't know. Maybe they prayed. Maybe they drank some. It is a holy lake, it has been holy for as long as people remember, even before the teachings of Buddha arrived."

"And his questions, how did you answer them?"

"It is always replenished, because it has no bottom. And of course we drink the water, even in winter, when we melt its ice. It freezes much later than other lakes."

"Because it is protected," Shan said, "because it is exposed to the south and heat is radiated from the huge walls."

"No," the monk said with a patient smile. "Because the mountain deities bathe in it."

Shan nodded. "And that is all he asked?"

The assistant abbot stared out into the sky. "He wanted to know about the animals in the ranges here. I told him the land below is thick with antelope and wild yak, that the mountains have wild goats and lynx and snow leopard. He wanted to know how many people could sleep in the gompa. He said workers might come to help us, and afterward important people might stay here sometimes."

"Help you?"

"Build things, I think."

"Did they come back after that?"

"Twice. Once to take many buckets of water out of the lake. Once to take many photographs. They brought us more of the sweet biscuits that the old ones like."

"Did you wear your robes when he came those times?"

"No. He asked us not to. He said it could be dangerous for now, that we couldn't trust every Chinese. But he gave me great hope."

"You mean because they are coming to—" To what? Shan wondered. To shoot animals, doubtlessly, but not just that. Not if workers needed to come first. "To build?"

"Of course not, we could not permit it. But I told the old ones," the monk said with a generous smile toward Shan, "I explained that it is a new time, we don't have to be afraid of all the Chinese anymore."

"Why could you not permit them to construct something?"

"We hold the valley and the gompa in trust. We await the return of the Yakde Lama. Maybe in ten years, maybe twenty, I told him."

"I don't understand."

"Only the Yakde Lama could give such permission."

Suddenly the ravens on the ledge shot into the sky, flying in a straight line toward those who circled the lake. They began to chatter, so loudly Shan could hear the echo down the valley.

The monk studied the birds silently for a moment, then nodded and turned to Shan, excitement mounting on his face. "You have luck," he said brightly, "the cloud riders are returning."

CHAPTER 16

Shan and Jowa jogged along the valley floor toward the trail the monks had described as the route of the herders. There was time if their visitors had to flee, the assistant abbot had confirmed, for the ravens always sensed the approach of the cloud riders from a great distance, in enough time for some of the monks to walk to the lake to meet the machine when it arrived. But there was nothing to fear from the men in the machine, he had insisted. What's more, there was no place to go. They had no more than two hours of light left and in the autumn night of the high Kunlun they would be blind, they would freeze. Sometimes travelers just shriveled in the cold, dry wind and blew away.

But Jowa and Shan knew there was danger. The Brigade knew their faces, and if the two of them were captured at the Raven's Nest the monks too would be in jeopardy. The assistant abbot had reluctantly shown his three visitors the ancient stairway cut in the rock face that was the only path to the valley floor and at the last minute had handed Jowa a battered old candle lantern, a small tin box with a handle of wire and a small glass window on one side.

When they had descended the stairs Bajys had collapsed on the last step with a forlorn expression. Jowa had impatiently urged him on but Shan had motioned for the purba to continue down the path, then turned to Bajys.

"It's a long climb back," Shan said after a moment, looking at the steep, narrow stairs that led up to the Nest. The Brigade knew Shan and Jowa, but they had never seen Bajys. One more unlicensed Tibetan in the gompa would make little difference to Managing Director Ko.

When Bajys looked up, the confusion had left his face. There was something new, a glimmer of gratitude in his eyes. "When we came out of that snowstorm," Bajys said, "it felt like my world had changed."

Shan sighed and looked up at the monks. They had gathered on the lower terrace. They were all wearing red nylon jackets over their robes and waving. Shan offered his hand. "I'd like to come back some day," he said, "and help you fix that window."

Bajys took his hand and smiled again, then began climbing back to the old monks.

Shan caught up with Jowa at the lake, which was as brilliant blue seen from its shores as from the gompa perched in the rocks above. But he paused as Jowa disappeared around the front edge of the ridge. He stepped to the shoreline, dropped to the water, and drank, then cupped both hands and washed his face. It was strangely sweet and caused a tingling sensation on his tongue. The holy water of the Yakde.

For a quarter hour they jogged down the face of the massive escarpment on which the Raven's Nest perched, then suddenly the sound of rotor blades filled the air. Shan lay beside Jowa on the path, the blanket thrown over them as the helicopter sped by and disappeared into the hanging valley above them. Then they sprang up and dashed recklessly along the narrow goat path, risking a plunge of five hundred feet with any misstep, until they reached a fork in the trail. Without hesitating Jowa chose the one that led to the south. Minutes later they crossed a narrow pass. Jowa paused to study the peaks once more, then, with the setting sun in front of them, cut a path to the crest of a long low ridge that descended to the west of the pass.

Jowa did not speak but jogged on, never once glancing back to see if Shan was there. After an hour, with the sun lost in a pink blush to the west, he stopped and stared at the terrain ahead, memorizing it in the last light. In another quarter hour he paused and lit the lantern. They could travel at no more than a fast walk in the dim light it threw, and finally Jowa stopped and said they would wait for the moon. They sat silently against a rock, huddling against the cold, each eating a handful of tsampa, until after nearly an hour the moon blinked over the eastern peaks. Jowa stood and studied the nearby hills, then moved briskly away.

Jowa extinguished the light as they began climbing down into a narrow valley, seeming more confident as he led Shan along the rugged terrain. He left Shan in the shadow of a large boulder by the bottom wall of the valley, handing him the blanket and instructing him in a grave tone not to move, not to leave with anyone but Jowa, as if danger lurked near.

Shan sat in the dark, clutching the blanket to his neck, watching the stars, shifting his view to the north, where Gendun and Lokesh roamed. Did they have shelter from the wind? he wondered. Had they found someone to give them light in the black of the night?

He had not heard the helicopter leave from the Raven's Nest, though it easily could have gone in the opposite direction without detection, back to Ko's home in Yoktian. What was it Ko was doing at the Nest? The question raged in his mind, it defied him, it filled him with a foreboding nearly as great as that he felt over the fate of Gendun and Lokesh. Ko had no authority in Tibet, no sponsor. In Tibet he would be as illegal as the monks at the Nest. But Ko was not like others Shan had known in authority. He was part of the new China. He did not yearn for higher government office, which had always been the source of power in the People's Republic. He wasn't interested in killing boys. He was interested in business, had perhaps been in the Kunlun that night in the truck, on some Brigade business Shan still did not comprehend. Ko saw gain elsewhere. He saw gain from a handful of old, illegal monks in a forgotten wilderness gompa.

He became aware of a noise and of movements in the shadows. He heard Jowa's voice through the darkness. "This way."

Two dark shapes, Jowa and a figure wearing a hooded cloak, emerged from the night and led him through a maze of rocks, wary of the moonlight, as if even in this high wilderness, in the black night, they feared being seen. They entered a cave, where Jowa's companion lit a butter lamp, and they walked for thirty feet in its dim light before the lamp was abruptly extinguished. There was the sound of a knock on a door and creaking hinges, a hastily blurted syllable that Shan could not understand—a password, perhaps—then a hand was on his back, pushing him through.

The door closed with a metallic groan, and Shan sensed that they had entered a new place. There were unexpected smells of metal and incense and damp fleece and onions. The lamp was lit once more, and to his great surprise Shan saw walls of concrete. Jowa and their guide moved rapidly away, and as Shan followed at a brisk walk he saw that the floor too was constructed of concrete. They passed sleeping forms on pallets of dried grass, then silent men and women sitting alone, bolt upright, at the intersections where other tunnels met their own, as if they were sentinels in some vast labyrinth. Several of the silent figures nodded to Jowa, then looked uncertainly at Shan as he passed.

It was an impossible place. It was a purba place, but it could never have been built by the purbas. As they passed through a central room that had wires hanging from the ceiling and cold, lifeless electric lamp fixtures on the walls, he saw dogs and children and several tables with small statues of Buddha and other teachers.

They went down a long stairway, not carved of the mountain rock but made of metal grating with rusty piping for railings, then followed a corridor that seemed to reverse their direction, as if they were now traveling under the valley floor. Jowa's face was fixed in a grim expression. Then, just as Shan was about to stop and insist on an explanation, they moved through a heavy metal door, spotted with rust. Old rubber seals, dried and cracked, hung from the door frame. They entered a circular chamber twenty feet in diameter, which Jowa walked through quickly, as if anxious to be away from it.

In the chamber was a ring of iron railing around a ten-foot-wide circle of deep shadow. Shan took a hesitant step forward and put a hand on the railing. A cold, hard thing grew in his belly, and he understood the essence of the place. It was not just a hole inside the ring. It was a concrete-lined silo.

"How is it possible?" he gasped, both hands on the rusty pipe as he stared down into the darkness.

"The first generation of missile bases," Jowa said in a low, unsettled voice. "Now the missiles are much bigger. Multiple warheads. Huge bases, like the Mushroom Bowl. But thirty years ago they built smaller facilities, as close to India as possible, half a dozen silos apiece. A small crew. Some, in the bigger valleys, were expanded for the new systems. Others like this were abandoned. They sealed the tops. They blew up the entrances to fill them with rubble. But a herder was watching here. He cut the fuse to the explosives in the one tunnel, so he could use it for his sheep in the winter. But later the Chinese made him surrender his herd to a collective."

"So he told the purbas."

"He became a purba. Not because of the sheep. Because they put his brother in prison on flour charges. Some July sixth, years ago."

Shan grimaced. For centuries throwing roasted barley flour into the air had been a traditional Tibetan expression of rejoicing. But July 6, the Dalai Lama's birthday, had been outlawed as a holiday, and those caught celebrating it with flour, even sometimes those caught carrying bags of flour on the day, were subject to criminal charges.

"But all these people," Shan said. "Not just purbas use it."

Jowa opened another heavy door and gestured Shan through it. "I was one of those who opened it years ago. It is one of the few safe places we have in the region. It became something of a sanctuary, for people in transit. They come usually at night, with a purba guide. Few know exactly where they are. Most stay only a few days and move on."

"Transit?" Shan asked as they started down the corridor.

"Sometimes people have to leave quickly," Jowa explained, "cross the mountains before they are arrested. Sometimes they can't take their families. But their families are known to Public Security, so their families must be protected." Public Security would use the families, Jowa meant, would take them as hostages for the return of the fugitive or just punish them in retribution.

"So, all these people—they are waiting to cross the border?"

"Some are. Some just come to help. Some come to rest or recover from injuries that can't be taken to a Chinese hospital. Others come for the quiet, to make plans."

As they walked past another group of reclining figures, a woman sat up and called to Jowa. "Thank you, thank you again," she said in a soft, shy voice, then looked at Shan with a tentative expression, as if she recognized him. As she raised her bandaged wrist, Shan realized who she was and halted.

"They were still very frightened when our people found them," Jowa explained. "Just sitting at the boy's grave, waving that charm. I said, at least give her time here, in safety, to heal her wrist. We sent people to watch their sheep."

It was the dropka woman, the foster mother of the dead boy Alta.

Shan stepped across a collection of sleeping forms to squat by the woman's side. "I hope your hand is better," he offered.

"Soon I will be able to use it, the healer here says," the woman said, bracing her broken wrist on her knee. She placed her uninjured hand flat onto something beside her as she spoke, as if she needed support. Shan glanced down. She was leaning on the charm, the sacred writing left by Gendun the day Alta had died.

"I wanted to ask you something important," Shan said. "I am sorry if the memory is still painful. But we are still trying to understand. The day when you found the killer, was the killer speaking to the boy? Asking him questions?"

The woman's brow knitted as she struggled to remember. She shook her head gradually. "Nothing. No words. Just noises."

"You said he was called away by lightning. Are you sure? Lightning is rare in the mountains this time of year."

"Of course. He saw the lightning and ran away with the boy's shoe."

"Did you recognize the noises he made?" Jowa asked her over Shan's shoulder. He spoke in Mandarin.

The woman looked at Jowa with a blank stare.

Shan glanced at Jowa and nodded. She didn't understand Mandarin.

"He did not speak," the woman said again. "Not in any language. Just noises, like an animal, when he saw the lightning."

"Can you remember the exact sound the killer made?" Shan asked.

The woman grimaced and hung her head. "I will always remember. I hear it in my nightmares now. One of the barking noises that demons make. Kow ni," she said, looking into the shadows now. "Kow ni ma swee. Like that."

"*Cao ni ma,*" Jowa whispered. It was a curse in Mandarin. Fuck your mother. Fuck your mother, Sui.

They nodded their thanks to the woman and began to walk away.

"We should have taken him to the other place," the dropka woman said in a hollow tone behind them. "Alta wanted to go there. Maybe he would be safe there."

Shan turned back. "The other place?"

"Where the shadow clans sometimes meet. The lama field, the children call it, but only the ghosts of lamas live there."

Khitai had shown the place to the zheli, Shan recalled. It was why Batu had insisted on going there. "Why did Alta want to go there?"

The woman shook her head with a sad smile. "Lau had given them work to do, a collection of autumn flowers. Some other boys told him many flowers grew there, that Lau would be pleased with flowers from the lama field. He said the boy Khitai liked to go there, that he often persuaded his foster families to take him to the lama field for a day, that Khitai would meet the new boy with the strange accent and play in the rocks there." She meant Micah, Shan knew. Khitai liked to meet the American boy at the lama field. When the dropka looked up at Shan he thought she was going to burst into tears. "It was for Lau. They thought they had to complete their last assignment from Lau, so she could rest in peace." She looked away, and her head dropped almost as if she were falling asleep. Jowa pulled him away.

"The ghosts of lamas," Jowa repeated in a haunted

voice. Shan took a moment to understand. The lama field had another dead lama now. The Yakde Lama.

"There was no storm that night Alta was attacked," Shan sighed. "We were only a few miles away."

"No," Jowa said slowly, as if fitting the pieces together as he spoke. "But the killer saw something like lightning, cursed Sui, and ran away. Which means it wasn't Sui who attacked Alta."

"She could have the words wrong," Shan suggested.

"I don't think so," Jowa said. And neither did Shan.

Jowa led him through another of the heavy security doors to a small room where four men sat at a wood plank table, studying maps. Planning. Shan recognized the young purba who had met them on the trail and driven away their truck. The youth looked up and nodded at Shan without rancor, a conspiratorial nod. The others looked at Jowa, not Shan, with unhappy, impatient expressions. A fifth man, at a table with thermoses, turned as they entered, a thin Uighur with a crooked nose. Fat Mao. Explaining that he had just arrived from Yoktian he filled two mugs with tea and handed them to the two new arrivals. Shan studied the room. Wires hung loose from several conduits along the ceiling. A tangle of pipes ran overhead, some painted red. There was a yellow sign warning of radiation exposure painted on the back of the door. The walls were almost covered with more maps, many bearing the legend *Nei Lou* across the top. Scattered across the maps were colored pins and bits of paper taped to their surface. Beside the maps on the table sat a portable computer.

"I told them about the boys," Jowa said. "About Gendun and Lokesh. They want to know where the murders took place, on the maps." As he spoke, one of the Tibetans pulled his chair back and gestured for Shan to join them. Together Jowa and Shan studied a map of the region and agreed on the location of the Red Stone camp, the road where Alta had been attacked, the canyon where Kublai was killed, and the lama field where Khitai was buried. The young purba inserted pins on penciled numbers on the spots, one for Suwan, two for Alta, three for Kublai, and four for Khitai. He ran the point of his pencil in the air over the pins as though to outline the route taken by the murderer, a pattern.

As he did so a hand reached over the table and inserted another pin. "Five," Fat Mao said, and he inserted the pin at the head of a valley ten miles from Yoktian. "Not killed," he said quickly as Shan looked up in alarm. "Jakli and her—" he began. "Last night Jakli and others were traveling to the valley because they heard one of the zheli boys was there, with a shadow clan. It was getting dark. They heard a sheep crying in great pain."

They. Fat Mao meant Jakli and her cousins, Shan knew. She had joined the riders from her clan who were searching for the boys.

"They looked down into a pass, where a rough road entered, and saw a sheep tangled in a vine by a tree. Or, that was the way it was supposed to appear. When they got lower they used binoculars and saw that the sheep was tied with wire to the tree and was lying on the ground, bloody." Fat Mao touched one pin, then another, as he spoke. "Suddenly a boy appeared, running to help the sheep. But the moment the boy reached the sheep, a man dressed in black clothes leapt on him. The boy fought back. One of the men with Jakli had a rifle, and they shot the boy's attacker when he stood up for a moment. He was hit somewhere by the bullet and ran into the shadows. A moment later a black utility vehicle raced out of the trees. The boy had been beaten," the Uighur continued, "and his shirt was ripped open at the neck, but he was not seriously injured. The sheep's rear leg tendons had been cut. They had to shoot it."

"Who was it?" Jowa asked urgently.

Instead of replying, Fat Mao inserted a disc into the computer and tapped a key. A screen appeared, with a heading that read *Yoktian People's Clinic*. He shifted the cursor and a list of recent patients appeared. "See for yourself. Last night, three hours after the attack, admitted for a minor gunshot wound to the forearm."

Shan and Jowa leaned forward and read the screen. Major Bao Kangmei.

"I thought," Jowa said heavily, "that I would feel better when we knew for certain."

Shan nodded silently. The knobs were untouchable. The Ministry of Justice would never prosecute the knobs. It would be suicide for the purbas or the Maos to act against Bao. Jowa was right. It did not feel like closure. It felt like they had crept into the beast's lair and glimpsed it, only to see how huge it was. Moreover, Shan was convinced more than ever that Bao was only part of the answer. He gestured toward the map. "There is one more," he said in a taut voice, and pointed near the edge of the desert, where he believed Karachuk lay. "Lau. The ani. She was the first to be killed."

The boy hesitated, then drew a number on the spot. A zero.

"It's been too easy for Bao. Most of the boys lived with known economic units," Jowa said. "The herding enterprises. Each enterprise has a registered set of pastures, a known set of camps."

"Known to the knobs," Fat Mao said.

"And to the Brigade, and to the prosecutor, and to anyone who can access the software reports," Shan added with a look at the Uighur.

"You mean you think it is not only Bao," Fat Mao said.

"Sure," Jowa interjected. "It's not. There's lots of knobs. A barracks full of helpers in Yoktian."

Shan shrugged. "Seeing him attack a boy last night still doesn't tell us his goal. But it means he's not stopping with Khitai. It means," he said in a hushed voice, expressing the thought as it entered his mind, "that he did not get the Jade Basket. Khitai gave it to someone else. It's still out there with the boys. And the key is still the death of Lau. The boys could be found, once Lau was exposed. Once the killer knew that Lau was Tibetan, that she was an ani, then he knew that the boy he wanted was one of the zheli. After that, finding the boys was easy."

"But after all these years," Jowa said. "Why now, why would they suddenly suspect Lau?"

"Because there was a meeting with a general in Urumqi," Shan said. "Everything happened after that meeting. Kaju was assigned to Yoktian, Lau's political reliability was questioned. Ko began his campaign to buy out the clans."

Fat Mao looked up. "The Poverty Eradication Scheme?" He spat the words like a curse. "Surely it's not connected."

"I think it is. The memo you took back from Xu. Did you read it?"

The Uighur nodded.

The oldest of the Tibetans, a man with the hard-bitten features of a khampa, stood and poured himself some tea. "You know his name?" he asked. "This general in Urumqi?"

"Rongqi," Shan said. "That's all I know. From the army. Now vice chairman of the Brigade. But they still call him general."

The man glanced at the youth, who quickly rose and left the room. Moments later he reappeared carrying a thick, oversized ledger. He laid it on the table and began leafing through its pages, Jowa looking over his shoulder as he read.

Shan had seen such books before. The Lotus Book, the purbas called it, the unofficial compilation of crimes against the people of Tibet, the expanding chronicle of the people and places and treasures lost since the Chinese invasion. It was compiled and copied by the purbas primarily from interviews with survivors as information became available and thus was in no particular order.

As the young purba and Jowa scanned the pages, Shan spoke of Gendun and Lokesh with the others. People would watch, they pledged, on both sides of the border. It was too risky to send more Tibetans into Xinjiang but Fat Mao promised he would take word when he left in the morning. There were places that were always watched by the lung ma. Glory Camp. Knob barracks. And hospitals.

"How will you go?" Shan asked.

The khampa answered the question. No one was allowed to leave a vehicle anywhere near the silo sanctuary. Two hours away, by foot, was a road, or what passed for a road, that connected to the road through Kerriya Pass. Sometime between six and seven in the morning a truck would go by carrying six wooden barrels and three sheep in the back. It would stop if three rocks were placed in a line at a certain spot in the road.

"I will go too," Shan said.

As the khampa silently nodded, there was a rap on the door and a man and a woman, wearing the fleece vests of dropka, carried in food on a plank of wood. A large bowl of tsampa and pickled vegetables. Shan ate quickly, then lay on one of the pallets along the wall. He sat up for a moment and looked for Fat Mao. The Uighur was missing, and a door at the rear of the room was slightly open. Shan stood and stepped into the doorway.

"No!" Fat Mao called as he saw Shan, putting his hands up as though to push him back. Shan quickly retreated as the Uighur emerged through the door and shut it.

"One more thing," Shan said. "The silver bridle from Nikki. Someone gave it to a Mao, to get it to Jakli and Marco. Can you find out who it was?"

Fat Mao shrugged, as if not understanding the significance, then nodded and turned to the maps.

Shan returned to the pallet. He closed his eyes but did not sleep at first, for he was replaying the scene he had glimpsed in the adjacent room. Four figures at a long bench, in front of a large chalkboard filled with translated words and alphabets. Two of those inside, a man and a woman, were carving slabs of wood into wedges. The other two were inscribing them with black ink. He had inadvertently discovered at least one of the ways the Maos and purbas communicated to their networks, using the ancient Kharoshthi text on simulated tablets. Ingenious, he thought. The knobs would not be able to translate the extinct tongue and they were so full of resentment for the tablets that they would simply destroy any they found.

He had finally drifted into slumber when the young purba cried out. Shan shot up and stood at the Tibetan's back as he read out loud. "The first entry says Colonel Rongqi, but that was twenty-five years ago." The purba read quickly at first, then more slowly, pausing more and more frequently as the words sank in. Rongqi had three tours of duty in Tibet, the last two especially requested due to what one file glimpsed in Lhasa said was his extraordinary patriotism and, perhaps, the fact that his father had been killed in 1961 by khampa guerrillas. He had become renowned in the People's Liberation Army for subjugation techniques, even to the extent of becoming a special lecturer on the topic at one of the PLA's training academies. During his first tour he had been notorious for forcing public copulation between monks and nuns, typically in the courtyards of gompas before they were leveled by his explosives experts. By forcing them to break their vows of celibacy, he forced them out of the church. Thirty-six gompas in central Tibet, north of Lhasa, had been looted and leveled on his orders, usually under his personal supervision. Pieces of two huge bronze Buddhas from one of the gompas had been seen by witnesses at a foundry in Tientsen, near Beijing. During his cleansing program, six hundred ninety-six monks and nuns had disappeared. Shan asked if Lau's nunnery, built beside the small gompa of the Yakde Lama near Shigatse, was on the list of those destroyed by Rongqi. The purba read silently, then looked up with a slow nod.

"She recognized him that day in Urumqi," Shan said with a chill in his voice. "The butcher had come back from her past." He shuddered, thinking of the horror that must have shaken the sturdy Lau, the momentary reaction that had given everything away.

The purba read on. During his second tour Rongqi had been commended by the Chairman himself for an initiative he called Sterilize the Seed, based on the principle that the Tibetan religious establishment was held together by its reincarnate lamas and that the death of every such lama represented a political opportunity for the people's government. Ideally, the government should assure the extinction of the reincarnate line by preventing the identification of the new incarnation. Rongqi accomplished this in over thirty documented cases, by destroying the tokens used to identify the new incarnation, imprisoning the lamas who traditionally were charged with the process of identifying new lamas, and, in one case, dynamiting and permanently draining the oracle lake consulted for the new lama.

During his third tour Rongqi, newly promoted to general, institutionalized his campaign by developing a catalog of all reincarnate lamas surviving in his military zone and all the identification artifacts, the signs—the favorite gau, the special robe, the ancient rosary—so that seeds could be sterilized not just in his immediate command district but in a region of hundreds of square miles in central Tibet. Where identification could not be blocked, Rongqi seized the incarnate child and dispatched him to special Party schools in eastern China. In the process the general had turned the Bureau of Religious Affairs in his district into a paramilitary organization, staffed with his own soldiers. The few local lamas who escaped sterilization were neutralized with riches: he offered military doctors to peasants, military equipment for working nearby fields, and an increase in the licenses granted to monks so long as the lama agreed to leave and to attend special Chinese schools for four or five years. Party bosses enthusiastically embraced the idea. A special institute for Tibetan studies had been opened in Beijing for this sole purpose.

Finally, the general had convinced Beijing of a new tactic for special cases, especially when lamas had a potentially important role in influencing economic activity: preempt the designation by declaring a new lama, one of the state's own choosing. By the end of his tour twelve years earlier, only four lamas had held out, keeping their independence—and of those, only one, a lama of a very old school with only a handful of gompas in all of Tibet, had passed on and was undergoing reincarnation. The Yakde Lama. The Ninth Yakde had died just before Rongqi had been reassigned to Xinjiang. His request to stay to finish his work, to stay and capitalize on the death of the Yakde, had been denied because his special skills in economic development had been needed in Xinjiang. But he had not given up. A copy of a memorandum sent by Rongqi in Xinjiang had been taken from a knob office in Lhasa five years earlier, asking Public Security to watch for evidence of a new Yakde Lama, for old informers had reported to him that a Tibetan nun was secretly nurturing a new incarnation.

Shan lay back on his pallet, feeling a strange numbness. What agony she must have felt, being thrown by happenstance in front of Rongqi, unprepared, knowing that Rongqi's involvement would mean the beginning of the end. Who would be able to hide their reaction on recognizing such a butcher? It would not have taken much to make the general suspicious. Rongqi might not even have known with certainty about Lau's connection to Khitai, might have simply suspected she was a disguised Tibetan. But a disguised Tibetan woman could be a secret nun, and a nun would be the link he sought to the new Yakde Lama. She had not been surprised when Wangtu had informed her that she was being replaced, just quietly made her arrangements to protect the Yakde Lama. But Rongqi had reacted much faster than she had expected, faster than Shan would have expected. Because, Shan realized, the Brigade was a much more efficient resource for Rongqi than the army. Lau's secret had been penetrated and the Yakde Lama finally had been killed, only weeks after she had met the only man in the world pledged to destroy the Yakde.

But Rongqi wasn't just after revenge. He was implementing his policies. Eliminate the line by eliminating all the indicators of the new incarnation, which meant the boys would still be stalked, for Khitai had given one of them the Jade Basket. Another piece of the puzzle had fallen into place. Now he had to discover who was serving as Rongqi's instrument in Yoktian. Ko was a businessman, too young to feel the enmity for Tibetans the killer must possess. Was it Xu, or did she just hate Tibetans for all the usual reasons? Or had it only been Bao all along? No. Bao was a knob, driven by knob ambitions and knob arrogance, unlikely to take orders from the Brigade, even its second-highest manager. Bao was following the trail of boys to find the Americans, a trail he had detected before Lau had been killed. Rongqi's agent was following the boys to find the Yakde Lama. Another piece of Shan's puzzle had fallen into place. But all the others were as obscure as ever. The only thing Shan knew for certain was that the killers still stalked the boys. And if Gendun and Lokesh got in their way, the two old Tibetans had no hope of surviving.

Suddenly he looked up and searched the faces of Jowa and Fat Mao. "Micah," he gasped with sudden realization. "The American." The boys were still being stalked, and the dropka woman said Micah may have been at the lama field with Khitai. Xu herself had confirmed that a second clan had been at the lama field. Micah had been given the Jade Basket. Bao and the boot squads were searching for the Americans. Another killer, sent by Rongqi for the Jade Basket, roamed the mountains. The paths of the killers had converged. And the American boy was their target.

CHAPTER 17

Fat Mao and Shan had been walking for an hour in the dim predawn light when Mao threw up his hand in warning. He pushed Shan toward a boulder and crouched behind another as a solitary figure came up the trail behind them. It was Jowa, running hard, his head raised high as though he struggled to see something, or someone, in the distance. Fat Mao stood after Jowa passed, and a moment later Jowa slowed, his hand going reflexively to his belt. But his dagger was gone.

"I thought you were staying in Tibet," the Uighur called out to his back. "Too dangerous for purbas."

Jowa stopped and spun about. "I told them," he said, panting hard as he looked at Shan, "this is different." His gaze shifted toward the mountains. "I have to find the lamas."

Shan did not ask him why he had removed his knife. This is different, he had said. Did he somehow mean this was a different Jowa?

Fat Mao nodded, glanced at his watch, and walked past Jowa to lead them down the trail. He walked faster and faster. Then, as the sun cast its first rays over the mountains, he broke into a jog. The men moved hard and fast, over the open plain now, in the face of the cold wind, back toward the Kunlun. Not because they were late, but because boys were being killed, the spirit of the young Tenth Yakde was wandering, lost, and Gendun and Lokesh were missing.

If they couldn't do anything else for the moment, they could run.

On they went, three small men in the vastness of the changtang, the wind sweeping the grass in long waves around them, the snow-capped peaks shimmering in the brilliant light of dawn. As they appeared over a small knoll they surprised a herd of antelope, which fled across the long plain. Except one, a small animal with a broken horn, which stared as if it recognized them, then ran beside them, alone, until they reached the road.

By late morning Jowa and Shan had been dropped at the side of the road to Yoktian, and an hour of walking brought Lau's cabin into view. Shan had decided the night before that he had to see the waterkeeper's chamber once more.

But Jowa held him back as they approached the clearing. Something was different. There were voices. A dog barked, then another, and they saw a big Tibetan mastiff charging toward them. Shan sensed Jowa's body tensing as it braced for an attack, then he threw his arm in front of the purba, pointing toward a figure walking up from the stream with a water pot. Jakli.

They emerged into the clearing. Someone shouted and the dog halted. Shan turned to see Akzu, and behind the headman, two yurts. Red Stone clan had moved camp.

Malik stood by a string of horses tied between the tents, with two young boys who had not been with the clan on Shan's first visit. He surveyed the camp. A pot of mutton stew hung over the fire, tended by Akzu's wife and another boy, who called out as Shan approached. It was Batu.

"They were coming back down," Batu explained as he ran to meet them. "They had fled at first, but they were coming back down."

"I don't understand," Shan said as he surveyed the clearing. He counted six boys, including Batu, all nearly the same age.

"They all had the same idea. Like an omen."

"Same idea?"

"That the only one who can really protect us now is Auntie Lau. We had to come back."

The zheli had returned to Lau. Of the eight survivors, six were in the camp.

A movement in the tree by the cabin caught Shan's eye. He looked up to see one of Akzu's sons sitting on a limb with a pair of binoculars, keeping watch. One of the man's hands was heavily bandaged.

"We're not leaving," Batu declared. "Not until her killer is caught. Not until we know she is in peace."

Jakli arrived at Shan's side. "It's too dangerous, I know," she said with a worried frown. "I found two of them walking on a path to come here. I told them stay away from the valleys. But then Azku arrived with the other boys. He said Red Stone had an obligation, because they had lost Khitai. And Marco agreed to stay." She gestured Shan back, out of earshot of the others. "The boys told me something else," she said in a hushed tone. "Lau was here, the day she died. With two boys and one of the girls. Riding horses. Then she sent them to sit alone, one of her reverence classes."

"Someone could come," Jowa pressed. "They have helicopters."

Shan followed Jowa's gaze toward the man in the tree with the bandaged hand, and suddenly remembered Xu's story of a Brigade truck that had been stolen and burned. He had almost forgotten their first encounter with Akzu and Fat Mao, when they had been interested only in speaking to Jowa about evading knob patrols. Red Stone clan might want a Brigade truck, not to sabotage, but to evade the Poverty Scheme.

"No one will come," Batu said defiantly. He reached into his shirt. "Not if we have this." He produced a piece of paper, which he unfolded into a large square. "A charm againt demons and killers."

With a surge of excitement Shan recognized it. Over twenty lines of Tibetan text in the elegant script used for religious writing covered the bulk of the paper, with renderings of the eight sacred symbols drawn along the edges. It was not exactly a charm but was called a Victorious Banner, an expanded form of prayer flag that invoked a special blessing on the virtuous souls who flew it.

"Who gave this to you?" he asked, suddenly looking

over the boy's heads, anxiously surveying the meadow behind the cabin.

"The holy men," Batu said. "They came yesterday. They went to the meadow, speaking with the deities. They wrote these magic words for us. They said it would protect us if we held Lau in our hearts."

Lokesh and Gendun had been there. He remembered Lokesh's words when they had first seen the beautful meadow behind the cabin. It was the kind of place where a boy's soul might linger. They had been seeking traces of the Yakde's wandering soul.

The man in the tree whistled, and moments later the mastiff barked again. Someone was approaching the camp, a tall man in a red Brigade jacket, a small backpack hanging from one shoulder. It was Kaju Drogme, wearing a nervous, uncertain expression, as if at any moment he might turn and run back down the trail.

Jowa seemed to growl almost as loud as the dog at the sight of the Tibetan. He ran to Kaju's side and grabbed the backpack off his back. Kaju held up his hands and let it go without protest as he surveyed the compound with a relieved smile.

"One of the teachers said she came to this place with the zheli in the summer," Kaju said awkwardly, apparently deciding to speak to Jakli. "I thought the children might remember." He pulled a paper from his pocket as he surveyed the boys. The list of the zheli. "I need to assure them, make sure they know we have class at Stone Lake tomorrow."

Jakli asked Jowa what he was looking for. "A radio," Jowa said, staring sourly at Kaju. "A weapon. A beacon. He works for Ko."

Kaju took a step closer to Jakli. "I work for the Brigade. I work for the people of Yoktian County," he said, pain obvious on his face. "All the people."

There was only food in the pack—a bottle of water, fruit, and a bag of chocolate bars. Batu spied the chocolate and called out excitedly. The zheli boys descended on Jowa as he knelt on the ground and held out their hands. Kaju smiled. "Go ahead," he offered to Jowa. But the purba grimaced and tossed the bag to Kaju.

When the candy was distributed Kaju held out his list and studied it, then looked up at Jakli. "I still don't know all their names," he said awkwardly. She stared at the list and shook her head. Kaju appeared hurt by the gesture and walked away from them.

"They took him from the camp," Jakli announced to Shan suddenly. "The waterkeeper. The instructors said he was too disruptive, but they didn't want to report it since they might be criticized. So they said he was sick and took him to the clinic near town."

"Is he—has someone seen him?" Shan asked anxiously.

"A Kazakh nurse who knows us. The doctors mostly give him medication to keep him asleep. He's in a secure ward, where they put injured prisoners sometimes. Not always a guard, but they keep the door locked."

But he was out of the camp, Shan thought. It meant there was a chance of rescue, a chance for him to at last speak with the lama. "Does he know about Khitai?"

Jakli sighed. "No one knows how, but he must. The Kazakh nurse speaks some Tibetan. He seems to trust her. He asked her in what direction the lama field was, because he had to pray toward the place now."

"Tell her not to speak any more Tibetan. It could make others—" He stopped when he saw Jakli was not listening. He followed her gaze toward Kaju.

"There is something you have to do for Kaju," Shan said after a moment. "Only you can do it."

Jakli looked at him with uncertainty and sighed, as if preparing herself.

"It may be," Shan said slowly, studying Kaju as he wandered among the boys, discomfort still obvious on his face, "the most important thing any of us could do. But I won't do it. She was your friend, your teacher."

"No," Jakli said slowly, almost like a moan. There was no uncertainty in her eyes now when she looked up. Only sorrow. "I couldn't."

"He won't accept that she was killed. And everything else he has done is based on that delusion." Shan looked up the slope. "Maybe he will find that he has something to say to her."

"And if he runs to Yoktian and brings them back? With

all the boys here? It would be just what Xu wants."

"I'm not sure what Xu wants anymore," Shan replied.

Jakli ignored him. "She would call it clear proof that the Kazakhs are conspiring. She will say we killed Lau and are covering up the evidence. She would take all the boys away, maybe all the zheli. Put them in a special school. Make them all Chinese."

"You can trust or you can distrust. Lau would choose to trust. It is up to you. I will not take him because to do so without your consent would be to dishonor you."

She looked at him with pain in her eyes, then walked slowly away, without reply, and Shan began to inch away from the group. Then, as he reached the shadow of the cabin, he moved quickly to the trail. In twenty minutes he was at the cavern. He lit one of the torches and stepped inside.

The waterkeeper's chamber appeared untouched. He walked around the room. By the tunnel he saw the words he had left for Gendun. *The way that is told is not the constant way.* With a spark of joy he saw that someone had written below it. It was Gendun's hand, unmistakably. *But a constant can be found in the way of the telling,* Gendun had written.

Shan turned and searched the room again. Under the sleeping pallet by the wall he found a large, soiled envelope, stuffed with papers. Government papers, routine paperwork for those paid to maintain streams. He scanned them quickly. They were separated in groups fastened with paper clips, dated at regular intervals. The waterkeeper apparently journeyed to town every other week, where he received his papers. All routine, except the very last paper. It was on special letterhead marked Poverty Eradication Scheme, Yoktian County, and sent by Ko Yonghong. The waterkeepers in the district were being privatized into the Brigade, it said. The Brigade would be presenting gifts in celebration of the event. And to facilitate the project, all keepers would be required to keep strict records of the movements of herders and others through their assigned watersheds. Because the Brigade felt special compassion for them, all orphans were to be especially noted and asked to report to Director Ko so they could be enrolled in a special benefit program. Continue to build socialism in pursuit of your duties, it said in closing.

Lau had been at the cabin the day she died, Jakli had discovered. The zheli had been given their solitary assignments and Lau had gone to see the waterkeeper. He had shown her the memorandum from Ko, and she had known it was the final sign, the beginning of the end. She had ridden to Karachuk that night, ridden at a desperate pace, to tell Marco that the Yakde and his protectors had to escape with Jakli and Nikki.

As Shan was leaving the cavern, two figures appeared at the entrance. Jakli, holding a torch, with Kaju. She looked at Shan with a sad smile. "Okay. I told him a true teacher would want to know the truth," she said.

Shan nodded silently and stepped aside to let her lead the Tibetan through the ice cave to Auntie Lau. Shan followed at a distance. He was at the entrance to the burial chamber when he heard Kaju groan and saw him drop to his knees. Shan stood at the back, by the frozen handprints on the wall, as Jakli showed him the bullet hole.

Kaju held his belly as if he were going to be sick. And then he sobbed.

Jakli knelt beside him, and they studied Lau without speaking.

"She left me files," Kaju said at last, very quietly. "Three days before she disappeared, she updated all the files about each of the children." The words came slowly, as if he were struggling to find them. "This one had pneumonia once, so keep a hat on her. That one likes to watch birds. This one is supposed to see a dentist in three months. It was as if she were going away." He looked down into his hands. "Not locations. She didn't tell me where to find them."

"Why would you say that?" Jakli asked, suspicion heavy in her voice.

"Major Bao asked. Twice, himself. And three days ago at the school, Comrade Hu asked. Said records had to be completed."

The words hung like a dark cloud over them.

At last Shan stepped to the Tibetan's side. "You should consider carefully who it is who lied to you," he said.

Kaju looked at him in confusion. "No one," he said in

a brittle voice. "This is just a terrible tragedy." He shifted his gaze to Jakli, then back to Shan. "Except you. She was missing, they said. But you had her body hid."

"It was all planned. Arrangements were made to bring you to replace her."

"Plans for her to retire, yes," the Tibetan said. "She was going to Urumqi." He fell back off his knees, sitting, as if he had lost his balance.

"Ko told you that she would definitely be leaving for Urumqi?"

Kaju nodded. "Ko said he was going to erect a plaque to her at the school. She will always be a hero in the Brigade." Kaju kept staring at Lau's face. "I will not let them stop me," he said. It sounded like a vow to the dead woman.

"Who?" Shan asked as he sat beside the Tibetan.

"The ones who did this. The reactionaries."

Jakli groaned.

"It's wasn't reactionaries," Shan said calmly. "It was someone looking for a boy. A very specific boy." He told them, as they sat in the chill burial room, about the Yakde Lama. He was careful not to let Kaju know about the Raven's Nest or the waterkeeper, but he spoke about General Rongqi and how one of the zheli had been the incarnation of the Yakde, and about the Jade Basket.

Jakli sighed heavily, then raised her hand slowly and rested it on Auntie Lau's shoulder. The Tibetan sat in silence, his eyes restlessly studying the corpse in front of him. "If I were to believe you, it would mean they all are lying, that they were all working together. Ko. General Rongqi and Major Bao. They aren't. I know that. That's not the kind of government we have now. Bao and Public Security, sometimes they don't understand. One of our assignments is to help them understand new techniques for—" His voice faded, as if he had lost his train of thought. "But the Brigade is different. I got a letter from vice chairman Rongqi congratulating me on my appointment. The People sent me to university," Kaju added, as if it explained much.

"To study integration of cultures," Shan observed. "Not annihilation of them."

"My training," Kaju said, as if in protest.

"Training for what?" Jakli interrupted. "To kill teachers? To murder boys?" She stopped, as if surprised by the venom in her own voice, and looked down, with pain in her eyes, at Lau.

"Of course not."

They were silent a long time. Jakli's head moved slowly up and down as she gazed at Lau, as if she were having a conversation with the dead woman.

Shan sighed. "It's a starting place. Just believe that. That someone has killed four boys, is still stalking them, and will not stop until he has the gau. Do you accept that the killer must be stopped? Whomever it may be?"

Kaju's eyes met Shan's and he nodded soberly.

"And understand this," Jakli added. "The boys are not safe with the Brigade for now. Or with Public Security. Not until it is over."

"I will—" Kaju said, confusion clouding his eyes, "I will not tell Director Ko about the boys being here. He might not understand, he might inadvertently say something to the knobs. I will not tell Major Bao. You can trust me. I have not told about the Americans."

Shan looked at him with surprise. "You mean the boy Micah?"

"Micah, and his parents. There was a class just after she disappeared. No one knew she was dead. Most of the zheli came. Micah was there. They played some American games, even tried speaking some words of English. One of them spoke about Micah's parents sometimes visiting classes, sometimes helping with instruction."

"Why wouldn't you tell about the Americans?" Shan asked. He considered the timing. Kaju had known about the Americans for nearly three weeks. When had Bao begun his search for the Americans?

Kaju looked at him and shrugged. "I don't know," he said, and Shan saw that he had struggled with the decision. "It's none of my business. The boy Micah is part of the class, and my business is to instruct the class, to help the class. He's—" Kaju shrugged again. "He's like the others, just a boy trying to understand the world." The Tibetan turned to Jakli. "But there are classes scheduled, at Stone Lake. Not all the boys have been accounted for. I am still going there." He stood and turned to leave, then after three steps stopped, looking at the wall, at the handprints in the ice.

"To pay homage," Jakli explained. "The ice wall will seal the cave. And then those who paid homage will be with her."

Kaju hesitated, looking at them with entreaty in his eyes.

"Those who paid her homage while she lived," Shan added. "And those who will pay her homage in her death."

Kaju cast a grateful glance toward Shan and pressed his own hand into the ice.

"It is a vow you are making," Jakli said behind them, in an eerily disembodied voice. "A vow to save the zheli."

"Then I give my vow," Kaju said in a small voice, pressing even harder against the ice. When he finished he stepped back and stared at the hollow he had made in the ice, then looked at Shan. "There was something I gave to Public Security. I mean, they took it. I was assigned to Lau's old room in the single teachers' quarters. Public Security was there when I cleaned out her things. I pulled something from under the pallet and they took it."

Shan sighed. "A poem."

Kaju nodded. "Just a poem about a teacher gathering flowers. I didn't—I wouldn't have given it to them but they were there and just grabbed it. No one should be put in jeopardy because of a poem."

Just a poem, Shan thought. But to Bao, a prime evidence of treason. He exchanged a glance with Kaju. It was why Kaju had not told about the Americans, he suspected, because he felt guilty about breaching Lau's confidence—or maybe, Shan thought, about violating the beauty of the child's poem.

Kaju took a step away as Jakli moved toward the tunnel, then stopped again. "I never thought about it, but maybe—" He began twisting his fingers together. "The schedule. Lau's schedule, and all the details I know about the zheli. I meant no harm. They told me her biggest fault was her secrecy about the children."

Shan considered Kaju's words and the pain on his face. "So you put it all on the computer."

Kaju nodded slowly.

Shan looked at the Tibetan uncertainly. He couldn't say it didn't matter.

Kaju sighed heavily, turned to face Lau, and walked, backward, out of the room.

Shan lingered behind in the cold vault as Jakli led Kaju outside. On his first visit, he had come to Lau the teacher. This time he had come to Lau the ani. He knelt at her side again. Speak to me, he wanted to say. Which of them came to Karachuk? Which of those in Yoktian were simply zealously performing their duties and which was working with Bao, which was a murderer? He sighed and pulled the tiny ceramic jar from his coat pocket, the jar that had been filled with sacred sands and sealed at Lhadrung. He held it cradled in his hands for a moment, then pried open the seal with his thumbnail. Lifting the robe, he poured the holy sands, making a small circle on her shirt, over her heart. Then he replaced the robe and placed the empty jar by her head. He stepped back, looking at the ice surrounding on the wall and back at the handprints. Jakli's hand was there, and Akzu's and Kaju's and his own. They could last a thousand years and more, preserving their shame that they had let a saintly woman die with a bullet in her brain.

When he arrived back at the Red Stone camp he realized that the boys had not told him everything about the visit of Gendun and Lokesh. He found Batu with Sophie, listening to Marco proudly explain her heritage.

"When they left," Shan asked when Marco finished, "where did the Tibetans go?"

"Last night, they left. On donkeys. Somebody had given them donkeys," Batu said with wide eyes. "It's what you do for holy men, Lau told us once, you give them things so their deities will smile on you. We asked them to stay, but they told us they had to go to another place. They were eager to leave."

"What other place?"

Batu shook his head, then called two other boys over. None of them knew. "In the desert," one of the boys said. "The old one who laughed a lot said he knew a place in the sand where souls collected."

Shan looked at Marco in alarm. "The Well of Tears,"

he gasped. "Where souls are collected by the wind when they become lost."

Jakli's hand shot to her mouth. "They are too old," she cried. "They could lose their way so easily. They could die in the wind."

"They came to the school, looking," Kaju interjected.

"Lokesh?" Jakli asked. "The lama?"

"No. Public Security. Knobs came this morning. They said they were looking for two old Tibetans who had escaped from prison."

Shan stared at Kaju with a clenched jaw, fighting the cold knot of fear that had suddenly gripped his stomach. The paths of the killers had indeed crossed. Bao had been looking for foreign subversives but now was asking about Tibetans. Someone must have seen Gendun and Lokesh, and reported them.

"Mother of God," Marco muttered and began harnessing Sophie.

When Jakli looked at Shan it seemed she was about to cry. "But we have to find the boys."

"Exactly," the big Eluosi said. "Which is why Sophie and I will go for the old Tibetans." He fixed Shan with a grave stare. "If the knobs take them, they won't last twenty-four hours. They don't want those old men for anything. Just want them gone."

Yoktian seemed in a state of seige. The town square was silent and empty, except for four squads of knobs, one stationed at each corner. Those few inhabitants who had business on the street scurried along, looking down, avoiding eye contact with anyone. The distant whinnying of horses floated through the air. Shan and the others had passed the pens on the way into town. Scores of horses were behind the heavy fences now, stamping the ground restlessly, looking wild-eyed and confused at the Kazakhs and Uighurs who watched them forlornly from a distance, not daring to approach the pens due to the knob guards at the gates.

Shan, Jowa, and Jakli followed Fat Mao along a side street that paralleled the square. With a grim set of his jaw the Uighur gestured toward two black utility vehicles parked near the square. "Another boot squad," he said. "Two new ones came in. One from Kashgar," he said to Shan. "And one just arrived from a base in Tibet." He looked to Jakli and grimaced. "They will start checking businesses soon," he said with an apologetic tone.

She sighed, then extracted a promise from the Uighur to keep looking for the Tibetans and turned toward her factory. She paused after her first step and turned. "Nikki could come looking," she said hurriedly. "Tell him to get back in the mountains. Tell him to just get to the festival on time," she added, then marched away to make hats.

Fat Mao led Shan and Jowa into a small restaurant in an old mud-brick building with a sign in Chinese, English, and the Turkic tongue that said *Closed*. Quickly checking the street for patrols, he led them to the rear of the building, then entered, stepping through the kitchen to the front dining room. A stout woman in a white apron, her hair bound in a red scarf, knelt on a small prayer carpet by a rear table. She glanced at them, grunted something that might have been a greeting, then reached up to flip a switch on the wall behind her. She flipped it twice, with no effect on the lights in the room, then Fat Mao led them through a doorway and down a set of rickety stairs to a musty cellar with a dirt floor. On one wall a set of shelves held blankets and clothing and many types of hats and footwear. Disguises. At a table under a single naked lightbulb a man and a slight woman with her hair bound in two small pigtails sat studying the screen of a portable computer. Shan recognized the man as the sullen, large-boned Kazakh who been on the truck to Glory Camp when Jakli and Shan had met it, who had driven Lokesh and Bajys to Senge Drak. Ox Mao. Fat Mao introduced the woman as Swallow Mao. Ox Mao was bent over something, studying it intently. He threw a paper over it when he saw Shan, but a corner could still be seen. It was one of the wooden tablets.

Half of Xu's detainees had been released, Swallow Mao reported, extending a sheet of paper, after the prosecutor had conducted interviews. Shan anxiously studied the list. The waterkeeper was not on it. He watched as they reviewed half a dozen computer discs taken from an envelope in front of the woman, with no change in the list. He realized after a moment that he had seen Swallow Mao before, sitting at a computer screen at Glory Camp.

"You said you follow people sometimes," Shan said to Fat Mao. "What about Bao?"

"The clinic, having his wound treated," Swallow Mao reported with a cold anger. "Then Glory Camp, talking to detainees," she volunteered. "The knobs collected old men for interrogation. Some of them look like Tibetans, from the hills." She looked up and seemed to recognize the pain in Shan's eyes. "Did I say something wrong?"

Shan sighed and shook his head slowly. Bao was looking for a lama. "What about Ko?"

"At the clinic yesterday," Ox Mao offered in a deep voice. "Meeting with the parents of newborns. Explaining the Brigade's new statistical tracking service, about why certain questions must be answered, to allow the pattern of health problems to be identified. He says."

Fat Mao and Shan looked at each other. "Since when?" the Uighur asked. "When did his questions start?"

"Two days ago."

Two days ago. Khitai had been killed three days before.

"What kind of questions?" Fat Mao asked. "What, exactly, about newborns?"

Ox Mao looked from the Uighur to Shan with confusion in his eyes. "I wasn't there," he said slowly. "I got the report from the Kazakh nurse. Ko said the most important starting point was the background of the parents."

"I need to go to the clinic," Shan said. But the Maos ignored him.

"The background of new parents," Fat Mao muttered heavily.

With a chill Shan remembered the struggle over identifying the reincarnation of the Panchen Lama. The government had carefully waited for a baby born to parents who were both members of the Party. Ko's questions could mean nothing. Or they could mean that General Rongqi was indeed involved and was already searching for the new Yakde Lama, the Brigade's tame lama, which they could proclaim as soon as they obtained the Jade Basket.

"Names," Fat Mao said with sudden urgency, and he began explaining how the Maos must obtain a copy of the data that Ko was collecting. Shan listened for several minutes, then told them he would be upstairs, outside, getting fresh air.

He walked slowly, to avoid attention, watching the windows for reflections of anybody following him. It took another quarter hour to locate the door he wanted, then he paused in the shadows of an alley, watching again, before darting across to it—the rear door of the old palace that housed the Ministry.

In a darkened hallway he passed a narrow door that hung open before a closet that smelled of cleaning chemicals, then another, wider door, with a cross-bolt lock. With a deep breath he pushed open the door at the end of the hall and stepped into the lobby. The bald man was there, sitting on his desk, reading a paper. His eyes grew wide at the sight of Shan, and he leapt off his perch with unexpected speed, grabbing Shan's wrist, pushing him back into the shadows of the rear corridor. But he did not hit Shan or call out for help. "Wait," the man said instead in a hushed tone and looked over his shoulder. Shan nodded and the man released his hold, then darted out to the lobby.

Five minutes later Prosecutor Xu appeared, accompanied by the bald man, who opened the bolted door and flicked a light switch. Xu gestured Shan inside. It was a stale, windowless room, with a small metal table and four metal chairs. Its single lightbulb was encased in a wire cage. On a shelf in the back was a tin basin, a flyswatter, a roll of heavy duct tape, and several long slats of wood, the size of rulers. An interrogation room.

At a nod from Xu the bald man shut the door, leaving Shan and the prosecutor inside. The door shook, and Shan realized the man had not locked it but was leaning against it. Xu sat in the chair nearest the door, Shan at the opposite side of the table.

"Public Security computers say Sui is on personal leave," Xu announced tersely. "Family leave."

"Did you ask Bao why he said Sui was transferred?" Shan asked.

Xu shot him a peeved glance in reply. Of course not, he realized from her expression. Because she had not asked Bao for permission to enter his document system. He looked around the room again. Xu was hiding; she didn't want Shan to be seen. Everyone in Yoktian had secrets. Everyone spied on everyone else.

"Bao expanded the file on Lau," Xu said. "Added two more witness statements."

"You mean, it's Bao's investigation now? A simple missing person case?"

"Public Security has the authority if they choose to exercise it. Two days ago he choose to do so, on the grounds that she was a former public official. We transferred our file and he inserted two more witness statements. No case anymore. He closed the file. Finding of death by accident."

"So all the detainees in the investigation can be released now."

Xu ignored him. "Bao contacted his Public Affairs Officer. There will be an expanded story in praise of Lau in the newspaper."

"What witnesses gave statements?"

"Comrade Hu, from the school. He reminded us that he had reported Lau for praising dissidents in her classes. Then he signed a statement. Walking to work the day after the reported accident he saw a woman's body floating down the river."

"Just like that, he suddenly remembered." What had Hu said at the camp? He had a family to think of.

"The other was a forensics expert in Kashgar. Said the wallet with the identity papers they recovered had traces of mineral consistent with the riverbank she reportedly fell down."

"I am endlessly amazed," Shan said with a sigh, "at what the resources of the People's government are capable of when properly motivated." He stared into his hands. "Did you verify how Sui came into possession of Lau's papers?"

"A responsible citizen." It was a familiar code for government files, referring to an anonymous source.

"I don't think so. I think Sui had them himself."

Xu rose and slowly walked behind him. He braced himself but did not look back. She reappeared holding one of the wooden slats and sat again.

"I thought Bao might pursue the other theory," Shan suggested impassively. Xu's eyebrows rose in inquiry.

"That Lau and Sui ran away together. Secret lovers, maybe. Or perhaps they both drowned, valiantly trying to save a copy of the Chairman's speeches that had fallen into the river."

Xu's eyes smoldered. She slapped the stick lightly in her palm, as if gauging its balance. "My chief investigator and Lieutenant Sui were friends. Sui would come here and wait for him sometimes by the stairs, at the end of the day." Shan glanced at the door. The bald man would be there, in the lobby, while Sui waited, listening to what Sui said. Perhaps, Shan thought, Xu's real investigator was the quiet, unobtrusive bald man. "Sui boasted a lot. He bought a new television, a new radio, a Japanese vacuum cleaner. He was going to buy a new car soon."

Shan stared at her. "The streets are paved with gold in Yoktian. You don't even have to be in the Brigade to get rich. But especially the Brigade. Comrade Ko, he's so rich he can give his sports car to Bao."

"Bao? Impossible. Complete opposites. They barely speak to one another. I've heard them argue in meetings. Ko says Bao is too rooted in the old economy. Bao says Ko does not sufficiently appreciate what the state has done for him."

"But he did," Shan said. "Should be simple enough to verify. A bright red car in a dull grey town." Xu's eyes stared intensely at the wooden slat, as if it might explain why Ko would do such an unlikely thing.

"Ko doesn't make enough in five years to buy such a car," she said slowly, speaking to the slat.

"But now he has announced he will buy another one, to take Loshi for a ride."

Xu looked up, her face clouded. "Loshi?" Xu asked, then nodded as if she had remembered that Shan had spoken with Loshi when he had visited the first time. Her hands became busy, playing with the slat, shifting it from one hand to the other. Then she abruptly laid it on the table and clasped her hands over it. "It's the bonuses," she said in a low voice.

"Bonuses?"

"You saw the memorandum from Ko. Economic incentives. It's the new world, comrade." Xu sounded unconvinced. "The market economy comes to Yoktian. Blend the best of capitalism with the tenets of socialism."

"Must be the Chinese characteristics that confuse me," Shan said with an exaggerated shrug, completing the slogan. It had been painted, bannered, and chiseled throughout China for years. Build for Socialism with Chinese Characteristics. He stared down at his own hands. "But Ko was just talking about disc players for students and teachers."

"There's more. It's the Brigade. They're so infected with capitalism," she said bitterly. "Bonuses to workers for achieving special goals."

"Special goals?"

"Bring in unregistered sheep, fifty renminbi. Bring in unregistered herders to be converted to Brigade employees, five hundred renminbi. Bring in unlicensed religious practitioners to be screened and licensed, three thousand, half in cash, half in Brigade shares."

"A bounty." Shan spat the word like a curse. Three thousand renminbi was more than a year's wage for many inhabitants of the region.

"Economic incentives. To help the growth of enterprise," Xu said in a hollow voice.

Shan placed his face in his hands, elbows on the table. What was it Marco had said that first day at Karachuk? The worker's paradise just keeps getting better and better. "Who," he asked in a taut voice, looking up, "who is eligible for this honor?"

"Only the Brigade, at first. They're a private company, they can spend their money as they wish."

"You said, at first."

"A month ago, it changed. General Rongqi is very influential, expected to be the head of the Brigade in another year. He arranged a telephone call with Ko and me, and Public Security. Bao couldn't attend so he sent Sui. The general asked that key enforcement officials in Yoktian be permitted to participate in his program. I refused. I said Ministry of Justice workers don't accept bribes. It was lucky that Bao was not on the call. Bao would have been furious."

But Sui had secretly accepted the invitation, Shan realized. And Bao, however angry he might have been at Rongqi's suggestion, had also eventually joined the program. Everyone had their price. Bao had gotten involved, not as Sui's superior, but as Sui's competitor. Bao would never have investigated Sui's murder if he himself were Sui's killer. But that didn't explain why Ko had surrendered his car to Bao.

Xu sighed. "Rongqi argued that having all of us join would help accelerate the Poverty Eradication Scheme, he said. The government supports the Brigade, and it's all Brigade money anyway."

"In some places, Comrade Prosecutor, it seems the Brigade *is* the government. Just without all the rules."

The comment seemed to wound Xu. Her head bent into her hands. "You know how campaigns work, Comrade Shan," she said sourly. "Two steps forward, one step back."

She had spoken his name. It confused him.

"You have no theory," she said. "You think everyone in government is guilty, is that it?" But her voice wasn't accusing, it was resentful. "Because of what the government did to you."

They were silent a long time. From outside, in the square, came the sound of a harsh voice over a public address system, announcing a curfew.

"Why have you been here so long, Comrade Prosecutor?" he asked at last. "Twelve years in Yoktian, it's a lifetime."

"I make a difference here," she said woodenly. "We've made historic progress."

Xu was a different woman, Shan saw, when the almost constant flame of her anger burned away. The Jade Bitch wasn't made of stone. She was made of gristle, tough, indigestible gristle, that bore the marks of having been chewed on for many years.

"I want to go upstairs," he said, to see what would happen. "To the records room."

"No!" she snapped, and stood. The audience was ending. She took a step toward the door, then turned with an unexpected look of regret. "That tape. The videotape I made of you that day. It's missing. Someone took it."

"Miss Loshi? You mean, the Brigade has it?"

"I don't know. Ko has asked questions about you. I said that you were a state secret."

Shan looked into his hands. "What's the bounty on secret videos these days?"

Xu's frown seemed to grow. She moved out through the door, the bald man ahead of her, checking the lobby. But before she disappeared she spun about to face Shan as he stood in the door of the interrogation cell. "The general expanded the program," she said hurriedly. "Five thousand bonus for those who can bring in orphans. But only if they're brought in by the end of this week."

"The end of the week?" Shan asked in alarm. It had a macabre sound. A sale on orphan boys.

"That's when he comes. General Rongqi is coming to Yoktian. For a final banquet, to celebrate the final stage of the Poverty Eradication Scheme." She spun about and had already put one foot in the lobby when he called her name.

"There is a way," he said with difficulty, not wanting to believe his own words. "A way to understand what's happening."

She stepped back and let the door close.

"Ask the general. Call his office to negotiate. Ask what you would get."

"Get?"

"Ask what the bounty is for bringing in a Jade Basket," Shan said, and he explained Rongqi's hunt for the Yakde Lama.

Outside, trucks with knobs were moving down the street. Worried faces looked from windows. A dog looked up at a truck and ran away, tail between its legs. Shan walked quickly back to the restaurant, as fast as he dared. The knobs were always interested in people who ran.

But the back door was locked when he reached the building. He nervously ventured back onto the street and tried the front door. Locked. A black car, perhaps a surveillance unit, turned the corner and approached from two blocks away. He ducked back into the alley. There was a fenced area behind the restaurant, a small yard of compacted dirt enclosed by a six-foot-high wall of mud bricks.

Against the back wall was a pen of chickens and a small shed with a door that hung partially open. He ventured toward it cautiously, remembering the cellar and how the Maos would prefer refuges with hidden escape routes.

As he swung the door open he heard running footsteps behind him. But as he turned something heavy hit his skull. He fell to his knees as the objects in the yard blurred, then there was blackness.

Shan regained consciousness in a new blackness, a small dark place that stank of nightsoil. Fighting the throbbing in his head, he explored with his hands and found that he was lying on a slippery cement pad, indented like a bowl, with a four-inch hole in the center. A toilet.

Dim light came up from the hole, meaning, he knew, that it opened to the outside, and under it was a short barrel into which waste dropped, to be hauled away to the fields. He tried to stand but was overcome with dizziness and only made it to his knees. His head throbbed in two places now, where he had just been hit on the back of his skull and from his temple, where he had fallen in the sandstorm. He pushed with his hands on either side of his head, kneeling, bent over, gasping for breath through the filthy stench. Gradually the dizziness faded and, still on his knees, he explored his cell, finding a single faucet in the center of the adjacent wall, a metal bucket below it, and a door in the opposite wall, only five feet away. In a corner by the door was a pile of towels, stinking of mildew. He pushed one against his nose, preferring its odor to the almost overpowering stench of the nightsoil.

It wasn't a knob cell, at least not an official knob cell. He had been lax, too absorbed with the questions in front of him to pay attention to anything behind him. It could have been certain knobs acting unofficially. It could have been Bao, or even Xu, with second thoughts about their strange relationship. He sat in the darkness, not in fear but in disgust, disgust that he had come so far and still did not know who his real enemy might be.

But when the door opened it revealed the Maos. Fat Mao and the two others from the cellar, with Jowa hanging behind him in a kitchen. The kitchen. He was in the restaurant. They had thrown him in the toilet of the restaurant.

A lightbulb switched on, and Shan threw his hands to shield his eyes as the pain flared again. As he did so something hard pushed his hands away, and he fell backward into the toilet again. He looked to see the large Mao, Ox Mao, standing over with him with a short, thick board. Shan wondered absently if he had splinters in his scalp.

"You went to the prosecutor," Ox Mao grunted. "You sneaked out like a thief, back to your protector. Your Han friend." He slapped the stick lightly against Shan's arm, as if to make sure Shan had noticed it.

Shan bit his lip as the pain surged through his skull once more. He seemed to be unable to keep his head straight. It kept wanting to tilt and drop down onto his chest.

They had said he might have had a concussion in the sandstorm. Now there might be two concussions. He had seen men die that way in the gulag, after being beaten repeatedly. Something would build inside their skulls that would just explode. They would squirm on the floor, making animal sounds, holding their heads, and then they would die.

Ox Mao swung the board toward him but stopped before hitting him. He tossed the board from hand to hand, then swung again, getting closer. When he swung a third time Shan caught it, jerked it out of his hand before he could react, and stuffed it down the toilet hole. "My head," he said, and heard anger in his voice. "My head hurts enough."

His vision was blurred at the edges. He saw Fat Mao put a hand on Ox Mao's arm. He saw the stout woman step forward. Carrying a pan of dirty dishwater, she squeezed in by Ox Mao and threw it in Shan's face.

"You Chinese," she said with poison on her tongue. "You killed my two sons."

Shan licked the water that dropped onto his lips. His throat had become so dry he could not swallow. Ox Mao was in the kitchen now, rummaging through cooking utensils. The Maos, a voice said in the back of his mind, had been trained in interrogation technique by the best. The knobs.

"Either you're working with Xu," Ox Mao said, reappearing with a heavy wood instrument that looked as if it were used to mash vegetables, "or you're incredibly stupid. Either way you're a danger to us."

"I came from Tibet," Shan heard some part of him say. His eyes seemed to be rolling about in his skull. He tried to look at Jowa, but the Tibetan seemed unwilling to make eye contact with him. "The lamas."

Ox Mao seemed not to have heard. "Xu killed Sui," he hissed. "Maybe she killed the others too. It's all about her power. More crimes, more arrests. More arrests, more glory. More glory, more power."

"I thought they called you Ox because you're so big," another part of Shan said. "Now I see it's because you have the brain of an ox."

The big Kazakh cursed and raised his new weapon. As if in slow motion Shan raised his arms over head, then another hand appeared and touched Ox Mao's arm.

"He said that his head hurts." It was Jowa. "Why did you go to Xu?" he asked Shan in a faltering voice.

Ox Mao uttered a sound like a snarl, but lowered his hand.

"Xu and Sui," Fat Mao said, looking from the Kazakh to Jowa, then to Shan. "They were riding together in the days before Sui was killed. They were at Glory Camp together. Sui didn't have a car when he died. He was riding with someone. It must have been Xu. She killed him to create a reason to eliminate all of us."

Shan sat up against the corner of the toilet, folding his knees to his chest. "Xu doesn't kill people," he said in a thin voice, gasping every few seconds. "She disgraces them. She imprisons them. She breaks them. Killing—" he said, and grabbed his stomach as a wave of nausea swept over him. "She doesn't need to."

"I thought you saw the cemetery at Glory Camp," Fat Mao said with a chill.

Shan tried to nod but the effort made his head explode with pain. "She doesn't kill people with guns," he conceded. "But Sui," he groaned, "Sui was killed by a competitor." Although he had not even formed the thought in his own mind until that instant, he knew he was right.

No one seemed to have heard him. Ox Mao was glaring at Jowa, Fat Mao was looking at each of the two men in turn. Jowa seemed to size the two Maos up, and took a step back.

Ox Mao turned with a satisfied grin. "You're going to tell us, tell us all about you and Xu." But as he took a step forward, a toe of a boot appeared in his groin and an arm suddenly appeared around his throat. The big Kazakh collapsed with a groan, falling back on the floor, and a figure flew past Fat Mao, who stood with his mouth open, as if trying to understand what had happened.

The figure stood in front of Shan now, shouting, facing the Maos and Jowa. "It's all you know, isn't it? Violence. Fighting. But you never know who your fight is with!" Jakli had returned from making hats. Her fury seemed a tangible thing. Her hands clenched and unclenched, like a tiger extending its claws. The stout woman appeared and pulled Ox Mao back into the kitchen, shaking her head.

Jakli bent over him, then grabbed one of the towels, moistened it under the faucet and wiped his brow. "I never should have gone," she said in a remorseful tone and helped him to his feet. "The gates were locked."

She took command. She arranged the Maos on one side of the table in the kitchen, found a coat for Shan to wear, told him to remove his soiled clothes, and dispatched the stout woman with them to be cleaned.

Jowa brought Shan a cup of fresh water, then found him a mug of hot tea. "I was going to—" he said to Jakli, but left his sentence unfinished. Jakli looked at him, and he hung his head. "How are we supposed to know?" the purba asked her, in a voice taut with pain.

"Know?" she asked tersely. "You come all this way because of Shan, and you don't know what to do?"

"No," Shan said. His vision was rapidly clearing. "Jowa came because of the lamas, not because of me. What we have to do is written nowhere. He has reason to be confused. I am confused." He pulled out the chair beside him, inviting the Tibetan to sit. "But not as confused as I was."

"What do you mean?" Jakli asked.

"I had to talk to Xu, I have to understand where she is in this. She told me something that makes me believe Sui was killed by someone over money, a competitor."

"There is only one lieutenant assigned to Bao," Fat Mao said with a frown. "Sui had no competitor."

"Not a competitor for rank," Shan said. "For bounty."

He swallowed more of the tea and explained what Xu had told him.

"The bastards," Fat Mao muttered when Shan finished. "They're unaccountable to anyone. It's not even about their socialism anymore. Just money."

"They can be accountable to us," Ox Mao grunted.

Jakli seemed to recognize the glint in the big Kazakh's eye and held up her palm as though to stop him. "Nothing. Don't do anything. Not until all the boys are safe."

"But you heard him," Ox Mao said with a conspiratorial nod toward Shan, as if he had decided to forget the episode in the toilet. "The general comes in a few days."

Shan looked at Jakli. The general was coming. The boys were being stalked. But the clans were gathering. One last time, the clans were gathering. And Jakli had to get to a new life.

The stout woman returned with Shan's clothes, still damp, and began cooking a meal for them. When he dressed and reappeared, she inspected him with a matronly air. Seeing dirt on his shoe, she rubbed it with her dish rag. It was her way of apologizing, Shan knew, and he accepted her hospitality with quiet nods as they started the meal, the woman serving Shan first.

When they had finished Fat Mao rose and pulled folded papers from a jacket hanging on the wall. "That truck driver," he announced, "the one who found Sui." He pushed the papers across the table to Shan. "We realized Sui had no money on him. We had the man's license number, so we tracked him down in Kashgar. After a couple of hours of persuasion he admitted stealing the money, but said he spent it all in a bar in Kotian. About a dozen drinks and a particularly enthusiastic *mai chun nu*." The phrase meant *girl selling spring*. A prostitute. "But when he grabbed the cash he grabbed some papers with it. He was glad to get rid of them, said they scared him when he finally read them."

There were only two sheets. One was a list of the zheli, the official list printed from the school computer, with Khitai's name underlined and a note beside it that said *Red Stone camp*. At the top of the page Lau's name had been written, with personal information. The room number of her office at the school. A description of her horse. *Brown horse, white face*, it said. There was another name Shan did not recognize. North Star Enterprise. He pointed to it.

"A garage," said Fat Mao. "Not just a garage—a blacksmith, a stable. Lau kept her horse there. Ox Mao checked it today. The afternoon before Lau died, she took her horse. Ten minutes after she left, a man who looked like Sui came in and rented a horse. In civilian clothes. Brought the horse back the next morning, drenched in sweat, worn out. The owner yelled at him, but Sui just smiled and threw him something that shut the man up. A piece of gold."

"A Panda?" Shan asked.

Fat Mao shook his head. "Gold in the form of a two-inch Buddha."

Jakli moaned and looked at Shan. They had seen the little solid-gold Buddhas before, in the sanctuary room at Karachuk, the room where Lau had died.

The other page held handwritten notes. In one corner was a series of numbers, sums of money, underlined repeatedly. Calculations of bounties, in multiples of five thousand. The price for an orphan. And in the center, a rough map, with a date on it. Over his shoulder Jakli gasped. "It's tomorrow. The map is to Stone Lake. Sui was going to Stone Lake for the boys."

"But he lost the competition to a better murderer," Fat Mao said grimly, "and now that killer is going instead."

CHAPTER 18

Stone Lake was an abandoned oil field camp, a place on the fringe of the desert where fossils were found in the outcroppings. As she drove, Jakli explained that Lau often took the zheli there in the autumn, between the summer and winter temperature extremes to collect fossils and imagine the world as it existed when the fossil forms lived. They drove on a rough track cleared and compacted for oil crews thirty years earlier, across a coarse, gravelly plain dotted with clumps of ephedra and the other tough stunted shrubs that, like some of the clans, had learned to survive where few other life forms could exist. Sand could be seen in the lee of boulders. Sometimes, as they crested low hills, Shan saw the endless white expanse of the Taklamakan in the distance.

As the shrubs began to disappear and the barren desert landscape took over, Jakli stopped the truck Fat Mao had provided them, paused to look for any approaching vehicles, then released air from the tires for better traction. She climbed back in and eased the truck off the road, cresting the dune that ran parallel to it, then drove for another mile in a trough between dunes before surmounting a second dune and stopping in its shadow.

They climbed out and she led Shan along the dune for fifty yards, then onto a low rise. At the top they stopped and surveyed a long bowl between the high dunes. Rock formations were scattered along the edge of the bowl and at the south end a cluster of cement foundations could be seen, with several sun-bleached timbers rising out of the sand, the ruins of the oil camp. Past them, near the south end of the bowl, was the frame of a building that swayed in the wind, and beyond it, fifty yards away, a dip in the encircling dunes where the road entered the camp. Several smaller structures, looking like tool sheds and housing for machinery, were scattered across the southern end of the bowl. The largest, big enough to garage a dump truck, was built of cinderblocks with two large rusted metal doors that opened at the center. It had survived the desert conditions better than the other structures. Beyond it against the dune on the opposite side of the bowl was a much older ruin, a stone foundation with part of a mud-brick wall still intact, its timbers no doubt long ago scavenged for fuel. To the north lay the desert, broken only by a single clump of shrubs perhaps three hundred yards from where they stood. Shan gazed to the far south, to the distant peaks of the Kunlun, where Jowa now searched. He was going to the lama field, with a Mao guide, to the grave of Khitai, in case Gendun and Lokesh visited.

A small dust devil spun around the bowl. A bird, a large carrion eater, floated overhead.

"No one," Jakli said, but as she spoke Shan pushed her down, pointing silently toward the road at the end of the bowl, where a man and a dog had just appeared at the crest of the dune.

As they watched, their eyes barely above the dune, the man turned and waved to someone behind the bowl, out of sight. Moments later two more figures appeared, another man and two boys wearing the dark, bulky clothes of herders.

They watched as the boys scampered down the dune toward the garage, the intact structure in the center, followed by one of the men.

"It's Kaju," Shan said. "But who's the other?"

"Akzu!" Jakli exclaimed, and she bolted over the dune.

Shan followed reluctantly, watching Akzu and the dog. Akzu could warn them of anyone approaching. But even if he did, where would they go? They had no place to hide.

They reached the building at the same time as the boys. A moment later Akzu arrived and greeted Jakli with an embrace, then turned toward the boys. One was Batu, who looked sheepishly at Jakli, then explained quite soberly that he had had a dream of a beautiful horse that had spoken to him and told him that as the oldest of the zheli he had the obligation to protect them. Akzu offered a silent nod, as if he was familiar with the power of such dreams. The second youth was introduced as Jengzi, a name that hinted of Tibetan origins. Jengzi offered a shy grin as he was introduced and tossed a stone against the metal doors. He stood close to Kaju, as if wary of Shan and Jakli.

Kaju watched the road with a worried expression.

"Is someone else coming?" Shan asked.

"I don't know. With Jengzi here, only one boy is left. High in the mountains, away from everything." He gave Shan a knowing glance. Micah, the American, had not come.

"I mean, from town," Shan said.

"No," the Tibetan said in an uncertain tone. "Director Ko said to bring them back when I was done, so he could present their gifts. I said after all that had happened I didn't expect anyone to come."

Shan nodded. He was watching Jengzi as he listened. Jengzi had come from one of the shadow clans. He might know where Micah was.

Kaju followed his gaze. "He speaks Tibetan," the teacher said quietly. "He has an old rosary, says someone gave it to him as a baby."

"Where did you find him?" Shan asked.

"On the road, five miles south. Walking. It's what his zheli family does, he says. His foster father will not be seen. He won't go on roads, treats them like they're poison. He distrusts everyone. They came out of the high mountains last night, to bring Jengzi, then went back into hiding in the foothills. They will return to pick him up at dusk."

As Shan took a step forward, Kaju touched his arm. "Ko said something else, as I left. He said to ask if the boys would like a helicopter ride. He said he might bring the Brigade helicopter here. Ko just wants to help," the Tibetan added in an uncertain voice.

One of the boys let out a cry of surprise. Shan turned from Kaju to see Jengzi pointing excitedly toward the shadows inside the building. In the darkness beside a broken window at the rear of the structure the outline of a figure could be seen, sitting on a steel barrel. Kaju jerked Jengzi back.

"Hungry, anyone?" a deep voice called out. "I brought us some multicultural cuisine. Peanut butter." Jacob Deacon stepped out of the shadows.

Shan watched the American as the boys greeted him warmly, as if they knew him already. They eagerly grabbed the jar from his hands, opening it to explore its contents with their fingers.

The American embraced Jakli and nodded at Shan, then extended his hand to Kaju. "Small class for the new teacher," he said.

Kaju grasped his hand with a nervous glance toward the road. "I didn't expect Micah's father today. Not with all the trouble."

"Trouble? What trouble? Lau wanted the class to hear about the archaelogy digs and hear about fossils. Weeks ago she asked, and I said I'd come. I came."

"But how? You came so far?" Jakli asked. "What if someone saw? The knobs."

Deacon held his palm up to silence her protest. "Not so far, if you go straight across the sand. With a good compass and a good horse, only four hours. I left at midnight. I'll be back before the sun sets."

"You've been waiting all this time?"

Deacon pointed to a small backpack at the foot of the barrel. "I've always got research to write up." He spoke in an absent tone as his eyes restlessly surveyed the dunes. Not for the danger, Shan knew. For his son. He had come for his son.

Shan watched as the two boys squatted at Deacon's feet, still excited about the American peanut butter.

"Micah," said Batu with a grin. "He takes peanut butter with rice. He makes balls out of it." The boy looked up at the American. "Let me take some back. I'll see him in the mountains this week, I know I will. Malik and I—" The boy cast a guilty look toward Jakli and Shan. "We're going to ride up near the glaciers to look," he said in a low voice. He pulled on the American's hand until Deacon looked away from the dunes. The American knelt beside the boy and began patting his pockets, as if searching for a container that might carry a few ounces of peanut butter to Micah.

Kaju glanced back toward Akzu, who had returned with the dog to squat on the dune overlooking the road. "People are scared," he said to Deacon. "The family he's with, they're so shy. Next class, it's the full moon. A few more days. I'll be here," the Tibetan added. "I'll come alone."

"Sure," Deacon said, his disappointment obvious. "Next class." He looked at Shan and winked. "Got a date on the full moon."

Shan offered a small grin. At least amid all the tragedy there were two good things. Jakli was starting a new life with Marco's son. And Deacon would be under the full moon with his son, listening to their insect orchestra.

Suddenly the dog started barking. They looked back to see Akzu rise. He raised his hand straight up, then lowered it to the back of his head as if scratching it.

Kaju gasped. "It's the signal," the Tibetan said urgently. "Someone is coming. Someone he has to warn about."

"Shit!" the American spat. "Shit and double shit." He began fumbling in the pockets of his baggy pants as Kaju herded the boys toward the shadows inside the structure, away from the line of sight to Akzu, who stood waiting for someone now, facing the road. The Kazakh was staying on the dune deliberately, Shan realized, so the new arrivals would come to him, so they would be visible from the building. Jakli and Kaju quickly pulled the doors shut, leaving a crack a few inches wide to see through.

A moment later a man appeared at Akzu's side, shorter and wider than Akzu. As he began speaking to the headman, he turned toward the bowl and his uniform came into clear view.

"Bao!" Jakli cried.

"It's all right," Kaju said, though his voice had no confidence. "Akzu has a plan. He will say he is checking the path for the Brigade herds to move to winter pasture. Sometimes there is water near here. If there is, he can save a day by cutting across the sand. He only wants to help the Brigade now, he will say, because he will be an owner soon.

Since there is no water here, he will ask Bao to look on his map for a better route. If Bao wants to help, Akzu will go with him. If not, Akzu will keep talking until they all drive away together. Then he will return in four hours. It is agreed."

But the words seemed to give little comfort to the boys or to Deacon, all of whom stood wearing grim expressions in the dim light. The American had something in his hand that he had pulled out of his pocket—a small battery light, the size of a pencil. He had strapped his pack to his back and stepped to the window.

Shan watched Bao with a cold intense stare, remembering their last encounter, remembering how Bao's slap had drawn blood. The man seemed like a dark planet that had captured Shan in its orbit. Who else was there, how many others waited behind the dune in a knob patrol car?

Shan turned. Jakli was in the shadows with the boys now, one arm around each of them, comforting them. What a land we live in, he thought, where ten-year-old boys not only know what Public Security is but know to be terrified of it. He looked from Jakli to Deacon, and somehow knew each was thinking the same thing. Bao could take them all and have enough glory to get noticed in the capital. Shan the fugitive. Deacon the illegal American. The orphan boys for whom there was a private bounty. Jakli, absent from her parole job.

Suddenly Bao was pointing at the building.

"We've got to go," Deacon said, and he began lifting Batu through the window.

"Go?" Kaju croaked in a desperate tone. "There is no place to go."

"Sure there is," Deacon replied. "We're going to become invisible." The American dropped Batu outside and climbed out himself.

Bao began slowly walking down the dune. Akzu hesitated, then followed, waving an unfolded map in the air, as if asking Bao a question. It took less than ten seconds for Jakli, Jengzi, Shan, and Kaju to clear the window.

Deacon was thirty feet away, at the remains of one of the small sheds, tearing away the floorboards. The shed was out of Bao's line of sight, blocked by the garage, but for how long no one could know. By the time Shan got to it the American had removed three planks and lowered the boys into a shaft underneath. Jakli and Kaju dropped inside, then Deacon pushed Shan in and jumped down himself.

"What is—" Shan began, but Deacon shoved him hard, pushing him into a darkness at the north side of the six-foot shaft. "As far as you can go!" Deacon ordered in a hushed, urgent voice, then he reached up to replace the planks.

Not until the American finished and began moving toward the others with his light did Shan see that they were in a tunnel lined with stone, nearly four feet high and perhaps five feet wide. Jengzi was crying, held by Jakli at the front. Kaju was next with Batu.

"Okay," Deacon said from behind Shan. "Today's archaeology lesson is about to begin."

"Archaeology?" Kaju gasped. Shan could hear the Tibetan breathing hard, as if he couldn't get enough air.

"Thirty more feet and it'll be safe to talk," Deacon said in a loud whisper.

The bottom of the tunnel was coated with a layer of sand, under which were the same square-cut stones that lined the rest of the tunnel. Every eight feet, wooden timbers, many still with their bark, stretched across the width of the tunnel, supported by small posts. As the group inched along in the dim light from Deacon's pencil lamp, sand trickled down from between the stones overhead.

"The karez," Deacon said when they stopped. "The ancient irrigation tunnels from the mountains, built to carry the melt water, like at Sand Mountain."

"Still intact?" Shan asked.

"Sure. See for yourself. Runs for miles in places. Up around Turfan, they still use them for irrigation, like some of the old Roman aqueducts in Italy. We found a map at Sand Mountain. Seemed to indicate a tunnel here. I checked it out this morning."

"But it's impossible," Kaju said, still breathing hard. "It can't be stable. We'll be—" He stopped, and Shan looked up the tunnel. The teacher's eyes were on his students.

"There were portals, all along the way," Deacon said. "Access for maintenance, access for taking out water. Just like what we came through. Just got to find the next one and out we go. Like pikas from their den."

The builders of the aqueduct had done their job well. For long stretches the stonework still fitted so tightly that the karez appeared to have been swept clean. In places there were small, stagnant puddles, meaning, Deacon pointed out excitedly, that at times of high water, in the spring thaw, some water was still finding its way down the old tunnels.

Shan began to recognize a pattern in the tunnel supports as they moved slowly forward. Every fifth set of beams was thicker and carved with scrolls and the shapes of plants, the plants once kept alive by the karez. In the center of each of the heavier beams was a small dragon head, facing north, ready in defense should demons seek to invade by subterranean means. To the front he heard Jengzi make a whimpering sound, calling out that there were spiderwebs. Shan felt like whimpering himself. There was no danger of Bao discovering them now, only the much more real threat of disturbing the fragile walls. If the roof collapsed, there would be no rescue, only blackness and enough time for horror to take hold as the oxygen was exhausted.

He heard Jakli speak calming words. *Khoshakhan*, he heard her repeat, the calming word for lambs. Jengzi, in front of Shan, stopped whimpering. But as they paused the boy began to inch forward to be beside Kaju. Shan was about to warn him that there was no room for two abreast when the boy's foot pulled against one of the ancient posts. There was a sound not of cracking or splintering, but simply a dry crunching noise as the bottom of the post fell away. The dribble of sand above became a steady flow, creating a thin falling veil that quickly accumulated on the tunnel floor.

"Go!" Deacon shouted. Jengzi scrambled forward, followed by Kaju and Shan. A stone fell onto Shan's back as he passed through the spilling sand. Before he cleared the breach, a second stone fell onto his leg. He paused to see if Deacon needed help.

"Go!" the American shouted again.

Shan shot forward ten feet and turned just as the entire roof around the weakened support collapsed. Deacon was halfway through as the stone and sand closed over him. Shan reached out and grabbed his flashlight with one hand, then grabbed Deacon's wrist with the other and pulled.

With a great heave the American came out of the rubble. He lay face down, gasping for a moment, then took the light and shined it forward, into the face of each of those ahead of him. "Okay," he said with a forced grin. "Guess Bao can't hear us now."

"Where exactly is the exit you promised?" Jakli asked slowly, each word sounding like a vast effort of self-control. The light barely reached her face. Beyond her was the vague shape of the tunnel extending a few feet, then blackness.

"There's access, has to be. There was a community here. You saw the stone ruins," Deacon said. "And cisterns. Almost all the cisterns have been sealed off at the top, but they might have only a foot or two of desert above them."

"But when?" Kaju said, unable to hide the fear in his voice. "Where is a cistern? It's hard to breathe."

"I think Mr. Deacon is saying we just keep going," Shan offered.

"Right," Deacon said in a subdued voice. "A few more days, maybe we'll come out in the northern mountains, with frogs in our pockets." He aimed his light at the boys' faces. "They say there's treasure in some of the old Karez," he offered with hollow enthusiasm.

Batu smiled. Jengzi looked at the American with skepticism, but they both began to crawl with new energy, following Jakli as she probed the darkness.

No one spoke for several minutes, as though fearful that a sound might shatter another of the frail supports. Then Kaju suddenly stopped. "Here!" he said, and pointed to the beam above his head. "We have protection."

As Deacon raised the light, an inscription painted with crimson pigment in Tibetan script could be seen. "The six-syllable mantra," Kaju said with a glimmer of hope in his voice. "The tunnel has been blessed."

"Again!" Jakli called out, pointing to a beam near her own head. The same inscription, in the same paint. She crawled ahead at a faster pace, as though the mark might portend a portal. As Shan watched, she faded into the darkness, but the sound of her movements continued. Then suddenly there was a sound of stones falling and a splash. Jengzi called out Jakli's name in alarm. There was no reply.

"Nobody move!" Deacon warned. "Not a muscle. Not a hair. I'll go."

"No," Shan said. "You're in the back. Pass the light to Batu."

The boy's eyes were wide with fear, but he took the light without speaking and inched forward. He moved twenty, then thirty feet in front of them. Jakli's voice could be heard in the distance, echoing as though in a hollow chamber. The muffled words of a conversation rolled down the tunnel and then, incredibly, laughter. Kaju and Jengzi shot forward, followed closely by Shan and Deacon.

Shan and the American arrived to find Kaju and the boys arrayed on a stone ledge, depressed along its bottom to continue the main course of the karez as it curved around a huge hole lined with stones. The cistern that had been designed to capture the overflow from the main channel was at least forty feet in diameter under a dome of tightly fitting cut stones, and had been built in four tiers, each several feet higher than the one below. Jakli stood below them, on the top tier, up to her waist in water, her head three feet below the top ledge.

Deacon whistled in awe at the construction as he shined his light along the ceiling and far wall. Roots pierced the stone at the apex of the chamber. Shan remembered the surprisingly vigorous clump of shrubs that grew near the far end of the bowl.

"With Jakli's permission," the American said, "I will record Batu and Jengzi as the discoverers. The solvers of the great mystery."

"Mystery?" asked Kaju.

"Sure. We just found out why this place has always been called Stone Lake."

The boys wore grins that nearly reached their ears. Jakli splashed them from below.

"If there was a cistern," Shan suggested, "there must have been access."

Deacon was already easing himself along the ledge toward the far wall. "Probably a stone stairway leading down from something like a bath house." He stopped and aimed his light at a point just below where the dome began on the opposite side. "Right about there," he said. A large stone could be seen, supported by two cut-stone posts. But the area below the lintel stone was packed with rock, sand, and timber debris. The entrance had collapsed.

As Shan and Kaju reached down and pulled Jakli onto the ledge, Deacon's light searched the side of the cistern. "It's too fragile here," the American concluded. "We could collapse the whole thing by moving the rocks. But the cistern would have been near the center of the settlement here. There will be more access ahead."

Just as his hopeful words rang out his light flickered and went dim. He shook it and it brightened, though not nearly to the brilliance it had a moment before. "Go!" he barked.

Two hundred feet past the cistern, Jakli, in the lead, asked for the light. A moment later she began describing in a shaking voice what lay ahead. But there was no need for words. The beam of the light told them everything. Several side posts were loose, three of them fallen and leaning across the tunnel. One top beam had fallen to the bottom and had a pile of sand and stones around it. Another small beam was rotted away, with little more than a few splinters holding it up. The tunnel appeared ready to collapse at any instant.

Time seemed to have a different quality in the tomblike stillness. The small party stared at the doom ahead, and Shan had no idea how long it was before Deacon spoke.

"Okay," the American said in a taut voice. Shan heard him breathe deeply, as if trying to calm himself. "It'll be like this. The light stays with Jakli. She goes first, then the boys. We need someone strong behind, in case there's quick digging to do, so Kaju goes, then Shan. Call back when you reach a stable zone, and I'll come. I'm the biggest, and so the most dangerous."

No one argued. Jakli began inching forward.

"You'll have no light," Kaju called back to the American.

"I got matches," Deacon said in a hollow tone. "No problem."

Shan urged the Tibetan forward with a touch on his leg,

and gradually the four in front made progress. Ten feet, proceeding with agonizing slowness, then twenty feet, and the light began to quickly fade, as if perhaps the tunnel had curved.

"I know you're here, damn you," Deacon said in the darkness. "You're smaller than Kaju. You can make it."

"I thought there might be crickets," Shan said. "Why should you have all the fun?"

There was silence for a long time. When he listened hard, Shan thought he could hear particles of sand turning over.

"How many do you have?" Shan asked. "Matches."

"I just counted. Ten."

"I've got maybe half a dozen." Shan said.

"Great. Run out for marshmallows. We'll have a roast."

"Marshmallows?"

"Never mind."

Silence again.

"I got Old Ironlegs to sing," Deacon announced through the darkness. "Big bass voice. I fed him some peanut butter."

They spoke of crickets again, of the ones the old monk had when Shan was a boy and those Deacon had collected so far for his son.

"Is this all we do?" Shan asked at last and heard the sadness in his own voice. The killer could strike again and he would be lying in the sand, chased into his grave by the knobs.

"Going ahead in the dark"—the American said quickly and urgently, as if forcing the words out—"it's suicide. A handful of matches, no better. So we wait. Jakli's going to send an army of pikas with lighted helmets."

"We could go back," Shan said.

"No better chance back there. This is where we told her we'd be."

Did he mean, Shan wondered, this is where they would dig for their bodies?

A match flared, hurting Shan's eyes. Deacon was looking at him, the American's head propped on one arm, a strange peacefulness on his face.

Do we just lie here until we die of starvation? Shan wondered.

"No, no," Deacon said, in an oddly calm voice. "There's no circulation of air in here. We'll die of suffocation long before that," he added, and Shan realized he had spoken his thought out loud.

The match flashed and went out.

Shan lay on his back, his head on his hands. He could hear the American's quiet breathing behind him. He reached and ran his fingertips along the stones, feeling a strange affinity for the builders of the karez. Other men had been here before him, worshipful men laboring in the dim light of oil lamps, tapping stones and supports into place, taking the measurements that assured gravity would move the water. Some paused to paint inscriptions in the tunnel, where no one would see them. No one but a small desperate group of castoffs, centuries later.

What would it be like when someone pulled his body out in a thousand years? Someone who would study his clothes and declare, How strange, this dried-up Han with an old Tibetan gau wore twenty-first-century textiles and had a tenth-century medallion in his pocket.

"Is it true," Deacon's voice came through the blackness, "that there are lamas who can speak with mountains?"

Shan smiled in the dark. "I think mountains might have much to say."

"A mountain is full of age," the American said very slowly, in English now. "And water and crystal and roots. I could learn from a mountain." He breathed silently for a few moments. The lack of oxygen was beginning to tell. "I used to walk in the mountains. I sat under huge trees and just absorbed everything. I stopped thinking, I just felt it. For hours."

"A meditation," Shan said.

"I guess. There are people in Tibet who do that for years, I hear. If I did that for years I would—I don't know. I wouldn't be me anymore. I'd be something better. Something more than just human."

"I've known people like that," Shan said softly.

"Then you're lucky. Me, I guess all I do is just hope that if I do real good—you know, acquire merit—that in the next life I can get to be a hermit in Tibet."

They were quiet again. Deacon lit another match and held it closer to the bricks, apparently studying the construction. There was no sound from the others. They could be lying in a cave-in, already dead. Perhaps that would be better than the torture of slow suffocation in the blackness. Shan felt something on his hand. Moisture. He wiped the sand from a bottom stone and laid his finger across it. After a moment the finger was damp. He pushed aside the sand and laid his cheek in the dampness on the rock. There was something of a miracle about it, he thought, something of great power in the dampness, something akin to the feeling he had known when he had touched the pilgrim's mummy, as if the dampness itself were a thousand years old.

Shan pushed his cheek down against the stone. He had been to a well outside an old gompa, where pilgrims came to drink. During the Chinese invasion, a khampa child had gone there, after being forced by the soldiers to shoot both her parents. She had cried for a week over the side of the well, and later the monks had covered the hole so the invaders would not fill it in. They opened it for visits by the faithful. Her tears were still in the water, the monks said solemnly, for once the tears had mixed in the well, no matter how many buckets came out, something of the tears remained.

He felt the moisture on his cheek and wondered how many tears had mingled with it. All those who had cried in the mountains beyond, for all the centuries, had something of their tears in these waters. He realized that though he had felt a great thirst earlier, the thirst was gone. A memory, a snippet of conversation with Malik came back to him. Is that how you know you are dead, Malik had asked, when you have no more thirst?

"If mountains could talk," Deacon asked through the darkness, "what do deserts have to say?"

"The same thing," Shan said, "only with sorrow."

"What do you mean?"

"Deserts are where the mountains go when they die."

There was silence again. His consciousness seemed to fade, as if he were falling asleep. He put his fingertip on his eye, unable to tell whether it was open or shut. He heard something. Music, and a falsetto voice. If bits of water could linger for centuries, he thought, maybe particles of sound could do the same, gathered into the karez by ancient winds. Maybe it was what the wind demons did, gathered up pieces of human lives and deposited them into quiet, shadowy places.

He smelled ginger and heard a voice that was unmistakably his father's. Not specific words at first, but tones, as if his father were humming, to comfort him. Then he heard his father speak, in a tongue he had never known. *Khoshakhan*, he was saying to Shan. *Khoshakhan*.

A trickle of sand fell into his mouth and Shan choked, coughing, awake again. "Back at the Stone Lake," he said wearily, "when it was an oasis, it would have been a good place for crickets."

A sound like a muffled laugh came from behind him. "We found a scroll last week," Deacon said. "An essay, on the proper diet to feed singing crickets. Ming dynasty. I'm going to show it to Micah. We'll mix up some of the recipes and see how they work."

"At the full moon."

"Yeah." The American paused before speaking again. "It's going to be hard."

"Hard?"

"When he hears about Khitai. The Maos told us what happened."

"You said they were friends?"

"Khitai was the best friend Micah made here. Lots of mischief together. We were excited about the news, that Micah would have a brother now. Warp was already expanding the house in her mind. Buying bicycles."

"I don't understand—" Shan began, then he realized Deacon was speaking of the future. He rolled over, pressed his back against the moisture, and extended his fingers into the darkness. There was nothing like being blind to make a man see. Marco had not known where Lau had planned to take the Yakde Lama. But Deacon did. "Khitai," he said. "I understand now. You were going to take him to America. You were going to take him after the full moon." It seemed odd now, talking about the future, as if they had become disconnected from it, as if they were speaking of other people's lives.

Deacon didn't answer.

"I know about it. The Panda. The medallions. I just didn't know how far he was going."

"Somebody told me once that no one should die with secrets. So I guess I can tell you mine and you can tell me yours." Deacon paused and breathed rapidly, as if speaking had become a great labor. "Micah and Khitai were hatching out ideas to be together long before the trouble started. Then a month ago Lau came to us all upset and explained about the boy, about who he was. Said things had changed, that she might have to find a new home, that she would have to get Khitai away. Maybe we could say he's our new adopted son from China. Warp acted like it was predestined, the perfect thing for us to be doing. Marco can get us out. Marco knows people outside, he has lots of money, in banks outside. He had papers made, good ones. U.S. passports he bought in Pakistan." Deacon sighed and seemed to sink back into his thoughts.

The silence of the grave. It was weighing on the American too, Shan knew. The silence seemed to shout. It seemed physical, as if pressing down, as if the tunnel were shrinking around them. He raised his fingers slowly, until they made contact with the top of the tunnel.

"I don't understand," Shan said.

"What?" the American asked. It seemed as though sound itself had slowed, as if ages passed between his words and the reply.

"I don't know. You. Why you and your wife came to Xinjiang. Why you would send your son to clansmen you don't really know."

Deacon was quiet so long Shan wondered if he had stopped breathing. "A splinter," he said. "It's all because of a splinter."

"A splinter?"

"We were in the Amazon jungle. It got infected, real bad. Warp was with me, and two Indian guides. We were doing an article on weaving techniques in one of the disappearing tribes. I was delirious off and on, I was going to die, I knew I was going to die. Fever. In and out of consciousness. She sat with me, wiped my brow, talked with me while the Indians looked for medicine in the jungle. I made a vow that if I lived it was going to be different. We were going to make a difference."

Slowly, sometimes pausing to draw in a deep breath of the depleted air, Deacon explained that he had spent much of his youth roaming the world, seeking adventure, spending most of what his father, an automobile dealer, had left him. "Kayaking for a month in Tasmania. Climbed four mountains in Alaska and Nepal. Bungee jumping in New Zealand. The Andes. A month in Peru. A month in Patagonia."

"Doing research?"

"Hell, no. At least, not often. After we got married, sometimes Warp would go on my adventures and pay her way by writing an article. I was just a thrill seeker. She settled us down for a while, said I had to grow up. Got jobs at the university, good jobs. Micah came. Then one day we're at a shopping center, a place where many stores are all together, in a cement maze. Had a big basket of toys, waiting in line. Suddenly I see she's crying, tears rolling down her cheeks. She says here we are, playing along. It's how everyone measures their lives, she said, when you have young children you go to the giant toy stores and buy expensive plastic things. They get older and you buy expensive electrical things at a different store. Then it's expensive clothes. If you're really successful, expensive shoes and expensive cars. It's called Western evolution, she says. You mark your existence, and your place in the herd, by what stores you shop at. I said it's just some toys, Warp. But when it came time to pay and she reached into her purse, her hands were shaking so much she couldn't hold her wallet. She couldn't move. Just cried and cried. Police came, then an ambulance. They put her in a place like a hospital for a week. Some fool heard about it and told Micah his mother had a breakdown in the toy store. He came to me—he was five—with all his toys in a big box and said he would give them up, never have toys again, if they would give his mama back. I went to the hospital and took her out, told them they were the goddamned crazy ones, not my wife. We agreed we would take every research project that came along, to get away from the world.

"Then months later I lay dying in the Amazon. I said to her, I married the wisest person in the world. You were right that day in the toy store, I told her. Nobody's accountable. People sit back and let bad things happen. Forests get leveled. Cultures get destroyed, traditions get cast aside because they're not Internet compatible. Children get raised to think watching television is required for survival and get all their culture from advertising. We pledged to each other if we got out of there we would make it different for us and Micah. We would be accountable, and we would find a place where we could make a difference."

"And here you are," Shan said distantly. "In an ancient tunnel under an ancient town, just waiting—"

"No regrets," the American shot back, as if he did not want Shan to continue. "Our government and the Chinese government doesn't want us here. Screw them. This is where it is, this is where we make the difference." Make a difference. Odd, Shan recalled, Prosecutor Xu had used the same words just the day before to explain why she was in Yoktian. "These people, Beijing thinks they're broken. They're not. They're just waiting. All we do is what you do. Help them find the truths."

"But your son." Shan tried to pretend that he was simply lying on a rock under the open sky, talking in the night.

"Two hundred years ago in America ten-year-old boys were out hunting food for their families. They were learning how to survive, how to build barns and cabins, how to ride, how to heal a sick horse, how to shear a sheep. That's what our boy is learning, essential things. The first things, Warp calls them. Hell, I couldn't even teach him some of them. But the old Kazakhs and Tibetans, they know. We trust them like family. After the first two weeks, Micah said he wanted to switch families, that his shadow clan didn't have any horses and he wanted to be with horses, like the Kazakhs, like his mother's ancestors. But we said stay up there, learn about the sheep for now. Lau said she would make sure he didn't switch among the zheli families. He's safer with them than anywhere."

Deacon's voice drifted off. But Shan knew what he was

thinking. Thank God the boy had not come to Stone Lake, to die with his father.

Shan was under one of the support beams. In the darkness he traced the contours of its carving with his fingers. A dragon head. A flower. He broke the silence a few minutes later. "What kind of New Zealand animal is a bungee?" he asked somberly, wondering whether, after a lifetime of questions, he only had a handful left. "And why would you jump over it?"

The sound that came out of the American was a rasping, wheezing noise that Shan knew was intended to be a laugh.

"Okay," Deacon said after he explained. "How about you? A secret."

Shan thought a moment. "I was a bad father."

"Come on. What man isn't? Every man with a child is a good father and a bad father, all in the timing."

"I was a disloyal worker."

"I hope so. You worked for the People's Republic, for chrissake. Not good enough."

"In my heart," Shan said at last. "There is constant pain. Because I am Chinese and China has forsaken me."

His consciousness seemed to flutter, and he wondered if perhaps he had passed out. He said Deacon's name, and the man made a small moaning sound. He inched forward, wide awake now, and touched the first of the rotten beams. He called to the American. "If we could ignite the fallen beam we could use it as a torch, see our way forward."

"And burn up what oxygen is left," Deacon said in a hoarse voice. "And if we move the wrong way, even in the light, it could collapse."

"Maybe," Shan suggested, "that would be better than slow death over the next few hours."

He could hear Deacon venturing forward. As the American approached, Shan found his hand in the dark and placed it on the beam. He produced one of his matches, lit it, and held it under the end of the beam. The wood smoldered but did not ignite.

"Not hot enough," Deacon said in a voice devoid of confidence. "Make a pile of the rotten chips, start them first."

They tried it and failed. Deacon had three matches left,

Shan had four, and they laid all the American's matches on the pile and lit one of Shan's. The pile sputtered, flared, dimmed, and burned out. Silently Shan pulled papers from his pockets, his notes, his evidence, and crumpled them into a pile and lit them. They flared into a small but steady orange flame. He fed it more chips while Deacon held the beam over the flame. In two minutes they had a torch and were moving down the fragile tunnel.

A beam sagged as Deacon passed, then broke behind him. They crawled like snakes over a pile of rubble that rose to half the height of the tunnel. Shan moved at a snail's pace, knowing that his next movement could be his last. Their progress was agonizingly slow. The wall shifted once, and buried Deacon's arm. Slowly the American dug himself out, then gestured Shan on. Twice the torch dimmed, as if about to extinguish, but Shan thrust it forward as far as he could reach until it found oxygen and revived.

Suddenly Deacon called out in a loud whisper, "The wall!"

On either side was solid stone, huge cut pieces, with long slabs of stone overhead.

"A building foundation!" Deacon croaked excitedly. "It would have access, a tap to the karez."

They moved faster. Then, twenty feet later, Shan froze. A spirit hovered fifteen feet ahead of him, a shape that glowed and shimmered. Deacon saw it and cursed. Shan crawled closer and his heart leapt. It was light, a small shaft of sunlight. But it came through a tiny crack in the stone, only a quarter-inch wide.

The tunnel curved as they proceeded, then suddenly Shan saw a fire with a face in it, a sight that frightened him so much he dropped the torch.

Then the face spoke, with a woman's voice. "Shan!" it called, and they saw it was Jakli, with a torch held below her face.

In five minutes they were out, gasping great lungfuls of fresh air as Akzu and Kaju pulled them through a two-foot opening in the tunnel ceiling, into painful, brilliant sunlight. They were at a ruin in the side of the dune at the northern end of the bowl.

"The flashlight was almost out," Kaju explained, extending a water bottle. "We couldn't use it to go back. Then it took so long to find wood for a torch."

They drank in great gulps as Jakli and the boys explained to Akzu their ordeal in the darkness and the miraculous appearance of Deacon and Shan.

But Shan wasn't celebrating. He was exploring for papers he hadn't burned, the ones that he hadn't reached in the tunnel. The small folded paper of abbreviations from the dead American was still there. He refolded it and stuffed it into his shirt pocket. The only other paper was the map he had drawn of Karachuk. He turned the map over. It had been in the trash, used by the Tadjik to wrap the baseball he had stolen. It had been nothing, he had thought then, just blottings from a pen, strange lines in different degrees of shading.

Deacon approached him and handed him the bottle. "I was thinking, Shan," he said, squatting by his side. "You should come. Next week. Under the moon, with my son and me. I want you to. I was gone down there. You saved my life."

But Shan only half listened. He was watching Jakli, who now stared at him with anguish in her eyes. She stepped away from Akzu and approached him. "Bao didn't leave because of what Akzu told him," she said. "He left because there was a report on his radio that two old Tibetans had been seen on the highway."

Shan felt his head sag. He stared absently at the paper in his hands, fighting a wave of despair, until suddenly the American grabbed the top of the paper and pulled it toward him.

"Where the hell—" Deacon exclaimed and bent to examine the line of tiny print at the top of the page.

"That Tadjik had it," Shan said, "the one at Karachuk. Do you know what it is?"

"Of course. Genetic mapping sequences. A copy of our lab results. What's the point?"

Shan thought a moment and looked up with alarm in his eyes. "That Tadjik was much smarter than I thought. He wasn't trying to steal your white ball. The ball was cover, a distraction in case he was caught. He was trying to steal this, to take it to someone."

"Jesus." Deacon sat down heavily on the sand and pointed to the print at the top of the paper. "A lab registration number, for our lab in the United States. Big secret, until we publish. This lab code gets out, everything gets shut down. The knobs will know who we are. Washington and Beijing will be all over us." Deacon gulped down the remainder of the water and tightened the straps on his backpack.

Shan had one match left. He used it to burn the paper, then watched the American with a pang of guilt as he jogged off to his horse. He hadn't told the American the worst of the news, that his son, the last of the hidden zheli, was now undoubtedly the next target of the killers.

Perhaps, he thought absently, there would have been advantages to being buried in the desert. Now, finally, he had to decide. Others were going to be taken, to be killed or imprisoned. He couldn't stop it all. He could try to save Gendun and Lokesh or he could try to stop the zheli killing. But he couldn't do both.

CHAPTER 19

It seemed like days had passed inside the karez, but it was only early afternoon by the time they reached the highway. Akzu embraced Jakli repeatedly as they departed, making her promise with each hug to be at the nadam early, until she began to smile, then softly laugh. Her aunts had secretly made a wedding dress, he told her, so she had to come early but act surprised. Before the Kazakh left, Shan asked Jakli if she knew the way to the camp where Marco had sent the Tadjik thief. She consulted her uncle briefly. Wild Bear Mountain, Marco had said, near the ford of Fragile Water Creek. They did not know the camp but they knew where to find a guide who would know.

"I thought a dust demon had taken you," Akzu said in a distant voice before departing. "They do that sometimes." He had listened in seeming disbelief when they had explained their passage through the tunnels, and now looked at the sand on their clothes, their skin, their hair and nodded solemnly, as though confirming his suspicion. "Sometimes, they bring you back just as sudden," the old Kazakh observed. "You wouldn't remember," he added solemnly.

Kaju studied the landscape with an unsettled expression, as if looking for other escape routes. He would have to come back in five days, for the next class. He had promised the American, for that was the appointed time for Deacon's son to return to his parents.

Jakli seemed to sense Shan's thoughts as they drove west, away from the desert. "He's out there, with Sophie," she reassured him. "Marco will find your friends. There is no one better for the task. He will take them to safety. They're probably on the way to his cabin now, singing Russian love songs with him."

Half an hour later Jakli eased to a stop at a crossroads jammed with people. Near the intersection was a shack with a wire fence behind it, holding a flock of goats. They stopped and walked to the gathering. More than two dozen people crowded the intersection, some carrying stones, others sitting in reverence before a growing cairn of rocks. Some were listening to a man who sat atop a broad log that served as a corner fencepost, speaking with great animation. A man on a horse rode up and asked where the holy place was. The man on the post pointed to the rocks and the other man dismounted, untied the wing of a large bird from behind his saddle, and walked to the rocks to fasten it to the cairn.

It was a shrine. For the miracle that had happened. The people were kneeling now. The rocks were arranged in a narrow pyramid nearly eight feet high. A rope was tied to a stick at the top, staked to the ground fifteen feet away, and a fragment of cloth was attached to it with Tibetan words. A prayer flag. Shan watched in confusion. Buddhists, down from the mountains, were putting on prayer flags. The Kazakhs and Uighurs were putting on feathers, pieces of fur, and the wing of a bird.

Shan walked through the excited throng, asking questions. The two Tibetan holy men had come through the day before, in the late afternoon, resting their donkeys at the crossroads. Others came with them, nine or ten others, old women, small children, a herder with a bad leg, some on horses or donkeys, some walking. Like a pilgrimage in the old days, a woman with grey hair said.

One of the holy men, the one in the Buddhist robe, had spoken with each of the followers, even the children. The other man, whose eyes twinkled when he spoke, had also listened to them, not to their words, but to their bodies, finding the words spoken by arms and legs and stomachs that no one else could hear. He had given herbs to some and advice for exercise of limbs to others. A dropka woman galloped up with a baby, asking the thin one with the red robe to give it a name. Once, Shan recalled, Tibetans had always asked lamas for the names of their children. Then the robed one had assigned journeys of atonement. This woman was to go see her brother whom she had not spoken with in ten years because he had given her a lame horse, that woman was to go a mountain lake and drink its waters, then build a shelter that wild animals might use in the winter. The lame man was sent to meditate where young colts slept. "A synshy," the man who had just ridden in said knowingly. "The man in the robe was a horsespeaker." Several in the crowd nodded knowingly.

But that had not been the miracle, the man on the post said. The miracle had come later, when the knobs arrived. Shan's head snapped up. A chill crept into his stomach. Only three young knobs, in a small truck. They seemed to have been searching for the holy men, and two stood guard with guns while the third, a woman knob, talked excitedly on the radio.

The people had gotten angry and told the knobs that they should be looking for the killers of children, not old men. The knobs had gotten out hand chains then, and somebody had thrown a rock at one of the knobs. They had pulled out their weapons and one shot a gun in the air, several shots, on automatic. The man with the robe—Gendun— covered his ears then, and when the gun stopped he lowered his hands and asked if the man was finished. You make it very hard to talk, Gendun had said, most earnestly, and the Chinese man who fired the gun had looked confused, then apologized.

Then Gendun had stood in front of the knob who had been hit by the stone and told the people not to hurt the young soldiers. He had spoken to Lokesh and Lokesh took the chains and fastened a pair on Gendun, then Gendun had fastened a pair on Lokesh. The lama had then asked the knobs to sit for a moment with them, to share some food. Two of the knobs had done so, and Gendun said a prayer while a herder handed out pieces of nan bread. Gendun had asked the knobs their names and he said the knob woman had a strong face and would make a good wife for a herder. People had laughed.

But even that was not the miracle, the man on the post

said dramatically. The miracle came next, when a limousine arrived and the Jade Bitch appeared. People had shuddered, some had run away. The prosecutor had stood silently, looking at the Tibetans and the knobs. Then Gendun had walked in his chains to stand in front of her, smiling. She had stared, a long time, as if in a trance. Then she had spoken on her radio and told the knobs to leave, to release the two men and leave. The woman knob had argued, and the protector had shouted at her. Before the knobs left the prosecutor made the knobs give her the chains used on the two men. People had thought she was going to take them away herself, to her prison camp at the foot of the mountains. But the Jade Bitch had walked to the two men, dropped the chains at their feet, and driven away. That was the miracle.

The chains, where she had dropped them, were under the cairn.

Shan looked in silence at the cairn, then at Jakli.

"She just doesn't want to share them with the knobs," Jakli said. "She wants them all to herself, without the knobs knowing."

"I don't know," Shan said, staring again at the cairn. "Sometimes miracles do happen." He walked away to find a rock for the cairn, then asked the man on the post what had happened afterward. Night had come, he said, and they had built a fire and talked under the stars. But when the sun rose the holy men were gone.

Shan gazed toward the desert. It would be night again in a few hours, and cold.

"They don't even have a compass," Jakli said with a tormented voice.

"No. They do," Shan assured her. "Just not the kind you or I could read."

"Marco and Sophie are at the Well by now," Jakli said, but her voice showed no certainty. "Sophie could find them. Sophie could smell them. Marco probably went to Karachuk. Maybe Osman is helping now. And Nikki," she added softly.

But thirty minutes later as they drove into the next village, Marco and Sophie were in the middle of the street, surrounded by Public Security troops.

Jakli eased the truck behind a building and they looked around the corner. The village was under the control of the knobs. They had erected a security checkpoint in the square and were checking the papers of everyone in the village and all those traveling down the highway. A queue of over a hundred people stood in front of a table where three officers examined papers and stamped the hands of those who had been cleared. Two knob soldiers with automatic rifles stood at the door of a blunt-nosed grey bus with heavy wire on the windows. Half a dozen forlorn faces looked out of the wire. Beside the bus was a grey troop truck, and two hundred feet beyond that a red utility truck sat with two men in the front seat. The Brigade was watching. Watching not the crowd, but the knobs.

Jakli desperately searched the faces of those in the line. She looked back at Shan anxiously, then searched again and sighed with audible relief as she noticed a teenage girl walking by. Jakli pulled the girl around the corner and spoke in low, urgent tones. She raised the girl's hand and studied the image placed there by the knobs. A circle of five stars in red ink. She released the girl's hand and spoke a moment more, then the girl walked briskly away and Jakli pulled Shan into the line.

Jakli asked the man ahead of them what the Eluosi with the beautiful camel had done. It was Marco Myagov, the man said in an admiring tone, with his silver racer. Marco, he explained, had done nothing except to refuse to leave his camel while he waited in line, so an officer had ordered him to wait until everyone else was done. As the man spoke the camel gave a small snort. She was looking directly at Jakli and Shan, cocking her head as if about to speak to them. Marco followed her gaze, gave a small frown as he recognized them, and looked quickly away.

Shan watched the officers at the table as they worked. They looked at faces first, then papers. Woman and children were passed through with a quick glance at papers and a nod. Shan saw a Han man go through with the same treatment. An old man got through without a second look, and another. The knobs were looking for someone in particular. Not a Han. A man, but not an old man. Shan's only hope was that they found him soon, or Shan would be on the bus, as one more illegal caught in the sweep.

There was a sudden commotion at the front of the line. One of the officers was standing, telling a man to take his hat off. He pulled the man to the side and questioned him while the other two officers carefully examined the man's papers.

"Who is it?" Shan asked quietly.

Jakli spoke to the man in front again. "He doesn't know. Some Tadjik. It's good. We need the time."

For what, Shan thought. Another miracle?

They were adjacent to Marco now. He was singing one of his songs, in the Turkic tongue, raising laughter among many of those in earshot.

Shan asked Jakli to explain.

She listened for a moment and blushed. "It is about camels. About camels making love and having trouble with their humps." As she spoke she breathed another sigh of relief. Shan followed her gaze toward a figure in the shadows of an alley that opened into the street ten feet from where Marco stood. Marco had seen the figure too. He cast a quick wink at Jakli, then spoke into Sophie's ear and dropped her reins.

The silver camel exploded into an ear-splitting bray and bolted straight through the line, scattering all those nearby. Marco shouted after her, then called for someone to catch her. More than twenty people broke into pursuit, including the figure in the alley, who ran headlong into Shan and Jakli, pushing them both to the ground while he shouted for the camel. Several hands grabbed Shan. Something moist touched his hand, and a hat was thrust low over his head. The instant he regained his feet Jakli pulled him into the crowd chasing Sophie. A moment later the camel quieted under the hands of an old Kazakh, who led her back to Marco. Jakli pushed Shan into the shadow of a doorway. He looked at his hand. It was stamped with a ring of five red stars. They wandered around the square, casually showing their stamp to the knobs they passed.

Another man was singled out for special attention at the table of officers.

"Ask someone," Shan said in a low voice, "if it is another Tadjik."

It was, a nearly toothless old woman said, and the chill returned. Suddenly, despite Bao's desperate rush to find the subversives, Public Security wanted a Tadjik.

"The fools don't know," the old woman added. "The Tadjiks have gone to Yoktian. Director Ko is giving all of them new clothes, American blue jeans. A special tribute to the social contributions of Tadjiks."

As Jakli pulled him into the shadows at the edge of the street, Shan stared at the old woman in confusion. The Brigade was not only watching to see what Tadjiks the knobs might snare, it was separately trying to entice Tadjiks to town. So they could turn over the Tadjiks to the knobs, Shan wondered, or so they could prevent the knobs from finding Tadjiks? Or at least one specific Tadjik.

Jakli brought them bottled orange drinks from a vendor who sold goods from a rug in the corner of the square, and they sat against the wall of a building, watching the knobs like almost everyone else in the village. In another thirty minutes the line was done, and Marco and Sophie were led to the table. The village began to close in, as if expecting an entertainment. But Marco stared straight ahead and spoke in low respectful tones. He had his identity papers. When the officer finished, however, he stood in front of Sophie, his face eighteen inches from her nose, and began a loud harangue about how undisciplined she was, how animals doing work for the people should respect the people, that she had wasted the valuable time of the Public Security Bureau. Shan had once seen a tamzing held for a horse by a furious Red Guard who had been delayed on a river bridge because of the slow horse and its cart, and wondered absently if this was the same man, thirty years later.

When the officer finished he lingered, glaring at Sophie. Sophie cocked her head as if to study him, put her nose closer, and erupted in a sound that was half snicker, half bray, an action that sprayed the man with her saliva.

Everyone laughed but Marco and the officer. Marco began to urge Sophie away, but the officer pulled his pistol and held it toward her head. With a chill Shan saw Marco's hand creep inside his coat. The crowd was instantly sober, and scared.

When the shot came Shan's head jerked back in the reflexive agony instilled by hearing so many knob pistols so many times before—in public executions in Beijing, where those seated nearest were sprayed with blood and particles of brain tissue. And in the gulag, where three times he had seen knob guards shoot monks as they calmly and defiantly recited their mantras.

But the shot came from behind, he suddenly realized, near the bus, where another officer held his gun in the air. The knob by Sophie scowled but lowered his gun, and the man who had fired in warning approached him. He had the same lightless eyes as the first man but more grey in his hair. He stared at Marco for a long moment, then ceremoniously picked up the ink stamp on the table and stamped a ring of red stars on Sophie's nose.

The knobs climbed into their trucks and in five minutes were gone, escorting the bus down the Kashgar highway. Moments later the Brigade truck eased out of the square, following the knobs.

Marco was at the village water trough when they reached him, where Sophie drank long as he washed away the red ink. "Four hours. Four damned hours wasted here," he groused.

With longing in his heart Shan watched Marco steer Sophie away into the Taklamakan at a brisk trot. Then he turned to Jakli with a new urgency. "That Tadjik Hoof holds the key. We have to find him before Ko or the knobs do."

Their sturdy horses climbed for hours, following a teenage girl from the camp where they left the truck. They rode hard, trotting constantly, their horses struggling, the girl's eyes always on the trail, where patches of ice could suddenly appear to trip the horses, or on the sky, where helicopters could materialize with even worse effect. Twice they stopped at small herding camps, where each time fresh mounts were given to Shan and Jakli. None of the herders argued. At the first camp the girl said it was for the zheli boys who were dying, and the horses were quickly offered with a cup of tea. At the second a man was talking about the holy men, and when Jakli said Shan was with them, the remounts were offered without their having asked.

They arrived at a solitary yurt so high that its water ran from a small ice field a few hundred feet above the camp. A middle-aged woman wearing a soiled red apron sat by a fire at the front of the yurt, threading kernels of sun-hardened cheese onto a string. A boy of no more than six stood close against the felt of the yurt, out of the wind, methodically working a butter churn. The woman nodded greetings, then broke a corner from a brick of black tea and dropped it into a kettle at the edge of the fire. Her face was friendly but sad, and Shan remembered. This was the camp of Osman's uncle, where a son had died recently of fever.

The woman poured the tea and said the herders would return by sundown, then pointed to the cushions and blankets piled high at the rear of the yurt. Shan felt desperately tired and knew his face showed it.

He was awakened from his slumber by a chorus of bleating sheep. A deep blush of pink over the western peaks was all that remained of daylight. The fire was blazing, and a grey-haired man squatted before it with a tin mug of tea. Sheep were everywhere. The yurt seemed to be an island in a sea of sheep. Shan saw two more figures in heavy dark chubas, moving among the sheep. One, an older woman, was walking toward the fire. The other, wearing a black felt cap, hung back, sitting on a rock, with a big mastiff guard dog.

There were more dogs, Shan saw. Two mastiffs lay near the fire, one with its head over the other's back, both watching Shan suspiciously as he stepped toward the fire. A smaller white dog, crawling under the sheep, emerged from the flock and ran into the yurt. When Jakli and their guide awoke they all ate bowls of yogurt with nan bread and some kind of dried meat, their hosts nodding politely but speaking more to their dogs than to their guests. Jakli provided a package of hard round candies from her bag, which were enthusiastically accepted and passed around. Finally, his hunger apparently outstripping his fear, the man in the black hat approached.

Shan was not sure he would recognize the man, but as soon as he entered the circle of the firelight Shan remem-

bered how the Tadjik had jumped on him. He recognized
the eyes, which had been so wild with emotion when the
man had pounded Shan's chest.

"We have come to speak with you, Hoof," Jakli said.

The Tadjik only grunted, and accepted a bowl of yogurt
from the woman.

"He knows sheep," the woman said, as if Hoof needed
to be defended. "Most of the dogs like him." Even more
dogs had appeared when the meal began. Shan counted
seven and wondered how many more might still be in the
shadows. If herders couldn't make their family of children,
they made a family of their dogs.

When Hoof sat beside Shan, he thought nothing of it.
But as the man gulped down his food, Shan noticed the
nervous way he looked at Jakli. The woman poured the last
of the tea and five minutes later, as he turned his head back
from watching the rising moon, Shan discovered that only
Jakli and Hoof were left at the fire.

"It's a long way from anywhere," Shan observed.

"They have a radio," Hoof said, "to listen to music." He
shrugged. "Mostly it doesn't work."

Jakli rose to push a stick into the fire. Shan saw that
Hoof tensed his muscles as she moved, as if he thought she
would hit him.

"Seems like a long time ago, when we were at Karachuk," Shan said.

"Seems like," Hoof agreed with a sigh, then he looked
up and spoke hurriedly. "I came here straight away, like
Marco said."

"We're not here for Marco."

The announcement seemed to confuse Hoof. His brow
furrowed and he stared into the fire. He muttered a syllable
Shan did not understand, and one of the mastiffs came and
sat by him, watching Shan and Jakli.

"Xinjiang, it's a hard place," Shan said with a sigh.
"People have to do a lot of things they don't want to do.
If we had a choice we wouldn't do things that hurt other
people."

"When I was young," Hoof said in a nervous, high-
pitched voice, "my father had a herd of sheep. But the
government took them away, they said no one could have

private property. Now you can have private property but I don't have my sheep. Someone else has them. I looked for my sheep, in the market, but couldn't see them anywhere." His voice had a slow, confused quality to it. He was not the same insolent man Shan had seen at Karachuk. "I asked a Chinese in the city. He laughed, and said probably they were sent to Beijing to feed the Chairman."

An owl called.

"My mother died last year but she lived in Tadjikstan," he said morosely, referring to the independent Tadjik homeland. "They wouldn't give me papers to go bury her."

Papers. Hoof meant travel papers, to go over the border. "You mean, you went out with Marco."

"My brother did. Not with Marco," the Tadjik said with a glance to Jakli. "Little Marco. I offered to pay for him to go, but Little Marco paid him, because he was so good with the animals."

"Nikki," Jakli said, in a hushed, emotional tone. She glanced at Shan with a smile.

"Right," Hoof said. "Nikki." He looked at Jakli and cocked his head, as if remembering something. "He paid my brother to go on more caravans. I like that Nikki. He laughs good."

Jakli smiled again and stroked the head of Hoof's dog.

"But someone asked you about it later," Shan said. "Someone in a uniform." If Hoof had been stealing information about Americans from Karachuk, it must have been for Bao.

"Not a uniform," Hoof shot back, as though anxious to correct him. "I mean not at first. I wouldn't have done it if I had known who he was on that first day. I thought he was a merchant, looking for Western goods. I was in the market in Yoktian. He just wanted to know about getting out, about the safe way for some friends of his to go across. He gave me drinks. We walked around the market. He gave me new shoes, just because I saw them and liked them. Said maybe if we became good friends, he could get me some sheep. Even get me a job. I never had a Han friend. I thought maybe I should have one. I think you have to have one," he said, looking to Shan as though for confirmation, "if you want to be successful in our world." Shan remembered when they had first met, how Hoof had boasted that he had Chinese friends in order to impress Shan.

"Maybe later you found out he was a knob in disguise," Shan ventured.

"A big one," Hoof nodded with a haunted expression. "An officer. I didn't know until later, when he wore his uniform once to meet me on the highway."

"Bao Kangmei?" Shan asked.

Hoof looked up with surprise. "Not that bastard. The other one. The thin one with the bad skin."

Sui. Hoof meant he had been recruited by Sui.

Hoof looked into the fire. "I had known a knob once before. He owned a gas station, after ownership was allowed. He ordered all the knob cars to come for gas."

"Later, though," Shan suggested, "this officer wanted other things. To know about Lau and people close to Lau. About foreigners."

Hoof shrugged. "He said he was going to leave the knobs, go into business. Business, it's international. Sure, he needed to meet foreigners. Americans especially. He really wanted to see Americans and things Americans did. I gave him an empty can of American soda once from Karachuk and he paid me more money than I can make in a month herding sheep. An empty can," the Tadjik repeated incredulously.

The sheep were all asleep, around the edge of the camp, a soft grey carpet under the moon. Beyond them one of the mastiffs sat upright on a rock, facing the darkness beyond.

"So you took him some more things from the Americans."

"Not much. You stopped me."

"But then you left Karachuk. The same night. You were planning to leave anyway, when Marco sent you here. You were planning to meet your friend from the knobs," Shan suggested.

Hoof nodded. "There were two of them there. The knob and another, who wore dark glasses even though it was after sunset. They were sitting in a red car waiting for me, drinking beer. The one with the glasses took me for a ride in the car while the knob sat on a rock and drank. As he drives he says he could help me. Says he was going to be my new friend, and he gave me money, for nothing. He asked me what I wanted most. I said sheep, and he said no problem." Hoof looked up at Shan. "If he can get some sheep for me, my brother and I can start our own camp in the spring. My brother needs to meet my new friend. Don't work for the knobs, I told him. They don't pay you as much."

It seemed to have gotten much colder. Hoof was working for the Brigade now. Shan moved closer to the fire. "So that night when you left," he pressed. "You saw both of them. Your friend who drives the red truck. Near the highway. Late."

"My new friend said he didn't have much time. But he said he wanted me to watch something. Said here's what happens to people who try to take away your business. The knob with the bad skin, he was just standing there smiling, like it was all a joke when the gun was pointed at him. But bang, the one with the red car just pulled the trigger. In the heart, two times. I ran. I came here, because Marco had said so."

Shan looked into the burning embers. Hoof had been a witness, he had seen Ko Yonghong shoot the man with the pockmarked face, Lieutenant Sui. Then Hoof had disappeared, making Ko nervous. He wanted Hoof. But so did Bao. With Hoof on his side, Bao could destroy Ko. But how had Bao found out?

Suddenly the dog leapt up and began barking toward the darkness on the north side of the camp. Jakli groaned and pointed. In the distance, on the horizon, two streaks of brilliant white light lit the sky.

"Flares," Hoof muttered. "We see a lot of them lately."

"Flares?" Shan asked. "From who?"

"The knobs. They like to search at night sometimes, catch people off guard."

As Shan looked at the fading streaks in the sky he remembered the dropka woman's words, how the demon had stopped attacking Alta because he was called away by lightning. It was how demons spoke with each other, she had said. She was right, he thought sadly. It *was* how demons spoke with each other. But if Alta's killer had been called back by Sui, if he had been working for Sui, why curse him when he saw the flares? Because he had not finished his work with the boy perhaps. Because the boy had still been alive.

They were silent a long time, watching the darkness where the flares had been.

"Before you came here," Shan suggested at last, "you saw your brother, didn't you?"

"On the way here. I said I'd be gone for a long time, to a secret place. But I wanted to tell him about my new business, about how we can get sheep. Good money, when I get done here," Hoof said. "Just cooperate, I told my brother, or you'll be like that dead Chinese."

But Bao, Shan realized with a sinking feeling, was already in business with Hoof's brother. Don't work for the knobs, Hoof had told him. They're not paying as well. That was how Bao had discovered that Ko was Sui's killer. That was how Bao had obtained a shiny new car from Ko, by divulging to Ko what he had heard about Sui's murder. Bao was learning about the new economy. Ko had killed Sui, but now Ko had a new competitor. And if Bao could find Hoof, if he could produce the witness to Sui's murder, he would have the means to destroy Ko, to take over all of Ko's lucrative bounty hunting.

Hoof sighed. "It's a hard thing, business," he said, his eyes lingering for a moment on Jakli, as if he had something to say to her. But he turned away, and after a moment spoke to the fire. "I only wanted to bury my mother."

In the morning Jakli was gone. She had said nothing, left no word other than to tell their guide that she would see Shan at the nadam. Everyone knew Jakli would go to the nadam, the Kazakh girl said with a flush of excitement, because her wedding was to be the main event of the festival. But not everyone knew that from there she would leave, from there she would start her new life.

And beginnings were always built on endings, a lama had once told Shan.

Shan described a place with a high cliff, with a meadow across the road, and asked if the girl could take him there. "Not far," she said, "maybe two hours." They rode hard until they reached the road, then walked the horses along the road until they found the spot where Jakli had left the flowers the day she had driven him to Senge Drak.

He thanked the girl, then found a trail that led up the high ridge and in half an hour he emerged on a small shelf of land that overlooked the road. He dismounted and tied his horse to a tree.

She was there, kneeling at a low, broad mound of earth on which autumn asters were blooming. He plucked a piece of reddish heather and dropped it on the mound beside her.

Jakli smiled through her tears. "The great detective," she said in greeting.

"I was worried about you."

"With you and Marco both watching over me, how could anything go wrong?" she asked, and began pulling away dried leaves that were caught among the flowers. "My great uncle who was the synshy, the horse talker, he said that horses have spirits that roam after death. That they may settle in another horse, far away."

Shan understood. "Even as far as America," he suggested.

Jakli nodded and continued clearing the grave of her horse, the horse that had been killed by the soldiers so many years before. There was no one else for her, no other way of saying goodbye. Her father had disappeared, her clan was leaving. This was her way of ending it, of leaving her old life behind.

"My uncle, the synshy, he rode a stallion until he was almost ninety, the horse almost thirty-five. When his horse died, he insisted on burying it himself, by himself. He dug for two days, a huge hole, beside the body, like I did here, to let the body slide in. But at the last moment the earth crumbled and the horse fell on top of him. It killed him. My aunt said to leave him there, it was the right thing for them to be in the same grave. At the funeral my father said that Zhylkhyshy Ata, the horse deity, had called my uncle away to work with his herd in the heavens."

When Shan looked, Jakli's eyes were full not of grief but of doubt. "I feel like I am just abandoning them all. Like I'm only thinking of myself."

"Red Stone clan is leaving too."

"I mean, all the Kazakhs. I mean the Maos and the purbas. Look at all the Americans have sacrificed to come here and help, and it feels like I'm doing the opposite."

"You're not running away," Shan said, but Jakli offered no reply. He knelt and helped her clear off the grave.

She thanked him when they were through and asked him to leave. He did, but only when she promised to go see her new wedding dress. "Only if you promise to be there," she said, playfulness back in her eyes. "Go to town. Find Ox Mao, he will take you to nadam, he's a good Kazakh."

"I can't. I must speak with the boys about Micah. We must find him, make sure he's safe."

"He is safe. If his dropka family is hiding, no knob will ever find him. And Marco," she added, more soberly, "Marco will be at nadam with Lokesh and your lama. Or he will know where we must go with the Maos to rescue them."

Shan found the big-boned Kazakh at the restaurant in town but did not immediately ask him to guide him to the horse festival. He had the Mao draw him a map and began walking toward the outskirts of town, staying in the shadows, wary of boot squads, ducking into doorways sometimes when the wind whipped sand against his cheek so hard it stung.

The People's Clinic of Yoktian was a shabby one-story building with a corrugated tin roof and mud-brick walls, marked by a truck near its front door that bore the weathered emblems of an ambulance. The truck appeared to have been abandoned. Its tires were flat, its sides corroded and rusted. A young girl in the front, playing with the steering wheel, ducked down as Shan walked by.

Inside, his first impression was that the clinic itself had been abandoned. Sand blew across the lobby as he entered, and a skinny dog looked up from where it lay in the center of the floor, then returned to its nap. Corridors ran to the left and right, the one on the left protected by a set of double doors with rubber seals.

The pungent scent of ammonia greeted him as he swung the doors open, and the only occupant of the hall, a grey-haired woman mopping the floor, looked up and gripped her mop tightly with both hands, as if he might challenge her for it. Stepping cautiously down the hall, he glanced into each room, looking for one with a lock on the door. Of the ten rooms in the wing, six were occupied, one by a sleeping nurse, but none had locks.

Shan found what he was seeking in the second corridor, a door with a lock that led to a small ward with half a dozen beds. He pushed and the door swung open. Only one bed, at the rear, was in use, and the old waterkeeper had been tied to it. One end of a long elastic bandage, the kind wrapped around sprains, had been knotted around a leg of the bed. The other end was tied tightly around the lama's hands. The waterkeeper had stretched the bandage enough to reach the floor, where he sat in the lotus position. The lama wasn't meditating, Shan saw, but staring with a curious expression at a window six feet away. A padlock was on the window, fastening it to the sill.

The old man simply nodded when Shan sat beside him, as though he had expected Shan, then gestured with his bound hands toward the window. "When the wind blows just right," the waterkeeper said in a rasping voice, "a tiny stream of sand blows in the top corner." He stared at the window and nodded. "If no one touched it there would be a dune across my bed in a few months." His voice was full of awe, as if the stream of sand was beautiful and his bed was predestined to be buried.

"Rinpoche," Shan said hurriedly, "is there a guard?" He looked down. The man's fingertips were blue. Shan began untying the bandage. "I can get you back to the Raven's Nest," he explained quickly.

"There has to be a crack," the old lama said serenely, "or nothing can get in."

Shan stopped and stared at him.

Suddenly there were feet running in the corridor. Fat Mao appeared, breathing hard, followed by Ox Mao, who shut the door tight and pressed against it, as if to hold off intruders. Fat Mao offered no greeting but darted to the window, extending a screwdriver, which he used to quickly pry up the hasp that held the window lock. He threw the window open and gestured for Shan. But before Shan could react Ox Mao had him, pulling him up, dragging him to the window. The two men lifted Shan and threw him onto the sand outside, then leapt out themselves. Fat Mao closed the window and pulled Shan around the end of the building, where a nurse stood at an open door, waiting for them.

Moments later they watched from an empty room as the waterkeeper was led outside by two knob soldiers, bound not by the elastic bandage but by steel manacles.

A thickset figure appeared behind the waterkeeper, wearing a satisfied smile. Bao Kangmei. He called out to the soldiers, who halted as Bao circled the waterkeeper. There was no fear in the lama's eyes. He simply stared at Bao with an interested, curious expression.

"Bao doesn't know," Fat Mao said, "he just suspects. He will take him to Glory Camp, to the holding cells the knobs use there." But Shan was not reassured by the Uighur's words. The waterkeeper was no longer a prisoner of the prosecutor, or the Brigade. It would not take long for Bao to understand which of the old men he had detained was a lama, which had been the subject of his subversive Tibetan poem.

Arms akimbo, Bao stood for a moment, looking at the clinic entrance as though hoping for a larger audience, then with an abrupt gesture he dismissed the men, who shoved the old lama into their truck. Shan watched the truck speed down the road with an ache in his heart, remembering the lama's words. *There has to be a crack or nothing can get in.* He had heard the words in a teaching, spoken by another lama in a gulag barracks. The waterkeeper hadn't been speaking about sand, but enlightenment. It will only be enlightenment that saves us, he was saying, enlightenment that reaches into some dark place through a crack that had not existed before.

As the knobs' truck drove away it revealed a small red car that had been parked beyond it. Bao lit a cigarette and surveyed the landscape with a satisfied smile, staring toward town, then at the clinic itself, staring so long that the nurse flattened herself against the wall in fear. Finally he stepped to the driver's door of the car, and paused. There was a beetle crossing the road not far from their window.

Bao marched to the beetle, bent to examine it, then straightened, smiled, and smashed it with a hard thrust of his boot.

It was late morning the next day when Shan and Ox Mao dismounted on the flat crest of a high ridge where updrafts kept dried autumn leaves hanging in the air, like chips of pigment on the palette of the sky. The Kazakh had pointed out a rider approaching along the top of the ridge. It was Akzu, Shan saw after a moment, wearing a red vest embroidered with horse and bird shapes.

"It's over," the headman announced with a broad smile as he dismounted. "All the zheli boys are safe. We had a message from that last shadow clan, a note sent on a dog. Their zheli boy is protected, they said. He will come to Stone Lake in three days. And some Maos stayed in the high mountains," Akzu explained, still grinning. "They were cutting down trees, causing small avalanches, blocking all the roads so knob patrols cannot pass through. The Maos are still up there, watching. That last boy is safe until we meet him there. We can celebrate." The old Kazakh appeared truly happy, not just because he thought the boys were safe but also, Shan suspected, because Red Stone clan had found a way to beat the Brigade's Poverty Scheme.

Akzu circled around Shan several times, then handed him a tattered fox fur cap and a pair of badly scratched sunglasses. "Nadam, it's a special thing, for Kazakhs," he said, shaking his head. "Once Han visitors came from Urumqi, a Party secretary. There was almost a riot." He inspected Shan, and pulled the fur cap lower on his head. "Your skin," he said. "It should be darker."

Before Shan understood his intentions, Akzu grabbed a handful of mud and began rubbing it on his cheeks. Ox Mao laughed. Shan looked at where the mud came from, a patch of wet soil where one of the horses had just urinated.

"You can at least smell like a horseman," Akzu observed with another grin. Shan stared at him a moment then, with a sigh of resignation, finished the task and, following Akzu's example, wiped his hands clean on his horse's tail.

The headman led them across the crest to a ledge that overlooked a long high valley. To the south and west it was bound by a vast wall of black rock, towering several hundred feet above the valley floor. To the north lay a turquoise lake, surrounded on three sides by evergreens and poplars. The impression created was of a vast chamber carved out of the mountains. The chamber was carpeted with olive-brown dried grass and furnished with perhaps fifty round cushions made of black, beige, brown, and white cloth.

Shan pulled the sunglasses from his face to better comprehend the scene. The cushions were yurts, arranged in groups of three and four, with rope corrals of camels and horses in the center of each group. Ox Mao let out a whoop of joy and left them standing on the ledge as he leapt on his horse and cantered down into the valley.

Twenty minutes later Akzu was guiding Shan through the nadam, leading their horses into a camp of three yurts. A boy called out, and Shan saw Malik and Batu running to greet him. They helped him remove his saddle and tether his horse, and then Malik, with a finger to his lips, stealthfully led him around the line of horses to a point where they could see between the first two tents. A group of six women were there, chattering happily, laughing, one even singing. A dress hung on a line between the tents and two of the women were fussing over the sleeves while another knelt at the hem. It was a beautiful white dress, onto which had been embroidered scores of flowers and horses. But there was no sign of the bride for the gown.

The other zheli boys were gathered in a tight knot around a squatting figure. Shan heard a familiar voice explaining to them how to make a whistle out of a willow branch. It was Jowa, who stood as he saw Shan and slowly shook his head. He had not found Gendun and Lokesh. And there was no sign of Marco.

The nadam was a portable Kazakh town, and the two boys were the perfect guides. Wearing an oversized felt vest with the fur cap and sunglasses to shadow his eyes, Shan wandered with them through the streets of the town. In the center of the camps a market had been organized. Loops of sweet dough fried in oil were hung on strips of vine and sold by old women; for an extra fen the loop was rolled in sugar. A mountain of green melons rose in front of an old man with one eye, who appeared to be selling very few since he was cheerfully distributing thick slices to all who passed by. Half of the vendors sold harnesses, hairwhips, or boots, the products, Shan suspected, of long solitary nights in dimly lit tents. He sat and watched the Kazakhs, nearly all of whom wore small, melancholy smiles. It was a time for celebration, but they all knew the one sad truth that no one dared speak. It was the last festival, the last time the clans of the region would be able to gather. Someone had nailed a board to a tree near the center of the encampment. On it were scraps of paper with handwritten messages and formal printed forms, announcing new Brigade work assignments for many of the Kazakhs. Small groups of two and three visited the board. Some gave sighs of relief as they read the board, and shook their friends' or clansmen's hands. Others read somberly then forlornly walked away to sit in the rocks. As he watched, Shan noticed Batu staring at the horizon with worry in his eyes. He too knew the killers had not stopped.

Beyond the camps extended a vast field. In other nadams, Malik said in a sad tone, there had always been a communal corral, with two or three hundred horses. But the Brigade had let them keep only their personal mounts. Hundreds of others had been collected by the Brigade in Yoktian, where they were being readied for shipment.

Riders were in the field, ten or twelve youths, galloping hard toward the north end of the valley. *Khez khuwar*, the boys explained, an ancient game of the clans. The girls would start twenty or thirty feet ahead of the boys, and they would race to the mark at the end of the field. If a boy caught up with a girl, she must let him kiss her, still riding, but once the girls reached the end of the field they were allowed to chase the boys to the other starting point, using riding whips to hit any boy who they passed.

They were interrupted by hoots and whistles from behind them, greetings for a rider approaching up the rough dirt road that led up the valley. Malik stood on a log and after a moment his face lit with excitement. "Jakli!" he exclaimed. Shan climbed up beside him and saw her reach the front of the camps on a lathered, exhausted horse.

As they turned back to sit on the log and watch the riders on the field, someone dangled a loop of fried dough in front of them. The boys laughed and began pulling away pieces of dough even before their benefactor could greet them. It was Jacob Deacon. He had come to record the events of the nadam, he said, and had brought more of the wooden tablets for the clansmen to keep with them when they were dispersed by the Brigade. But also, Shan knew, because he had hoped Micah might have come down out of his hiding place.

"They got a note," he said brightly, as if reading Shan's thoughts. "Just three more days."

The American was about to sit beside him when another round of jubilant shouts broke through the camps. Deacon laughed and pointed to the north. Marco was coming down from the trail by the lake, already so close they could see he was wearing an outlandish hat of felt stuffed with tall flowers and feathers. He led a heavily laden camel. "Presents from the groom's family," Deacon explained. "An old Kazakh custom."

People cheered louder as Marco approached, and then a minute later another excited murmur swept through the camps as two more riders came out of the trees. Not cheers this time, but a hushed call of important news, in a reverent tone. Two old men, one in a maroon robe, had emerged from the trees, following Marco.

Almost no words were spoken. Shan walked up the trail to meet the Tibetans, and silently took the reins of Gendun's horse to lead him into the Red Stone camp. He had found them at the Well of Tears, Marco confirmed, where they were fastening tiny red prayer flags into the rocks. Shan looked at Gendun's robe. The hem had been ripped open and the fabric torn away. The lama himself looked like something had been torn away from him. His eyes, glazed with fatigue and sadness, briefly acknowledged Shan, then settled back into his hundred-mile stare.

"Helicopters began looking in the desert," Lokesh said in a weary voice. "Marco said wandering souls would flee from the noise of helicopters, because they sound like demons." The old Tibetan sighed. "And his camel kept pushing us with her nose. Gendon said this Russian and his camel are wise about spirits, so we agreed to go with them." He looked over the mountains, toward the desert. "It felt as though we were close to the Yakde Lama for a while. We will go back soon. There're so many lost ones out there," he said forlornly, and he let Shan lead him into one of the yurts, where Jowa was already arranging a sleeping pallet for Gendun.

Shan sat by the two old men until they were lost in slumber. When he looked up, Marco was there too, quietly watching the Tibetans. He looked as if about to speak, but seemed unable to find words. The Eluosi knelt and pulled the blanket over Gendun's shoulders. "I thought they were just old fools when I first met them," Marco confessed. "Now . . ." He shook his head and looked into Shan's eyes and shrugged. "Sophie walked around them again and again when we found them, like she didn't recognize what type of creatures they might be. They wouldn't leave at first, and I wasn't sure what to do. I made as if to go, but Sophie went and sat with them. She wouldn't budge. She was ready for me to leave but she was going to stay with them." Marco scratched his head and creased his bushy eyebrows, as if still wondering about what his camel had done. "Then she heard a helicopter in the far distance and began pushing them toward me." He gazed at the two old men. "It's important they're here, isn't it?" he asked in a self-conscious tone. "I don't mean here, I mean . . . I don't know."

"Important that they are in the world," Shan suggested. As he spoke he saw a movement in the shadows at the back of the tent. The wild-eyed woman was there, the one who had thrown stones at him. She was rocking back and forth, a rolled blanket in her arms, giving no sign of having seen them.

As Marco rose, Shan saw Jowa standing at the tent flap. What was it Jowa had said that night so long ago? If the lamas didn't survive, what was the point of continuing? The thought brought a pang of pain, as it reminded him that there was another lama still out there, unprotected, with the knobs now at Glory Camp.

It was a day of celebration, a day of joy. The clans flowed in a steady stream into Red Stone camp to see the gifts brought for the bride's family and to present gifts of their own. They drank toasts to Nikki, the jokester who could be counted on to be late, just for effect. Horses were raced, in pairs and in fours, and even as many as twenty at a time, and skins of kumiss were passed about the jubilant onlookers.

After the races Batu pulled Deacon out onto the field. Another of the zheli threw a ball to the American, a baseball. Macro appeared with a bat, one he had brought from Nikki's room, and the youths of the camp began playing the American game. Jakli appeared and, making an exaggerated bow of greeting to Shan, ran to join the game, chiding everyone about how Nikki would hit balls into the mountains when he arrived. Deacon and Marco had declared themselves coaches, and the air was filled with laughter and shouts of "First base! Second base! She's out!" as Shan leaned back on the log, drowsy in the sunlight studying the game. Half the camp wandered to the field to watch, until suddenly there was a shout from the back, then a hushed silence. The crowd parted as a magnificent white horse pranced onto the field, led by Wangtu, the Kazakh driver Shan had talked with at Glory Camp.

Jakli was pushed forward by Marco, and with a shy smile Wangtu handed her the lead rope of the white horse. "I know when Nikki comes," he said loudly, so the crowd could hear, "he will bring five more like this. But," he said with a shrug, "at least I'm first."

The horse, Shan was certain, was the one they had seen at the rice camp. The fiery creature looked at Jakli and its eyes softened, then it stepped forward and she extended a hand. As it pushed its muzzle into her palm, the Kazakhs cheered. Malik shot away and a moment later returned with the silver bridle.

For the next hour many from the camps watched as Jakli raced up and down the field on her white horse, while others mounted and rode alongside her. At last she consented to a game of khez khuwar, and though many youths galloped forward for a kiss, none could catch her.

Shan found Malik under a tree at the north end of the field, sitting with one of the dogs resting its head on his legs. He sat without speaking, and they watched the riders in silence.

"I keep thinking about that day you found him," Shan said at last. "I keep thinking, what if there was something else? Something Malik decided to keep, something he didn't put back on the grave? That would be a sad thing, because Malik would start feeling he had done wrong, even though it was because he just wanted a remembrance of Khitai, and his memory of his friend might have a cloud over it."

"So many things have happened," Malik said, his eyes on the dog. "It's hard to understand." He sighed, and pain clouded his face. "I only wanted something because we were friends. I have almost never had friends. I mean just another boy. He was so gentle with the lambs." Malik unbuttoned the top of his shirt and removed the object that hung around his neck. A large silver gau, with a top of woven filigree.

"I didn't lie to you," the boy said. "You asked did he have anything on him. This was in the dirt, thrown by the rocks. I never looked inside," he added, then he handed it to Shan, rose with a small smile, as if glad to be free of the object, and walked with the dog toward the lake.

Shan took it to Lokesh, who now sat upright, watching the sleeping form of Gendun. The old Tibetan studied the gau reverently without opening it, but shook his head and handed it back. It was not the Jade Basket.

"Khitai might keep the Basket in a special place sometimes, to protect it," Lokesh said, then he grimaced and looked up at Shan. "That's why he gave it to the American boy, isn't it? To protect it."

Shan nodded. There was no other possibility now. Prosecutor Xu had been the one to confirm it. Two clans had been at the zheli field, two zheli friends, meeting in the lama field, to look for flowers. Khitai, sensing the danger and knowing the importance of the gau, had passed on the Jade Basket for safekeeping. Just for a few days, he probably told Micah, for they would be together soon, on the way to America.

Lokesh's head turned and twisted in several directions as he looked at the gau in Shan's hand, as if he had to get a precise angle on the mystery. "That last boy, the American boy, he has the sacred Basket," he said, as though needing to persuade himself.

And by now the killer knows it, Shan almost added. He

remembered the flares in the mountains. Bao's patrols were out, still searching. Akzu had been wrong about one thing. Micah wasn't safe, or at least would not be when he left the mountains to go to Stone Lake.

Lokesh looked up, his eyes clouded. "How do these things happen?" he asked, and he seemed about to cry. Fires were lit as the sun went down, and still representatives of the other clans arrived at the Red Stone camp, bringing skins of kumiss to drink by the fire. They ate mutton stew and hard cheese, singing songs, some of the old women dancing ritual dances that none of the young generation knew. Marco and Deacon freely drank the fermented milk and taught each other new songs. Inside one tent Shan found Ox Mao with the slender woman, Swallow Mao, who held one of the small computers on her lap. She acknowledged Shan with a nod and kept busily tapping the keys as he sat nearby.

"That newborn program," she announced. "I downloaded files from the Brigade onto a disc. It's not just local, but all over southern Xinjiang. Not administered by Ko. It's higher up than Ko. Two hundred babies registered so far, with detailed notes on all birthmarks. Some parents are being asked to take examinations."

"Examinations?" Shan asked.

Ox Mao grunted angrily. "Administered by political officers," he whispered, as though speaking the words more loudly would violate the sanctity of the festival.

The moon was high overhead when sentries came down from the hills and new ones rode out. "Don't shoot anyone who's bringing white horses," Marco called after them, and everyone laughed. Jakli excused herself to go to the sleeping tent but as Shan watched from the fire she slipped around the yurt and sat in the moonlight by her new horse, who nuzzled her and made soft wickering sounds, sounds of contentment. A piece of paper was in her hand, and somehow Shan knew what it was. The letter she always carried, almost in tatters from being so often folded and unfolded. A letter from her Nikki.

Thunder woke them in the dawn, followed by shouts, then jubilation. Every Kazakh in the tent seemed to recognize the rumbling sound and rushed outside, leaving Deacon and Shan and the Tibetans alone, sitting up in their blankets, rubbing their eyes.

It was horses, scores of horses galloping through the camp, more horses than Shan had ever seen. Or maybe not, as he listened to the cries of the clans. He had seen them in Yoktian. The Kazakh herds had been freed. The gates at Yoktian had been opened despite the guards, and the animals had come home.

The excitement was palpable. Children leapt in the air. Dogs yelped. Guns were fired in the air. Everywhere people were embracing each other. The Brigade had not won after all, people were saying. It was Zhylkhyshy Ata, someone shouted, the horse deity had not forgotten the southern Kazakhs.

"This day will be written in the history of our people," an old woman called out, and her eyes flashed with the excitement of a young girl.

The celebration in the camp lasted through the morning. Shan was watching the zheli boys, who shone with delight as they walked through the herd, when Gendun touched his arm and pointed up the hill. Lokesh was waving at them from a large rock on the slope above the camp. When they arrived, he pointed excitedly to a beautiful circular pattern of lichen growing on a rock face above where he sat. It was a mandala, a mandala made by the deity who lived in the mountain.

The two Tibetans sat to contemplate the lichen rock as Shan found a perch on a boulder near the bottom of the ridge. He watched Jakli on her white horse, spontaneously laughing as she rode back and forth on the valley track below him, then took out the piece of paper he had taken from the body at Glory Camp. He stared at the strange abbreviations again, trying to make sense of their odd code.

He was leaning back on the rock in the sun when someone spoke his name.

"There is a feast tonight," Jakli said in an oddly shy tone. He looked up and saw the white horse tethered to a tree at the base of the ridge. "I would like you to sit with my family."

Shan nodded. "You honor me."

"It's not over, is it?" she asked after a moment, kneeling beside him.

"The general is coming," Shan said. "The killer is still free. The last boy is still unprotected. The Americans—" He stopped, seeing the anxious look in her eyes. She had felt guilty that she was leaving her people at such a time. "We can get word to you through Marco," he assured her. "Marco will know what happens. Everything will be all right," he said, doing his best to sound hopeful for her. He gestured toward the herd in the pasture beyond the tents. "The herds are free again."

"I was thinking about Marco," Jakli said. "He's going to be lonely. Everyone will be gone. He likes you. He would never say it, but I know it. Sometimes maybe you could write to him, from wherever you are."

Shan offered a thin smile. "Sure. Write him," he said, knowing it was impossible. Outcasts and fugitives didn't correspond.

"I wish—" She abruptly stopped and raised her hand. Rifle shots could be heard, not the random volley of the nadam revelers, but regularly spaced shots several seconds apart, each louder than the one before it. The last came from the top of the ridge above the encampment.

"The sentries!" Jakli shouted in alarm and stood. "Warning shots."

The encampment burst into frenzied activity. Shan could see children being herded toward the trees beyond the pasture. One group, a tight knot of boys with two Kazakh men carrying hunting rifles, ran from the Red Stone camp. The zheli were fleeing. Men collected in small groups at the entrance of each clan camp.

Shan looked up the slope and saw Lokesh, standing beside Gendun, waving at them. Shan gestured for them to get down and the Tibetans disappeared behind their rock. Moments later a moan escaped Jakli's lips as a sleek black utility vehicle appeared, followed by a troop truck. As the vehicles stopped at the first circle of tents and the troops leapt out, the knot tying itself in Shan's stomach grew ice cold. Knobs. One of the boot squads. He pushed Jakli toward the cover of a boulder.

"Maybe," he said without conviction, "it's just a security check."

Jakli just shook her head.

The knobs, clutching the compact submachine guns used for riot control, flanked their officers, as if expecting resistance, and marched forward, shouting at the inhabitants of the first camp to present papers. A line formed, but no papers were collected. One of the officers broke away and walked alone along the front of the encampments, studying the faces of those in line. Not walked. Strutted. It was Bao. He made a dismissive gesture and the first group of Kazakhs were ordered to go into their tents.

The knobs repeated the process at two, then three camps. Shan's mind raced. It could take an hour or two, and he and Jakli would have to stay on the hill, hidden, until they were done. He looked up the hill, wondering if he could steal his way to Gendun and Lokesh.

"Marco got away," Jakli said in a hollow voice. "I saw Sophie slip into the trees."

The knobs got no further than the sixth camp, the Red Stone camp. They did not bother to ask for papers, but just marched Akzu, his wife, and Malik toward the center, a hundred feet from their trucks. Bao paced around them, shouting at them. Shan glanced at Jakli. She had a knuckle in her mouth, and was clenching it so hard in her jaw that she seemed about to bite it off.

Bao barked at a soldier, who climbed into the truck and reappeared with chains in his hands.

When he looked back Jakli was looking at the mountains to the west and her eyes were full of tears. The knobs began to herd Jakli's relatives to the trucks.

Jakli slowly stood, still watching the mountains, as if Nikki might ride across a ridge at any moment. "It will be a good day for the races later," she said, the way she might make conversation over a mug of tea. Her tears were gone, replaced by a cool glint of determination.

Shan stood too, uncertain but scared.

Jakli began walking down the path to the camps. He stood alone for a moment, then caught up with her.

"You have been like an older brother, Shan," she said. "You have taught me things."

"We should stay back," Shan warned. The large rocks that hid them from view were thinning out. In another fifty feet they would be at the valley floor, in plain sight.

Jakli pointed to a rock. "There's a place with cover. The knobs will be gone soon."

She picked up Shan's hand and dropped something in it, then pushed him toward the rock. "Use it," she said urgently. "Get out of here. Go to your new life." She took a paper from her pocket and dropped it by her feet. "Nikki and I, that was like a dream. It could never have been part of this world. It will have to wait for another time." She took a step and paused, then spoke in a whisper, looking back up the slope toward the Tibetans. *"Lha gyal lo."* May the gods be victorious.

He darted to the rock but when he looked up she was not there. Jakli was walking to her white horse. If she rode hard, he realized, rode up the ridge where trucks could not go, she would make it.

But a moment later she slipped the saddle off, then the bridle, and slapped the horse's flank hard. It bolted away, up the ridge. Then Jakli stepped toward the knobs. There was a movement beside him, and suddenly Fat Mao was there, out of breath, shaking with exhaustion.

"I told her, don't do it," he gasped. "The knobs were all over Yoktian. Some in the school, dressed like teachers, waiting for the zheli. Some were secretly watching the horses, hoping the zheli would pick up their prizes so Bao could snare them. But she did it anyway. She said she didn't see any knobs, that she would make it look like an accident, like a gate was just left open. I told her these were boot squads. They had special techniques, they could hide and watch. Electronic surveillance. And you have three bowls already. If they take you, I told her, then you're gone, off to Kashgar, in some coal mine the next day. For the next few years."

The herd. Shan remembered how she had arrived late, her horse lathered, and recalled her words at the horse's grave. She had wanted to find a way to say goodbye, a gesture for the Kazakhs, and her uncle the horsespeaker. She was the one who had freed the herd.

"Jakli!" Shan called as painful understanding flooded

over him. He stood but she was already seen by two knobs, who were running to intercept her. The knobs had her family. They had come for Jakli, who had openly defied them at Yoktian. If Jakli didn't go they would take her family to prison.

The soldiers grabbed her arms and roughly pulled her toward Bao.

"Jakli!" someone else called out. Wangtu emerged from the crowd and ran toward her. A knob slammed the butt of his gun into Wangtu's belly and the Kazakh crumpled onto the ground, groaning in pain.

Word seemed to spread through the encampment like a surge of electricity. Men, women, and children, some on horseback, converged around the knob trucks. A hundred Kazakhs, then two hundred, surrounded the knobs, who stood, weapons ready, as Bao strutted about her, ignoring the angry shouts. The knobs let go of her family and Malik charged a knob, jumping on his back, beating him with his fists. The soldier flung him to the ground and held him under his boot until two of the clansmen dragged him away. As they did so Akzu pointed. The white horse was on top of the ridge now, standing proudly on a ledge overlooking the camp. It seemed to be watching.

"Niya!" someone shouted. "Niya Gazuli!"

The knobs put chains on Jakli, at her wrists and her feet. Wangtu was on his knees, gasping, crying, holding his belly. The soldiers began to pull her by the chains, but she resisted and called out to them defiantly. The soldiers dropped the chains, and she picked them up herself, walking on her own, her head held high, to the truck that awaited her.

The murmur of Niya's name swept through the clans, which began to form a long line along the road out of camp. More horsemen began to appear on the slopes, where they had been hiding. At the north end of the valley, below the lake, Shan glimpsed a solitary man watching, astride a silver camel.

"Niya! Niya! Niya Gazuli!" the crowd chanted, until all the Kazakhs picked up the cry and it reverberated down the valley.

Bao glared at the crowd, then cast a poisonous look at

the horse above them. The truck with Jakli began to move. Then Bao climbed into the black vehicle and it followed.

"Niya! Niya!" The riders on the horses stood in their stirrups and raised their fists high, the defiant shouts echoing through the mountains as the truck moved down the road.

Then, a hundred yards from the crowd, Bao's truck stopped. The major climbed out quickly and stood at the hood of the truck, bracing himself with a long-range rifle, aiming up the ridge. He fired twice and the chant stopped. A woman screamed in pain and the majestic white horse stumbled. Then it dropped and its body fell off the ledge, rolling down the slope.

Major Bao called out and Jakli's head was shoved from the back of the other truck, her hair roughly held by a knob, forcing her to see the dead horse as its body slid into the rocks below. Then Bao strutted back to his truck and the knobs drove away. Shan found himself on his knees, clenching his belly, as the wise, joyful Jakli disappeared into the gulag.

CHAPTER 20

Marco did not come back to the encampment. He and Sophie had disappeared up the valley. An hour later someone had called and pointed to a small dot moving at the top of the high ridge to the west. Marco was going home.

Gendun and Lokesh had not spoken with Shan but followed Jowa to the Red Stone camp as Shan stood watching the dust cloud of the knob trucks. Ten minutes later the three Tibetans appeared, leading horses. Shan saw but did not hear Malik giving directions to Jowa, pointing toward the high ridge Marco had crossed. At the last minute, as the four of them approached the lake, another rider raced to join them. Fat Mao.

By the time they reached the last valley Shan had taken the lead. There was no sign of Marco above as they began climbing the final steep switchback, no sign even when they reached the plateau. But Sophie was there and greeted them with a shallow bray. Jowa pointed as Shan was removing his saddle. Marco was sitting by the waterfall on the far side of the pasture.

Lokesh took Gendun's arm. "We can make food," he announced, and the two men disappeared into the cabin.

Marco finally saw Shan and Jowa, and he lumbered across the meadow like an old, weary ape. "There were to be races today," the Eluosi said to Shan. His voice sounded empty. "You would have liked the races."

"We had to come," Shan said. "We have to be sure the

plans go ahead." Marco looked wearily from Shan to Fat Mao, as though for an explanation.

"The Americans have to leave," the Uighur said. "Nikki can still go. Give her something to hope for, to live for. We can watch out for Jakli, find out what prison she was sent to. We can get news to her then. That's what will keep her alive."

Marco was silent a long time. "Right," he said at last. "Day after the full moon it starts. There's time."

Shan followed Marco into the house and watched him go down the back hallway, not to his room but to Nikki's. He took an envelope out of his pocket and laid it by the samovar. It was what Jakli had dropped when the knobs came. A letter from Nikki he was certain, that she read whenever she was lonely, a letter she would never allow the knobs to see. He heard Gendun ask Jowa to come with him, and the two Tibetans went outside. He watched from the doorway as they wandered over the meadow, pausing, bending to pick up things. And then, because he realized what Gendun was doing, he went to the pool at the waterfall and brought back a clay pot full of water.

Shan sat with the three Tibetans in front of the cabin in the last rays of the sun with the pile of stones collected by Jowa and the lama. Gendun picked a rock from the pile, gazed upon it, and passed it around their small circle. It was a small, ugly thing, crusted with dirt and what may have been camel dung. Jowa watched uncertainly, but accepted the rock from Shan and looked it over before returning it to Gendun. With the rock in one hand, the lama took a dipper of water and poured it over the rock. The dirt fell away, and the rock became brilliant, with a swirl of oranges and browns, and a tiny seam of something green. The lama handed the rock around the circle, and Shan and Lokesh studied its complex beauty. When Jowa took it he passed it quickly on to Gendun. But the lama handed it back to the purba. Jowa looked at it a few seconds, turning it over, and passed it to Gendun. The lama handed it back to him and Jowa accepted it back, more uncertainly, then began to study the rock in earnest.

It was an exercise Shan had seen often in the gulag. The crust of life, one of the imprisoned monks had called it.

They would just sit sometimes on their brief eating breaks, and wash rocks, sometimes using their only water ration for the day, wash away the crust that accumulated from living in the world, to reach the true nature of the rock.

They ate a vegetable stew in silence, and Jowa and Fat Mao left to speak in hushed tones outside the front door. The cold, clear night fell quickly. Lokesh and Gendun stayed in the kitchen, on the floor, saying their beads.

Shan leaned against a tree outside and watched the stars for a long time, letting the chill wind wash away his crust. He had the paper with the abbreviations in his hand and stared at it even though he could not read it in the darkness.

The house was quiet when he went inside and found his way to the tower. Marco was there, in a dark, brooding silence.

Shan offered small talk, about the sky and the sound of an animal far away. Marco joined with quiet, terse words.

"They are hollow, empty things," the Eluosi said suddenly, "the bastards that would put Jakli in prison. Their world is a desert far crueler and more heartless than the Taklamakan. And you," he said to Shan in an accusing tone, "you think you are like the old monks who lived at Sand Mountain, trying to take water to the desert. But whatever is planted in the soil where such men live just shrivels and dies."

"So we keep alive the seeds," Shan said after a moment. "Sometimes, when a drought goes on for years, all you can do is preserve the seeds. That's what Jakli does. Preserve the seeds. She will survive. The drought won't last forever."

"You mean the government can't last forever."

Shan did not reply.

"My boy, he reads many things. Once he read that a group of Western writers, in the spirit of revolution, claimed that the best form of government was no form of government, where people could be free. He laughed when he told me this, he said we had found the highest form of government, here on our mountain."

After a long silence Marco spoke again. "Try it, Johnny. We can wait here while Nikki goes to university in America. He will have to go. She will want him to go, go and make a place for her when it is time. He will send us a telescope. We will stand here and look at the stars."

"No," Shan said, his voice cracking with pain.

"The choice is yours."

"No. I mean, he will not send a telescope." In the moonlight Shan could see the fear in the big man's eyes.

Marco buried it with a snort. "You will see. I will name a star after him. He speaks English like the president."

Shan did see. He saw with excruciating clarity, excruciating empathy, the worry that had been building in Marco. It wasn't the danger of the caravan, of the chase. These were realities he had lived with for years. It was something alien to his huge, ebullient spirit. Like a worm with an insatiable appetite, it had been gnawing away within him, trying to reach his soul. As Shan searched for words, Marco fled down the stairs.

He found him in Nikki's room. "It's a mess," Marco said distractedly, and began arranging the books on the shelf. "He likes things neat. Didn't get it from me. Must be his mother." His voice was hollow and small.

In that moment Shan would have preferred to be at the bottom of a cell in the gulag under a life sentence, than to be standing there searching for the words he knew he must say.

"I know where your Nikki is."

Marco paused in his work only for a moment. He did not look at Shan. "He is on caravan. Back soon," he said in his thin voice. "You saw the silver bridle."

"He was taken by the knobs."

"No!" Marco picked up a stack of books from the floor, then dropped them. He lowered himself to his knees to retrieve them.

"I saw Nikki."

Marco seemed to move in slow motion, lowering the book in his hand, as if it had grown too heavy to hold. "You never said this before," he said, looking up with a wooden face.

"I did not understand before. It was the baseball at the nadam camp that finally made me see. Then I began to realize. I had seen Nikki. I saw him shoveling coal at Glory Camp."

"I don't think so. . . ." Marco said in a voice spiked with

fear. Shan realized that somewhere, deep inside, Marco knew.

"They captured him and took him to Glory Camp. There was a white horse there. Nikki had brought a white horse for Jakli from Ladakh. It was the horse that Wangtu brought."

The worm that had been gnawing inside was nearing the surface. Agony began to twist Marco's face.

"Then I saw him later," Shan said in a very quiet voice. "There was a scar on his right shoulder."

"A border patrol rifle, during his first caravan," Marco said in a whisper. "I told him not to move during daylight, so close to the border."

"The second time I saw him . . ." Shan clenched his jaw until it hurt. "He had a piece of paper in his pocket, with English letters. I thought it was code. I thought he was American, he spoke English to me so well. But the paper was just about baseball. First base, second base, third base, written in abbreviation so he could remember all the places." The baseball game at the nadam had broken the code for him. Shan had been reading the abbreviations wrong—it wasn't rows of letters, it was clusters of one- and two-letter abbreviations in columns. *FB* was first base, *SB* was second base, *SS* stood for shortstop. He reached into his pocket for the slip of paper and unfolded it.

"In America," Marco said in his tiny voice, "he thinks he will be asked about baseball on his citizenship test. He tries to play all the time, so he will know."

"The second time," Shan continued, "it was that night at Glory Camp. I wiped off his hair. There was black boot polish in it. It was blond. I saw a birthmark, at his hip. He was dead, Marco." He dropped the paper beside the Eluosi.

"No," Marco insisted, with a flash of anger. "You can't know that. He's coming back. He's going to America to make babies with Jakli. . . ." His voice trailed off.

Jakli had known too, Shan was certain. Her parting words had haunted him during the long ride to Marco's cabin. Nikki and I, that was like a dream she had said. It will have to wait for another time, she had said, and it sounded like she meant another life, another incarnation. And her eyes, before she had gone to surrender to Bao. It had not been fear he had seen there, or hatred, he realized later. It had only been emptiness, for she had already discovered in her heart what Shan could only prove later. In a way he had shown the terrible truth to her, when they had gone to the Tadjik camp. She had not responded, only ridden away later to her special place of mourning, when Hoof had admitted to Shan that his brother who rode with Nikki worked for the knobs.

"Bao killed him. I was sure he was an American. Blond hair and blue eyes. I never understood." Shan seemed able to speak only in short bursts. But it was his heart, not his lungs, that was gasping. "They had been closing in. Bao had the scent of the Americans. He was desperate to catch them, it would mean promotion for certain. He hatched a plan to catch them when they were leaving, a trap for the caravan that took them out. He captured Nikki, when Nikki was bringing in the white horse and silver bridle. He had to be sure only one caravan would go out with the subversives, yours, so he could track it and capture it with his helicopters. He paid one of Nikki's men to help, the Tadjik who brought the bridle to town, to make sure you didn't grow suspicious of Nikki's absence."

"No! Damn your eyes, no!" Marco shouted. His face seemed to collapse. "No!" Marco cried. There was no anger left. "He'll be here soon." The tiny voice returned. "I love my boy."

"It has been a season for losing boys," Shan said in a faltering voice. He pulled the steel ring from his pocket, where he had kept it since that night at Glory Camp, and placed it on the log table beside Marco, then left the room.

He climbed the tower, into the night. Five minutes later came an enormous, wretched sound that Shan hoped never to hear again in his life. It was the sound of the worm eating through the thin shell, burrowing into the man's soul. It was fury. It was misery. It was confusion and despair, all in one long inhuman howl. It was the sound of complete desolation.

Shan found himself trying to see the stars through the moisture in his eyes, desperately hoping for a distraction. The horrible sound seemed to echo through his mind, making his flesh crawl. For a moment he longed to be able to howl the same way, to give release to the agony in his own heart.

He stayed on the tower past midnight, trying not to think or feel. In the small hours of the morning he found Marco sitting in a corner of Nikki's room. The big man looked as if he had been fighting all night, as though he had been beaten, and broken, for the first time in his life. He let Shan help him into his bed, as feeble as an old woman.

The others were awake, in the kitchen, on the floor by the stove. A pile of dirty rocks sat in the middle of their circle, and a pot of water was beside Gendun. But they appeared to have stopped the exercise long before. They had heard and understood. Gendun and Lokesh were saying prayers. Jowa sat with a confused expression, looking into his empty hands.

Fat Mao was angry. "It's just this thing, this ugly cloud that gets bigger every day," the Uighur said suddenly, and looked at Shan. "And you know it can't be stopped. What do you do about it? You just make it more painful."

"The Yakde Lama. We came to help the Yakde Lama," Shan said quietly, looking at the rocks.

"To hell with the Yakde Lama!" Fat Mao snapped. "One little boy, is that all you care about? Nikki was a friend of mine, and Jakli. What about the clans that have to disband? The big investigator, you don't do anything! You didn't save the Yakde Lama, he's dead. The wizard from Lhadrung, come to solve it all. Four boys dead. You didn't save them. All you do is get involved. All you do is discover bad news." There was something close to rage in the Uighur's voice. "You have no logic! You have no rules!" The Uighur glared at Shan, who sat across from him in the circle, leaning forward, tensing his muscles as if he might attack Shan. Then he grew silent as he seemed to remember the others.

Shan returned Fat Mao's smoldering gaze for a moment, then looked into his own hands as the great tide of sadness surged through him again.

They sat without speaking, in the cabin, on the distant mountain, the wind moaning around the rock walls of the tower, the fire cracking. After a long time the lama moved. He raised a ladle and slowly poured water over the pile of stones. "These are Shan's rules," Gendun said somberly as the dirt washed away. "The properties of water."

They left when there was enough light to see the trail, with no words to Marco. Nearly an hour later Shan saw the smoke. He called to the others and began to urge his mount back, but Lokesh raised his hand. Marco was burning his cabin. There was no time to save it, no time to save him if he had gone into the flames. Shan dismounted and watched helplessly as the flames rose over the ridge, silhouetting the stone tower. Even from their distance he could hear the cracking of the big logs as they fed the inferno, and Shan thought he saw a figure on the top parapet. Then the wind shifted and fire and smoke engulfed the ancient tower and Marco was gone.

At the restaurant in town the stout woman was cooking a sheep's head while Fat Mao hit the keys of his computer at the kitchen table and yelled at Swallow Mao for not having the latest admission records for Glory Camp. It didn't matter, she said, Jakli had been seen twice on the road to Kashgar. The boot squad took her to the special processing center they operated in Kashgar. It was lao gai after that, the young Kazakh woman said, as if to deliberately goad Fat Mao. Glory Camp was like a hotel compared to where they would take Jakli, she added.

Fat Mao stared with venom in his eyes until suddenly a hard rap on the door sent the Maos scrambling for their cellar chamber. The woman admitted Ox Mao and another man, who pulled in a third man roughly, a burlap sack tied over his head.

They silently led the man down the cellar steps, past Gendun and Lokesh, who sat meditating in a pool of light by the front window. Shan quietly followed as Jowa rose from the table and disappeared down the stairs. The Maos sat the man in a chair at the table and wrenched the sack away. Their prisoner's face was badly bruised along one side, and a trickle of blood ran from his nose into his moustache and down his chin. It was Wangtu.

Fat Mao paced around the table in silence.

"I was released," Wangtu said quickly, in a voice full

of fear as he searched each of their faces. "The prosecutor questioned me about Lau and I was released from Glory Camp. I didn't have a way to town. I knew they were rounding up horses. I said, Let me ride that horse to the sheds, I'll leave it there."

"No," Fat Mao growled. "They gave it to you for something. You paid for it. Told them something."

Wangtu looked at the floor. "I hate them," he said in a hollow voice. "They are my enemy. I was going to look for you, for the lung ma. I can help you. I hear things when I drive the cars."

Shan felt the Uighur's stare and expected Fat Mao to order him to leave or have the others take him away. But the Uighur turned back to Wangtu.

"Which is the lie?" he barked. "That you didn't cooperate with them or that you want to help?"

Shan rose, took a towel from a pile in the corner and wiped the blood from Wangtu's face. No one, not even Wangtu, seemed to notice.

The blank stare remained on Wangtu's face. "Sometimes I know when people are coming on the highway. Important people," he said weakly. "Sometimes I could make cars break down." He looked up at Fat Mao. "That horse was magnificent. Jakli loved that horse. I just wanted her to have it. In the old days, when I was a boy, friends would bring horses to weddings. Don't you understand?" he croaked. "It was the last nadam." He looked into the Uighur's grim face, then turned to Shan. "Did you see her face when I brought it? Like the old days . . ." His lips curled up as if he was trying to smile, but the effort ended in a grimace of pain. "He gives it to me, then he shoots it," he said in a desolate voice, staring at the floor.

"I don't think you told him anything," Shan said. "Because you didn't know anything. I think you agreed to do something for him."

"A stupid thing. A small thing. A lie to the prosecutor. Bao acted like it would be a good joke." Wangtu tried to smile again and grimaced once more.

"What kind of lie?" Fat Mao demanded.

Wangtu looked at Shan as he spoke. "About the boys.

See that Xu got word tonight that another boy has been killed, high in the mountains."

"What boy?" Jowa gasped.

"Any boy. Not a real boy. Just say it, make her go to the mountains."

"An ambush against Xu?" Fat Mao suggested.

"Did Bao tell you where to say it happened?" Shan asked.

"No. Just a place in the Kunlun, on one of the bad roads where you have to drive slow. A place two or three hours away. Bao didn't care where."

"Not an ambush," Jowa concluded. "A distraction."

"Because," Shan said with a chill, "Bao doesn't want her anywhere near Stone Lake."

The Brigade compound on the south side of Yoktian was like a private club compared to the rest of the town. Its stuccoed walls wore a fresh coat of white paint, and its courtyard was covered with that peculiarly Western convention, a grass lawn. Red vehicles abounded, sedans, utility vehicles, and heavy trucks, all bearing the gold emblem of prosperity.

Fat Mao had refused to go, refused to risk any Maos in such a foolhardy venture. "Go home," he told Shan in a taut voice. "You found your old men. You're all still alive. You've done better than the rest of us. Quit before the knobs reach out again." It wasn't simply that Fat Mao was angry over Jakli's arrest, Shan realized as the Uighur watched Jowa and Lokesh join Shan. He was humiliated.

The compound seemed deserted. Shan stepped past the empty gatehouse. It had the feeling of a trap, but he could not stop. He quickly turned to Lokesh and told him to wait with Jowa across the street. The old Tibetan nodded agreement, but as Shan put his hand on one of the double doors leading into the office building, someone reached out and held it open for him. Lokesh was standing at his shoulder.

There was an unexpected noise from nearby. Shouts. Cheers. The sound of a crowd, but still there was no one in sight. They ventured into the lobby and saw an elderly Chinese woman sitting stiffly at a reception desk. As they walked by her she smiled and nodded repeatedly, and Shan saw she was wearing blue work clothes. A mop and bucket of water sat behind her.

There was no mistaking Ko's office. Its entrance consisted of a garish imitation of French doors, with red plastic grilles set over sheets of clear plastic. On one of the chairs near the entrance was a pile of American magazines, and above it hung a poster of a towering building, a nighttime skyline, over which was written *New York, New York*, in English. On the opposite wall was a banner, which Shan assumed held a political slogan until he glanced at it, then read it twice. Get Rich with the Brigade.

The office was empty. Shan rushed past a secretary station into a large room with a gleaming desk made of chromed metal and glass. There was nothing on the desk but a red telephone and a photograph of a red sports car.

Lokesh, at the large plate glass window behind the desk, made a quiet chuckling sound. Shan pulled the Tibetan back from the center of the glass and peered around the edge. The window opened onto the center of the compound, a yard framed on three sides by buildings. A baseball game was being played. Vehicles had been pulled to the side, and at least two dozen spectators sat on the hoods and roofs of the vehicles to watch the spectacle. Ko was there, running about the way Deacon had at the nadam field, directing the players to stand a certain way, showing them how to hold the wooden bat.

Shan stepped back to his search as the batter hit the ball and the onlookers cheered again. The enterprising Ko did not appear to be involved in the details of his enterprises. The two drawers in the narrow table under the window held paper clips and pencils. Bookshelves held an assortment of mementos and books on management, including several in English. *Thriving on Chaos*, one said. The mementos were mostly familiar political tokens. A bust of Mao tse Tung. A piece of wood into which the words *Persist Unswervingly* had been carved, an abbreviation for a favorite motto of a past decade. Two cigarette lighters mounted in polished stone with brass plates noting Party conferences. Several pen and pencil sets. And a string of dingy plastic beads. Shan picked them up. A mala. Remembering that the demon who killed Alta had taken the boy's rosary, Shan put the beads in his pocket.

There were no lists of boys' names with calculation of bounties. There were no notes on Lau. On the wall was a photograph of Ko standing under a banner announcing the Poverty Eradication Scheme, shaking hands with a nearly bald man with a thin, hatchet-like face. Shan studied the man. On his suit coat was a large pin in the shape of the Chinese flag, with a battle tank underneath it. A memento for retired soldiers.

Shan wandered back to the secretary's desk. On it was a large envelope, return address Brigade headquarters in Urumqi, with Ko's name scrawled on it. Below Ko's name was a note. *I wish all my managers understood the new Chinese economy as well as you, comrade. This will be our model project to explain what a market economy with Chinese characteristics really is.* It was signed *Rongqi*.

Inside the envelope Shan found a glossy label bearing an image of mountains and the Potala in Lhasa, the traditional home of the Dalai Lama, now converted by Beijing to a tourist shrine. Superimposed over the image was the word *Oracle*, with a trademark symbol. *Fresh from the sacred spring*, it said underneath and then, at the bottom, *ten ounces*. On the side panels were more marketing words. *Healing. Fortifying. Better Dreams. Taste the magic of Tibet.*

Shan stared at it in confusion at first, but then he read the cover note again, and his throat went dry. The oracle lake at the Raven's Nest. The Poverty Eradication Scheme. Rongqi's hatred of the Tibetans. The assimilation of lost minorities into the economic process. The subversion of the Yakde Lama. Ko and his general had found the perfect project. The model for their new economy. Distribute the sacred waters of the Raven's Nest to the newly affluent Chinese of the eastern cities. Rongqi was a man who evolved with the economy, but not all the way. He would have his vengeance on the Yakde Lama, paying rich rewards for the boy's death and also for the Jade Basket, even annoint his own Yakde Lama, then he would rub his victory in the faces of the lama's survivors.

Shan's hand trembled as he lifted the simulated label

that covered a series of index cards. *Suggested marketing slogans*, someone had ambitiously penned on the first card. *Print image: sexy woman in a nightshirt*, it said. *Caption: "Psst! I've got a Tibetan sex secret for you!"* The second said, *Print image: Monk raising a bottle with a big smile. Caption: "In Tibet we say, lha gyal lo! Victory to the gods. Now I say Victory to you!"*

There was more, but Shan could not bear to read them.

Suddenly horns blared from the vehicles at the baseball game. Shan dropped the envelope and pushed Lokesh toward the door. "Don't run," he said urgently. Don't look Tibetan, he almost said. He grabbed a heavy coat hanging on the back of the door and a baseball bat leaning in the corner. He threw the coat at Lokesh, who slipped it on, pulling its hood over his head. They walked down the hall, past the smiling janitor watching the desk, Shan in the lead with the bat on his shoulder. The woman waved goodbye. As they reached the door a group of men entered, a tall big-shouldered one in the center boisterously speaking of the game they had just played. Shan glanced at him and quickly looked away, then slowed to listen to the man's deep voice again. As he passed the man and exited the building Shan realized he had seen him before, wearing a white shirt that glared in the night, standing on the road in the Kunlun mountains.

Twenty minutes later they were in the cellar of the Maos' restaurant, Lokesh grinning as he offered the coat to the Mao's wardrobe. He paused to point out the gloves and hat in the pocket and the rich lining inside, synthetic fur in the pattern of a leopard. Shan smiled at his friend, feeling in debt to the deities who protected the old Tibetan, then began explaining to the Maos what he had learned. Wangtu, slumped in a chair in the corner, sat up and listened.

Moments later Lokesh called out in a somber tone. Shan turned and looked at him with a puzzled expression. The coat was reversible. Lokesh had put it on, leopard skin out, brown gloves on, a brown balaclava over his face, showing only eyes and mouth. He was holding the baseball bat, not as a batter would, but in one hand, raised over his shoulder. In his other hand was a long thin object which Fat Mao took for inspection. The Uighur pressed a button on its side and with a loud click a long blade appeared. A switchblade.

Shan gasped and stood as he realized what Lokesh had discovered. The demon in leopard form that had attacked the boy with the dropkas. The demon without a face. The demon had paws, and a shiny stick like a man's arm, the woman had said, without the fingers. He looked at the bat, wide at the top and ending like a wrist at the bottom. Jowa groaned loudly and turned to Shan with a look of shocked understanding. The boy had met the demon in mere leopard form. But Shan had to deal with the demon in Ko form.

Shan turned to Wangtu and studied the sullen Kazakh. "You have to make it happen," he said with a glance to Fat Mao, "you have to get the lie to Xu." He quickly explained what he had to do, then called the prosecutor's office from the pay phone at the post office, three blocks away, with Ox Mao listening. He asked for Miss Loshi and left a message with the secretary saying he was going to the town square, where he wanted to meet Prosecutor Xu with important information about Director Ko. A minute later Ox Mao left with a message to give to the bald man in the lobby, as Fat Mao gave hurried instructions to the others.

The sirens started five minutes later as the knobs converged on the square. Had Loshi bothered to call Ko first, Shan wondered, or had she contacted Bao directly? Ox Mao was behind the Ministry palace by then, watching the Red Flag limousine. Swallow Mao, the shy Uighur woman, stood in an alley a block away, where she could see Ox Mao. Jowa sat on a bench on the street opposite Shan, where he could see Swallow Mao. The signal came quickly. Jowa dropped the paper he was reading and raised both arms as if stretching. Shan stood, walking slowly, until he saw the shadow of the big car in the alley and stepped in front of it.

No one spoke as he climbed inside. The bald man drove fast, out of town, as Xu looked out the window, her eyes restlessly surveying the streets. Five minutes later they pulled onto a rocky track and climbed to the top of a small hill. They were at the edge of the desert, looking west toward the late afternoon sun. Xu silently walked to the edge of the knoll and down the other side. Shan followed, and found a short set of wooden stairs in severe disrepair. At the bottom Prosecutor Xu sat on a decrepit bench, beside a sign that leaned against the wooden post it had apparently fallen from. It had the flowing script of the Turkic language, but no Chinese.

"The old Muslim cemetery," she said, looking out over row upon row of identical sunbaked tombs, long cylindrical mounds of mud and cement, curving to a slight point along the top ridge. The scene gave the impression of scores of columns from a temple that had been toppled in symmetrical rows. Here and there were small beehive shapes of baked mud, the home, Shan suspected, of cremated remains and several large beehives, where bodies were buried sitting upright with their knees folded against their chests.

He quickly explained about the evidence linking Ko to the attack on the dropka boy.

"Circumstantial," she said.

"Ko must have been in a Brigade truck in Tibet with others that day, just like the next night when we saw them. It shouldn't be hard to find some of those who were with him. You could interrogate them. Get statements. It's one of your specialities, I hear."

She did not rise to his bait. "Bao found Lau's body," she said instead. Shan's head snapped up. "Or said he did. So we called, said an autopsy should be done. He said the Bureau already did one, confirming drowning was the cause. Body was cremated in Kotian."

"The body?"

"He had a body. But he didn't know my office uses the crematorium in Kotian too. We called, and the technician said the job had been delayed, that they were just about to start. I said we needed one last check of the woman's identity, and he called back five minutes later, all upset. Wasn't a woman at all. It was a young man, and he hadn't drowned, he had been shot twice in the chest. Mistakes happen I said, just put him away in the morgue. We'll be in touch."

"Lieutenant Sui." Shan spoke toward the graves, as if their occupants deserved to know.

The prosecutor nodded. "It's a strange sort of coverup. If Bao shot Sui he would have been more careful, there would have been no body. He's cleaning up someone else's mess. Someone he won't prosecute."

"Ko. Ko shot Sui. I met a witness. Bao found out, and Ko gave him his car to quiet him. Now they're business partners, thanks to Rongqi. Bao is protecting Ko, at least for now."

"Ridiculous. Bao and Ko, they're totally different. Never been friends. I've known them ever since they arrived in Yoktian."

"I saw a banner for the Poverty Eradication Scheme," Shan said. "Unify for Economic Success. I think Rongqi created a bond between them, a mutual interest."

"Like finding your boy lama?" Xu asked in a skeptical tone. "You're talking about the Brigade, one of the biggest companies in China, and the Public Security Bureau."

"No. Not the Bureau, just two renegade officers. Sui hid what he was doing from Bao. Sui killed Lau and got a lead on Ko in trying to find the boy. Ko killed him, because Sui was getting too close to the big prize. Then, later, when Bao discovered what had happened, he stepped into Sui's role. Unify to maximize the bounties. They can collect more if they work together. Rongqi increased the prize, too much to ignore for someone like Bao, stuck in Yoktian on a knob's salary. Creating a false record in the Lau investigation, that would be nothing for someone who kills boys for money," Shan sighed wearily. "Arrest them both. You'll be a hero."

Xu grimaced. "There's still no hard evidence."

"A body in the morgue is a good start. And there's a witness to Sui's murder, hiding in the mountains." Shan studied her. "You just mean there is no political explanation."

Xu was silent, looking out over the field of tombs. The wind blew sand in drifts along the rows of graves.

"Corruption is political," Shan suggested. "Bring down Rongqi, and you can get out of Xinjiang."

She made her grimace again. "I need books. I need ledgers. I need evidence. Offering economic incentives with private money, that's no crime."

"Offering a bounty to kill a boy is."

Xu shook her head. "One word from Rongqi to a boot

squad and we can all wind up in lao gai. You don't possibly think I could touch the general."

Shan stared at her. Her eyes remained as hard as pebbles but she would not meet his gaze. "I think you can. I think you're just scared."

"Sure. Next he'll have a bounty on uncooperative prosecutors."

"No. You're not scared of Rongqi. I think there is only one thing that truly scares you." She looked at him. "I think you're scared of becoming me."

The sound that Xu made seemed to start as a laugh, but ended more as a whimper.

"It's possible to stand up to them," he continued. "But if you do, it's also possible to end like me." He spoke in a matter-of-fact tone, as if speaking of some strange lower life form, not of himself.

She stood and abruptly walked away, down a row of tombs. The wind picked up as the sun began to sink behind the mountains. It shifted and filled with the acrid smell of the ephedra bushes that grew along the desert fringe. It was cool, almost cold, a sign of a shift in seasons.

He followed, but not all the way to her, stopping six feet away to bend at a grave. He began clearing away the dead leaves that had gathered against its wall. One of the traditions lost to most modern Chinese was Chen Ming, the festival when one swept the graves of ancestors and placed a branch of willow over the door to ward off evil spirits. When the government outlawed graves, it had effectively outlawed the festival day. Once Shan had found his father trying to fasten a tiny willow twig to the frame of their door, and his father had made an awkward joke about it and walked away. But in the night the twig had appeared over the door.

"You are going to get a report of a crime in the next few hours," he said in a loud voice as he worked. "Bao arranged it. Someone will say another boy has been attacked, maybe even killed. In the mountains. The kind of call the prosecutor's office must respond to. You will need to go immediately, or in the morning, early."

Xu gave no sign of having heard. She wandered away. A few minutes later she appeared on the other side of the tomb where Shan worked. "You mean a trap?"

"A distraction, I think. Because tomorrow morning is when Bao and Ko plan to catch the last boy. The one with the Jade Basket. It's timed perfectly for the general's visit. The big prize at last, presented to him when he arrives."

"He's here," Xu reported. "Came this afternoon, staying at a special Brigade guesthouse. Has boot squad bodyguards."

Shan sighed. "Perfect. Arrest them all."

"Lunacy," she shot back. "You've lost all sense of the bond between the government and its citizens." The words came out forced and hollow.

Shan just stared at her.

"You've been in Tibet too long," she accused him.

"I read something on the bond between the government and its people," he replied. "It's called the Lotus Book."

The words had a strange effect on the prosecutor. Xu seemed to stop breathing for a moment. She looked out over the tombs. "It's not like that," she said after a long time, in a taut voice.

"When you're in prison," he said quietly, speaking toward the horizon, "you always wake up without making a sound. People learn to have nightmares with silent screams, because of what the guards do if there is noise." The woman looking at him now was not the prosecutor. It was someone he had never seen before. The stone in her face seemed to have shattered. "But one day I woke up to the sound of a beautiful bell. Not loud, but true and harmonious, resonating to my bones, a perfect sound. Later I asked a lama who rang the bell. The lama said there was no bell, but at dawn he had watched a single drop of water drop from the roof into my tin cup. He said it was just the way my soul needed it to sound."

"I don't understand," Xu whispered, toward the graves.

"It's only that it changes you, Tibet. It makes you see things, or hear things differently. It marks you, it burns things into your soul." He looked at her. "Or sometimes burns through your soul."

Xu turned to put the sunset wind in her face. "In that book," she started, as if trying to explain something.

"Know this," Shan interrupted, for he would not deceive

her. "I read nothing about you in the book." But he remembered the strange look on her face when she had stared at the Kunlun, and how Tibetans worried her.

She seemed relieved for a moment and turned toward the stairs. But when she reached them she sat on the bench again. He worked on the grave a few more minutes, until it was clean, and still she just sat, staring over the weed-bound tombs.

Shan walked out of the graveyard and stepped past her. He was on the first stair when she spoke. "There're three hundred forty-seven graves here," she said, in her whisper again. "I counted them once."

He sat on the stairs. A large bird soared over the graveyard and roosted on a far tomb. An owl. Keeper of the dead.

"I was only sixteen," she blurted out, almost a sob. "We made a truck convoy from Shanghai, gathering more and more cadres as we went. They elected me officer. I never asked for it, but they said I could recite more of the Chairman's verses than the others in my unit. We traveled for weeks. We broke down fences to liberate livestock. We burned schools to liberate children. We burned libraries to liberate knowledge."

The Red Guard, Shan realized. She was talking about the Red Guard and the Cultural Revolution.

"When we got to Tibet they assigned me a district and a quota. Ten percent of all citizens were declared bad elements, and I had to identify my ten percent and submit them to struggle sessions, public criticism, violent criticism. Sometimes fatal criticism. Gompas had to be eliminated. The reactionaries had to be punished. Fourteen times our unit forced children to shoot their parents." She paused and surveyed the graves again as if she were thinking of counting once more. "We were only children ourselves. Sometimes they stripped lamas naked and made them dance in the town square."

"They?"

Xu was silent. She ran her hand over her lips. It trembled. "We," she said at last and pushed a knuckle into her mouth. She took the finger out after a moment and stared at it, as if not understanding what it had done. "I wanted

to stop. I wanted to go home. I was tired of the brutality.
I was worried about my family. But if you spoke about
family you were criticized. Sign of a reactionary, sign of
addiction to the tradition of oppression. All I could do was
continue. We got awards. A model unit. I kept getting promoted. There was a gompa far in the hills, a big gompa
past Shigatse. The Revolutionary Committee came with
photographers from Lhasa to watch us do our job. We surrounded the gompa and sang songs of the Revolution. I
gave the order to burn it. I thought the monks would come
out, they had time to. But they didn't. Some of them stood
in the doors and looked at us as they burned. But most just
stayed inside, saying their mantras. For a long time we
could hear them, louder than the roar of the flames. Afterwards we found the bodies in rows, because they had carefully sat in their sanctuary with their lamas facing them.
Rows and rows, like a cemetery. We celebrated and sang
our songs again. Three hundred forty-nine. The Chairman
sent me a letter of commendation. It's how I got my first
job in the Ministry. Because I had the letter from the Chairman. It just said I did a good job, that I was a model
worker. It didn't say it was because I had killed three hundred forty-nine monks."

Shan had no words. A history teacher had once told him
that the only problem with modern China was that people
lived too long, that too many millions lived to old age,
when they began to cultivate a conscience. For Xu the
nightmares had come early, and her conscience had trapped
her. It's not like that, she had said of the Lotus Book.
Meaning, It was like that, but now I am a different person.
She was as surely a prisoner as those she sent behind wire,
self-exiled in the borderlands where she thought she might
make a difference.

She seemed not to notice when he rose and climbed the
stairs. He passed the car without looking at the bald man
at the wheel and walked back to town, the wind throwing
sand across the road, his soul so heavy he thought he might
never hear a bell again.

CHAPTER 21

Sand blew down the streets of Yoktian, obscuring their broken curbs and other imperfections, blurring the cracks in the walls. It was as if the entire town had been airbrushed for a cleaner, more wholesome image. Perhaps on the general's orders. But Shan was not fooled. There were still holes in the street that would break your ankle and fissures in the walls where rats waited.

A cargo truck was at the rear of the restaurant when Shan arrived. Gendun and Lokesh were asleep in the front room under two tables that had been pushed together, as if the Maos expected an earthquake. Jowa sat beside them, lotus fashion, watching them. As the stout woman extended a mug of tea and a bowl of noodles toward him, the truck's engine started.

"Rice camp," she said in response to his look of query, and he bolted out the door, jumping into the cargo bay so quickly that he did not realize until he sat down that the tea was still in his hand.

Fat Mao, sitting in the shadows behind the cab, was not happy to see him. A quick trip, he said, to pick up the order for the next week's food delivery, although Shan knew better. They were going because of Red Stone clan, because the next afternoon the clan would be disbanded, because Akzu and Fat Mao had a plan they would not explain. But Shan did not care. He was going for the waterkeeper. There was nothing else to do except wait for the dawn, wait for the meeting at Stone Lake, for the final confrontation where the killers would come to collect their last prize, where Shan had to be before the knobs, to whisk the boy away if he and the herders guarding him eluded the Maos, who would be trying to intercept the boy on the roads leading to Stone Lake.

The adminstrative compound at Glory Camp was deserted. The gatehouse itself was empty and the gate locked. But Ox Mao climbed out of the driver's seat and quickly unlocked the padlock. They parked by the warehouse and a woman followed the big Kazakh out of the front seat— Swallow Mao, wearing a severe-looking business suit. The woman carried a large envelope and marched toward the administrative building with an air of authority.

Shan stood by the inner wire, studying the barracks with the holding cells, inside the prisoner compound. He had no plan, no idea, no confirmation even that the lama was in the barracks. Even if Swallow Mao could find his hut assignment the Maos could not risk entering the second wire, which was where the real security started. He bent to a small clump of dried asters that had managed to survive in the sandy soil at the base of the inner wire. Plucking one of the stems, Shan tied it to the wire at the closest point to the holding cells. Maybe, he thought sadly, he had come just to say goodbye. The old Tibetan would not last long once Bao, or Rongqi, discovered he was a lama. He looked back at the administrative building and slowly, reluctantly, turned his head toward the small shed where he had found Nikki, then the boilerhouse.

He started walking, without conscious effort, and found himself under the boilerhouse roof. From twenty feet away he could feel the heat of the furnace and he stood there, the image of the spirited blond youth by the boiler door burning through his mind. Not much older than his own son. He walked out the far side of the building and stopped at the edge of the cemetery. In the dim light of the cloud-covered moon the graves seemed endless. With small, uncertain steps he started toward the far end, where the freshest mounds of earth had been.

Then he saw the animal. A low shadowy hulk, it moved along the graves as though following a scent. Shan looked down for a spade, a stick, anything he might use as a weapon. The creature lingered at one of the freshly dug piles of earth. With a pang of fear Shan wondered what he would do if it began to dig for the dead. Scavengers preferred rotten meat. Feebly, he stepped forward. The beast paid him no attention. It pawed idly at the earth in long motions that gave the impression of a great and reckless power.

After a moment the animal leaned back and sat up on its rear haunches. As the moon appeared from behind a cloud Shan gave a half-choked cry. The animal was Marco Myagov.

He stood in silence for a long time before venturing a step forward. Marco tensed and seemed about to pounce on him, then eased back as he recognized Shan. Shan spoke no word of greeting but instead began to range among the graves himself, surveying the mounds, trying to remember how they had looked on his first visit. After a few minutes he stopped at a group of three fresh graves. "Here," he said. "This is where he would be."

Marco seemed to require great effort to rise. He wiped his hands, caked with soot and the dirt of the cemetery, and joined Shan.

"He is—" Shan struggled to find words. "He is with many good men." Despite their miserable deaths in a forgotten wasteland, many of those laid to rest before them were men who defied the dictators, who had been true to their beliefs.

Marco gave no sign he had heard Shan's words.

"I thought you were—" Shan offered tentatively. "I saw the flames, I thought you had died." What if this was not Marco, he thought with alarm, what if it was some frail shadow of Marco, some wraith left after he had lost his soul that night?

But then the man spoke, and Shan sighed with relief. "She burned," Marco said in a hoarse voice. "God's breath, how she burned."

"But why are you—"

"I have talking to do with my Nikki."

"Then what?" Shan asked after a moment.

"I told you before. I get bastards. It's what I do."

The words somehow made Shan sad. "They need you.

The Americans still have to get out. They're in great danger."

Marco looked at Shan, with an expression of confusion, as if he had not thought of it before.

"They'll kill you here. There're soldiers. You won't have a chance."

Marco did not reply. He selected the middle of the two graves and sat on the earth by it, then patted the soil beside him as though gesturing for Shan to join him. Shan knelt by the end of the mound.

"I would not fear to stay here with Nikki," the Eluosi said, almost brightly. "I have nothing left. I have no country. I have no family. I have no home."

"But what would Sophie do without you?"

Marco's eyes rested on a patch in the darkness, in the shadows of the knoll by the camp. He sighed heavily and pulled something out of his pocket. In the moonlight Shan recognized it. The Russian medal he had seen in Nikki's room. The medal from the Czar.

Marco scooped loose soil from the head of the grave and buried the medal, then spoke in Russian for a long time, looking first at the grave, then at the sky.

When he finished Marco shifted his gaze toward the compound. His eyes had a new, sharp glint, a warrior's eyes. Suddenly he rose and began jogging toward the boilerhouse.

By the time Shan caught up, he was at the open boiler, rapidly shoveling in coal. He motioned toward the loaded barrow at the front of the shed, and Shan pushed it toward him. Soon the boiler was packed with fuel, almost overflowing with coal. The heat was nearly unbearable before Marco closed the door. The Eluosi darted to the tool bench and returned with a long spike and a pair of pliers. He jammed the spike through the holes designed to hold a padlock on the door when not in use, and bent both ends so the door could not be opened. He quickly studied the simple controls above the door, then shut off the relief valve, opened the air intake to maximum, and smashed the temperature warning gauge. He turned away, then paused and turned back, pulling something out of his pocket and plac-

ing it on the top of the door. Shan recognized it. The plain
steel ring that Nikki had worn.

There was no point in protesting, no way to stop what
Marco had set into motion, no possibility of asking the
Maos to stay and find the waterkeeper in the chaos that was
to follow. If any of them were found near the camp they
would probably be held, even summarily shot, for com-
mitting sabotage.

The Maos were waiting at the truck. Shan stared into
the inner wire once more, and sighed.

"I'm sorry, Johnny," Marco said. "It's what I do. Now
go. Go quickly."

The Maos were ready when he returned. He said nothing
about the boiler until several minutes after they had left the
gate. Fat Mao listened, then rapped on the window and Ox
Mao slowed the truck. Just as he rolled down his window
to speak, an explosion shook the valley. The truck rocked.
A boulder on the slope above dislodged and rolled past
them. Ox Mao accelerated up the hill at the end of the
valley and stopped the truck. They could see the camp
clearly, no more than three miles away. Huge flames
reached into the night sky. The boilerhouse and warehouse
were engulfed in flames. Burning debris could be seen
blowing across the compound. Moments later the administration building began to burn.

Thirty minutes later the Maos were pacing anxiously
around their cellar, arguing among themselves, offering
plans and rejecting them, suggesting what the knobs and
Brigade might do next, seeming to make themselves more
nervous with each suggestion. Fat Mao kept reminding
them that the Red Stone clan was being processed for dis-
persion within hours and now their plan was impossible.
Ox Mao said they should be celebrating. Swallow Mao sat
at the table, staring at the blank computer screen.

Shan watched for a quarter hour from his seat on the
stairs, then took a stool at the table. "Your plan. If it is
impossible now, then you can tell me what it was. I know
it had to do with trucks, like the one Red Stone tried to
steal."

Fat Mao frowned but shrugged and explained. The herds
were being shipped to the north, in four big livestock

trucks. All of the personnel assignments were finalized—
the Kazakhs were to go to towns, to Brigade factories,
mostly. Swallow had obtained all the details from the Brigade computers. Mao drivers had been arranged for the four
trucks. "But the trick was this," the Uighur said. "Truckloads of livestock are sold by the Brigade to Kazakhstan
all the time. A dozen trucks are booked to go across the
Kazakh border this week, west on the highway to Alma
Ata. Swallow got the shipment numbers, the travel permit
numbers, which have all been approved and processed. The
border guards have the numbers, for verification. Jowa
helped us plan everything. Tonight Swallow put in a new
disc, for when the office opens tomorrow. Swallow's name
will not be attached to any file. Some other clerk will get
the file and transmit the travel confirmations to the Brigade
headquarters. The four Red Stone trucks will be cleared by
the computers to go to Kazakhstan. Those four will arrive
at the depot that is receiving the Red Stone sheep, because
Mao drivers will take them."

"And when the trucks leave with the sheep, the clan will
be with them."

Fat Mao shrugged. "It's a small clan. There's land in
Kazakhstan for those displaced from China. They will get
new pastures, with other Kazakhs."

"But trucks get inspected. First the papers are checked,
then the cargo is checked."

"Which is why timing was so important. Border guards
get bribed all the time. At a certain time two days from
now a certain guard sergeant was going to be in charge of
inspecting four trucks. He would handle the clearances himself. The papers would be fine, he just won't look at the
cargo. He's used to black market goods. Marco recom-
mended him."

"Except now the data won't get sent because the disc
burned in the fire," Shan said.

"All they can do now is take their factory jobs and hope
we can find some other way later."

Shan studied the faces of the Maos. The excitement that
had been there when they first saw the flames of Glory
Camp had been replaced with expressions of defeat.

"The copies of records from Glory Camp," Shan said to

Swallow Mao. "Do you have the cemetery records?"

She nodded slowly.

He turned to Fat Mao. "Can you get money? Maybe four Panda coins."

The Uighur nodded. "We use them with people across the border. They all prefer to deal in gold."

Shan quickly outlined his plan. "The only problem," he concluded with a sober tone, "is that Akzu and the others, they all have to die." Marco would take the Kazakhs out with the Americans, with four more gold Pandas for four more boats. The difficulty was that the Brigade couldn't know, Rongqi couldn't allow anyone to think the Kazahks could defy the Poverty Eradication Scheme. So the names and identity numbers for the Red Stone members would be switched with the names and identity numbers of long-dead prisoners. Recordkeeping would be chaotic in the aftermath of the fire, Swallow Mao confirmed. An emergency operations center would be created, and she would be assigned there, giving her a chance to replace the cemetery records with the new disc. The Kazakhs would have officially disappeared. And the records would be changed to show that the correct number of names were transported with the others as part of Rongqi's program, transferred onto Brigade factory headcounts. In his Beijing career Shan had investigated more than one government factory system where favors were distributed in the form of payroll identity numbers for nonexistent employees, since managers could keep the wages and no one would complain. It took no stretch of imagination to believe that Rongqi already distributed patronage in the form of such profitable ghosts.

The Maos debated the risks for nearly an hour, then Swallow chided them all. "The biggest risk is mine," she announced and sat at the computer with a new set of discs. A moment later the Glory Camp cemetery list was on the screen, then the list of Red Stone clan members assigned to the Poverty Scheme. They watched as she began tapping the keys, and one by one the members of Red Stone clan were buried at Glory Camp.

*   *   *

When they arrived at Stone Lake just after dawn, a silver camel stood in the shadow of the long dune that ran along the western edge of the bowl, beside a large shape under a blanket. They let Marco sleep and sat thirty feet away, near the top of the dune, three hundred yards from where the road led into the camp. Fat Mao had brought them and offered to stay, looking toward a toolbox in back of the truck. Shan had seen the cold anger that had settled over him and suspected the box contained weapons. He asked the Uighur to leave.

"You need a plan, in case the boy makes it here and the knobs come," Fat Mao protested.

Shan stared at him for a moment. "The boy won't come here because the Maos will find him first."

"There's been no sign of him. Those dropka he's with, they're like wild animals. Stealthy. We may not intercept them."

Shan sighed. "Then everyone will flee with the boy and the Jade Basket," he said quietly, so only the Uighur could hear. "I will distract any knobs who come."

"Distract?"

"There is something else Bao wants in addition to the gau or the Americans."

Fat Mao studied him a moment. "You."

Shan shrugged.

"Not everyone has to be a victim," the Uighur said with a frown. "Not every time." There was frustration in his voice and, oddly, a tone of apology.

"Look for the boy for another hour," Shan said, "then go to Red Stone clan. They need you today too."

Fat Mao frowned again, then turned and left.

The last day had arrived, the day Rongqi and Ko had dreamed of, the final implementation of the Poverty Eradication Scheme. Akzu had to be found and told of the new plan. The Red Stone herds had to be surrendered, with their tents and everything else being taken over by the Brigade. For the only way for the clan to be free, and together, was to give up everything in life they had valued, except life itself.

Gendun laid back on the sand and exclaimed over the shapes of the clouds. Lokesh, as he had countless times before, laid out the possessions of the Yakde Lama and studied each one. They had all their bags, ready to leave for Tibet. Shan pulled out their old pair of binoculars and cleaned the lenses on his shirt, then handed them to Jowa, who crawled to the top of the dune and began to watch.

After an hour Jowa whistled. Kaju had appeared, walking alone down the road. They lay on the sand behind the crest of the dune and watched as he stopped at the building skeleton that swayed in the wind, tied something to one corner post, then tightened it and secured it to another post. A string of Buddhist prayer flags, the flags, Shan suspected, from Lau's office.

The Tibetan stopped and stared at the flags after he had fastened them, as if seeing prayer flags for the first time in his life, then turned and walked slowly toward the garage building. Shan stood and waved and in a few moments Kaju had joined them.

He greeted them in Tibetan, not Mandarin, and for the first time since Shan had known him continued the conversation in his native tongue. There had been no contact from Micah, he reported, no chance to warn him away. But in the night, Kaju said hopefully, there had been many sirens and many knobs had rushed out of town. Maybe they were gone, or at least distracted. Maybe Bao would forget one small boy in the face of whatever Public Security emergency had arisen.

They were sitting in a circle, listening to Kaju explain how he planned to one day return with all the zheli and truly see the fossils, when someone threw a plastic bag of raisins into their midst. They looked up to see Marco's broad face, looking grim but determined.

He squatted by Shan with a handful of raisins. "Took an hour for them to decide to let the prisoners out to fight the fires," he reported without emotion. "Fools. By then all they could do was throw sand on the embers. Nothing left but smoldering bags of rice where the warehouse was. No administration building. The little house at the gate, even that." There was no victory in his voice, but when he looked at Shan an odd glint rose in his eyes. "Nikki approved," he said in a low tone, and nodded as though to acknowledge that although it might not feel like victory, it did feel like completion.

As Kaju stood and walked along the top of the dune, watching for Micah, Lokesh lifted the raisin bag and passed it around. Breakfast. "You'll see," Kaju called out to Shan. "It's only Bao. If he comes and tries to take the boy it will be the proof I need. I'll go to Ko," he said as he stepped nearly out of earshot. "Ko will know what to do." Shan and Jowa exchanged a glance. Kaju still refused to accept the truth.

As Marco ate his raisins Shan explained the new plan for the Red Stone clan. The Eluosi didn't argue. "That old Tibetan hunter at the border, the one with the coracles, only way he'll do it now is if he sees I'm with them," the Eluosi said and looked at Shan. "I'll need help."

Shan didn't understand at first. The words weren't spontaneous. They had been chewed over by Marco and he meant them.

"Come with me, Johnny," Marco said in English. "I'm leaving this forsaken land. You should too. I've got buckets of money in banks outside. We'll go to Alaska. Catch big fish. Build a cabin by the ocean."

Shan's mouth opened and closed again. He looked at Gendun and Lokesh, and explained to them in Tibetan, but they offered only small serene smiles and nodded.

"It isn't over," Shan said. "There's no time—"

As if Shan's words were a cue, Kaju shouted. Two riders on horseback had appeared from the desert, leading a heavily loaded packhorse and an empty saddle horse along the back of the dune they sat on. "The Americans," Kaju announced brightly, as if somehow the arrival of Deacon and his wife assured their success.

But Shan just looked at the sand by his feet. He realized that unconsciously he had hoped they would not come.

Deacon's wife seemed to overflow with energy and excitement. She had brought a large jar of peanut butter, which Kaju explained to Gendun and Lokesh, offering samples to them as they examined it with schoolboy curiosity. She spoke to Marco, to make sure the bags on the horse were not too big, then flattened an area of sand and laid a towel on it, then arranged things on it. One of the leather gloves used for baseball. A small green toy truck. A pack of chewing gum. And a red can, battered and dented from heavy travels, an unopened can of American soda. Then, with a puzzled glance from her husband, who just stood and stared down into the bowl, she untied a narrow wooden box from the top of the packhorse, digging a recess for it so that it was shaded. She pulled away the cloth that covered the top of the box and Shan saw that it was perforated with holes. Deacon's insect singers.

Marco took over like an officer instructing his troops, moving them all down into the shadow of the dune, on the opposite side from the bowl. No one was to go on top, in plain sight, except Kaju. He sent Jowa with Gendun and Lokesh even further, to a place two hundred yards to the north where a small outcropping provided some cover. If anyone came for the boy, the Eluosi announced, he and Sophie would grab the boy and take him into the soft desert sand where trucks could not follow.

Twenty minutes later, at the far end of the bowl, where it flattened and opened into the desert, three figures came into view, riding horses, less than a mile away. Lying flat at the crest of the dune with the binoculars Shan could see that it was two men in the garb of herders and between them, on a pony, a boy. Two large mastiffs ran on either side of the horses.

"Micah!" the American woman called out, and stood as though to run toward the distant figures.

"Warp—no!" her husband yelled, and pulled his wife back behind the dune.

In the same moment, over the dune on the opposite side of the wide, sandy bowl, a vehicle appeared. Not a red Brigade truck as Shan had expected but one of the sleek black utility vehicles of the boot squads. It inched to the top of the dune and stopped. A figure in a red nylon jacket climbed out of the driver's seat. Even without the binoculars Shan knew it was Ko Yonghong.

"The bastards," Marco spat at his side as the remaining doors opened. Two men in grey uniforms, carrying submachine guns, darted half a dozen paces in opposite directions to flank the vehicle, then each dropped to one knee, guns raised, as if prepared for combat. A third man, a barrel-chested figure who walked with a swagger, moved to Ko's side. Major Bao.

A gasp escaped from Kaju, standing halfway down the dune below Shan. The Tibetan stared in disbelief, glanced at Shan with an anguished expression, then looked back as one more figure emerged, a tall, thin, older man with an imperious bearing. Ko solicitously handed him a pair of binoculars and the man studied the approaching riders, then patted Ko on the shoulder. Shan studied the stranger with his lenses. He had seen him before, in the photograph at Ko's office. "Rongqi," he heard Kaju gasp. It was the general himself, come to witness his ultimate triumph over the Tibetans.

"Dammit, no!" he heard Deacon's urgent whisper from behind, and he turned to see Lokesh and Gendun walking toward the end of the dune, as if to intercept the riders, waving them toward the outcropping as though it might hide them from the men in the truck. Shan felt a hand on his arm. Marco pointed silently toward the entrance to the oil camp, where another car had appeared, a Red Flag. It stopped and backed up, out of sight, then Prosecutor Xu appeared, alone, aiming a pair of binoculars toward the black truck.

Bao's attention was fixed on the riders. He raised his hand and seemed to snap out a command. The two knob soldiers sprang back to the truck.

"No!" Kaju moaned. He stumbled forward, his face twisted with pain. His eyes moved from the riders to the truck and then drifted back into the center of the bowl, where the single shrub grew between him and the truck. He stared at it curiously for a moment, then he began tearing at the neck of his shirt. He pulled a chain from his neck, a chain holding a large silver gau.

Raising the gau over his head, he leapt forward, bounding down the side of the dune, calling out, shouting Ko's name, then shouting for Major Bao, running hard toward the center of the bowl as if trying to meet the truck there. The men at the black truck stared at him for a moment, then jumped into the vehicle, the soldiers leaping on the sideboards, guns still at the ready, as Ko drove over the crest of the dune.

As he ran Kaju kept gesturing with an emphatic energy, as if he urgently needed them, dangling the gau as if they should recognize it. As if it were the Jade Basket. His pace slackened as he approached the bush, stopping for a moment thirty feet away from it, then starting again with a much slower movement, still waving the truck toward him.

Suddenly Shan understood. "No!" he gasped and began to rise. But a beefy hand settled over his shoulder. Marco pushed him down.

"You don't understand—" Shan protested. "He remembers the shrub. He saw the roots before! Deacon!" he called out desperately. The American would know.

Kaju had arrived at the bush and stopped, in the center of the bowl, still waving desperately as the truck sped forward. For a moment he turned, and looked back, as though seeking Shan, then he lowered himself into the lotus position, the gau now clutched at his chest, his head raised not toward the truck but toward the sky.

Deacon appeared at Shan's side. "Jesus!" he bellowed. "No! The cistern!"

The truck lurched to a stop beside the Tibetan and the soldiers jumped off. As the doors opened the truck began to sink and the soldiers shouted frantically at the men inside, one stumbling toward the door where the general had climbed in. Then the soldiers themselves began to drop as if being consumed by the sand itself.

It seemed to happen not in slow motion, but in fast motion, in a blurring sequence, as the desert opened up and swallowed the vehicle into the depths of the ancient cistern, then the sand of the bowl and the adjacent dunes swept inward in a great violent surge. A deep crater appeared for an instant where the huge cistern had been built centuries before, and Shan thought he saw arms and legs swimming in the sand and rock rubble. Then the desert filled the crater, the dunes shifting and sliding with a dreadful hissing and swirling as the tons of sand moved in.

Then, abruptly, there was stillness.

Deacon stood beside him. Shan had not had time to rise from his knees. At the road Xu stood staring, the binoculars at her side, then slowly she disappeared from view, walking backward, still facing the empty bowl. A moment later

Shan heard the engine of the car as she drove away.

They walked silently, in shock, toward the shallow depression that marked where the cistern had been.

"We have to dig!" Abigail Deacon shouted repeatedly as she leapt down the dune and began scooping the sand with her hands.

"It's forty feet at least, Warp," her husband said quietly, as he and Shan reached her. "Thousands of tons of sand. Not a chance."

They stood, paralyzed, for a moment as the American woman, still kneeling, pounded the sand forlornly. The desert had claimed more dead. The karez had become a tomb after all. Ko who worshipped money. Rongqi who worshipped power. Bao who worshipped force. And one Tibetan who, however wasted in life, had been steadfast in his death.

A horse whinnied and they looked up to see the riders standing beside their horses now, with Lokesh and Gendun. They did not advance, but stood two hundred yards away, as if frightened.

"Micah!" the American woman called out, and jumped up to move toward the figures. Deacon started after her but stopped and looked back uncertainly as Shan called his name. Shamed by his weakness, Shan handed the American the gau he had taken from Malik, the gau from the grave at the lama field. The American's face went stiff, and his arm drooped when he reached for it, as if it had lost its strength. Shan pushed the gau into Deacon's hand and stepped away. He remembered the stab of pain in his heart when he had opened it the first time, the only time, the day after Malik had given it to him. For inside there had been no Jade Basket, no secret prayer. There had only been the shriveled remains of a small brown cricket.

The American woman kept stumbling in the soft sand, calling her son's name even as she fell. Deacon stood a moment staring at Shan, then at the short, slender figure with the two herders, his face growing dim, as if a veil were descending over it. Then he made a gasping sound as though he were back in the suffocating karez and stepped forward, calling his wife in a voice no one could hear at first, then louder, until as she stumbled to her knees again he caught up with her.

There was no need to explain, Shan saw, for Jacob Deacon understood. The American had been glimpsing another of the nightmares that had shadowed Shan since the nadam. Two mischevious boys had fooled their foster parents, their shadow clan guardians, because one had wanted to move to the lower pastures to be with the horses, while the other had been trying to reach the high Kunlun, the land of the lama field. Khitai had already played the same innocent game by trading places with Suwan at the Red Stone camp. Only for a few days, Khitai and Micah would have said, for everyone would meet at Stone Lake on the full moon. Malik had been certain Khitai died at the lama field but Malik had seen only a battered boy with dark hair already in his shroud, in possession of Khitai's belongings, at the place he expected Khitai to be.

"Micah!" the American woman called again, when her husband pulled her up from the sand. "Our boy!" she cried to her husband, as if Deacon did not understand. But Deacon held her from the back, his arms locked around her, as she faced the riders, keeping her there as Shan and Marco passed by, their pace slower and slower as they approached. The two herders, holding the horses, looked at the Americans with wild, confused expressions.

When they reached the horses Lokesh was sitting on the sand with a slim Tibetan boy, chanting a mantra with him, pointing out the possessions that he had recovered for him at the lama field. Tears ran down the old Tibetan's cheeks.

Gendun stood, his eyes wide and sad, looking from Shan to Khitai and back to the Americans. "Thank you, friend Shan," he said, his voice cracking. "For raising our Yakde Lama from the dead."

CHAPTER 22

No one discussed staying at Stone Lake. But stay they did,
for hours, Shan staring in silence at the shallow depression
that marked the tomb, Deacon and his wife alone with their
grief, Marco introducing the boy lama to Sophie and offering him a ride. Fat Mao came to find Marco and left
after speaking with Jowa, taking the Americans to the grave
at the lama field. By midday people began to appear, Kazakhs and Uighurs mostly, some on horses, some walking
down the road from the highway. They gathered around the
depression in the sand with puzzled expressions. Shan
heard someone point out the holy man in the robe, and
many nodded, as if Gendun's presence explained everything. They raised a small cairn at the site of the collapsed
cistern, using rubble from the oil camp buildings and stones
from the old ruins. Shan and Jowa removed the prayer flags
from the building frame where Kaju had erected them and
fastened them to the cairn.

The boy lama seemed to avoid Shan at first, then finally
came and sat beside him as he contemplated the bowl of
sand that had become Kaju's grave. The boy appeared
about to speak, and Shan leaned forward as if to say something himself, but neither of their tongues found words.
They sat silently, for an hour, then the boy moved in front
of Shan and slowly lifted Shan's hand. He spread Shan's
fingers to make an open palm, and then placed the palm
over his heart.

When the boy raised his hand Shan reached inside his

shirt and pulled out his gau. "I met one of the old ones at Sand Mountain," he said to the boy as he opened the gau. "Before he returned to the sand he gave me this," Shan explained as he pulled out the feather. He stared at it, cupped in his hand. "I gave him a new one, to take back." Shan looked up to see the boy lama staring reverently at the feather, and he extended his hand toward the boy. "I want you to take it now."

The boy did not take the feather at first, but pulled his own gau from his neck, opening the finely worked silver filigree lid to reveal a similar filigree worked in jade. He lifted the top of the Jade Basket and Shan dropped the feather into it.

The Yakde stared at the feather, his eyes filled with emotion. "Micah loved owls," he said softly. "When we were together we would stay up and listen for owls. He had learned from his shadow clan how to call to them. One night he grew very still and said there was one old owl calling for him now, that it felt like the owl was trying to call him somewhere." The boy shook his head slowly, then gently lifted the box close to his face to study the feather. "It will become one of the treasures," he said.

He meant, Shan realized after a moment, that it would become a permanent part of the Yakde Lama's chain of existence, one of the treasures that would become an indicator for future incarnations of the Yakde.

By late afternoon the Maos returned with two trucks, and spoke again in hushed tones to Jowa. They helped Shan and the Tibetans into a truck, then loaded Sophie into the other. Shan jumped out at the last minute and climbed in with Sophie and Marco. They looked at each other without speaking, stroking Sophie as the truck lurched down the road.

"Where will you leave her?" Shan asked. "When you go across the ocean."

Marco's face still had no cheer but it seemed to have found a certain peacefulness. "Leave her?" The Eluosi grunted. "Sophie never leaves me. She goes, she always goes."

"To Alaska? They don't have camels in Alaska."

"They will now," Marco declared in a loud voice. "We'll

take her on a big ship, one where we can walk with her on the deck. You and me."

It was such an impossible thing that Shan wanted to laugh. But it was an impossibly wonderful thing. He was young enough to start a new life. Jakli had given him the medallion because she too wanted him to go. Tibet, the lamas always told him, was the starting point for his new incarnation, but no one could know where it would lead. He had missed the trip to Nepal and the new life in England, but now another path was unfolding.

They were close to Yoktian, Shan saw, and suddenly they were passing a familiar set of hills on the edge of the town. At the top of a hill was a boxy black car. Shan pounded on the window for the truck to stop, then jogged up the hill, past the empty Red Flag.

He spotted her in the middle of the cemetery, slowly sweeping a grave with a ragged broom, dust on her clothes. She could have been a groundskeeper or a mourner.

Xu showed no surprise at seeing him and continued sweeping around the grave before speaking. "Glory Camp is dead," she said, huddling over the broom. "Can't use it after the accident, not for weeks at least, probably not until spring." All the prisoners sentenced to six months or more were being transferred to other facilities, she explained, all the others released.

"And those taken by Bao?" Shan asked.

Those too, the prosecutor confirmed without looking up, then she walked to a bag by a grave ten feet away. She pulled out a videotape and tossed it toward Shan's feet.

"I told Loshi to get it, to make them get it back for her. I told her she was fired if she didn't get it, because she had tampered with an official file, that she'd never have a chance for a transfer back east. I was going to bury it." She kicked it closer to him, then, as if impatient with his indecision over touching it, smashed it with her foot. An end of the loose tape broke free of the cassette and the wind grabbed it, unwinding it with such force that it broke when it reached the end. The tape slithered across the graves like a snake, then blew out into the desert.

"They've all been reported missing by their offices," Xu said stiffly. "Someone said they saw Bao pick up Ko and the general at the Brigade compound, in one of the boot squad trucks, but no one saw them afterward. This afternoon the knobs from Kashgar took a look at the Brigade offices. Found a storeroom of contraband. Smuggled goods. Someone said maybe they caused the accident at Glory Camp, to cover up evidence." Nikki's goods, Shan thought. The goods they had stolen from Nikki when they seized his caravan would condemn them.

"People could be convinced that they fled," he suggested. "That they were corrupt and ran in fear of being discovered."

She sighed. "There're campaigns for that too," she said with a slow nod, holding the broom tightly, as if it were all that kept her from blowing away. "Must have fled to America. Everyone knew Ko liked American cars." She appeared much older than her years. She had bags under her eyes, as if she had not slept. "The Poverty Scheme won't stop," she said with a tone of apology.

"I know."

"But those horses, they're too much trouble. We're not going to round up the horses again." She bent with the broom and swept some more.

"There was a hatmaker," Shan said to her back, and found he had trouble swallowing, "who loved those horses."

Xu halted and slowly turned. "Apparently," she said with a frown. "I read the reports. She went north, to a coal mine prison."

"Maybe a mistake was made," Shan suggested. "Maybe she was helping you in your corruption investigation, helping prove that Bao killed Sui over money. You still have Sui's body to explain and the morgue can testify that Bao falsified records." It would be a solution. Not perfect, but he had never known justice to be perfect. Sui could become a posthumous hero, killed by those he was investigating for corruption.

"Just a hatmaker," she said in a near whisper, with her distant look. "What does a hatmaker know about mining coal?" She frowned again, then sighed. "I couldn't just have her freed. Everyone knew she was breaching probation. It would be a transfer to a lao jiao camp. For a few months."

Shan nodded, and she grimaced, then nodded back as if to seal an agreement.

She fell silent, then continued sweeping. He watched her work. She seemed to have grown smaller. "If I had a letter from the Chairman," he said after a moment, "a letter about killing monks, I think I know what I would do with it."

She stopped and looked back at him.

"I would write a reply on the bottom of it," he explained. "Maybe I would say it was wrong what I did, and wrong for you, Comrade Chairman, to pretend it was good to kill monks. Maybe some night I would go alone out to the place where the Tibetan died today and I would light a fire of fragrant wood. Then I would burn the letter to send it to the Chairman, and watch the ashes fly away to the heavens."

Xu stared at the ground by Shan's feet. "It wasn't Kaju's fault," she said in her distant voice. Then she raised her broom and swept again. "There's a little suitcase," she said after a moment. "We found it in Rongqi's room, like it was packed to take back to Urumqi." She gestured toward the bench on the hill above the cemetery, and said no more.

When he said goodbye, she only nodded without looking up. He stopped on top of the hill and looked at her small, bent figure among the neglected graves, the empty desert beyond, slowly moving along the long, desolate landscape.

He found the suitcase beside the bench and opened it. It was a sleek, black leather case with an Italian label, and inside were Rongqi's trophies, the proof he had required for payment of his bounties. Four small, dusty, tattered shoes.

The Maos drove south, through Yoktian, onto the main road into the Kunlun. Marco talked with Sophie about the long trip they were to make, then talked with Shan about how they might cook all the fish they would catch. They stopped unexpectedly, behind the first truck, which was pulled to the side of the road. Jowa and Fat Mao were talking to a group of mounted Uighurs. Some of the prisoners from Glory Camp had passed the riders on the way home, they reported. There would be celebrations in the hill camps that night as Uighur families were reunited. Kazakh prisoners, Fat Mao added, were rushing to join the clans now dispersed by the Poverty Scheme. The Maos would see that they found their families.

An old man from the rice camp had been walking up the road into the mountains, one of the riders added. He had been offered a ride in a truck but declined, the man explained with a laugh, because he said he had to watch a butterfly.

Jowa darted to the rider's side. "Where?" he asked urgently.

The Uighur shook his head with a grin, then stood in his saddle and pointed. On a ridge half a mile away a tiny figure could be seen, walking hurriedly through the high brown grass.

"Crazy old—" the Uighur began, but broke off, openmouthed. Jowa was gone, leaping through the grass, running toward the distant figure. In the back of the truck, Lokesh began to laugh. Fat Mao called out that he would send one of the trucks back before dusk.

In the late afternoon they arrived at a small cabin a hundred yards from the road, surrounded by a grove of poplars. It was a surprisingly busy place, with the cheerful noise of boys. Half the Red Stone clan had already passed through, Fat Mao explained, and would be at the silo sanctuary by nightfall, where they would meet Marco and the remainder of the clan the next day. Six of the zheli boys—Jengzi, the Tibetan, and the five surviving Kazakh boys—had been left at the cabin with Akzu and the others. The boys were listening attentively to Malik, who was trying to arrange a game of baseball.

Fat Mao looked at Jengzi. "I know of two dropka at the silo," he said to Shan. "They buried a boy named Alta."

Shan smiled, remembering the forlorn words of the herder the day the man had found them hiding in the rocks. All they had wanted was to have a son and live in peace. They needed a son, and Jengzi needed parents.

Shan surveyed the clearing by the cabin and its jubilant population. The stout woman from town was there as well, cooking a giant pot of stew and baking stacks of nan bread, assisted by Akzu's wife. The Yakde Lama was watching from the trees, his eyes clouded, staring at the opposite side of the clearing. Shan followed his gaze toward a path through the trees. He quietly followed it past the small stream that ran by the cabin to a ledge with a long, high view to the desert. He was about to step onto it when he saw the Americans sitting there, holding each other, Micah's mother still weeping. He backed away without speaking.

At the meal, before the food was served, the two women who had cooked it made an announcement. They had decided that the surviving zheli boys would go with the Red Stone, as well as the stout woman who helped the Maos. The woman looked at Shan as the news was told, and nodded, as though she were apologizing again for what she had done to him in town. He smiled back, remembering what she had said, that she had lost her two sons to Chinese. Akzu stepped close to the fire, his face drawn, as if he were in pain. He had been that way, Shan suspected, since Jakli had been taken. His wife had not consulted him, Shan saw from the surprise on the headman's face.

The leathery old Kazakh looked from boy to boy and shook his head. "It's too dangerous, to go out with us," Akzu said, looking at his wife now. "And much hardship after that. I have buried enough children. They can go to the Chinese school. At least they'll be alive."

"With so many new sons," his wife replied in a strong, proud voice, "Red Stone can become a clan again."

Akzu stared grimly and shook his head again. "Woman," he began, then broke off as two figures appeared from the path by the stream, a woman and a boy. Shan saw in Akzu's face the same confusion he himself felt as he stared at them. They were strangers, but somehow familiar. The boy, smiling brilliantly, led the woman forward until they were a few feet in front of Akzu. The woman stepped behind the boy and began to gently stroke his head, with the serene affection of a mother.

Akzu gasped and looked at his wife, then turned away a moment and wiped his eye. As he did so Shan recognized the two figures. It was Batu, a clean, happy Batu in fresh, bright clothes, and the crazy woman who had thrown stones at Shan. But she was crazy no longer. Her hair was washed and neatly braided, her dress free of the debris that had clung to it, and her eyes were no longer wild, but filled with hope and love for her new son. Malik, staring in disbelief, dropped the ball in his hand. The woman stepped forward to retrieve it, and tossed it to Batu, who caught it and laughed. It was a simple thing, a small sound of joy, but somehow it resonated through the clearing, drawing the attention of everyone there. Because, Shan realized, it was just a boy sound, a sound not of a tormented youth who had been running from killers but the sound of a child, and perhaps of an entire clan, learning about joy again.

The clearing was silent. Every eye fixed on the headman as he solemnly looked into the faces of each of the orphan boys. "It's going to take a lot of new saddles," Akzu declared at last, and his wife rushed forward to embrace him.

After the meal, when the sun had been down two hours and most of the camp was asleep, Shan went back to the ledge. Deacon was there alone, under the full moon. Not quite alone, for he had his singers with him, arrayed in a semicircle in front of him. Shan did not join him at first but returned to the cabin to speak to the Yakde Lama, then ventured back to the ledge.

The American did not speak when Shan arrived but moved to the side to make room for him.

The moon was so brilliant they could see the glow of the desert miles away. One or two of the crickets sang, uncertain chirps, as if frightened perhaps.

"There was a compass there," Shan said quietly. "A black metal compass." He reached into his pocket and handed it to the American.

Deacon took so long to reply that Shan thought he had not heard. "I gave it to him. He was brave and independent, but that day he first left with the zheli he asked where we would be. I told him and said we would always be there waiting for him." Deacon's voice cracked and he stopped speaking for several long moments. "I said, Take my compass, and I showed him on a map where Sand Mountain would be. So if he ever wanted to talk to us or shout out goodnight he would know which direction to face."

Shan closed his eyes and fought away the image of the terrified boy as Ko came for him with the bat and knife, pulling out the compass to know which way his parents were, which way to go to find safety.

They were silent again, for a long time. More crickets sounded. "Ironlegs won't talk," Deacon said absently. "Never has, since that night I caught him." The moon rose higher and brighter. From somewhere an owl called. And then, behind them, a twig broke. The Yakde Lama stepped into the moonlight, looking down, wearing a sad, shy smile.

"There is someone I want you to meet," Shan said.

"I know Khitai," Deacon replied in a hoarse voice.

The boy took a step closer.

"There is someone I want you to meet," Shan said again.

The boy took another step forward.

"You said you were going to buy a bicycle for him," Shan said.

The American made a choking sound and then a sob wracked his broad shoulders. He put his arms out, the boy ran forward into them, and the American finally cried. In long groaning sobs he cried, and the boy clung to him and cried too. Until finally they began to quiet. Because all the crickets were singing.

He was awakened by a light touch on his shoulder, just as the sun was rising. "Is it true," Gendun asked in almost a whisper, "that the Yakde still wishes to go to America?" Shan only nodded, and Gendun rose and moved back to a small group sitting by the trees. Shan threw his blanket off and rose. The camp was still quiet except for two Maos at the fire who had been on guard all night. He walked to the trees. Gendun, Lokesh and an old, nearly bald Tibetan were listening to Jowa as he drew with his finger in the earth, a map of how to go from Senge Drak to the Raven's Nest. Shan looked back to the stranger and froze.

It was the waterkeeper. The old lama seemed to sense Shan's stare. He looked up and nodded warmly, then patted the earth between himself and Lokesh, inviting Shan to sit. As Shan returned the waterkeeper's smile he remembered the lama's last words to him. There has to be a crack or nothing can get in, he had said at the clinic. In the end, that was all Shan had been able to do, to help open the cracks, first in Kaju, and then in the hard brittle shell around Prosecutor Xu.

Lokesh leaned toward Shan and explained that Gendun was going to take the waterkeeper to Senge Drak and then the waterkeeper would take Gendun to the hidden gompa.

Gendun was beaming at Shan when he looked up. "There's an old teacher at the Nest," he said with a tone of great satisfaction, "who knew my father."

"But, Rinpoche," Jowa said. "Who will go with the boy? The Yakde needs a teacher until he is ready to return."

Gendun put his hand on the waterkeeper's shoulder. "The gompa has been without their abbot for too many years."

"What is needed," the abbot of the Raven's Nest said in his raspy voice, "is someone younger and stronger. Someone trained as a monk but also trained in the ways of the world."

"The Americans spoke to me before they slept," Jowa said. "First they are going with the Eluosi, to help him buy land and build his cabin by the ocean. The boy will stay there. They can do their work there, they say, for a year or two at least. It would be a quiet place a Mao could come visit, when there are more samples to bring from the desert."

"It could be difficult to navigate from a gompa to the world, but perhaps more so to go from the world back to the life of a gompa," Gendun observed enigmatically.

Lokesh made a chuckling sound and Jowa cast him a puzzled glance.

"In the mornings," the waterkeeper said with a contented sigh, "the boy is always distracted until he eats. Just a bowl of porridge, then he studies his sutras." Jowa looked away, around the clearing, as if he expected to see another monk arriving at any moment. "But if he does well, a reward is following butterflies. One time we followed a butterfly for three hours. Someone young, with stronger legs than mine, could do it for six."

Lokesh chuckled again. Jowa looked to him, then to Shan.

The waterkeeper touched Jowa's leg. "He hates to wash his socks," the old abbot said. "Make him wash his socks."

Jowa froze and stared at the waterkeeper's fingers. "Rinpoche," he said in a whisper. "I am not—" He could not finish the sentence, but just stared at the lama's hand.

The waterkeeper leaned forward and put both hands on top of Jowa's, resting on the purba's legs. "I hear this Alaska is a wet place." He shook their hands, one on top of the other, hard, as if to make sure Jowa understood. "Dry him off sometimes."

The old lama and Jowa gazed at each other for a long time. "When he is ready," the abbot of the Raven's Nest said at last, "you must bring him back to us. There will be much work for him, in the new Tibet." He squeezed Jowa's hands again. "We will watch the oracle lake for signs."

As Jowa looked at Shan, the Tibetan's mouth slowly turned up in a grin, and Shan remembered a night that seemed long ago, standing under the moon in the Kunlun, when Jowa had spoken in despair about how the lamas would eventually disappear, about how there was no point in continuing without the lamas, and how he could never become a lama because of what the Chinese had made him. But there would be a new generation of lamas, a different breed, but lamas nonetheless, and Jowa would help nurture them.

The Yakde had risen and was standing at the fire. Fat Mao nodded at Gendun.

"We are going now," Gendun announced to Shan, and the Tibetans rose. The waterkeeper and the Yakde embraced, and the waterkeeper gestured for Jowa and embraced the Yakde's new teacher as well.

The lamas followed Fat Mao up the trail, and Shan walked the first hundred feet with them. There were no words to say. Fat Mao stepped to Shan's side, and with an awkward, sober expression, dropped something into his hand, then darted away. Gendun, then the waterkeeper, stood in front of Shan, each grinning brightly, and each in turn placed his palm over Shan's heart. Shan nodded gratefully and watched until they were out of sight, then looked into his hand. Fat Mao had given him a small, brightly colored stone, newly washed with water.

In another hour the rest of the company was on the road, waiting for a truck that was taking Lokesh into Tibet. Lokesh was full of smiles and kept holding his bag tight against his chest. More than any of them, Lokesh was certain of where he was going and what he was doing. He was going to Mount Kailas, where he would complete a pilgrimage started a thousand years before to honor a dead mother and daughter. "It's going to be cold," Shan said awkwardly, and Lokesh just smiled. "There are dangerous places, I hear," Shan warned, "where you can lose your balance." Lokesh just kept smiling his crooked smile and embraced Shan, then moved onto the road as the Maos began calling him.

Sophie was grazing on the bank of the road, where Marco lay basking in the sun. As Shan sat, the Eluosi studied him as if measuring him for something. "I'll buy you a coat in Alaska. One of those big fur coats, for the winter that Russia sends there. And a fur cap. A ushanka. You'll look like a little bear. Johnny Bear." He smiled, the first smile Shan had seen since the terrible night on the parapet, and a new thought seemed to light Marco's eyes. "We'll build a sweat lodge in the winter. Take off your clothes and get heated like the desert. Then we run out and roll in the snow. Bare Johnny." Marco laughed a small laugh, then paused with a surprised expression, as if he had not expected to ever laugh again, and the laugh erupted once more, until he was holding his belly, and Shan laughed, and laughed some more, and marveled at it, a laugh of a kind he had not felt in years. And with it came a realization of why. Because to Shan Marco was not a teacher, not a prisoner, not a student, not a warrior. Marco was only a friend.

Shan watched as Jowa, his eyes burning with a brightness Shan had never before seen in them, threw a ball with Deacon and the boy lama. Sophie nuzzled his ear and Marco spoke again of the cabin he would build. A butterfly passed by and Shan turned to see Jowa pointing it out to the boy.

The sound of a struggling engine reached his ears and a moment later a decrepit vehicle came into view, a decades-old cargo truck. Its rear bay, covered with a soiled, torn canvas, was nearly filled with crates of chickens. Lokesh laughed as the Maos helped him on board, into a space between the crates.

Shan could not take his eyes off the old man, going alone into the inhospitable Himalayas. He realized suddenly that he was standing, and his hands were trembling. He felt his mouth open and shut, but no words came.

At his side he heard Marco sigh heavily and saw him rise to work on Sophie's saddle, where their bags were tied. "On the other hand," Marco boomed out, as if for dramatic effect, "it can rain for weeks in Alaska. Hard place, if you're used to looking at the sky." Something landed at Shan's feet. His bag.

Lokesh was settling into the truck. Chickens were squawking irritably and fluttering in their crates. The Maos were waving at the old Tibetan, fond smiles on their faces. The engine sputtered back to life in a cloud of smoke and with a groan the truck began to climb the mountain again.

Shan looked into the Eluosi's eyes. "It's a lot of chickens for one man," Marco said in a grave tone, and something seemed to catch in his throat. He grabbed Shan's hand and clasped it hard for a moment, then handed him his bag. Shan only nodded, then took a small step, and another, then began to run. As he jumped on the bumper of the moving truck, his shoulder swung back, pulled by the weight of his bag. Then, just as Shan was losing his balance, a thin hand, spotted with age, reached out and pulled him inside.

AUTHOR'S NOTE

While the characters and most of the places in this book are fictional, the struggle of the Tibetan, Kazakh, and Uighur people to maintain their culture and identity is very real. Many elements of this story are distilled from actual events in that fifty-year struggle, and from the rich and fascinating heritage of the Silk Road. The sands of the Taklamakan desert do indeed sometimes part to reveal ruins of lost Silk Road cities and tombs, and dedicated archaeologists from many nations do indeed work among the ruins, and do find ancient mummies and textiles, despite the political storms which rage around their work. Genetic research in the region and even scholarly assessment of scraps of cloth have attracted such political controversy that the simplest quest for knowledge in those distant quarters can be an act of heroism. And sadly, in Tibet the government of modern China has repeatedly interjected itself in the identification of reincarnate lamas.

For those readers who wish to learn more, many excellent sources are available, and deserve recommendation. Perhaps the most comprehensive works describing the Tibetan experience are John Avedon's *In Exile from the Land of the Snows*, and *The Dragon in the Land of the Snows* by Tsering Shakya. The many excellent firsthand accounts by or about Tibetan survivors include *A Strange Liberation: Tibetan Lives in Chinese Hands*, by David Patt, *Ama Adhe: The Voice that Remembers*, by Adhe Tapontsang and Joy Blakeslee, Palden Gyatso's *Autobiography of a Tibetan*

Monk, and *In the Presence of My Enemies*, by Sumner Carnahan. The details of the most public of Beijing's interventions in the selection of Tibetan reincarnations are set forth in Isabel Hilton's important work *The Search for the Panchen Lama*.

The fascinating horse-based culture of the Kazakh people is well described in *Kazakh Traditions of China*, by Awelkhan Hali, Zenxiang Li, and Karl W. Luckert, and *China's Last Nomads*, by Linda Benson and Ingvar Svanberg. Elizabeth Wayland Barber captures the remarkable archaeological discoveries being made in the Taklamakan in her *The Mummies of Urumchi*, which are explored even more comprehensively in *The Tarim Mummies* by J.P. Mallory and Victor H. Mair. Lastly, for any readers inclined to learn more about the world of cricket singers, Lisa Gail Ryan's *Insect Musicians and Cricket Champions* provides a lyrical introduction.

GLOSSARY OF FOREIGN TERMS

Terms that are used only once and defined in adjoining text are not included in this glossary.

Aksai Chin. A border region located where the Kunlun Mountains meet the Karakorum range, in the far southeast of Xinjiang, on Tibet's far northwestern border. Ownership of Aksai Chin is disputed between India and China, although it is occupied by the Chinese.

ani. Tibetan. A Buddhist nun.

ashamai. Turkic. A special soft saddle traditionally presented to Kazakh children when they reach the age of five, the age at which they typically stopped riding with their parents and began riding alone.

bumpa. Tibetan. A treasure vase, or ceremonial water pot, used in Buddhist ritual.

besik zhyry. Turkic. A cradle song.

changtang. Tibetan. The vast high plateau which dominates north central Tibet.

chuba. Tibetan. A heavy cloak-like coat made from sheepskin or sometimes thick woolen cloth.

dombra. Turkic. A two-stringed lute-like instrument.

dopa. Turkic. A round brimless cap often worn by devout Muslims.

dorje. Tibetan. From the Sanskrit "vajre," a scepter-shaped ritual instrument that symbolizes the power of compassion, said to be "unbreakable as diamond" and as "powerful as a thunderbolt."

dorje bell. Tibetan. A bell with a dorje handle.

dropka. Tibetan. A nomad of the changtang, literally "a dweller of the black tent."

Eluosi. Mandarin. A Russian, used to describe the Russian émigrés who live in Xinjiang.

gau. Tibetan. A "portable shrine," typically a small hinged metal box carried around the neck into which a prayer has been inserted.

gompa. Tibetan. A monastery, literally a "place of meditation."

jinni. Turkic. A type of evil spirit.

karaburan. Turkic. A sand storm, specifically used for the "black hurricanes" that plague the Taklamakan desert.

karez. Turkic. The underground water system, consisting of tunnels, cisterns, and access shafts, which uses gravity to transport water from mountain springs to distant farms and communities. Some elements of the karez system in Xinjiang date back two thousand years.

khampa. Tibetan. A native of the Kham region of what was traditionally eastern Tibet.

khata. Tibetan. A prayer scarf, traditionally of white silk or cotton, often offered to a lama at the end of a ritual.

Kharoshthi. A language of Aramaic origin dating to the fifth century B.C., which was commonly used on the early Silk Road.

khez khuwar. Turkic. A Kazakh riding game, traditionally played between girls on one side and boys on the other.

khoshakhan. Turkic. A calming call made to lambs.

kumiss. Turkic. Fermented mare's milk, often carried in a leather drinking skin.

Kunlun. The high, long mountain range that defines the northern border of the Tibetan plateau, extending from the Pamir and Karakorum ranges on the Pakistan border for several hundred miles to the east.

lama. Tibetan. The Tibetan translation of the Sanskrit "guru," traditionally used for a fully ordained senior monk who has become a master teacher.

lao jiao. Mandarin. Literally "reeducation through labor," referring to a less severe incarceration facility where prisoners receive intense political education.

lao gai. Mandarin. Literally "reform through labor," referring to a prison labor camp.

lung ma. Mandarin. Traditionally, a "horse dragon," a mythical beast, part horse, part dragon, that brought justice to the common people.

lha gyal lo. Tibetan. A traditional Tibetan phrase of celebration or rejoicing, literally, "Victory to the gods."

mala. Tibetan. A Buddhist rosary, typically consisting of 108 beads.

mani stone. Tibetan. A stone inscribed, by paint or carving, with a Buddhist prayer, typically invoking the mantra Om Mani Padme Hum.

mani wall. Tibetan. A wall made of mani stones. Traditionally pilgrims visiting a shrine would add a mani stone to such a wall to acquire merit.

Mei Guo. Mandarin. America, literally, "Beautiful Country."

mudra. Tibetan. A symbolic gesture made by arranging the hands and fingers in prescribed patterns to represent a specific prayer, offering, or state of mind.

nadam. Turkic. Traditionally, a Kazakh horse festival, where Kazakh clans gather for several days to engage in horse racing and other athletic competitions.

nan. Turkic. Flat bread, traditionally baked on a stone.

nei lou. Mandarin. State secret; literally, for government use only.

pecha. Tibetan. A traditional Tibetan book of scripture, typically unbound in long, narrow loose leaves which are wrapped in cloth, often tied with carved wooden end pieces.

purba. Tibetan. Literally "nail" or "spike," a small dagger with a triangular blade used in Buddhist ritual.

Rinpoche. Tibetan. A term of respect in addressing a revered teacher, literally "blessed" or "jewel."

Sekset Ata. Turkic. The deity who protects goats.

sundet. Turkic. In Kazakh tradition a boy is circumcised between the ages of five and seven, in a ceremony called *sundet toi*. Often a pony is presented to the boy by his family at this time. Later in life this is referred to as the boy's *sundet* horse.

synshy. Turkic. A "knower of horses," or "horse speaker," who is thought to have special abilities to communicate with a horse and discern its personality, attributes, and illnesses.

Taklamakan. Turkic. A vast desert in south central Xinjiang, between the Tian Shan mountains in the north and the Kunlun range in the south, known for its extreme temperatures and treacherous shifting sands.

tamzing. Mandarin. A "struggle session," typically a public criticism of an individual in which humiliation and verbal and/or physical abuse is utilized to achieve political education.

tsampa. Tibetan. Roasted barley flour, a staple food of Tibet.

tsingha. Tibetan. Small cymbal-like chimes used in Buddhist ritual.

thangka. Tibetan. A painting on cloth, typically of a religious nature and often considered sacred.

torma. Tibetan. A ritual offering made primarily of butter and barley flour, shaped and dyed in many shapes and sizes in homage to Buddhist deities.

Urumqi. Mandarin. The capital of Xinjiang.

Xinjiang. Mandarin. The Xinjiang Autonomous Region, the name given by the People's Republic of China to the huge region bounded to the northeast by Mongolia, on the east by the Chinese provinces of Gansu and Qinghia, on the south by Tibet, and on the west by Kazahkstan, Kirghizstan, Tajikstan, Afghanistan, Pakistan, and India.

zheli. Turkic. The rope stretched between pegs or trees to tether young animals.

Zhylkhyshy Ata. Turkic. The deity who protects horses, also called Khambar Ata.

Keep reading for an excerpt from
Eliot Pattison's next compelling mystery

Bone Mountain

Coming soon from St. Martin's Minotaur!

"Sift the sand to find the seeds of the universe."

The voice that came to Shan Tao Yun through the night was like wind over grass. "Let them reach the original ground then plant them," the lama said as Shan's gaze drifted from the white sand in his palm to the brilliant half moon. He knew his teacher Gendun meant Shan's original ground, the seedbed of his soul, what Gendun called Shan's beginning place. But on such a night he could not shake the sense that Tibet itself was the true original ground, that the vast remote land was the world's beginning place, where the planet, and humankind, never stopped shaping themselves, where the highest mountains, the strongest winds and the most rugged souls had always evolved together.

Ten feet farther down the river's edge Shan's old friend and former cellmate, Lokesh, chanted quietly, beads entwined in his fingers, his mantra almost indistinguishable from the rustle of the water. Shan breathed in the fragrant smoke of the juniper branches they had brought to burn at the water's edge and watched as a meteor flew over a low distant shimmering in the sky, the only hint of the snow-capped mountains that lined the horizon. It seemed he could reach out and touch the moon. If the earth had a place and a season for growing souls this was surely it, the chill moonlit spring of the high Tibetan wilderness.

Shan watched as though from a distance as Gendun gently opened Shan's fingers and lifted his hand toward the moon, then lowered it and turned Shan's wrist to empty the sand into the small clay jar they had brought from their hermitage ten miles away.

"Lha gyal lo," a voice murmured on Shan's opposite side. It was the caretaker of the hermitage, Shopo, his voice cracking with emotion. "Victory to the gods." They had arrived at the river at dusk, and only now, after the lamas and Lokesh had spent two hours speaking with the *nagas*, the water deities, had Gendun decided Shan could begin collecting the special white sand.

"Lha gyal lo!" an excited voice echoed halfway up the slope behind them. It was one of the four *dropka*, Tibetan herders, who had escorted them to the river and now stood guard, nervously watching the darkened landscape. Gendun and Shopo were outlawed monks engaged in an outlawed ritual, and the patrols had grown aggressive.

Without even sensing the movement, Shan found his hand back in the water, and when he lifted it out it was full of the white sand again. In the moonlight he saw Lokesh's eyes widen and gleam with excitement as, slowly repeating the motions Gendun had shown him, Shan washed the sand in the moonlight then emptied his palm into the jar.

Gendun's face, worn smooth as a river stone, wrinkled with a smile. "Each of the grains is the essence of a mountain," the lama said as Shan's hand dipped into the water once more, "all that is left when the mountain has shed its husk." Shan had heard the words a dozen times during the past two months as they had ventured into the night to collect sands from places known only to Shopo and the herders. In their turn each of the vast peaks that lined the horizon would be reduced to such a grain, Gendun explained, and so it would be for all mountains, all continents, all planets. It would all end as it began, in such tiny seeds, and humankind in all its glory could never match the power reflected in a single grain. The words were a way of teaching impermanence, Shan knew, and of showing respect for the nagas from whom they borrowed the sand.

Shan sensed a distant drumming noise in his ears and the moon seemed to edge even closer as he gathered another handful for the jar. His hand reached toward the clay jar then froze in midair as a frantic voice split the stillness.

"*Mik tada*! Watch out! Run!" It was one of the dropka sentinels on the ridge above. "The fire! Dowse the fire!"

Shan heard feet scrambling over the gravel of the slope above and looked up to see two men silhouetted in the moonlight, realizing in the same moment that the drumming was not in his head. It was a helicopter coming in low and fast, the way Public Security operated when raiding Tibetan camps.

One of the guards, wearing a black wool cap, darted to the water's edge, futilely pulling on Lokesh's shoulder, then moving to Shan's side to tug on his collar. "You have to go patch that god!" the man shouted. "We must flee!"

Shan let himself be pulled to his feet, his spine chilling as he looked first toward the helicopter, then at the lamas, who only smiled and continued their homage to the river. Gendun and Shopo were accustomed to risking imprisonment for simple acts of reverence. And though Shan and the dropka might be disturbed by the increased pressure from Public Security, there was only one mystery that ever concerned Gendun, the mystery of growing and strengthening souls.

"If it is Public Security, they will drop soldiers over the ridge to surround us!" the sentinel groaned as he kicked sticks from the small fire. "They will have machine guns and devices to see in the night!"

Shan studied the man in the black cap warily. He had more than a mere herder's grasp of Chinese weapons and tactics. Shan suddenly realized that he had not seen the man before, that he had not been part of their escort.

Gendun replied by raising a finger to his lips, then gestured toward the water. "There are nagas," he observed quietly.

"The sand will be useless if you are arrested," Shan whispered, his hand on Gendun's shoulder.

"There are nagas," the lama repeated.

"It's only sand," the stranger argued, casting a tormented glance in the direction of the approaching helicopter. Public Security had its own ways of teaching impermanence.

As Gendun turned back to the water, Lokesh was suddenly at the stranger's side, pulling him away from the lama. "We are creating something wonderful with that sand," Shan's old friend whispered, the white stubble of his whiskers glistening in the moonlight. He placed his hands on the man's shoulders to be sure the young Tibetan was listening and gazed into his face. "When we are done," he explained in a solemn, confiding tone, "it will change the world."

The man in the black cap illuminated an electric lantern and aimed the beam into Lokesh's face as if doubting he had heard the old Tibetan correctly; then, as the sound of the helicopter surged to a crescendo, he snapped off the light and dove to the ground. A moment later the machine was gone. It had skimmed the ridge above but had been traveling too fast to deploy troops.

The man in the cap lit his lantern and muttered under his breath, casting an accusing glance at the other guards, who had gathered behind Lokesh with sheepish, even embarrassed expressions. He aimed the light beam into each man's face, settling it on Shan's, which he studied with a frown. "You are supposed to be delivering an artifact," he said to Lokesh, his voice heavy with impatience. He did not move the light from Shan.

"We are," Lokesh agreed. "We are preparing for the journey," he added with a gesture toward the two lamas, who continued to speak over the swift dark river.

"Preparing?" the man scoffed. "What have you been doing for two months? You're not preparing, you're taking root! You will ruin us!"

Shan stepped beside Lokesh and pushed the man's lantern down. "Those who brought the artifact agreed that the lamas will decide the proper way to return it." He knew now the stranger, like those who had brought the sacred artifact to Shopo's hermitage, was a *purba*, a member of the secret Tibetan resistance.

"You mean Drakte agreed."

"Drakte is one of you," Shan asserted. He and Lokesh had met Drakte nearly a year earlier aiding prisoners in the gulag camp where they had served. It had been Drakte who had intercepted them two months ago and taken them to Shopo's hidden hermitage. "We will go when the lamas and Drakte are ready. He is coming to show us the way. A few more days at most."

"We don't have a few more days," the purba groused. "And don't expect Drakte. He's not keeping his appointments."

"Missing?" Shan noticed a bulge under the man's jacket, at the waist, and looked back at Gendun. If the lamas thought the man had a gun they would insist he leave.

The purba shrugged. "Not where he was asked to be."

"And you've come in his place?"

"No. But I was hoping to find him at that hermitage. There is news. And I brought something he had asked for," he added in a peevish tone. "He said the lamas needed it. He said if we did not agree to retrieve it he would go himself, all the way to India if necessary." The purba lowered a long, narrow sack from his shoulder and produced an eighteen-inch-long bamboo tube, which Lokesh eagerly accepted.

"What news?" Shan asked.

Before he replied, the man pointed to one of the herders, then to the top of the hill where the guards had been watching the road beyond. The herder sprang up the slope. "A man was killed. An official, in Amdo town," he said, referring to the closest settlement of any size, nearly a hundred miles away. "Public Security will sweep the hills and detain people. When they interrogate, they will learn of the hermitage." He cast another frown toward the lamas. "You may call it sacred, what you are doing, but they will call it a crime against the state." He took a step toward Gendun as though to try again to drag him away, but a herder in a fleece vest stepped forward with a hand raised in warning.

"Do you have any idea how dangerous this is?" The purba's hands clenched and unclenched repeatedly. He seemed ready to do battle with them. "No one told us you would wander around the mountains like this. You could go to prison, all of you. For what? You can't fight the Chinese with sand and prayers."

Lokesh uttered a hoarse sound that Shan recognized as a laugh. "I have known Chinese prisons," the old Tibetan said. "Sometimes sand and prayers are the only way."

The purba fixed Shan with a bitter stare. "You are the famous Chinese who fixes things for Tibetans. You know better, but still you let them do this."

Shan paused to study Gendun and Shopo. "If these lamas asked me to jump into this river with my pockets stuffed with rocks," he said quietly, "I would thank them and leap in."

"Lha gyal lo," the herder in the vest whispered, as if to cheer Shan on.

Lokesh touched the warrior's arm. "It is difficult for one so young to understand these things," the old Tibetan said. "You should return with us to the hermitage and see."

"Unlike Drakte, I obey my orders," the man snapped. "I am needed elsewhere."

Lokesh raised the bamboo tube in his hand. "Then look now," he suggested, extracting a roll of cloth from the tube. As Lokesh straightened it Shan saw that it was an old *thangka*, one of the cloth paintings used to depict the icons of Tibetan Buddhism.

When the purba's light hit the painting, the man grimaced and retreated a step. One of the dropka guards moaned loudly. It was the image of a fierce demon, with the head of a bull garlanded with human skulls, surrounded by swords and spears and arrows, holding a cup of blood. The flayed skins of its victims lay at its feet. Lokesh studied the image with a satisfied grin, then motioned the purba forward.

"Look carefully," the old Tibetan said, pointing to the head of the terrifying image. "This is what we are doing. This is how we win without violence. This is how the artifact will be returned, how that deity is going to be repaired. Because this is what he is becoming."

"Who?" the purba asked, the anger in his voice now tinged with confusion.

In the dim light Shan thought he saw surprise on Lokesh's face, as though the answer were obvious. Then Lokesh gestured from the skull-clad demon to Shan. "Our friend. Our Shan."

The spell cast by the words silenced the purba and the dropka, all of whom stared uneasily at Shan. Shan searched Lokesh's face for an explanation, but his friend just grinned back expectantly, as if he had given Shan a great gift.

Suddenly another desperate cry split the air. The guard at the top of the ridge frantically stumbled down the slope.

"A patrol! Knobs!" he cried, meaning the soldiers of the Public Security Bureau. The purba and Shan leapt up and moments later gazed down at a troop transport half a mile away, edging its way slowly toward their position.

"That helicopter spotted us," the purba said. "Last month they used infrared to find an old hermit who only came out at night to pray." Shan sensed the fierce determination rising in the warrior's voice and shuddered.

At the river three of the dropka were in a cluster around the lamas, facing outward, as if preparing to engage the knobs with their staffs. The fourth, the man wearing the fleece vest, stood apart, staring into the black water. As the purba marched purposefully toward the lamas, the herder in the vest spun about and hurled himself on the purba, shoving him to the ground, then just as abruptly pulling away. In his hand was a large automatic pistol.

"You fool!" the purba spat. "They have to be taken away! We can't fight those knobs."

Shame crossed the herder's face as he looked at the pistol in his hand, and he held the weapon clumsily, fingers around only the grip, not touching the trigger. "You see that one," he said, nodding toward Gendun, who still communed with the river. "My mother stays at that tent by the hermitage. She calls him the Pure Water Lama. You know why? Not just because he never registered with the bastards at the Bureau of Religious Affairs, but because he took his vows more than fifty years ago, before the invasion. Before the Chinese scoured our land and changed it forever. He has never gone into exile, never been captured. His words are uncontaminated, my mother says, because they flow from a stream the Chinese never discovered." The man spoke slowly, with a tone of wonder, as if he had forgotten the knob patrol. Beside him two of the herders knelt at the river and began collecting pebbles.

"I need my gun," growled the purba, still sprawled on the ground. He was scared, Shan saw. Sometimes traditional Tibetans hated the purbas as much as the Chinese. "We need to get them out of here."

The herder shook his head. "I have never done anything with my life," he said in a hollow voice. "The Chinese would not let me go to school. They wouldn't let me travel.

They wouldn't let me get a job. I'm like a little stunted tree that can never grow, and that one, the Pure Water Lama, he is like the towering survivor of a forest where everything else was leveled."

He cast a smile toward Gendun, then looked at the purba, his face hardening. "Here is how we protect such men," he said, and he threw the gun into the black water. The two herders at the river's edge rose and stepped to his side, pulling slings from their pockets. "We have heard how to do this from others. We will smash their searchlights and fill the air with stones. If we are lucky they will not see us. Chinese soldiers get scared in the night. They hear stories of demons." He glanced at the thangka, still in Lokesh's hand, then at Shan. "The lamas must fill the jar," he said to the purba, "and then you will take them back. My younger brother knows the way," he said, gesturing toward the remaining herder. "If we do not stop the patrol, you are the one who best knows how to evade the soldiers."

When the man lifted, his sling his hand shook. "Patch the deity," he said in a rushed whisper to Shan, then faded into the shadows with his companions.

As Shan helped the purba to his feet, the man looked into the darkness, in the direction the herders had gone, a mixture of anger and awe on his face. "That artifact," he said in a hollow voice, "I hear it's just a little piece of stone."